I forced myself to think of the many valid reasons the Urabi despised Arin.

He had no friends, no confidants. He handled people like lines on his maps. Shifting them subtly, strategically, without giving them the chance to feel the ground moving beneath their feet. His father's charm was natural; Arin's was carefully cultivated. Logic led his life, leaving emotion to fester at the sidelines. Even to his own people, he was an enigma. A dangerous one. Supreme Rawain could tear apart kingdoms, but Arin could destroy worlds.

As long as magic was his enemy, so was I.

Water misted across the shore as a wave barreled into the mountain.

How unbearably pathetic that the person whose advice I trusted most, whose counsel I wanted so badly in that moment, was the same one preparing to kill me.

A tear slid from the corner of my unblinking eye. I let it roll to my chin before catching it with my thumb. Raising my hand to blot out the moon, I studied the droplet.

The first and final tear I planned to shed for Arin of Nizahl.

Praise for

THE JASAD HEIR

"A remarkable, razor-sharp debut that cuts straight to the heart. Steeped in intrigue, tension, and dangerous magic, *The Jasad Heir* is a thrilling read that held me captive past its heart-pounding ending."
—Chelsea Abdullah, author of *The Stardust Thief*

"A stunning fantasy debut that deftly examines the burdens of political responsibility. With a morally complex heroine and an incomparable enemies-to-lovers arc. A compelling tale of self-discovery, found family, and the meaning of justice."
—Hadeer Elsbai, author of *The Daughters of Izdihar*

"*The Jasad Heir* takes familiar fantasy plot elements—a destroyed kingdom; a hidden heir to the lost throne—and gives them a thrilling extra layer of political complexity. The slow burn between protagonist and antagonist will have you turning pages in a frenzy. Sara Hashem is a talent to watch!"
—Shelley Parker-Chan, author of *She Who Became the Sun*

"Hashem weaves a complex tapestry of magic, danger, and violence set against some vividly atmospheric worldbuilding in her mesmerizing debut." —*Publishers Weekly* (starred review)

"Beautifully creates a story of intrigue and high stakes.... Hashem's debut is enemies-to-possible lovers that fantasy romance readers will eat up." —*BuzzFeed News*

"A compelling fantasy saga that's one part political treatise, one part slow-burn enemies-to-lovers romance, and one part survival competition.... A summer fantasy banger." —*Paste* magazine

"*The Jasad Heir* will have you on the edge of your seat and eager for the sequel. Evocative and layered, this Egyptian-inspired debut features a formidable heroine, a kaleidoscopic backdrop, a slow-burn romance and endless intrigue." —*Ms.*

THE JASAD CROWN

By Sara Hashem

THE SCORCHED THRONE

The Jasad Heir
The Jasad Crown

THE JASAD CROWN

THE SCORCHED THRONE: BOOK TWO

SARA HASHEM

orbitbooks.net

This book is a work of fiction. Names, characters, places, and incidents are the product of the author's imagination or are used fictitiously. Any resemblance to actual events, locales, or persons, living or dead, is coincidental.

Copyright © 2025 by Sara Hashem
Excerpt from *The Foxglove King* copyright © 2023 by Hannah Whitten

Cover design by Lisa Marie Pompilio
Cover illustration by Mike Heath | Magnus Creative
Cover copyright © 2025 by Hachette Book Group, Inc.
Map by Tim Paul
Author photograph by Sara Hashem

Hachette Book Group supports the right to free expression and the value of copyright. The purpose of copyright is to encourage writers and artists to produce the creative works that enrich our culture.

The scanning, uploading, and distribution of this book without permission is a theft of the author's intellectual property. If you would like permission to use material from the book (other than for review purposes), please contact permissions@hbgusa.com. Thank you for your support of the author's rights.

Orbit
Hachette Book Group
1290 Avenue of the Americas
New York, NY 10104
orbitbooks.net

First Edition: July 2025
Simultaneously published in Great Britain by Orbit

Orbit is an imprint of Hachette Book Group.
The Orbit name and logo are registered trademarks of Little, Brown Book Group Limited.

The publisher is not responsible for websites (or their content) that are not owned by the publisher.

The Hachette Speakers Bureau provides a wide range of authors for speaking events. To find out more, go to hachettespeakersbureau.com or email HachetteSpeakers@hbgusa.com.

Orbit books may be purchased in bulk for business, educational, or promotional use. For information, please contact your local bookseller or the Hachette Book Group Special Markets Department at special.markets@hbgusa.com.

Library of Congress Cataloging-in-Publication Data
Names: Hashem, Sara, author.
Title: The Jasad crown / Sara Hashem.
Description: First edition. | New York, NY : Orbit, 2025. | Series: The scorched throne ; book two
Identifiers: LCCN 2024047270 | ISBN 9780316478243 (trade paperback) | ISBN 9780316478342 (ebook)
Subjects: LCGFT: Fantasy fiction. | Novels.
Classification: LCC PS3608.A789747 J365 2025 | DDC 813/.6—dc23/eng/20241021
LC record available at https://lccn.loc.gov/2024047270

ISBNs: 9780316478243 (trade paperback), 9780316478342 (ebook)

Printed in the United States of America

LSC-C

Printing 1, 2025

To the difficult girls who built their armor early.

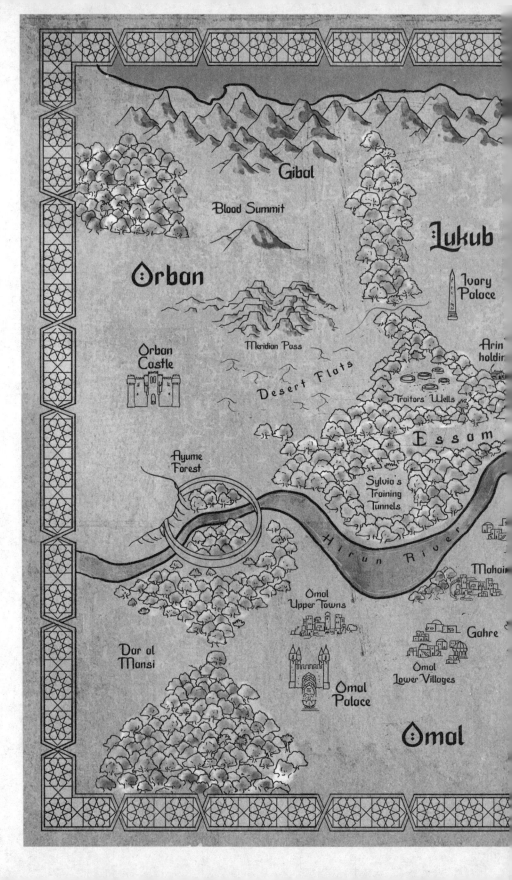

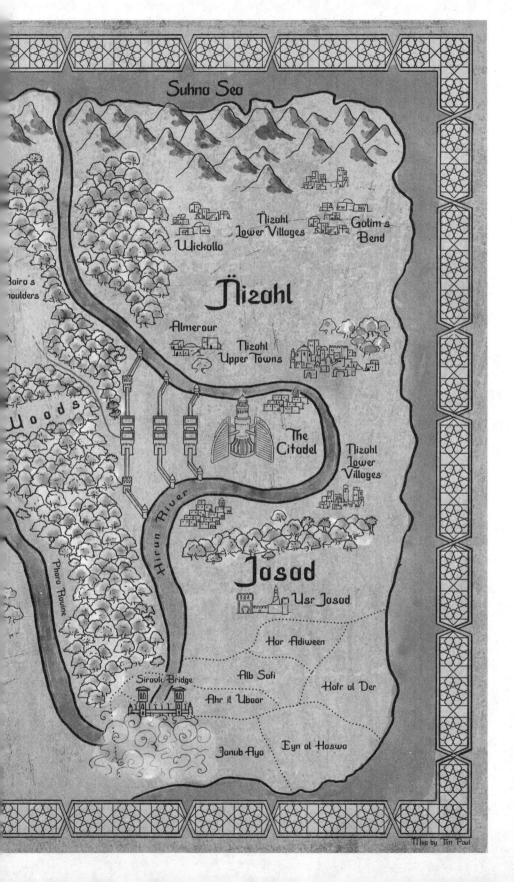

CHAPTER ONE

ARIN

Arin firmly believed an attempt on one's life was the highest form of flattery.

Becoming a threat by the very virtue of your existence, inspiring the sort of mad dedication that drives men to murder... what could be more of an accomplishment?

His father endured at least two dozen assassination attempts a month—more than the rest of the rulers combined.

Arin had waited impatiently for his turn. On the eve of his tenth birthday, it came.

A commotion had erupted outside his chambers, and Arin followed it into the hall. His guards had shouted for him to return to his room, occupied trying to hold back the intruder.

Preposterous—as if Arin were some fragile bird in a glass cage. Only cowards hid.

Besides, he had waited for this. Planned for it. At ten, Arin had begun to grasp the role he played in his kingdom. The power he stood to inherit. The fact that someone had come to the Citadel seeking to kill him meant others had begun to realize his power, too.

Later, he'd learn the assassin was one of fifteen sent to infiltrate the Citadel on the eve of the Champions' Banquet, which was being held in Nizahl that year. The others were apprehended before they ever reached the Citadel's grounds.

When the assassin spotted the Nizahl Heir, a manic light had brightened in his eyes. He darted around the guards and reared his arm back.

The knife flew.

Arin could have avoided it. Unlike his graceless guards, Arin could measure exactly what movements he needed to avoid injury. One twist to the right, a collapse of his right knee, and he would have been out of harm's way.

Except, Arin didn't want to avoid the knife.

Arin knew his flaws—they were frequently recited to him. Cold, heartless, stubborn. Arin's mother called his shortcomings by kinder names than Arin's tutors. To Isra, his shortcomings were *a keen regard for precision*. A personal standard that demanded nothing short of perfection.

But his worst flaw, universally agreed upon by all, was Arin's curiosity. Once a question blossomed in the Heir's mind, he could not rest until he found an answer. His curiosity eclipsed everything—his sense, his reason, his very sanity.

So Arin stood still for the knife. He pulled his arm over his chest, drawing his shoulder over the fatal points of entry. The knife cleaved into him. The suddenness of the impact temporarily whitened the world.

Arin had screamed. He barely registered the guards jumping onto the assassin or the heavy thud of bodies hitting the ground. His arm hurt. Everything hurt terribly.

The next time he had opened his eyes, he was in his own bed, the wound hidden beneath a thick bandage. His mother was fast asleep next to him.

"You scared her," Rawain said. He stood in front of Arin's window. "You know I detest when she cries."

Tear tracks had indeed dried on Isra's cheeks. Arin moved to wipe them away and stopped when Rawain glanced over. The Supreme disliked it when Arin showed his mother affection or let her fuss over him.

Without ever being told, Arin understood that Rawain did not love her.

Arin withdrew his touch, because loving his mother meant losing a little bit more of his father.

"You let him hurt you," Rawain said, staring out the window again. His hands were clasped around his scepter, fingers tight above the glass orb. Arin did not have to peer closely to make out the raven's wings, the black feathers unfurling above the two swords clashing at its feet. The symbol of Nizahl, cast in exquisite gems at the head of his father's scepter, always seemed alive enough to glare at Arin.

His heart pounded. "I did not *let*—"

"Arin," Rawain interjected lightly. Too lightly. "What is my first rule?"

An all-too-familiar weight pressed down on Arin. He fought to breathe through it. "I am not lying, my liege."

"One last chance." Rawain turned, moving from the window to hover over Arin's bedside. Terror closed Arin's throat, the slow suffocation rendered infinitely worse beneath his father's knowing gaze. The raven's beady glare pierced into him. "Why did you let him hurt you?"

Resignation settled like a shroud over Arin. Punishment was inevitable. The only variable Arin could control now was its severity. Telling the truth would mean months of grueling training and the confiscation of his books and maps.

But lying would sentence Arin to the Capsule.

"I wanted to know how it would feel," Arin said. He knotted his fingers into the blanket, ignoring the pull on his arm. "The injury."

"You've been injured by many knives in your training."

"Never stabbed." Arin swallowed. "I wanted to see if I could survive it."

A heavily ringed hand settled on Arin's throat. His father's finger ghosted over Arin's pulse. It beat sickly fast, betraying its owner.

"Do you think if you put yourself in the path of what you fear and let it hurt you, you will somehow be stronger for it? That you will know your limits better?" Rawain's hand moved to Arin's arm.

Without hesitation, he dug his thumb into Arin's bandage.

Pain roared through him, and Arin barely remembered to trap his gasp behind his teeth. He couldn't risk waking his mother. Rawain did not tolerate her interruptions when he was teaching his Heir a lesson, and Arin hated it when she was punished because of him. "Those who survive longest never put themselves in a position to be hurt. They see the threat coming and *they step aside.*"

Red leaked beneath the bandage. His father pressed harder. Arin tasted blood. He had bitten into his own tongue.

"You are my sole Heir. You will inherit my kingdom, my throne, and my enemies. How can I trust you if you cannot command your impulses or quash these infernal curiosities? How, Arin?"

Black dots swam in Arin's vision, and only then did Rawain withdraw his hand. He wiped his thumb on his robes. "Your lessons resume at dawn."

His mother woke two hours later and fought with the servants who came to dress Arin for his training. "Can't you see he's hurt? He cannot train today. He is only a child! Please, he's in pain." The servants moved around her while she wept, ignoring her attempts to hold them off.

And Arin, who still felt the imprint of his father's thumb, had found himself disgusted by her tears.

She put herself in a position to be hurt, he thought, suddenly and without much emotion. *She loves me too much. She will see the threat coming and stand perfectly still, if only to let me live a minute more.*

Arin put his hand on the bandage and pressed.

The pain grew, and grew, and grew.

He would become familiar with this pain. He would learn to think through it.

And then he would never see it coming and stand still again.

Rain pattered against the window, obscuring the sight of a sleeping Nizahl from its watchful Heir.

The stormy evening possessed every hallmark of nights his mother called *sieges of the Awaleen*. The wind picked up, its mournful howl cutting through the stone walls. Arin could almost hear his mother's phantom sigh, the tap of her thin fingers against the shaking glass. *Sleep is the space between life and death. A space where anything can happen,* she would say, in the faraway tone Arin had grown to fear. *The Awaleen have dwelled in their dreams for centuries. Look at the sky, Arin, and tell me you cannot see them in the clouds.*

In her last few years, she had developed a habit of speaking such nonsense where others could hear. Persistent superstition was a relic she carried over from her village in Nazeef, and his father hated any reminders of Isra's lowborn origins.

A crackle of lightning washed Arin in shades of blue. If the Awaleen truly slept, down there in their eternal tombs, then their sleep knew only nightmares.

A knock came at the door. Arin smoothed a palm over his vest, dispelling the phantom of his mother. He had plans with the living to oversee.

"Enter." Arin didn't move from the window as the door creaked open behind him.

"Your Highness. You summoned?"

"Have a seat, Counselor Rodan."

Arin turned from the window. The High Counselor bowed deeply, gaze meeting Arin's for a brief instant before darting away.

Rodan moved to the chair nearest to the door and hesitated. The seat would be close to the head of the table—within Arin's reach. Executing a shuffle unbecoming of anyone above the age of five, the High Counselor instead chose a chair at the center of the table.

As though Arin would ever expend the effort to physically assault him. There weren't enough gloves in the world. The entire episode had taken less than a minute, but it told Arin what he needed to know.

It didn't end there. When Arin lowered himself into his chair, the High Counselor flinched. *Flinched.*

"Peculiar weather tonight." Rodan picked at his thumb, seemingly indifferent to the blood crusted in the hinges of his nail. The thought of replacing his table because the High Counselor bled on it irritated Arin to distraction.

Arin's silence only further aggravated the High Counselor. Over the years, Arin had found silence a most effective tool for excavating the inner workings of someone's mind. To some, silence scraped and clawed and screamed. Others settled in it, content to float on its ebb.

Save for a bottle of talwith and two glasses, the table lay empty. Arin uncorked the bottle. In each glass, he poured two fingers' worth of the lavender liquid. Rodan watched the bottle, wiping his knuckles across his chin. A smear of blood from his thumbnail caught on his whiskered jaw.

When Arin placed both glasses in front of Rodan, the High Counselor blinked. "None for you, my liege?"

"I have had more than my fair share as of late," Arin said genially. "I presume you're familiar with talwith?"

The High Counselor regarded the glasses with transparent unease. "The Orbanian beverage. Quite difficult to import to Nizahl, isn't it?"

Her teasing voice cut across Arin's thoughts like a well-aimed blade. *Wait, are you important or something?*

Arin's fingers curled.

"Your Highness?"

Arin sat back in his chair, elbows balanced on the armrests as he folded his hands together. Rodan still hadn't touched either drink. It always amused Arin how careful fickle men became when it was their own life on the line. "You've worked for the Citadel for many years. Since the start of my father's reign."

The High Counselor nodded, relieved to be back on familiar footing. "Nearly twenty-four years."

Arin considered the man sitting at his table with the same level of interest he might afford an insect on the bottom of his boot. He'd rarely had cause to deal with Counselor Rodan in the past. The High Counselor's role positioned him as an advisor to the Supreme and gave him a seat on the council—powerful privileges, but not ones that made him notable to Arin.

Twenty-four years. Decades Rodan had slithered around the Citadel, privy to the secrets of the most powerful kingdom in the land.

Arin couldn't fathom it. Nothing about the High Counselor marked him as anything more than another dull, crown-kissing sycophant. Age lined his narrow face, and his hairline's backward march had reached his ears. He was thin as a stalk of barley. Just as easy to snap.

Utterly unremarkable.

"I see." Arin tilted his head. "And how many of those twenty-four years did you spend molesting little girls?"

The question hit the High Counselor with the force of an open-palmed slap. His breathing changed, turning shallow and quick. Arin's vaguely bored expression did not change.

"S-sire, a grave misunderstanding is afoot." Rodan's trembling voice steadied. Just as abruptly, the lines carving across his graying skin eased. As closely as Arin was watching, he still couldn't see them. The signs of his deception.

In any other situation, Arin would be impressed. Long and sustained deceit required a certain finesse. The fidgety man in front of him hardly seemed capable of it.

"I cannot imagine what tales that licentious, traitorous Jasadi spoke, but you must know better than to believe her."

Arin heard the words the High Counselor didn't dare say: *You should have known better than to believe anything she said. You should have known better. You should have* known.

There was a time when the provocation would have evaporated on contact, dispersing against the unyielding wall of Arin's focus. A time when nobody but Rawain had the right weapons to get under Arin's skin.

A time before a dark-eyed Jasadi became the fastest blade under which Arin could bleed.

Arin took one breath, long and slow. Anger needed embers to catch—stone against which the flint might strike. The most efficient way to dispose of an inefficient reaction was to keep moving. Crush it underfoot and never look back.

Until five days ago, the strategy had worked. Arin devoted a lifetime to designing the lay of his own mind—crafting every valley and bend.

But now, there were breaches. There was the blade.

Arin reached into his coat and extracted a tiny bottle containing four ivory beads, each roughly the size of a fingernail.

"Why did Sayali Barakat flee your home when she was fourteen?"

A flash of surprise, wiped in an instant. The High Counselor opened his mouth, and Arin lifted a finger. "Think through what you say next. I offer you one chance, and one chance only."

Rodan's palms flattened on the table, leaving Arin with no choice but to observe the dirt creased into the other man's knuckles. "I have nothing to think through, my liege. She is a thief. She abused my kindness and broke her mother's heart. She stole everything I'd saved for her future to run away with her fair-haired lover."

One bead rolled from the bottle into Arin's palm. "Strange. Your wife told a different story."

Leaning over the table, Arin dropped the bead into the glass on Rodan's right. It dissolved with a hiss. The two of them watched ivory flecks settle at the bottom of the glass.

Neat. Predictable—like this entire conversation.

Rodan didn't take his eyes off the tainted glass. "Time has diminished the truth of her daughter's treachery. She cannot be relied upon when it comes to Sayali."

"I am sure Sayali felt similarly."

Meeting Sefa's mother had been a strange experience. She'd wasted an hour preparing tea and honey cake, jittery with apologies as she rushed to accommodate Arin and his guardsmen. It was almost, *almost* a perfect replica of her daughter's endearing mannerisms. Except where Sefa's eyes were always warm with mirth, a void tunneled through her mother's. The rumors of her long-lost daughter appearing with the Nizahl Champion had unsettled her, and as he'd anticipated, Arin's careful questions rattled the last of her defenses. He finished dissecting the truth from her before his untouched tea went cold.

Arin crossed his legs. "Sayali—Sefa—spent much time in my company. What I know of her is this: she is entirely led by her sense of right and wrong, she hates to be watched while she eats, and the only obstacle interfering with her loyalty to her friend was her fear of you."

"I can assure you, sire, I would never—"

Counselor Rodan absorbed the impassive set of Arin's features.

Then, a marvel.

Like a canvas stripped of its paint, the panic drained out of Rodan. In its stead waited a chilling blankness. "Well, here we are."

Arin's lips curved in a humorless smile. He considered it a personal victory every time he convinced a beast to show him its teeth.

"You have a choice," Arin said. "A kinder choice than you deserve, but a fair one." He nodded to the twin glasses. "Drink from the glass on the right, and your atrocities die with you. Your wife will give you a decent burial, and your name will not be stricken from our records. My father and the other counselors will lay the royal wreath on your headstone. You will have a grave for Sayali to spit on."

Rodan licked his cracked lips, fixing on the poisoned glass. "And if I drink from the left?"

"A drink from the left is your death delayed. You will live—for a time. But when your death catches up to you, it will not be gentle. I am a creative man, Counselor, with limited opportunities to properly express it. Your killers will arrive with instructions to exact horrors upon you that your very worst nightmares cannot fathom. Those who bother to mourn you will remember you as a traitor and thief who stole from the Citadel and vanished. And when you eventually die, it will be with tears of relief on your lips. What remains of your body will be disassembled, burned, and cast into the river."

And since Rodan had paid him the courtesy of showing Arin his true face, Arin repaid him in kind. His voice hardened, crystallizing beneath the force of the violence clenched behind his teeth. "Personally, I hope you choose the second. Sayali may have haunted you, but I will hunt you. I will see to it that every shadow in your wake takes my form. Every sound you strain to hear in the night will whisper in my voice. I will feed you your death in doses and enjoy watching it rot you from the inside. The glass on the right, Rodan? That is your one chance at mercy."

Rodan stared at Arin, frozen.

After a lifetime, a laugh shuddered out of the frail High Counselor. "I warned them, you know. Even as a child, it was clear what you were. What you are."

This conversation had already taken longer than Arin allotted for, but he supposed he could indulge a dead man. "What am I, Counselor Rodan?"

The High Counselor regarded Arin as one might gaze upon ropes hanging from the gallows. The terror was the first genuine emotion Arin had seen from him tonight.

"Nizahl's doom," Rodan whispered. "The end of everything we have built."

The High Counselor gripped the poisoned glass. "My only regret is dying before I see my prophecy fulfilled."

Rodan drained the talwith in one pull, slamming the empty glass on the table. "But it won't be long now, Arin of Nizahl. Your legacy is death, and I am merely the first sacrifice."

Outside, the rain pummeled the side of the Citadel, pouring over the windows in a dull roar.

Mildly bemused, Arin arched a single brow. "Do not grant yourself such credit, Rodan. If death is my legacy, it was anointed long ago, by adversaries far more worthy than you."

Rodan went rigid before Arin could be regaled with further pontification. The High Counselor's chair screeched across the floor as he bent forward, gripping his stomach with a groan.

Reaching for the glass on the left, Arin observed the sweat pouring from Rodan's shiny head. Drops splattered on the table, which shook beneath the dying High Counselor's tremors.

Arin took a sip, greeting the burn of the talwith like an old friend. "The night of the Victor's Ball, I made a decision."

Five days ago, a wing of the Citadel burned.

Five days ago, the Malika of Jasad stepped forward in Sylvia the village apprentice's skin.

Five days ago, Arin strangled Sultana Vaida until blood broke in her eyes. One more second, and the ruler of Lukub would have been dead in his hands.

Control. For others, it was a pillar. Something steadfast to hold them up, to hide behind when the pressure became too much.

For Arin, control was a cliff.

One step too far, and everything that made him who he was shattered on the rocks below. One step too far, and a beast would rise from his remains. Arin had fought his entire life to remain on the right side of the cliff. To turn his sights away from the temptation of what waited just beyond the edge of his control.

White spittle foamed between the High Counselor's lips. Rodan toppled from his chair with a clatter, clipping his head against the table leg. His body seized in rapid tremors. A wet patch spread over his groin.

"My people will not suffer another war while the likes of you walk freely in the heart of the Citadel. While I live, those in Nizahl's court must prove every day that they deserve their place. Power hoarded where it doesn't belong is power borrowed, and I intend to collect on the debt."

In the wild, savagery was survival. It took only what it needed when it needed it and did not ask for more. But behind the walls of the Nizahl royal court, savagery was an art. As a baker might measure out ingredients for the perfect dish, so Arin measured each move he made. He bided his time. He gathered information.

And when he struck, he struck to kill.

CHAPTER TWO

ARIN

When the High Counselor finally lay still, Arin walked to the door and rapped twice. On cue, Vaun and Jeru slipped into Arin's chambers. The door quickly closed behind them.

Jeru took a step forward. Vaun matched it. Jeru bowed, and Vaun bowed lower. Their hostility toward each other had devolved into what Arin could reasonably call a children's game.

So long as they did what they were told, their tantrums hardly signified. Arin lifted an ink-spattered map he'd ruined in a burst of frustration last night and began to tear it into even strips.

"Arrange him in his bed within the Citadel. The swelling should disappear within the next hour. You will say he was unwell when he took to bed. He drank a tonic to help him sleep, sold to him by an unlicensed street merchant. Death came for him in the night. An unfortunate reaction to the benign tonic." Arin handed them an empty bottle the size of his thumb. "The tonic."

His guardsmen curled the High Counselor into as small a shape as they could manage. All the harm and pain this man had caused, and he was little more than gray flesh, stuffed into a sack of grain for inconspicuous transport to the other end of the Citadel.

"Go through his belongings before his wife does," Arin said. "Anything of note, anything he kept hidden, bring to me." Eyeing the droplets of sweat drying on Rodan's side of the table, Arin gestured to his ruined furniture. "Have someone see to replacing this table and rug."

The guards bowed. They turned to the door, Jeru reaching for the handle, when Arin spoke again. "I'd like you to stay a moment, Jeru."

His youngest guard swallowed. Vaun shouldered the sack and shut the door, leaving Jeru waiting stiffly in Arin's chambers.

Arin pushed aside the curtain separating the front room from the rest of his chambers. Jeru followed him into the cramped space, watching silently as Arin pulled out the keys for the thick steel door behind the curtain. The locks fell open one by one. At the very bottom, a tiny bottle slipped from where Arin had affixed it beneath the last lock, falling into Arin's waiting palm. If spilled, its contents would burn through skin and bone—the last defense against an intruder if they somehow managed to find all six of Arin's keys.

His father would call it excessive; Arin preferred thorough. It would be a much less onerous affair to identify the culprit if half their foot was melted off.

The chains fell from the door in a clanking symphony of metal.

They crossed Arin's bedroom, the large bed consuming the majority of a space originally intended as an antechamber. Arin had had his bed moved here from the main chambers shortly after Soraya's assassination attempt. He was at his most vulnerable asleep—it defied logic for his bed to be accessible behind one single door.

At the last door, Jeru waited while Arin repeated the process of opening it. An old exchange flitted through Arin's mind as he worked through the last of his wheel of locks.

"Caution is an area where I am prone to excess," Arin admitted. "My faith in my guards has taken a beating."

She grinned. "You? Paranoid? Steady me, sire, I may keel from my mount."

Arin didn't realize he'd gone still, key halfway inserted into the last chain, until Jeru cleared his throat. "My liege?"

The key cut into Arin's tightening fist.

Jeru wanted to talk about it. About *her*. Arin had caught him and Wes exchanging furious whispers outside his door the morning after the Victor's Ball. It seemed they had been too worked up to remember Arin's unusually sensitive hearing.

"The Heir does not need your coddling," Wes had snapped. "He can handle his own affairs."

"He has no one to confide in, Wes! No friends, no siblings." Jeru was the youngest guardsman at twenty-two, and he had been raised in a close-knit family that discussed their problems.

Wes, who was thrown into a military compound at fifteen and had no connection with his family beyond the percentage of his earnings he sent them once a month, snorted. "He has plenty of people to talk to."

"You know as well as I do the only person he ever let come close enough to confide in was Sylv—"

Arin had chosen that moment to interrupt, startling the guardsmen apart.

"Sire?" Jeru's tentative touch on Arin's shoulder jolted him back to the present, and Arin drew away from the guard, pushing open the door.

"By Hirun's glory…" Jeru whispered, raised brows threatening to disappear into his curly hair.

Maps covered every inch of the room. Precious maps, maps Arin traded from Orbanian khawaga, collected in Omalian markets and smoke-filled Lukubi gambling houses. Maps he'd been gifted as a child from diplomats visiting from Jasad.

On the ground, an entire armory lay organized in twenty-seven neat rows.

"Sire…" Jeru trailed off, raking over the hundreds of blades Arin had sharpened to a deadly gleam; the arrowheads he had stacked into bundles of fifteen, each triangular point perfectly matched to the one beside it. "Were the Citadel's blacksmiths unable to accommodate you?"

"They are working on another assignment for me," Arin said.

Arin could predict each revolution of Jeru's mind as he worked through the sight before him. It would have taken weeks to fix and organize this many weapons. Arin had done it in days, which meant Arin was not sleeping. In one room, Arin destroyed maps in a flare of temper. In another, he fixated on the precise edge of weapons older than the Heir himself.

Jeru opened his mouth. The question shaped on his tongue.

Before it could fall, Arin supplied one of his own.

"Where are Sefa and Marek?"

It worked. Chagrin flushed over Jeru, and he bowed his head, addressing his shoes. "No one has seen or heard from them, sire. I am still waiting on word from the soldiers I sent to Mahair, but I suspect they will return empty-handed."

Arin's palm flattened against the map to prevent it from curling. "Have I made myself less than clear, Jeru?"

"I'll find them, my liege, I swear it. I plan to extend the search into Essam Woods."

"You shouldn't have waited this long to extend your search."

The guard continued to study the ground. The stubborn angle of his chin reminded Arin of the day he'd found Jeru, head lowered in preparation for the executioner's sword.

Jeru and Wes believed Arin saved Jeru and began the nimwa system out of a desire to see the lower villages at least as well fed as they were well punished. A sign of Arin's mercy.

Perhaps. Arin liked to think he would have inevitably interceded to save Jeru from his idiocy, regardless of the potential he saw in the young man.

But in that moment, Arin saved Jeru because he saw something more rare than reckless courage and renegade justice: conviction.

"This week, the council will meet to discuss ending the conscription pardon on the lower villages."

Jeru went white.

"If they see fit to end it, young soldiers will flood our training compounds, and many will not come willingly."

"Sire—"

"Five days." The words were a condemnation. "Five days ago, I asked you to bring me Marek and Sefa. Each day the Jasad Queen evades our capture is another day closer to war. Five days, and you have nothing."

"Sylvia sent them—"

"*Sylvia* doesn't exist." Rage buckled in the void where Arin had thrust it, straining against its chains. "There is only the Jasad Heir." A dry curl of his lips. "The Jasad *Malika*."

Jeru swallowed. "My apologies. The Jasad Malika used her magic to send Sefa and Marek away during the Victor's Ball, sire. They could be anywhere."

The Jasad Malika. Oh, it was enough to make him wish he remembered how to laugh.

When Arin thought of the former Jasad Queen, a murky image of Malika Palia surfaced. He'd met the former Malika once as a child. She'd carried an air of authority that could not be taught, brimming with poise and power.

How could the Jasad Queen be a mouthy crook who would sooner wrestle a rabid bear than hold her temper for ten minutes? The Jasad Malika couldn't be vicious and loud and unreasonably confident in her comedic skills—

"Lukub has closed its borders." Arin spoke over his own thoughts, an action he was loath to have grown accustomed to. "Orban has collected dozens of Jasadis under the guise of other crimes and executed them. The khawaga have taken the crisis as an opportunity to pillage any village they see fit. Felix's raids…" Arin exhaled softly, collecting his fury before it could unravel. "That imbecile is indiscriminately raiding his own lower villages. The last report said seventy accused Jasadis had been murdered—by his own men or by the people around them, who fear potential Jasadi presence will invite the Omalian forces down upon them."

It hadn't come as a surprise to Arin, who had already taken steps to account for the recklessness of the other kingdoms. Nizahl soldiers were threaded throughout Essam, planted at strategic trade routes, and holding vigil from Nizahlan strongholds at the nexus of each kingdom. Not to find the Urabi, whose intelligence Arin valued much higher than that of his fellow rulers, but to ensure the other three kingdoms did not engage in any action too catastrophic for Arin to fix.

Little had he known catastrophe was the very first item on their agenda.

Jeru cleared his throat. "I will leave no stone unturned, sire."

"Stop turning stones," Arin said. "Start throwing them."

Before the guard could answer, Arin pushed out the words souring in his throat. "If the council votes for conscription, you will need to ride against any town that resists."

Jeru turned his eyes down, but not before Arin caught the spill of pain. Arin understood what he was asking of his guardsman. His family had lived in the lower villages for generations, only lifted out of poverty thanks to Jeru's position with the Heir. Arin's orders would see him enter his former home on royal horseback, a sword in hand, fighting against the people he'd almost died to protect.

"It is not certain yet," Arin added. If Arin had his way, it wouldn't even be close. "If I fail, can you be trusted in this charge?"

Thunder cracked outside as Arin waited. This was the moment he'd foreseen when he took a mud-streaked village boy and dressed him in the Citadel's uniform. A crossroads of duty.

When Jeru faced Arin again, his features were resolute. "I won't fail you again, my lord."

"Good." Arin turned to his maps. "Now get out."

The Citadel's library was useless.

With a groan, Arin flipped the cover of *The Marvelous and Macabre Histories of the Awaleen* shut and pushed it aside.

Piles of books lined the table, several left open on pages he had deemed worth a second glance. He rubbed the pads of his fingers, where dust had settled into his calluses. Hours and hours of poring over these books had so far yielded nothing but a faint headache and a guttering candle.

Arin set his elbows on the table and pressed his knuckles to his temples. His gloves were folded beside the latest four-hundred-page waste of his night. None of the books he spent his evenings leafing through discussed Jasad or the Jasad War beyond a few paltry, self-censoring lines.

He had also spent hours searching for verified accounts of magic-madness over the last several centuries. When it became a recognized affliction, how it presented in different kinds of magic, how quickly it accelerated. And once again—nothing.

Arin stood, scraping his chair back, and picked up the book to return to its shelf. It would serve a better purpose as kindling for his hearth. He studied the rest of the row, frown deepening into a scowl. So many spines were cracked with age, lines running over the leather like rings around a tree. How could such a wealth of information exist at his fingertips, but so much of it contain nothing of actual use?

Returning to his seat, Arin poured another glass of talwith, the thud of the bottle echoing in the spacious library. When he flipped the cover for the next book, Arin stopped short.

The Slow Death of Rovial: A History of Magic-Madness Then and Since.

Arin set aside his glass, drawing the book toward him. It sounded entirely too good to be true. There were only fifty pages in the entire text, and all of them were in Resar.

By the time Arin finished reading, black smoke curled from the candle by his elbow. Long shadows slipped across the walls, trailing over the shelves like curious ghosts. Dust motes swirled above the pools of moonlight spilling through the open window.

Arin wished he knew the author. The person responsible for a work of such scholarship deserved recognition—they deserved a name. They had managed to condense a lifetime of study into a text a fifth the size of the intellectually destitute tomes Arin had been reading all week.

He flipped through his notes, cross-checking them against the text to make sure he'd captured the right details.

Every hundred years, one notable case of magic-madness emerges. Every time, in every century, it was a Jasadi whose magic would drive them to madness.

The author had tracked the cases over the last five thousand years. The earlier legends were recorded through carvings in Essam's trees, and some of the pages were sparse where a particular story had been passed down orally in lower villages, since the communities were either not literate or avoided keeping records in fear of the higher courts.

The first known case after Rovial was a girl named Lena. A welder's daughter who loved to chase the cats around her village until she turned thirteen, when they found Lena covered in scratches after hanging every cat in the village from her favorite tree. When they located the remains of the woman who tried to save the cats, her body had been turned inside out. The next morning, they caught Lena in the middle of skinning the dogs. The villagers killed her and burned her body.

The following century, a nineteen-year-old named Rath was imprisoned for putting a horde of Ruby Hounds under his thrall and compelling them to slaughter everyone in the Ivory Palace. The Sultana managed to regain control of her Hounds eventually, but it stood as one of the largest massacres to ever occur in a royal court.

They only managed to keep Rath imprisoned for two hours—his magic, which should have been temporarily drained from such an expenditure, tore apart the guards. It also wound up destroying the entire dungeon and burying Rath beneath the debris.

The stories continued, each more gruesome than the next. Only three variables remained constant: the magic-mad Jasadis were typically young when they were executed, they carried a staggeringly high quantity of magic, and nobody seemed to notice the signs of their sanity slipping away until it was too late.

Two of them, three hundred years apart, had disappeared into the Mirayah, never to be seen again. Arin had needed to stop and reference a different text when he saw the long-forgotten name. The Mirayah was a void for magical monstrosities—a shifting realm buried in Essam where the rules of magic did not apply, where beasts fled after the purge of Essam and escaped criminals sought refuge. Few who found the Mirayah were ever seen again. After magic had passed from the kingdoms, it seemed reasonable to assume the Mirayah had disappeared along with it.

Arin rubbed his eyes and stood, stretching his bones until they popped. He moved to the only window in the library. He took a deep breath, filling his chest with fresh air, and forced his circling thoughts to settle.

Beyond the three towering iron gates protecting the Citadel, the wilderness of Essam Woods waited with a predatory anticipation. Magic may have run dry in the rest of the kingdoms, but Essam... Essam had played host to countless wars between the Awaleen. To bloodshed and magical atrocities Arin's generous imagination could never stretch far enough to accommodate. If the Mirayah had existed, it wouldn't have faded like the magic of Lukub, Orban, and Omal. It would not have weakened like Jasad's.

Like a parasite, the Mirayah would sustain itself on the bleeding magic of the woods. It would be the eyes of Essam, staring back at

Arin every night as he fought not to saddle his horse and ride into its waiting teeth. Its voice, whispering blood-tipped promises in his ear.

Arin couldn't shake the feeling that if he struck out on his own, he'd find her.

Arin exhaled harshly, his breath misting the window. He hated this—hated fighting a force that could not be reasoned with, that refused to surrender any ground in Arin's mind. He would give anything to reach inside his chest and tear out the rot of her. To close his eyes without seeing her face.

Unusual cruelty is your specialty, she had said once, her tone accusatory and full of spite. And maybe she was right, but one thing Arin knew: He would never have done this to her. He would never have let her step toward this precipice with a lie wrapped around her neck. He would never have watched her willingly drop herself over the edge.

Arin took a handkerchief and wiped his breath from the window. Easier for the woods to keep watch.

Lighting another candle, Arin opened the book again.

CHAPTER THREE

SYLVIA

Children's laughter skittered in the dark.

Ugh. More brats. Didn't the keep have enough mouths to feed already? Raya insisted on taking in every dusty, nose-picking little orphan Mahair coughed out. There were more cows than people in this Omalian village; where did she keep finding these children? Under a hat?

A voice broke through the chatter, soft and melodious. Sefa?

In the emptiness, Sefa's name sparked like flint skating across stone.

This woman wasn't Sefa. She couldn't be. I sent Sefa away.

How did I send Sefa away?

"Many, many years ago, there once lived a brave and honorable Awal. His name was Rovial, and he was the kindest of all the Awaleen. Do we remember how many Awaleen there were?" the voice that wasn't Sefa's said.

"Four!"

"Five!"

"Minna wins! The four Awaleen of our earth were Dania, Rovial, Kapastra, and Baira. Before there was us, there was them. Kapastra became the mother of Omal, known for her terrifying rochelyas and glorious weather magic. Baira was the beacon of beauty, and she built Lukub in her image. Battle beat in Dania's bones, and she sang its bloody song through Orban. But Rovial was different than his siblings. He wasn't searching for a place he could shape to mirror his own spirit. More than anything, Rovial wanted the land to speak to him in its own language. He wandered for years and years, looking for such a land. All his siblings found his plan ridiculous, but Rovial wouldn't give up. Some say Rovial's heart was molded from the lights that hang in the night sky, and it lit a path only he could see."

My fingers twitched. *Oh.* I had fingers.

"One day, Rovial grew weary from his travels. He found a sturdy tree to rest beneath for the night."

A date tree. The shape sprouted in my head. I could almost feel the rough bark scratching my palms. Suddenly, it wasn't a strange voice telling the story, but Hanim's.

No. Hanim was dead. I killed her twice.

Tension knotted between my shoulder blades. The darkness rippled.

"Rovial slept deeply and soundly. The best sleep of his whole immortal life. When he woke, a rabbit stood near his head. It was chewing on a fallen date and watching him. He stroked its ears and marveled at its tranquility. The air filled his chest with new life. He ate from the tree that had watched over him through the night. 'This land is for me, and I am for this land,' he said. But the first problem appeared when he tried to find water to wash down his date. The river cut too far north of the land, and the seawater sweeping the other shore couldn't be swallowed. So Rovial walked until he found the nearest spot where Hirun flows and pulled it south, stretching the river until it ran all the way down to Janub Aya. This way, the people of his land would never need to travel too far for water."

Water. I needed water. My mouth tasted awful. I probed the darkness for a way out, but it held firm.

"That land, Rovial's land, is our true home. It was peaceful before they burned it to ash."

"Is there anything left?" a child's voice asked.

"We are what's left of Jasad."

I am what remains.

My eyes flew open. I was moving before my body remembered how.

I hit the ground in a crouch. A group of children sitting in a circle shrieked, rushing to their feet and stampeding to the door. The young woman at the front froze, watching me with wide eyes. I reached for the knife in my boot without thinking. No boot. They'd taken my clothes. My knives. A simple brown dress covered my body.

With the attention I wasn't using to take stock of my surroundings, I assessed the willowy stranger. She couldn't weigh more than my left leg. Black hair fell in a frizzy curtain around her pale, round face. Bright brown eyes roved over me with too much fascination and not nearly enough caution. My fists would be more than enough to get her out of my way.

"I can't believe it. You woke up. We were so afraid you wouldn't. They had to put more than a dozen arrows of sim siya in your body before your magic stopped. A normal person just needs one." She paused. "I'm Omaima, by the way. You can call me Maia. If you want."

Had she just offered me her nickname in the same sentence she described tranquilizing me like a feral animal?

"Where am I?" I ground out.

If possible, the girl's eyes grew rounder. "You don't remember?"

I took a step toward her and nearly crumpled. Maia backed to the door, fumbling for the handle. My legs—they were shaking. My hands, my jaw. A clacking sound scraped in my ears, and I recognized it as my teeth knocking against one another.

I reached for my legs—and stopped short.

My wrists were bare. Not a single remanent of the cuffs I'd worn almost my entire life showed itself on my skin.

The world bucked and heaved as I struggled to understand.

I remembered kneeling before Rawain to plead for Sefa and Marek's lives. My cuffs falling to my feet when I rose, declaring my true name. The kitmer borne of my magic roaring in the center of the Citadel's ballroom and the entire wing of the castle crashing around us. The sting of arrows dissolving into my skin and the strange faces surrounding me as the world faded to black. Had it all been real?

"Malika Essiya."

I snapped to attention as a woman appeared in the spot Maia had occupied. The girl must have taken advantage of my stupor to fetch her. The newcomer's hair was gathered in a severe bun, and a series of white scars forked through the brown skin of her throat. A dagger the length of my forearm dangled from the belt at her waist. The muscles on her arms bulged as she crossed them over her chest.

My fists would not be enough against this one.

"You're one of the Urabi," I said accusingly, scouring the room for anything I could use to protect myself. If I could get her close, maybe I could wrestle the dagger from her.

"I am. My name is Namsa. It is a pleasure to meet you, Malika Essiya."

I flinched. She kept calling me that, and my nerves were too raw to tolerate the added scrape of the title.

"You drugged and abducted me from the Victor's Ball."

"We see it as drugged and rescued."

"Oh, well if *you* see it that way." I balled my fists. "Let me leave."

"I'm afraid that's not possible." Namsa didn't bother with the pretense of regret. She stayed cool in the face of my unraveling temper. "Your safety is our highest priority."

My nostrils flared. She had unwittingly stomped right on one of the few threats someone could make to drive me straight out of my sanity. The last time I had felt trapped, I fled into Essam and dangled my bleeding body over the rocky bank of a river. The time before that, I'd left behind a corpse.

"Get out of my way." My muscles, sore from disuse, bunched in preparation.

She set her feet. "Mawlati—"

I swung, fist colliding squarely with her right eye socket. An odd whine slipped from her mouth before she raised her arm to block my next blow.

She defended against each blow I tried to strike, not ceding a single inch. I couldn't get close enough to reach for the dagger, nor could I maneuver around her to the door.

It took me longer than it should have to notice she hadn't raised a hand against me once.

"Fight back!" I snapped. "What game is this?"

Namsa wiped the blood under her nose. "We aren't in the habit of striking our leaders here, Mawlati."

"Stop calling me that!" I shoved her shoulders. She went back on her heels, but again, her arms remained poised only to defend.

The resigned set of her jaw, the weary pull of her brow. I stopped in my tracks, furling and unfurling my stinging knuckles.

She wouldn't fight me. No matter how hard I hit or for how long, she wouldn't strike me back.

In the realization, I heard the ghost of my own voice, teasing and inquisitive.

"Do you train the new recruits yourself?"

Arin sighed. "Rarely. They are too frightened of me. They will simply obey."

"Is obedience not what a Commander should seek?"

"Obedience should be conscious, not instinctual."

Something vast and sickening cracked open inside me.

Arin.

I staggered back, catching the edge of a dresser.

My mind curled into itself, shutting off the memory before it could spawn more. I couldn't think about him. I couldn't remember the way he'd looked at me before my cuffs fell away—the depths of the betrayal reflected in the eyes that only moments before had been gazing into mine as though they might never be convinced to look away.

"Are you all right?" Namsa lowered her arms, taking a cautious step in my direction.

A mistake.

I hit her in the stomach and shoved her to the side as hard as I could. Without waiting to see where she landed, I sprinted toward the door.

Pretty as Arin's notions of honor and responsibility were, they were Arin's alone.

My rules were simpler: survive, survive, and survive. Feel guilty about the means later.

A grip on my hair reeled me backward just as I crossed the threshold, dragging me into the room by my curls.

Namsa shoved me to the ground, releasing her absurdly tight grip on my hair. She scowled down at me, her nose a mess of clotted blood, twin streams running over her lips and chin.

"Since we're playing dirty," she said, and proceeded to kick me in the stomach like my organs had done her a personal disservice. She did it without fanfare, without even pulling her leg back far enough to give me warning.

Pain erupted in my middle. I gasped, curling around my stomach and coughing violently.

"I think you ruptured something," I choked out.

The coughs turned into ugly hacks. Concern hedged out Namsa's wariness, and she knelt by my side.

Baira's blessed hair, it wasn't fun if it was this easy.

I swiped Namsa's legs out from under her and rolled, shoving my knee against the bone between her breasts. "Are all Urabi this gullible, or did they send me the exception?" I snarled.

Namsa struggled against my knee, but I held firm. Even weakened from days of sleep, I could execute this hold without trouble. Three different guards tasked with protecting the Nizahl Heir had forced me to perfect it or risk getting flung into the wall.

The facade of deference vanished as Namsa spat, "The only simple-minded thing any of us have done is trust you. Doing so killed my uncle, and by Rovial, it will be the death of us all."

I raised my arm, planning to deliver a hit that would rearrange the inside of this Jasadi's skull.

Wait. "Your uncle?"

"Of course you wouldn't remember him. Just another servant to you, wasn't he? He spent his whole life mourning you, and you *killed him*." Rage seemed to build into an inferno within Namsa. The stone features burned away, revealing a depth of pain that froze me in my tracks—and a face that, but for a few adjustments, was unmistakably inspired by someone else's.

My breath stuttered. "Dawoud."

"You don't deserve to speak his name!" Namsa bucked. Shock had loosened my limbs, and I didn't resist when she hurled me to the side. My head hit the dresser, sending a clay ula tipping to the side. Water splashed over my legs.

I barely noticed. I was standing in the middle of Dar al Mansi, wading through monsters and the bones of my people. Al Anqa'a had its claws in my clothes, beating its powerful wings against the barrier I'd erected in the sky. Below, Dawoud was smiling at me with resigned eyes. He lifted the knife. Turned it toward his chest.

From the sky, I had screamed.

Namsa rolled to her feet. Blood smeared her torn bottom lip. The beginning of a truly terrible bruise bloomed around her right eye, purpling her brown skin.

"I didn't kill him." My voice emerged like a burr from a dog's paw. Painfully, scraping skin along the way. "I swear I didn't. I wanted to leave Dar al Mansi with him."

My gaze went to my hands, as though under close examination they would turn red, glistening with the blood of the man who raised me when a dead father couldn't. When a living grandfather handled me at arm's length. A man who devoted his life and loyalty to Jasad and its Heir.

An Heir he'd believed to be dead after she spent years hiding in an Omalian village, leaving him and the rest of Jasad to rot in a well of unwanted memories.

"Don't lie to me. You handed his body to a Nizahl guardsman. You called him a trophy," Namsa hurled out. "He spent years in a Nizahl dungeon because he served your family. Served *you*."

Frustration sparked beneath the weight pressing onto my chest. Dawoud had been physically weakened, but Nizahl hadn't stolen his spirit. Namsa described him as one might a newborn calf, stumbling in the direction of its owner's prod. "He chose to serve the royal family. He chose to turn the dagger on himself in Dar al Mansi. He was one of the bravest men I knew. Dawoud was many things in his life, but he was never some bumbling victim of circumstance."

Namsa went still. I realized what I'd revealed a second too late. "What do you mean, he turned the dagger on himself?"

I clenched my teeth, the tension ricocheting through my jaw. Would Dawoud have wanted his niece to know the truth?

The truth...another of Arin's pretty notions. To him, the truth was absolute. A measurable quantity with a beginning and an end. He accepted nothing short of it, and offered the same in return.

I held the notion of truth in little esteem. For my entire life, I had bent and broken it in more ways than I could count. Truth was little more than clay, molded and reshaped in the hands it passed through.

"Please," Namsa whispered. The Jasadi I'd tossed around the room slid to the floor. "I ask for your honesty. What happened to my uncle?"

I can't, I almost said. *My memories are not to be trusted.*

But she had asked for my honesty, not the truth.

"They wanted trophies of our kills." I rubbed my arms. "Three trophies from three monsters."

I told her everything about the second trial of the Alcalah. Dar al Mansi and Al Anqa'a, how hard I tried to convince Dawoud to run while he still could. How he had stayed to fight with me, knowing it would get him killed.

"Supreme Rawain sent him to test me. He suspected I might be Jasadi, but I wouldn't have—I swear on Sirauk, I would never have hurt Dawoud."

I didn't mention how I had destroyed my room in the Omalian palace after the trial. Magic ablaze, rare tears dripping from my chin. And I certainly didn't mention that the person who held me as I wept, who brought me back to reason, was the man whose father sent Dawoud to his death.

"Oh" was all Namsa said. She stared at a spot behind my shoulder. I took the opportunity to study her, searching for Dawoud in more than her appearance. Dawoud's valiance, his bravery. Those were not traits I associated with someone willing to work under the Urabi. Were they forcing her? Holding some threat over her head?

"You thought I killed your uncle, and you were still willing to serve me."

Namsa's eyes snapped back to mine. "Without question."

Tension feathered along my neck. They knew I had acted as Nizahl's Champion. They knew I had been helping the Heir lure them into his trap. What could I possibly represent to them to overcome such betrayal? It couldn't be just a royal name.

Dawoud had died for my family—for me. The least I could do was give his niece a chance to explain before I started swinging again.

I scrubbed my face. "What do you want from me?"

Namsa stood, wiping her cheeks. Blood spatters marred the front of her tunic. "Let me show you."

Before we'd moved a foot to the door, Namsa raked a disapproving glance over my bedraggled sleeping gown and shook her head. "You need to change first. Our seamstress left you clothes in the wardrobe. She took your measurements while you slept."

I went rigid. "Is she the one who undressed me?"

There were few touches I tolerated, and even fewer I welcomed. A stranger touching me in my sleep, even if just to take my measurements, raised every hair on the back of my neck.

Namsa read the murder on my face and quickly clarified, "Not the way you're thinking. She doesn't have to touch someone to dress or measure them. She looked at you for two minutes and walked out."

My muscles relaxed. Magic. It had been so long since I was around other Jasadis that I'd forgotten how differently life operated with the use of our powers.

Namsa stepped outside while I tossed through the clothes. I picked up a pair of pants and frowned. The material glided between my fingers, much softer than what I would have expected. Shouldn't they be preserving their magic for more important uses?

Shaking my head, I pulled on the pants and slipped my arms through the billowing sleeves of a black abaya. Teta Palia had always worn hers loose, but I cinched the fabric belt securely under my ribs.

Thumbing the embroidered edges, I thought of the ratty cloak I'd left in the Citadel. The poor thing had been practically begging to die for years, but it was the first garment I'd ever bought for myself in Mahair. The cloak had seen me through five years in the village and six weeks of underground training for the Alcalah. Through kingdoms and murders and agonized confessions.

I would never wear it again.

I would never be just Sylvia again.

Swallowing past the lump in my throat, I turned my attention to a problem I could solve. My curls, for one. I negotiated the biggest knots apart as I parted my hair into three and wove the strands into as tight a braid as I could bear.

Satisfied, I lowered my hands—and paused.

A gold vein ran from the bone at my wrist into my palm.

I wiped my hand on my leg and checked again. Still there. What in the Sirauk-damned waters was *this*? Some colorful scarring from the cuffs?

I curled my fingers over the inexplicable gold vein. A deep foreboding settled in my belly.

I had unfettered access to my magic.

It had taken approximately two seconds for my freed magic to cause irreparable damage. I could still remember how light and free I'd felt with the magic flowing through me, how inconsequential the chaos I'd unleashed had seemed. The boulder hurling toward Sefa and Marek, who in the melee had escaped the clutches of the Nizahl soldiers trying to haul them to prison.

My head snapped back to the mirror, reflecting my widening eyes.

Dania's bloody axe, where had I sent Sefa and Marek?

The door cracked open. Namsa scanned over my outfit without much interest. "Shall we? Many people are eager to meet you." She pivoted before I could reply, striding in the other direction. I shoved my feet into the slippers she'd left by the door and hurried after her.

Sefa and Marek were in Mahair. They had to be. Where else would my magic have sent them? I had never seen where they lived in Nizahl—or in Sefa's case, Nizahl and Lukub—which meant the only home my magic knew for them was Omal.

They were fine. They had to be fine, because I could not think through any possibility where they were not.

"I don't understand," I said, frustrated. "Why would they be eager to meet me? They should be eager to dangle me over a den of hungry lions. Eager to run a sword through my belly and roast me over an open flame. Eager to—"

"Nobody is planning to harm you, Mawlati. We need you."

"For what?"

She sighed and sealed her lips into an unimpressed line.

Not very forthcoming, was she? I made a note to corner the tiny woman from earlier. She had the countenance of someone who'd tell me what I wanted to know without a fuss.

The hall narrowed the farther we walked, until Namsa had to walk slightly behind me to fit. The top of my head brushed the roof, sending pebbles tumbling into my hair. I struggled to identify anything I could place: a smell, a sound, even the color of the dirt. But the odor tickling my nose wasn't one I recognized. Not the mildew or mold found near the river, but something sweeter. Less pungent.

My head sent another shower of pebbles crumbling from the soft stone ceiling. Namsa glanced up with a frown. "Apologies. You're taller than most."

I shrugged. My height served me too well to quibble about its inconveniences. "Are we underground?"

"Not quite."

I pressed my tongue against the point of my sharpest tooth, resisting the urge to throttle the woman. Unlike my body, my patience was famously short.

Fortunately for her health, she kept speaking. "The Silver Serpent doesn't know the truth. We aren't killers, and we only abduct those who give us no other alternative. As much as we wish it were otherwise, it is not always possible to win compliance from those comfortable in their secrecy or who believe our cause is doomed. We bring them back here. They meet the others and learn of our plans. They see that Jasad is not gone. Its spirit still fights, and so must we. Once they understand, we send them back. There are some who prefer to remain here, and those are the individuals flagged by the Nizahl soldiers. The rest reintegrate quietly, working for us from the inside."

"They can't return." I twisted, blocking her path. "Once you take them, they become targets. Ar—the Nizahl Heir hunts you and the Mufsids through the people you take." He had recruited me as his Champion for the express purpose of luring the groups close.

"We do not send them back to the same place. They are scattered across courts and kingdoms."

"So you strip them of their homes and force them to spy for you?"

"*Jasad* is their home," Namsa said, anger finally bleeding into her tone. "As it is yours. They are glad to serve it."

The implication couldn't be clearer: *They are glad to serve. Why aren't you?*

Sultana Vaida's wall of suspected Nizahlan spies flashed through my mind. I had thought no one could possibly rival Arin in paranoia until I met her. If she knew the Urabi were taking our people from Lukub and bringing them back as spies, she would never sleep again.

Namsa moved around me, rounding the bend at an irritated clip. For someone who brought me here as a captive, she was certainly self-righteous.

The hallway ended, opening into a cavernous space vibrating with hundreds of voices.

I stopped walking. An unfamiliar panic surged through me, catching me off guard.

How many people were out there? Did Namsa say?

I braced my shoulder against the wall. I'd been chased by mutated dogs without experiencing this much panic, and certainly not this fast.

I slid my hand over my heart, counting out the beats.

One, two. I'm alive.

Three, four. I'm safe.

Five, six. I won't let them catch me.

Nothing happened. My heart continued to beat wildly beneath my palm, heedless of the mantra I'd recited to myself for years.

And why not? It wasn't true anymore. I was alive, but I wasn't safe. I was alive, but I—Essiya—had finally been caught.

"Mawlati?" Namsa reappeared in front of me. I dropped my hand from my heart and fixed on the little divot in her right brow, its arch clearly sharpened by an expert thread.

I needed a new way to calm myself down, and fast.

"If you stop calling me that," I ground out, "then I'll walk out with you."

Namsa considered. "Come along, Essiya."

My stomach rolled unpleasantly, and I almost recanted. *Essiya* came with its own knives.

I shuffled out behind Namsa, flinching as bright light replaced the gloom of the hall. I raised a hand to shield my eyes—and immediately stepped back.

The cacophony of voices quieted as hundreds of people turned at our entrance.

More Jasadis stared at me than I had seen in one room since I was a child. Which…there were *children* here. Not just the handful from my room, but dozens of them, toddlers and infants and sullen adolescents. Generations of Jasadis. Generations of magic.

Namsa gestured at the cavernous space around us. Alabaster stone walls rose into a high peak, the bumpy pattern of the pale rock face reminding me of freshly kneaded bread. Blankets covered the ground, and colorful hand-stitched cushions were strewn around low-rising wooden tables.

"Welcome to the Gibal."

Maia waved shyly from behind a makeshift stone counter.

"We still don't know for certain she's the Heir." A girl roughly my age approached us alongside an older man. "Just because an insane Mufsid tried to kill her? It proves nothing."

The Mufsids had hunted me alongside the Urabi, but the Mufsid the girl meant could only be Soraya. My former attendant who killed my mother and conspired with the rest of the Mufsids to overthrow Usr Jasad. Who hated my family enough to defect from the Mufsids and poison me during the third trial in a desperate effort to kill me before either the Mufsids or Urabi could put me on the throne of Jasad.

"Enough, Kawsar. I tire of this conversation. The Mufsid who tried to kill her knew her family—she worked in the palace. Soraya served the royal family and helped orchestrate the Blood Summit. Besides, Essiya is not the Heir." The gravelly voiced older man stopped a few inches away, peering down at me with kind brown eyes. "She is the Malika."

A ripple ran through the room. The intrigue in their eyes, the tentative hope... it hit me harder than any anger could.

I can't do this. I can't do this.

"Malika Essiya," Namsa affirmed. She shot an apologetic glance when I grimaced.

The man put a hand to his slim chest. "My name is Lateef, Mawlati. We are so grateful to have you here."

Lateef knelt. My hand went to a dagger that wasn't there, but he didn't swipe my feet out from under me or stab at my tendons. He simply knelt.

One by one, the others joined him on the ground. I balked at the sea of bowed heads, my stomach churning. After a minute, Kawsar huffed and joined the others.

Every bone in my body screamed at me to run. Blow a hole through the side of this mountain and crawl to freedom through the debris. I didn't deserve reverence. I was not a leader of kingdoms. I was barely a leader of *me*.

Namsa knelt last. My chest contracted, and I struggled to draw air. Rovial's tainted tomb, I was about to throw up on all their bowed heads.

"Welcome home, Malika Essiya," Namsa said.

I wasn't home. I didn't know these people, and they didn't know me.

My heart beat faster, faster, diverting the route of every drop of blood in my body to sustain its speed. My airways constricted, forcing me to breathe in shallow sips. Heat gathered at the back of my neck, the most damning warning signal.

I couldn't breathe. I couldn't breathe, and they wouldn't let me go, and they were looking at me like I was the answer to their problems, like fate had finally paid them a favor.

My grandparents betrayed the Urabi. I had little doubt most of the people before me were farmers and merchants from the southern wilayahs, Jasadis whose magic had been secretly mined for decades to satisfy the greed of the northern wilayahs. The Mufsids had reaped the reward of my grandparents' atrocities—*their* desire to restore me to the throne, I understood. I couldn't fathom why the Urabi wanted to place a crown in my hands.

I didn't need Hanim's voice to remind me of the colossal failure I represented to these people. The failure I had made of myself.

The thought of proving Hanim right sobered me. The exiled and disgraced Qayida of Jasad had tried to mold a warrior, a woman fit to fight for a throne. For five years, I had endured her expectations. Her punishments when I fell short. Killing her had freed me of her physical presence, but I had carried the rot of her voice, her insidious influence, for years.

I knotted my hand above my heart. Sweat damped the fabric clutched in my palm.

Malika Essiya.

I was not a natural leader. I would have to fight my instincts every step of the way. I would fail again and again, and the cost of my failure wouldn't be more scars on my back. The cost of my failure would be the lives kneeling before me. The lives waiting in other kingdoms, their magic hidden and their destiny unknown.

I had understood the consequence of my decision the night of the Victor's Ball.

When I gave Rawain my true name, I chose Jasad. I chose to give everything I could, no matter how imperfect the offering or how shaky the hands holding it.

There was nowhere left to run. Either Jasad would rise in victory, or we would all burn with it.

"Thank you." Though I barely spoke above a murmur, it echoed across the vast room. "Thank you for letting me come home."

CHAPTER FOUR

SYLVIA

As soon as she shoved a platter of food into my hands, Namsa abandoned me in the dining hall.

I watched her depart, resisting the urge to trail after her like a lost child. How bad would it look if I took my meal to my room?

I chanced a look around the tables, shoulders hiked up to my ears.

Rovial's tainted tomb, what if someone wanted to have a conversation?

Longing for Marek and Sefa weakened my knees. For five years, they had been my safe landing. They had offered a space where I could rest my bones and breathe, and it took me far too long to appreciate how rare a thing it was to simply *be*.

I could still scarcely comprehend how quickly everything had changed. It felt like minutes had passed since I danced at the Victor's Ball, not six days.

Maia appeared at my side. She had gathered her formidably long hair into a ponytail. "Mawlati, would you like to join me outside to finish our supper?" She held a large plate, bouncing from foot to foot. At my suspicious squint, she tipped her head in the direction of the observers. "Where we can perhaps enjoy a bit of solitude?"

"Yes," I said, too quickly. I followed her through a narrow doorway carved into the right side of the dining hall. As soon as we ducked through the opening, a wave of noise hit our backs.

I snorted. At least they waited until I left before unleashing the gossip.

I kept pace with Maia easily, eyeing the uneven stone beneath our feet. "How are we going outside? I thought we were inside a mountain."

"We are. There are passageways here that open into Essam Woods. But we also have an outdoor area for trainings and celebrations behind the mountain."

The mountain had passages into Essam Woods. The temptation hiked again, a battering ram at my feet urging them to leave this place and find Sefa and Marek. I weathered the hits, wincing, until they faded. It wouldn't be the last time the urge to escape swept me, but I had no intention of indulging it unless the Urabi left me no choice.

Still, I made note of the information. Maia shouldn't have shared it with me.

We rounded the corner, and the ground grew even bumpier. "Couldn't someone on the other side see us?"

The passage ended at a solid iron door, nearly invisible in the gloom. The familiarity of its design caught me off guard. I had seen the same plaited pattern on the doors in the underground complex where I'd trained for the Alcalah.

Maia pressed her hand to the metal and murmured under her breath. A silver-and-gold glow lit the outline of the door, identical to the colors swirling inside Maia's eyes.

I watched her longer than I should have. It would take a while before the sight of magic stopped slamming terror into my bones. I had not knowingly encountered Jasadis while living in Mahair; the last person who had openly used magic around me was a Mufsid. Even my own magic had been hidden from me, suppressed by my cuffs. Learning how to draw it out had been a battle. The Urabi exercised their magic casually, with as much forethought as they probably gave to breathing, and I couldn't help but be a little envious.

Maia kicked the door, sending it creaking open.

"After you, Mawlati."

As a rule, I preferred not to be the first to walk through an unknown entrance. Fortunately for Maia, her bouncing was giving me a headache. Any threat on the other side of the door couldn't be more frustrating than watching her roll from her heel to her toe again and again.

The smell slapped me as soon as I stepped outside. Salt and fresh rain.

Wind stung my cheeks. I cradled my plate to my chest, shielding it with an arm. Endless skies moved in shifting colors above us. Heavy clouds hung close enough to touch, swirling like warm breath exhaled on a winter day. Streaks of red and orange seared the horizon, glimmering across the rippling surface of the—

No. It couldn't be.

Pebbles rolled beneath my feet as I lurched forward, my embarrassing gasp stolen out of my mouth by the wind.

"Careful, Mawlati," Maia murmured, but I ignored her.

The breeze raked freezing fingers through my hair, whipping it away from my neck. My feet carried me to the edge of the cliff, determined to confirm what my mind refused to believe.

Over the side raged the sea of a hundred names; the sea few had dared cross the mountains to explore and fewer still had survived the journey.

I couldn't believe it. It had been a century since anyone had laid eyes on the sea beyond the mountains. Even when every kingdom had had its magic, it was widely considered an act of lunacy to undertake the journey to Suhna Sea. Why bother, when you could access it through any of the wilayahs in southern Jasad? The lower wilayahs generated half their income from those visitors. Pay a fee to pass through the Jasad fortress and visit the sea, or potentially go through the mountains and pay with your life.

Blue stretched as far as the eye could see. Waves dappled in the receding orange of the setting sun crashed against the side of the mountain, spraying foam dozens of feet into the air. An ancient force colliding against an ancient fixture in a rhythm as old as time itself.

"No one can see us here but the skies and the sea," Maia said. I jerked, nearly upending my plate over the cliff. What kind of shoes did this girl have that she moved without making a single sound?

Oblivious, Maia continued, "I like to come out here at night. Namsa thinks it's dangerous, but the stars are always bright enough to see the edge. We practice the children's magic over there. It looks like a hole, but the dark space is a flat canyon between our mountain and the next one."

I barely heard her. My fingers had gone cold and numb around the plate.

I was in the mountains. Miles and miles away from everything and everyone I knew.

I tasted salt on my lips and knew it was not seawater.

"I will be inside if you need me." Maia's voice softened. Without waiting for acknowledgment, she retreated on her ghostly feet.

The door shut behind her, and I released a stuttering breath. The waves splashed noisily below, the reflection of the crescent moon the only point of illumination left in the dark sea.

I lowered myself to a seat, wincing at the damp stone digging into my skin. For all the weight piling in my chest, my head felt clear for the first time in years. Clear and eerily quiet. Before the Victor's Ball, even when Hanim's voice had been silent, I'd always known it was there. Lurking in wait, biding its time. But I couldn't sense it anymore—that throb of her disapproval and loathing creasing my every thought.

I was finally alone. Completely alone, just like I had always wanted.

With the sea as my only witness, I eased my grip around the memories rattling in the back of my mind.

Six days ago, Arin discovered my true identity. The horror on his face...I would never forget how he looked when he saw my cuffs and heard Rawain call me Essiya. In one stroke, hundreds of my lies had imploded between us.

He had covered his face before my magic ruptured, the fig necklace swinging around his neck, the only spot of bright color on the Commander's stiff and formal ensemble. Gifting it to him, watching him smile while he slipped it around his neck, had healed one of the many fractures in the tattered thing masquerading as my heart. To know he would see it as just another lie...

One of my slippers fell from my foot, disappearing into the undulating waves below me.

He was always my enemy. When he turned his horse around in Lukub to heal me after Soraya put her knife in my chest. When he cradled my tearstained face and told me to run. When he kis—

Enough.

I forced myself to think of the many valid reasons the Urabi despised Arin. He had no friends, no confidants. He handled people like lines on his maps. Shifting them subtly, strategically, without giving them the chance to feel the ground moving beneath their feet. His father's charm was natural; Arin's was carefully cultivated. Logic led his life, leaving emotion to fester at the sidelines. Even to his own people, he was an enigma. A dangerous one. Supreme Rawain could tear apart kingdoms, but Arin could destroy worlds.

As long as magic was his enemy, so was I.

Water misted across the shore as a wave barreled into the mountain.

How unbearably pathetic that the person whose advice I trusted most, whose counsel I wanted so badly in that moment, was the same one preparing to kill me.

A tear slid from the corner of my unblinking eye. I let it roll to my chin before catching it with my thumb. Raising my hand to blot out the moon, I studied the droplet.

The first and final tear I planned to shed for Arin of Nizahl.

Once I had collected myself and scarfed the cold and seawater-sprayed food on my plate, I went back inside to find Namsa. Most of the dining hall had emptied out, and I tried to smile at the remaining individuals who openly stared as I walked past. What a reversal of fate, that someone staring at me should be met with a smile when four months ago they would have been met with my swinging blade.

The dining hall failed to turn up Dawoud's crotchety niece. I ducked into the hallway again, my irritation brewing rapidly toward anger. After her grand speech and the dramatics in the dining hall, I thought there would be more planned for the evening. Thanks to their sim siya arrows, I had slept enough to last me the rest of the year.

I ran my hand over the dips and ridges of the stone wall as I walked, trying to memorize my path. Halfway down the hall, the texture turned spongy, and my fingers disappeared into the wall with a sucking sound.

I recoiled, yanking my hand out of the wall. I cradled my fingers to my chest as I gaped.

What were these halls made of? As a matter of fact, what was *any* of this made of? It must have taken the Urabi years to carve the insides of these mountains into a sanctuary without being discovered.

No wonder Arin hadn't found them in any of the kingdoms or Essam. The Urabi had chosen to hide in the one place Arin's plethora of maps could not follow.

I cautiously palpated various points of the wall, massaging the crevasses for any hidden keys. I considered trying to use my magic and instantly discarded the thought. Without my cuffs, I had no idea how far my magic could go or how much control I could wield over it.

A spiderweb caught on my thumb when I crouched, a palm braced against the pockmarked wall for support. I wrinkled my nose and tried to draw my hand back.

My shoulder slammed into the wall. I gasped, pulling away only to discover the web pulling with me. The string had wrapped around my thumb and held it fast.

Oh, *absolutely* not.

I braced my foot on the wall and heaved. The web stretched, the threads thinning into translucency, but refused to snap. I put my other foot on the wall, yanking with the weight of my entire body.

A hand appeared from my left and stroked the web. In a flash, it released my thumb—and sent me sprawling onto my rear.

I contemplated staying on the ground. Maybe if I hoped hard enough, the floor might also attempt to swallow me whole.

A shadow fell over me, and I drew myself up on my elbows, red-faced with exertion and not an insignificant amount of mortification. At this rate, they would be calling me the Witless Heir before the end of the day.

I lifted my head to offer a mumbled thanks to my rescuer and promptly shut my mouth again.

A man glowered down at me. I had seen him—and that spiteful glare—before. But where?

"You don't remember me, do you?" He swiped the back of his hand over his nose like the scent of me might stain. "I wish I could say I was surprised. I imagine you betray your own too frequently to keep track of individual faces."

It hit me like a thunderbolt. The man at the Meridian Pass. The Urabi had been shooting arrows into the canyon, unaware that Arin had neatly walked them into a deadly trap. I'd split the canyon of the Pass wider to scatter the Nizahl soldiers and give the Urabi time to escape, but I remembered the shock and betrayal in this man's eyes when I said I wouldn't leave with them.

You agreed to help the Silver Serpent lure us to our deaths?

"Erfa," I said. He watched me trip over the length of my abaya as I climbed to my feet, his scowl defying the limits of facial physics to deepen even further. Despite the valiant efforts of the worst living barber, the haphazard cut of the man's thick brown curls took little away from his natural good looks. His eyes were a mossy green and brewing with disdain. He was more powerfully built than I'd prefer for a man who despised me, and the only victory was in our matched heights.

"*Erfa* means cinnamon. My name is Efra."

My smile broadened to include too many teeth. Framed by unfairly long lashes or not, his eyeballs would bleed under a knife just like anyone else's. "My mistake. The sweetness of your disposition must have confused me."

Kicking the spot I'd been caught against, I asked, "Do the spiderwebs in the Gibal understand the difference between humans and flies?"

"Trespassers will be trapped until someone apprehends them or the web senses an authorized signature. It doesn't recognize the magic of strangers." The last word dripped with enough scorn to put even a brat like Felix to shame.

His efforts to get under my skin were adorable. I'd lived in a cramped underground training complex with four Nizahlan guardsmen who took pleasure in finding new ways to test my willingness to commit murder before breakfast. If Cinnamon wanted to glare a hole through my skull, I certainly wouldn't stop him, but he'd have to try much harder to provoke a reaction.

"Where is Namsa?"

He crossed his arms over his chest. "At the Aada."

I pursed my lips. Maybe he wouldn't have to try too much harder. *Aada* meant seat in Resar, so unless Namsa had a designated chair I should know about, the answer was as useless as him.

"Where. Is. Namsa."

"If she wanted you to know, she would have told you," he said. "Find someone else to cower behind."

With that last parting shot, Efra walked past me, his shoulder bumping mine and rocking me on my heels.

It should probably bother me more that I had managed to make an enemy out of someone within hours of regaining consciousness, but I understood Efra's antipathy more than I understood the reverence in some of the Jasadis' gazes. I thrived under loathing, whether it was my own or someone else's. It slipped over my shoulders like a custom coat, whereas devotion suited me like shoes to a snake.

I pointed at the web. "Next time, I'm bringing a knife."

CHAPTER FIVE

SYLVIA

Three days had passed with sleep failing to find me in the Gibal, and tonight, I did not bother giving chase.

Like most Jasadis, the Urabi seemed to be largely nocturnal, which meant I couldn't pace the inside of the mountain without running into someone around every corner. The last time I had lived under the same roof as so many people was at Usr Jasad, and I'd had the benefit of my own wing. Here, every covert stare and whisper pricked at the back of my neck, leaving me twitchy and increasingly on edge.

So, engaging in the perfectly rational actions of a woman missing two nights of sleep, I snuck back onto the pitch-black cliffside to explore the outside of the mountain.

The mountain quickly made its opinion of my presence known. In the last twenty minutes, I had swallowed a bug and fallen face-first onto the frozen surface of a lake. The ice hadn't broken, thankfully, leaving me with only a bruised cheekbone and saving me from drowning under the most idiotic circumstances imaginable.

Despite the mountain's passionate efforts to repel me, I seemed to have developed an appetite for near-death experiences, because I took one look at the edge of the cliffside and decided a bruised cheekbone was merely the introductory soup in my supper for fools.

Swearing under my breath, I tightened my grip on the rocks

slipping beneath the frozen flesh formerly known as my fingers. The gloves I'd had the presence of mind to wear before leaving my room had already saved me three times over. I swept my boot across the rocks, groping for a solid place to land as I dangled over open air.

The lake hadn't just gifted me with a giant, throbbing bruise. It had knocked loose a tale Soraya would read to me on nights as dark and overcast as this one. A tale of adventure and perilous journeys, of magic-rich waterfalls on the other side of the mountains that spilled into Suhna Sea.

Waterfalls flowing from Hirun River.

The waterfalls are the mountains weeping for the Awaleen, Soraya would say. *All along Orban, Nizahl, and Jasad, they shed their tears into Suhna Sea to mourn the magic that has left this earth.*

I climbed lower, digging the toes of my boots into the crumbling side of the mountain in lieu of a stable foothold. Considering Soraya had poisoned my mother for years in Bakir Tower, helped the Mufsids sack Usr Jasad, and accidentally brought down the Jasad fortress, I wasn't inclined to place much weight onto a single word out of her duplicitous mouth. Not to mention the absurdity of believing Hirun River flowed beneath Orban—beneath the Desert Flats.

But Soraya had spoken about the waterfalls with such genuine emotion. The longing in her voice…it couldn't hurt to check, could it?

I huffed a laugh, pressing my forehead to the inside of my arm to catch my breath. Even now, alone in my head, I couldn't resist hiding from the truth.

Waterfalls sounded wonderful, but I wasn't clinging to a sea-slicked mountainside in the dead of night because I craved a pretty view. The other part of Soraya's story brought me out here. Specifically, the part about adventurers sneaking across the mountains into Suhna Sea by sailing through Hirun, which poured into the waterfalls and became the tears the mountains shed.

And if someone could find their way into the mountains through Hirun, maybe they could find their way out.

I was *not* planning to escape. Not just because I had nowhere to go, but because I had made a vow.

Still…time was the enemy of intention, and it couldn't hurt to know what my options were.

It would be so much easier if the clouds would just *part* and let the moonlight through. I had always been a good climber—the trees in Usr Jasad's courtyards had seen me dangling from their branches more than any leaf. A tiny, little bit of light would change everything.

Slowly, I scaled my way down the side of the cliff, the memory of Ayume Forest too near for comfort. But my hands were not raw and bloody from poisoned sap, and the stones were less punishing than the rope I had used to climb out of the forest and over the cliff.

I gritted my teeth. The climb in Ayume hadn't just wreaked havoc on my body. My magic had been pounding against my cuffs, fighting for release, and managed to conjure a childhood version of myself to taunt and scold me.

I think even if your magic was free, and you had every advantage to reclaim our kingdom, you still wouldn't save Jasad.

I flexed my fingers, holding tight as my boot found the flat of a protruding stone.

Power is a choice. When you choose who you are willing to fight for, you choose who you are.

Absurdly, just the memory of that snide little Essiya sparked my indignation. I *had* chosen. In the heart of Nizahl, I had declared my true name to every royal in the land and exposed my magic. I knew choosing just one time would not suffice; one time would not make up for the thousands of times I hadn't chosen Jasad. But did it mean I could only choose to fight for Jasad for the rest of my life? Did it mean I could never choose myself again?

My ears caught a sound sweeter than any harmony, slightly louder than the cacophony in my head.

Rushing water.

The mountains curved along the sea, the night sky draped over their silhouette like a velvet shroud. If not for the dull roar of waves smashing into the mountainside, the darkness beneath me might have been the doorway to another world, waiting to catch me as I tumbled off the side of the cliff and into an entirely different realm.

Swallowing, I forced myself to focus on my climbing without contemplating the impossible vastness of these mountains. The strange sense that I was disturbing something sacred—something better left unseen.

Droplets of water clung to my eyelashes, cold against my lips. I was getting close.

I considered releasing one of my hands to wipe the moisture from my eyes and thought better of it. The rocks had grown too slippery to risk leaving even an inch of air between myself and the surface.

Besides, I didn't want to see the vein on my palm again.

I'd toyed with the idea of asking Namsa about it before she frolicked off to the "Aada" but thought better of it.

More likely than not, the vein was merely a remnant of the cuffs. Nothing worth drawing attention to, and certainly not worth alarming Namsa. She might consider it an ill tiding of my newly freed magic, and I wouldn't know how to prove her wrong. I knew my cuffs as well as I knew my right arm, but my magic?

I caught my breath as I shuffled from stone to stone, heading in the direction of the rushing water.

Hanim had tried to draw out my magic and failed, thanks to the cuffs.

Arin had drawn out my magic in limited amounts only, thanks to the cuffs.

My cuffs had protected me from the very worst of what I could do, and without them...

In the wrong hands, I could become a weapon turned against Jasad. I wasn't like Dawoud, able to withstand years and years of torture without breaking. I wasn't like my grandparents, knowledgeable in every way magic could be stolen, restrained, and withheld.

History had shown that I could be broken. I could be used. That, in fact, I seemed to accept my place most readily in circumstances where I lost the illusion of control. When I surrendered my choices to someone else to make on my behalf.

If Arin caught me, the war would end before it began.

At least with the Urabi, I could be used for Jasad. The choices they would make—the control I would surrender—would be on behalf of the kingdom I had failed.

The Urabi needed me, but I needed them, too.

I raised my leg to the next stone and nearly tipped sideways onto a long, flat surface holding firm beneath my boot. I tested its strength, shifting more and more of my weight onto it without releasing the rocks under my hands.

After reassuring myself it wouldn't collapse and plunge me into the sea, I settled myself onto the ledge. The gush of fast-flowing water surrounded me. My hands prickled as I shook them out, stiff from hours of clinging to slippery stone.

The night refused to relent. I was clearly close to some kind of moving water, but without light, it was impossible to tell how close. Resigned to waiting until the moon reared its stubborn head, I slid to a cross-legged seat on the ledge.

I knew what Arin would say. I could use my magic to illuminate my surroundings. In fact, I could have used my magic to scale down the side of the mountain. Each time the idea occurred to me, I brushed it aside.

Without any other distraction, I reluctantly unchained the thought I had held captive the instant I saw my bare wrists.

"I can't know for certain what would happen if your full magic was accessible. I might be able to drain it normally. Maybe I'd never reach the bottom of your magic's well, so to speak, and could only temporarily drain portions of it," Arin said. *"But if you want my strongest theory, I suspect touching you while you can fully express your magic would kill me."*

If I started laughing at the irony, I might never stop. Arin's touch had brought forth my magic and saved my life on at least two separate occasions, and now my touch could end his life.

The Urabi could never know. They already suspected my loyalties, and if they knew I had this ability and refused to use it, they would begin to doubt my heart, too. And I wouldn't use it—not unless Arin left me with no other choice.

Perhaps growing jealous of the clouds I had collected over my own head, the moon finally decided to show its face. Wisps of white melted from the dissipating clouds, and I blinked against the brightness of the crescent waiting behind them.

I saw the sea first, churning much closer than I expected. The moonlight spread to the mountainside, revealing the uneven stone face I had climbed down in the dark. It shifted to my right, casting its bluish hue over the source of the rushing water I'd been hearing for the last hour.

I gasped.

Streams poured over the side of the mountain, flowing in dozens of different directions as they cascaded over gleaming black ledges identical to the one beneath me. They rushed toward the sea like a traveler eager to reunite with an old friend.

I tasted the water the wind had generously whipped onto my face and grinned. No salt.

This was Hirun. The river truly did flow beneath the Desert Flats—all along, through droughts and dying crops, Orban had had access to Hirun just under its feet.

I tried to gauge how far I would have to climb to reach the middle of the waterfall. Once I confirmed the entry point, I would go back to the Gibal. The Urabi wouldn't need to know I had ever left, and I would sleep easier having found a place to run if the need ever arose.

I turned around and went stiff. A scream lodged in my throat.

A woman stood on the ledge behind me, leaning against the rocks.

"So," she said, "are we leaving?"

I was hundreds of feet from the top of the mountain. It would have been impossible for anyone to follow me unseen or appear without making a sound.

Displeased at my long silence, she heaved a sigh and jumped to the ledge under me. "I don't mind if we stay. I like the little bouncing one. Omaima? Her magic intrigues me."

A blur of motion as she twirled to another ledge, and when she glanced up, another woman's face had replaced hers, thickly lashed green eyes dancing mischievously. "What do you think?"

My fingernails cut into my palms as I ran through my options. I was on a ledge in the middle of the mountainside. To my right, a waterfall ready to sweep me directly into the depths of Suhna Sea if I made a single misstep. To my left, a deranged apparition.

I inched closer to the waterfall.

"I think we should stay," the green-eyed apparition said. "For now, at least. They are our best chance of winning our crown."

Our crown?

My sleeve caught on the stream behind me, soaking my arm instantly. The blast of cold shattered the last of my shock, and my heart began to pound with sickening speed. What had I been thinking, coming down here? If I vanished—if this thing killed me—

I glanced up in a last feat of desperation, scouring the cliffside, and nearly choked with relief at the sight of a figure looming over the edge. The bad haircut, the slim frame—Efra. Thank the Awaleen. A real person who knew where I was, knew I needed help.

I waved my arms. "Find help!"

Efra didn't move. He stood on the cliffside and simply watched. What did he think he was doing?

"We can punish him later," she said.

I tore my gaze away from Efra. "Who are you?"

I lost sight of the apparition as it leapt onto another ledge.

"You know who we are."

I startled. The voice, sea-deep and smooth as the finest glass, belonged to a man.

"Allow me to rephrase," I growled. "What are you?"

I careened back as the stream nearest me erupted with movement. A hand closed around my wrist, and I gazed into bright gold-and-silver eyes identical to my own.

No, not identical—they *were* my eyes.

"What we are depends on you," he said.

Before I could retreat, the hand on my wrist yanked me forward.

I tumbled into the waterfall.

I'd plummeted from great heights before. For most of them, blood loss and exhaustion shadowed my memories of the drop.

I knew I would remember this fall in excruciating detail. The sudden weightlessness, the surge of terror in my hollowing stomach, the frigid wind battering me as the waterfall swept me toward the frothing surface of the sea. I would remember shutting my eyes as my muscles tensed to prepare for impact. My magic, sluggish in my veins as it pumped with my panic.

I plunged into the sea, and pain washed my world white. My limbs disconnected from my command, and for a minute, I could not tell where I began or ended. My lips parted beneath the freezing cold, accidentally inviting a surge of salt water to sear my throat. The waves battered me, each choppier and more forceful than the next.

I clawed to the surface in time to vomit before another wave drew me down again.

The weight of the water closed in, wrapping icy fingers around my thrashing limbs.

I didn't want to die.

Sensation left my extremities, until I no longer knew where to find my legs to keep them kicking. I drifted deeper into Suhna Sea's embrace, my body growing lax as I choked on the last of my air.

Drowning in Suhna Sea, at least, was less embarrassing than drowning in the lake.

Wake.

My eyes flew open, shock tearing apart the settling shroud of sleep. What the—

The tide is strong. The next wave will hurl you against the cliff. You will not heal from a broken neck.

I didn't recognize the voice; I hesitated to even describe it as one. It was more akin to a series of sentient—and uninvited—vibrations in my head.

Bubbles floated out of my mouth. If I still had air, I wasn't dead.

Yet.

I jerked. What *was* that?

My legs struggled to push me toward the surface, shoving pitifully against the unyielding weight of the sea.

I sank.

My vision blurred for a terrible second. Between Hanim and training for the Alcalah, I could hold my breath for a significant amount of time, but I wouldn't last much longer.

I needed my magic.

The vein on my palm brightened to a throbbing gold. Light poured from the vein, cutting through the black dots dancing in my vision. My feet hit an invisible barrier, and the light pushed out, forming a bubble around me.

I drew a desperate breath as air filled the bubble. A fist pressed to my chest, I hacked out buckets of seawater. My magic pumped with my pulse. Waiting. Eager to serve.

I would have preferred to be taken to the surface, but this would do while I collected myself. Sitting back on my haunches, I fixed my streaming eyes on the edges of the protective circle to check how far I would have to swim.

Odd. I squinted, trying to pierce through the prism of my magic's light to the other side of the bubble. It almost looked like—

I screamed so loudly I threw myself into another coughing fit.

The light emanating from my vein illuminated dozens of creatures floating in the dark. They pressed against the outside of the bubble, staring at me. One of them, red-scaled and bulbous, unhinged a jaw large enough to swallow Raya's keep. Its fangs were unlike any I had seen before, twisted and curled around one another like a nest of thorns.

Baira's blessed hair, was it...smiling?

Hello.

No amount of practice or training could corral my fear this time. It tore through me, obliterating any rational thought. My vein brightened again, and I acted without thinking, thrusting my arms to the sides and throwing my magic with every ounce of strength I possessed.

I intended to widen the bubble. Enough to push me to the surface, or just push the monsters back.

Instead, it burst.

CHAPTER SIX

SYLVIA

Water rushed over me once more, bringing the creatures on the other side of the barrier with it. My magic had failed me, and now legendary sea beasts were about to take turns tearing me to pieces.

Something hard collided with my wheeling feet, halting my descent. I caught a glimpse of red scales and giant black eyes. Before I could scream again, the creature surged forward. My knees buckled, flattening me against its back as I scrambled to hold on to its slippery skin.

Was it carrying me back to its home? Was I about to be dropped over a cradle of baby sea monsters?

The water parted above me, and beautiful, wonderful, *freezing* wind slapped the gasp of relief straight from my lips. The clouds parted, a ray of hazy dawn light catching on the scales beneath me and casting millions of red diamonds over the churning waters.

I dug my fingers between scales larger than my body, wincing at the gooey squelch, and held tight. If it planned to throw its head back and eat me in midair the way I'd seen Marek toss a roasted pumpkin seed into his mouth, it would have to throw me *hard*.

Please cease your wriggling. I am earnestly endeavoring not to dislodge you.

I jerked, nearly losing my grip. "Are you talking to me?"

No response, although the vibrations in my head seemed to shape themselves into a sigh.

Where were the waves? The slap of waves against the cliffside had vanished, the sting of its spray noticeably absent.

I immediately regretted glancing back. My mind frayed like the hem of a poorly sewn blouse. Maybe I *had* drowned. Maybe my dying brain was rewriting reality to comfort me in my last moments.

The sea level flattened as a red island rose out of the water. A spine longer than the tallest mountain blotted the horizon as its iridescent scales emerged from beneath the waves. On either side of its enormous body, two powerful fins propelled the creature through the water. Each fin could flatten an entire village.

I whipped my head forward. My wet braid slapped me across the cheek. If this was what I thought it was...

In Jasad, we called this creature Sareekh il Ma'a. Omal referred to it as the Scream of the Sea, and the other kingdoms just called it a legendary nightmare.

One of Rovial's first acts upon founding Jasad had been to swim the length of Hirun. A brisk thousand miles later, Rovial stood in the shadows of the mountains, captivated by the sight of the setting sun gilding Suhna Sea in golds and reds.

A precocious lizard had raced over his foot, and Rovial scooped it up, studying the little red reptile. Baira had her Ruby Hounds, Kapastra her rochelyas, and Dania her bulls. Unlike his siblings, Rovial didn't see the need to create an army of creatures at his beck and call, but one...just one creature, something to appreciate the beauty of the sun as it disappeared beneath the sea and protect Hirun from ever being dammed.

I was not a "little" lizard. I was a burss the size of your leg.

I managed not to yelp this time, which should be lauded as one of the most impressive feats of my existence.

Sareekh il Ma'a stopped lifting us halfway up the cliff. The shimmering scales beneath my hands quivered and slid apart. I lost my hold and tumbled down its back, grappling for purchase.

A dozen vines shot out from the Sareekh's back. Attached to the end of each one was a large bone-white knob, not unlike a rosebud before its bloom. One of the claws unfurled, spikes of bone stretching open to catch me before I had slid more than a few feet. It wrapped itself around my middle like a skeletal corset. The spikes tightened when I tried to wiggle my fingers between them and my torso.

They held me fast as the rest of the Sareekh's spine separated, revealing a spinal column covered in a heavy gelatinous sheath. Beneath the layers of goo, hundreds of furled bone claws formed the knobs of the Sareekh's spine.

I shrieked as hundreds of those spinal buds speared through the gelatinous sheath, blooming like death's bouquet.

Had I not watched my family burn before my eyes, this would have been the most frightening sight of my life.

I touched one of the spines wrapped around me like a second set of ribs. Warm and hard to the touch, it shivered but didn't unlatch. Even if I managed to pry them off without one of them skewering me, I'd just slide right into the next one.

The vine lifted me through the air, and I was so occupied watching the distance between me and the Sareekh grow, I almost didn't notice when my feet made contact with a hard surface.

The cliff.

The bones relaxed, unceremoniously dropping me into a heap on the ground. I crawled away from the edge on all fours, abandoning any notions of dignity. I turned in time to watch the stems retract into the Sareekh and the bone claws coil back into a hard knob before being absorbed into the gelatinous layer of the spinal column. Its scales rippled as the panels of its spine closed once more.

I patted my body, absently checking for any wayward pieces as my heart heaved back to life. It hadn't dropped me. It *saved* me. "Thank you," I whispered.

You may call upon me at any hour of need.

I shivered. My magic hadn't betrayed me. It broke the protective bubble because it knew my best chance of survival was waiting behind it.

But it had also made the decision on my behalf.

I sensed a presence behind me, but I couldn't peel my gaze from the Sareekh's. It regarded me with an intelligence I could live ten thousand lifetimes without equaling.

Wrapping my arms around myself, I dipped my chin in a slow nod. Of gratitude, of respect. This creature was as old as Sirauk Bridge, as ancient as the Awaleen sleeping in the tombs beneath it.

The Sareekh sank into the darkening waters. Its spine arched, casting a shadow over the side of the mountain. I threw my arm over my face as a wave slammed into the cliffside.

The surface of the sea smoothed. The only evidence of the Sareekh were the thin, symmetrical bruises forming on my sides from the bone claw. The presence behind me shifted closer.

Because of the Sareekh, I would live another day.

Because of Efra, I almost hadn't.

I got to my feet. I was trembling, but it had nothing to do with the cold. I greeted the rage flooding through me like an old friend. It wasn't the livid, impassioned rage that led to the Victor's Ball collapsing around Supreme Rawain and the other guests. This rage was cold. Cleansing.

Efra lingered a few paces behind me, open-mouthed with astonishment. "That was Sareekh il Ma'a!"

"You saw me before I fell! I waved to you for help, and you ignored me!" I seethed. "You watched that thing jumping around the ledges before it pulled me into the waterfall."

Efra's brows furrowed. "Thing? What thing?"

"Do you think lies will save you? I *saw you*."

"I am not lying," he snapped. "Yes, I watched you standing by the waterfall, but you seemed fine on the ledge. And you were completely *alone*."

I stopped short. He hadn't seen the apparitions?

If none of that had been real... if I had imagined it all...

But the voice I'd heard behind the water. The glowing gold-and-silver eyes that may as well have been plucked out of my face, the hand yanking me into the waterfall.

Later—I would dwell on the questionable state of my sanity later. "Even if you thought I was alone, why didn't you get help?" He had still seen me completely stranded in the middle of the mountain, clearly panicked.

Brown curls tumbled over his brow, victims to the restless wind. The nervous way he swept them back reminded me of Sefa. If Sefa were here, she'd note Efra was only a year or two older than me. We had absolved Marek many a foolhardy mistake, and he had weathered much less damage in his life than Efra probably had. Sefa would try to forgive him.

But Sefa wasn't here, and I hadn't gone to find her because for the first time in my life, I was trying to keep a vow. To break a pattern. I had run after the Blood Summit, after I killed Hanim, after I killed the Nizahl soldier. I'd even run away my first night in the tunnels.

For once, I was trying to *stay*.

"You didn't use your magic," Efra said, and I stopped short.

"What are you talking about?"

"You didn't use your magic to climb down. You didn't use it to light your way. You didn't even use it when you stumbled into the waterfall."

"How long were you watching me?" I balked.

Efra's lips curled back. "I told them it was a trick, what happened at the Victor's Ball. Another hoax delivered by the same hands that ruined our kingdom."

Frustration rolled like a rock between my teeth, and I forced myself to swallow it down. I hadn't remembered the truth about my grandparents' magic mining until after the second trial, but the Urabi had suffered under it their entire lives. Magic mining wasn't some theory or whispered secret. To them, it was a family member who never came home. A friend whose death couldn't be fully explained, whose body went missing.

"I'm sorry for what my grandparents did," I said, because I was. I was sorrier than he would ever know. "But my magic is not your concern."

"It is when our survival relies on it."

I looked at Efra for a long moment. "Consider your next words to me carefully, Cinnamon. I do not take kindly to being manipulated to suit someone's ends, regardless of how noble those ends might be."

I moved to walk around him, but he shifted into my path. "You lack a natural connection with your magic."

Without missing a beat, I shoved him with my full strength, sending him sprawling. "Of course I do," I hissed, looming over him. "I didn't have access to it for over half my life. It failed me every time I needed it. Where was my magic when Hanim flayed my back raw? When she sent monsters after me in Essam, when they ripped into me with teeth and claws the size of your ego? All this time, it was right there. What if I rely on it and it betrays me again?"

The confession caught us both by surprise.

Efra reclined on the ground, offering me a venom-tipped smile. "Perhaps it didn't feel inclined to bend to the will of the Silver Serpent's traitorous whore."

Someone gasped, and I belatedly realized Maia had emerged from the mountain. I didn't have to check to guess what her face would read: shock and horror. Not because of what Efra had said, but because he had dared say it. He had dared speak the thought circulating in everyone's head.

For a dizzying moment, I stepped out of time to stand in a cabin many miles from here, Arin across from me and a dead Nizahl soldier's body at my feet.

I offer you a new life.

My freedom in exchange for competing as his Champion in the Alcalah and luring the Urabi and Mufsids into his trap. I had foreseen this moment, accepted the title of Nizahl Champion with full awareness that it would forever tarnish my true name. I hadn't cared then. Essiya was a stranger to me, and I would have done anything to ensure Sylvia lived free.

"The last person who called me a whore was a guardsman named Vaun," I mused. My waterlogged boot kicked out and caught Efra's temple, snapping his head to the right. "We fought, and my magic erupted over me like fire—scorching him and leaving me untouched. I wanted to kill him. I should have killed him. It was a mistake to leave someone like Vaun alive."

Efra leapt to his feet and swung, his fist careening wide. I grabbed a handful of his hair as his pathetic blow passed me by a mile and slammed my fist into his jaw, knocking him back into the dirt. Was this the caliber of fighters among the Urabi? Maybe if Efra hadn't relied on his magic so much, he wouldn't have the fighting instincts of an inebriated raccoon.

"I never make the same mistake twice."

I fisted the front of his tunic and grabbed a heavy rock, preparing to deliver a blow he wouldn't recover from. But first, I drew him forward, softening my voice to say, "In the next life, be more wary of us traitorous whores. Especially, sweet Cinnamon, when we're the ones wearing the crown."

My elbow bent, lifting the rock over my head. Efra's eyes squeezed shut.

"We need your magic to raise the fortress!" Maia screamed.

Efra's head twisted, alarm blaring through his battered features. "Be quiet, Omaima!"

Maia appeared behind Efra, crouching behind his shoulders. She threw her arms around his head. "Please! Efra was born this unpleasant, he can't help himself. But he isn't taunting you about your magic to be obnoxious, Mawlati. He asks after your magic because the Aada—our council—plans to invade the Omal palace to present you to Queen Hanan. As Emre's only child, you have a higher claim to the throne than Felix. If you become Omal Heir, you control the armies of the largest kingdom in the lands."

Disbelief tinged my laugh. I didn't lower my arm. Their grand plan, the reason for hunting me down across four kingdoms… was to try to take Omal's throne? "Why would you want Omal's armies? Felix has rotted them. They have no battle skill, no tactical intelligence."

"They have numbers," Maia said. "We need numbers."

Dumbstruck, I stared at Maia. It dawned on me that she was telling the truth. If Efra's petulant silence hadn't convinced me, the sheer absurdity of this plan would have.

Title and magic. I'd thought I had the answer for what my title offered them, but clearly I had underestimated the Urabi. I was the daughter of Niphran of Jasad and Emre of Omal.

Born Heir of Jasad *and* Heir of Omal.

"Queen Hanan disinherited me at birth." I thought of the dull-eyed, fragile woman drowning in her finery at the head of Omal's banquet table. She'd barely had the strength to hold a conversation, let alone strip her monstrous nephew of his title and pass it to the human equivalent of political suicide. "Giving the title to me would turn her own council against her. It would mean war with Nizahl. Queen Hanan helped tear our kingdom to pieces. She signed the decree against magic. What makes you think she would have any interest in reinstating me?"

"She was grieving her son and her husband during the war," Maia said. "She may feel differently now, knowing her granddaughter lives."

Rovial's tainted tomb. Sequestering in the mountains had bred their delusion, unchecked, and developed it into a plan guaranteed to annihilate us.

I went back to Maia's first remark. "What does Queen Hanan have to do with the fortress?"

Maia hesitated. She glanced at the rock still clenched in my fist. "If our plan to regain your title in Omal fails, we will have no choice but to stand on our own in Jasad. Even if seventy percent of the Jasadis in hiding come out to fight with us, we will not triumph against the forces of Nizahl, Omal, Orban, and Lukub. We are already running out of time—the kingdoms have been purging their lands of magic, bypassing Nizahl's laws to execute anyone suspected of having it. Hundreds are already dead, and the rest will be too frightened to risk traveling to Jasad without assurance of their protection. Our only chance of survival would be to resurrect the fortress around Jasad."

Was this some sick attempt at humor? "It took thousands of Jasadis to raise the fortress. The effort of channeling their power burned Qayida Hend alive, and that was centuries ago, when magic was still rich in our blood." My grip tightened on the rock. "The Jasad fortress cannot be raised."

Eyes entirely too sincere for someone protecting an idiot pleaded with me. "I swear to Sirauk, Namsa and the Aada have been meeting to figure out how we can prepare you to raise the fortress by Nuzret Kamel."

Nuzret Kamel? The name rang a distant bell. Some holiday the lower wilayahs had celebrated. What did it have to do with raising the fortress?

Maia placed her hand on the rock and gently pushed my arm down. "We were going to tell you once you became more comfortable in the Gibal, but circumstances have changed. Efra acted without thinking, but it wasn't out of malice. We're desperate."

I dropped the rock, disgusted with myself for entertaining any of this. "What do you mean, circumstances changed?"

Efra's purpling lips curled into a sneer, and he finally broke his silence. "The Silver Serpent thinks he can hide your existence and wage this war in the shadows."

I didn't move my glare from Efra as the door to the mountain scraped opened.

"Maia, Efra, what's happening?" Namsa appeared in my periphery. "Mawlati, you're soaked!"

"Efra," I said quietly. Dangerously. "What did you do?"

He wiped the blood dribbling from his nose. "The first strike of this war, *Mawlati*, goes to us."

CHAPTER SEVEN

SEFA

Close to six years had passed since Sefa's survival depended on tricking lecherous men out of their coin.

A spoon of mahalabiya nudged her lips. "Open your mouth, darling," said a man at least thirty years Sefa's senior. "A sweet for my sweet."

"Oh, I don't eat milk desserts. They make my stomach sing. You wouldn't wish to be a one-man audience to its special melody, trust me." Sefa patted her middle.

He blinked, as befuddled as if she'd started barking. Docile, sweet lap girls did not turn away the hand that fed them, no matter how catastrophically its contents would implode in their bellies. He nudged the spoon against her mouth again, and Sefa reluctantly parted her lips, pulling the creamy mahalabiya onto her tongue.

Treacherously delicious. She could almost forget the consequences.

On the substantial list of schemes she and Marek had used to swindle their way across the kingdoms, seduction had always ranked last for Sefa. They usually avoided it unless they were on the brink of starvation, especially since Marek's own charms could usually save them from a predicament or ten. The difference was Marek had no qualms following through on his illusions of seduction, whereas Sefa had never allowed it to go so far.

But Marek wasn't here, and Sefa hadn't eaten more than four stale pieces of bread in the same number of days. What she wouldn't give to squeeze a lime over a steaming bowl of fūl speckled with black pepper. To plunge a piece of freshly baked aish into a bowl of molokhia. Bless Baira, she'd even settle for Maya's eggshell omelets.

Corpse Walker's hand landed on her head. She'd forgotten his real name within minutes of hearing it. Balanced on the edge of a small stool at his feet, Sefa forced herself to stay motionless as he petted her hair and ran proprietary fingers along her neck. Just another Lukubi courtesan for the garden of debauchery.

Sefa glanced around the Ivory Palace's verdant estate. Lush green vines wrapped around the ivory pillars encircling the palace. The stone-forged skulls of Ruby Hounds glared from the cornices over the archways, the torchlight glittering across their bejeweled eyes.

With so much to observe, nobody but Sefa seemed to note the peculiar dent in the patch of poppies. If Sefa unfocused her eyes, she could almost see Sylvia, broken glass surrounding her and a knife protruding from her chest. *Gah*—the memory still made Sefa nauseous. Despite possessing the height of a centuries-old tree, Sylvia had looked so small lying there.

It was also the moment Sefa saw the relationship between Sylvia and the Nizahl Heir was more dangerous than anyone recognized. Arin had been shouting—him, *shouting*—and the look on his face. Oh, that look. Sefa had never seen anything equivalent to it in her twenty-three years. It had sent foreboding shooting straight through her.

Sylvia had the power to make the most careful man in the kingdoms reckless.

"Fetch me another drink," Corpse Walker said.

Sefa shook herself back to the present and compulsively checked behind her for Marek. But Marek had wound up somewhere else after Sylvia's magic whisked them out of the collapsing ballroom. Sefa was alone.

She climbed off the stool, wincing at the twinge in her back. Corpse Walker snapped his fingers, summoning a courtesan to warm his lap while he waited.

Decadent desserts and chalices brimming with a honey-gold liquid tempted Sefa at the table. Corpse Walker had forbidden her from eating unless it was his hand feeding her, but maybe he wouldn't notice if Sefa snuck a few bites.

As soon as the evening ended, Sefa planned to skulk away, a handful of stolen coins the well-earned compensation for her troubles. She needed him drunk and oblivious, which meant not drawing unwanted attention to herself. It was already risky returning to the Ivory Palace after what happened in the Citadel. Surviving the night hinged on the hope that no one remembered the small, quiet seamstress accompanying the Nizahl Champion's team. As far as she knew, none of the guests at the Victor's Ball had seen past her glamor except Arin and the High Counselor.

Bile burned in Sefa's throat at the memory. Seeing the face of her nightmares after so many years had invited Sefa to a rage she didn't recognize. She had imagined seeing him again, of course. Everything about the day she would cross paths with her stepfather had been rehearsed and rewritten down to the most minor detail. What Sefa would say, how she would stand, the exact set of her chin. She'd even planned out *his* response.

But when the moment came, all Sefa had felt was disgust. He didn't deserve her rage or her defiance. He didn't deserve to know she had become someone she was proud of despite what he had done to her.

She'd spat at his feet, and it felt better than anything she'd prepared.

A man bumped into her, jostling Sefa along the dessert table. He grabbed a platter of ruz bil laban without hesitation, his spoon cutting through the film of cooled milk with confidence Sefa envied.

Dania's sacred skirt, Sefa was not going to be intimidated by a man who was one strong exhale away from disintegrating. If she wanted dessert, she would take it.

Glancing furtively behind her, Sefa heaped as many sweets as she could fit onto a plate and scurried across the garden, weaving between clusters of other guests. She needed a private place to eat. If Corpse Walker questioned her absence, she'd describe in graphic detail what the mahalabiya had done to her insides.

Servants bustled out of a small door on the eastern side of the palace. Sefa waited for a break in their stream and slid inside. She didn't recognize this side of the Ivory Palace. Then again, she and Marek had barely left their room during their visit.

The splendor of the Ivory Palace was muted here. The sconces holding the torches were still in the shape of Ruby Hounds, the flames dancing inside their unhinged jaws and reflecting red crystals onto the floor. But the walls were a bland white instead of ivory, and soap and dust replaced the cloying smell of dying flowers.

Checking over her shoulder, Sefa turned down a narrow hall and ran right into a guard.

Positioned in front of a stairwell, the guard raised her brows at Sefa's appearance. "Wrong way, girl."

Sefa's stomach growled. She couldn't linger down here for long—sooner or later, Corpse Walker would come searching for her and his missing drink.

Sefa drew herself to her full height—which, admittedly, didn't amount to much. "What are you doing here? Tayra said tonight was her shift. I am meant to bring her a plate."

Suspicion clouded the guard's face. "How do you know Tayra?"

She was somewhat certain Marek had slept with the giggling guard while she and Sylvia looted the Sultana's bedroom. "She recommended me. I am the new kitchen girl."

"Then perhaps you should stay in the kitchen." The guard

assessed Sefa for another endless minute before rolling her eyes and stepping aside. "Go. Tayra's probably napping on the third floor."

Sefa gave a curt nod of thanks and tried not to trip in her rush up the stairs. She kept climbing until the only sound she could hear was her own labored breathing.

When her legs turned to jelly, Sefa found a quiet hidden spot behind one of the countless tapestries strewn across the Ivory Palace and collapsed. Without waiting to catch her breath, Sefa consumed her plate in minutes.

Four days, four pieces of bread. Breathing could wait until later.

She was dabbing at her mouth when a clatter whipped her head to the right.

"You know where to find me when it's done," said a gruff voice. "Make sure she doesn't scream. Her guards are crawling all over this place."

Sefa squeezed her legs to her chest and flattened herself against the wall.

A second man spoke. "There are dozens of guests downstairs. Are you sure this is the best time?"

"Dozens of guests means dozens of suspects. They won't know where to start searching for the Sultana's killer."

Sefa went still. They were talking about assassinating Sultana Vaida. Tonight. *Right now.*

"Do you remember where her chambers are?"

"I turn right here and walk to the end of the hall."

"Good. Don't get lost."

Sefa was directly in their path. There was no scenario where they let her live after eavesdropping on a plot to kill the Sultana.

"The guards will be drawn away. You will have minutes before they return. Do not waste them."

"What if she isn't there?"

Sefa crawled backward until they fell out of earshot and climbed to her feet. Hurrying in the opposite direction of the assassins' voices, panic replacing her sugary euphoria, Sefa didn't slow at the bend of the hall.

A corridor came into view, lined with guards dressed in the elaborate uniforms marking them as the Sultana's highest guard. At the end of the short corridor, twin drapes covered the doors leading into the Sultana's chambers.

If she could tell the guards in time, maybe they could—

A scream rang from behind her. "Someone help! Help!"

The front set of guards glanced over, attention bypassing Sefa entirely. They made no move toward the voice.

Sefa started to relax. These guards were likely instructed not to deviate from the Sultana's doors under any circumstances. The assassins would never be able to get past them.

An explosion shook the ground beneath her. Sefa slammed into the wall as rocks cascaded from the ceiling, tearing through a tapestry. The statue of Baira at the end of the hall tipped over, crashing beside Sefa. The Awala of Lukub's severed head rolled.

Dust formed a gray haze throughout the hall. The guards ran toward the source of the scream—and presumably, the explosion. There was no other point of entry to the Sultana's chambers, and she wondered how the assassin would evade the sudden rush of guards.

Sefa took tentative steps to the Sultana's unprotected door. Her pulse rioted, sensing the danger on the other side. What did Sefa care if someone killed the Sultana? Vaida was no ruler of hers. She had orchestrated the death of her Champion and threatened the lives of everyone in Mahair. Half-Lukubi or not, Sefa owed the Sultana no loyalty.

Yet it was her hand that found the door handle and pushed it down.

CHAPTER EIGHT

SEFA

The door opened easily. Sefa entered and slammed it shut behind her.

A bedroom twice the size of Raya's keep and decorated with more color than Sefa had previously known existed assaulted her senses. The chaotic explosion of craft wasn't what Sefa would have expected. One would think a ruler who tossed her enemies in open graves and let the world watch them starve wouldn't sleep on bright yellow blankets.

"Hello there."

A woman in a silk shift sat across a vanity heaped with creams, fragrances, and ornate bottles. White-lined eyes nearly as dark as Sylvia's met Sefa's in the mirror, remarkably collected given the circumstances. Gold cream smeared one of her eyelids, the other light brown. Powder glittered over her high cheekbones, stars shining on her dark skin.

Vaida arched a brow. "I don't imagine you're lost."

Not lost, but certainly speechless. Sefa hadn't laid eyes on the Sultana in person before. Well, she had seen slivers while hiding in Vaida's wardrobe, but she had been preoccupied with the possibility of being caught and executed at the time. The beauty of the Sultana was legend throughout the kingdoms, and Sefa could finally confirm it had not been exaggerated. Sefa must have caught her in the middle of experimenting with her cosmetics.

Another commotion outside unstuck Sefa. "You are in grave danger, my lady."

"I'm always in grave danger." Sultana Vaida turned on the bench, facing Sefa. Dozens of braids cascaded over shoulders like sharply honed blades. "Are *you* the grave danger? If your aim is to kill me, don't dawdle. I loathe trite conversation."

Sefa's mouth opened. She thought Sefa wanted to kill her? Sefa wasn't even armed. Crumbs clung to the front of her dress, which Sefa hadn't taken off in days. She would be the world's most slovenly assassin. "Sultana, I can assure you I was not dispatched to kill you. I am, however, stupid enough to barge into your chambers to beg you to hide before—"

A scratch came from the door. Sefa's eyes widened. Uncertainty flickered over Vaida. She glanced at the door and back at Sefa.

The options presented themselves to Sefa in the endless stretch of the next minute. She could scurry somewhere and hide, leaving the Sultana like a sitting duck for whoever burst through the door. It was what Sylvia would do. Sylvia wouldn't have entered the room to begin with. She might have even tossed the assassins an extra knife for good luck. Her friend didn't indulge indecision over whether to save the life of someone guaranteed to make hers more difficult.

But Sefa had always believed that most decisions, no matter how complicated they might seem, could be clearly categorized as right or wrong. The decision to leave a weaponless woman to die in her own chambers was not the exception.

Another rattle of the door had Sefa darting forward and catching the Sultana's wrist. The fearsome leader of Lukub proved surprisingly easy to manhandle. Sefa threw open the doors to one of the many wardrobes tucked around the chamber and shoved Vaida behind a rack of coats bigger than the animals they were skinned from, hopping in after her. As soon as she closed them inside the wardrobe, she heard the creak of the bedroom doors.

Vaida, too deep in the wardrobe to hear the sound, opened her mouth. Frustration bubbled through Sefa. For someone obsessed with preserving her safety, Sultana Vaida appeared determined to resist Sefa's efforts to keep her alive.

Sefa slapped her hand over the Sultana's mouth. They were squeezed behind the coats, close enough that Sefa saw the exact moment Vaida registered the sounds of a person rummaging through her chambers.

They held themselves still as the assailant drew closer. Angry mumbling filtered into the wardrobe. "Told him she wouldn't be here. He's put me in a bind this time, damn him."

Something slammed to their right. The assassin was opening the other wardrobes. Vaida's panicked eyes swung to Sefa and held.

She was afraid.

Sefa wasn't sure why the revelation came as a shock. Perhaps she'd spent too much time with Sylvia, who seemed to believe she feared death until she encountered an opportunity to run toward it like a bull with a branch up its rump. Or Arin of Nizahl, who unflinchingly stood toe-to-toe with Sylvia even at her worst—a decision that would have seen a normal man slain ten times over.

Thanks to the company Sefa had kept in the tunnels, she'd forgotten what the normal response to an impending possibility of murder looked like.

Another slam, closer this time. Their wardrobe would be opened next. Sefa released a silent exhale. She and Marek had been in similar situations in the past and escaped unscathed. Granted, the last time they were in such a position, Sefa was nearly beaten to death, but she doubted the assassin would have time to get more than a couple of punches in. Sefa moved much faster than they expected.

She spoke directly in Vaida's ear. "Stay here. Do not move."

Red-tipped fingernails caught Sefa's sleeve. Sefa patted the Sultana's hand before gently prizing it off.

With as much stealth as she could manage in the cramped space, Sefa slid the most expensive-looking of the furs over her stained dress. If this didn't work, at least she would die in luxury.

Sefa reared her leg back and kicked the wardrobe doors open. Sultana Vaida was still obscured behind the other coats, and Sefa avoided rustling the rack when she careened out of the wardrobe.

The assassin jumped a foot in the air. His knife swung toward her. "You aren't the Sultana."

Sefa quickly shed the coat, glancing around guiltily. "Are you one of the new guards? I'm so sorry. Sultana Vaida went for her bath, and I—her clothes are so beautiful, and I only wanted to try—you won't tell anyone, will you? Oh please, please don't. I just started working in the kitchen. My mama won't take me back if I'm dismissed." Tears slid down Sefa's cheeks. She gazed at the assassin from under wet eyelashes. With her ratty gown and generally unkempt appearance, Sefa certainly looked the part of lowly staff.

His confusion grew while she babbled, but she was handing him an excuse with a bow and a scented rose. Was this the caliber of assassin being sent after one of the most powerful people in the kingdoms? Sefa was almost offended on the Sultana's behalf.

"Yes, I'm a guard." He puffed up his chest and lowered the knife. "There was a noise."

"I heard it! From down the hall, I believe. I got so scared, I hid in the wardrobe. Would you like me to fetch the other guards to accompany you? It can't be safe traveling alone with the assailant still wandering."

"No!" The assassin pursed his lips. "No, you stay here. Don't leave this room. Understand? It isn't safe."

Too, too easy. Sefa squeezed out another tear. "As you see fit."

"Where did you say the Sultana's baths were?"

"Walk down the hall and take two rights. The door is covered with rose petals." Sefa had no idea where the hall led. Into the clutches of an armed guard, hopefully.

He pulled open the door a crack and glanced out. After checking Sefa hadn't moved from her spot, he slid outside, pulling the door shut behind him.

Sefa immediately dragged the velvet bench in front of the door. The odds of him returning were slim, but she never underestimated the brainlessness of some men. He'd broken the lock, but she turned it anyway.

In the middle of assessing whether she could topple one of the wardrobes to block the door, Sefa jumped a foot in the air when a hand settled on her shoulder. Sefa whirled around to find the Sultana directly behind her, dark eyes regarding her with no trace of the fear Sefa had seen in the wardrobe.

Sefa could almost convince herself she had hallucinated it.

"He won't return. The palace gates close during an attack. There is no escape for him." She removed her hand and walked to an overstuffed emerald chair by the window. "You are quite a capable performer. I am impressed."

Sefa swallowed. Without the imminent threat of harm, her nerves failed her. What if Sultana Vaida recognized her? Sefa did not harbor a shadow of a doubt that the Nizahl Heir had guards searching for her and Marek. They had proven themselves the best leverage against Sylvia during the Alcalah. If the Sultana knew who Sefa was, she'd either order her killed or use her as a bargaining chip with Arin.

"It is a necessity of my station in life, Your Majesty."

Vaida smiled. "Mine, too. What is your name?"

Her name? She had too many names. Sayali was hunted in Nizahl, and after the Victor's Ball, so was Sefa.

"Zahra. My name is Zahra." Her heart jumped to her throat.

"Zahra." The word rolled from the Sultana's tongue without a hint of recognition. "Tell me, Zahra, why are you in my palace? Do not mistake my inquiry for ingratitude, as your service to me tonight cannot be faulted."

"It is a service anyone would have gladly performed, my lady."

Sultana Vaida's lips twisted wryly. "I am flattered you think so." She lifted an expectant brow.

Embarrassment tripped the words into a mumble. "I am here as an escort to one of your guests."

A glance at Sefa's tragic attire would determine exactly what kind of escort she meant. Sultana Vaida tilted her head. "Which guest?"

Sefa opened her mouth—and stopped. Oh no. Oh, she had forgotten his real name. If she didn't answer quickly, Vaida would think Sefa's lies hadn't ended with the assassin.

She hung her head. "To be perfectly honest, Your Majesty, I don't recall. I have been referring to him as 'Corpse Walker' in my head."

A burst of laughter drew Sefa's gaze up. Sultana Vaida pressed slender fingers to her mouth, holding back a grin. "Ah yes, Heilan. Corpse Walker is... terribly appropriate."

Full of relief and lightheartedness, Sultana Vaida almost looked her age. A clever young woman, power brimming from her very pores.

Sylvia had told Sefa once, during one of her strange introspective moods, that Arin and Vaida were cut from the same cloth. *They could set fire to the world and convince us to dance in its ashes.*

"I should leave," Sefa said, shaking Sylvia's ghost.

Vaida stood. Her full height unfolded, until she stood a head above Sefa. Fortunately, after years with Sylvia and Marek, Sefa's neck had adjusted to a life of looking up.

"I'd like you to stay, Zahra."

Her stomach turned to ice. Vaida knew. She would throw her in one of the pits outside the Ivory Palace, and then she'd feed her remains to the feral cats crawling all over the gardens—

"Stay and work for me. I need someone I can depend on in my employ. We are living in dangerous times, and you will be well-protected in the Ivory Palace."

The shift from imagining herself as cat cuisine to the offer of employment dizzied Sefa. "Huh?"

Vaida's hand found Sefa's chin, pushing her gaping mouth shut. "You'll catch flies."

"Why would you want—I am honored, Sultana, but—"

"Are you happy with your current employ?" Vaida easily interrupted Sefa's disjointed babbling.

Robbed of coherent speech, Sefa could only shake her head.

"I need a new personal attendant. Someone who can think quickly and critically, even in the face of their superior." Vaida pressed her lips together, and Sefa recalled what Sylvia had told her of the incident at the Omal palace, how the Nizahl Heir's proximity had disoriented a Lukubi servant enough for him to slip the two ghaiba dolls into her pocket.

Marek's ability to seduce the guard assigned to Vaida's chambers the night of the festival probably hadn't reinforced the Sultana's confidence in her staff, either.

The offer strained every limit of absurdity. As personal attendant, Sefa would have nearly unfettered access within the Ivory Palace. She would be privy to every aspect of Vaida's life, empowered with decision-making ability over everything from the Sultana's meals to her social calendar.

The rest of the staff would surely despise her. A stranger with nothing to her name stealing a role someone else would kill for.

Sefa shook her head again, utterly bewildered. "How do you know you can trust me?"

"Trust you? Dearest, if you're going to say something that silly, save it for a stage." A chillingly discerning gaze roamed over Sefa. "You had no reason to save me. Even less reason to put yourself in harm's way to hide me. This leaves me with two possibilities: either you are a self-sacrificial simpleton, or you have your own intentions against me. I could always use more lambs willing to feed themselves to the lion."

The words were out before Sefa could rethink them, propelled by a sharp burst of indignation. "And if I am not a lamb? If I have my own intentions?"

Vaida smiled. "Even more reason to keep you close, isn't it?"

Ice trickled down Sefa's spine, and she took a step back. Sefa *wished* she had insidious intentions. It seemed the popular thing to do. Maybe she could develop one or two after she left this place. "I respect Your Majesty too much to accept a position I know myself to lack the qualifications for," Sefa said, steeling herself. "Your efforts would be better directed at a more suitable candidate."

Sultana Vaida paused, a complicated array of expressions chronicling her surprise. The room fell into a contemplative silence while Sefa braced herself for Vaida's reaction.

And there *would* be a reaction. People like Marek and the Sultana, who used their looks like currency, never took it well when they realized beauty didn't carry a universal value. Marek had apologized over and over for how he reacted after Sefa told him she would never be able to reciprocate his feelings. He'd be crushed to learn that the memory of waking up to find Marek gone still haunted Sefa. Three days. Three days she spent in terror and regret, wondering if he'd return. Trying to understand when their definitions of *love* had taken such drastically divergent meanings.

Marek had come back with a basket of apples and a flimsy slew of apologies. A miscalculation of time, he'd said. But Sefa, fearful she'd wake up the next morning to find him missing once more, hadn't been fooled by his newfound forgiveness. "I love you so much," she had sobbed. "If you let me, I will live and die at your side. But I don't—I can't love you the way you asked me to. I don't think I can love anyone that way."

He'd held her while she wept, his mouth shaping promises against the top of her head, vowing never to leave her again. A promise he kept.

But sometimes, in dark moments like these, Sefa couldn't help but wonder if Marek's acceptance came too readily. If he only forgave the rejection because her heart and body would never belong to *anyone*, so he wouldn't have to witness someone else succeed where he had failed.

Sultana Vaida merely regarded Sefa thoughtfully. "You're searching for someone."

Sefa's blood ran cold. She knotted her hands together to keep them from trembling. It was just speculation. A mere guess shot out like an arrow at a board, nothing more. If Vaida knew the truth, Sefa would be in chains.

"Friend, family member? A lover?"

Sefa stayed silent.

"Here is my last offer. Work for me at the Ivory Palace for one month. You will serve as my eyes and ears in the court, and I expect nightly reports of the whispers winding through my palace. In exchange, I'll help you find whoever you are searching for."

Sefa's breath caught. Vaida would help her find Marek and Sylvia? The resources at the Sultana's disposal were staggering, and her influence was second only to Nizahl's. With Vaida's help, Sefa could scour through the ends of the earth for Marek and Sylvia.

Not Sylvia.

Essiya of Jasad. Also known as the most wanted woman in the kingdoms.

Sefa didn't care about any of the scheming and maneuverings of the royals. She'd grown up with a ladder-climbing mother and a well-spoken scoundrel for a stepfather. The games of these courts were blood-soaked and savage; Sefa wanted nothing to do with them.

Except that if Arin was chasing Essiya, then Vaida would be, too.

Sultana Vaida raised a hand to adjust the white lace trim under the neckline of her dress. The craftsmanship temporarily distracted Sefa, who had always prided herself on an ability to replicate any design she encountered to near perfection. Every garment she'd spotted in the Sultana's closet left Sefa questioning her own years of training.

It took Sefa several seconds to stop thinking about how she'd re-create the lace's pattern and notice the ring on Vaida's third finger.

It was the ring she and Sylvia had tried to steal in the Omal palace. The ring that had scorched Sefa's fingers when she tried to pick it up; the ring Arin of Nizahl had rolled into a mold after rendering the Sultana unconscious.

She thinks she can win a war against Nizahl, Sylvia had said.

Sefa stood before the Sultana of Lukub with the memory of Corpse Walker's spoon knocking against her resistant mouth, and she wondered if the Sultana had ever felt powerless. She wondered if Sefa's mother had been right, and Sefa would always be led by her heart instead of her head.

Her mother meant it as an insult. Most people did. But it was Sefa's heart that told her to pack a bag and flee Nizahl with the golden-haired rich boy who'd inexplicably stayed by her side since they were children. The same heart that saw the hostile, lonely girl skulking around Raya's keep and decided to make her a friend. The best decisions Sefa had ever made—the bravest decisions—had always come from her heart.

It protected what it loved better than Sefa's mind ever could.

"If you give me funds to find my companions instead of searching for them yourself, I will agree to remain as your attendant and bring you news of your palace."

Sefa didn't let her gaze linger on Vaida's ring. The first rule of any royal court: never let them see you coming.

The phantom Sylvia would shake Sefa until her teeth rattled out of her mouth if she saw Sefa bargaining with a woman so dangerous—so prone to fatal whimsy and sadistic retaliation—that she unsettled even the Commander of Nizahl.

Sefa was tired of being the person everyone constantly needed to protect. The weakness in a room of warriors. That ring was leverage. A bargaining chip.

Power.

Vaida stared at Sefa. Her lips eased into a smile.

"Consider it done."

CHAPTER NINE

ARIN

Arin reclined in his seat at the head of an excessively long table and imagined setting fire to the room.

Wishful thinking, but the idea tempted Arin more the longer he watched the council bicker. A particularly opaque Nizahlan proverb came to mind, one his father had been partial to when teaching Arin about the foils of pursuing a plan out of passion instead of strategy. *Those with hunger and no vision will catch the duck and gorge themselves on its feathers.*

He hadn't understood it until this moment, sitting silently while men and women of supposedly advanced intelligence scrambled to ensure their horrible ideas were heard louder than the horrible ideas of the person next to them.

The war wing of the Citadel was the only one of the three—formerly four—wings of the Citadel strictly forbidden to anyone other than the council, royals, and their guards. The first time he walked into Hatem Hall, shortly after the Victor's Ball, Arin had counted no less than seventy-seven active spiderwebs.

Lanterns hung above the iron-banded table, dangling from a peaked glass ceiling. The chairs were built many millennia ago from the oldest trees in Essam, and the austere wood had seated thousands of increasingly foolish counselors passing through Hatem Hall. Basalt had been carved into sharp, long raven feathers and forged to the back of the Commander's chair at the head of the table. Their shadow stretched like raised wings on either side of Arin.

When the counselors' blathering finally breached the outer limits of Arin's patience, he spoke. "Sama, correct me if I'm mistaken, but are you suggesting we rip apart every kingdom's poorest population with an overwhelming show of military force on the slight chance we'll capture members of a rebel group I have already scoured those same kingdoms for?"

"What other choice do we have, sire?" Sama asked. Her pin-straight hair fell in an assertive cut around her square jaw, giving Arin the impression of a soldier playing at accountant. "The rebellions in Omal's lower villages have made it impossible to search for the Jasad Heir without meddling in Omal's affairs."

Three schools of thought—*thought* being a word Arin hesitated to apply to the intellectual backwash spewing from everyone in the room—had solidified in the last several hours. The longer Arin considered them, the harder it became to mask his scorn.

Arin tapped a finger against the edge of the table, counting the ridges. Disdain dripped from his voice. "There will be no Nizahlan interference in the lower village rebellions. The chances of the Jasad Heir hiding in the Omalian lower villages are negligible, and I will not violate our own laws on a poorly calculated gamble."

Rebellion had been brewing against the Omal crown for some time, and it had only grown stronger after Felix saw fit to interrupt Mahair's Alcalah waleema by hurling a child in front of his horses.

In this, Nizahl's founding laws had always been absolute: unless it involved magic or directly compromised Nizahlan lives, they would not interfere with the internal affairs of another kingdom. The villagers could dismember Felix and hoist him on the spires of his own palace, and if it did not involve magic, Arin would execute any soldier who walked onto Omalian soil to intervene.

A few other counselors wanted to gather Sultana Vaida, Queen Hanan, and King Murib to secure their support and convince them to give Nizahl complete freedom to search their territories until the Jasad Heir was found.

Arin crossed one leg over the other. He affected a tone as lazy as his posture, befitting the value of the proposition. "King Murib hasn't strategized beyond what he plans to have for breakfast since the Jasad War. Sorn runs most of the army's operations. And as we know, the whole of the Orban Heir's time is dedicated to searching for a cure for his comatose Champion."

Sorn's continued grief over his Champion had surprised everyone, including Arin. Rarely did Champions live to see the end of the Alcalah—a fact Arin would have thought Sorn needed no reminding of.

Even now, Sorn's frantic bellowing while his Champion hung limp in his arms rang in Arin's ears. The sound had played in the background of his own consuming panic as Arin dragged the Jasad Heir out of the sand. Though her head hadn't gone under like Diya of Orban, her limp body and shallow breathing had been sufficient to strip Arin of any sense of relief.

Arin shook off the uninvited recollection. Until Sorn gave up on finding a cure for Diya, he was useless.

Arin continued, "The Zinish Accords are the only reason Sultana Vaida has not instigated war with us. I see no worthwhile reason to offer the Sultana a way to implicate Nizahl in a breach of the accords by involving her in our search."

"The Sultana has a long history of running right up against the barriers of the Zinish Accords before backing down," Layla added, speaking for the first time. The Nizahl emissary had been quietly taking notes since she sat down.

Arin nodded. "Layla is right. For years, Sultana Vaida has tested the limits of the Zinish Accords like a cat with a mouse under its paw: too clever to risk removing its grip entirely and too mischievous to resist pressing down."

"What about Omal? Are we positive Queen Hanan holds no sway over her nephew?" Faheem asked. The newly appointed High Counselor ran the pad of his thumb over his brow, studying his notes with a weariness Arin knew all too well.

Faheem was the second person Arin had appointed to the council. The first was Layla. One by one, Arin's people were replacing his father's.

It had not gone unnoticed.

Gersiny, the oldest counselor in the room, shook his head. "Queen Hanan barely leaves the Omal palace, and reports have come back saying her health has taken a turn for the worse. The shock of seeing her son's daughter alive has been difficult."

"What does it matter? She's been obsolete since the Blood Summit," said Sama. "Felix should be our target. He helms the kingdom and its substantial resources. He has every reason to want the Jasad Queen captured. Her father was first Heir of Omal; her blood gives her a direct claim to his throne."

"Felix is a spoiled child," Faheem replied. "The magnitude of an allyship is beyond his comprehension, and we cannot rely on the support of a vacillating ruler who holds his power like a rattle in a baby's fist. We already have access into Omal and the rest of the kingdoms through the Madeen Declaration—as long as the soldiers do not exceed their bounds, we have written authority to search for the Jasad Queen as we see fit."

"We don't even have enough soldiers to spare," Bayoum said, and thus arose the third—and most grating—school of thought.

Years of practice kept Arin's expression smooth and unreactive. Bayoum's proposal seemed simple on its face. Reinstitute mandatory conscription across Nizahl, including in the lower villages, and eliminate the middle two tiers of training so the soldiers graduated faster.

Ham-fisted, lazy, and full of flaws. Just like every other idea Bayoum had proposed.

Under Nizahlan law, Arin couldn't remove a previous appointee to the council without cause. The rule allowed council members to speak truthfully on divisive matters without fearing the loss of their position or wasting time with flattery of the next Commander. Ordinarily, Arin would find the rule useful. Since it guaranteed the continued presence of Bayoum in the council room, he hated it.

Faheem cleared his throat. New as he was to his role, he hadn't quite found his footing among his new colleagues. "We can't risk what would happen if news of the Jasad Heir's existence spread."

Bayoum groaned. Dishwater-brown hair curved over and behind the counselor's head like a peeled banana, as slippery as his ever-shifting eyes and too-ready smile. "As I've repeated, the news will spread eventually. If not today, then tomorrow, or the day after, or the day after. The Urabi did not risk their necks breaking into the Citadel to abduct her so they could tuck her away and let her go to waste."

"We still don't know it was an abduction. She probably snuck them onto the Citadel's grounds before the third trial and gave them the signal to attack during the ball," Sama interjected. She firmly believed the Victor and the Urabi had been in communication the entire time.

Arin's fingers curled instinctively, his gloves sparing his fingernails from splintering against the table.

It wasn't the first time Sama had shared her theory. In fact, she wasn't even the first person to entertain the possibility that the Urabi and the Heir had been colluding throughout the Alcalah.

The Jasad Heir had been lying to him since the beginning. It would make perfect sense that she'd been lying about more than just her identity.

Except, Arin didn't see the use of it. He didn't see what she stood to gain from enduring the Alcalah and risking her life in each trial if she was merely waiting for the right moment to join the Urabi.

If escape had been her goal all along, she would have taken it when he offered.

Run. Take a horse and get as far away as you can.

Be free.

Faheem cleared his throat, reclaiming Arin's attention. "If we conscript half the lower villages, they'll find out about her much sooner than if we let nature take its course."

"It's not nature that'll decide!" Bayoum threw his arms into the air, and the conversation promptly devolved.

Arin counted the table's ridges.

Five years ago, Arin's elimination of non-wartime conscription in the lower villages had been met with outrage. He had explained it just once: nobody should be wearing Nizahl's uniform or lifting a sword in its name who did not wish to.

Bayoum had made a career of attempting to reverse every policy Arin implemented. The existence of the Jasad Heir had given him a perfect opportunity to take aim at conscription.

As long as Arin remained Nizahl's Commander, his word on all military dictates reigned. No amount of impassioned arm-waving from Bayoum could change the simple fact that unless Arin died, appointed his offspring as successor, or was found guilty of treason against Nizahl, the forces of this kingdom answered to him, and him alone.

The only other way to remove a sitting Commander was to hold a Nitraus Vote.

The legal mechanism had been put into place in 930 A.E. in response to the actions of a particularly maniacal Commander, and it had been used exactly three times throughout history. The Nitraus Vote allowed the council, with the support of the Supreme, to override a Commander in order to instigate or end a war. A Nitraus

Vote meant all faith had been lost in the authority and judgment of the Commander.

The Nitraus Vote was a relic. A few paltry lines among thousands in Nizahl's legal texts. Arin had forced himself to consider the option—to unravel that particular future within his mind's eye—until he felt comfortable setting it aside.

To his right, Layla yawned just as she caught Arin's eye. She blushed a bright red and straightened in her seat.

She turned back to the squabbling with an attentiveness bordering on comical, clearly embarrassed. Not as though Arin blamed her for losing interest, but Layla took immense pride in her work. Most people were surprised when Arin introduced Layla as the interkingdom emissary, since everything about her radiated guilelessness. Her round, heart-shaped face and wide eyes. The golden hair drifting around her shoulders like a cloud of sunshine, left loose to give her the opportunity to demurely tuck the strands behind her ears.

The impression of softness and vulnerability was one she had wielded with expert skill across a variety of scheming courts. Her subtle approach had taken Arin longer than usual to recognize. She did not assert her opinions or forcefully impress her will upon a higher authority. Instead, Layla would press against their resolve, over and over, a gentle wave eroding the most unyielding rock. The style required a patience and stability of temperament Arin admired.

Layla glanced at Arin again, and he remembered to avert his eyes too late. Her flush deepened, prodding at a tension Arin would rather leave forgotten.

Arin had known Layla since childhood, and any romantic interest Arin may have contemplated faded soon after it sparked. For as expertly as Layla navigated the twisted games of royalty, Arin had the sense she had never crossed the line into experiencing the true savagery leashed at its core. Hers was a high-collared life of perfume politics and deals struck over lavish meals in gilded manors.

If I were a sensible woman, I would slit your throat while you slept.

Arin thrust the memory aside with an impatient hand. He did not need to scour his own mind to understand that a certain kind of violence appealed to him—that the Jasad Heir's oceans of wrath had called to Arin like a poisoned fountain to a parched man.

With a strained smile, Faheem interrupted the latest round of bickering to suggest, "With Your Highness's leave, let us disperse and reconvene later in the day. After sunset, perhaps, if it should please the council."

When Arin gave a short nod, Faheem melted into his chair.

"Sunset, then," the new High Counselor said.

CHAPTER TEN

ARIN

At the door, Layla stepped into Arin's path. "Your Highness, might I have a word?"

No, Arin wanted to bite out. He had had enough of other people's words today.

Layla wound and unwound her hands together—a nervous tic or a clever impression of one.

He exhaled through his nose, casting a glance upward at the statue of Nizahl's founder.

Molded to appear as if he were bursting through the wall and growing over the ceiling was Nizahl's first Commander and Supreme. Sculpted in mid-motion, Fareed loomed over the top of the door to the council room. The two swords he had carried in countless battles were crossed above his head. Flying from between the clashing swords, a raven spread its wings wide, the feathers fanning across the ceiling.

Under the watchful gaze of Nizahl's founder, Arin thrust aside his impatience and gestured for Layla to walk with him. He moved at a steady clip, more than ready to put distance between himself and the council. In a typical month, he saw the council once a week to review petitions and hear updates on the provinces they controlled. Since the Victor's Ball, Arin had been subjected to their presence almost twice a day. A rusted sword through his extremities would be a more welcome experience.

Servants stopped to bow as they passed Arin, but he dismissed them back to their duties with a wave. At the corner, Arin slowed, allowing Layla to catch her breath. Two guards pushed the front doors open at Arin's approach.

As soon as Arin stepped out of the war wing, his chest expanded with its first full breath of the day. He pressed two fingers to the ache in his jaw, borne from hours of clenching his teeth. By nightfall, it would travel upward and pound between his temples while he tried to sleep.

Temporarily ignoring Layla's jittery presence, Arin tipped his chin toward the sky, searching idly for the sun. It would be nice to feel it on his skin, if just for a minute. He felt, strangely, as though he had forgotten what it was to be warm.

"Sire?"

Arin cast one last sweep over the unyielding slates of gray. "What is it, Layla?"

Perhaps sensing Arin's dissipating interest in their conversation, Layla jumped straight to the point. "The Omal Heir is conducting raids on the lower villages, Your Highness. His soldiers have slain fourteen Nizahl soldiers at their outposts in Essam, but the palace claims it was the lower villagers' doing."

"I see." Arin tucked his hands into the pockets of his coat. "Send a troop of fourth-year soldiers to the Omalian nobles' quarters. Station them outside their homes and say it is for their protection."

Layla blinked. "We are sending soldiers to protect the Omalian nobles?"

Arin carefully pinched the spark of irritation between thumb and forefinger. Should it be allowed to land, Arin had a sense he would ignite.

"Seeing Nizahl soldiers strewn around their property will anger the nobles. Angry nobles keep their purse strings clasped tight. Felix will either cease his raids on the lower villages or find his capital city at odds with its richest inhabitants."

"You've already thought about this." She laughed a little. "Of course you have."

What else would Arin think about? Capturing the Jasad Heir and preventing magic from tossing them into another war? No, no, his time was much better spent strategizing ways to keep the kingdoms from cannibalizing themselves.

Layla clasped her hands in front of her, the six delicate gold bracelets around her wrist clinking with the movement. Last time he saw her, she had been wearing five.

"Are congratulations in order?" he asked, offering a ghost of a smile. Normally, he wouldn't have asked. He wasn't sure why he did now. Lingering solidarity from their shared misery at the council meeting, perhaps.

After a bewildered beat, Layla glanced down at her wrist and sighed. "Not this time, I'm afraid. Our courtship only lasted a month. My parents weren't fond of him; they said a structuralist from Ukaz would eventually want a wife more interested in homemaking than negotiating with 'lecherous nobles in smoky dens of iniquity.' Poor man denied it, but their suspicions got into my head." She rubbed a thumb over the sixth bracelet. "Just more bad luck for me, I suppose."

"I'm sorry to hear it," Arin said, and he meant it. Nizahl's southwest provinces had a history of despising their northern counterparts. They found the pettiest ways to spite each other. Firras, Layla's hometown, took part in the old Nizahlan tradition of collecting a gold bracelet from each suitor who came knocking. In Ukaz, they collected silver rings. If Firras hosted a festival, Ukaz flooded the roads. Ukaz ate sardines to celebrate spring, so Firras broke multiple laws to dam a section of Hirun and collect as many sardines as they could.

"I am not worried for you, Layla." Arin did not make a habit of commenting on the personal lives of those in his employ, nor was he regularly offered anything to comment on. "The man worthy of calling himself your match will find you when the time is right."

"I wish he would find me faster." Layla smoothed the front of her blouse, shaking herself off. They resumed walking across the Citadel's lawn. "I'll send the fourth-years riding to Omal by nightfall. With any luck, Felix will reconsider the wisdom of his actions."

Arin's shoulders relaxed a fraction now that they were back on familiar footing. He didn't share that he very much doubted Felix had any wisdom to reconsider.

A brisk wind lifted his hair from his neck. Arin tilted his head, indulging the breeze, and made the mistake of glancing at Layla.

His emissary's gaze transformed with resigned longing, not unlike how Arin might have looked as he searched for a glimpse of the sun amid the clouds.

The tension returned to Arin's jaw. She typically hid this… problem…better. She was out of sorts today, and Arin didn't have the time or patience to manage another conversation.

Arin stopped walking, turning fully to face her. As soon as she met his eyes, the longing in hers dimmed, retreating as Arin knew it would.

A strong leader played every advantage they were given to its greatest potential. Arin's looks were nothing more than a lure, and one he rarely bothered to use. Unless he devoted himself to the deception, Arin's eyes would always give him away.

Cold. Removed. Inhospitable to anything tender or soft.

Movement slid into his periphery just as he opened his mouth to ask Layla if she had any further matters to discuss.

Arin went still as stone.

It couldn't be.

In the shadow of the east wing, a woman stood on the grass. Her back was turned to Arin. Black curls cascaded over her broad shoulders, loose in a way Arin knew she disliked. She turned slightly, facing the tower, and a rough sound scraped and died in his throat.

No. No, she wouldn't be this stupid. She knew better.

The woman who couldn't be the Jasad Heir stepped toward the side of the east wing and poked it.

Arin took a step forward. His hand slid into the left pocket of his coat, closing around the thin, needlelike blade. It would immobilize her long enough for the right restraints and reinforcements to arrive.

His hand spasmed around the knife.

This wasn't real. She would never be this reckless.

Fighting the dryness of his mouth, Arin said, "Layla, turn around slowly and tell me what you see."

The Jasad Heir–shaped hallucination crouched and pressed her palms to the grass. She patted the ground with increasing panic.

"Um, there are guards patrolling the gate. A bluebird hiding in the bushes. A cloud of gnats by the garden's archway."

Layla couldn't see her. Layla couldn't see her, which meant she wasn't here. Either Arin had gone mad in the last ten minutes, or some strange magic was afoot. But Arin's sensitivity to magic meant he never failed to see the edges of a glamor or sense the charge of it in the air, and everything aside from the hallucination of the Jasad Heir remained perfectly normal.

"My lord, are you all right?"

Capturing Essiya of Jasad at the Citadel's door after she managed to hide her identity from Arin for months defied every tenet of logic. It made more sense to assume he'd gone mad.

The hallucination scrunched her face in familiar frustration.

"Sire!" Layla's shout sent the bluebird into flight. Sylvia's head snapped up. Arin's hand went still against the knife as wide dark eyes found his. Eyes he'd watched light in anger and dance with humor, eyes that were never cold or removed.

Eyes that had once felt warmer against his skin than the sun ever could.

A small hand closed around Arin's forearm. His attention snapped to the point of contact, and whatever expression he wore was severe enough for Layla to retract her hand instantly.

In the split second of distraction, the hallucination vanished. Arin scanned the courtyard. Nothing. As though she was never there.

Pale breath shuddered out of Arin. After another minute, he tore his reluctant gaze from the grass.

He didn't have time to lose his mind. He had a war to avoid.

"Forgive me," Arin told Layla. He adopted a soothing, intimate tone. It would derail several of Arin's plans if Layla joined the ranks of those who believed his judgment was impaired. "I slept little last night and thought I saw a stranger on the premises. I did not intend to handle you roughly."

"There is nothing to forgive, Your Highness. You can handle me however you like." As soon as the words left Layla's mouth, a fierce blush stole over her cheeks. Arin pretended not to notice.

The bell tolled the hour, and Arin firmly guided his attention away from one dangerous realization.

His first instinct when he saw *her* wasn't to reach for his blade or summon the guards.

It was to shout *run*.

Red sparks arched over the blacksmith's worktable as the chisel slammed against the base of the steel sword. The same sound rang from every smithery in Nizahl, echoing from the upper towns to the lowest street in Galim's Bend.

Vaun shifted restlessly beside Arin, watching the blacksmith work with no small amount of disdain. The guardsman had never been keen on lowering himself to learn the mechanics upon which the working society made its living. He never wondered where the food on his plate came from, never dwelled on why the hilt of his sword was rounded instead of squared. When Arin felt generous, he interpreted Vaun's disinterest as a narrow focus, which left little quarter for curiosity.

Another clear example—Vaun had insisted on joining Arin for each visit he paid to dozens of blacksmiths across Nizahl. Vaun was in plainclothes, his guardsman's pin—the symbol of his role in Arin's service and rank in the Citadel—tucked in his pocket.

Arin's mission was Vaun's. Arin's safety, Vaun's sole interest.

"Do you think they will be necessary?" Vaun watched the blacksmith rush to the orange maw of the furnace.

The blacksmith's assistant offered Arin a petrified bow before hurrying past. He whispered in the blacksmith's ear, pointing to the drawing Arin had provided every blacksmith and welder in the kingdom. They traced the carving Arin had paid handsomely to have forged into hundreds of swords across Nizahl.

"I hope not," Arin said.

If these particular swords were ever placed in the hands of Nizahl's armies, it would mean the Zinish Accords had been broken.

It would mean for the first time in over a century, Lukub and Nizahl were at war.

"The Sultana wouldn't risk war with Nizahl now. Not with the threat of magic hanging over our heads." Vaun's lip curled, and Arin watched him swallow back another remark. In an unspoken agreement, neither of them discussed the Jasad Heir or their time in the tunnels. By the same token, they avoided invoking the memory of Vaun betraying Arin to his father shortly after Arin terminated him from his employ.

"It is a waste of time to try to predict which impulse Vaida might indulge on any given day," Arin said. "All we can do is plan for every outcome."

The blacksmith and his assistant bowed once more as Arin and

Vaun left the shop. With regret, Arin noticed the blacksmith's shaking hands finally still as soon as Arin's eyes were no longer on him. Perhaps these visits were not as productive to the task as Arin hoped. If their Heir's presence unnerved the blacksmiths, then he would send Wes in his stead.

A cart rumbled past them, two women and six children seated in the open wagon. Piles of barley surrounded them. The smallest child had his arms wrapped tight around a chicken as the wagon rocked over the uneven road.

Arin took one last look at the sigil engraved in the newly forged swords piled at the corner of the blacksmith's bench.

For now, they were just a precaution. An untested theory.

Arin did not hold much faith it would stay that way.

CHAPTER ELEVEN

SYLVIA

I woke up on the ground, Maia and Namsa sitting cross-legged on either side of me. They sipped from steaming reddish glasses, casual as a sunny day.

Battling the dizziness in my head, I pushed myself onto an elbow and tried to convince the muscles in my stomach to contract and pull me the rest of the way up. "Where…" My throat tightened, rippling with pain. "Where am I?"

"The Geneina," Maia answered. "We like to bring the children here to celebrate the holidays. Youm il Fark, Zeenat Hend, you know. We thought it might be less jarring for you."

Gold and silver light whirled around the domed ceiling, creating an imitation of the sun that hurt to look at for longer than a second. Though the sun might have been false, the rows of green crops rustling around us were very real. So were the flowers—more colors and kinds than I could count, wrapping around the walls, dangling in vines from the ceiling, blossoming over the ground.

I stared at the gently rotating sun. The hall I had trained in for the Alcalah had had a moving sky just like this. Instead of flowers, the opposite wall had showcased a looping scene with Usr Jasad and my grandparents.

"What happened? The last thing I remember is trying to kill Efra." I perked up. "Is he dead?"

"No," Namsa said.

"He is in quite a bit of pain, though," Maia reassured me, earning herself a quick frown from Namsa.

"Maia put you down before you could do serious damage. It took every drop of her magic," Namsa scolded.

"Put me down," I repeated slowly.

"I have a... specific kind of magic," she said. "Many of us in the Gibal do. One of my abilities includes severing someone's consciousness without causing them harm."

"You were going to kill Efra," Namsa added. "We had no choice."

My body finally remembered it could function, and I pushed myself the rest of the way upright. I slapped aside the ropes of flowers trailing dozens of feet from the high ceiling like a suspended waterfall of color. Petals carpeted the ground.

Sultana Vaida would drown a hundred children to get her hands on these flowers.

"So the dream—it was your doing?" I demanded. "It wasn't real?"

Maia and Namsa exchanged another glance. One more secretive look, and I would start biting. They had already put me down like a feral animal twice. I may as well reap the benefits.

"Dream?" Maia folded a long, wavy strand of hair behind her ear. "I was very careful to keep your mind clear, Mawlati. I didn't want to risk causing your magic to react against mine."

"What kind of dream? What did you see?" Namsa set aside her glass, watching me intently.

I saw him.

The words clogged up in my chest, restrained by a caution I didn't entirely understand. It had just been a dream—what harm was there in sharing a dream?

The Citadel had looked as dread-inspiring and terrible as the first time I rode through its gates. With seven stone wings curving out from a sky-high central tower, the Citadel's architecture resembled a nightmarish spider waiting to pounce. Except for the wing I had destroyed the night of the Victor's Ball, every grim detail had been the exact same.

My dreams were always vivid, but this... I'd prodded the wall of the central tower, and when it didn't dissipate into smoke, I'd fallen to the ground, tearing at the grass. Trying to break the illusion, because it *had* to be an illusion. I'd escaped from the Citadel. I was in a mountain many leagues from this accursed place, bracketed by the woods and the sea.

Then I'd heard a woman shout.

A woman stood at a less-than-respectable distance from him, her petite features colored with worry.

There he was. Blue eyes like a cold fire, fixed on me.

An illusion could perfect many aspects of Arin. The cut of his black coat falling to his boots. The matching gloves, as synonymous with the Nizahl Heir as his shining silver hair. Even the tiny violet ravens etched into the sleeves of his coat could be conjured by a creative and observant bit of magic.

But his eyes. The steadiness of his gaze. The iciness of it, nearly impossible to penetrate or crack.

No magic could re-create Arin of Nizahl's eyes.

The woman had grabbed Arin's arm. He'd turned his head, removing me from the shackles of his attention, but it was too late. Half a second was all it took to understand that either I'd suffered a critical loss of sanity or my magic had gone awry.

Seeing the woman take Arin's arm as I disappeared had also inspired a fury I wasn't familiar with, and I was familiar with many, many flavors of fury.

I rolled my shoulders, dislodging the dream like a stray piece of lint. "What Efra said on the cliffside. Is it true?"

Namsa sighed. "The plan was in motion before we captured you at the Victor's Ball. Otherwise, we wouldn't have authorized it without your input."

I staggered to my feet, grabbing one of the dangling flower ropes to steady myself. The world blurred, and I squeezed my eyes shut as my stomach revolted. "Someone needs to warn him."

"Warn who?" Namsa shot to her feet. "The Silver Serpent? Are you mad?"

"This breaks the rules." I could hear the nonsense spilling out of my mouth, and despite my full awareness of how it would sound to the other Jasadis, I couldn't bring myself to rein it in. "We have rules."

Maia grabbed Namsa's arm when she took a step toward me. Namsa's glare would have shriveled another person, and I shrank from the force of her disgust. "Awaleen below, maybe Efra is right. Maybe she cannot be trusted."

"Of course not!" I exploded. "You abducted me, shot me full of tranquilizers, and then knocked me out *again* when I wasn't behaving the way you wanted. Your rules are clear: keep the Heir docile, keep the Heir away from any important decision-making. Guess what? I have my own rules, too. I know the Nizahl Heir better than any of you, and our greatest chance at success is by staying within the parameters he ascribes to. Arin follows the precise letter of his laws—what do you think will happen when we use magic to unleash a slew of magical beasts onto an unsuspecting Nizahlan lower village?"

Maia held her arms out to the sides, trying to wedge herself between me and Namsa. "Efra acted recklessly, but the strategy is sound. Disarray allows us to move undetected."

"No, it allows *them* to move unchecked."

Namsa's teeth clicked together. Were I not so profoundly furious, her silence would have been gratifying. "These kingdoms have decree after decree dictating their every decision. Hundreds of internal and external agreements and accords. In all of them, you will find a provision basically stating that none of it counts if a kingdom faces an imminent risk to its security. What you are about to cause is anarchy. It is imminent risk."

"How do you know this?" Namsa regarded me strangely.

"How do you *not* know this? Doesn't half your ridiculous plan hinge on reinstating me to the Omal line of inheritance? You should have tracked down copies of every important document and memorized them front and back."

Hanim's specter rose, looming over me. She had known reviving Jasad would require more than just magic, more than effectively swinging a sword. The most lethal acts in a royal court often happened without shedding a single drop of blood. Words were the currency of the powerful.

"Is there any way to stop it?" I forced out.

Namsa shook her head. "I don't think so."

I wrapped my hands around two of the vines and yanked with all my might. A plume of petals rained over us, and the vines went slack in my grip as they tore at the root.

"Gather your Aada, Namsa." I tossed aside the vines, shoving past the pair. "Maybe we can prevent our first strike in this war from being our last."

While Namsa gathered the council, I hunted down Efra. It took some time, since the architecture of the Gibal was governed by magical logic instead of structural coherency. Each layer of the mountain served a separate function: the top was reserved for bedrooms and the dining hall, the middle three for recreation and strategy rooms, and the bottom for basic functions like bathing.

I tracked Efra to the lowest level. Steam billowed over me as soon as I entered the washroom, soaking into my tunic. The walls curved around the heated spring like a stone raindrop, a hole punched into the side for the steam. The spring took up the space of a modest lake, and I wagered it could hold forty to fifty people at a time. With the lake frozen on the cliffside, Maia had mentioned the children loved to swim here during the winter. I had been taking my baths upstairs, where nobody could see the scars forming a second skin over my back.

Efra leaned over the edge of the spring, shirt discarded and fingers hooked at the waistband of his pants. A giant black-and-blue bruise in the shape of my boot decorated his torso. His lip had stopped bleeding, but the stretched skin around his eye had blackened and sunk.

Maybe Maia had had the right idea, knocking me out.

When I materialized from between the clouds of steam, Efra jumped, dropping his shirt into the spring.

"Damn it," he growled, fishing out his sodden garment. "Can you wait? I'll be done in fifteen minutes, and I would much rather not spend those fifteen minutes sharing a bath with you."

I rolled my eyes. "I would sooner bathe with a corpse."

"If you finish what you started earlier, you very well might."

My lips twitched. Were Efra not the equivalent of a walking migraine, I could see myself enjoying his company every now and again.

"Maia said you could have prevented me from killing you, but you chose not to." I crossed my arms over my chest. "What kind of magic do you have?"

Efra scoffed. "The better question is why I would have rather died than used my magic on you."

I blinked. "The same reason Namsa refused to fight me when I woke up in the Gibal. I am your Malika."

"No."

I waited, but he did not elaborate further. I thought about pushing the matter, but frankly, I was more interested in Efra's magic than in his philosophy about its use. "It cannot be defensive magic—not with how feebly you fight."

He wrung his shirt out in the spring. "I can show you, if you'd like."

I shrugged. "All right. Do your worst."

Gold leaked into Efra's eyes. Silver streaked over his irises just as he lifted a hand and said, "I thought you would never ask."

Rage.

My fingers curled as rage roared to life inside me. I itched to feel Felix struggle beneath my hands as I strangled the life he didn't deserve to live out of his pampered body. I would carve Fairel's name into his corpse and leave his decaying remains on her doorstep. I wanted to rip my knife into Supreme Rawain. I'd aim for his face first, open him from cheek to cheek like prize meat at a festival. I would take my time. For his death, I would master patience. Draw out his agony until the walls rang with it. He—

"Wow," Efra said. "Certainly potent and ready with your rage, aren't you?"

He flicked his hand.

Grief.

Tears filled my eyes. I missed Marek and Sefa almost more than I could bear. I didn't know where they were, if they were safe. Their friendship had weakened me. Before them, I hadn't known what it meant to be lonely. I just was, and life went on. Fairel, Rory, Raya—what did they think happened to me? It felt like Dawoud dying in my arms all over again.

Efra cleared his throat. A single tear had slipped out. My fingernails tore slashes into the heel of my hand. He could enhance my emotions, but could he see the reasons behind them?

I didn't know the name of the next one. Suddenly, I was at the head of the stairwell in the Ivory Palace, placing my gloved hand into Arin's as we descended. I was watching him arrange my clothes by the door so I would be ready in the morning. Holding me as I wept in my burning room in the Omal palace. *I am just a man*, and the tenderness spreading over him as he hovered over me, the vulnerability in his eyes as I smiled and drew him down for another kiss. His face as the cuffs slid from my wrists and magic ruptured through the Citadel.

"Sad little broken heart." Efra flattened his palm, and I gasped, freed from the choking misery of missing a man I didn't dare name.

"There is something back there I don't recognize." It sounded like Efra was talking to himself. "What *is* that?"

The next wave had the opposite effect of the others. Instead of a barrage of intensified emotion, I relaxed. The furrows in my forehead smoothed, and my arms loosened at my sides. Frost chased away the residue of pain in my heart.

The man near the spring watched me with alarm. "Essiya?"

The vein in my palm was glowing again. I tilted my head, bemused. I had known this man's name at some point. I also vaguely remembered he had tried to harm me.

This is for your own good!

I sneered. That voice! I knew it as well as I knew that the name this insect had just spoken wasn't the right one. I needed to find the voice and finish it once and for all.

Before I had taken a step, the panicked boy swept his hands apart, threads of magic sparking in the space between his fingers. The net flew toward me and melted against my skin.

I coughed and massaged my ribs.

"Impressive," I said, straightening from my hunch. "Enhancing and diminishing emotions. A nice trick. Unless it extends to physical sensations like hunger, I think you overestimate its value."

I may as well have spoken in a foreign tongue for the attention Efra paid my remark. "What in the tombs was that?"

"What?"

"What I amplified...I've never experienced anything like it. It felt—" Efra passed a shaking hand over his forehead. "Whatever that was inside you, it is completely devoid of any humanity. If I hadn't pulled my magic back, I think you would have killed me."

"I wouldn't have killed you." But even as I said it, a seed of doubt caught in my teeth. Already, the memory of the strange coldness was retreating. I'd wanted to go somewhere. Find...something.

I shook my head, casting it aside. I had enough real problems without inventing new ones. "The steam addled your limited senses. Make yourself decent and be present at the Aada so we can fix the catastrophe you created."

I left, Efra's gaze heavy on my neck, and crushed the seed before it could root.

CHAPTER TWELVE

MAREK

Marek's lifelong trouble was this: unless someone stopped him, he was liable to find himself on track to be expeditiously murdered.

He turned on the cot, mindful of jostling the soldier sleeping in the bunk below him. Finding himself on the wrong side of a sleep-deprived Nizahl soldier had taught him how to dodge a punch better than any formal training could. His brothers had taken swings at him more times than Marek could count before his parents finally let him have his own bedroom.

Years of stealth informed Marek's movements as he climbed down the ladder at the end of the bunk. The soldier—Zaid? Zain?—didn't stir as Marek gathered his shoes from the pile by the door and slipped into the hall.

Marek closed the door behind him and released his breath. He tugged on his shoes.

As he strode past rows of closed doors, vigilant of the sleeping soldiers stacked into rooms that hadn't known the pleasure of a mop since the dawn of the Awaleen, Marek thought of his family.

Amira, Hani, Binyar, Darin—all of Marek's older siblings had slept in a clustered, morbid compound just like this one.

Amira died at twenty-one while stopping a riot in Nizahl's lower villages. Most of Marek's memories of his sister were foggy, but oh, did he remember her smile. A smile not even their humorless mother could ignore. Despite the two crooked bottom teeth Hani would mercilessly tease her about, Amira never let her smile shrink. "You're jealous your teeth are plain and boring," she'd toss back. Marek's chubby five-year-old fingers often dove toward her mouth in a childish attempt to straighten her teeth and shut Hani up. *How dare Hani mock her smile,* Marek would think. *When I get big and strong, I'll make all of Hani's teeth crooked so he can never be mean to Amira again.*

Amira never got to see Marek get big and strong. They buried her after Marek's sixth birthday, and it wouldn't have mattered if Marek had knocked all of Hani's teeth out right then, because Hani left his smiles in the grave next to their sister.

Marek walked faster, his chest growing tight. The ghosts of his siblings were everywhere in Nizahl, especially in these Awaleen-damned training compounds. He glanced down at his stolen uniform and felt ill.

The guards stationed at the front of the compound nodded to Marek as he exited into the chilly night. "Water's hot if you're angling to beat them to the bath," one of them said, gesturing across the field to the squat, single-story building surrounded by clotheslines. "Sun's up in twenty."

"Twenty minutes?!" He'd overslept! Tombs-damned Zaid/Zain and his unnaturally quiet breathing. Marek usually roused to the sound of Sefa's predawn snores.

Change of plans. Marek would walk far enough to get out of their line of sight and *then* get to the fence.

His paranoia proved unnecessary—the guards didn't watch as he moved in the direction of the baths. Like the other soldiers, their trust had been easily won. Marek possessed the right kind of confidence, his accent held a trace of Nizahlan upper society, and his familiarity with military procedures had only aided in helping him blend in. In Omal, he'd needed to fight to keep his Nizahlan accent from slipping through.

About a week ago, Marek had materialized in a storage closet deep inside the Nizahlan military's training compounds. He'd still been in the middle of reaching for Sefa, intent on knocking her out of the falling boulder's way, and he'd wasted an embarrassing number of minutes panicking in the closet. Sefa was gone, a gold- and silver-eyed Sylvia had waved her hand and apparently transported him across Nizahl, and he had no idea what he would find when he opened the door.

When Marek finished gathering his wits, he'd swiped an oversize uniform from the wash basket and slipped out. Every glance had felt like an accusation, and Marek's sweat could have refilled Hirun twice over.

Luckily, too many new recruits passed through the compounds for his arrival to trigger any alarms. Entry into this sector of Nizahl was heavily screened, nearly impossible to breach, so nobody doubted his presence.

Marek lifted his head to the breeze, relishing the fresh earthiness of it. In Mahair, he'd be lucky to find a single spot in the village untainted by the scent of manure from Yuli's farm. He'd forgotten what it was like to wake up and smell something other than excrement.

Nobody intercepted Marek on his way to the farthest corner of the gate. Marek wasn't sure where in Nizahl Sylvia had dropped him. The kingdom had at least sixteen compound communities just like this one for new recruits, and more for each subsequent level of training. Maintaining the most skilled army in the kingdoms certainly ate up the acres.

If he had to guess, Marek would say this compound was somewhere east. Remote enough to grant them privacy, but not more than four or five days' ride to the nearest village.

By the time he reached the fence, Marek's nose was running from the cold. He checked over his shoulder for the hundredth time. Nobody had followed him.

Marek's heart catapulted into his throat as he knelt, palms slipping against the grooves in the fence. A few feet from the bottom, a hole the size of his thumbnail punctured the hard metal. Marek had found it after days of scouring for a means of escape. Three times a day, Marek came to this spot and pressed his eye to the fence.

The only thing waiting for him on the other side was the same gnarled tree. Tears of disappointment sprang into Marek's eyes too fast to counter. He let them fall.

Rationally, he knew Sefa wouldn't find him here. Sylvia's magic had been whipping around the Victor's Ball without any measure of premeditation, and she could have sent Sefa anywhere in the kingdoms.

He leaned back on his haunches, staring unseeingly at the fence. He hadn't left Sefa's side since they were twelve years old, and now Sefa was out there alone. Marek wanted to ram himself against the fence until either it broke, or he did.

Light crawled under Marek's bent knees. It stretched over his uniform and began its steady and unstoppable climb over the compound.

His knees cracked as he stood. The frost had seeped into his pants, but he hardly felt it.

At the sight of soldiers spewing over the field like ants, Marek sloughed off his bitter sorrow and cast it aside. He was going to escape from this compound and find Sefa. The minute the opportunity to leave presented itself, Marek would be gone, leaving behind nothing more than a dazzling memory.

If they caught up to him, he would be executed for a bevy of different crimes, not the least of which was desertion, but what good plan didn't involve at least some risk of beheading?

The halls strained with the cacophony of disgruntled shouts, creaking floors, and wet feet slapping their way back from the baths. Someone rammed into Marek, nearly sending him to the ground. "Sorry," the soldier mumbled, his wet hair plastered to the sides of his head like a second skin.

Marek shrugged affably. "What's your hurry?"

"Didn't you hear? One of the Commander's personal guardsmen is visiting. We need to be in formation at Fareed Mill in ten minutes."

The blood drained from Marek's face.

The fresh-faced recruit rushed around Marek, eager to meet one of Arin of Nizahl's personal guardsmen. Why wouldn't he be? Only four highly qualified men in the world held the coveted role.

No, not four. The quiet one had gotten an arrow through the eye during the Meridian Pass ambush. So just three men who would take one look at his face and either cut him down on the spot or drag him to the Citadel, where their Commander would do much worse.

Marek didn't think before he started running. Their superior officer would be furious with Marek for missing the guardsman's visit, but his wrath paled against the risk of encountering one of the Heir's trained murderers.

He dove into the first empty room he came across and slammed the door shut. Twisting like a sheet on an unstable clothesline, Marek searched for a window. But without knowing which part of the fence the guardsman's cavalry would enter through, he couldn't risk hiding outside.

Marek dropped to the floor and squeezed under the bunk. It was a good day not to have the brawn and barrel chests of the other soldiers. He sipped the air, trying not to jostle the bedframe with the rise and fall of his chest.

Eventually, the scurry in the hall went quiet.

Marek breathed, and he waited.

While his body lay trapped, Marek's mind wandered.

The flurry of new recruits, the visit from the Commander's guardsman... it had to be about Sylvia. The creature she'd conjured at the Victor's Ball had featured in Marek's nightmares more than once already. If the gold wings and black eyes hadn't clued Marek in, the horns on either side of its enormous skull would have (Marek may not have paid much attention in school, but even he recognized the symbol of Jasad).

He could hardly bring himself to believe that a kitmer the size of a building had been animated by the same Sylvia he'd seen blow her nose in a dirty tunic ("It's going to be washed anyway!"), hide loaves of aish feeno in her waistband, swear and swing at moths that flew too close to her head, and rant about frogs until Marek begged her to stop.

In the hall, a leather boot creaked.

The bottom of Marek's stomach dropped. He scooted away from the side of the bed facing the door, pressing his back to the wall.

Through the crack of the door, the light dispersed around a shadow. It lingered long enough for the spit to dry in his mouth. Before he'd done more than bunch his muscles in preparation, the shadow moved.

Away from the door.

Marek went loose-limbed with relief. Thank the Awaleen.

Marek didn't intend to stick around for the shadow's encore. He pulled himself out from under the bed and stood, wincing at the painful pull in his lower back. He was only twenty-three years old, but his back felt every one of those years.

Pressing his ear to the door, Marek listened for any sign of movement. Silence met him when he cracked open the door. He cast a quick glance through the part of the hall he could see. Still nothing.

Relief slackened his shoulders. Just an absent-minded recruit.

Marek opened the door the rest of the way and stepped outside. Maybe he'd try hiding under Diran's bed; Marek had heard Diran's parents regularly sent him the best food, and Marek doubted the kitchen had saved him a plate at breakfast.

Before he had taken more than a step forward, a tanned hand materialized from his right and grabbed his collar. The world blurred as Marek flew back into the room. He slammed his knee against the bedpost and swore so loudly, it nearly masked the click of the door shutting behind him.

Marek whipped around, raising his arms to bar any further grabbing, and went still.

"Uh-oh," Marek said. His heart pounded. "The Commander's good little boy is far from home, isn't he?"

CHAPTER THIRTEEN

MAREK

Jeru stared at Marek like he'd seen a ghost. Except for a row of violet ravens stitched along his right lapel and a pin of Nizahl's crest carefully obscured beneath the flap of his chest pocket, Jeru was dressed like the rest of the soldiers. The hidden pin marked him as the biggest threat in the room, the one all arrows should take aim at.

"You tombs-damned idiot" were the first words out of Jeru's mouth, exhaled in a disbelieving rush. "What are you doing here?"

Marek frowned. "Don't call me an idiot."

"Don't call—" Jeru touched the top of his curly hair, perhaps to ensure there wasn't blood seeping out of his head. "Marek, why are you in Nizahl? In a *training compound*?"

"I could ask you the same thing." Marek could feel himself begin to devolve with defensiveness, his grip on maturity deteriorating under the weight of his panic. Sefa considered it one of his worst habits. Faced with the urge to mock the man likely tasked with murdering him, Marek couldn't disagree.

"A guardsman has to pay a visit anytime a compound welcomes more than two hundred new recruits! His Highness almost sent *Vaun*. Do you understand what Vaun would have done if he found you here?" Jeru sounded faintly nauseated. From a Nizahl guardsman, who had seen more bloodshed and horror than most men encountered in ten lifetimes, the unease was no small thing. "And you closed the door. Recruits are instructed to leave their doors open during a visit to permit ease of inspection."

Oh. Maybe relying on the stories he'd heard from his siblings wasn't a foolproof method of blending in. The blunder made Marek's voice rough with aggression. "Well, it's not Vaun who found me. What are *you* going to do?" Marek still hadn't lowered his arms from their defensive pose.

"What am I going to do?" Jeru sank into the only chair in the room and clasped his hands together. Strain showed itself in the lines creasing his face. "Excellent question."

Marek measured the distance between Jeru and the door. Jeru had the muscles and the training. Even Marek wasn't brash enough to believe he could win a fight against the Heir's guardsman. He had exactly one option.

Marek bolted for the door.

He managed to open it an entire inch before Jeru grabbed his collar and yanked him back. Marek, reacting on pure instinct, swung without aim or finesse. His fist connected with the hard resistance of a jaw, eliciting a hiss from Jeru.

His satisfaction enjoyed a short life. Jeru, who had been holding Marek's writhing form at arm's length as one might keep a grip on a rabid cat, reared his arm back and struck Marek so forcefully that for a minute, Marek wondered if he'd swallowed his own teeth. If Jeru didn't still have a grip on his collar, Marek would be a human-size hole in the ground.

"Stop. Fighting!" Jeru dragged Marek until they were almost nose-to-nose. "He wants me to bring you back to the Citadel! *Alive.*"

The world stopped.

No.

The floor of Marek's chest disappeared, plunging his heart straight to his feet. The fight drained out of him. No wonder Jeru looked so tortured. Much as Marek loathed to admit it, Jeru was a good man. He'd treated Sylvia kindly, even when the rest of the guardsmen barely acknowledged her. When the arrows had begun to rain down at the Meridian Pass, Jeru had immediately ridden for Sefa and Marek and led them to safety.

He was a good man, which meant it wasn't easy for him to deliver Marek to a fate worse than death.

"I'll ask again. What are you doing here?"

A new terror gripped Marek, and he clapped his hand over his mouth as bile surged in his throat. Jeru released him—quick thinking that narrowly saved him from the delight of Marek's vomit spewing over his uniform. Marek hunched over, his arms going around his contracting middle.

"He doesn't have Sefa. Right? Tell me he doesn't have Sefa, Jeru, *tell me that mad, coldhearted bastard doesn't have—*"

"No one has Sefa!" Jeru regarded Marek with an exhaustion hedging on pity. "But he's looking for her."

The relief crushed him. Marek slid to his knees, shoulders bumping against the chair Jeru had knocked over. "He wants to use us to lure Sylvia, doesn't he?"

Jeru said nothing.

Fighting another wave of nausea, Marek shut his eyes. "If he tries to use her against Sylvia, Sefa will let him kill her."

The guardsman blanched. "She wouldn't—"

"She would. If she feels escape or rescue are impossible, if she knows the Heir is planning to execute Sylvia, she will not be a pawn to it. Sefa will remove herself from his game board." Tears gathered behind Marek's closed eyes. His brave, loyal, self-sacrificing fool of a friend.

Pushing to his feet, Marek thought fast. If Jeru had been instructed to capture them, perhaps he had an idea where Sefa might be. Maybe he could even get Marek out of this compound.

"I woke up in a storage room in this compound after the Victor's

Ball. I don't know where Sefa went. I can't leave the compound, and even if I could, I don't know where to start looking for Sefa and Sylvia."

Jeru winced. "I wouldn't recommend trying to look for Sylvia. The Malika of Jasad is a part of an entirely different game now—one neither of us is qualified to play. Pursuing her will get you killed, and you will be no use to anyone dead."

Part of a different game? If Marek had anything left in his stomach, he would be donating it all over Jeru's shoes. "Is that your sorry attempt to calm me down?" Marek lowered himself to a seat at the edge of the bed before his legs gave out. "I love that girl."

Jeru paused his pacing to raise his brows. Marek rolled his eyes. "Like a sister," he snapped.

"Good," Jeru muttered. Marek couldn't be sure, but he could have sworn he heard the guardsman grumble, "We don't need to give him another reason to kill you."

"You can't let him find Sefa, Jeru. At least Sylvia has her magic and the leverage of her title. People to support her. Sefa doesn't have anyone but me."

"I told you, we don't know where Sefa is. I haven't found her. But I did find you, and I don't—" Jeru scrubbed a hand down his face. "I don't know what to do. His Highness isn't... he isn't himself. The prospect of war haunts him, and Sylvia's betrayal cut him deeper than anyone knows. If I hand you to him, there's no telling what he might do. And if he kills you knowing how it would destroy Sylvia, we may lose him altogether."

"You're worried about how killing me would emotionally impact him?" Snorting, Marek wondered why he was surprised. The guardsmen always put their Commander first. Frankly, Marek was shocked Jeru was still talking and hadn't already summoned the carriage to haul him to the Citadel.

Jeru stopped pacing. He pivoted on his heel, taking stock of

Marek with an inscrutable expression. "You were a crook before Mahair."

Marek raised a blond brow. "Looking for a career change?"

"Shut up." Jeru ran his thumb over the row of embroidered ravens, lost in thought. "You managed to hide in Mahair under a false name for seven years."

Marek eyed the door longingly, touching his throbbing jaw.

"I'll help you find Sefa."

The scattered pieces of Marek's attention gathered themselves, welded into a steely focus, and aimed their combined force at Jeru. Marek stood slowly, a dangerous pulse in his veins. "Do not toy with me."

"Shouldn't you know what a proposition sounds like, Lazur?" Jeru crossed his arms over his chest. "I'm searching for a relic I believe to be hidden with a Nizahlan noble family. An insignia that vanished around the Siege of Six Dawns. It was once used as a token of favor, and I suspect they have it."

Marek racked his memory for the Siege of Six Dawns. His attention span in class had ranged from abysmal to abominable. "The siege where they burned all the fields in Omal?" Marek didn't consider himself an expert on the kingdoms' many, *many* conflicts, but he had passed the scorch marks on the wall dividing Mahair from Essam a thousand times. A long black streak stretched right under the words *May we lead the lives our ancestors were denied*.

Even hundreds of years later, the land remembered what had been done to it by the Orbanian invaders.

Orban used a nasty—and more importantly, prohibited—curse to transform a regiment of Omalian soldiers into ravenous cannibals. The Omalian soldiers turned on one another, leaving eviscerated and half-eaten corpses strung from Abeiyla to Mahair. For six agonizing days, Orban had reigned over the lower villages of Omal, their horde of feral soldiers left to feast on the helpless population.

A victory as briefly enjoyed as it was horrifically earned.

They had broken the laws of war to win the battle, and the arbiters of magic swiftly marched to level the crime. Nizahl soldiers flooded the villages to expel Orban, summarily executing the cursed soldiers. Omal had hailed Nizahl as its hero, despite the fact that Nizahl would have allowed every single lower villager to die if Orban had been smart enough to attack them with a sword instead of a curse.

When he was a child, Marek had suffered nightmares about those cursed Omalian soldiers. Not all of them had been caught. Several had fled from the Nizahl soldiers into Essam Woods, disappearing without a trace. Nobody knew if those soldiers had found the Mirayah, or if it had found them.

Overly pleased with himself, Marek grinned as he leaned against the bedpost. "What does an insignia have to do with the Siege of Six Dawns?"

"That's not for you to concern yourself with. When the next rotation leaves to quarter in the noble towns, I will send you to the Shinawy manor. Find me the insignia, and I will help you find Sefa."

"Consider it done," Marek said, shrugging. Stealing from a spoiled Nizahlan noble family? Marek had expected a challenge. "Aren't you worried about defying your Commander? If you're caught, I imagine he will greet your deception with a nice sturdy noose."

A wall sprang up behind Jeru's eyes. A wall Marek had bloodied himself against anytime he tried to speak ill of the Nizahl Heir during those weeks in the tunnels. Even Sylvia, who held nothing sacred beyond the coin in her pocket and the aim of her blade, had fortified herself behind it.

It was the wall Marek recognized from his childhood, as one after the other of his siblings signed their lives to the Citadel.

"Focus on your own neck," Jeru said. "I will arrange your visit to take place at the next available opportunity, and you will report to me what you discover. Hide a single detail, and our arrangement terminates. Understood?"

Unspoken between them was what else the termination of the arrangement would spell: the termination of Marek's time among the living.

He flipped Jeru a glib, easygoing smile. Living as a fugitive for nearly ten years had increased Marek's threshold of what properly qualified as a dilemma. He had grown up as Caleb Lazur. For a very long time, he'd called the world of upper Nizahl home. He may not be able to fight like Jeru or use magic like Sylvia, but damn it to the tombs, nobody could charm a sophisticate like Marek.

"Deal."

CHAPTER FOURTEEN

ARIN

Of the myriad of unpleasant ways Arin had spent his evenings lately, the prospect of dinner alone with his father was the worst.

Dusk painted the Citadel's gardens in muted pinks and blues. Arin strolled through the groves, dry leaves crunching beneath his boots. He'd been circling the gardens for twenty minutes and passed Isra's Fountain, the reason for his visit, twice. His feet carried him past the statue of his mother each time he tried to stop.

Arin had not been alone with his father since the night of the Victor's Ball. A night where Arin had expected a reckoning from the Supreme the likes of which he had never seen before.

But Rawain hadn't mentioned the small matter of the Jasad Heir. Not then. All he had said was, "You are a Commander. My Heir. No son of mine succumbs to his *feelings* in the presence of company. No matter how very tempting it is to kill the Sultana."

This dinner would be the true trial. What Arin had known about the Champion, the circumstances of her selection, the nature of their relationship. Arin would have to sit across from the Supreme and decide whether to reveal the depths of his own dishonor or lie through his teeth.

On his fourth circuit around the garden, Arin finally stopped beneath the shadow of Isra's statue. Hers was one of seventeen in the Citadel's sprawling groves, each statue erected like a guard post across the miles of greenery.

The statue of Arin's mother gazed out over the gardens. Freshly picked stone flowers bloomed between her curled hands. She was kneeling on the pedestal, her gown flowing over its sides and touching the ground. A delicate sadness lingered in her features.

It was always her sadness that hit Arin the hardest. How telling that a sculptor had mused over which of the late Isra's most distinguishing characteristics to mold for eternity, and they had chosen her sorrow. Not the fear permanently lurking behind her eyes or the skittish dance of her fingers, both of which Arin remembered just as keenly.

"Forgive me for not visiting sooner," Arin said. He plucked loose the branches trapped in the folds of her stone dress. "I was away."

The wind ruffled Arin's hair. He should start walking to the tower if he wanted to reach the dinner table before Rawain.

Curiously, the idea of turning his back on Isra unsettled him more than arriving late to the dinner.

Ridiculous. A slab of stone did not care that he hadn't come to see it in months. A slab of stone was not his mother.

"I am still away, I think." The confession slipped out before Arin could stop it, hiding itself in the fading light. Arin stared at Isra and tried to find the words to explain how the pit of dread in his stomach grew larger each day. War haunted his thoughts, weighed on his bones. Half of Arin was fixed in the future, the other half in the past. It left nothing to spare for the present.

"There was a girl." Arin's gaze dropped to the bottom of the pedestal, and he had never felt more like a child in his entire life. "You've met her."

Strange to think of Isra meeting Essiya before Arin, but his parents had paid Usr Jasad multiple visits throughout his childhood. Arin hated himself for wondering whether Isra had liked her.

It didn't matter. Sylvia would probably have terrified Isra, since everything but Arin had terrified Isra. Arin had sometimes thought his mother weak for the way she loved him, the anguish she endured on his behalf. None of which Arin had appreciated at the time, having dedicated the whole of his focus to pleasing Rawain. Isra's love was guaranteed, easily won, so Arin had set his sights on the unobtainable.

I do not know if I am the right man for this kingdom, Arin wanted to confess. *What if I cannot do what must be done?*

The last of the sun disappeared, draining away the dregs of color left in the sky. Within seconds, the windows of the Citadel brightened with freshly lit lanterns.

Arin stood in front of Isra, and he shared none of the things he wanted to say. They were useless to a dead woman. A woman who'd died at the Summit besieged by the Malik and Malika of Jasad.

He pulled a cloth from his pocket and ran it over the contours of her face, removing the dust collecting in the creases. The gardeners hadn't bothered to maintain the statue in his absence.

When he was younger, Arin would sometimes imagine Isra's stone face softening when he touched her cheek. Warmth replacing the chill of her, and the eyes that stared unseeingly into the distance finally turning toward Arin. Those moments when hope had melted into disappointment were the only times Arin ever wished for magic.

He folded the cloth and tucked it back into his pocket.

"I won't be gone so long this time," Arin said.

Arin turned, leaving his mother in the shadows.

Only the reflection of the lanterns from the Citadel illuminated Arin's path. Rosebushes bordered the cobblestone track, the branches nurtured to magnificent heights on either side of Arin. Navigating the gardens in the evening didn't bother him, but he knew the mazelike pathways intimidated the servants. They rarely wandered after nightfall.

Which was why when the bushes rustled, Arin halted.

Another rustle, closer this time. Arin reached inside his coat and quietly withdrew a small blade. It barely spanned the length of his palm, but it would slash a throat as effectively as any dagger.

He turned the corner, blade tucked above his thumb.

A woman materialized inches away from Arin, nearly ramming into his chest.

The breath shuddered out of Arin. He stared, and then stared more.

Velvet brown eyes widened in wonder. "You again," she said.

Blood pounding in his ears, Arin took a step back. The prudent move, the intelligent one, was to close his eyes and wait until the hallucination passed.

"You aren't real," he whispered.

"Funny," the Jasad Heir said. "I keep thinking the same of you."

Her tunic didn't ruffle with the wind. The iridescent fabric of her sleeves cinched at her elbow and draped loose around her wrists. Against his better judgment, Arin remembered how he'd grasped those arms as he drew her close. His swell of pride and admiration at the strength there.

Once again, her curls tumbled loose down her back. His delusion didn't seem to care that the real version rarely wore her hair in anything other than a braid.

"Have I gone mad?" Arin asked.

She smiled. "The world will fall to ruins long before your mind does."

"Don't." It tore out of Arin.

"Don't…?"

"You aren't real. These hallucinations are symptoms of… exhaustion. Yes. Exhaustion."

Arin was not sure who he wanted to convince. In an instant, Arin stood inches away from her. Like a chemist teetering on the brink of creation or catastrophe, Arin couldn't bring himself to take the final step toward discovery.

"Probably," she agreed, not seeming to mind his close scrutiny. "But what would you say to me if I *was* real?" She offered the question on a platter of humor, and Arin burned beneath a surge of his old frustration. She was a mere figment, but a bitterly convincing one. The real Sylvia had the same avoidant tactic of threading sincerity with comedy, masking fear with aggression, sorrow with coldness.

If Arin was stone, then she was a river. Always moving, always flowing, no matter how fast the tide or how frequently she broke against its shores.

The wind ruffled his hair. It left hers still.

"That bad?" she whispered at his rigid silence.

Bad? Bad was the greeting. Bad would be the first sentence of a book Arin planned to fill with blood and agony and words so heavy with cruelty they would pin down any tongue that tried to speak them. The page where he would record her fate would wrinkle to escape the horror of his pen, and he would ink it with the blood he poured from her.

Sylvia's gaze dropped to the knife in Arin's grip, then swung back up to him. She huffed a short laugh.

He struck fast, but she had seen it coming. The knife went airborne as Sylvia reared back and kicked Arin's wrist, sending a spasm of pain through his arm. Before he could reach into his coat, she collided into him like a bull, slamming his back against Isra's statue.

"You still don't think I'm real," she heaved. Her hands bunched in Arin's lapels, pinning him to the statue. "You wouldn't fight me so leisurely if you truly believed I was here."

Arin studied the collection of freckles on the underside of her chin. Interesting. The pattern looked remarkably identical to her real freckles.

Not freckles—hasanas.

It was ludicrous to argue with a hallucination, but this woman—and apparently, even her apparition—frequently compelled Arin to the ludicrous. "Were you truly here, I would have felt your magic the instant you entered the Citadel's grounds."

She was pinning him to the statue so earnestly, her arm a solid bar against his collarbone. Arin almost smiled. Fine, then. If his hallucination wanted an actual fight, Arin may as well indulge her.

Sylvia wheezed when Arin's knee slammed into her stomach. He grabbed her wrist and twisted the arm she'd used to pin him behind her back. "Is this satisfactory to you?"

He launched the hallucination into the rosebushes.

She careened into the bushes and hit the ground. Slapping off the burrs caught on her sleeve, she leapt to her feet. "You stubborn, tombs-damned man, I am trying to *warn you*—"

Footsteps farther up the grove drew Arin's attention. Urgency burst across Sylvia's features, and she spoke fast. "Arin, you need to listen. Evacuate Galim's Bend. The cages—"

"Sire?" Wes turned the corner, a lantern held aloft to ward away the encroaching shadows. "There you are. Is anything the matter?"

Arin didn't move his gaze from Wes. He knew she was gone.

"I should ask you the same," Arin said. Calmly, smoothly, as if Wes hadn't interrupted Arin in the middle of his flight from reality. "Did my father send you?"

"The attendants said they saw you enter the groves without a torch. I worried you might lose your way back."

Arin was the last person who would get lost anywhere, never mind in the Citadel's gardens, and Wes knew it.

"Wes." Light, congenial. "I advise you to exercise extreme caution before lying to me."

Wes set his feet, moving away from the throng of branches he'd begun to subtly disappear into. His chin jutted forward, resolve replacing his wariness. "Your Highness. Arin. I have served as your guardsman for more than ten years. My life has always been forfeit to yours, and I bear the sacrifice with pride. It is a sacrifice you have always respected. Until now."

The number of times Arin had been caught off guard tonight could be counted on more than a finger, and Arin didn't much care for it. "If you wish to lodge a complaint, be clear with it."

The light from Wes's torch cast long shadows over the brush. If the torch tilted four inches to the right, it would catch on the branches in seconds. Winter had not yet loosened its hold on the gardens, so the blaze would be contained to the areas where the frost had melted. But it would reach his mother. It would lick hungrily at the bottom of her pedestal, confusing stone for skin, until futility smothered the flames. Its glory—its potential—foiled by its own determination to consume the only thing in the garden it could not burn.

Rawain is cruel by nature, but you? You are cruel by choice.

"Sire? Are you listening?"

Arin passed a gloved hand through his hair, sweeping out the Jasad Heir's voice. He needed to get out of these groves. "Unfortunately."

"The whole of your evenings are spent in the library. You rise to meet the council at dawn. The shadows under your eyes grow darker each day."

Arin did not wish to be curt with his guard. Wes was ten years Arin's senior, and his temper wasn't as fractious as Vaun's, nor his heart as easily won as Jeru's. He wouldn't be addressing Arin with such gravity were it not a matter Wes considered of the utmost importance.

But Arin was tired, and he needed to reserve his restraint for supper with Rawain. "I imagine you're hiding your point somewhere in this observation."

"Jeru thinks you need to talk."

A humorless smile touched Arin's lips. So the young guardsman had finally won the elder to his side. Arin started walking. "Explain why I should care about Jeru's opinion on my needs."

Around the bend, the path opened into the Awaleen's memorial courtyard.

Three towering figures loomed in the center of the courtyard. Green vines twined through the wood and wicker limbs of Baira, Dania, and Kapastra.

Dania held an iron axe over her shoulder, its weight against the hollow wooden frame of its owner a defiance of logic. Baira's hands curved around her face, the red roses blooming from her empty eye sockets rustling in the breeze. Thick vines snaked through Kapastra's ribbed chest, winding around the interlocking branches like one of her beloved rochelyas.

Arin always went out of his way to avoid this courtyard. Six and a half hundred years ago, the Supreme had seen fit to invite architects to build a monument to the Awaleen. A gesture to commemorate Nizahl's roots in magic. The architects had lived in the newly built gardens for months on end, knitting branches together, coaxing vines to grow. Their magic had saturated the courtyard—and the creations left behind. The thin branches working like tendons in the Awaleen never rotted. The vines never browned or withered.

Magic still lived in this courtyard. Arin could feel the soft thrum of it all around, raising the hairs on the back of his neck.

The Awaleen's heads blotted out the moon. A red petal floated from Baira's right eye, landing on Arin's boot.

When Arin became Supreme, this courtyard would burn.

"My liege?"

Arin clenched his teeth. Without looking at Wes, he resumed his walk. The petal slid from his shoe.

The crunch of their footsteps was the only sound for long minutes. The brightness shining from the Citadel's tower lit the night like a falling star.

If even his guardsmen were having doubts, Arin was in more trouble than he realized.

At the end of the grove, Arin turned to address his guard. "I apologize if I've given you reason to doubt how much I value your service, Wes. Your concern is appreciated, but I assure you it is misplaced."

"Sire—"

"Do you think I would still lead our kingdom if I truly believed my judgment compromised?"

Wes hesitated. After a minute, he dipped his chin—an acknowledgment, an acceptance. "I should not have spoken out of turn. Perhaps I've spent too long in Jeru's company."

Arin forced himself to smile. "Jeru grew up with seven siblings. He thinks every thought—no matter how benign—should be a token for discussion."

At the door to the east wing, Wes broke off from Arin. "Enjoy supper, my liege."

Arin shot him a sour look, and Wes grinned.

Servants startled from their card games at Arin's entrance. He waved them down. The east wing was usually reserved for the recruits' ascension ceremonies, which only happened three or four times a year. The staff came here to relax, and Arin wouldn't begrudge them their not-so-secret hideaway.

Given the tripling rate of conscription, Arin ventured their opportunities for leisure were rapidly dwindling.

Arin laid a hand on the banister. He'd always dreaded dinners with Rawain, but never quite to this level. The thought of sitting across from his father and telling the truth made him sick. But the thought of lying...

Arin had climbed exactly one step when the sirens went off.

The walls shook, sending the servants' playing cards sliding across the floor. Dust rained over them as the siren shrieked from the tower, its reverberations thundering beneath them. Shock suspended Arin for a fraction of a second before he burst into motion.

Arin grabbed a frazzled servant. "Get everyone to the cellars. Go!"

Outside, chaos had erupted. Swarms of recruits flooded from the compounds and pooled around the foot of the tower. Only a handful were in proper uniform; the rest looked like they'd run out while preparing for bed.

The first row saw Arin and snapped to attention, and the awareness rippled over the crowd until each recruit stood perfectly still, awaiting orders.

Orders Arin couldn't deliver, since he did not have the faintest clue what was happening. He'd only heard the tower's siren once before in his life—the day of the Blood Summit. The alarm was engineered alongside the wicker figures of the Awaleen centuries ago, seeded with magic to go off only when Nizahl was under severe attack. The thought of what the alarm might have deemed threatening enough to the kingdom's security to sound for the second time in two and a half decades turned Arin's stomach.

A swell of guards stormed out of the tower, Rawain sheltered between them. "Arin!" he called.

The guards parted to allow Arin into their circle of protection and swiftly closed again.

"You are unharmed?" Rawain raked a panicked gaze over Arin.

Arin paused, momentarily thrown off-kilter. Had Rawain been worried? "Yes." He almost added *thank you*.

It was difficult to hear over the unyielding siren. "Is there an intruder in the Citadel?"

Rawain's mouth tightened to a grim line. "No, this alarm wouldn't sound for a mere assassin. Something terrible is afoot. You need to get into the cellar."

Rawain may as well have dealt him a resounding slap across the face. Arin took a step back. "You want me to hide?"

"You are the Heir and the Commander, Arin. You cannot be risked." His father huffed an indulgent laugh. "This is what armies are for, son."

Past the ring of guards, the recruits still waited on Arin's instructions. This siren would ring throughout Nizahl, sending villages and towns into frenzied panic. And somewhere in the chaos, a danger worthy of rousing a centuries-old alarm walked.

Humiliation burned in his chest. Rawain truly thought so little of him? He thought Arin would willingly hide while…

It didn't matter. There was no time.

"Is there a mechanism within the alarm that can alert us to where the threat is?"

"No, but the soldiers will find it and exterminate it. You need to—"

But a different voice cut through Rawain's.

Arin, you need to listen. Evacuate Galim's Bend.

But it couldn't be. She was just an apparition.

Arin shoved through the guards, ignoring Rawain furiously shouting his name. The recruits weren't looking at Arin anymore. They had turned east, facing the hills curving above the valley of villages. Horrified gasps rang in the air, joining the siren, as a familiar winged beast burst into the horizon. They were too far to hear the gentle clinking of its glass feathers, but the colors of its wings—the white and pink of dawn tapering into the blazing red of dusk—shined above the flames roaring along the valley.

Someone had unleased Al Anqa'a from its cage. And if they had unleashed the most fiercely guarded of the Alcalah's monsters…

The cages—

Arin broke into a run. "Evacuate Galim's Bend!" he ordered the stricken recruits. "Get everyone to the Wickalla!"

Al Anqa'a's wings were clipped to fly short distances at a low radius. Useful for the second trial of the Alcalah, when they wanted to test the mettle of hard-trained Champions in an abandoned village. Not so useful in a teeming neighborhood of easily accessible prey.

A symphony of huffs and whinnies erupted from the stable as soon as Arin threw open the doors. The horses weren't enjoying the siren any more than the rest of them. Arin headed straight to Ehal and unlocked the stall. The black horse hadn't joined the others in voicing his complaints, and he allowed Arin to lead him out without a fuss. In a stroke of fortune, Ehal was already saddled.

The black warhorse took Arin's weight easily. Arin wrapped the reins in his fist and leaned forward.

I did not have to lie to my father, Arin thought, darkly triumphant. *Not tonight, at least.*

With a snap of the reins, Arin and Ehal charged toward the hills of Galim's Bend.

CHAPTER FIFTEEN

SYLVIA

A black lake stretched between two mountains at the edge of the world.

On our right, the cliff disappeared into the familiar shroud of darkness. If I squinted, I could make out the surface of Suhna Sea gently undulating, the twinkle of hundreds of stars glimmering over its waves.

The Urabi had gathered at the lake's perimeter. Three figures stepped from the crowd, treading lightly over the lake's icy surface.

"I was frightened the first time they did this," Maia murmured. "It's rare to find one Visionist, so we are very fortunate to have three. When they store enough magic, they can pull sights from anywhere in the world for our display."

At the current moment, their aim was to pull forward the scene in Galim's Bend. Excited murmurs passed between half the circle; the other half waited in silent vigil. Efra stood with the first group, watching the ice with gleeful anticipation.

I licked my lips. "Can they pull... any sights?"

The Silver Serpent's traitorous whore. Had they watched us the night of the Victor's Ball?

They couldn't have. My cuffs had resisted magic, including the strongest of tracking spells. Any Visionist trying to conjure an image of me would have run straight into their barricade.

I rubbed my wrists. I never thought their nakedness would leave me so bereft.

"Not any, no." Maia yawned, her trimmed nails tapping lightly against her upper lip. "It is not a reliable science."

Still, three Visionists? Not to mention Maia's mysterious specialty and Efra's annoying one. Who knew how many others among the Urabi had unique magic?

Arin was wrong. He'd thought the Urabi targeted Jasadis at random unless they were competing with the Mufsids for someone who'd held an important post in Jasad. He couldn't have known the Urabi were targeting rare and unusual magic. Maia still hadn't specified exactly what her specialty was, just that it included an ability to sever a consciousness without hurting the recipient.

I scanned the assembled Urabi and wondered how many other exceptional types of magic dwelled in our midst. It stirred a strange pride in my chest. Even after the siege, even after ten years of persecution—nobody could tamp out the spark that left Jasadis with magic and the other kingdoms barren. Our magic lived through Rovial's sacrifice, and it had adapted new ways to survive in an environment hostile to its existence.

With the pride came a rush of dread. The Mufsids had been determined to prevent the Urabi from gaining power. Both groups must have been tracking Jasadis with specialized magic, which explained why the Mufsids never allowed those who refused recruitment to live past the rejection. "How many Jasadis did the Mufsids kill?"

Namsa and Maia glanced around me at each other. Namsa massaged the corner of her jaw. "Too many."

"You must have been relieved when the Nizahl Commander captured the bulk of their operation."

She glanced at me sharply. "They are ours to punish. A common enemy does not make Nizahl our friend."

Maia nodded. "And it bodes very ill for us that they haven't been executed yet."

At my quizzical glance, she continued, "Our spies alerted us that none of the Mufsids have been killed or made to stand trial. Either the Commander and the Supreme cannot see eye to eye on how to proceed, or they want something from the Mufsids."

"Our location, our spies, and our numbers," Namsa said. "The Mufsids are useless to Nizahl dead."

The three Visionists locked hands in the center of the lake. I became poignantly aware of the fragile shell of ice supporting their weight. With a chill, I realized why the tableau looked so familiar. My old nightmare had featured Niphran burning on a lake just like this one while I stood helplessly by.

"Where is your coat?" Maia asked, wincing sympathetically at my chattering teeth. "I thought you went to fetch it."

"I got lost finding my way back to my room," I sighed, the lie blooming easily between my lips. I raised a finger and drew a zigzag in the air, my nose scrunching in slight embarrassment. "Just wandered around the halls until I circled back out. I have an awful sense of direction."

Maia giggled, launching into a story about her first week in the mountains and how she'd walked in on a naked couple chasing each other in the Geneina. I listened with one ear, relieved neither she nor Namsa had questioned my story.

It was partially true. I had entered the mountain and gotten temporarily turned around. But I possessed a keen sense of direction—I would've been an embarrassment of a crook and a Champion otherwise. Once I'd found my room, I spent ages pacing, panic ravaging through me.

Sefa and Marek could still be in Nizahl. I had no idea where I'd sent them during the Victor's Ball.

Arin was in Nizahl.

As soon as I thought his name, the world had vanished. I'd found myself on a gloomy garden path, penned in by rosebushes on either side. Then Arin had turned the corner, blade expertly tucked under his thumb for quick slashing.

I had known as soon as I saw him that this was no dream. No imagination of mine could conjure the complexity of the reaction that twisted across his face at the sight of me. The rough plea in his voice when he said, *Don't*. The way he'd looked almost resigned when he asked if he was going mad. At the end, before Wes arrived, he'd hardened into the man I remembered from the Relic Room. From our first days of training. As though everything that happened in between was the real hallucination, and our only lingering truth was the promise of violence.

I had tried to warn him. Whether or not he believed me... we were about to find out.

Part of me recognized that the others would consider this a betrayal. I couldn't care less. They hadn't batted an eye when Efra decided to let me drown as some demented test of magic, leaving me to either climb up the side of a cliff or become a morning treat for the waiting monsters. They had also agreed and executed a release of the Alcalah's monsters—monsters only *I* had faced—into the poorest string of villages in Nizahl, where they were housed.

"It isn't our problem Nizahl saw fit to harbor those creatures beneath active villages," Efra had said. "They knew the risk of storing them there."

"Those cages were built centuries ago," I'd snapped. "Long before a village formed on top of them."

The Visionists broke apart, arms extended on either side. In a single, uniform line, they stepped backward. A crack formed in the spot where they had stood and raced toward the Visionists, ice collapsing in its wake. I glanced at Namsa in alarm, but none of the Urabi seemed to share my concern.

By the time the Visionists were back on solid ground, the rest of the ice had collapsed. The lake churned, and a whirlpool formed at the spot where the Visionists had stood, funneling the lake down until we were staring at a dry, empty canyon.

The ground quaked. With a dull roar, the water shot upward, a pillar rising high above our heads, and unrolled itself like a scroll beneath an impatient palm. In a blink, the sloshing surface solidified into the scene at Galim's Bend.

My hand flew over my mouth as a nisnas chased a screaming girl down the street, dragging itself after her with jarring speed. The creature Wes had once charmingly described as *what happens when you crush a body like a walnut and soak the remains in sewage.*

"What *is* that?" Maia covered her mouth, horrified.

Another nisnas flung its arm around the ankles of a man and unhinged its jaw, revealing spikes of teeth covering the entire roof and bottom of its mouth. It clamped them around the screaming man's face. Maia turned green at the crunch of bone.

A figure leaned against the side of a wagon, watching the chaos with leisurely interest. Between one blink and the next, its features shifted, rearranging themselves to resemble the man lying bloody beneath the nisnas.

A chill of recognition swept through me. But it couldn't be. I'd buried my axe in his neck during the second trial.

"Is that a…" Namsa trailed off as the man caught the reins of a fleeing horse and laid a comforting hand on its nose.

His neck pulsed. The tendons thickened, pushing out like veins in a tree trunk. He swallowed, and his neck solidified once more.

"Dulhath," I hissed. Magic Eater. They must have kept multiple of them imprisoned.

The dulhath swung onto the horse and snapped the reins. He rode into the carnage and disappeared.

I wanted to storm around the lake and shove Efra's head into the water. He'd released a *dulhath*? That idiot—a dulhath had no interest in Nizahl or random violence. It just wanted to eat. It would ride straight for the nearest source of magic and drain it dry. Efra may as well have unleashed a sentient compass pointing straight toward Jasadis.

In the distance, a zulal burst between the rows of flaming roofs. I'd never seen the worm extended to its full height before. When it killed Mehti, it had been tightly wound around the Omal Champion as it absorbed the moisture from his desiccating corpse. The yellow of the zulal's fleshy body split the horizon.

Several of the Jasadis jumped when it suddenly struck, diving between the houses in an impossible burst of speed. Dirt sprayed in long arcs through the air, landing on the thatched roofs of the flaming village.

I lost track of the number of monsters razing through Galim's Bend. I recognized a mere handful, many of which I'd thought had gone extinct during the purge that wiped monsters from Essam Woods decades ago.

The scene shifted, expanding outward, and I saw Efra whispering to the Visionists.

Above the wreckage, the sunrise wings of the creature that haunted my nightmares unfolded in the sky.

My insides went cold. Maia touched my shoulder, but I shoved her off. I was going to kill him, and no one would stop me this time.

"You unleashed Al Anqa'a?!" I roared.

Al Anqa'a weaved low over Galim's Bend, its clipped wings forcing it into a low loop around the village. Its beady eyes scanned the screaming villagers. Hunting.

Namsa's grip on my elbow halted my progress around the lake. "Mawlati, the kingdoms recapture Al Anqa'a every Alcalah. As soon as the Supreme's soldiers arrive—"

"Dawoud died protecting me from Al Anqa'a." I tore my arm

away. "It nearly killed me. And now you've unleashed it on villages of people without a trace of magic or training!"

Namsa had gone white at the mention of her uncle. I hoped she felt the judgment of his ghost heavy at her neck.

"Look!" came a shout. I whirled around, and my heart leapt into my throat at the image in the water.

At the crest of a low hill, thundering down on a black horse, was Arin.

He believed me.

I waited for the soldiers to come pouring down the hill behind him. Reinforcements with the weapons and tools needed to take down Al Anqa'a and hordes of monsters, more of them than the kingdoms had handled in decades.

No one came. Arin was the single spot of color on the dark hillside, and he rode toward the wreckage of Galim's Bend without slowing.

I was fixed to the spot as I watched Arin swing from his horse and survey the rubble and smoke. A nisnas lashed its arm around his knee, but he slashed through its joint before it could tighten its grip. Arin had trained me for the Alcalah; he had prepared other Champions before me. He knew that walking into Galim's Bend without help would spell his quick and brutal demise.

Arin swung onto his horse and turned it back up the hill.

"Coward," I heard Efra hiss.

Tension lined my body. Arin wouldn't leave his people in distress. I knew that look. Damn it to the tombs, he had a theory.

At the top of the hill, Arin stopped. The Visionists joined their fingers at the tips and pulled them apart, moving the scene closer to Arin. We watched, soundless, as he stripped off his gloves and tossed them to the ground. He shrugged off his coat and undid the buttons at his wrists, rolling his sleeves over his elbows.

His gaze lifted. Al Anqa'a had spotted him. A lone figure on the hill; much easier prey than the crush of villagers darting between fire and other predators.

My stomach curled into a pit of dread as Al Anqa'a folded its wings and soared toward Arin. He pulled a dagger from his pocket and waited. What was he *thinking*? Awaleen below, I was about to watch Arin have his conniving head torn from his shoulders.

"Does he think he can conquer Al Anqa'a with that little knife? He's going to get torn to pieces," someone remarked cheerfully.

"Good work, Efra."

"Wait," Namsa snapped. "This is the Silver Serpent. He would not usher in his own death. There's something…something we are not seeing."

The shadow of Al Anqa'a cast Arin in darkness. Its beak opened. Talons unfurled. And still, he didn't budge.

Just as pearly white claws were about to curl around Arin, he dropped to the ground and rolled. Before Al Anqa'a could close its claws around the empty spot where he'd stood, Arin stabbed into its underbelly. It bellowed, the powerful beat of its wings sending trees crashing and boulders hurtling down the hill. It burst into flight, weaving along the peaks and hollows of the valley overlooking Galim's Bend.

"Why is it flying like that?" At some point, Maia had joined me and Namsa on the edge of the lake.

I had no answer for her. When I'd sliced into Al Anqa'a, it had merely shaken me off like a persistent mosquito. Not dipped and weaved like a drunk leaving his tavern chair.

It skimmed dangerously close to an outcropping of sharp stones, and only then did I see him.

Silver hair whipping in the wind, features set with determination, Arin looked like lightning molded into a man.

He must have used the knife to hike his way to the creature's neck without being thrown off. An elbow was crooked around the blade to hold him in place, leaving both his hands free to press against Al Anqa'a.

I covered my mouth to hide the wild laugh threatening to burst free. That cunning, brilliant man knew the best weapon against Al Anqa'a wasn't a knife—it was his touch. The same curse that allowed him to drain magic from Jasadis apparently allowed him to drain it from other creatures. Had he known before he hurled himself onto Al Anqa'a whether his plan would work?

Al Anqa'a looped around, wings slowing, as though it had lost the energy to carry their weight. It flew too low to avoid the outcropping of stone this time, and it bellowed as the rocks shattered the feathers on its underside.

It was going to crash. Al Anqa'a was going to crash with Arin still on it.

The beast had returned to the spot where Arin had stabbed it. It swerved right and flew toward the flaming remnants of Galim's Bend.

"Get off, get off," I heard myself whispering. Namsa and Maia glanced at me, but I couldn't find it in myself to care.

On top of Al Anqa'a, Arin glanced at the hillside rapidly vanishing beneath them and the approaching wreckage.

I held my breath.

Arin slid down Al Anqa'a's spine, gaining speed as he raced past the glass wings. He tumbled from Al Anqa'a just as it cleared the bottom of the hill. It kept flying, the ends of its fiery wings sweeping the ground, before it slammed into a row of shops. The shops exploded, wood and detritus flying in all directions. Al Anqa'a skidded, toppling at least a dozen structures before it finally slowed to a halt. The path of its destruction cut wide, and at its end the great beast shuddered, completely colorless, and lay still.

"He killed Al Anqa'a," Maia whispered, voice thick with disbelief.

On the hillside, Arin drew himself up on a knee. Blood wept from multiple gashes on his arms, pouring through his uniform. Shards from Al Anqa'a had slashed his palms, and a patch of his hair was matted and red.

Hundreds of shadows assembled at the top of the hill, blotting out the moonlight.

The Nizahl soldiers had arrived.

Rovial's tainted tomb, what had taken them so long? How could they have left their Commander to fight alone?

Behind Arin, a single arm dragged a heap of oozing flesh and filleted bone with chilling speed in Arin's direction.

The nisnas gained on Arin, soundless in the grass. The Heir still knelt, his sight fixed on his soldiers, who were too far to see or help him.

Turn around, I wanted to shout. The scream I swallowed tore my throat raw. He couldn't defeat Al Anqa'a and then fall to a nisnas. *Turn around, turn around!*

Arin went still. Very slowly, his head turned, neck tight with tension.

Blue eyes looked directly at me.

Gasps sounded around me. Maia and Namsa skittered back, cursing in Resar.

Somehow, I wasn't surprised he had heard me. That across mountains and hills and trees, my voice reached him.

Turn around!

Just as the nisnas snapped its arm forward, Arin whirled.

The vision went black. The suspended water crashed into the lake and sprayed me, Maia, and Namsa. The three Visionists collapsed, narrowly saved from falling into the lake by their companions. They must have emptied their stores completely.

I found myself once again at the center of attention as all eyes left the Visionists and turned to me.

"How did you do that?" Namsa demanded.

"Do what?"

"He looked right at you!"

"She summoned him!" another voice cried out. "She created a portal!"

The murmurs grew, rising until I couldn't pick out individual voices.

"The Visionists can't create portals," Efra shouted. I braced myself for his barrage of accusations. "The Silver Serpent is sensitive to magic, remember? The Visionists always refuse to conjure visions of him for fear he would sense the trace of their power. They held up this vision with him at the center for nearly twenty minutes, and indeed, their fear was confirmed. The Malika just happened to be standing in front when he sensed it."

If someone had asked me at the start of this week whether it was more likely I'd plunge into a sea full of ancient monsters, watch Arin ride Al Anqa'a, or experience Efra defending me, I would never have chosen the last option. I would probably have jumped out of the nearest window, but I wouldn't have predicted this.

"We can't risk casting a vision near him again," Lateef agreed. He'd been standing behind the Visionists when they collapsed. "What if he manages to see into our side?"

"We learned our lesson," Efra said gruffly. "But our goal has been accomplished. The kingdoms will turn against one another. The careful order the Silver Serpent sought to maintain is broken."

Their moods lifted, the Urabi started filtering back into the mountain, chatter of food, war, and sleep mingling among them. Efra, Namsa, Maia, and I remained at the lake.

I crossed my arms over my chest. "I don't need you to defend me."

"I do not intend to repeat it." Efra cast a hard glance at the crushed ice floating over the lake. "Your power fills them with hope. Hope is all that has sustained us through years of horror and desolation. I will not let you tear it from them by revealing the dark underbelly of your magic."

Namsa held up her hands. "Efra, consider your accusations. The Commander *is* sensitive to magic. It's entirely possible your story holds truth."

Efra scoffed. "Don't be naïve. She was watching the nisnas approach him like her heart was on the Awaleen-damned butcher's block. We have no idea what her magic is capable of because she *refuses to use it*. But let us review, shall we? Her magic conjured a kitmer in the middle of the Victor's Ball, it destroyed a wing of the Citadel, and it summoned the Sareekh—the *Sareekh*, Namsa—to her rescue. She could have easily started to create a portal without realizing it."

Maia cleared her throat. "Portalists are extinct, though, aren't they? The only known one allied with the Mufsids."

"Am I speaking to a wall?" Efra threw his arms wide. "Her magic doesn't follow any accursed rules!"

"All magic has rules. Consequences." Namsa turned to me, a speculative gleam in her eyes. "We just need to find out what hers are."

CHAPTER SIXTEEN

SYLVIA

Namsa delayed me, waiting until the others had vanished into the mountain before she spoke.

"They are gathering for the Aada in there." She inclined her head toward the entrance. "They'll be expecting you."

"What more is there to discuss?" I brushed a crusted strand of my hair away from my mouth. I hadn't had a chance to wash up since last night. Thanks to my luxurious soak in the brine and sediment of Suhna Sea, I could pick up a curl and crack it between my fingers. "Nobody listened to me earlier. Any tidy scheme you might've had before won't survive Galim's Bend. In hours, Felix will have soldiers posted up to his hairy nostrils. Orban will likely declare a curfew and arrest anyone out past the hour. Who knows what Lukub will do? Vaida might start throwing anyone whose name ends with an *a* into the Traitors' Wells."

"It was a mistake to authorize the attack without your input. Don't give us an opportunity to repeat it. Come listen to what we have to share with you, Essiya."

I could spend an eternity plummeting through the depths of her audacity without reaching the bottom. "I repeat: I went to your Aada this morning. I waved my arms, I shouted, I begged them to find a way to reverse this disaster Efra set into motion. Now you want me to come back and listen to another doomed plan?"

"It isn't doomed. We—"

"Go to your Aada, Namsa." I tried to maneuver around her. "If you decide to invade the Omal palace, let me know what time we ride to our deaths."

A lightly muscled arm thrust itself in my path. "Leadership comes to you naturally. Why do you insist on walking away from it?"

I tipped my head to the stars and sternly advised myself against hurling Namsa into the lake. Leadership couldn't be more unnatural to me. I was short-tempered and impatient, and I firmly believed compromises were an empty solace for the unwittingly defeated. Toss in the voices in my head, the unpredictable magic, and the random hallucinations? They would be better off flinging my crown into the sea.

"He will win," she said.

The stars winked.

"You can anticipate problems we cannot. You know how these rulers think. He showed you maps of their palaces, trained you in the ways of their courts. Before the Alcalah, you were already a formidable force, but now?" Namsa's laugh floated, disembodied, over the dark mountains. "Arin of Nizahl created his own worst enemy."

Sefa's soft voice swallowed Namsa's, as though whispered from the clouds. *The way he looks at you sometimes. Like you are a cliff with a fatal fall, and each day you move him closer to its edge.*

A shudder entirely unrelated to the cold worked its way down my spine, and I forced my gaze back to the mountains. To Namsa.

He may have created his own worst enemy, I wanted to say, *but I am my own worst enemy, too.*

"I will sit in on the meeting," I said. "But do not expect me to do more than observe."

"My, my!" I raised my hands over my head and clapped. "If the goal is to expedite your own gruesome murders, I must say—you have all applied yourselves to the extreme."

The members of the Aada regarded me with varying levels of indignation. Thick cushions covered the ground, arranged in a loose semicircle around the room. The aim behind removing the table and chairs was supposedly to strip away barriers to communication. Or, in my hands, potential weapons.

"Queen Hanan does not care a whit about me. Felix could pulverize me into soil for their gardens, and she wouldn't stop to smell the flowers growing from my carcass."

Dust motes drifted across the speechless room. After a minute, Lateef cleared his throat. "Your...vivid...objection is noted, Mawlati. We understand your doubt, but we have reason to believe Queen Hanan may be easier to persuade than you think."

The urge to draw out the knife hidden in my boot and stab it into the nearest hard surface nearly overwhelmed me. Hours we had spent in this fashion. *Hours*, while my hair took on a texture akin to burnt bread and the members of the Aada exerted themselves to incinerate every last one of my nerves. I took solace in my putrid smell. In this coffin of a room, they were probably choking on it.

"Reason, reason, reason." I drew my wrist across my nose, wiping the layer of dust settling above my lip. Awaleen below, but I was tired. "A reason you refuse to share, but continue to cite as a valid rebuttal to any of the points I raise. Tell me, then: Why am I here? You do not treat me honestly, you will not hear my counsel, and you expect me to join you in a pointless death based on a trust you will not return."

Lateef and Namsa glanced at each other. On the other side of the room, the three Aada members I didn't know avoided my eyes.

"Oh, just tell her!" Maia burst. She pushed off the wall she'd been slouching against and strode over to Lateef. She held out her hand.

"She's right. How can we ask her to trust us when we will not do the same?"

Namsa leaned back with a slight smirk. She shrugged at Lateef. "You know where I stand."

"Why should we trust her? She—"

"Be silent, Efra." Lateef scowled. "You have become unbearable since the Malika arrived. If you intend to drown yourself in childish petulance, do not drag us down with you."

I wouldn't laugh. I absolutely would not laugh at the affronted look on Efra's contemptible face.

Properly chastened, Efra huffed, but did not speak again.

A bundle of parchment rolled together with twine dropped into Maia's hand. "Give it to the Malika," Lateef sighed. To me, he said, "Dawoud brought this to Namsa six years ago. He recovered it from a high-ranking general in Nizahl's army in the first month of the siege."

I dragged a lantern closer to my lap as Maia handed me the bundle. The current state of my vision did not easily lend itself to reading, and it blurred double at the tiny script squeezed onto the pages.

Already dreading the headache this would shepherd my way, I sifted through the bundle. The damaged edges of the parchment crackled beneath my fingers. If Dawoud had taken this in the first month of the Jasad War, then it was nearly half my age. "What am I looking at?"

Namsa threw her arm over the back of Lateef's cushion, one leg spread and the other bent at the knee. She was different in these meetings. Cockier. Namsa in the Aada was a relaxed woman of thirty, and I barely recognized her.

"Reason," she said.

I sighed. Relaxed or not, she was still Namsa.

Settling back, I lifted the first parchment and forced myself to focus on the tidy blocks of script.

I have been lied to. We have all been lied to. Should these pages be found beyond my possession, know this—they have killed me, and they will eventually kill you, too.

The fortress fell before the messenger did.

Rawain knew the fortress would fall. He knew what the messenger would say.

We rode for Jasad two days before the fortress fell—before the slaughter at the Summit.

It is my belief that Supreme Rawain of Nizahl, to whom I have pledged my loyalty and led regiments of men to their death, worked in league with Sultana Bisai of Lukub and King Murib of Orban to orchestrate the events precipitating the Jasad War.

No—this is not a war.

This is a siege.

I straightened, gripping the parchment with too much force. My pulse juddered to life, a pounding drumbeat of disbelief rolling through my body.

The others stayed silent as I read. My hands shook harder with each page I flipped.

The author described how the armies of Orban, Lukub, and Nizahl were sent out before the messenger at the Blood Summit had delivered the news of Niphran's death. *Before* the massacre supposedly launched by Malik Niyar and Malika Palia against the other rulers. It had been planned all along, from who would die at the Summit to when the strike against Jasad should come.

The only kingdom that had refused to ride against Jasad was Omal.

Queen Hanan and King Toran despise the Jasad throne as much—if not more—than the other rulers, but they refused to ride against the kingdom of their granddaughter without grave cause.

King Toran is dead. His son, Emre, was killed in Jasad a decade ago. Supreme Rawain has stripped Queen Hanan of everything she loves and left her with one option only: war.

The author went on to detail his confusion about how the kingdoms had facilitated the destruction of the fortress; who did they have inside Jasad who could destroy a centuries-old magical barricade? Niphran was the Qayida at the time—could her death have led to the fortress's fall?

I glanced at the watching Jasadis and wondered if they knew what Hanim had done to them. What she had tricked Soraya and the Mufsids into doing.

Sentence by sentence, the knot in my stomach grew. Here was the validation for what I had known all along. My grandparents weren't responsible for the Blood Summit. In this, if in little else, their conscience had been clear.

But this document failed to answer the only question that mattered. How could Supreme Rawain, a man without an ounce of magic in his blood, summon enough magic to destroy the Summit and kill the two most powerful Jasadis in the land?

The last page was brief.

Rawain is searching for something. He will not stop until he finds it. Magic may have been the face of this war, but it is not the heart.

A scrawled signature followed.

Binyar Lazur, First General of the Southern Regiment of Nizahl.

I dropped the parchment. I knew that name.

I had lived with this man's brother. Fought for him. Listened at his side while he confessed why he fled Nizahl at fourteen, changing his name and severing his ties with what was left of his family.

My last brother, Binyar, rose in the ranks quickly under Supreme Rawain. He was among those chosen to lead the siege on Jasad's fortress after the Blood Summit. He never returned.

The Nizahl general who'd written down his doubts and safeguarded them with Dawoud. Who pieced together Rawain's lies and never returned from the battlefield.

It was Marek's brother.

CHAPTER SEVENTEEN

ARIN

Arin waited until he was alone to throw up. Gripping the rim of the wastebasket, he sank to the floor. With his forehead pressed to the permanently chilled wall, Arin did his best to breathe through the pain. The healers had tried to attend him after the soldiers finally descended on Galim's Bend, but Arin diverted them to the villages. They were still pulling bodies from the wreckage. Any survivors would need far more care than Arin. These wounds wouldn't kill him. He was almost certain.

One more minute, and he would stand up and find his medical kit. Just one more minute.

The spot where the nisnas lashed its arm around Arin's ankle had been stripped red and raw, burned by the acidic excretions from the creature's skin. It could have been much worse. It *should* have been much worse. Arin had been on his knees at the base of the hill, the damage to his head making him see double, and he'd heard it.

Turn around.

Not many things had the privilege of frightening Arin. He had been the kind of child more likely to set a trap for the imaginary monster under his bed than tuck his feet beneath the blanket in passive surrender. Losing control of his mind, losing faith in his own judgment...

He knew what his mind was capable of. He knew what shadows it kept.

The voice had been real. It had to have been real—Arin's talent for foresight did not translate to prophetic power.

By now, the council would have ridden halfway to the Wickalla, where survivors of Galim's Bend would be living until new arrangements could be made. Bayoum had insisted on riding to meet them and giving a speech.

Arin couldn't find it in himself to scrounge even a scrap of surprise. A massacre and the release of centuries-old monsters into Nizahl? It was the perfect opportunity for Bayoum to argue against the conscription protections without directly crossing Arin. The wreckage fit into Bayoum's agenda so neatly, Arin might have wondered if the councilman was its architect. Fortunately for Bayoum, the only keys for those cages were in Arin's possession, and he hadn't touched them since the Alcalah.

The cages had been broken by magic.

With a white-knuckled grip on the table, Arin hoisted himself to his feet, a groan escaping his pressed lips. Each step toward his bureau whipped fire across his skin. He removed his emergency supplies and lined them up on the table by order of use. Talwith to clean the injury, a towel for the blood, a thin blade to cut out fragments stuck inside any open wounds, a needle and thread, and bandages to cover anything too small or hopeless for stitching.

Arin sank into a chair. He peeled off his vest and discarded the remnants of his torn shirt. They dropped in a wet heap at his feet. Another time, the sight would bother Arin more than the pain.

The chill air breathed a sigh of relief across Arin's wounds. He poured talwith onto the towel and down his throat in equal turns and set to managing the smallest gashes first. Time crawled, content to relish Arin's discomfort. By the time Arin reached the biggest wound, black spots danced in his vision and a metallic rust coated his tongue.

Arin had miscalculated his stunt at the hilltop by a fraction of a second. After he lured Al Anqa'a away from the village, he'd dropped to the ground too late. Al Anqa'a had grazed his chest with its claws and gouged three parallel lines into his torso before Arin plunged his knife into its underbelly.

Lifting the talwith over the first of the shredded marks, Arin hesitated. Reaching toward the bureau, he opened the middle drawer and pulled out another towel to slide between his teeth. He didn't trust himself not to bite off his tongue.

Arin gripped the talwith like a man holding on to his last breath before dumping its contents over his chest.

The towel depressed between Arin's teeth. He couldn't tamp down a strangled gasp. He tried to reach for the bandages only to discover his arm refused to cooperate.

The black spots on the edges of his vision grew. The empty bottle dropped from Arin's numb fingers to the carpet, and the thud was the last sound Arin heard before the darkness closed around him.

"You left him bleeding in here alone? What kind of guardsman are you?"

"I'm so sorry, sire. I thought he was in the infirmary, he ordered me to stay in Galim's Bend to guide the recruits, and I didn't realize his injuries were so—"

Arin stirred, fighting the pull of sleep.

"You have been in my son's employ for ten years. How could you not know he wouldn't go to the infirmary during an emergency? His utter nonsense about taking resources from others—as if he isn't the Commander! As if the loss of a hundred thousand lives could ever be worth the loss of his! And for what? Some farmers and vagrants in Galim's Bend?"

Arin became aware of a pressure on his chest. Someone was touching him.

Arin's hand struck out. He opened his eyes to a petrified medic leaning over him, her wrist caught in Arin's grip.

Behind her, Wes and Rawain whirled toward Arin. Relief poured over his guardsman, and he pressed a shaking hand to his pin. "Sire. You're awake."

The medic hesitantly tugged at her wrist. Arin released her, shifting his attention to the rest of the room. He was still in the chair he'd bandaged himself in, supplies haphazardly strewn across the table by his elbow. How long had he been unconscious?

"Well, if it isn't my martyr of an Heir." Rawain brushed the medic aside and peered down at Arin. "In your fit of heroism, did you notice you forgot to bandage your head wound?"

"I didn't forget," Arin said. "The blood had already clotted, and the injury itself was nothing of note."

Rawain glanced at the healer for confirmation. Her timid nod only seemed to heighten his irritation.

"I need to speak to my son. Alone."

She looked stricken. "But I haven't finished—"

Rawain cut her off with a cold glare. Wes guided the unhappy medic from the room, pausing briefly at the door to aim a small smile at Arin. Wes's relief made Arin guiltily aware of the position he'd put the guardsman in. If Arin had died, the consequences would have fallen heavily on Wes's head.

As soon as they were alone, Arin forced himself upright. Though predicting the changes in Rawain's mood was a lifelong exercise in futility, Arin did not need to stretch his imagination far to guess Rawain was furious. Not only had Arin disobeyed him by riding to

Galim's Bend instead of sheltering inside the Citadel, he had gone alone.

Rawain arranged himself on the other end of the table, tucking his scepter inside his elbow as he propped his chin against his fist.

"The Mufsids will be executed in Antar Square at dawn."

The words hung, a lit match in a dark room, and imploded.

Arin set his hands on the table, splaying his palms open. He focused on the grain of the wood beneath his hands as he aimed for a measured tone—Rawain would be utterly unreachable if he sensed even a hint of emotion or anger in Arin's voice. "I thought we decided there was still time."

The question of what to do with the Mufsids had become a strong source of contention between Arin and the council. The Mufsids weren't responding to interrogation, and Arin wasted precious time every day visiting the highly secured jails to drain their magic.

But the Mufsids had also successfully evaded Arin for years. They knew the Urabi's patterns, their movements. The crispness of their accent hinted at noble backgrounds, which meant they might have had access to Malik Niyar and Malika Palia. The Mufsids could be the key to finding the Jasad Heir. Enough pressure, enough time, and one of them would break. They'd held spies and traitors for much longer.

The rush to execute didn't make sense. The right piece of information could be more powerful than a thousand armies.

Rawain rolled the head of the scepter between his hands, leaning back in the chair. "The cages in Galim's Bend were impenetrable and heavily guarded. Someone found their way through our barriers. Someone familiar enough with our protocols to know how to sidestep them. This was a message from the Urabi to show their magic can defeat our strongest defenses, to announce their presence to the rest of the kingdoms. You spend so much of your waking hours searching for a way to avoid this war—have you even considered how to win it? Because the Urabi have. Do you plan to stand in front of your kingdom and inform your people you haven't a notion of how to find the ones responsible for this?"

The last sentence hit Arin with a force to rival Al Anqa'a. "I will find them."

"Not quickly enough." The note of finality warned Arin that any further argument would not be kindly met.

Arin couldn't let it go. They would be playing right into the Urabi's hands if they blamed the Mufsids for a crime they didn't commit. Nizahlans were not fools, and the rest of the kingdoms would see right through the distraction. How could Rawain agree to lose critical sources of information in a clumsy attempt to save face?

"It is a shame we couldn't sit down for supper tonight," Rawain went on. "It has been too long since you and I had a conversation without the intrusion of politics. Perhaps we could have still salvaged it, had you decided to listen and stay in the Citadel."

For all his father's flaws, the artistry of his threats was beyond reproach. Arin's gut usually recognized it first, tightening uncomfortably from nothing more than a passing word or glance. Rawain's first language was intimidation, and Arin had learned how to translate its hidden symbols long ago.

Rawain got up, adjusting the cascading layers of his robes, and laid a hand on Arin's head. His sigh traveled like a rumble in the clouds, promising thunder. "I am glad to see you returned alive and whole, Arin."

Every muscle in Arin's body corded tight. He wished he could close his eyes and pretend the conversation ended there.

His father's hand shifted to the other side of Arin's head, pausing inches from his wound. "You have the most aggravating habit of measuring the worth of your life as equal to those around you. They were not born to rule. I have not wasted my life preparing *them* to lead my kingdom. You are more clever, more skilled, more determined than any of them could ever hope to be."

The shock of pain as Rawain's thumb pressed against the bandage on his head wasn't reflected in Arin's stony face. He made certain of it. Even when red trickled over his right temple and dripped onto his cheek, Arin showed nothing.

"Magic will never deserve your mercy, son. Again and again, I have tried to teach you this lesson. I have tried to prepare your heart against the forces which might twist it in their favor."

Arin deserved much worse than this. What he'd done, the wreckage he'd facilitated by allowing the Urabi to capture the Jasad Queen... Arin deserved so much worse.

"Such a fine mind you have, Arin. If only you would lend it to more worthwhile matters. Aren't you glad your mother is not here to suffer seeing you like this?" Rawain's thumb dug deeper, and Arin's hands curled into fists. "To see her son suggesting we offer her killers clemency?"

Blood caught on Arin's eyelashes. The world faded in and out of focus. He set his attention to the raven rising from his father's scepter, anchoring his swaying consciousness to its upraised wings. Its beady eyes seemed to mock him.

After an eternity, Rawain removed his hand and pulled a handkerchief from inside his robe. He cleaned his thumb and tossed the cloth onto Arin's lap. "Don't be late to the execution. I expect you to stand tall in Antar Square and show the council's decision the same deference you waste on the villagers. Is that clear?"

"Yes, my liege."

"Good." Rawain patted Arin's cheek. His gaze softened, warming with affection. "My brave boy. I will send the healer in to finish patching you up."

Rawain swept from the chambers, the swirl of his robes sending the shredded pieces of fabric on Arin's floor flying. When the medic returned to finish fixing Arin, he didn't allow her to rebandage his head or wipe the dried streak of blood down the right side of his face. "Leave it," he ordered.

Later, he sat on the edge of his bed and touched the scar on the underside of his jaw. He traced the divot where Soraya's blade had twisted up.

A drop of red fell from his temple, seeping into the rug.

Arin closed his eyes. Some wounds were best left to bleed.

CHAPTER EIGHTEEN

SYLVIA

An hour ago, I would have gladly maimed everyone at the Aada for the chance to go to sleep. After Lateef dismissed us, my singular concern had been walking to my chambers without fainting in the hall.

That is, until I had started undressing for bed.

Blanket drawn to my chin, I stared at the ceiling, more awake than I'd been in years.

There was a new vein. Silver this time, traveling from the back of my knee to the top of my ankle. I spotted it by accident, twisting to adjust the back of my sleep pants, and it had led to frantically stripping and searching my body for more hidden veins. Just the two, fortunately—gold on my palm, silver on my leg. If it hadn't been for the late hour, I would have hunted down Namsa and asked her to explain why my body appeared to be cracking like a statue under a clumsy chisel.

Tomorrow. Tomorrow I would show Namsa the veins.

I turned, pulling one of the pillows to my chest. Half the times I closed my eyes, I saw Soraya and the Mufsids attacking Usr Jasad, their victory cut short by the collapsing fortress. The other half, I saw Supreme Rawain winking at me from across the table at the Blood Summit, seconds before the screaming began.

It was almost a relief to think about strategy instead.

The Urabi had collected a truly impressive fleet of Jasadis with specialized magic. Twenty Jasadis with Hayagan magic, a specialty my grandparents had disdained unless someone needed to urgently throw a loud party. Apparently, the Hayagan could use their powers to unsettle animals from miles away. If we needed horses, the Hayagan were our best bet for stealing them from any patrols in Essam. Their ability to release pulses of chaotic energy into the air had the dual effect of fueling an excited crowd as well as summoning animals, oddly enough.

Stranger still was the number of Sahirs in their midst. Sahirs were notoriously reclusive; many of them hated the hierarchical structure of Jasad's wilayahs and left for other kingdoms long before the war. The Urabi must have expended every resource at their disposal to find and recruit fifteen of them. Sahirs could transfer their magic between elements: mold steel from dirt, fashion a blade from mere branches. With them alongside the Hayagan, we would have however many weapons they could create before their magic ran dry. They did, however, require three times the recovery period of other specialties.

Eventually, even war strategy lost its appeal. I yanked a pillow over my face and drew my arms over it, stifling my groan. The furnishings in my room were meager, but they were still double what the others here had. They were treating me well, bestowing me with comfort they themselves lacked, and I didn't even have the decency to enjoy it.

The pressure in my chest built. I pressed my hand to my heart like a child listening to a once-beloved story.

One, two. I'm alive.

Three, four. I'm safe.

Five, six. I won't let him catch me.

When the roil of dread in my stomach only increased, I tried again.

One, two. I'm alive.

Three, four... Where was I?

My room vanished, its outlines blurring and liquefying before me. Panic instantly turned to cold comprehension. Not this. Not again. Not *now*.

When the walls solidified, they were nothing like mine. My bare feet landed on soft carpet.

An enormous and startlingly austere room surrounded me. A candle flickered above a table strewn with empty vials and bloody cloths. Sickly trickles of moonlight traveled through the rain-streaked window and caught on a magnificent four-poster bed at the head of the room. I paused, a bit idiotically, to admire the lush covers. Not even I could stay awake on a bed like that.

The shadows in the room shifted as the oil in the lantern popped, and I started at the sight of a bare back hunched on the edge of the bed. Its owner faced the wall, hands braced on either side of him, broad shoulders drawn.

I knew that spine better than I knew my own. How many times had I marveled at the grace in his body, the fluidity in his movements? Arin moved like an unfinished song, answering to a rhythm the rest of us couldn't hear. Even the blood matting the side of his head, darkening the silver strands to a dark maroon, couldn't diminish him.

I wished I could look away, but in a room of beautiful things, Arin of Nizahl outshined them all.

He hadn't seen or heard me yet, which meant I still had a chance to disappear. Of all the times and all the people. What was my magic thinking, bringing me here? In fact, why was my magic thinking at all? Maybe it would please Efra to know I *had* been using my magic over the last few days. Excluding, of course, how it had been used and how little I'd been involved in the process.

He still hadn't sensed my presence. He hadn't sensed it in the garden, either. Arin's attunement to magic should have given me away as soon as I came near.

Were you truly here, I would have felt your magic the instant you entered the Citadel's grounds.

I checked my palm. The gold vein hadn't disappeared, but its glow had dimmed. I dug deep for my magic, scraping every corner and crevice, and came up empty-handed.

Was I here... without my magic?

On the table to our right, a dozen silver tools lay scattered haphazardly among the blood-soaked bandages. Expensive tools, tools a healer would have taken with them when they left.

Had he tried to fix himself?

A horrified laugh punched out of my throat. "You tombs-damned fool."

Arin's back snapped straight, each muscle pulling taut. He didn't turn around.

Not a reassuring sign. Really, it was a sign shrieking *Danger! Danger!*

"Al Anqa'a could have killed you. Is that how you wanted to go? Sliced-up bird dinner?"

The bandages wrapped around his torso and side came into view, and I inhaled sharply. The damage from Al Anqa'a's claws hadn't appeared nearly so dire in the Visionists' illusion.

Arin was hurt. Badly.

A line of blood had dried from his hairline to the bolt of his jaw, but the rest of his wound dressings were clean. Why hadn't he wiped this bit of blood away?

My hands curled into fists in my tunic. If my magic was here, now would be the moment to whisk me away. Now, before the dust settled over my crumbling resistance or my reaching hand—

—touched the back of his bare shoulder.

It happened instantly. My skin had barely grazed his when an iron grip caught my wrist. The room flew as I was flipped backward and slammed against the wall, my traitorous hand pinned above my head.

Arin loomed over me, inches away, murder ripening on his lovely features.

"Hello to you, too." I grinned. I wasn't one to prod hungry lions, but damn if my asinine instincts hadn't convinced themselves that this one wouldn't bite me.

The hold on my wrist tightened. I huffed. "Yes, you're very intimidating. Let me go."

I yanked, trying to dislodge him, but even injured and bleeding, Arin was Arin. I'd have a better chance pushing past a wall. "You are being unreasonable."

Nothing.

I took a deep breath. Before the kindling of my irritation could blaze into anger, I caught sight of his wardrobe, its carved wooden doors thrown open. The chaos distracted me from the Heir glowering a breath away from my face.

The mess on the table was a symptom of his injuries, but the wardrobe? The skewed drawers on his bureau? The three empty cups on his nightstand?

I met his eyes, brows pinching in concern as I studied him. Arin would sooner let rats gnaw on his fingers than show even a hint of weakness, but the condition of his room spoke louder than his implacable features.

In the wardrobe, Arin's clothes were organized in neat, symmetrical rows. Only one item stuck out, its shoddy craftsmanship a far cry from the tailored sleeves and intricate hems of its neighbors. Surrounded by Arin's immaculate clothing, a moth-eaten, threadbare old cloak had been carefully hung in the back.

My chest swelled to a point of pain.

Though I was the one pinned to the wall, I suddenly felt as

though I had cheated. I had seen what was not meant for me, stolen an advantage in our game.

"Let me go," I said hoarsely. "Let me go, and I'll leave. I swear it."

He flipped me around at dizzying speed, twisting my arm behind my back. Instead of pressing my face to the wall, Arin pushed us a step toward the door.

"Are you trying to *arrest* me?" Appalled, I couldn't help a laugh. "Arin, we both know my body is miles away."

Again, nothing. Arguing with Arin when he had closed himself off was a waste of time. He would respond to only one language.

My unrestrained arm shot backward, driving my elbow into Arin's stomach.

Not quite as painful as hitting a wall, but close.

His grip loosened the barest fraction, but I capitalized on it, twisting my restrained wrist down and out.

My victory lasted mere seconds, sliced in half by the dagger glinting in Arin's hand. I marveled at the frequency with which this man hid a blade on his person.

We moved in a sadistic mirror of the moments before the Victor's Ball when we'd exploded into motion toward each other. Except then, he'd drawn me close with his mouth over mine, and this time—this time, he swung a knife at my heart with deadly accuracy while I rammed my shoulder into his chest at full speed.

Were Arin less grievously injured, he would have used the force of my run to overturn me and sink the dagger into my chest. We'd practiced the strategy together a million times in the tunnels. But blood had starting weeping through his bandages, and we went down in a heap.

We grappled. I tightened my knees around Arin's hips as he twisted on top of me. As soon as he raised the knife, I dug my fingers into the bandages at his side until he gasped. Blood stained my nails.

"Sorry, I'm sorry—" I grabbed his wrist, knocking it into the ground by my head, but he wouldn't drop the knife. His other fist drove into my side, and the pain shot me straight into a coughing fit.

Bastard. I grabbed a handful of his hair and yanked him close.

I had a hard head—a useful detail Hanim uncovered during her long tenure of torture. Arin learned about it in the training tunnels, and I paid him another reminder by smashing my forehead against his.

I recovered quickly and used his momentary disorientation to throw my weight forward, flipping us once again. I leaned over him and clasped his wrist, grinding it into the floor. His fingers wouldn't unclench.

"Let go, you stubborn fool! You're bleeding and I don't want to hurt you."

"Don't want to hurt me?" The growled words, the first he'd spoken, caught me off guard. Strands of silver hair slipped over his forehead, catching on the blood newly flowing from his temple.

He heaved with the effort of speaking with me atop his torn chest, sweat shining on his collarbone. But he'd stopped resisting. He wasn't trying to buck me off or pursue any of the vulnerabilities my position above him granted.

I looked at the trail of dried blood along his cheek and thought of the way I'd found him sitting. Hunched and drawn.

"I didn't know about Galim's Bend."

Lightning cracked through the impenetrable frost in his eyes, brightly furious.

"Arin, I would never have released Al Anqa'a. You know I wouldn't."

"I know nothing about you," he said, harsh and low. "Essiya."

Uttered with contempt, clearly meant to injure, my name in his mouth had the opposite effect. Hearing it filled me with a shapeless wonder. I didn't have to battle the instinct to correct him or grimace at the sound. It didn't feel like an ill-fitting piece of clothing someone else had chosen for me. I wanted him to say it again.

Our shroud of secrets had fallen, and we knew each other truly for the first time.

"Be careful how you address a Queen," I whispered, legs tightening around his waist as I leaned forward, "little Heir."

He went still, and I realized my mistake in shifting forward. Arin's free hand—the one I'd pinned against his body, between my knees—came loose. In seconds, I went airborne, a powerful shove sending me halfway across the room.

By the time I hit the ground and rolled to my feet, Arin was stalking toward me. I darted behind the table and threw an inkwell at his head. He dodged, so I started hurling everything within reach. Bandages, clothes, scrolls, and books rained on Arin. He batted them aside without slowing.

Physically, Arin was unimpeachable. Every muscle on his finely honed body had earned its way there through hard labor, wrapping around a broad and powerful frame. The Commander of Nizahl had trained since childhood, and his ironclad will made it so nothing beyond death would slow his blade or alter his aim. Even now, with so much blood leaking from his bandages, he would keep coming until one of us was in pieces.

To know Arin of Nizahl was to know the real force—and the real vulnerability—lived beyond his body.

I blurted the words that had been circling in my head since the Aada meeting. "The fortress fell before the messenger did!"

It was a gamble. A match tossed in a dark well. I grabbed a bottle and held it between us like a sword, waiting for him to cross the last of the distance.

Instead, a miracle happened.

Arin paused.

I had never encountered anyone whose mind worked like Arin's.

Once cut with curiosity, it would not heal. Any uncertainty would fester, spreading like poison, consuming him.

Ignoring the ache behind my ribs, I reached for his weakness, and I dug my fingers deep.

"Haven't you asked yourself how it was that the Jasad fortress, which had stood for centuries, fell within hours of the Blood Summit? How four armies were already in place to strike as soon as the fortress fell?" The questions tripped over one another, rushing to liberation. These doubts I had bottled for years, finally shared with the one person who would be as tortured by them as me. "If my grandparents had planned to attack the Blood Summit, why would they bring me? Why would news of Niphran's death—the daughter they threw to rot in Bakir Tower, whose lover they murdered—affect them so greatly that their magic would react to destroy the entire Summit?"

I took a cautious step toward his motionless form, bottle still raised between us. He tracked me closely, flinty gaze never leaving mine.

He was listening.

"Think of how cleanly it happened," I urged, and it was reckless to speak like this, drawing unseeingly from a well of my own suspicions. I didn't dare mention Binyar or his confession, but otherwise, I didn't know what I would say next. A wrong move, a misstep, and the cage of his curiosity might break. "Magic-madness has been a discredited theory for over a hundred years. Your own kingdom cast it aside as unsubstantiated fearmongering. Your father is patient, I will grant him that. He spent decades slowly shifting Nizahl from the kingdom created by the Awaleen to arbitrate magic to a kingdom galvanized to destroy it."

Invoking Rawain was risky, and I feared the worst when Arin took a single, precise step forward. The bottom of the bottle pressed against his sternum. He wrapped a hand around the center, but made no move to pull it out of my grasp.

Still silent. Still watching me.

My heart pounded. It would have been less terrifying if he had unsheathed a sword.

My time was running out.

"I met your mother at the Blood Summit," I said. "Isra knew she was going to die. She walked into that Summit knowing what Rawain planned to do."

Talwith bottles, one of which I was keeping pressed to Arin's chest, were crafted to endure rowdy khawaga and treks across trade routes. Dania's kingdom of warriors had pooled their talent and created a bottle sturdy enough to survive long campaigns through Essam and fearsome battles. A bottle that, for all intents and purposes, could outlast time itself.

Arin's knuckles turned white around the bottle, and the glass shattered.

I barely had a second to process—*he broke a talwith bottle with his bare hand*—before he was stepping over the puddle of broken glass toward me. My back hit the wall, and I exhaled with ill-timed amusement. Arin's repertoire of skills should include a singular ability to corner me against walls.

I raised the bottle's neck, still clasped in my grip, and pressed the jagged ends to the underside of Arin's chin before he could take another step.

My voice hardened. "I know he is your father. I know what I ask of you."

I wished I understood less. I'd torn myself apart from the inside out trying to please Hanim's ghost. To be the Heir and Jasadi she wanted. I had recoiled from the simplest touch; fought against any tenderness or friendship that might wrap itself around my neck and drag me to the mud. I'd spent a mere five years in Essam, but neither the scars on my back nor the influence she had cast would ever fully heal.

Arin had never known a day in his life without Rawain. The Supreme had drawn the constellations of Arin's world, dictated the parameters of his universe. Another son would have probably contented himself with living in a predetermined reality. That son wouldn't have allowed anything so troublesome as doubt to crack the comfortable foundation upon which he rested.

Though Arin had grown up in the world Rawain devised, Arin had a quality—a miraculous, almost spiteful strength—that was a nightmare for those whose bloody hands built our skies and earth.

Arin wondered.

"It took one lie for you to lose faith in me," I whispered. "Tell me, Your Highness: How many will it take until you lose faith in your father?"

I dropped the bottle's neck. It landed at our feet, rolling out of sight.

"Will it be before or after one of us dies at the other's hand?"

The colors in the room began to fade, the surfaces dipping and swirling. Our time had ended.

"Ask him about the fortress." My stomach churned, and I fervently hoped I hadn't just committed a fatal error. In Arin's hands, a thread of information, no matter how thin, could unravel significantly more than intended.

Still, it was my last chance. A final arrow across the stars.

By most estimates, it was a colossal failure. Arin hadn't softened. He'd spoken only once.

The Commander blurred, disappearing like a stone dropped in a river, but the feeling I carried away was not despair.

Because I did not lie when I said I knew Arin.

And I knew what it looked like when the Heir's mind began to twist.

CHAPTER NINETEEN

SEFA

Servants rushed around Sefa, bumping her shoulder and shooting her harried scowls.

"My apologies," she mumbled, pressing herself into a corner. The chaos in the kitchen reminded her of mornings at the keep, except here she didn't understand how to navigate the flow.

Grease popped and fizzled as fried eggs slid onto plates. An eggplant, its skin softened over a low flame, was peeled and mashed. A dash of oil, salt, and tahina later, and the plate went into a running servant's hands.

They forgot to squeeze lemon over it. People always forgot the lemon.

Frozen fiteer flipped on a hot pan until the dough flaked golden brown. To Sefa's surprise, the cook drizzled honey and molasses directly onto the fiteer. Sefa had always poured the honey in a separate bowl for dipping.

Once the kitchen had emptied save a handful, Sefa stepped toward the most senior-looking staff member and said, with a confidence she didn't possess, "I wanted to bring the Sultana's breakfast to her quarters. Could you help me?"

The woman glanced at her, then at the rest of the servants. A girl no older than seventeen opened her mouth. "Of course," cut in the senior servant, speaking over the girl. "We would be more than happy to assist you in delivering breakfast to the Sultana's quarters."

"But—" tried the girl again.

"Salwa, gather a tray for the Sultana's attendant. Now." The glare quieted Salwa. The girl hastily collected a tray from the counter and began to pile it with food.

The servant cocked her hip against the counter. "Your name is Zahra, correct? I am Birta, head of the southern kitchen."

The man standing next to Salwa inclined his head. "Radwan."

They spoke with a thick Lukubi accent Sefa hadn't heard since she was little. Her father's accent had never faded, even after they moved to Nizahl. Sefa closed her eyes against the rush of nostalgia. She usually tried not to think of her father if she could help it.

Sefa had never quite worked out how to forgive him for dying.

On the bright side, the reminder had done away with Sefa's hunger. She accepted the tray from Salwa with a gentle smile. The girl averted her gaze and retreated behind Radwan.

Sefa opened her mouth to ask for directions to the Sultana's wing and paused. Radwan and Birta were exchanging smirks; Salwa had placed her nails between her teeth and appeared intent on gnawing to the bone. They were awaiting her question, noses already turned up to avoid the stench of her ignorance.

"Thank you for the food," Sefa said, and left.

Luckily, finding the Sultana's wing took significantly less effort than finding the kitchen. The tapestries grew more elaborate, the rugs plusher, the air sweeter.

At the end of the short hall leading to the Sultana's door, Sefa faced her third challenge of an increasingly long morning. She couldn't knock without putting the tray down, and the guards on either side of the hall wouldn't twitch a muscle to help her. But what if she put the tray on the ground and the Sultana opened the door right away? She would see Sefa standing with the Sultana's breakfast by her feet. Since the guards refused to move, maybe Sefa could balance the tray on their heads.

Sefa cleared her throat. "Sultana? I have your breakfast."

The silence on the other side of the door turned the ball of nerves in Sefa's belly to a boulder. What if in the cold light of day, the Sultana had changed her mind about needing an attendant? What if someone had already brought her food and the servants had neglected to mention it to Sefa? This might not be the Sultana's room, even, and the story of Sefa's mistake would turn her into an overnight laughingstock.

A rustling, followed by a low chuckle, emerged from behind the door. "My breakfast."

Thank the Awaleen. Sefa bent down, peeling exactly two fingers from her grip on the tray to push the handle.

"Good morning, Sultana!" The door opened a sliver, and Sefa rejoiced as she shouldered it the rest of the way. Overcome with victory, she walked into a pitch-black room and immediately tripped.

She fell and landed elbows-first, the tray still clutched in her panicked grip. The clatter of rolling dishes pained her almost as much as the tea splashing over her hands. At least she could confirm it hadn't grown cold.

Sunlight spilled into the chambers, illuminating Sefa in all her glorious humiliation. A naked man blinked down at her from next to the parted curtain. Oil smeared over his chest and shoulders, gleaming on his dark skin, and Sefa made the mistake of following it down to—*oh*. Oh no.

Abandoning the tray, Sefa lurched to her feet. Sultana Vaida sat up in her luxurious bed, in a similar state of undress as her guest. Instead of oil, bright red streaked the regal column of her throat, swirling along her jaw and the cut of her cheekbone.

Not blood, Sefa determined after a pause. Just paint.

Vaida turned on the bed, covers slipping as she settled her feet on the ground. The man by the window switched his attention to Vaida, a lecherous hunger ripening in his features.

Shoulders sharper than twin blades folded back as Vaida stretched, drawing her robe over her arms and looping the belt lazily around her waist.

Sefa studied the high ceiling, counting the virulent colors painted on the stone beams braided into the wall. She had not seen so much bare skin since she'd lived on the streets with Marek. The small issue of vagrancy hadn't stopped his adolescent self from tumbling a new girl every time Sefa left the tent for more than ten minutes.

"Your Majesty?" the man murmured, still unabashedly aroused by the window. Sefa may as well have been a sentient pile of buttons.

Sultana Vaida rose and poured from the water pitcher by her bedside table. She took a long drink. Without glancing back at the man, she said, "The day wastes, Ajil. Lace your trousers and go see to making the most of it."

"My name isn't—"

The Sultana's neck rotated, the knives in her eyes slashing the rest of Not-Ajil's sentence to ribbons. He gathered his clothes, his haste to leave an ironic replica of Sefa's entrance.

The door shut behind him. Sefa became freshly conscious of the food splattered all over the bone-white rug. "Sultana, I am so sorry." Sefa rushed around the bed and swallowed a dismayed hiss at the sticky honey saturating into the carpet's fibers, sharing company with flakes of overturned fiteer and soaked tea.

"Leave it." Vaida glanced over the mess dismissively. "Someone will take care of it."

Sefa blinked. "Am I not the someone?"

The corner of Vaida's mouth indented. "Not for this. Come. My head is splitting, and I distinctly remember being warned against sleeping with this"—gesturing at the paint streaks—"on my skin."

Vaida settled herself in the chair across from her dresser. A slim leg shifted under her robe as she crossed it over the other. Vaida tipped her head back, eyes shut and fingers lightly tapping at her temples.

Not eager to commit another misstep in a morning full of them, Sefa sprang into action. More bottles, powders, tubes, and vials cluttered the dresser than Sefa had seen in her entire life. The volume of beautification products displayed on this one surface could destroy the self-esteem of at least a hundred girls. What did Vaida need all this for? It wasn't as though anyone had a hope of competing with her.

Sefa uncorked the bottle sitting next to a stack of folded cotton squares and brought it to her nose for a cautious sniff. Lime and eucalyptus.

"Lightly pour it onto a square and dab." Lethargic eyes opened and settled on Sefa. "Sometime today would be excellent."

Sefa soaked a section of the cotton square. Clear liquid splashed onto her fingers, the bottle quivering beneath her unsteady grip.

Applying the cotton square to the base of the Sultana's throat, Sefa pretended she didn't notice the Sultana openly studying her. She dragged the cloth upward.

A delicate clasp of her wrist. "I said *dab*."

"Apologies." Sefa dabbed.

Vaida's throat vibrated in a hum. "I make you uncomfortable."

After a brief pause, Sefa drew a breath. The cloth traveled to the spot where jaw met ear. "Of course. You are the Sultana."

The cheek under the cloth drew up in a smirk. "Merely a healthy respect for my rank, is it?"

"Yes."

Before Sefa knew what was happening, the Sultana's arm struck out. A strong hand closed around her throat, and Sefa was yanked down to eye level. "That was your first lie."

Nails dug into the back of her neck. "I brought you here to serve as my eyes in the palace. In my presence, the truth alone may fall from your tongue, or I will have no recourse but to liberate the muscle from your mouth."

Vaida's grip slackened, and she returned to her languid sprawl. Sefa rubbed her throat, frustration warring with fear. "I didn't lie."

"Oh?"

Sefa was painfully aware of the fragile fate of her tongue. But Vaida had demanded honesty, and Sefa could afford this piece of it.

"Even a trained botanist would hesitate to stroke the petals of a poisonous flower without knowing when its toxins may burst."

Sefa deliberately dabbed the corner of the Sultana's eye, staining the rest of the cloth red. "I am cautious, not uncomfortable."

When Vaida remained quiet, Sefa worried she had overstepped her bounds. But Sultana Vaida, Sefa was quickly coming to understand, rarely encountered a bound she didn't cheerfully tear apart.

"What kind of flower do you think I would be?" Vaida asked with great interest. "It isn't typically the petals you should fear when it comes to poison, unless you plan to eat them."

Sefa spent the next several minutes listening as Vaida described the different personalities of the plants growing in her garden. She had to wait for Vaida to pause in her rant about how lilacs had the attitude of roses but the market value of sunflowers before she could speak. "All done."

"Perfect!" Vaida tossed her arms over her head and yawned. "My skin feels absolutely refreshed. You did an excellent job, Zahra."

Thrown, Sefa twisted her lips into a hesitant smile. The Sultana's moods shifted like spring rain. The whiplash between storm and sunshine left Sefa wishing she could duck for cover.

Vaida strolled to a curtain at the left of her bed and pushed it aside. A cavernous room stuffed with more colors, fabrics, and fashions than any human should ever possess struck Sefa speechless. Goodness, were the external wardrobes just for overflow?

"Oh, and darling"—Vaida pivoted in the doorframe, as though struck with a sudden thought—"the servants are toying with you. I never eat breakfast in my chambers, and I don't rise until the sun is at its peak."

Mortification flooded Sefa in a hot wash. She tried not to press the back of her hands to her overheating cheeks. That explained the smirks and derisive tones. Salwa must have been trying to warn her. "Oh."

"Zahra."

Sefa looked up, meeting Sultana Vaida's thoughtful gaze. It was a moment unmarked by slyness, whimsy, or any of the other strange traits Vaida flipped through like a gambler with a trusty roll of coins.

"My palace was built by an Awala who crafted illusions more perfect and persuasive than any reality. Baira...she was never just one thing. Unpredictability made her dangerous. If you wish to last in the Ivory Palace, I suggest you fiercely guard that heart of yours. Its softness is an irresistible temptation to those of us with teeth."

CHAPTER TWENTY

ARIN

An hour before dawn, Arin visited the prisoners.

Mildew and stale sweat wafted over Arin as he took the narrow stairs one at a time. Carved into the wall, the steps descended into the Citadel's basement at a steep angle. Anyone in a rush would hurtle over the side and break their neck on the stone floor below.

A gate mottled with rust creaked when Arin fit his key into the lock, and the tendrils of conversation floating from the basement abruptly ceased. The lock groaned, scraping metal as it turned. Shoving the gate into the wall with his boot, Arin wiped his gloves on his handkerchief and walked into the prison.

Moss wreathed the torches molded to the walls, the corroded bases struggling to maintain a flame in the damp, airless space. Rivulets of yesterday's rain dripped from the low ceiling, slicking the stones under Arin's boots.

"Sire." Bul appeared around the corner, flanked by two new recruits. Afan and Ladar rubbed sleep from their eyes and hurriedly tried to fix their uniforms. The sight of the dried blood on Arin's head and the bruises shading his face stopped them in their tracks.

"Don't let me interrupt a good night's sleep," Arin said.

Afan turned the color of an overripe plum. He opened his mouth. Nothing emerged.

"Has anyone been to visit?"

Bul straightened. "No, my liege. Should we be expecting someone?"

Rawain's envoys hadn't alerted the guards to the coming execution. The Mufsids had no idea they were spending their last night among the living.

Perfect.

"Go to the gardens and help the recruits prepare the Wickalla. Take Afan and Ladar. Pack a wagon with as much water as you can fit. They'll need it."

To his credit, Bul hid his surprise at the abrupt turn of events. "Shall I also summon the next guard rotation, my liege?"

This time, when Arin pinched the spark of irritation, it scorched his fingers. "Do you feel my orders are deficient, Bul?"

"No!" The guard flushed. "I only meant—"

"I did not ask what you meant. No one enters until I leave."

The soldiers sprang into motion. Arin didn't move until he heard their shuffling footsteps on the stairs vanish. As soon as the gate creaked shut behind them, Arin placed a hand against the wall, waiting for the wave of dizziness to pass.

You're bleeding and I don't want to hurt you.

Arin did not know where to begin to make sense of how the Jasad Heir kept appearing near Arin without her magic. He had wondered if she knew, back in the garden, but she must. However little Arin may esteem some of her general choices, there was no faulting Sylvia's sense of self-preservation. She had touched his naked shoulder with her bare hand—something she wouldn't have risked even with the safety of her cuffs, let alone with her full magic freed.

She was real. If the incident at Galim's Bend hadn't convinced him, then how ready she'd been to stab the broken end of the tal-with bottle through his throat would have.

The fortress fell before the messenger did!

Grim, Arin pushed away from the wall.

Some of the Mufsids slept, lying on threadbare cots pushed against the wall. A few jeered and shouted as he passed. Most, however, watched with sullen resignation. Arin had entered the basement every night since the third trial to drain their magic.

Six cells from the end of the block, Arin stopped. The Mufsid lounged on the cot, his back to the wall and a leg swinging over the side. Unwashed hair fell over his face, catching on the edge of an old scar gouging his cheek from nose to ear.

At Arin's arrival, the Mufsid slid from the cot. His bare feet padded silently on the floor. Arin didn't flinch as the Jasadi wrapped his hands around the bars. Yellow ringed the whites of his eyes. "Late for silver serpents to be slithering about."

Arin studied the white crust around the man's peeling lips, the nail marks scattered around his chin. Coming down here may very well have been a waste of time. This Mufsid had been mad for years. Maybe decades.

"At dawn, you and the rest of your coconspirators will be put to death." Arin delivered the news without inflection. Pity would fall falsely from his tongue. If it hadn't been for Arin's interference, the Mufsids would have been put to death two weeks ago. Their lease on life had ended the day of the third trial.

The prisoner laughed. A white-coated tongue darted out, licking a long stripe in the air. "Do you know what I'm tasting in the air tonight, young man?" He grinned. "The sweet, sweet flavor of desperation."

"I've come to make you an offer."

The Mufsid wagged his finger. The remarkable length of his own nail temporarily stole the man's wafer-thin focus before he returned to Arin. "You walk into our grave and try to steal secrets from the dead? Slither back to your den, boy."

"No, I don't believe I will," Arin said thoughtfully. "Who destroyed the Jasad fortress?"

The reaction was instant. A clawed hand struck through the bars, falling inches short of Arin's face. The Mufsid strained, clawing at the space in front of Arin's nose.

Arin waited.

The Mufsid snarled. "How dare you?"

Arin's smile was colder than the mist melting down the walls. "Are you ready to hear my offer?"

Distrustful yellow eyes darted around the cell, but the man stayed silent. It was as close to a *yes* as Arin expected from him.

"Tell me what you know of the fall of the fortress. Every detail. In exchange, I will leave this basement without draining a single one of you. When you are taken to the gallows, you will possess whatever meager amounts of magic you can build up by dawn."

The Mufsid curled his lip. "Why should it matter if we die with or without magic?"

"It doesn't."

"Our magic will not be enough to escape."

"No," Arin agreed.

"Your soldiers will descend on us as soon as we break from our restraints. It will be a slaughter."

"Indeed."

The Mufsid scuffed his nail against the manacle, considering, and Arin silenced the warning bells in his head. Why was he here? He didn't have a plan, nor a theory he needed confirmed.

Standing on the other side of treason, Arin only had doubt.

"Come into my cell, boy King, and I will tell you the tale of how an unassailable fortress falls." The mania seemed to drain out of the Mufsid, leaving only an intent so quiet, so singular, that it steadied the very ground beneath him. The Mufsid retreated into the dank space and waited.

The challenge was clear. Arin tipped his head, a mirthless laugh silent on his lips. He supposed it was fair play. The Mufsid's magic wouldn't hurt him. To demand honor from a man, the same should be offered.

Turning the lock, Arin stepped into the cell and closed it behind him.

The Mufsid sank to the ground and gestured for Arin to join him. Arin remained on his feet.

The Mufsid shrugged. "You should sit. It can be disorienting the first time."

"My patience with your games wears thin. If you intend to speak, do so now."

The Mufsid tilted his head, an eerie mimicry of Arin from moments ago. "Dear Commander, who said anything of speaking?"

Unease pricked along Arin's neck.

"I kept asking myself why you never demanded to know what we are," the Mufsid said. "But you did not even know to ask, did you? You don't know what a Bone Spinner is. You don't know that we had a Portalist, a Visionist, a Hayagan, a Sahir. Then again, I suppose he never expected his favorite sword to start cutting the hand that forged it."

Arin's eyes narrowed. He slid his hand into his coat pocket, closing his fingers around his blade.

Gold and silver erupted in the Mufsid's eyes.

"Now, now," the Mufsid said. "We made a deal."

The cell disappeared.

CHAPTER TWENTY-ONE

ARIN

A dead body stretched out by Arin's boots.
Body wasn't the right term. Body implied a semblance of structure still existed. A body was something recognizable—something that had once dwelled among the living.

Shards of crystallized bone tore through skin translucent as glass. Where a face might have been, a caved-in bowl held empty eye sockets and blackened teeth, thin red tendons wrapped around the mash of what might have been a nose. Rib bones pierced his chest, facing different directions like the sterns of sailing ships. Red spikes covered his stomach, drops of blood sharpened into thorns puncturing through his belly.

His legs had splintered from thigh to ankle, the bones of his calf peeled backward like cornhusks. Layers of crystallized flesh and bone overlapped in thin fillets, and a single shard of white bone held the limbs to the rest of his body.

By any definition, Arin was not an easily shaken man. He had spent years crafting the fortifications necessary to withstand the horrors of higher command, to hold firm against any assault.

But he had not accounted for the sight of a magic-mined body lying at his feet.

Brutal, isn't it? They feel every minute of it, too. They don't stop screaming until their tongue turns to glass, the Mufsid hummed, the disembodied voice ringing in the back of Arin's head.

Arin exhaled, tearing his gaze from the mangled body to the wailing girl crouched beside it. Decadence had trailed its fingers across every surface of the room they were in. Billowing ivory drapes hid the gaps in the walls where shutters should have shielded against the wind. Rubies glittered along the crown molding. Tapestries woven with breathtaking detail covered the right side of the room. In them, Arin found his first answer.

He was in the Ivory Palace.

"How did you bring me here?" Arin uttered, low. The girl paid him no heed. "What magic is this?"

Pleased to make your acquaintance, Your Highness. I am Waid Entair, Bone Spinner of Crowns.

Neither the name nor the title held any meaning to Arin. He wasn't sure which unsettled him more: that the Mufsid had blown a crater into Arin's understanding of magic in less than two minutes, or that a magic capable of affecting him existed.

Your lack of enthusiasm wounds me. I am the only Bone Spinner in two hundred years. I see the stories of the dead. I divine secrets from the magic left in their bones, and I travel through time while my feet stand still.

Bone Spinner. Arin tucked aside the information for later examination and returned his attention to the problem at hand.

He was in a memory stolen from the dead. Whose bones had Waid used? Whose memory was this?

The door burst open, and two guards spilled into the room. They assessed the space, gazes sweeping straight past Arin.

A woman strolled in behind them, and any doubt about his location disappeared. The type of beauty this woman possessed—a beauty capable of leading men to murder and stopping a battle in its tracks—was reserved for one lineage, and one lineage only.

The lanternlight winked off of her towering crown, crafted in the shape of a rising sun. Rubies crusted the rim, which supported three rays of alternating heights composed of...white quartz? Onyx?

Loose curls gathered around her head like a spring cloud, brushing the collar of an elaborate gown trailing several feet behind her. Intelligent brown eyes stared out of a face that sent a chill of recognition down Arin's spine. It was a face crafted by a supplicant at the altar of Baira, capable of rending hearts from chests while still beating and bloody. He had seen its likeness in another.

Sultana Nafeesa. It took me seven years to find her bones. She had decoy tombs set up all over Lukub.

Impossible. If the woman staring down her nose at the corpse was Sultana Nafeesa, then the Mufsid had taken Arin to a four-hundred-year-old memory.

It meant Arin was in the presence of the ruler who brokered the Zinish Accords. Vaida's ancestor.

"She dragged the body into the courtyard, Your Majesty," one of the guards murmured. He nodded to the sobbing girl. "We apprehended her before she could bother the guests, but some of the servants saw her."

"How did she get past the obelisk?" Nafeesa snapped.

Right. Four hundred years ago, Lukub still possessed its magic. If Arin recalled correctly, the ruby obelisk had originally been designed to signal to the Ruby Hounds if any danger ventured toward the Ivory Palace from Essam Woods.

The age of monsters was still in full swing, which meant nobody dared enter or travel through Essam save for the most urgent of necessities, and Ruby Hounds still prowled the perimeter of the Ivory Palace.

Arin held himself still, perilously aware of the precipice upon which his calm teetered.

"You killed him," the sobbing girl finally managed. She couldn't be more than nineteen years old. In her fraying green frock, she looked completely out of place in the palace. "I told him not to believe you. I told him it wasn't possible to gently drain a little magic. You tore him apart. You took *everything*."

Lashes tipped in red swept the top of Nafeesa's cheekbones in a slow blink. "Your husband made a deal, and I kept my end of it. Your farm is thriving now, no?"

"My... farm?"

"Besides," the Sultana continued, "his magic allowed six of my Hounds to stay alive. Six! You should be proud of him."

"May the Awaleen damn you." Rage crackled over her, twisting her youthful features into a snarl. "May you meet your justice, you lying wh—"

"Now, now." Nafessa lifted her hand. At the sight of the ring on her second finger, Arin took an involuntary step forward.

Vaida's ring.

"If you want your husband back," Sultana Nafeesa said. "By all means, darling. Have him."

White bloomed in Sultana Nafeesa's eyes, encircled by a glowing red ring. Her magic didn't churn like the gold and silver of Jasadi magic, but unfurled like the petals of a poisonous rose.

This is my favorite part, Waid said.

The rage melted from the girl, sloughing off like a lizard's skin. She beamed at the broken remains of her husband. "Hani! Oh, you silly man. I was so worried."

She gripped the fractured sides of her husband's head, and the shards of his cheekbones pierced through her hands. The smile didn't leave her face as she bent to bathe the cavern of his face in kisses. The crystallized skin shredded her lips, her cheeks, but her bloody smile never faded.

It is a merciful fate. There are worse illusions the Sultana could have created.

The girl kept going until ribbons of her skin clung to her husband's corpse. Arin couldn't do anything but watch, spellbound with revulsion, until a shard of rib bone impaled her right eye. She slumped over the corpse, finally limp.

Sultana Nafeesa gave the bodies a disdainful sniff. "See if they assigned next of kin for the farm. If not, slaughter the animals and empty out the house. We need a new den for my Hounds."

She turned, the tail of her gown trailing across the blood spreading over the rug. "Get them out of my palace."

Arin moved to follow her into the hall.

Ah ah ah, Waid tutted.

The floor beneath Arin sank, caving like a house of sand. He could feel the Mufsid's magic around him, its oily residue thick on his skin.

Waid groaned. *So obsessed with your rules and reason, aren't you? Rest assured, you are still draining my magic, just much slower than you would if I wasn't aiming most of it at the space around you instead of at you.*

But I am the Bone Spinner of Crowns, and you still have much to see.

The ground hardened beneath Arin. Fighting through a surge of nausea, he braced himself on his thighs.

When Arin straightened, he found himself inches away from his mother.

Fidgeting toward the end of a long table, Queen Isra's fingers twisted in her lap, knotting in the sleek fabric of her dress. The sun glowed across her tawny brown skin. A delicate chain bearing the Nizahl crest hung from her neck. Her gown was a perfect fit, but from the way Isra pinched at it, it may as well have been suffocating her.

Arin struggled to draw his breath. This was no lifeless stone statue.

Whose memory was this?

Under the table, a ringed hand squeezed Isra's wrist until her restless fingers spasmed and lay still.

Rawain subtly drew away from his wife and smiled across the table. Age had yet to leave its mark on his father, and untamed power rolled off the young Supreme.

"Be reasonable, Niyar. What can any of us do with five percent of the magic? That will hardly sustain us a single winter." Rawain tucked his scepter under his arm, the other propped on the table.

"You are not in a position to quibble with me over the terms of how we divide our people's magic. You get what we give you," Malik Niyar said. The ruler of Jasad leaned forward, raising his brows at Rawain. "If you need more than five percent to survive a bitter winter, you should consider whether your kingdoms have greater problems to handle."

No. Arin couldn't be hearing this.

Sultana Bisai, Vaida's mother, scowled. "These agreements have been in place for nearly five hundred years. Why are you changing them now? It used to be an even split."

Five hundred years?

Arin took a step back, every inch of his being recoiling from the scene in front of him.

Peals of laughter echoed across the table as Malika Palia clapped. "Yes, and five hundred years ago, you still had magic to trade. Today, you sit here with nothing. This is not a transaction, Bisai. You come here as beggars, and you should mind how you address us."

"Beggars? You foul wretch," King Toran snarled. He leapt to his feet, smacking the shoulder of the young man beside him. "Emre, draw your sword."

Emre of Omal. Sylvia's father.

Emre glanced up from the book on his lap, blinking owlishly behind his spectacles.

"Sit down, Toran," snapped the woman on Emre's other side. Arin barely recognized Queen Hanan. The scowling ruler looked nothing like the sorrowful cloud of a Queen sitting on the Omal throne.

What he was witnessing didn't meld into any plane of reality Arin understood. It repelled comprehension. Every time Arin tried to process it, he slammed into the iron resistance of his mind.

Arin needed to exercise care. It was an inopportune time to implode.

Settling back, Arin scanned the table once more. With an impassive hand, he began to take the scene apart.

The rulers of each kingdom had assembled here to discuss how they should divide stores of mined Jasadi magic between themselves.

The trade apparently began five hundred years ago, before Sultana Nafeesa's lifetime. In the age when the kingdoms still carried their own magic, every ruler had apparently mined from their own people. It would have cost thousands upon thousands of lives.

The practice had continued into Arin's lifetime, and his father had engaged in it. Rawain, who pummeled into Arin never to rely on or trust magic, had sat across a table and complained about only receiving five percent of magic brutally mined from its Jasadi owners.

The Malik and Malika of Jasad were not the original magic miners. They were just the last.

"Whose memory is this?" Arin asked flatly. "Whose bones did you use?"

Patience, young King.

Queen Hanan held her head high. "Consider it compensation for Jasad's raids, Palia. Are the three hundred of our soldiers you slaughtered last month not worth more than five percent?"

Palia leaned back in her chair, affecting an innocent mien. "I am sure I don't know what you mean, Hanan."

"Orban will accept five percent," King Murib bellowed. He clapped hands wide as paws together. "It will be enough to lift our drought, and we can handle the rest."

Groans around the table. The arguing resumed in full force, but Arin had ceased listening.

He knew who this memory belonged to.

Seated beside Niyar and Palia, dark eyes dancing as she watched Emre read, was Niphran. The first Heir of Jasad, and Sylvia's mother.

After a moment or two, Emre glanced up. Arin watched as Niphran arched a brow at the skittish Omal Heir, who managed to look spellbound and nauseous at the same time.

See? Waid said. *Your patience will be rewarded.*

The visions were coming faster. The Mufsid's magic was waning.

My magic is only partially at fault, Waid muttered. *Not all the bones have stories. Some of them just like to scream.*

Footsteps pounded down the hall. Arin barely had a second to step aside before Niphran barreled past him, an older man close at her heels.

It took Arin a second to place him. The last time he had seen the man pursuing Niphran, Arin had ordered five of his most trusted fifth-year recruits to transport his body to Jasad for burial. The time before that, Essiya had been carrying his corpse out of Dar al Mansi and handed him to Jeru as her third trophy.

She'd wept for the first time that night.

"Niphran, stop!" Dawoud panted. "This is childish."

"Stay away! I won't let you touch her." Niphran spun around, and Arin caged his breath.

The child in Niphran's arms giggled at Dawoud, seemingly delighted with their game. Black curls bounced around her round face. "Go, Mama, go!"

Dawoud raised placating hands as he approached Niphran. "The Malik and Malika merely want the second Heir to join them for supper. No harm will come to her. I promise you."

Sweat dripped from Niphran's forehead. Fear had stripped away the carefree confidence of the woman in the last vision, leaving a pale and shaking parent in its stead. "I know what they want to do to her."

Dawoud glanced around them, lips pursed in disapproval. "They would never harm an Heir of Jasad."

Kicking her feet, Essiya tugged at her mother's earlobe. "Mamaaaaaa."

"They didn't even want her, Dawoud. She links them to Omal permanently. Her existence obliterates their bargaining power."

Dawoud's brows knit together. "Omal disinherited her."

"Only after my father offered them three percent more magic from our stores, and because Emre's fool parents still don't understand how powerful she is," Niphran whispered, and the terror in her voice shredded through to Arin's core.

"Are you willing to stand there and swear that Niyar and Palia would never think to mine a magic as potent as hers? That in a time of crisis, they would not turn to the readily available resource living under their roof?"

Dawoud hesitated. When Niphran took off in a sprint, Essiya's gleeful squeals ringing behind her, he did not give chase.

A bearded man crouched over a sleeping Essiya, holding a cuff.

"Are you certain, Mawlati? Once I place these on the child, nothing and nobody can access her magic—including her." The man ran his thumb over the etchings on the cuffs. Letters Arin had memorized front and back. "They may never come off."

Niphran's gaze didn't waver from her daughter. "Put them on."

She was more cunning than the stories gave her credit for, Waid said. *Soraya and Hanim invested a small fortune in poison to keep the first Jasad Heir docile.*

Poison?

The first cuff closed around Essiya's wrist. The bearded welder's eyes swirled gold and silver as the seams of the cuff sealed together. The etchings shined a brilliant white before the cuffs thinned, melding into Essiya's wrist like a second skin.

As soon as the second cuff had sealed, Niphran withdrew a dagger from her boot and slit the welder's throat.

His body thumped to Arin's right. Niphran stepped over him and crawled into bed with her daughter, drawing her into her arms.

As I said. Waid chuckled. *Savage little creature.*

When Arin landed this time, he knew the Mufsid's magic was nearing its end. He could see the gray of the cell behind the vision, fading in and out.

A muddy creek flowed around the trees of Essam Woods, their branches lush with summer leaves. The texture of the vision was off, not as vivid or heavy as Niphran's had been.

I had only a single fingerbone to draw from. It is a testament to my talent that I was able to pull anything at all from such a tiny bit of bone, let alone a whole memory, Waid sniffed. *Unfortunately, Essiya is just as clever as her mother. We have never been able to recover more than a finger from Qayida Hanim's bones. Wherever Essiya buried that wretched traitor, it was far from wherever Hanim had imprisoned her.*

A whip split the air, and Arin whirled around.

A girl knelt in the mud, a red line bisecting her naked back. A woman stood tall behind her. One hand held the whip, and the other deftly knotted her wavy hair into a bun at the base of her neck.

The girl's arms hugged the tree, her wrists tied around the other side of it. A band of black fabric covered her eyes.

Arin had weathered fires and stab wounds, poisons and beatings. He'd begun training to become a soldier at an age most children were learning how to sound out their letters. His very existence as Commander necessitated a close and familiar understanding of the many ways he could be harmed.

In short, Arin thought he knew pain.

He thought he knew rage.

The whip fell again, Sylvia jerking silently beneath it, and it became abundantly clear Arin didn't know a thing about either. His real education came in that moment, eviscerating the tentative hold on his stability he'd managed to maintain throughout these visions.

Arin would find the body of Qayida Hanim and kill her again. He would hunt down each of her bones and crush them between his bare hands.

The lashes on Sylvia's back multiplied until a curtain of red poured from her neck to her waist.

She never made a single sound.

This memory is how we knew she was still alive, Waid murmured. *This is how we found the Jasad Heir.*

Arin didn't hear him. His entire being had narrowed to the lift and fall of the whip against Sylvia's back. He thought of a room in Orban, a towel easing to reveal layers upon layers of brutal scarring.

I have a legacy of disappointing people, you see.

Bile built in Arin's throat until he thought he might retch. After an eternity, Qayida Hanim moved behind the tree and cut through the ropes around Sylvia's wrists. The Jasad Heir slumped forward, curling in on herself.

"You may take it off," Hanim said.

Sylvia swept off her blindfold, red-rimmed eyes rising to Hanim's. Softly, she whispered, "Do you forgive me?"

Her teeth clattered. Arin couldn't fathom how they weren't rushing to clean her wounds, to stop the blood loss.

"You were a good girl." Hanim held out the whip. "Clean it off in the river. When you're done, we can bandage you by the fire."

"Thank you." Sylvia took the bloody whip.

The Citadel's cell materialized around them, and Arin finally saw the Mufsid. He was slouched on the cot, skin sallow with fatigue.

"Can it be?" Waid chuckled weakly. "Is that a glisten I see in the Silver Serpent's eyes? Now, now. That was only the story of a single finger. How might you weep if we had recovered the rest of Hanim's bones?"

Arin let himself have just one minute. One minute to re-collect as many pieces as he could from where he'd left them scattered by the magic-mined farmer, across the rulers' trading table, and in the woods by Sylvia. He wanted nothing more than to leave this cell, to go—anywhere else.

But in less than an hour, Arin would watch dawn rise on the death of Waid Entair, Bone Spinner of Crowns. He would leave Arin with more questions and die with the answers inside him.

Even now, the Mufsid's temporary lucidity was fading; the roving eyes had returned, the restless twitching.

"What did you want from the Jasad Heir's magic?" Arin's voice hardened. "Did you hope to mine it?"

The Mufsid had rearranged himself onto his cot once more, obscuring himself in the gloom of the windowless walls. Only the yellow of his gaze was visible, piercing Arin with a chilling intelligence.

"Naughty Commander." The whisper floated on the back of a caustic laugh. "Mining magic, draining it. Same thief in a different hat. What matters is not what is taken, but where it goes."

The Mufsid gave Arin his back and spoke no more.

CHAPTER TWENTY-TWO

SYLVIA

"If you don't try using your magic before we leave, we may as well order everyone in the mountains to line up on this cliff and start leaping into Suhna Sea," Efra said.

"Interesting idea." I gestured toward the waves smashing against the side of the mountain. "Perhaps you should provide a demonstration."

"You two bicker like infants," Namsa sighed. She adjusted the blanket beneath her, surrounded by the clothes I'd helped her collect from the clothesline earlier in the morning. "I thought I'd managed to avoid child-rearing."

Efra strolled in a loop around the canyon between our mountain and the next, pacing to the foot of the refrozen lake and back. "The informant will be here in a matter of hours. If she gives us the news we're expecting, we will need to mobilize our team toward Omal immediately. We can't afford to sit around and coax her sweetly."

My nails bit into my palms. Tombs below, but I loathed it when Efra spoke like I was some disagreeable pet and not ten feet and one insult away from incinerating him.

The worst part was he had a point. They were anticipating a report from one of their spies about the kingdoms' reactions to Galim's Bend. It had been a little over three weeks since the cages were opened. Since our options for sneaking into the Omal palace relied on trade routes staying open and minimal sentries along the border, everyone was on edge, waiting to see whether Queen Hanan would follow Sultana Vaida's example and shut down access to her kingdom.

Efra had spun us into an impossible situation and then had the sheer gall to accuse me of trying to sabotage the Urabi's plans by withholding my magic.

"You chose to announce our presence to the kingdoms by releasing centuries-old monsters and destroying an entire village, and you're surprised the other rulers have taken up defensive positions?" Anger, bitter and wild, thrashed in my belly. "I follow fools in this mountain, don't I?"

Efra bristled. "How many other options did you leave us with?"

My hands curled at my sides. The chafe of the Urabi's demands had scraped me bloody, a persistent stone sanding off my skin, and it was only a matter of time before I reacted.

After a minute, my fists loosened. The fury dissipated, muffled beneath the resignation settling around my shoulders.

I hadn't been taught how to lead. I understood next to nothing about the right way to rule.

What I knew better than anyone was how to obey.

"What would you like my magic to do, Efra?" I asked, toneless. "Choose your trick."

Namsa frowned, rising to peer at me with concern. Efra did not bat an eye. "Summon the kitmer again."

"You do not have to do anything you don't wish to," Namsa urged.

My smile, cold and bloodless, propelled the Jasadi a step back. Her well-meaning nonsense bothered me more than Efra's barbs, sometimes. At least he did not dip his blade in honey before swinging it at my head.

"A kitmer," I repeated. His interest in having me call forth a kitmer bordered on obsession. I had done it exactly once, and it had not been voluntary.

I faced the sea, drawing its stinging air deep into my chest. With the cuffs, my magic had reacted to threats against the people I cared about. To threats against Jasad.

Not a perfect starting point, but as good as any other.

Dropping my chin, braid heavy between the brackets of my shoulders, I thought of the kitmer raging through the Victor's Ball. The streak of silver and gold as it shot above the Citadel, a beacon in the night sky.

Sefa and Marek could be anywhere. I had no idea if they were alive, if they were safe. They had been perfectly content in Mahair before I upended their lives. I should have stopped them when they decided to follow me into Nizahl. I should have forced them away.

A lazy heat spilled in my veins, thawing the tips of my chilled fingers.

Dawoud would have left Dar al Mansi if it weren't for me. He would be here with his niece, probably leading the Aada. Taking his tea in the evenings with a piece of cream kunafa or basboosa, despite how I would harangue him about his health.

The heat crawled over my arms.

It was because of me that—

The woman screamed, clawing at the hand I'd wrapped around her throat.

Even though I could turn my chin and kill her where she stood, never having soiled myself with the throb of her slowing pulse beneath my palm or the smell of her choking breath, I enjoyed the sensation of her struggling beneath my grip. The close and personal view of the life draining from her dumb eyes.

She landed in a heap in the mud. I wiped my hand on my hip.

Hmm. This sight would grieve her husband, but it wouldn't break him. It would not reduce him to the barest components of a living man.

I cocked my head, and cracks formed along the youthful bronze skin. Her flesh began to peel in thick, fat strips. Layer after layer, curling into spirals as it landed in the dirt, until the meat barely clung to her exposed ribs, and the panels of her skin were splayed open like flipped shutters.

I left her face untouched. The effect would be lost if he couldn't recognize the pile of flesh and blood lying in his farm, after all.

I washed my hands in the creek and smiled at the gold and silver veins webbing out of the corners of my eyes.

Too late, I realized that the heat of my magic had enveloped me, trapping me in a burning seal. To withhold it was to suffocate in it.

The face reflected in the creek—it wasn't my face, but I recognized it. It had been one of the hallucinations from the waterfall. The woman with green eyes.

The ground shook. Pieces of the cliffside tumbled into the sea. I heard Efra and Namsa cry out as though from a great distance.

Threads of silver and gold spun between my fingers, crackling with power. I dropped to my knees, my hands sliding into the dirt. In seconds, the colors flowed from my skin and poured into the earth. Mist rose from the ground like steam from a boiling pot, coalescing into a rapidly swirling cloud of magic.

"Step back!" I shouted to Namsa and Efra.

I shielded my head as the mist spun faster. Awaleen below, my first significant act of magic as Malika, and it was going to blow apart the mountain. What had I been thinking, listening to Efra? He was no better than a little boy kicking his heels to see a vicious animal. He didn't consider the consequences—

The mist erupted.

Namsa wheezed, bent over double as she shook with laughter. She hadn't stopped in the last twenty minutes, and I was beginning to worry she had suffered a mental collapse. Every time she glanced at Efra, she'd begin howling anew.

In Namsa's defense, Efra's expression after the baby kitmer had hopped out of the cloud of magic would reduce the most disciplined stoic into hysterics. A kitmer barely taller than my knee, staggering under the weight of its own wings, wasn't the majestic beast he'd imagined.

He had asked me to try again, and I obeyed. I tried ten more times, and each attempt brought forth another miniature kitmer. Two with fluffy golden wings and silver beaks; one with alarmingly sharp feathers; several more with misshapen horns curving in different directions behind their heads.

All of them had my eyes.

Your beautiful kitmer eyes, Niphran would always say. *Dark and deep as the vastest sea.*

A shiver ran through me. Had I given these kitmers my eyes, or had the resemblance always been so uncanny?

The sun sank, casting the surface of Suhna Sea in shimmering reds and golds.

"Do you think they would bite the children?" Maia asked from my right, her sudden appearance startling an undignified squeak out of me. "They would be so excited to play with them."

The kitmers hopped around the cliffside, showing no sign of fading out like their predecessor. One pecked at Maia's ankle, and she patted its scaly head. "Best to give it some time, I think," Maia said.

"Yara is here," Maia added, almost as an afterthought. "The informant."

I inhaled. "Did she say anything?"

Maia shook her head. "I came to get you first. The rest of the Aada will be assembling. Is Namsa all right?"

One of the kitmers wandered toward Efra, and he scrambled away when it hopped closer. For someone scared of a bird half his size, he managed to call upon a shocking amount of indignance. "Is this it?"

he demanded, stabbing a finger at the flock of small kitmers. "This is the limit of your lauded magic?"

Efra almost died, then.

The moment came and passed. The sun barely sank an inch. Namsa hadn't finished wiping the tears from her cheeks. Maia had just bent down to rub the beak of a fatally feathered kitmer.

But the moment stretched, cords of my magic arching tight. My magic wanted him dead. If I had ordered it, Efra's heart would have beat its last, and he would have fallen dead to the ground.

Like the woman in the vision.

What I had seen was impossible. It was *me*, but not me. The face reflected in the creek belonged to a stranger, but the things she had done had felt so real. The way that poor girl had been dissected, left open like an animal pelt to dry in the sun...I couldn't have done that, not in my very worst moments. I could be brutal, and I could be cruel, but I was artless about it. My rage took the shape of a rabid brute force, too focused on simply making impact to notice or care how it reached its destination. The detached, musing sort of savagery I'd felt in the vision was beyond my capacity.

At least, I thought it was.

Your mind is a maze of mirrors, reflecting only the memories you choose to save.

My nails dug into my elbows, and I shoved my mounting alarm deep into the recesses of my chest. My magic was strange—it had always been strange, even before the cuffs. The visions, the figures I had seen at the waterfall? None of it meant anything. None of it was possible.

Efra was still rattling off objections to the kitmers, my magic, and everything about my general existence. The impulse to kill him had passed, but that did not mean Efra had not burst through the limits of my patience.

The pulse of magic came smoother this time. I flicked my wrist, and four of the kitmers dove toward Efra. Garbled shrieks ripped through the air as the kitmers' claws grabbed Efra's limbs and they took flight. I waved cheerfully as they carried him off the side of the cliff.

"Well." Namsa joined me by the edge, watching the kitmers weave and bob over the sea, Efra held beneath them like a particularly unwieldy log. The best kind of sunset view, in my opinion.

"I tried my best," I said stiffly. If she planned to deliver a soliloquy about my failures, I wouldn't order her tossed around the surface of Suhna Sea like Efra, but I would not stay to listen. "That is all I can do. It is all I can offer. I will keep trying, but I don't understand my magic yet. It may take time."

A light touch to my elbow sent shock waves up my arm, and I barely remembered not to flinch. My aversion to touch may have abated, but unexpected contact still rattled me.

Stricken brown eyes studied me. "We have done this all wrong, haven't we? We ask you to lead, then treat you like a criminal. We demand your magic, then hold you in judgment over it. It is no wonder you possess such a low opinion of us. Awaleen below, you might have found more mercy from the Nizahl Commander himself."

Stupefied, I could only blink.

"You are twenty and one, Essiya," Namsa offered gently. "What you know of Jasad is a mere impression, yet you have been consigned to carry its burden since the moment of your birth. The rest of us—the point of having an *us*—should make it easier. Duty is a weight we should carry between us, not a weapon we use to crush each other." She pushed a lock of hair behind her ear, dropping her gaze to the ground. "I should have done more to smooth the way for you, but…"

I wrapped my arms around myself, battling an unexpected surge of emotion. "Dawoud."

"Holding you in judgment for his death was small and weak of me. You loved him as dearly as I." The hand on my elbow traveled to my shoulder. "I am so sorry we failed you, Essiya."

Braced as I was for admonishment, the kindness left me wrong-footed and unbearably raw. I tried to return us to familiar ground. "I failed you, too. Far more frequently."

She squeezed my shoulder once before releasing me. The warm imprint of her hand lingered. "I will agree to forgive myself, if you agree to do the same."

In the distance, Efra screamed as one of the kitmers dropped his leg, briefly submerging the limb into the sea.

I moved my jaw from side to side, trying to round out the words I wanted to say. As comfortable as I was around Namsa, I was still her Malika. I was someone she expected to exude inner strength and steadiness.

Loneliness had become a rope around my neck, and the noose tightened each time I put on the mask of Malika. No matter how comfortable I became around the Urabi, they were not Sefa and Marek. They were not Rory, Fairel, Raya.

They were not Arin.

I exhaled slowly, already guilty at the thought. Despite the chasm of secrets between myself and the Nizahl Heir, he'd inspired a rare honesty out of me. Around him, I could be sullen and quiet, vicious and loud, careful and cunning. Any mask I wore crumbled beneath his scrutiny, so what was the point of trying to hide myself?

"I am resentful," I said, and those were *not* the words I'd so carefully crafted in my head. They poured free before I could dam the river. "I resent my crown. I resent you for asking me to storm the Omal palace knowing Queen Hanan will reject me. I resent myself for missing my old life."

"It is perfectly natural—"

"I resent you for asking me to burn alive for Jasad."

Stupefied silence replaced whatever platitude Namsa had been ready to offer.

"We are at war. If—when—Queen Hanan refuses to reinstate

me to the line of inheritance, we will have played our last hand. You will ask me to raise the fortress, to give Jasad its only fighting chance. We both know what will happen when I raise the fortress, Namsa. What happened to Qayida Hend is legend for a reason."

Maia's shout reached us from the door. "Mawlati! Are you coming?"

The harsh set of Namsa's features softened. Guilt, maybe, or pity. "We don't know what will happen, Essiya. Qayida Hend became a legend for burning, but I truly believe you will not meet her fate."

I turned away from Efra and the swooping kitmers, gazing dully at the silhouettes of the mountains, their jagged peaks tearing through the star-strewn sky. "Oh?"

"You, Essiya of Jasad, will not be known for burning." A shiver went through me at the force of Namsa's conviction. "You will always be known for surviving."

CHAPTER TWENTY-THREE

SYLVIA

In the face of catastrophically bad news, the mountain decided to throw a party.

I watched in bemusement as Maia's husband—a title which, upon introduction, had shocked me speechless—spun her in the middle of the dining hall. The low tables had been pushed to the sides of the room, leaving plenty of empty space in the center for dancing.

Lateef reclined on the ground, his back propped against the long stone counter in front of the kitchen. He'd gone around the room collecting the hastily tossed cushions and piled them into his corner, where he lounged like a bird guarding its nest. A gaggle of children sat cross-legged in front of him, listening raptly as he regaled them with the tales of Goha and his silly donkey. On the kitchen floor, a row of young girls scooped warm rice out of the enormous pots they had carried in from the firepits outside and rolled it into thinly cut and steamed grape leaves. At the counter, six boys traded insults as they chopped piles of parsley and onion. I winced sympathetically at their watering eyes.

"We save mahshy for special occasions," Namsa shared with a tone of great magnanimity. We were clustered on the single cushion Lateef hadn't managed to steal, observing the revelry and hustle from our own quiet corner.

"Probable death is a special occasion?" I curled my legs in time to avoid a stampede of boys running past, cackling at the top of their squeaky, prepubescent lungs.

"Well, yes." Namsa shot me a sly smile. "When death lives around the corner, you learn to pay no attention to its shadow. Besides, we finally have a plan. A goal to put into motion. Soon, change will come. One way or the other."

In the center of the room, Efra played the tubluh with flabbergasting skill, drumming as though he hadn't spent the better part of an hour screaming himself hoarse as he was flung around the surface of the sea.

"I don't understand why everyone is so calm," I said. "The informant was nearly in tears. Omal's lower villages are overflowing with soldiers, and Felix has patrols posted across the borders. Vaida is expanding her territory by miles in every direction within Essam, and she floods each gained acre with her soldiers. Orban closed their trade routes—their trade routes, which I might remind you, are the only way Jasadis in other kingdoms can even cross to Jasad." I massaged my forehead, ignoring the faint echo of Raya ranting about wrinkles. "And Nizahl…"

"We don't know what the Silver Serpent is commissioning. It could be nothing."

"Nothing, Namsa? Yara said every blacksmith in Nizahl was asked to fashion a special kind of weapon. Rawain spent half his early reign amassing an arsenal beyond any the kingdoms could compete with. What kind of new weapon would the Heir need thousands of?"

Namsa picked at the dirt under her nails with a marked lack of nerves. "Do you know what Nizahl can't commission?"

I narrowed my eyes. "What?"

"Magic."

I groaned. "I'm serious. The Jasadis are trapped. If they manage to survive leaving their kingdoms, they will be killed on the way to Jasad. If not by soldiers, then by the creatures we unleashed at Galim's Bend."

"The creatures will just disappear into the Mirayah."

A plate appeared in front of me, heaped with a mountain of mahshy, missaka, and a grilled tomato. My mouth watered embarrassingly fast. Maia mistook my pause as dismay and immediately began rocking on her heels. "We usually use ground beef with the missaka, but beef is difficult to transport or preserve in the mountains. Potatoes make a decent alternative, and I have always thought the key part of the dish was the spiced tomato sauce, of which you will find plenty—"

I took the plate from Maia, curtailing what was sure to be the start of her long saga on sauce. "Thank you," I said. "It looks delicious."

She beamed, sliding down the wall to join me and Namsa on the ground. "What were you talking about?"

"Namsa appears to believe that the Mirayah is a real place," I said, with the sort of patronizingly indulgent tone one reserves for speaking in front of children or the senile. "Next, we will discuss if she sees the Awaleen standing at the foot of her bed while she sleeps. Do they lean over and whisper sweet prophecies in your ear, or—"

An elbow caught me in the side, rocking me toward Maia. Gathering my plate close, I glared at Namsa. "My mahshy!"

"The Mirayah is real, Essiya," Maia said, slicing into a baked potato circle soaked in her beloved sauce.

I stared. One was funny, but two was worrisome. "Surely, you don't believe there are pockets of ancient magic scattered around Essam Woods? Actual realms of rogue magic?"

"What would you call Ayume Forest? You were there. You must have felt the perversion of Dania's magic left over from the Battle of Ayume. That battle happened several millennia ago, yet to this day, the very air in Ayume can kill you." Namsa snatched a finger of mahshy from my plate before I could swat her away. "I don't believe there are entire realms of rogue magic in Essam, no. But magic was born in those woods. It is in Essam's very soil, the roots that stretch across our kingdoms, the river we rely on for life. Who knows what other worlds it sustains?"

"I lived in Essam for five years," I said tersely. "The woods are disturbing and unsettling, but they pledge no power of their own. If there was a realm of rogue magic wandering around, I would surely have stumbled upon it."

"How?" Oil glistened at the corner of Maia's mouth. She wiped it on the inside of her wrist. "You were hidden from the strongest tracking magic for a decade. The Mirayah is as ancient as Essam. If you couldn't be found and it did not want to be found, you could have walked straight past each other."

I opened my mouth to argue and reconsidered. Flimsy as it might be, she had a point. The cuffs had protected me against most magic, repelling it as strongly as it trapped my own. It was not entirely impossible that a similar force existed to hide some pocket of magical fluctuation in Essam.

It was just mostly impossible.

I changed the subject before they could jump on my hesitation. "When do we leave?"

Namsa shot me a knowing smirk. I squinted, not entirely convinced the woman I'd brought back from the cliffside was the same woman who had kicked my liver into my skull the first day we met. Who knew she had such emotional range? Until this morning, I would have said she was capable of two expressions: scowling and lightly scowling. "Ten hours. The journey to the Omal palace will take roughly five days, if we push our magic to its limits."

Our. Foreboding tightened my throat. "Who else is coming with us?"

"Me!" Maia grinned. "Lateef, of course, and Medhat. Efra, Namsa, Kenzie—"

I held up a finger. "There it is."

Maia paused. "There what is?"

More and more, I marveled at how the Urabi had managed to evade capture for years. "The limit to how many people can move together in Essam Woods without alerting a patrol. In fact, I would be more comfortable if we stripped out two, but I could be persuaded otherwise."

Maia's gaze slid past me to Namsa, and my lips compressed into a flat line. Yet another silent look. Malika this, Mawlati that, all the airs and none of the actual authority.

"I agree with the Malika," Namsa said lightly. "The kingdoms are on alert. We will need to move inconspicuously."

"Speaking of moving." I stood, keeping an eye on the platters of food maneuvering around the room. "How exactly are we getting to the Omal palace? You said five days, but Omal is nowhere near the mountains. It would take two weeks to cut across the Desert Flats, travel around Ayume, and move through Essam. If we factor in the added patrols and border sentries…" I tipped my hand side to side as I estimated how long it would take seven people to navigate the new obstacles. "Closer to three weeks."

For the first time, a hint of nerves showed itself in Namsa's restless fingers, picking at a loose thread by her pocket. "Right. Under normal circumstances, you would be right. Our method of transport to Omal might be a bit… disconcerting. It is difficult to explain, but we will reach Omal much faster than three weeks."

She yanked at the thread as though it had spat on her mother's face, so intent on avoiding my gaze that I couldn't help but comfort her. "As long as it isn't the spine of the Sareekh, I will not be disconcerted for long."

Maia giggled too loudly and slapped a hand over her mouth.

"Not quite the Sareekh." Namsa tore the thread loose and

gestured at the crush of Jasadis entering the dining hall. "If you want more stuffed squash, you'd better hurry."

Sitting naked on the floor of my room, I stared into the mirror and counted the veins a third time.

It had taken a while to hunt them all down. One was a mere strip of gold under my right breast; another curved quietly along the joint of my hip. My belly, my leg, the inside of my thigh. All visited by a fresh vein.

A vein for each time I used my magic.

I dragged the blanket from the bed and wrapped it around myself, unable to move from the floor, petrified to leave the mirror and rise to a new reality where my paranoia became fact.

Nobody could see the veins but me. I'd tested it three times since the last vein appeared. When I held out my hand to take the plate from Maia, I'd kept my palm open and exposed. The vein was impossible to miss.

I traced the lines on my skin. A vein for each time I appeared to Arin. A vein for the magic I'd thrown around while drowning, before the Sareekh arrived. A vein for each kitmer I created on the cliffside. A vein for the magic I'd used to catapult Efra around Suhna Sea.

I had seen the veins multiply, and I had ignored them. I had felt the strange presence of my magic, pressing against the back of my head, and I had brushed it off.

My breath shuddered, growing shallower. The worry I'd throttled into submission over the last month broke from its captivity, submerging me into the panic I had fought so hard to avoid.

The figures from the waterfall. The memory of the woman dying at my hand. The visions my magic produced each time I asked for more of it.

Something was wrong with me.

I bent forward, pressing my forehead to the cold stone floor. The lifelong habit came on instinct, and my palm covered my wildly pounding heart.

One, two. I am alive.

Three, four. I am safe.

Five, six. I am not losing my mind.

My teeth chattered, shaking along with the rest of me. I reared away from the floor, gasping for air. The last time panic had consumed me so wholly had been the day after the first trial, when Supreme Rawain walked into my chambers to congratulate his Champion and call me a merit to Nizahl. It had taken hours to regain myself afterward, and I didn't have hours. We were to leave for Omal in an hour. I was supposed to pack.

If we failed to convince Queen Hanan to reinstate me as the Omal Heir, we would have no choice but to raise the fortress. I would have to read the enchantment that burned Qayida Hend alive. The amount of magic it would demand—the amount of magic I would need to expend—

I tipped my head back, averting my gaze from the mirror, and focused on taking tiny sips of air.

Magic-madness was not real.

I exhaled shakily.

I was not losing my humanity like Rovial.

The fear, once ignited, started dripping in the back of my mind. Staining each thought, bleeding my world red.

The bands around my lungs tightened. I tried to remind myself that there was an array of possible explanations for the veins. I barely understood anything about magic, let alone a magic that had been trapped beneath my cuffs for most of its existence. For all I knew, I was terrified of nothing more than a cosmetic quirk.

I curled against the ground, drawing the blanket over my head. My breathing, already slowing, stopped.

Magic-madness wasn't an option I could calmly think through and plan for. This was not a reality I could navigate even in theory.

In the cover of dark, it was much easier to notice the pinch of magic at the back of my skull.

I shoved my head out from under the blanket in time to see the room disappear.

CHAPTER TWENTY-FOUR

SEFA

Nothing good could come out of joining the Sultana in a midnight excursion through the streets of Lukub, yet here Sefa was—fully dressed and incredibly disturbed.

The chill nipped at Sefa's bare cheeks. The stories of Lukub's nocturnal proclivities had clearly been exaggerated. The street stretched empty before them, devoid of any signs of movement beyond the lanternlight dripping its shadows over the pale stone roads. Domed two-story buildings lined the sides of the street, reminding Sefa of eggs arranged in a basket. They passed one dome with red stripes, the bottom faded into strips of paint peeling onto the grass. Emerald tiles swirled across the sides of the dome beside it.

Vaida strolled along the empty road in a tight cotton sheath, her fingers curled around the sides of her white cloak. The hood was pulled over her braids and drawn low over her forehead. Without her signature ruby-red lip paint and kohl, the Sultana looked startlingly young.

She had taken off all her rings except one. *The* one. The ring Sefa had begun to fixate on with worrying regularity, the ring that never left Vaida's finger no matter how frequently Sefa checked.

The Sultana's ensemble had clearly been chosen with anonymity in mind, and Sefa fought to stifle her amusement. A lion would have more luck masquerading as a ladybug. If someone took one good look at Vaida's face, the ruse would be over in an instant.

"You never mentioned you were a seamstress," Vaida said, speaking for the first time since she'd had a servant wake Sefa in the dead of night and summon her to the carriage.

Sefa nearly tripped over her own boots. Fear breathed fire over her skin, and she itched to press the backs of her hands against her cheeks to push back the blood rising to her face.

"Your Majesty?" was all Sefa could think to squeak.

"My servants speak of the gowns you've been working on in your chambers. Are they for me?"

The half-finished gowns in her room. Relief slackened the muscles in Sefa's stomach. "They are not worthy of you, Sultana," Sefa said. "Just a silly task I busy myself with when sleep fails me. A distraction."

"I see. Has serving me been so awful that you need a daily distraction?" The Sultana's bottom lip quivered.

"Of course not!"

"Good." Like the tide sweeping away letters spelled into the sand, her pout faded into boredom. "What do you need distracting from, then?"

Baira's blessed beauty. Every hair on Sefa's body stood on end.

Emotions weren't meant to be so...fleeting. They didn't have clean lines and discernible edges. But the Sultana tried on emotions like hats, modeling them for the occasion, and cast them aside with an ease that chilled Sefa to her bones.

"My own head," Sefa answered. She could hardly reveal how much the servants loathed her. How they went quiet when she entered the room or plated her food on dirty dishes. Given Sefa's entire role in the Ivory Palace was to gather information for the Sultana, the animosity of the staff wasn't a mark in Sefa's favor.

"Hmm," Vaida said. The noncommittal sound stoppered any further discussion, and Sefa gratefully sank into the silence.

Over the past several weeks, Sefa had thought she was getting better at predicting Vaida. Giggling could either mean someone's imminent destruction was upon them, or she had just made a joke only a ten-year-old would find amusing. If her sigh lasted longer than five seconds, anyone in her immediate vicinity needed to evacuate.

The most consistent habit was the Sultana's fixation with her appearance. She spent several hours a day under the attention of experts; Sefa had witnessed everything from leeches to hot wax entering the Sultana's chambers.

At first blush, it came across as extreme vanity. But Sefa had watched Vaida as she watched herself in the mirror. The intensity of it had been an unpleasant reminder of the days following Sylvia's stabbing in the Ivory Palace. After Sylvia had woken, she asked Wes for the knife they'd pulled out of her chest. When the reluctant guard handed it over, Sylvia had wiped the blade against her pants and traced her thumb over the sharp end before tucking it into her boot.

Vaida regarded her reflection with the same cold determination Sylvia had for the knife that almost killed her.

Sefa hurried to keep up with Vaida's long stride. "Sultana, are you certain this is safe? I can catch the driver and ask him to summon your guards."

The narrow-eyed look Vaida shot her invited Sefa to shut her mouth.

They turned the corner, and Sefa gasped as the Sultana grabbed her arm. "Watch where you walk," Vaida hissed.

Sefa had nearly stepped onto the lawn of one of the dome houses, where several tall bushes with... were those arms?

Vaida, once again demonstrating a disturbing affinity for reading Sefa's mind, offered, "Lafa Souda. See those vines? Each has its own spine keeping it upright. They trap any trespassers within reach and hold them until the owner arrives."

"How do they know not to trap the owner?" Sefa studied the turgid vines warily.

"The gardener mixes a quart of the owner's blood into the watering pot while the Lafa Souda is growing. It won't trap what it recognizes."

Sefa shuddered. The plants in Raya's garden may have been unremarkable and overwatered, but they'd been a source of joy. Sefa couldn't imagine growing a living thing out of anything but love.

They walked until Sefa could feel the pulse in her legs.

"Would you like me to intervene?"

Vaida posed the question like they were in the middle of a conversation Sefa had forgotten to take part in.

"Intervene?"

Vaida gestured above her neck. "Your head. The *distractions*. Would you like me to intervene?"

An arched brow confirmed Sefa's suspicion. Vaida knew the truth. Somehow, she had figured out the staff were making her miserable. It shouldn't have come as a surprise. Sefa's very presence in the Ivory Palace was evidence of Vaida's unrelenting surveillance.

Sefa imagined what would happen if she answered *yes*. If the staff disliked her now, they would positively despise her for tattling to the Sultana. The antics wouldn't stop; they would only get more discreet and creative.

Sefa shook her head. "I can take care of it myself."

"Good." A wan smile played at the Lukub ruler's mouth. "A bit of advice, darling. You have no talent for deception, and my staff has no tolerance for weakness."

Vaida's gaze drifted over the tapestry of stars stitched over the night sky. "Do you know that before Rovial unleashed his madness on the kingdoms, it was Baira who was the most hated of the

Awaleen? Her illusions terrified them. She could create worlds within our minds, and her enemies were bound to whatever reality she spun for them. What they loved, what they feared, what they hated... she would thread it all through the eye of her magic. Some even think her beauty itself was an illusion, shifting to appeal to whichever eyes beheld her."

Sefa stared at Vaida. A claim so egregious could get someone killed in certain parts of the kingdoms. To hear it coming from Baira's descendant herself...

"Do you?" Sefa heard herself ask. "Think her beauty was an illusion, I mean."

The light from the string of lanterns swaying between the domes flickered in Vaida's dark eyes like trapped flames.

"I think knowing what is real is beyond the reach of mortals and Awaleen alike."

They veered into a tight alley, forcing Sefa to fall a step behind the Sultana. The walls lengthened, curving around them like a steadily closing jaw. Rocks rolled forward as the clean white stones gave way to pebbled dirt.

At the end of the alley, a hooded figure stepped out of the shadows. Startled, Sefa caught Vaida's sleeve, tugging her back. Vaida peeled her fingers off. "Don't *grab*, Zahra. It's uncouth. Come, you can meet a friend of mine."

Tempted to engage in further uncouth behavior and sprint out of the alley, Sefa forced herself to follow the Sultana to the hooded figure.

The lanky man bowed deeply, sweeping down his hood. A crop of reddish-brown hair sat above a hawkish face. Grayish-green eyes momentarily swept over Sefa before returning to the Sultana. "Your Majesty."

"Did you find it?"

"Not yet. I came to ask your permission to expand the search east."

"I already gave you permission to claim whatever you want." Impatience punctuated the sentence. "Essam is uncontested territory."

"There is a Nizahl holding at the nexus of these coordinates, Your Majesty. If Lukub claims the territory, it would mean laying claim to the holding, as well."

Vaida ran her tongue along the inside of her bottom lip. "It would certainly get Arin's attention. The question is, is now the best time for it?"

Sefa had heard the whispers about this even before she came to Lukub. Vaida had been steadily expanding into Essam for years, claiming more and more territory for Lukub as she did. Nobody had stopped her—who would waste soldiers to protect the woods?—but it had not gone unnoticed. So long as she didn't impede on a trade route or compromise access to Hirun, the rulers did not seem inclined to curb the Sultana's ill-advised expansion.

Why had Vaida brought her along for this?

"You are confident in these coordinates, Bausit?" Vaida narrowed her eyes. "Or will I need to come down here in another three weeks to grant you further leave to waste my time and claim more useless land for my kingdom?"

Bausit wrung his hands together. "Kera traced seventeen disappearances to that location in Essam, Your Majesty. He saw the links of their life chain wind through Essam and sever within ten miles of the holding."

Sefa's heart, which had not enjoyed a moment's respite this entire night, broke into a gallop. Surely she couldn't be hearing what she thought she was hearing.

"You have my leave to capture the territory Kera wants," Vaida said. "Try to stay as far away from the holding as you can, but if you must claim it under our flag, do so without violence. Capturing the land around a Nizahl holding is one thing, but Arin will not ignore a slaughter of his soldiers."

"Understood, Your Majesty." Bausit bowed, and as suddenly as he had appeared, the tall man melted into the shadows once again.

Vaida chewed on her lip for a second, deep in thought. Then, "Should we have the driver fetch us halawa? I prefer it with pistachios, but we can get a plain square for you, if you object."

Maybe Sefa should have walked into a Lafa Souda, just to confirm this wasn't a terrible dream. It certainly seemed like one, with the Sultana musing about a breakfast treat in a dark alley while a hooded man ran off to potentially trigger an act of war.

"The man he mentioned, Kera..." Sefa's imagination had never been anything impressive, and she simply lacked the creativity to have dreamed this night. Which meant it was horribly, jarringly real. "Is he Jasadi?"

"Half." Vaida tightened her cloak around her frame and strolled in the direction from which they'd entered. "Jasadi father, Lukubi mother. Fascinating magic. Terrible taste in hats."

"He uses his magic for you?" Sefa hurried to catch up, wary of the darkness collecting at the other end of the alley.

"Who else would he use it for?"

"I don't understand. Magic is forbidden."

"Then you should probably stop talking about it, dear. You wouldn't want someone to get the wrong idea."

The next words died on Sefa's tongue. Vaida's tone had shifted ever so slightly. Sefa was pushing against the fragile barrier between Vaida's good humor and the wrath responsible for throwing people into wells.

After a stretch of climbing, Sefa cleared her throat.

"I like pistachios."

CHAPTER TWENTY-FIVE

SYLVIA

My knees hit the dirt. I careened forward, the blanket weathering the worst scratches from the tree I caught myself against.

I ran a quick check. Ten fingers, one nose, all my toes.

Smooth as a heated blade against butter, instinct cut through the haze of my panic; I used the tree to heft myself to my feet, listening closely for any movement.

Where had my magic taken me?

I scanned the crop of trees and scraped my heel against the soil. Crumbling, cracked dirt, and no evidence of mosquitoes, so I wasn't near Hirun. The close cluster of trees placed me somewhere in the north, probably in the sector of Essam Woods between Nizahl and Lukub.

I searched for black raven marks on the trees or any northern vegetation I could use to identify my whereabouts. It did not stand to reason I should be dropped in a random corner of Essam. What was I missing?

I went stiff at the sound of voices and pressed behind the tree.

They ventured close, and the bottom dropped from my stomach. Oh, but my magic had a *sick* sense of humor.

"Are you certain you won't take an additional regiment?" Rawain asked, and my nausea from earlier surged back to life. "I worry you are leaving yourself exposed."

"I am already bringing more men than I would prefer," said an even, melodious voice. I dropped my forehead against the bark, the rough fibers digging into my skin. Of course. "We risk sending the wrong message if we arrive in great numbers. King Murib is precariously on edge."

"They all are. Their tantrums are becoming untenable." Rawain sighed. The voices stopped nearby, and I held myself perfectly still. I had not forgotten the Heir's keen hearing.

"Untenable was two weeks ago, when closing the trade routes was an idle threat. Since Galim's Bend, they have been rounding up and executing anyone suspected of using magic, and it is only escalating," Arin said. "We may not have set an ideal precedent by executing the Mufsids."

The slight note of censure in Arin's tone would go unnoticed by most, but my brows lifted in surprise. The decision to execute the Mufsids clearly hadn't been unanimous.

A frosty pause, then, "What further information had you hoped to draw from the Mufsids, Arin? If they knew where the Jasad Heir was, they would have found her first. When a tool no longer serves its intended purpose, you either discard it or put it to a different use. In one stroke, we rid ourselves of the Mufsids and soothed the hurt of those crying out to see someone punished for Galim's Bend."

I shifted my weight just enough to angle my view around the tree.

I saw the scepter first. The glass raven's beady eyes caught mine, the hideous head partially obscured under the cover of Rawain's ringed fingers. The Supreme looked unchanged from the last time I had the misfortune of laying eyes on him. A broad and physically powerful man, only the streak of gray in his wavy black hair marked his age. He oozed charm like pus from a wound, catching the unwary in its slimy trail.

The other speaker had his back to me, but even if I had not heard his voice, if I couldn't see the waves of thick silver hair, I would have known him by his back alone. I had spent hours studying the breadth of those shoulders; counted the notches of that spine as it bent over a map. Envied the way it maneuvered with grace, unburdened by the creaks and cracks of my own.

With a touch of amusement, I realized I'd grown more accustomed to meeting Arin's back than his front.

"Besides," Rawain continued, "I would have thought your final visit to the cells would have answered any lingering questions."

Had I not already been staring at Arin's back, I would have missed the tension feathering across his muscles. Rawain tilted his head at Arin, and I restrained a shudder. Every action I admired in the son reflected so monstrously in the father.

"I thought it strange that the Mufsids retained enough magic to break free of their restraints before reaching the gallows. Imagine my surprise when a guard mentioned your visit to the prison mere hours before the execution. Impossible, I thought. Why would you visit the cells without draining their magic? It isn't like you to allow such a detail to slip your mind."

"Details are difficult to track with a head injury," Arin said flatly. It hung in the air, oddly loaded, and I remembered the streak of blood running from Arin's temple the night of the Galim's Bend attack.

"So they are," Rawain mused. "I gather you were hoping the prisoners would be more forthcoming with their secrets on the eve of their deaths. As always, you afford them more honor than they deserve. Did you learn anything useful?"

The beat that followed reverberated in my own chest, Arin's second of hesitation unspooling a glow of disbelief around me.

It could just be Arin's measured way of speaking, I reasoned. It didn't necessarily mean he was hiding anything from his father.

"One of them told me a story," Arin said. "You were correct, of course, in that there was nothing of value to gain."

I went absolutely still, rivaling the tree upon which I leaned. Again, Arin sounded perfectly normal, but the cadence of his voice...the lack of a thoughtful pause between his sentences. As though he had memorized the words, practiced them for this performance. I may not have been born a liar, but I had certainly grown into an excellent one. I knew the right way to shape a good lie, the best moment to offer it. I had never heard its likeness from the Commander.

I pinched my arm. Nothing happened.

Rovial's tainted tomb.

Arin was *lying*.

"I suppose I should have considered your concerns more," Rawain sighed. "I know you were only trying to find answers about that Jasadi rat."

Ha! Rat, was I? I hoped I scurried around the attic of his nightmares.

"The Mufsid did raise an interesting question," Arin said, level and dispassionate.

"Oh?"

"We never recovered the stores of magic Palia and Niyar mined from their people, did we?"

Both Rawain and I paused.

The lines on Rawain's forehead smoothed, his shoulders easing into a casual slump. The feigned relaxation of a performer stretching before the stage. Were I less repulsed, I would be inclined to take notes. *This* was how you told a lie.

"No, we didn't. How could we? None of us knew the Malik and Malika were mining magic until shortly before the Blood Summit. They had been conducting the practice with the utmost secrecy, concealing it as workplace accidents in the southern wilayahs. As soon as the rest of us learned of their heinous deeds, we convened the Summit."

"Of course."

"As for the mined magic, it is anyone's guess where they hid it. It may still remain somewhere in Jasad. Mined magic—indeed, any magic removed from its source—does not last very long without an external force to anchor it. The profanity of the practice is one our ancestors fought hard to contain, Arin. I did not seek to uncover the mined magic lest the other rulers succumb to avarice."

"I see."

Rawain took a step toward Arin, the bottom of the scepter leaving a perfectly round imprint in the dirt. "I hope the Mufsid did not unsettle you."

"I am not easily unsettled," Arin said.

"No, you aren't," Rawain agreed, still studying his son. "That is what worries me."

The moment stretched, thinning until I wanted to quake beneath the tension. I felt as though I could reach out and touch Hanim, so forcefully did Rawain's quiet menace invoke her.

A third voice spliced through the clearing. "I am sorry to interrupt."

Wes! I grinned, giddy at the sight of the somber older guardsman. Who knew I would miss that frown and glaringly bald head?

"The supplies have been loaded, and the horses are ready. The soldiers await your instruction, my liege."

Rawain clapped Arin on the arm, the menace disappearing like mist on a warm summer day. "Off you are, then. Come back with open trade routes or Murib's head in a sack, I care not which." Rawain laughed. "I want you returned whole and unharmed, Arin. Your notions of honor have no place in a time like this. If your soldiers return to Nizahl without you, if you commit some asinine act of bravery at your own expense, I will hang every man, child, and horse who allowed you to do it."

Wes stared at Rawain, nonplussed, but Arin's expression didn't change. A speech he had heard before, I gathered.

The Supreme bid his son another farewell before striding through the trees. I hoped whatever carriage awaited him on the other side broke down and launched him face-first into a stony riverbed. Wrath pounded against the walls of my heart, and I pleaded with my body to relax before the rest of my equilibrium crumbled. The panic had finally eased, and I would rather not give my mind any reason to restart.

"Sire, shall I—"

"Wait."

I counted three long minutes before Arin exhaled, turning away from the juncture where his father had vanished. "I have a favor to ask of you, Wes."

"My lord, there are no favors between us. Your will is my command."

Arin held up a hand, cutting off the guardsman. Wes's eagerness seemed to pain him.

Obedience should be conscious, not instinctual. But why would Arin worry that Wes's obedience might be instinctual? He had been Arin's guardsman for half the Heir's life. If anyone knew Arin, if anyone would follow him for the strength of his leadership over the strength of his blood, it was Wes.

"No—no. What I ask of you trespasses the bounds of your duty to me. It imperils your life and liberty. If you do not wish to grant this request, I will hold you in no less esteem."

I probably looked as bewildered as Wes. The guardsman shifted, his knuckles ghosting over his collar. In the training tunnels, I had noticed how the Nizahl guardsmen wore their unique insignia on different parts of their uniform. Jeru kept his hidden under the flap of his chest pocket. Wes, the collar of his shirt. Ren had worn his on the inside of his sleeve. Vaun wore his pin on his chest; I remembered tearing it off his uniform when we fought.

"Ask, my liege. My answer will be my own."

Dread lined my stomach at the rigidity of Arin's profile. Whatever this task, he vehemently did not want to ask it of Wes.

"I cannot figure out where they are," Arin said in a rush, half defeat, half aggravation. "I have spent days scouring my maps, but I would have felt them. I should have felt them."

I shifted forward, straining to hear.

"I suspect that after our conversation, my father might detour to the mines before returning to the Citadel. I hope I'm wrong. I truly do." Arin fell quiet, his struggle palpable.

"I don't have the time to explain magic mining to you, nor do I believe it in your best interest to know the details. It will suffice for you to understand these mines were used by Malika Palia and Malik Niyar to store the magic they drained from the Jasadi people—the magic my father and the rest of the kingdoms secretly divvied between them in a practice nearly as old as the woods we stand in."

If I had doubted the absence of my magic during these appearances to Arin, this moment would have confirmed it. If I had my magic, the tree bearing my weight would be in flames. In fact, every tree in my proximity would be in flames, and I would spread the inferno until it reached Supreme Rawain and charred him alive.

I tried to fight past the roaring in my ears. Supreme Rawain—Queen Hanan, King Murib, Sultana Bisai—they had all traded in the magic my grandparents mined from the lower wilayahs? They had been participants of the very practice they torched our kingdom for?

Any illusions I had held of my grandparents had been most effectively shattered over the course of the Alcalah, but this was another level entirely. Not only did Gedo Niyar and Teta Palia murder our own people and redistribute their magic to the already-wealthy upper wilayahs, but to hand it over to Omal, Orban, Lukub, and Nizahl? To trade it like jewels or land?

And what did Arin mean, this was an old practice? An old

practice of Jasad or of all the kingdoms? Sweet Sirauk, how far back did this go?

I was not in a state to think through this revelation, and I could already feel my insides squeezing, the bottomless void of my panic roiling. The earlier lull must have been a false calm. I pressed my knuckles to my mouth before Arin heard me gasping like a land-stranded fish.

Arin looked at his guardsman for a long moment. "When my father leaves, I want you to follow him."

The reason for Arin's solemnity eluded me a minute longer than it did Wes. Comprehension settled over the older man. The lines in his forehead smoothed.

Entirely too calm for someone who had just been asked to accept a death sentence.

If Wes was lucky, spying on the Supreme would see him thrown in prison and executed as a traitor. If he were less lucky—if Arin was right and Rawain planned to leave the Citadel's grounds to determine the security of highly illegal magic mines—then getting caught meant Wes would never return to Nizahl. The guardsman would not be permitted to live long enough to send word back to his Commander.

Wes knelt before Arin and folded his hands over his bent knee. "I serve you, Arin of Nizahl, freely and of my own will. It is my honor and my duty, to whatever end."

Arin caught Wes's arm, hauling him back to his feet. They stood like that, arms clasped, a lifetime hanging between them.

"Do not get caught," Arin said.

Wes grinned, briefly. "I won't."

"Thank you, Wes."

They separated, and Wes reminded Arin of his regiment's readiness to depart before taking his own leave. We watched him go.

I rested my forehead against the tree, grimacing at the scrape of sap dried into the bark. Part of me wanted to follow Arin to the soldiers' encampment, but what was the point? I knew where they were going, and I could hazard a guess how many were accompanying him. In many ways, this visit was an enormous boon—if Arin was headed to Orban to persuade Murib to open the trade routes, then I could predict his path and ensure ours would not cross it.

I should feel glad. I should feel anything other than the horrible pit in my stomach. The molten panic in my chest, steadily burning through me.

I needed to get a handle on myself before Namsa came to collect me for the journey. They couldn't see me like this. I had barely begun to find a place with them, to feel like a real leader. Falling apart because of a couple of veins? Because there was a small, *tiny* chance that when the cuffs fell away, the sudden resurgence of magic in my body after a lifetime of suppression had accelerated symptoms of magic-madness?

One second I was alone, and the next, my shoulders stiffened beneath the sharp point of a sword.

CHAPTER TWENTY-SIX

SYLVIA

I didn't flinch, the tree and its dried sap the only witnesses to my tired smile. "What gave me away?"

"Turn around."

I rolled my eyes. At least he had graced me with speech this time. I wasn't sure I could tolerate another wordlessly spiteful interaction. "Care to remove your sword? I will not rotate at the end of it like a pig on a spit."

After a second, the pinch between my shoulders disappeared. I took a breath meant to fortify me, but it landed awkwardly behind my ribs, refusing to dissipate. I was still in the throes of the panic that had brought me here, and any air I tried to draw floated in my chest like oil poured over water.

Gathering the blanket closer, I faced the grim Commander, raising a sardonic brow. "Did they not teach you greeting etiquette in little Heir school? Perhaps instead of pinning me to walls or introducing me to your plethora of blades, you could try saying hello."

I would have had more satisfying results taunting a rock. The sword still raised between us, Arin studied me, eyes raking over my exposed legs and the red-and-black wool blanket strung around my bare body. Winter-blue eyes met mine and held them fast. My heart, already operating at an accelerated rhythm, began to pound. Arin had always possessed an uncanny ability to see straight through me, no matter how practiced the lie or polished the performance. I was not in the mood to be known today.

I returned the attention in kind. Silver hair was tied back behind his head, the fine strands sliding from their captivity to curve like crescent moons around his cheekbones. The bruise on his temple had gone from blue and black to a mild yellow, and my gaze drifted over the perfectly laced column of his vest to where the gashes I'd dug my fingers into had bled. Had those healed enough for him to ride a horse to Orban?

He wore his infamous black coat, the tiny ravens stitched in violet embroidered on the sleeves and the hem skimming near the top of his boots.

The very image of power and self-assuredness. Every detail crafted to immaculate perfection. The kind of leader that lived in legends.

My hands curled into the blanket. Maybe my magic hadn't brought me here to listen in on Arin's conversation with Rawain. Maybe it wanted to prove to me how low my measure fell against the Nizahl Heir; his lifetime of standing straight beneath his responsibilities held up like a mirror to reflect my own bent back.

Busy sinking into the whirlpool of my head, it took me a second to realize Arin was speaking.

"What. Happened." The question—if one could call it that—came torn from between his teeth.

"What happened with what?" He probably wanted to know how much I had overheard or how I found him. Would he find it aggravating if I said, *My magic decided to bring me here*, or would he find it as terrifying as I did?

The sword plunged into the dirt beside me. So quick was the strike, it took me an entire twenty seconds to notice the hilt vibrating inches to my right.

A shiver worked down my neck. All my training, all my years with Hanim. Pointless.

If Arin and I fought—truly fought—I would not emerge the victor. He had never shown me the full range of his skill, never exerted the limits of his strength in my presence.

I probably would have tried harder to kill him if he had.

It became clear why Arin had disarmed himself when he took a step closer. "Your eyes are bloodshot and your breathing is shallow. You can track what I say, but your mind is straying." His lips pressed together. "I have seen you like this before."

Impossible. I would never have let him witness me at my most vulnerable, especially not in those early days. Maybe afterward, but during—

The Nizahl Heir's gaze found me through the dim of the hall. How long had he been there?

"Have you returned?" he asked.

"I never left." Hoarse, as though I had been screaming instead of sitting silently on the ground.

"Yes, you did."

Right. I exhaled on a bitter chuckle. I had forgotten about my fit in the hallway after discovering one of the trials would take place in Nizahl. Arin had seen me break so many times, in so many different ways. If he wished, the Nizahl Heir could pull at a single stitch and unravel me. I had given my enemy the designs to my destruction.

"It will pass," I replied. "It always does." Even if it took more of me with it each time.

My shoulders tensed, prepared for him to ask what had caused it. Prepared to lie and prevaricate and launch us out of the first conversation we had had without the embers of rage lying between our feet, threatening to blaze.

I had been away too long. The singularity of Arin's attention, his unwavering focus, discomfited me nearly as much as it had those first weeks in the tunnels.

"Why are you naked?"

I glanced down at the blanket, taken aback. Suddenly, the absurdity of the situation struck me, and I had to bite my lip to restrain my laugh. My magic had really dropped me, naked and barreling toward a veritable meltdown, into Essam Woods. Into Arin's path.

"Did someone—" Arin paused, and my flash of humor dissolved. I could rarely recall seeing the Nizahl Heir struggle for words. He closed his eyes. When they reopened, icy shards of deadly intent pierced through me. "Are you naked of your own will, or of someone else's?"

It took me longer than it should have to understand. Arin had taken my nakedness and mental state and pieced together a horrible conclusion. I extricated a hand from the blanket to wave it in vehement denial. "No, no! Nobody tried to force me to do anything. I am naked of my own volition."

Relief melted the rigid contours of his face. He released a heavy breath, while I flushed at the potential double meaning of my words.

"To clarify," I added, feeling unbelievably absurd, "I was not engaged in any activity where nakedness is expected or customary. Not that you *must* be naked to take part in those, uh, activities. In any event, I wasn't. Taking part, I mean. In any activities."

"But there *were* activities?" Arin asked, straight-faced.

"No, no activities! I was alone and fully intending to stay that way. I—why are you smiling?"

The corners of Arin's mouth had curved upward. The humor in his smile, though invoked at my expense, spread through me like warm honey. I hadn't thought I would see it again.

"You lied to your father," I blurted.

Why enjoy a moment when I was just so good at ruining them?

As much as I hated the resurgence of caution wiping Arin's features clean, I would have hated it more if my magic swept me back without an opportunity to understand what I had witnessed between the Heir and the Supreme.

"What did the Mufsid say to you?" I pressed. "They were executed the day after Galim's Bend, so if you saw him the night before his execution, then you must have visited him right after I saw you. Did you ask him about the fortress?"

Arin didn't retreat, even when I bridged the gap between us. This close, his beauty hit me like a blow to the gut. The aftershock of it rippled into an unpleasant awareness of my own disheveled appearance.

It made my tone sharper than necessary. "Tell me, Arin of Nizahl. How does it feel to doubt?"

Fury flashed over Arin, splitting his carefully placid features like a clap of lightning through the clear blue sky. "Do you think doubt is new to me?"

I opened my mouth and came up empty. The answer must have been clear on my face, because a muscle in Arin's jaw clenched.

"For all the horrors you have lived through, *Essiya of Jasad*, you understand nothing of what it means to lead. All I do is doubt. Myself, others, the very reality we occupy. Every day, I take the facts as I understand them, and I make a choice. When those facts change, I make a different choice. Doubt forces me to confront what I know and reassess it as the circumstances demand. The day I stop doubting, the *moment* I submit myself to convenience over clarity, I pray my crown rusts in my hands."

It was the second time I had ever heard Arin speak so much in a single fell swoop. Our gazes collided and held fast. Two swords locked on the battlefield, neither willing to yield.

"You say 'facts' as though the word means something. I've told you before, my liege—life is not an equation you can calculate over and over again. Every choice won't be perfect, but you still have to make it." I shook my head. "If you've allowed doubt to become indecision, your crown has already rusted."

Arin's eyes narrowed, but I held firm. We'd flung our daggers, and there was little left to do but stand there and bleed.

Unfortunately, I had forgotten that no amount of injury could force Arin still. "Who is Hanim?"

I blinked, breath catching in my lungs. Oh, but it almost worked. Hanim's name was *almost* sufficient to destroy the trajectory of my thoughts, to leave me off-kilter and bewildered.

It would have worked had I not just witnessed him play the very same tactic against his father.

"What a chatty Mufsid you found." I leaned back against the tree, the blanket tightening around my body as I crossed my arms over my chest. "I doubt he recalled her very fondly. Hanim was their leader for a time, you know. Before her exile for conspiring with your father against the Jasad crown, though I imagine you haven't stumbled across those records. Supreme Munqual went to great lengths to cover up Rawain's misdeeds when he was Commander."

His silence lengthened. It was another of his tactics, inviting the other person to keep speaking until he had what he needed or they incriminated themselves. Historically, it worked with embarrassing success against me.

Several strands had escaped my braid, curls frizzing near my ears and tickling my neck. I tried to tuck them away and nearly dropped the blanket.

Damn him. "I bet the Mufsid blamed Hanim for the fortress falling. Richly ironic, if you ask me. Hanim didn't sack Usr Jasad. She might have written the false enchantment, but who read it?" I wondered how much Arin knew about what had happened on the other side of the fortress the day it fell. It wasn't until Soraya's vision that I learned Usr Jasad had fallen before the fortress, ravaged at the hands of its own people. "Soraya was working for Hanim, by the way. They were poisoning my mother in Bakir Tower and passing it off as an affliction of her mind."

At the mention of Soraya's name, Arin's face went curiously still. My former attendant was the same woman who had given him the scar on his throat. She had managed the impossible and infiltrated the Citadel under an assumed identity, but instead of targeting Rawain, she had tried to kill his adolescent son. I still didn't understand why; had I been in her position, I would have shoved Rawain's scepter through the other side of his skull while I could.

Despite the sumptuous temptation I'd laid before him, Arin didn't bite. It seemed he had hit his limit of human conversation for the day.

"What I know for certain is that your father expected it to fall. The Blood Summit, the march on Jasad, the fortress—he planned every moment, accounted for every detail. An artist of destruction, that man. I nearly admire it."

"Is this how you amuse yourself?" My triumph at prodding him out of his pen of silence faded fast. His voice stayed crisp and infuriatingly even, as though my insults were as insubstantial as a raindrop hitting the surface of a river. "You lie awake at night and run in the same circles of suspicion until you tire?"

The same strategy, but applied to much greater success. He wanted to provoke, to fluster. At this rate, he'd probably succeed much faster than I would, so I pressed my tongue to the back of my teeth and reassessed my approach.

There was one method he wouldn't see coming. One front where our weapons hadn't previously crossed, where our moves had not yet been charted.

Years of proximity to Marek caught up to me in an instant. I let my head loll against the tree as the blanket slid below my bare shoulders, and I twisted my lips into a taunting smile. "I have nothing better to tire me at night. How would you suggest I amuse myself, Your Highness?" The question emerged low and inviting.

When Arin stared at me, momentarily dumbstruck, my laugh blew a cool breath over the last embers of panic still flickering in my chest. I crossed my legs at the ankle, and the blanket parted around my knees. Arin's gaze flicked to my calves, and I belatedly remembered the veins. Fortunately, the one on my right leg ran up the back of my calf. Out of sight.

The reminder doused me in cold water. It would be an absolute disaster if Arin discovered the veins. If the exchange I had witnessed between Rawain and Arin was any indication, the Nizahl Heir had stepped over a line and into a territory of unspeakable danger.

Arin had begun to question the Supreme.

Discovering that my magic was manipulating my memories, superseding my will, and leaving traces across my body? There was only one conclusion Arin would come to, and why wouldn't he? I had no other conclusion to offer. No other explanation for why my magic and I interacted like strangers who had not quite decided whether the other meant them ill.

"So much time you have spent worrying about where we're hiding," I said. "Perhaps you should have spent some of it worrying about what your father is hiding right under your nose."

A distant shout echoed past the throng of trees. "Your Highness!"

I inclined my head toward the sound. "Your men await you, my lord."

Arin didn't glance in the direction of his camp. In one of his long-legged strides, the gap between us suddenly closed. Startled, I stumbled away from the tree and tripped over the sword he'd driven into the ground.

Two things happened at once. The blanket, which slipped when I tried to catch the sword's hilt, was caught in a gloved fist. Before I could careen to the ground, Arin's other arm went around my waist, hauling me into his chest.

Pressed together from shoulder to knee, I counted the rise and fall of his chest as though it were my own breath traveling through him. Eventually, I tipped my chin back, meeting the patient gaze above me.

"There you are." His chuckle brushed my forehead, sending heat racing over my skin. "You want my suggestions on how you should amuse yourself?"

I gripped his lapels, viscerally aware of the brush of leather at my collarbone where he held my blanket aloft.

"I have some thoughts on the matter." The silky pitch wrung a shiver out of me.

I shouldn't have offered this new angle to our game, not when I was just as likely to lose. Just from standing pressed against Arin, my heart had apparently decided the inside of my chest was no longer its preferred residence and was attempting to pound its escape through my ribs.

As though he could read every thought warring in my head, a slow smile curved over Arin's lips. I could feel every single strap of his vest against my chest. I had a notion that if I dropped the blanket, I might find their impressions stitched into my skin.

He thought he was winning.

The thought annoyed me back to myself. Seduction might not come as naturally to me, but then, seduction rarely worked on Arin anyway. How many stories had I heard in Mahair about the Nizahl Commander's rejection of perfectly suitable royals or the most coveted women of the season? Arin's control over himself was merciless. He allowed himself no quarter for error. As long as he remained so tightly wound, no one could ever snag a thread to unravel him.

I remembered the snide remarks I'd made to Jeru and Wes as they escorted me to the training tunnels.

Oh dear, did you think lust *overcame your Heir?* My caustic laugh. *Are you calling your Commander frigid?*

Despite the tight fit of our bodies, I drew my arm out to grab his chin and yank his face toward me.

He offered no resistance. He let me cage his jaw in my hand, his eyes rapt on mine.

What I understood of desire wouldn't fill the eye of a thimble, but

I knew mine didn't feel like what Marek described or what the girls at the keep gushed about. I wanted to taste his pulse and trace the sharp curve of his hip. I wanted his poison-tipped tongue and his moon-stricken hair, my nails in his thighs and my lips at his throat.

But I also wanted to crawl into his chest until the rest of the world went dark and quiet. I was losing the battle against my dread, flagging beneath the force of my uncertainty. I had been fighting alone since I was ten years old, and the thought of trusting someone else to fight for me, to fight alongside me... the force of my wanting pulled me apart, exposed every crack and scar where the world had taken a swing.

"Come back, Suraira." Arin tilted his chin in my grip. Something seized my spine when the corner of his mouth brushed my thumb, his lips too soft for a man who rarely used them for anything other than chiseling daggers out of every conversation. "You're hiding again."

Suraira. Two names in my possession, yet Arin chose to name me after a Nizahlan demon of mishap said to haunt Sirauk Bridge and lure the unwary to their doom.

I rasped a laugh, and with no small amount of force, welded myself back together. Maybe someday I could rest behind someone else's armor and trust it to hold the world away, but it wouldn't be today.

"Hiding is what I do best." I flashed him a grin. "You and your ocean of maps still haven't found me."

He offered me an arch look. "Is that what you think?"

"It's what I know. You can try to track me until my hair is as silver as yours, but if you could have found me, you already would have." I slid my hand from his chin to the back of his neck.

Arin swallowed, and for a second, I wondered if he had ever wanted to rest behind someone else's armor. If he would ever trust me to hold the world away.

"Why should I bother tracking you when I need only to wait?" He pressed the words against my temple. "The moment you leave the mountains, you're mine."

CHAPTER TWENTY-SEVEN

MAREK

Covered in soot and the remains of a shredded zulal, Marek had gained a newfound respect for Sylvia.

Even with hundreds of soldiers at his side, battling the creatures infesting Galim's Bend had taken every last ounce of his strength. The fact that Sylvia had fought her way through Dar al Mansi alone, carrying nothing more than an axe and a knife? Oh, and Al Anqa'a hadn't been conveniently incapacitated for her, either.

Thank the Awaleen he and that girl were on the same side.

The wagon hit a bump, jostling the group of them shoved in the back. Marek groaned when his bruised arm hit the side of the wagon. Galim's Bend had wrecked him. Holes riddled his boots, the leather eaten through by the nisnas's corrosive blood. His hair dripped with a variety of eviscerated organs.

It shouldn't be long until he fell into a hot bath and a warm bed. The upper towns had opened their homes to some of the recruits while the recovery at Galim's Bend continued. Several of the more experienced recruits had been annoyed to learn Marek was assigned to the same block of nobles' houses as them. "Who sent you to *this* neighborhood after you've only muddied your boots once? Your mother must have left a feather by the bridge for you," Zane had grumbled, clapping him a little too hard on the shoulder. The reference was lost on Marek, though not the general sentiment.

The road smoothed beneath them. Conversation ceased as the moonlight disappeared behind houses grander than Marek had seen in a long time. Verdant gardens grew beside immaculate entryways, each step behind their wrought-iron gates glittering with incandescent glass tiles. Lanterns flush with oil burned over soaring stone walls, illuminating the gilded nameplates at the front of each gate that declared the household's name, many of which Marek recognized as well-known dignitaries of the Citadel.

The soldiers dropped off one by one. Marek remained in the wagon as they passed decadent estates eating up the same amount of acreage as a sizable Omalian village.

As uncomfortable as he found such ostentatious displays of wealth after the massacre in the kingdom's poorest village, a small part of Marek...relaxed. For a very long time, this had been his world. Though he would happily spend the rest of his life in a tent with Sefa rather than a single hour in his former home, he sometimes missed those days of luxury.

Until he remembered the cost.

Those names carved onto each gate? The Lazurs had one, too. They'd varnished theirs with the blood of Marek's siblings. Amira, Hani, Binyar, Darin. The gravedigger's shovel never had a chance to leave the ground before the next Lazur body arrived.

How tragic for his parents that their spoiled, spineless, vain son was the only one left to survive them. They shouldn't have been so hasty to turn their other children into heroes. Maybe they would have noticed that their youngest had been born with a deficit of bravery. If it came down to dying a hero or living a coward, Marek would do whatever it took to keep himself aboveground.

The wagon juddered to a halt. "Out," called the driver.

Marek shook himself out of his reverie. The house the driver stopped in front of couldn't be the right one. It was the last in the neighborhood and the most magnificent by far.

"Out!" A canvas bag hit his chest.

"Easy!" Marek clutched the bag carrying his meager overnight fortifications and hopped out of the wagon. The driver barely waited for Marek's boots to hit the ground before snapping the reins.

Marek eyed the long path to the front of the manor uncertainly. He had more viscera coating him than the buckets in the back of a butcher's shop.

Nerves danced in his belly as he knocked on the door. What if whoever waited on the other side recognized Caleb Lazur? He should have stopped to glance at the nameplate on the gate—was there enough time to run back and check?

A woman roughly one or two years Marek's junior opened the door. Fiery red hair cascaded past her shoulders, curtaining her slim frame like the sun blazing around the horizon. Freckles kissed the rounds of her cheeks. A mouth Marek could write poems about widened into a grin.

Marek's nerves melted into a slow smile. A beautiful woman staring at him in wide-eyed curiosity. Familiar territory at last.

"Hello, soldier. Welcome to our home."

She stepped aside, and Marek didn't take his eyes off her as he crossed the threshold. "And what a beautiful home it is," Marek said. They could have been standing in the middle of a sinking cesspool for all he cared.

A throng of servants appeared out of nowhere, whisking off his filthy coat and dabbing the sludge caked into his hair. A bout of shyness stifled the girl's momentary confidence, and she pointed at the stairs without lifting her gaze to Marek's. "The attendants will see you to your chambers. Once you've had a chance to freshen up, please join me and my mother in the sitting room. We have the most luscious cake prepared for you."

Before Marek could get the girl's name, he lost sight of her in the flurry of attendants. They hustled him across the manor and into an empty room, where he was stripped bare and scrubbed nearly to the bone.

Once Marek had been cleaned to within an inch of his life, he buttoned his white shirt into a pair of high-waisted black trousers and tied the leather ends of his suspenders into the belt loops.

Marek smirked at the mirror. Sulor, the section leader at their compound, had ordered Marek to get his hair cut to issue length, but Marek had convinced the barber to leave a little extra. Wisps of gold fell over his forehead. His skin glowed, having miraculously survived the fabric of the compound's cot. The bruise on his chin, while not the most attractive injury in his new collection, would remind the hosts of Marek's noble and brave endeavors on their behalf. (Never mind that he had gotten the bruise by tripping over a basket and hitting his chin on the buckle of a saddle.)

The servant outside Marek's door led him to the sitting room. Decadence draped every facet of Marek's temporary accommodations, from the hundreds of lanterns flickering in empty rooms to the carpets and curtains dyed in more shades of violet and black than should ever exist in one place. Marek passed a steel door bearing Nizahl's insignia and grimaced at the gilded raven flying from between the two clashing swords.

Two people stood at his entrance. One was the girl who'd greeted him at the door. The other woman shared similar features to the first, but bestowed with age's loving touch. Silver streaked her short red hair, framing the sharp cut of her chin and the bow of her lips.

Marek couldn't believe his luck. *I have passed into death, and eternity has met me with bliss.*

He took his host's hand and bowed, brushing his lips lightly over her wedding band. "My lady. I have marveled at my privilege to be hosted at the loveliest home in Nizahl, and now you grant me your company? The blood I shed on the battlefield is not worth half this honor."

"Leave your formality at the door, soldier. You may call me Mira." The orders fell naturally, as prim as the rest of her property. "You've already met my daughter. Gigi, did you say hello?"

"Hello." Gigi blushed. Adorable.

Marek kissed her hand, too, and straightened with a smile. "A pleasure."

Had there ever been a more delicious dilemma? If Marek were a smarter man, his gaze would stay with the daughter. He would subtly coax her from her shell with a mixture of humor and rapt attention, and when the time came to retire, he would restrain himself to a kiss on her cheek and a gentle good night.

But Mira cocked a brow at Marek, pointing at the chair in silent command, and Marek was lost.

He could almost hear Sefa cajoling him. She would call him a jelly-kneed obsessive who couldn't resist a pretty smile. She'd ask if he had developed a taste for the fists of cuckolded husbands. *The one trait all these women share is their unavailability*, Sefa would scold. *When will you find someone who can love you the way you deserve?*

The answer was never. As long as Marek drew breath, he belonged to Sefa. What woman would accept second place? Marek never treated his lovers cruelly. He didn't pretend to offer his heart or feign interest in a future where he wasn't at Sefa's side.

A steaming cup of a greenish tea passed into his hands. Marek took a sip and valiantly managed not to spit it back out. The tea tasted like shredded grass and the pungent seed Raya would drop in their stew for seasoning and forget to fish out before serving.

"Zangabeel," Gigi said. "It calms the nerves."

Marek forced himself to swallow. "Then I may need a second cup to ease myself into an evening in such lovely company."

Conversation with Gigi flowed easily. The girl was chattier than Marek had guessed, and he nodded along more often than he contributed. To Marek's right, Mira's gaze had stayed steady on him since he sat down. A thrill tingled at the base of his spine. The hunt was always most fulfilling when Marek felt hunted in turn.

Jeru had no idea the favor he'd shown Marek, assigning him to this neighborhood.

The thought momentarily shorted Marek's attention. He missed what Gigi said about her favorite scouring method for restoring a rusted short blade.

Jeru wouldn't do Marek a favor. He had sent him to this neighborhood—this *house*—for a reason.

"My lady, if you would forgive my impudence," Marek said. "Which household name do I have to thank for my excellent accommodations?"

Mira arched a brow. "You didn't check the gate?" She clicked her tongue. "I suppose the oversight can be forgiven in these circumstances."

"Our household name is Shinawy," Gigi supplied, scowling at her mother.

When the next rotation leaves to quarter in the noble towns, I will send you to the Shinawy manor. Find me the insignia, and I will help you find Sefa.

Meeting Mira's unflinching stare, Marek's smile turned predatory. For all of Jeru's buttoned-up village-boy virginity, he hadn't been shy about using Marek's particular talents to win a way into the hearts—and confidences—of the noblewomen. If Mira had information about the missing insignia from the Siege of Six Dawns, Marek would work tirelessly until he got it. He would stay up all night long if he had to.

Once Gigi excused herself for the night, the real fun began. Mira took the cup from Marek, set it delicately onto its platter, and straddled his lap.

"We owe you a great debt for your efforts tonight, soldier," Mira purred against his cheek.

Marek weaved his hand through her hair and tightened his grip.

He hooked a smile against her forehead. "How would you like me to collect on this debt?" His voice dropped to a low rumble.

Mira shivered. With a quiet laugh, Marek kissed the corner of her mouth and murmured, "Brace your knees for me, my lady."

Marek stood, Mira clinging to his shoulders, her knees hitched on his hips. With the directions she provided in between bites to his ear and throat, he navigated to her chambers on the third floor. The servants blowing out candles politely averted their gazes.

Marek chuckled. Always a pleasure to offer a juicy piece of gossip for the staff.

The door had scarcely clicked shut behind them before Mira shoved Marek against it. She yanked his suspenders off his shoulders and worked through the buttons on his shirt with the vindictiveness of one greeting an old enemy.

"Patience." Marek caught her hands and flattened them to his chest. "Time is on our side." He popped a button toward the bottom, exposing a strip of his stomach.

"Or…" Mira promptly ripped Marek's shirt open. She gazed at his naked torso with a hunger Marek found deeply flattering and a dash frightening.

Marek hadn't been intimate with anyone since the second trial of the Alcalah. It was the longest he had stayed abstinent in years.

He'd missed this so much. The tension in his muscles melting under a warm touch. The riptides of pleasure, climbing and cresting, dragging him to exquisite depths. The shattering bliss on his enthusiastic partner's face.

Mira pulled off the straps of her dress and went to work undoing the lace over her breasts. How rude of Marek. He stopped her with an open-mouthed kiss. "Let me."

In minutes, their clothes were a combined pile near the door, and Marek clasped Mira's wandering hands together while he drew her to the bed.

He landed in pillows infinitely softer than the atrocities in the compound, which would have snapped his neck on impact if he'd fallen on them so heavily. Candlelight cast its dancing shadows over the walls. In their light, Mira's fiery hair glowed.

She pinned his wrists over his head, a wicked smile on her rosy lips. And Marek, who had always known he'd make a terrible soldier, easily surrendered.

CHAPTER TWENTY-EIGHT

SYLVIA

There was nothing I loved more in this life than being proven right.

Drops of water pelted us from the roaring waterfall. Soaking wet and standing knee-deep at the westernmost part of Hirun River, I allowed vindication to warm me through my damp clothes. "I *knew* this was how you were all moving in and out of the mountains!"

Lateef's brow furrowed. "When were you down here?"

"When she tried to escape," Efra said.

"When Efra decided to watch me drown instead of calling for help," I said at the same time. The current gently tugged at my legs as it tipped over the edge of the opening, joining the streams cascading toward Suhna Sea.

"When the Sareekh rescued her," Maia piped in, avoiding the glares Efra and I shot her.

The waterfall gushed behind us, a powerful deluge curtaining us off from the steep drop into the sea. Ahead, the river snaked beneath the mountain, rising higher the farther it traveled. In a mile or so, our supply of air would probably narrow to a couple of inches above our heads.

If legends were true about Hirun running beneath the Desert Flats, was the other part of the story true? Had hiding Hirun been Rovial's punishment for Dania's strike against his kingdom? The Orbanians would always be in drought, always be reliant on creeks and streams, because the river that nourished the rest of the land had been hidden from them.

"Do you use a boat?" I asked, glancing around. "Or does one of you know how to help the rest of us breathe underwater?"

One of the Urabi I hadn't interacted with much sloshed forward and cleared her throat. The river rippled around her, six long shapes rising to the surface.

"About that," Kenzie said.

"Stop shouting!" Maia pleaded. "Efra, can't you calm her down?"

Efra shuddered. "I told you—I will not use my magic on her. I nearly let her beat me to death on the cliffside rather than have my magic collide with the toxic vat of power roiling around inside her."

"*Let* me," I hissed. "A moth with its wings tied back could beat you to death."

"She's hysterical. I will handle it," Medhat announced, and lifted his hand to presumably strike me.

Two seconds later, he wheezed, grabbing at the throat I'd just punched.

"Essiya!" Namsa grabbed my elbows. I put up a token struggle, but truthfully, my hollering had turned to shrieking curses a while ago, and I didn't particularly wish to strike Namsa in the throat. "It won't hurt you. Kenzie can control beasts of the river—it is why we brought her with us, despite her abysmal fighting skills."

Kenzie gasped. "I'll fight you right now, Namsa!"

Namsa's eyes, so very like Dawoud's, bored into mine. "Breathe. Collect yourself. We would never put you in a position to be harmed."

The frenzy drained slowly, leaving me loose-limbed and embarrassed. I didn't shake Namsa's grip off right away. "She's never lost control of them?"

"Never."

Kenzie nodded. She crossed spindle-thin arms over her chest, drawing herself tall. "I will have you know I was the premiere River-tamer in my—"

I spoke over her. "And her magic will last until we reach the Omal palace?"

An outraged huff from Kenzie, but Namsa nodded. "She has been saving up her magic for weeks, so she's brimming with it."

It would have to do. I finally shook Namsa off and retreated, bracing myself before I glanced down.

Slitted bulbous eyes peered up at me, attached to seven monstrous crocodiles twice the width of my body and three times its length. Rows of hard scales studded their backs, cresting over the menacing lash of their tails. Spiky ridges ran in parallel lines between the gray and brown tiles of their tough skin. I tried not to wince at the teeth protruding from their closed jaws, too long for the confines of their snouts.

I exhaled, reaching into my coat to palm Binyar's journal. The critical piece of this journey, the evidence the Urabi had hinged their hopes on.

"We will reach Omal in three days. The palace in five," Efra said. I bristled at his snide tone, wishing I hadn't left my little kitmers hopping along the cliffside. "Unless you'd like to spend weeks stomping around Essam Woods, that is."

We didn't have weeks to spare. Even if we did, we were sharing Essam with Arin. Sooner or later, he would find me. He always did.

He told me he would come for me as soon as I left the mountains, and I believed him. It hadn't even surprised me to learn he'd known where I was. Arin was methodical, slicing apart a problem the way Rory opened a frog beneath his knife. He had spent years searching for the Urabi and Mufsids across the kingdoms, across the woods. There was only one option left.

"*You have a map of the mountains?*" I asked faintly. "*A detailed map?*"

"I have several, but they're far from finished."

He had known where I was—he just hadn't known how to get to me.

I took a deep breath, forcing myself to study the creatures again. A crocodile lashed the point of its tail, sending water arcing at my feet. I winced. I had ridden the Sareekh. These crocodiles were barely the size of one of the Sareekh's scales. And yet—

I shuddered and turned to Medhat. I'd met the man briefly my first day in the mountain and instantly wanted to saw off his tongue. On his worst days, Marek could talk for several hours straight, but Medhat—the Jasadi possessed a bottomless well of energy and an eagerness to wield it against every unwitting fool in his path. Fooled by his youthful demeanor and gangly limbs, I had given him seventeen years of age until Namsa revealed he was older than me by eight years.

Mere minutes in his overwhelmingly cheerful presence, and I already wanted to lie down for a week. I pointed at him. "If you try to slap me again, I will liberate your hand from your body and feed it to my kitmers as a treat."

The group made a disgusted face. I pressed on, puffing my chest. "With that said, I'm afraid you are going to need to tie me to the crocodile."

It took sixteen hours to reach land. Sixteen hours traveling by water beneath the Desert Flats, slipping in and out of the river as the crocodiles swam at top speed.

Marek and Sefa were *never* going to believe me.

In the back of my head, I had been keeping a collection of all the stories I wanted to share with them when I saw them again. Stories from the mountain, certainly, but also from before. Stories from my childhood and Usr Jasad. About the Blood Summit and Rawain and Hanim. They had learned I was Essiya minutes before my magic destroyed the wing of the Citadel.

The minute they knew me completely was also the minute I lost them. How very consistent.

I wrung my hair out for the third time, grimacing at the twinge in my sore arms. We'd made camp for the night on the outskirts of Essam Woods. The trees this far northwest were more scattered than I was accustomed to, the wide gaps between them forming doorways of darkness around the perimeter.

The seven of us huddled next to the crackling fire. Maia passed around soggy feeno sandwiches, the fluffy bread sliced down the center and filled with gibna rumi. I hadn't had gibna rumi in *years*. Not much of a loss, since the overly salty flavor and crumbly texture of the cheese always dried out my mouth. But food was food, and I was ravenous.

Someone scooted closer, an arm slinging onto the log braced behind me. "I think I saw you shiver earlier. If you need anyone to warm you up, I've been told my services are more than adequate," Medhat said. Mischief glittered in eyes bluer than a spring sky.

I squinted suspiciously.

Silver and gold swirled in his irises. Flames danced on the ends of his fingers and melted into his calluses, flowing like red rivers through the lines of his palm. "Think about it."

The other reason meeting Medhat exhausted me: he was yet another of the Urabi with a rare magic. They'd called those with the ability to draw forth fire and manipulate it a wakeel el-nar. Their services had been highly coveted in the Jasad military, but of those blessed with the terrifying power, most had the personality of a butterfly. They preferred to flit through life using their fire for festival tricks and royal entertainment instead of lending it to battle.

"Medhat," Namsa groaned from her sprawl near the fire. She had curled into a ball as soon as we trudged out of the river and hadn't unfurled. "Leave the Malika alone."

"We are only having fun," Medhat pouted. "As a rule, I don't irritate women who threaten to feed my body parts to their pets."

He ran a hand through his wavy, sand-brown hair and shot me a grin. "Despite the insult to my honor, I do still try to make sure those women don't freeze to death."

"How about you check on the rest of us first?" Efra groused. He had been the most active in our group, gathering wood and arranging makeshift bedding out of scattered leaves, moss, and weeds. An admirable effort, if a wasted one. The upright among us certainly couldn't unclench our frozen limbs long enough to lie down.

"You will have to forgive Efra," Medhat shared in a conspiratorial whisper. "He's usually much better mannered."

My nostrils were too frozen to produce a respectable snort. "If you say so."

Victory flashed in his toothy grin, and I stifled my groan. He had tricked me out of my stoic silence, and now he had a better notion of what buttons to push.

"Just sleep, Essiya," Namsa mumbled. "He won't shut up until you do."

I rolled to the ground, cushioning my head in the crook of my arm. I was too nervous to sleep, but I could pretend.

After a stretch of petulant silence, Medhat shuffled in Efra's direction, and I heard him muse, "Do you think I have the right chin shape for a beard?"

Curiously, I didn't have to fake for long. I breathed the comforting stink of rotten eggs and moss wafting from Hirun; listened to the chirps of crickets buried in winter-eaten tree trunks and self-assured frogs who no longer had a reason to fear a hooded chemist's apprentice ruining their night. The lullabies of my youth.

Soon, my act became reality, and I slipped into the best sleep I'd had in weeks.

I roused to the sound of hushed voices.

"There is no point telling her." Still mired in the fog of sleep, I grimaced at the unwelcome intrusion of Efra's voice. "We don't have the time or the ability to do anything about it."

"What do you think she will do if she finds out we knew and withheld it from her?" Namsa hissed. I opened my eyes without moving a limb, mapping the sound of their voices. The fire had burned down to crackling embers and ash. Medhat and Kenzie slept curled near each other, hands and knees almost touching.

I raised myself onto my elbows and quietly crawled away from the campsite.

"Namsa is right." Maia. They were on the other side of the perimeter, where the edge of the woods flattened into the desert. "It is bad enough we didn't tell her in the mountain."

A mournful sigh that could only belong to Lateef. "We didn't tell her because it's entirely too dangerous. You know what she will do."

"What will I do, Lateef?" I stepped around the trees, enjoying the fissure of shock traveling through their secret circle. "Enlighten me."

Perhaps sensing the aggression skating beneath my skin, Namsa pushed forward, her tunic stretching tight around her defined arms as she elbowed the men aside.

"Mawlati—"

"You're making a mistake," Efra sighed.

"*Mawlati,*" Namsa persisted, louder. "When the informant came to us in the Gibal, she told us of the Omal Heir's raids upon the lower villages. In the last two weeks, Felix's soldiers have destroyed Gahre and Alyub as retaliation for the uprisings in the lower villages."

"Yes, I know," I said impatiently.

"We believe the Omalian offensive is targeting Mahair next."

The world halted, teetering on the brink of a great fall.

Lateef twisted his hands together. "Mawlati, you must understand our position. We can't allow you to put yourself in harm's way for a battle that doesn't pertain to us." A distressed palm swiped over the crown of his bald head. "This is not the first time the Omal throne has suppressed dissent with violence."

"*Allow* me?" Rage vibrated between each letter like the chords of an oud. My magic responded, surging with an eagerness I would have found daunting in any other circumstance. I barely recognized the ragged sound of my voice. Sefa and Marek might be in Mahair. Fairel, Rory, Raya. The girls in the keep. "Am I here by force, then? Has this been an elaborate trap from the start?"

"Essiya—" Maia reached for me. I smacked her hand aside. If she touched me, I would incinerate her where she stood.

"Malika Essiya," I snarled. I rounded on them, the pressure of my magic turning painful. "If there was a grain of worth to that title, you wouldn't have hidden this from me. I am not some tool you can pick up and point when it suits you. You can take whatever you want from me, but not this. Not them. What I want *matters*." To my horror, there was a sob caught in my throat.

"Of course it does!" Maia appeared on the brink of tears.

"Mahair is mine. It's mine, Felix knows it's mine—" I put a white-knuckled fist to my breastbone. Dread trailed icy fingers over my insides. "This is his revenge. Arin stopped him from killing me time and time again, and now he plans to claim the blood he feels owed from Mahair."

"Be that as it may, we cannot lose this opportunity to reach Queen Hanan. We are running out of time, Essiya. If we fail, we will have no recourse but to raise the fortress during Nuzret Kamel." The sympathy in Lateef's gaze, as though his truth was absolute and beyond reproach, infuriated me nearly more than his pitying tone.

"There is no 'we.'" I stormed to the campsite, ripping my coat from the branch I had hung it on to dry. "How long until the Omalian soldiers reach the village?"

"We didn't think you would care," Efra said, and I went still. "You have not established a reputation for being someone who runs *toward* a fight."

Gold and silver flooded my eyes. The restraint it took not to impale Efra against the highest branch of a tree was more than I thought myself capable of. The gold vein on my palm glowed, reminding me what would happen if I used my magic.

What I might see.

"Get out of my sight," Lateef snapped, shoving Efra away from the campsite. "Go collect our bags while you ruminate over the hardships of being an imbecile."

Medhat stirred, propping himself up on an elbow. "What's happening?"

I shoved my arms through the coat and collected my boots. "Apparently, the lot of you have no qualms asking me to beg for an army from the woman who rejected me and my mother, sent her soldiers to destroy Jasad, and lives in permanent supplication to her useless nephew. If she rejects me again, why, the only other reasonable option is that I should cast an enchantment to raise the fortress that, if I am lucky, will burn me alive before I have finished the first recital!"

Namsa, who had heard this from me already, glanced away. The rest of the Urabi blanched, and their surprise felt like its own insult. "You are worse actors than you are liars. Every one of you knows what will happen if I raise the fortress on Nuzret Kamel. You knew what asking me to raise the fortress meant. You have no trouble asking me to die. No trouble demanding my magic and my mind. Yet if I asked you to fight on my behalf—"

"Ask us." Namsa shoved between the throng, shoulders squared and chin raised. "Ask us, Essiya."

My chest heaved with the effort of barring my magic. I searched her for signs of duplicity. Namsa was my weak spot; Dawoud's niece had managed to sell me on the quality of her character, and now I had to work twice as hard to think ill of her.

Behind me, Kenzie and Medhat had risen, glancing at each other in mutual bewilderment. Efra sighed, clearly opposed to Namsa but resigned to her course of action.

I pushed out the question before it could curdle on my tongue. "I am going to Mahair. Will you come and fight with me?"

Namsa smiled, revealing three of her chipped teeth. "Even better." She reached for my arm, and I held still this time. She squeezed my elbow once. "We will come and win for you."

As soon as the decision settled, the campsite was cleared and our belongings gathered. Medhat and Kenzie crouched around a map of Hirun, with Medhat pointing out where our original path would need to divert into Mahair.

Lateef appeared beside me, clad in a heavy beige overcoat that would probably drown him in seconds if he fell off his crocodile.

We stared at the others in silence.

"His route to Orban is not far," Lateef said. The wind picked up, and he folded his hands under his armpits. "He will have heard about Mahair. He will come for you."

The veins pulsed.

"Yes."

"If he captures you, we are lost."

I smiled. "He won't."

Let Arin bring his strongest men. His best maps.

Let him come, and I would show him what it meant to hunt Essam's favorite monster.

CHAPTER TWENTY-NINE

SYLVIA

I traced the faded words chiseled into the wall partitioning Mahair from Essam Woods.

May we lead the lives our ancestors were denied.

I was home.

Or at least, an impression of it.

At high noon, the streets should have bustled with activity. The ruckus of market preparations should have echoed all the way down to the raven-marked trees.

I glanced around, dread mounting the deeper we ventured into the empty village. Shutters had been drawn shut. The metal hooks outside the butcher's shop swung in the breeze. I studied the ground beneath them. The dirt was still wet with the blood of whatever animal Nader had had strung up.

"Where is everyone?" Medhat whispered loudly. Kenzie slapped her hand over his mouth and shot me an apologetic glance.

I didn't like this.

Even Rory's apothecary had been bolted shut, the bell hanging limply from its wire above the door. Empty seed shells littered the stoop, and I fought the swell of nostalgia threatening to overtake me.

"Maybe the Omalian soldiers already came?" Kenzie asked.

The stab of fear was an instinctual reaction, but I didn't allow it to pierce anything vital. I leveled a stern glance at Kenzie, reassessing her. A village pillaged by soldiers would not lie quiet and abandoned. It would be torn apart between the two opposing forces; homes broken, carriages stolen, horses slain. Bodies and blood, at the very least. Violence screamed in a million different voices—even its silence was loud.

I shook my head at Kenzie, once. I made a note to keep an eye on her during the fight.

"There are people nearby," Efra said suddenly. Gold and silver churned in his eyes. "I can feel them. They're nervous, unsure. Angry."

A comforting combination. I scanned the dormant buildings ahead. We were in the center of the main square, and I had yet to spot any sign of life. Even the stray animals permanently wandering Mahair seemed to have vanished. "Where?"

Efra turned in a slow circle, head cocked. "Nearby."

Dust floated over Medhat. He sneezed, the sound jarring in the stillness. "Omal is much dustier than I expected," he grumbled. "It can't be good for my skin."

I wasn't listening. My gaze had flown up, following the source of the unsettled dust, and landed on a hooded figure crouching awkwardly on the edge of a rooftop.

Notched into a bow and trained directly on us, an arrow quivered, recentered, and flew.

Directly at Medhat.

As haphazard and fractious as my magic could be, it had yet to fail me when I needed it on someone else's behalf. Magic rolled through me, and the arrow buried itself in the ground by my feet instead of Medhat's chest.

The figure turned, as if to run, and their hood shifted. I caught a glimpse of upturned braids and a familiar chin.

I stopped breathing.

"Fairel?"

She paused. Pulled her hood from her face and squinted down. "Sylvia?" she shrieked.

Fairel whirled around on the edge of the roof, sending alarm shooting straight to my head.

"It's Sylvia!" she hollered.

Efra groaned, tips of his fingers pinching into his head. "People are coming. Many. They are... excited."

The shutters over the halawany's shop trembled as they were rolled up and the rope knotted around a catch. Faces pressed against the glass.

They came in sweeps. Raya, Yuli, Odette, Rory, Daleel, Zeinab, even Zeinab's contrary mother. Floods of Mahair's citizens. I glanced behind them, but no one else appeared. Where were Sefa and Marek?

"It takes Fairel a little longer to move," Raya said, misinterpreting my frown. Heavy hands landed on my shoulders. Streaks of white shot through her light brown hair, loose around her stooped shoulders. Lines pressed indents around her tired brown eyes, adding years beyond her fifty.

It occurred to me that they must have heard the news about the Victor's Ball. I had just used magic right in front of them. These people had been the closest approximation to family I had had for five years, and I had lied to them for every one of those years.

Yet Raya assessed me with the same keen maternal concern that had chafed my nerves so much when I lived under her roof. To see it now brought a lump to my throat.

She flicked my temple. "You had magic at your disposal and still couldn't manage to wash your own dishes?"

A startled laugh spilled past my lips. "I wash my dishes!"

"She hasn't touched a single one," Namsa said from behind me. I scowled.

Fondness softened the lines in Raya's forehead. She pinched my cheek. "Always such a shameless little liar."

A cane appeared out of nowhere, prodding Raya in the side. She smacked it away with a glare. "Stop shepherding us, chemist. We aren't goats."

"Goats would have better survival sense," Rory growled. "Why are we standing here in the open? Should we lie down and make ourselves easier targets for the soldiers? Get inside!"

The sun might fall, the earth could sink, and the moon might dim, but never would Rory know a good mood a day in his life.

Laughter bubbled in my chest. "Stop ordering everyone around, old man. They aren't your apprentices."

"As if I had an apprentice capable of following my orders." He raked a critical gaze over me. "Life as the most wanted fugitive in four kingdoms suits you."

Awaleen below, but I had missed the cantankerous mule. I took his hand, surprising us both. He recovered quickly, squeezing my fingers with a small smile. "I have missed you, Essiya."

"Essiya?" Raya repeated. Her brows furrowed, likely struggling to place the name. It rippled through the crowd, growing louder. "Baira's blessed hair, the rumors are true."

The second Heir of Jasad. Niphran's daughter.

Rory drew me close, out of earshot of the others. "I need to speak to you." Urgent, tinged with worry.

Before I could respond, a hostile voice sliced through the din.

"Why are you here?"

With a cane tucked under her right arm and a bow hanging from the left, Fairel glowered at me.

In the four or so months since I had last seen my favorite of Raya's wards, she had shot up to Maia's height. Her twin braids lay docilely over her shoulders, the long strands much more amenable to braids than her short hair had been.

I remembered a pout, a petulant kick to the ground. *Twelve is big, you know.*

"Fay. You've grown." The admission stung. I had never particularly cared when one of the wards left the keep or marveled at their transition into womanhood like Raya and Sefa had. Youth held nominal value to me. What was there to celebrate about entering a new era of pain, of starting to learn yourself and hating what you found? Seeing the choices before you clearer than ever and realizing you had no real choice at all?

But then, it had been at fifteen that I chose to survive and slit Hanim's throat. Twenty that I broke a Nizahl soldier's neck and snapped his spine.

Twenty-one that I came to Mahair knowing what it might cost.

I looked at Fairel's flat braids, the new length in her limbs, and in each change, I saw a universe of different futures.

"You haven't grown at all," Fairel said. She held herself with an uncharacteristic aloofness, staring at a point somewhere behind my shoulder. Had it not been for the tiny quiver in her bottom lip, I might have believed she wanted to notch a new arrow at my head.

"It looks like I might need to start," I remarked lightly. "Especially if you plan to be taller than me. It would be terrible for my reputation."

Her mouth twitched. "Sylvia, your reputation couldn't be worse if you tried."

"Is that a challenge?"

She swung her cane at me, hitting my knee. Kenzie gasped, but I only had eyes for Fairel.

She sniffed, and her voice turned heartbreakingly small. "Are you leaving again?"

I bent down, waiting until Fairel met my gaze and registered the truth in it. "I'm not going anywhere until you're safe."

The stubborn set of Fairel's chin finally eased, and I grabbed the back of her neck and pulled her into my arms when she began to cry. She shuddered and clung to my waist, the cane and bow dropping to the ground. I didn't pay attention to Lateef quietly collecting them.

When she had calmed, Fairel drew away, dragging her sleeve across her nose. "I replanted your fig seeds. I knew you would come back."

Despite a new assortment of arrows and murderous intentions, Fairel still shined with an optimism I almost envied. I had thought she would outgrow it. With someone like Fairel, maybe hope would need to be taken from her by force.

I would break every bone in the hand that tried.

I glanced at the seemingly abandoned village and understood the last-ditch effort a desperate Mahair had concocted to protect itself from the wrath of its own ruler.

Play dead, let the predator prod at the corpse to its satisfaction. Pray it doesn't see you breathe.

"Save your tears for tomorrow, Fairel." I took her bow and cane from Lateef and passed them back to her. "Today, let me teach you how to make your enemies weep."

The main road teemed with activity. They had accepted my orders with a surprising lack of protest. I supposed the plan to hide hadn't sat too well with Mahair, especially after everything Felix had inflicted on them over the years.

The Jasadis worked side by side with the Omalians; Namsa beside Raya, Kenzie next to Zeinab, a rambling Medhat by a laughing Fairel. Efra hadn't stopped rubbing his temples and wincing since the rest of the village had emerged. The onslaught of new people and their accompanying emotions must be wreaking havoc on him. I celebrated each time he flinched.

My plan was simple. Mahair might lack the advantages of a more war-ready village, but we were not without our strengths. Thanks to the wall surrounding Mahair, the village was already fortified against entry from Essam.

If the soldiers came from the west, we would be in more trouble.

I was observing Maia struggle to empty a sack of sand and wondering if she had used her magic for anything other than knocking me unconscious on the cliffside when the end of Rory's cane prodded my hip. "Stop dawdling and come with me," he ordered. "I told you we needed to speak."

I rolled my eyes and followed Rory to his apothecary. He stepped under the awning and surveyed our surroundings. When he was assured we were alone, he slammed his cane into the pane of his shop's window.

The wood cracked, and Rory hit it again. "What are you *doing*?" I exclaimed. The chemicals must have finally cooked his head.

Rory reached into the hole and withdrew a package coated in dust and specks of hardened clay.

Sweat glistened on the chemist's forehead. "I found this while we were preparing to evacuate. If I had known I still had it—if I had even suspected—" Rory cut himself off and thrust the package toward me. "Here."

I evaluated Rory as I tore the wrapping. What if he was legitimately ill? He distrusted healers—an irony that flew straight over his head—and I wagered he would rather dwindle into death than allow those "ham-fisted crooks" to treat him.

The wrapping finally fell away. "A book?" Leather-bound and thick, it had the semblance of a journal kept by a politician obsessed with the sound of their own opinions or a poet with more whimsy than talent.

I had read through plenty of the first under Hanim's tutelage.

"It may be an unfamiliar concept to you, but you do this remarkable trick with books where you *open them*."

I snorted. He was in perfect health. I would probably die before he did.

I flipped the cover. The script was slanted, written with a balanced hand.

After many years of research and reflection, I have found only one absolute truth to share: time is the enemy of knowledge.

A poet, then. Great. I paused to raise a brow at Rory. "I think we should discuss reading preferences."

Rory beseeched the skies for patience.

It is important to understand that when I undertook the study of magic, my interest was of a purely scholarly nature. I had little inclination toward its political relevance, nor was I in possession of any overruling opinion as to the merit of its existence. All I wanted was to learn.

But the pursuit of knowledge never takes the straight path, and I could not have predicted what waited around the bend.

Reader, I urge you to read these records thoroughly and with an open mind. Discard your preconceived notions. Fight your instincts to deny a narrative that does not suit the world you know.

For the truly enlightened among us are those who understand that the realities we build were already built for us.

I dropped the book with a strangled gasp. It landed at my feet, still open to the same page. The same sentence. The *impossible* sentence.

Shivers raced up and down my arms, connecting at the peak of my stiff spine.

Those words were nearly identical to the ones I had said to Arin in the training tunnels. They were too specific, too exact.

Pressure built behind my temples. Whose mouth had I stolen these words from? What memory had I suppressed this time?

I crouched in front of the book and tried to focus my burning gaze on the page.

At the bottom, in tiny script, was the author's name.

Emre Faluk, Heir of Omal.

My father.

I lifted my head. I looked at Rory as if seeing him for the first time.

"You never answered me," I whispered. "When I asked you how you recognized me. You didn't say."

"I wanted to find the right time. A fool's excuse, I know. The time is always right, and it is the rest of us who are wrong." The sigh Rory released shrank him in half, seeming to rattle his very bones. "The name I held before Mahair was Rusheed Osman. Royal healer and personal physician of the Faluk family."

My head spun. Physician to the Omal royal family? *Rory?*

I wiped my features clean. He could be lying. I had no way to verify the account. "You knew my father?"

"Knew him?" Rory stared off at a point beyond my shoulder, the scar of an old grief bleeding behind his eyes. "I held your father the day he was born, and I held him the day he died. I loved that boy." A choked laugh. "He was permanently confined to his books, determined to chase the most obscure and pointless pieces of knowledge the world had to offer. His father despaired of him, but his mother doted on him. Queen Hanan was happy if Emre was happy, and it did not take much to make your father happy."

I was afraid to breathe and miss a word. If he was lying—if Rory was leading me by my nose on some merry tale—

My grandparents had never spoken of my father. Neither had Niphran, beyond an incoherent sentence or two during her fits. Emre was a mystery I had made peace with leaving unsolved, and the entire time... the entire time, Rory had known him better than anyone.

"When he fell in love with your mother, he became like a man possessed. He would have laid down his life to please her. But your mother wasn't like him. She *was* a warrior, an Heir, slotted to be the future Qayida. Emre could offer her little in the world of warfare and combat, and he had no magic. So he threw himself into the one way he might support your mother: a study of magic. How it might be strengthened, manipulated, transformed. I don't know if he wanted to find a way to draw magic into himself or merely to enhance Niphran's."

I exhaled slowly to conceal my dawning comprehension. Emre was not merely researching magic; if he had wanted to aid my mother, he would have been researching magic mining.

Niphran could roar astride the biggest horse in the kingdom, swing a sword three times her size, and kill someone without dislodging a strand of hair from the neat bun at the nape of her neck. She was more likely to use a book as firewood than to crack one open. Emre would have had to know pretentious drivel about magical history and long-forgotten artifacts would not earn her respect.

But a solution to her parents' profane practices? A way to rectify the harm they had done and prevent its repetition?

"When he learned she was pregnant with you, everything changed," Rory continued, unaware of my racing thoughts. "Niphran could feel your power, and it terrified her beyond measure. Emre applied what he had learned about magic to try to understand yours, but it defied reason. Your parents were planning to take you and flee Jasad as soon as you were born."

"But my grandparents killed him," I said tonelessly. This part of the story never changed. "And Niphran went mad." Rory didn't need to know Niphran's madness had been a result of Hanim and Soraya's yearslong poisoning. The spindle of this tale kept turning, and the threads were already too tangled.

Rory nodded. "I retired from my post after the Omal Heir's death and came here. But I still cared about Queen Hanan, and long journeys took a toll on her health. Before the Blood Summit, I would join her on those trips. Several of which were to Usr Jasad, where I had the dubious pleasure of watching a peculiar little girl climbing trees in the courtyard and sending the palace staff into hysterics." Rory cocked his head. "Ten years later, she wound up at my door, covered in blood."

I clutched the journal to my chest. I knew this history—had vividly and brutally lived it—but hearing it alongside the truth of Rory's identity shook me. Of all the places I could have gone, all the doors I could have darkened, why Rory's? It couldn't have been a coincidence.

After I killed Hanim, I had barely been alive myself. I had walked without seeing, focused solely on putting one foot in front of the other. I could have wound up anywhere. Mahair hadn't been the closest village, not by several miles.

I thought of the Sareekh. My magic had destroyed the protective bubble because it knew my best chance of survival was on the other side. Could it have led me to Rory? Had it wielded some control even behind the cuffs and guided me to the only person capable of keeping me safe?

My heart plummeted into my stomach. The appearances to Arin—they always happened near the peak of my panic. My magic had been whisking me away to the one person who could pull me back from the edge.

Terror raced through me.

You speak as though your magic has a will of its own.

I tightened my grip on the journal. "Thank you for this," I said. I didn't own anything belonging to my parents. I escaped the Blood Summit with the clothes on my back, and the war had scorched the rest to the ground. "Rusheed."

"My pleasure, Essiya." He tapped the top of the book. "He would be proud of you, you know. You're like him. Passionate. Committed. Reckless for the people you love."

I crooked a sardonic smile at the chemist. Such sweet nonsense. "We both know Emre would be horrified by me. He was a bookish royal incapable of so much as swatting a fly. He would have expected a daughter who read poetry in a garden and played with frogs instead of serving them to you in buckets." I traced the edge of the journal with dirt-crusted fingers. "I am his blood, but I am no one's daughter."

CHAPTER THIRTY

SYLVIA

Raya emptied two rooms for the Urabi, settling in her guests with an overwhelming show of hospitality. The warm welcome had clearly unnerved Efra, and he kept eyeing Raya like she might fold his body into the furnace if he relaxed a single muscle.

I found Lateef in my old room, reading in the chair by the corner. Since I wasn't a guest, Raya had graciously tossed me into a room with four other girls, so I would be sleeping on the rug in front of the hearth tonight.

"Essiya," Lateef said, surprised. He closed the book, setting it on his lap. "Are the preparations finished?"

"Mostly." I scuffed the toe of my slipper against the carpet. "Medhat and Namsa went out to finish the rest."

"Good, good. The Omalian soldiers will have a real fight waiting for them."

When I continued to linger in the doorway, Lateef gestured at the journal hanging by my side. "Is it yours?"

"My father's." I lifted a shoulder. "I was wondering if I could read it in here. I wouldn't be a bother. It's just, the girls keep asking me questions, and I need a moment of silence."

"Of course. I am hurt you felt the need to ask." Easy as that, Lateef picked up his book and resumed reading.

I took my spot at the head of the bed as though I had never left.

I propped my back against the wall, knees against my chest and my feet tucked under the covers.

Time to see what my father had to say.

Frankly, it was a miracle my grandparents hadn't tried to kill Emre sooner.

So far, my father's journal consisted of countless pages of poetic nonsense about the magic in my mother's eyes, the gnats over Hirun on warm summer nights, the mist on Sirauk. If he had meant to speak in some sort of riddle, it was lost on me. Fiddling with the shape and structure of words to unlock a deeper meaning had never been my strong suit. I could lie my way through a den of thieves and gut a beast three times my size, but ask me to sit around and poke at lines on a page? I would rather fashion myself a necklace out of live leeches.

Namsa had joined me and Lateef three pages ago, dropping onto the other side of the bed and closing her eyes. "I'm waiting for Kenzie and Medhat to fall asleep," she'd said. "If I have to listen to them pretend to bicker for another hour, I'll rip both their tongues out."

Lateef muttered something about a lack of emotional intelligence while Namsa buried her face in the pillow.

I flipped Emre's journal to the back cover and opened to the last page. It was always easier to understand a story when you knew how it would end.

Sentences clustered together, squeezed tight onto the page. He must have realized he was running out of space to record a worthwhile thought after wasting so much ink simpering. I skimmed, one leg swinging idly off the side of the bed as I read.

In the center of the page, the sight of my name stopped me cold.

Essiya isn't safe. Niphran, Dawoud, Rusheed, please. If I am killed, whoever finds this journal must send my daughter out of Usr Jasad before it is too late.

Jasadi magic is running out. In two generations or less, it will vanish. Like the rest of the kingdoms, they will still carry the ability to wield magic, but the source will be gone. Palia and Niyar know it, and they are draining the southern wilayahs with impunity to fortify themselves against the inevitable future. It is not just about strengthening the nobles or trading their stolen magic with the other kingdoms.

When magic fades from Jasad forever, what happens to the fortress?

Palia and Niyar do not believe me. I told them what the Nizahl Heir truly is. I begged them to listen, but they will not cross Rawain. The boy is not a threat to them now, not while the fortress still stands. If they drain enough magic to protect the fortress for the coming generations, the Nizahl Heir will eventually die, and the fortress can fall without the horror of what waits behind it. In a sense, it is comforting to know their brutality toward the southern wilayahs is not mere greed. They do want to protect their kingdom—even if it is at the expense of its people.

The boy cannot be saved. What has been done to him cannot be undone by any mortal means. Killing him is the only choice left.

Rawain created the ultimate weapon against magic. They are fools to think he will not use the child against us. The only question is when.

I leaned back. He'd crammed all of that on the *last page*?

My thumbnail scraped the cramped lines of ink while my mind raced. So Palia and Niyar weren't just draining the southern wilayahs' magic to enrich the northern wilayahs' nobles. A threat on the other side of the fortress scared them so much that they hoarded the magic they mined to ensure the fortress would withstand the weakening of our magic.

A threat so terrifying to my gentle, bookish father that he demanded they kill it—kill a six-year-old Arin.

What had he told my grandparents that they ignored? It had to have been about Arin's ability to drain magic. But Arin's ability was limited by touch, and nobody whose magic he drained wound up dead. Compared to magic mining, what danger could some inopportune side effect of a musrira's curse pose to the Jasad throne?

I chewed my lip, a headache whispering at the back of my skull. I flipped through the rest of the journal, but if it wasn't agonizingly sappy poetry, it was a page full of numbers and mathematical figures completely unrelated to the passage before it.

Damn it to the tombs, why couldn't anyone in this land speak in a straight line? I couldn't just receive terrible news, no, I had to spend hours deciphering it first.

At my wit's end, I stormed over to Lateef and held out Emre's journal, opened to the last page. "Read this."

Without missing a beat, Namsa rolled off the bed and moved to read over Lateef's shoulder. The curiosity must have been killing her.

"I don't understand. The Nizahl Heir would have been six at the time of this writing, possibly even younger," Namsa said, a harshness to her voice I hadn't heard in weeks. She swiped angrily at the corner of her eye, and a pang of guilt shot through me. Of course reading about my grandparents draining the southern wilayahs would hit her harder. Nearly every member of the Urabi had come from the wilayahs Palia and Niyar treated like their personal treasury. "What was your father so afraid of?"

"It's true, isn't it?" Lateef closed the journal, hurriedly passing it back to me as though it were contaminated. "About the Commander's ability to drain magic with a touch. We had heard rumors, but I thought... Even after I saw it with Al Anqa'a, some part of me still didn't believe it."

"It shouldn't be possible," Namsa murmured. "The only person capable of sensing magic so acutely, of draining it, was Fareed."

"Fareed, the founder of Nizahl?" My brows tried to disappear into my hairline. Fareed had lived in the time of the Awaleen.

"Yes, but he could only drain and sense magic because Dania, Baira, and Kapastra needed him to safeguard against abuses of magic between the kingdoms. How would an Heir hundreds of generations later have the same ability?"

"A musrira tried to kill him. He said it was the side effect of her failed curse," I said, dumbfounded.

Namsa and Lateef glanced at each other. "It is... possible," Lateef said.

"Be honest." Namsa elbowed him. "Mawlati, the amount of power a musrira would need to not only infiltrate the Citadel but to then craft a curse so deadly that it imbues the Nizahl Heir with a lifelong side effect... if such a musrira existed, she would not have failed. He would have died."

A shiver traveled down my spine. "I don't understand. Are you saying Arin's abilities and magic mining are connected?"

Lateef had clearly missed his evenings regaling the children with his long and winding stories, because he eagerly grabbed hold of the question. "To understand the difference, you must first understand the basic composition of our biology. All of us—Lukubis, Orbanians, Omalians, Jasadis, most Nizahlans—we were born with a pool of magic built into us. A well, you could say."

I cracked a smile. I wondered how Lateef would feel if he knew he shared metaphors with the Nizahl Heir.

The leader of the Urabi gestured animatedly as he spoke. "We, the individual, contain a lifetime's supply of magic in our blood, but the well produces a limited amount of it at a time. How fast the well replenishes depends entirely on the individual. For example, Namsa's magic is unique; right now, she could emit a sound capable of bleeding the ears of everyone within a mile of us. The amount of power it takes for her to do so would likely drain about half the well, and it might take her a day to recover. If she pushed her radius out to two miles, she would drain the well entirely and need two days to recover. I have generalized magic, and given my age, my magic takes twice as long to recover when my well runs low. Every single one of us possesses this well—this space where magic could be carried inside you—including the kingdoms whose wells have run dry over the centuries."

I crossed my arms over my chest. "I am aware of the basic anatomy of our magic. My question is how magic *moves*. If it can be drained, can it be transferred?"

"Transferring magic from person to person is impossible," Namsa said.

"Engage in some intellectual exercise, Namsa," Lateef chided. "Transferring magic is distinct from draining or magic mining, you see. Magic came to this land through transference. When the Awaleen tried to give their progeny magic directly, it killed many—brutally. Their magic was too powerful for our bodies to contain on its own, so they carved a separate space for it."

"The wells," Namsa said.

"Precisely. The wells store our magic, and they have limits. Caps to how much magic we can expend and wield at any given time. Once the Awaleen gave us this function, their next step was to sow magic into their population's blood."

I dropped to the edge of the bed, tugging on the ends of my fingers in an old habit Soraya had tried to break. "Magic is carried in the blood, which is why it can be passed down from generation to generation. The well acts as a cap to prevent anyone from drawing too much magic from their blood at once. Transferring magic requires magic in the blood *and* the well to siphon the magic safely?"

Lateef grinned. "Yes. All of us have the well, but only Jasadis still have magic in their blood. As you can imagine, nobody is capable of infusing magic into someone's blood. If someone tried to transfer their magic into a dry well, they would risk killing themselves as well as their target."

Interesting, but not entirely related to my original question. "Why does magic mining kill its victims while Arin can drain them without any physical harm?"

"When you mine someone's magic, you don't just drain the well—you strip it out completely. Imagine this: You stand waist-deep in Hirun on the other side of a dam. Once the dam is torn away and the water bursts toward you, you must collect as much water as you can before you're swept away in the current. It's a craft, magic mining. The instant they strip out the wells—the spaces in our bodies meant to safeguard against magic ripping us apart—they have to drain as much of the magic as possible before the gush of magic annihilates the victim's body and kills them."

I remembered the glass bones of Soraya's father, the hollow cavern of his face and his mangled limbs. To think he had lived through even a *moment* of that process—had experienced the agony of his magic tearing free inside him just so someone could scoop handfuls before it completely killed him—

I ground my teeth together. My grandparents were dead. I couldn't do anything about their past actions except mitigate the harm they left behind.

"I think what the Heir does is different." Namsa spoke up. "What he drains is the reserve of magic. So when he touches someone, he is only draining what we have in our well at any given time. Right now, I am at full power—he could drain me down to nothing, and I would need two days to completely recover. When I recovered, he could drain it again. In a sense, magic mining tears out the base of our powers, whereas the Heir only siphons the output."

"You don't think a musrira could have given him this ability?" I checked.

The Urabi shook their heads in unison.

Unhelpful. If it wasn't a musrira or the Awaleen, what had brought about Arin's ability? In the vision I saw after Soraya stabbed me, Isra had clutched a black-haired baby while she begged Rawain to wait until he was older. Wait until he was older to do what? Rawain didn't have magic. Arin's talents were perfectly suited to Rawain's scheme against Jasad, but how could Rawain have caused it?

"I do think we are forgetting the most important question," Lateef said. He reached for the bridge of his nose, pushing up invisible spectacles. "Once the magic is drained, whether by mining or otherwise, where does it go?"

The question bloomed like a toxic cloud between us, staining our fingers when we reached out to touch it.

Where does the magic go?

"I don't know," I said honestly. Right now, Wes was following the Supreme to determine the answer to that question. "But it won't be long until we find out."

I sat on the floor watching the flames flicker in the hearth, my palm heavy over my heart, and wondered which kind of madness was worse.

Was it the erosion? The slow and steady pressure of a wave breaking against a boulder, both bound to the other by forces beyond their control. Feeling every scrape, every piece of you the tide carried away.

Perhaps it was the instant death. A mind lost with a single stroke, tearing it from its tether to reality. You wouldn't know you had gone mad, because you did not remember an existence before it.

I rubbed the vein on my palm. A tiny silver web snaked out from its center. It had appeared after I stopped the arrow aimed for Medhat, feathering out to the tip of my thumb.

"You frown any harder and you'll carve your chin right off," Raya said. I didn't turn as she settled on the carpet beside me, our backs propped against the armchair. "Odd, seeing you without Marek or Sefa. When the Nizahl Heir declared you Champion and took you from Mahair, I knew it was only a matter of time until those two followed. I swear on the mists of Sirauk itself, they were gone by supper."

I squeezed my eyes shut. They stung, reminding me of how long it had been since I last rested them in sleep. The darkness blanketed me, and in its confines I found my voice.

"You should go to sleep," I murmured. "The battle could be upon us at any minute."

"The same could be said for you."

"I don't need rest to fight capably, especially against some pathetic Omalian soldiers. I will do what needs to be done, no matter how fit I feel for it."

"Tombs below, that tongue of yours has only grown longer," Raya huffed. "You think you have the world figured out now because someone gave you a royal title and a shiny bit of jewelry? A crown can sit on an empty head just as easily as any other, girl."

I blinked, finally glancing at Raya. She arched her stubbed brows into a disapproving slant.

"I didn't even get the jewelry," I said. "You are speaking to the first ever crownless Queen."

We stared at each other for a long minute.

I laughed first, and then Raya was slinging her arm over my

shoulders and tucking me against her side. I curled against her, laughing so hard that it took me a while to realize I was also sobbing, and even longer to figure out I wasn't laughing at all.

Raya rocked me like I was one of the new orphans rescued to the keep, weeping uncontrollably at the memory of a life lost.

"I don't want to die."

The arm around me tightened. "You will not die, Sylvia."

"I am not Sylvia." I wanted to be. I wanted to be her so badly.

"Be Essiya with your Jasadis, be powerful and fearless for them. Tonight you are Sylvia, and you are home, and you are allowed to be afraid."

Raya didn't understand.

If Queen Hanan does not reinstate me as her Heir, I will have to raise the fortress.

If I raise the fortress, I will either burn alive or the magic will consume me. Should it be the latter, I will go mad, and every Jasadi who rallied behind me will be trapped behind the fortress with a mad Malika.

My magic has its own memory that I do not understand.

What if Arin was right about magic-madness?

"When I was seventeen, I begged my mother to let me marry the butcher's boy," Raya said suddenly. She stretched her slippers toward the hearth, and I lifted my head from her damp shoulder to peer up at her. As far as any of us knew, Raya had never taken a husband. "I had already made a name for myself as the best seamstress in our village, and I did not see the need to wait around for a wealthier suitor when I pocketed more coin than most of the men around me. I wanted to marry for love, and I loved Baheeg. He was...sweet, you understand, in a way boys as big and strong as him rarely are. He would talk about helping me open my own store, how I could work next door to him after he inherited the shop from his father. Finally, when it became clear to everyone in our village where my heart lay, my mother relented. She said I could marry Baheeg, but never to come crying to her if the ring on his finger changed him from a man to a beast."

Riveted, I watched the fire with her, as though the rest of the tale might manifest in the flames. "Did it?"

"I don't know. I never married him. A week before we were set to be joined as man and wife, I went to deliver a gown to one of my patrons and found her house empty. Clothes gone, furniture stripped, kitchen bare. The only thing left was a bundle on the carpet, shaking its tiny fists and bellowing red murder."

"She abandoned her baby?" Though I hadn't imagined every single girl in the keep had wound up here by having a set of dead parents, it still shocked me to think of someone willingly casting aside their child, let alone an infant.

Raya hummed. "Happened all the time, and not just in our parts. Pregnant girls come into a village, make up a tale about a dead husband, and stay long enough to dispose of the infant before they go back to wherever they came from. Sad state of it, really. Anyway, I took the child home—what else could I do? Leave it for the vagrants? Baheeg and my mother were furious, trying to force me to give her up to the Omalian patrol, but I refused. I liked the squalling, red-faced little thing. I would have a home and food to eat soon enough, why shouldn't I share it with this child? When it became clear I wouldn't be parted from her, Baheeg ended our engagement and told me to enjoy life as a spinster. No man would come near a woman 'loaded with the cast-off spawn of whores.'"

"I hope you told him you wouldn't spit on his face if he was on fire," I said emphatically.

"I didn't have your way with words." She chuckled. "That's the problem when you're young. Sometimes you mistake stupid for sweet."

"What happened to the baby?"

"Ah, she was the light of my life. I would wear dresses to the shop so I could bundle her on my lap while I worked. When she was three, I took her to her first Alcalah festival." Raya rubbed my arm absently. "The sickness came out of nowhere. One day she was writing out her letters on the kitchen table, and the next I was laying her to rest beside my mother."

My heart squeezed. "Oh, Raya—"

"It was a long time ago," Raya said. "I left our village and came to Mahair, and I opened the keep. I made raising you girls my life's work, and it is the best life I could have asked for. Could I have been happy with Baheeg and the life we imagined for ourselves? Maybe. Maybe. But I will never know. Life does not allow you opportunities to travel down every path, to see the outcome of every choice. You can spend your entire existence frozen in one spot, squinting into the future, or you can decide to move. Pick a path and never look back."

I wiped my dripping nose. "What if I know where every path leads?"

"Are you a prophet, girl?"

"No, but—"

"Then all you have are suspicions and worries, just like everyone else."

I huffed a laugh. Leave it to Raya to imply a possible descent into madness and a war capable of ripping apart the four remaining kingdoms were *boring*.

Eventually, as I absorbed the warmth from the hearth and Raya's steady presence, my breathing evened out. I slumped into her lap.

She stroked my curls, gathering them away from my face. When sleep finally caught me, I surrendered with ease.

CHAPTER THIRTY-ONE

SEFA

The staff had finally warmed to Sefa, and it was for one reason and one reason only: nobody else was willing to approach the Sultana during one of her moods.

Sometimes, it was a volley of insults and threats. Other days, she would hover over Sefa while she cleaned or mended a piece of clothing, as though Sefa was a fascinating spider she was wary of releasing from her sight.

But Sefa's favorite of Vaida's spontaneous moods was the adventurous one. "Get your coat and meet me by the carriage," she would snap to Sefa on more than one occasion. "I have business to attend to in the city."

Sefa had not forgotten about the Jasadi in Vaida's employ or the troublingly tall man in the hat. Every time they left the Ivory Palace, Sefa wondered if it would be the day Bausit reported that Kera had found the Mirayah. From what Sefa understood, the Jasadi was able to follow trails of magic—see its imprints in the air as Sefa might see footprints in the mud. The goal, Vaida had explained, was to follow the trails of magic to the Mirayah.

"The Mirayah is constantly moving," she'd sighed, lounging in bed with a bowl of cherries balanced on top of her breasts, studying a painting of her scheduled for a ceremonial framing later in the week. "Magic does not function normally in the Mirayah. When someone disappears into it, their magic's trail cuts off. Kera follows those lines to see where they disappear, but they have usually gone stale by the time he reaches the other end."

The conversation had ended when Vaida abruptly threw the bowl of cherries at the painting, splattering her image in crimson.

Sefa still didn't understand *why* Vaida wanted to find the Mirayah. What could a realm of lawless magic offer the Sultana of Lukub? What was in the Mirayah that could convince Vaida she would win a war against Nizahl?

Whatever the answer, Sefa was almost positive it involved the ring. However many secrets Sefa had uncovered, Vaida still had a vault of them locked away.

It wasn't all bad. Sefa rather liked exploring Lukub in the carriage of its ruler.

Not the bowing everywhere she and Vaida went—she never knew where to look when people prostrated themselves to the woman walking ahead of her. But the buildings they visited, resplendent with painted mirrors cloaked in gold veils, walls covered in elaborate and colorful tapestries, tables bursting with delicacies and food Sefa would have sworn had passed harvest seasons ago. Even the people they met—eccentric, fabulously dressed, and polished to a lethal point—left an impression on Sefa.

Each time, Vaida introduced Sefa as her personal attendant. Sefa thought it was strange, forcing so many of her council members and nobility to acknowledge someone leagues beneath their station.

Not a day had gone by without longing stirring at the base of every new experience Sefa collected. Sefa missed evenings in Sylvia's room, sighing as Marek singed his fingers picking around the coals for the seeds he'd tried to roast. She missed the smell of the keep— a swirl of tea and bergamot that had become more familiar than her own scent. Sefa missed knowing that if she was struck dead, someone would care. Vaida would probably step over her body and then run it down with her carriage.

The carriage jerked, bumping Sefa into the window. Retaliation for her uncharitable thought, probably. Vaida had her moments of bizarre kindness. They were vastly outnumbered by her capricious and thoughtless ones, but still—Vaida could be sweet. During their last trip, she had stopped the carriage suddenly and ordered the driver to run into town and procure a pair of wool slippers. Slippers she had abruptly handed to Sefa without looking at her, remarking that she had tired of the sight of Sefa's feet poking through her cheap shoes.

The other most notable instance had taken place at the manor of Ashraf Abira, the former head of Lukub's council and a close friend of Vaida's mother. His giant mustache should have been a jarring contradiction to his sparklingly bald head, but he carried an air of wisdom Sefa implicitly trusted. Perhaps more men should be bald and mustached.

They had been in his gardens, and Vaida had momentarily stepped away with Ashraf to speak in low tones, leaving Sefa awkwardly standing by the fountain beside Ashraf's own attendant. A statue of Baira loomed behind them, rose-scented water pouring from her hands and splashing into the wide pool beneath her.

The attendant had inched closer to Sefa, either oblivious to her discomfort or choosing to ignore it, and leaned in to proposition her for a romp in the garden while they waited. She had been rigid with mortification as the attendant described in graphic detail what he would like to do to Sefa there, reluctant to move away and encourage him to follow, unable to remember how to lift her tongue to hiss vitriol at him.

Sefa still wasn't sure how Vaida had rounded the fountain and come up in the rear without either of them noticing. All Sefa recalled was wanting to sink into the earth, and then gasping as

Vaida grabbed a handful of the attendant's hair and shoved his face into the fountain. Despite her willowy frame, Vaida maintained an easy hold on the thrashing man, humming under her breath as he struggled. Water splashed, soaking Vaida's sleeves and the front of her dress.

Ashraf had returned and cast a curious glance at his drowning attendant. "Would you mind terribly if I relieved you of an attendant?" Vaida had asked.

After some thoughtful stroking of his mustache, Ashraf had nodded. "I'm afraid so. My mother is coming to visit next week."

Vaida had pouted and released the attendant. Coughing and spluttering, the soggy idiot dropped to the grass, crawling away from Vaida on his elbows.

Sefa and Vaida hadn't remarked on the incident until they were safely ensconced in the carriage. Sefa had tried to offer her thanks for the rescue only for Vaida to snap, "If anyone speaks to you like that again, you have my full permission to saw off their tongue with your dullest blade. Don't wait for me or someone else to step in on your behalf. Much as you seem to despise it, sometimes violence *is* the answer. Sometimes, it is the only way you can save yourself."

No one could call Vaida warm.

But Sefa would insist with her last breath that yes—the Sultana of Lukub could be kind.

CHAPTER THIRTY-TWO

SYLVIA

Death arrived at dawn, dressed in the blue and white of the Omalian flag.

The ground rumbled with the pounding of hundreds of horses. Light dispersed in front of the woods as a horde of Omalian soldiers rode toward the wall at full speed.

In the main road, the villagers had crowded together, their weapons pressed dangerously close to the backs of those in front of them.

Terror itself could not have found a more fitting homage to its name; from eldest man to youngest child, it ravaged the Omalians. They stood beneath the fading painting of the Awaleen, the siblings regarding the proceedings from the side of the building with their usual indifference. The older villagers pressed their hands to the painting of Kapastra, the Awala of Omal, for strength.

As if Kapastra would lift a single finger to help anyone in this village. I gave her my back.

"Do you think it will work?" Namsa murmured. I belatedly noticed the grip she had on my sleeve, the whiteness of her pinched lips. Namsa might have killed before, but I doubted she had seen serious combat. There was a reason Arin had been chasing them across the kingdoms for years: the Urabi were experts at avoiding capture, and their reliance on those survival skills had prevented them from cultivating others.

On my other side, Efra grimaced. Unlike the others, I had not given him any instructions on when to use his magic. I watched his hands tremble with the urge to ease the buildup of emotion pressing in on him from the Omalians.

I needed Efra's magic at full strength. I couldn't express that if what I feared came to pass, his power might be the only thing to save us.

As one, we held our breaths as the first riders raced through the gap in the wall. This was it. The fate of Mahair, hinging on a single minute.

Shouts rang out as soldiers tumbled from their horses. Hooves strained to free themselves from the netting hidden beneath mounds of mud at the wall's entrance. The snap of frenzied reins struck a chord of relief through us, music to our ears.

I shared a triumphant grin with Namsa. We had just enough time and netting to put a small bank of mud around the perimeter of the wall. I had reassured the village the mud would hide the netting, and felling the riders at the front would give us a precious advantage. I didn't need the surge to fall back.

I just needed them to slow.

As the fallen set of soldiers tried to push their horses from the net, the next dozen rode in at full speed and collided with the stuck soldiers. They flew from their saddles, taking one another down in the impact. Horses huffed, stomping on the underfoot men.

"Go over the wall!" shouted one of the soldiers. "One at a time!"

Horses began to leap over the wall, clearing it in a single bound. The village shook as they landed.

"Medhat, now!" I bellowed.

Medhat stepped away from the crowd. He touched the inside of his wrist to the other, the tips of his fingers kissing as flames gathered in the space between his palms.

The Omalians watched him, spellbound, while I watched them. A revived Jasad would not last long without allies. One day, we would need them, just as today they needed us.

Medhat crouched, cords of fire linking his separating hands and pulsing between them. He turned his palms outward and *hurled*.

Howls saturated the air as fire erupted at the top of the wall, racing along the perimeter. A horse screamed as it cleared the wall and found its underside scorched, landing on its knees and sending its rider pitching forward. The crack of his skull against the earth echoed over the burning soldiers' screams.

I lifted my sword and signaled Fairel, who had taken cover at the top of the building bearing the painting of the Awaleen. An arrow sliced the air, and a soldier staggering to his feet crumpled as it buried itself in his heart.

At the signal, motion finally burst in the crowd. They rushed at the soldiers, every weapon we'd scrounged lifted high, along with some pans and wicker carpet dusters.

"Medhat, can you hold it?" I asked. Rivulets of molten red flowed in the cracks of his hands. As long as Medhat prevented them from leaping over the wall, they could only enter through the front opening. At most, it fit five riders at a time. Without the benefit of their numbers, we could pick them off as they came.

He blew me a kiss. "Anything for you, Malika. I am but your humble subject."

"I'm telling Kenzie you said that."

"Wait, wait—"

Spear aloft, I bolted toward the fighting. The others had their instructions, and I had to hold faith they wouldn't choose such a precarious moment to defy me. Even Efra.

More soldiers poured through the opening, and swords collided in an ear-piercing howl of metal behind me.

Screams rang out from our side of the wall. My stomach

churned as I cut down a soldier running toward the keep. If I had miscalculated... if it would have been better for everyone to hide...

I couldn't think about it.

A soldier rode directly for me, his sword swinging toward my neck. I ducked, the tip of my dagger slicing through the ropes of his saddle. He pitched to the side as his own momentum betrayed him, and I dragged him the rest of the way to the ground and rammed my knife through his throat. I had left the axes and spears—anything with a longer range—to the less experienced among the villagers, which meant the deaths I delivered today would be nice and close.

I yanked the sword from the soldier's slack grip and stepped over him. Grabbing a handful of his horse's mane, I pulled myself onto its back. Rovial's tainted tomb, but I had missed riding astride an animal without scales.

Most of the fighting had concentrated close to the entrance. Mud churned beneath racing feet. Cries shot through the fighting, their origins lost in the crush of swords and horses. My heart thumped painfully, and I checked to ensure Fairel hadn't left her post on the building. She had wanted to join us on the ground, but I told her we needed someone to raise the alarm and shoot if the soldiers found the other entrance to Mahair, since they would come up behind us.

I steered the horse toward the fray and held tight to the reins with one hand as it galloped. Wind brushed my neck, frosted my lashes, but I felt none of the cold. I blocked blows with my stolen sword and sliced through the fools who came close. Exhilaration carried away my earthly worries, drowning them beneath the beat of my heart and my coursing blood.

No Emre, no Palia or Niyar, no twisted magic. Just the ache in my muscles, the soreness of my thighs gripping the horse's sliding flank, the tackiness of the blood soaking in my clothes.

My magic heated me from the inside, eager to join the fight, but I didn't need it. Not for this.

My sword clashed with the one swinging toward Lateef's head. I lunged forward, yanking the soldier from his horse onto mine and plunging the dagger strapped to my waist into his chest.

I threw the body to the ground as Raya called my name, but as I slashed and shouted warnings, I was Essiya and I was Sylvia. I was both and none, the perfect Heir and the brutal orphan, the living and the dead. I was two imperfect wholes melding into one.

Soaked in blood, brimming with magic, the severity of the disservice I had done myself dawned. How terribly I had minimized the enormity of all I contained. How much I had feared everything I could become.

You have the potential and power to be worse than any who have come before you.

I wasn't bound to be the person Soraya feared. Her fears would not be my fate. What if that potential and power meant I could be *better* than those who came before me?

A bloodcurdling scream rent the air, raising the hair on the back of my neck.

I turned the horse, knuckles white around the reins. Daleel and three other girls from the keep were lowering Raya to the ground as she gasped for air, clutching her chest. I leapt off my horse, casting my sword aside as I ran.

Why was she outside the keep? I had told her to stay put!

I hurled to my knees beside Raya, shoving aside the other girls. The seamstress's skin had taken on a grayish cast. White lines traced the ridges of her colorless lips, parted for her shallow breathing. Her eyes were half-lidded, flickering with movement.

"Is she going to die?" wailed one of the girls. I didn't know this one. She must have arrived recently.

"Get Rory," I ordered. "Go!"

A wide gash stretched over Raya's right shoulder, slanting over her collarbone and chest. Blood had soaked into her undershirt.

My body went cold. I had seen these kinds of injuries.

I knew what they meant.

"You can't die," I gasped. "Who will take in these girls if you die? Nobody else will tolerate them. Nobody else knows how to love difficult girls. They'll be vagrants. They will all become vagrants because you couldn't listen to me for *once* and just stay inside the keep!"

I was in Dar al Mansi, and Dawoud was dying in my arms.

A cane tapped my shoulder. "Move aside, child," Rory murmured. "Let me see."

Daleel helped lower Rory into a kneel beside Raya. He examined the wound, palpating the bloated edges. Two fingers went under her chin, finding her pulse.

For all the years I had known him, Rory's hands had always kept busy. Swinging his cane, shaking his fist, or assassinating the frogs I brought him for his potions and ointments. Even when he fell asleep over his table, his fingers would twitch toward an invisible target.

When he withdrew from Raya, his hands lying still in his lap, I shook my head before he could say a word. "No."

"Essiya—"

"No!" Who did he think he was speaking to? I could fix her—

—I couldn't save them—

I could make her whole.

—they did this—

When the magic swept through me this time, I welcomed it. I greeted an old friend with open arms.

I kneel in the mud, rain sluicing over my hair and shoulders. I failed. I failed. I failed.

The figures from the waterfall appeared beside me. We wouldn't let her die. We would save her. We would not lose her the way we lost Dawoud. They knelt in a circle around Raya, shoulders touching.

"Essiya," Rory repeated, low. "My child, magic cannot reverse death."

"She lives, chemist," we said. "Death has not laid its claim."

One hand closed around Raya's wound. The other, we pressed to the center of her chest. Together, we counted the beats.

One, two. She will live.

Three, four. She will be safe.

Five, six. She is ours.

Light bloomed in the center of Raya's chest. It built, a sun burning through its mortal skin. Gold waves lapped over one another as it grew, searing into the eyes of the girls crouched around Raya. They cried out, turning away, but my eyes held steady.

I pressed down against her chest, her heart trapped between her spine and the heel of my hand, and her wound began to bleed. Silver blood poured from Raya's chest and trickled onto the ground. Gallons and gallons of silver, pooling around us. Soaking our knees and swords.

Once given, it cannot be returned, the others whispered. Billows of gold unhinged like a ravenous mouth, unspooling out of Raya. *If you make her ours, we cannot take it back.*

I didn't want anything back. There was no Mahair without Raya. These girls would not become vagrants at my hand. Raya's story would not end today, not like this.

We pressed until a bone cracked in Raya's chest.

A drop of silver slithered back into Raya's wound. Then another, and another. Sliding into her skin, brightening her veins as we watched. The golden light flared in tides that could reach the ends of the world, rise as tall as the mountains on the edge of the sea.

We pressed our wrists together, the memory of silver cuffs trapping us never too far behind, and threw our arms open.

The face in the bucket of water smiles. Behind her, the mutilated bodies of the cats that wouldn't play sway from the branches of her favorite trees. The gold and silver in her eyes hold perfectly still, and she is too busy admiring them to notice the shadow stretching over the water, nor the shovel hurtling toward the back of her head.

As suddenly as they had flooded forth, the tides of gold receded, shrinking until they were a single glowing ember floating in the air.

Soft as a feather, it melted into the center of Raya's forehead.

I gasped as my magic waned. The figures disappeared around me, emptiness following in their wake. I wanted to cry at the loss.

"What did you do?" Rory whispered, and his fear finally drew me away from the aching nothingness. Rory had an arm out as though to shield the girls from me. They cowered behind him, and two thoughts collided as one.

Why would he think I would hurt them?

Does he think he could stop me? I can strip their bones dry in the same time it takes him to waste my name on his lips.

A shudder rolled over me. I scrambled off of Raya, startling my horse. Rory and I stared at each other, wide-eyed, and I opened my mouth.

Except, I didn't trust my voice. If I spoke, I wasn't sure who would shape the words.

Me, or *it*.

The answer would remain unknown to us both, because Raya groaned. I crawled toward her, hovering without touching. Terrified of what my hands would do if they reached for her.

"Raya?" I said, tentative. "Can you hear me?"

A guttural groan. "I wish I couldn't."

The girls embraced one another, knees weakening with relief as we gathered around our fallen guardian. Everyone except Rory. He watched Raya as though she might grow claws and swipe off his head.

"Her wound is gone," Daleel murmured in wonder. "Dania's bloody axe, Sylvia, you healed her."

"No cursing," Raya admonished.

When she opened silver- and gold-streaked eyes, something inside me relaxed.

Ours, it said.

To avoid spiraling, I did what I knew best—I threw myself into battle.

I twisted in my saddle and sliced into a soldier's spine just as he yanked his sword from a villager's chest. The soldier collapsed atop the villager he had slain, and I spared a second to hope someone would pull him off.

Raya and Rory were safe in the keep with the other girls. Rory had tried to speak to me, but the battle still raged. I couldn't hear what he had to say. I had no answers for him. No explanation for how Raya was not one of the many corpses strewn over Mahair.

Her eyes…

The back of my neck prickled. I froze as a soldier barreled toward me and earned a deep slice into my arm.

"Ihzary!" Namsa. Maia, maybe. I didn't know. I didn't care. The warning meant one thing.

I turned to the entrance.

Black-and-violet uniforms swarmed the edge of Mahair and formed even rows along the border. I counted forty-six Nizahl soldiers—far fewer than the Omalian force still battling inside Mahair, but ten times deadlier.

At the front, his arm thrust to the side to halt further forward movement, stood Arin.

The world narrowed, reshaping itself around the Nizahl Commander.

Unbelievably foolish, to lose touch with my surroundings when those surroundings contained soldiers valiantly attempting to run me through. Beyond stupid, to grip the reins of my horse so hard the leather cut into my palms. I couldn't convince my chest to unfreeze long enough to draw in air.

He found me.

Silver hair brushed his collar, longer than the last time I had seen him in the flesh. The end of his coat lifted in the wind, setting flight to the ravens embroidered on the hem. Every lace on his vest perfectly tied, every stitch of his black pants neatly trimmed.

No chaos dared lay a finger on Arin of Nizahl. The icy Heir, the untouchable Commander, as pristine on the battlefield as in a royal court.

But when I looked into his eyes, there was nothing cold about them. Arin stared at me as though inches separated us, as though the sea of fighting did not merit a second's attention. I felt scraped raw and exposed, more aware of myself than I had been in a long time.

My pulse pounded, the frantic thrum drowning out any competing sound. I needed to snap out of this. If he got ahold of me, it was all over. Queen Hanan, the fortress, Nuzret Kamel. Every option would be lost.

Even if Arin had begun to question his father and the truths he had grounded himself in his entire life, it wouldn't stop him from apprehending me while he searched for the answers.

Arin scanned the flames leaping over the wall, the mudslide, the soldiers hemmed into the front entrance. Piecing together my strategy.

When his gaze met mine again, it glinted with pride.

Someone grabbed my sleeve. I only just managed to slow down in time to avoid ripping Efra's arm from its socket.

"Do you know what you're doing?" he hissed. He looked ahead, fixing on Arin with an expression somewhere between bone-deep fright and burning hatred.

My barrel of patience had scraped bottom, but I summoned enough to clasp the hand he had over my arm and say, "He will not enter unless we pass the wall or use magic. Chasing us now would require killing the villagers or the soldiers in their way, and it would be viewed as a declaration of support from Nizahl to the Omal crown. Nizahl absolutely forbids involvement in nonmagical conflicts within and between kingdoms."

I glanced at Arin. He hadn't moved, but his eyes had ticked to the spot where my hand covered Efra's and gone curiously blank. "Arin would allow us to escape before he broke his kingdom's laws. Unless we give him an opening, we are safe."

An explosion behind us rattled through our bones, shaking the earth. Efra tackled me off the horse, using his body as a shield as flaming debris rained around us.

I shoved him off, swiping at the wood shavings burning through my clothes. "Damn it to the tombs," I swore. "Just once, I would like to be *wrong*."

More Omalian soldiers had arrived, entering in through the unprotected western borders of the village. They swarmed from the back of the main road, the flag of Omal hoisted at the fore. We were about to be penned in by Omalian soldiers on both sides.

"You need to use your magic if you want to save your precious village!" Efra snapped. "Otherwise, we need to evacuate the survivors and get away from here. We cannot risk your capture."

Do not ask me to use my magic, I wanted to plead. *You have no idea what it might cost.*

I couldn't ask them to leave. They wouldn't. They would stay and fight until their bodies stacked over one another.

"Listen!" Dirt crusted Efra's hair, muddying his clothes. "We can't defeat them all."

I knew Efra didn't care about Mahair. He saw this as an unfortunate Omalian conflict with no bearing on Jasad or magic.

But this was my home. Mahair and everyone in it were *mine*. A piece of me would always remain here, and I wouldn't let Felix take it.

"Not on our own." I raised my head, meeting Arin's unwavering gaze. I would need to run back to the keep and fetch the gloves I'd packed. "Tell me, how many people can your magic influence at the same time?"

CHAPTER THIRTY-THREE

ARIN

Lives were ending a handful of paces away from him. On the horizon, flames crackled over thatched rooftops. Gray smoke billowed into the placid sky. The acrid scent of burning straw smothered them.

These were events demanding Arin's full and undivided attention. He should be devising methods to circumvent the laws preventing him from marching into the mayhem and extracting the Jasad Queen. He should be attentive to any opening they would give him to cross the border into Omal.

But Arin couldn't seem to focus beyond the way the man had put his hand on her arm. How she had covered it with her own.

A girl no older than twenty screamed as a soldier on horseback grabbed a handful of her hair. He thrust his sword, and the sound cut off abruptly. Her body dropped, joining the rising number on the ground.

"Sire—" One of the third-years, Riddah, stepped forward, only to meet the resistance of Arin's arm.

"Hold," Arin ground out. He loathed standing and watching as much as they did. It was a massacre. Felix had sanctioned an execution of entire villages, extinguishing livelihoods and families in minutes. They had committed no crime. The only danger they posed was to Felix's image, which had already gone through the mud and back again. A massacre on this scale was purposeless cruelty, solely intended for massaging his ego and sending a message.

But Nizahl could not intervene. This line *could not* be crossed.

The longer Arin watched Sylvia, the harder it became to remember why.

Her sword sliced through a soldier's neck, severing it in one neat swing. She leaned back in her saddle, narrowly avoiding another soldier's sword. It pierced the empty air where her torso had been, and she grabbed the hilt, trapping the soldier's arm as she brought her sword onto it. He screamed as his hand fell into her lap, the hilt spasming from his orphaned fingers. She silenced his cries with his own weapon, shoving his sword through his chest and kicking him out of his saddle. Her braid swung from one shoulder to the other as she moved with ruthless efficiency to her next target.

Arin could watch her fight until weeds grew around his boots, and he had the sense he would never tire.

"Uh…"

The dumb sound from Riddah forced Arin's attention back to the village's entrance, where a row of Omalian soldiers had gone still as stone. Snarls rippled over their faces. Fingers clenched and unclenched around sword handles.

As one, they veered to where Arin and the Nizahl soldiers stood.

A current of magic vibrated in the air, pricking Arin's senses to high alert.

The Omalian soldiers kicked their horses into motion, swords aloft and pointed in their direction. Attacking Nizahl soldiers on neutral ground while they stood by, doing nothing?

A small smile touched the corners of Arin's lips.

Why… it tasted like political pandemonium. So delicious Arin wanted seconds.

"Hold!" Arin shouted. Laughter bubbled in his chest. Clever,

clever Suraira. "If they attack, you have my clearance to enter the village and drive out the Omalian soldiers. Do not throw your spears unless it is in close contact—if any of you kill a villager out of carelessness, I will leave your fate to their family."

The Omalian soldiers burst through the entrance and vaulted over the bodies half-buried in the mudslide. In seconds, they would be upon them. A ripple of anticipation flowed between his men.

Arin dropped his arm. "Now!"

His soldiers streamed around him, steel crashing into steel, horses rearing as their riders tumbled from their backs. Arin picked his way around the mess, tucking his hands into the pockets of his coat, and entered Mahair.

Another vibration of magic preceded a swarm of shrieks coming from the main road. Arin spared a glance at the people bent in half, hands pressed to their ears. The magic slammed into him and dispersed, as insubstantial as smoke barreling into a wall. An interesting tactic from one of the Jasadis.

Ash blanketed the sky, gray specks gently raining over the bodies of the fallen.

Where was she?

A sword slashed Arin's sleeve. He ducked the next swing and struck out, hauling the soldier attached to the arm off his horse and to the ground. The soldier struggled, but Arin held him fast. His hands framed the Omalian soldier's head and twisted. A hard crack, and the soldier's struggling body went still.

Arin tossed him aside and frowned at the tear in his sleeve.

By the time he had reached the middle of the main road, he had disposed of another four soldiers without catching sight of her.

"Kenzie!" The bone-chilling cry tore across the melee. A fair-haired man raced to the collapsing body of a woman. A red glow poured from his cupped hands, and Arin stopped short at the twin spheres of flame that shot through the air. They landed on an

Omalian soldier, enveloping him in fire. The horse reared, unseating its burning rider, and galloped in the opposite direction.

Three unique magics Arin had encountered in the last ten minutes alone. How many did the Urabi have among them?

He walked toward the crouched Jasadi, who sobbed as he tried to stem the blood pouring from the young woman's stomach. Arin didn't need to get much closer to deduce she had already passed. Another Jasadi?

"Medhat, watch out!"

Arin whirled around. There she was—leaping over the bodies of the fallen, clothes tattered and bloodied. An Omalian soldier rode past Arin, raising his broadsword to lop off the weeping Jasadi's head.

With no real urgency, Arin picked up the spear lying beside the torched soldier and dusted off flecks of crisped flesh. He leaned against the wall, watching her sprint toward the pair on the ground.

Arin raised his arm, shifting his weight to the back of his foot. He waited until the Omalian soldier's sword curved down, the momentum guaranteed to slice the sobbing Jasadi's head clean from his shoulders.

Arin threw.

Three-pronged and short-handled, the spear had been designed to pin wild boars at short range. Arin had thrown high, hedging the weight of the spear against the distance. A howl tore from the Omalian soldier as the spear skewered him through the shoulder, sundering through flesh and bone. The sword dropped inches from the weeping Jasadi as the soldier tumbled from his horse.

The impaled soldier's ankle caught in the stirrup, and his hoarse shouts echoed behind him as the horse took off, dragging his body over the burning debris and scattered corpses littering the village grounds.

Arin had barely lowered his arm from the throw when he was

raising it again, this time to slam aside the knife barreling toward him. Arin grabbed her wrist, holding firm as she tried to jerk free, and dragged her back against his chest. He twisted her arm so her own knife balanced at the underside of her throat.

"Found you," Arin murmured in her ear. She tipped her chin up to glare at him, ignoring the blade at her throat. This close, Arin could see every fleck of brown in her velvet dark eyes, read every emotion like it was written in a language he was born to speak. "I warned you what would happen if you left the mountains."

"It would have been embarrassing if you hadn't found me," she said. "I was worried I might have to start drawing signs."

Amusement swelled in his chest. "Is this my thanks for saving your weeping friend?"

"I had it handled. I didn't need your help."

Arin did not have a hope of stopping his grin, any more than he could halt his lungs from drawing in the scent of her. She smelled terrible—like mud and river mold—but underneath it was the unmistakable sweetness of Sylvia. She was here. Not a ghost in his head or a magic-made apparition in his chambers.

"I suppose you didn't need my help driving out the Omalian soldiers entering from the west, either. It was mere good fortune they attacked my men under the persuasion of magic, facilitating our intervention."

An elbow drove into Arin's middle in the same instant that a set of teeth clamped around his gloved wrist. He withdrew before he accidentally sliced into her, allowing Sylvia to spin out of his arms and face him from the safety of a few feet's distance. He rubbed the teeth marks in his glove, his ridiculous grin widening.

Malika of Jasad or not, she still had the temperament of a deranged goose.

"I will not let you take me," she warned. She raised a sword, adjusting her grip on the hilt. She wore gold gloves nearly identical to the ones she had kept during the trials. "Don't force my hand, Arin."

Arin took a light step toward her. "I thought I taught you better than this." Another step. "Never extend a challenge to an opponent you cannot defeat."

"Baira's blessed hair, you think highly of yourself." Sylvia stepped as he did. They circled each other. "We aren't sparring in the tunnels anymore. I am not the same girl you prepared for the Alcalah."

"Good." Arin considered and discarded the spear, picking up the broadsword from the slain soldier instead. Not an ideal weapon for close combat, but he may as well give her a lead. Arin swept an inviting hand in the space between them. "It is about time you showed me who you really are."

To her credit, her first strike nearly caught him by surprise. Low and diagonal, a well-met aim would slash him open from right shoulder to left hip. Arin twisted out of the way, and in the same movement, pulled a dagger the size of his longest finger from his coat and threw.

It embedded itself a hairsbreadth away from her foot. She froze, and Arin said, "Your first and only warning. You bend your knees before you swing; it gives you away and instructs me of the direction you intend to pursue."

Sylvia yanked the dagger out of the dirt without taking her eyes off him and tucked it into her boot. "Still fond of throwing knives, are you?"

"Only when my target is so very good at catching them."

Arin flipped his sword to block her blow, the clang of metal music between them. Asserting enough force against her sword to keep it raised, he marched her against the wall and pinned her sword beneath his own. Caught between the wall and the weight of Arin's broadsword, she strained to maneuver from the trap.

"How many times have I taught you to avoid this hold?" Arin's voice cooled into deepest winter. "Do you think because your eyes glow a little now, you have no reason to keep with your training?"

Arms lifted above their heads, inches apart, they glared at each other.

"By the end of this, you will call me Mawlati with a smile," Sylvia vowed.

A thrill tumbled through Arin. He had forgotten this feeling, this reckless abandon only she engendered—as though the rest of the world was nothing more than noise at the back of his head and true reality began and ended in the space she occupied.

"Prove it," he enunciated, lips less than a breath from the crown of her hair.

Suddenly, the swords clanged into the wall as Sylvia slid down and threw her weight against Arin's waist, taking them both to the ground. Before they landed, she slammed her fist into his stomach and tried to grab the sword.

Not bad.

Not good enough, either.

Arin swung, slamming the broadsword's metal hilt against her temple. She twisted in time to avoid the brunt of the blow, but it still dizzied her long enough for Arin to throw her off him.

A horse galloped past them, its rider slumped forward with an axe between his shoulder blades.

Sylvia wiped her forehead with the back of her wrist. "Is this all you have to offer me, Silver Serpent?"

She rolled out of the way of his dagger. In the two seconds it took Arin to shift back, she'd hurled a handful of pebbles and dirt directly into his eyes and lunged.

They grappled on the ground without any sort of finesse. Blows flew, blood flowing between them until it became difficult to tell who it belonged to. If Arin had seen his recruits fighting like this, he would have called them undisciplined children and ordered them to spend a week digging in the Wickalla. Arin never put his hands on anything without a clear plan, without strategy. She had dragged him into something raw and brutal, and if Arin weren't viscerally aware of what might happen if any of her bare skin accidentally brushed his, he would relish every minute of it.

But one slip of their gloves, the wrong tear in her clothes... Arin couldn't risk it.

She slammed her fist into his jaw, knocking his head so hard into the ground it echoed in Arin's knees.

He spat out red. "I am not one for pointless musings, Suraira, but I am starting to wonder if whoever built my skull built it for the express purpose of surviving you."

Arin's eyes flared open as gloved fingers raked through his hair, gathering it at the nape of his neck. Sylvia crouched above him, and he would have regretted the split in her full lips or the blood dripping from her nose if she hadn't paid him the same. If they couldn't truly touch each other, this approximation of it... the intimacy of this violence between them almost sufficed. It almost satisfied the hunger that sparked at the base of Arin's spine as she pushed a lock of his hair away from the seeping wound near his cheekbone and murmured, "Just your skull?" Her hair had come loose around her, black curls spilling around her strong shoulders, and she leveled a dagger against Arin's heart. "Not the rest of you?"

Arin dug his fingers in the dirt and reminded himself what would happen if he twisted out from under her and pinned her to the earth. If he kissed the infuriating smirk off her face and let her tear into him a different way, unravel him in pleasure instead of pain.

All of me is written in your name, he wanted to say.

The earth rumbled beneath Arin, and a shadow blotted out the sun. He saw the metal glint before he saw the soldier wielding it.

Arin whipped off the ground, tossing Sylvia behind him just as an Omalian soldier hurled a dagger straight at her.

It tore across Arin's thigh and landed, wet with his blood, beside a startled Sylvia.

Arin didn't feel the cut. He didn't even glance down to see how deep it had sliced.

If it had met its mark, it would have killed her.

A strange fog descended over him, cooling his injuries to a pleasant numbness. Picking up the soldier's dagger, Arin wiped it against his vest and stood. He walked toward the soldier unhurriedly, avoiding the frenetic swings of the incompetent fool's sword. Imagine—a foul urchin of an Omalian soldier felling Sylvia of Jasad. Killing her while she was distracted. Killing her while she was quite literally in Arin's arms.

Essiya, not Sylvia. Essiya, who has never been safe—will never be safe—because she is the Malika of Jasad. Sylvia would have run the moment you walked into Mahair, but Essiya stayed. Essiya fought, and she will keep fighting until there is nothing left of her.

The girl who'd grin at him with blood smeared in the cracks of her teeth and the ruler who'd tear kingdoms apart for her people. One and the same.

Without thinking, Arin stabbed the dagger into the hollow of the soldier's throat and dragged it down: over the ridge of his breastbone, through the soft fat of his belly, and into the sponge of his pelvis. The handle juddered in his grip as it severed muscle from bone. Innards spilled over Arin's gloves, dirtying his sleeves, but he didn't care.

They do not get to take her from me.

It repeated in Arin's head, a mantra ringing louder by the second. He gutted the soldier, and for a brief moment, it was the woman who raised the whip against a blindfolded Essiya on the other end of his dagger. Qayida Hanim whose bloodcurdling screams ripped through the air, Qayida Hanim whose eyes glazed over with the first frost of death.

The soldier dropped to his knees. When the body pitched forward, head cracking against Arin's boot, it once again belonged to an Omalian soldier.

Red rivers poured from the corpse, watering the thin patch of weeds beneath it. The dagger dropped from Arin's hold, landing in the puddle.

When he turned, she was fixed in the same spot on the ground. For the first time since the battle had started, she looked afraid. *"Oh."*

"He could have killed you."

Without removing her gaze from his, Essiya climbed to her feet. A fundamental shift had taken place, but Arin hadn't calmed enough to identify it yet.

"And?" Instead of anger, Essiya's voice roughened with frustration and something akin to grief. "Were you upset at losing the opportunity to do it yourself?"

"You will not die at the hands of a cowardly soldier who strikes at you from behind."

"So you eviscerated him over the nature of the attack?" She scrubbed her forehead with the heels of her hands. "You once taught me that the only true honor in the world lies with the dead, because survivors strike first and repent second."

Arin stiffened. Beyond her, the tide had turned against the Omalian soldiers. Arin hadn't doubted it would—a horde of butchers in uniform was no match for a handful of disciplined and well-trained soldiers. Buoyed by the prospect of victory, the villagers stopped retreating. As Arin watched, Nizahl soldiers, Jasadi rebels, and Omalian villagers marched toward Felix's fleet, who had begun to edge toward Mahair's outer wall.

When was the last time the kingdoms had stood as one, aligned under a common cause?

Essiya raised trembling hands, open palms pointed toward Arin. "The Supreme is lying to you."

Arin's teeth came together, and it took a concentrated effort to unlock his jaw. "As you keep saying."

"You keep not hearing it. Arin, he is lying about—"

"My father has been lying since the day he learned how to sound out letters," Arin said. "If we stood here and reviewed them from start to finish, we would disintegrate alongside your village."

"Excellent! If you know he's lying, then *why* are you still fighting me?" she demanded.

Arin ran a hand through his hair, heedless of the blood dried into the grooves of his glove. Heedless of anything other than the pounding in his head, the aggravation gnawing at his bones with hooked teeth. He should never have opened the door to this kind of conversation with her—never allowed her hazy accusations to cross the threshold of his mind. She was a flame sparking on the kindling of his doubt and breathing small suspicions into an incoherent blaze.

"The Supreme might have lied about the Blood Summit. He may have lied about who was party to the Malik and Malika's magic mining." Arin exhaled, a tranquilizing frost settling over the inferno in his chest. Her way was not his: Arin did not need to set himself on fire to see through the dark. He would move through it, step by step, assured of where his foot would land before he raised it. "But he did not lie about magic-madness. Every atrocity, every massive loss of life—it has been at the hands of magic-madness."

"How many cases have there been in all of history?" she snapped. "One or two hundred since the entombment?"

"One case every century since the entombment."

Essiya stared at him, shell-shocked. "That is...what, a little over seventy? Are you telling me seventy people went magic-mad, and you decided the whole of magic was to blame?"

"Ask me how many deaths each case caused. How much carnage."

Essiya didn't react, her gaze unfocused past his shoulder.

"Magic-madness is your foundational truth, isn't it?" she murmured, barely audible. Another without the privilege of Arin's hearing would have missed it. "Is it what Rawain built everything else on top of?"

Arin's skin tingled just as plumes of gold and silver shot through her eyes. They swirled into a deadly pool.

He cocked his head. She knew her magic would pass through him. Even if she exerted enough of it to hurt him on the way through, it would be a waste of her energy. She would need all her strength to evade him.

As if reading his mind, she said, "You may be immune to magic." Pebbles knocked against Arin's boot as the ground trembled. Gold and silver whirled faster. "But the world around you is not."

CHAPTER THIRTY-FOUR

ARIN

The earth rocked. The patch of dirt under Arin shot backward. He dropped to a knee, the tips of his fingers braced against the ground as it shifted beneath him on invisible wings. Arin slid across the dirt and hit the stone porch beneath the awning of the apothecary. The sudden inertia sent Arin hurtling through the door, wood splintering and exploding against him. Glass jars shattered, shards flying in the shop like sparks from a freshly lit hearth. Arin's head slammed into a bench, and he blinked away black dots.

She appeared in the doorway, outlined in the smoke of the burning village. Before Arin could move, the cushions on the bench rippled. Two of them flattened and twisted, springing to life. They weaved around his forearms and fastened him to the shelf behind him. Arin tugged, and the shelf quivered in warning. One strong pull would bring the entire row crashing on top of him.

He rotated his wrists, testing the restraints, as Essiya approached him. In the dim of the shop, she might have truly been Suraira, arriving to lure him into the mists of Sirauk.

"You're thinking about ways to get loose, and I highly suggest you save yourself the effort. You can't out-strategize my magic, and I would hate to see you exhaust yourself." Her knees settled on either side of Arin as she straddled his chest.

"The others have all these plans. Plans they think will save Jasad, save magic," she mused. "They think our greatest strength lies in numbers. But the kind of Queen who would allow her nephew to commit these atrocities and destabilize half their kingdom... what use will she be to us? If she cannot even stand up for her own kingdom, why would she bother making the effort for another?"

Arin turned the information over, rotating the pieces until they formed an image he understood. The Urabi wanted Queen Hanan to rally behind Jasad? Why would they think—

Ah.

"You see it, too, don't you?" Essiya asked, studying his face. Were Arin bleeding less, he might find it alarming how quickly she could glimpse the rotations of his mind. "Appealing to her is futile."

Arin raised a brow. She wouldn't be sharing the Urabi's grand designs with him if she believed it was their best chance of success. "I gather you have a better idea."

"Me? No, no. I am not the planner," she sighed. "I am always the plan. But you see, I do have a theory."

Essiya bent toward him, close enough for Arin to count the flecks of brown still visible in her magic-drenched gaze. "I think the only way we win is if we win you, Your Highness."

Arin's second brow joined the first, arching in twin peaks of mockery. "Win me," he repeated slowly, tasting each absurd word. "And how exactly do you propose to do that?"

The outer wall of the shop shuddered. The ground rumbled beneath the beat of dozens of horses riding along the main road. A cheer went up, a cacophony of lively sound that unclenched the tense furrow in Essiya's forehead.

"They won," Essiya murmured. Her gaze softened. "We won."

"Congratulations," Arin said. "Let me go."

She ignored him, biting her lip. "I imagine it won't be long before your soldiers come looking for you." She tilted her head back, nose scrunching in thought, and Arin emphatically refused to find it endearing. "Do you remember when I tried to stab you in the cabin and you broke my wrist?" Her gaze traveled unseeingly to the next row of shelves. "I knew if I immobilized you, your guardsmen wouldn't be able to chase me. Their first dictate is to protect their Commander. To secure his safety above all else."

Finally, her attention returned to his carefully impassive face. "Your soldiers will start rounding up the Urabi. I brought them here, Arin. I asked them to save Mahair, and now I need to save them, too."

The desperation in her voice gave Arin pause. Did she think his soldiers would start killing the Urabi? With their magic drained from the fight, they posed no danger. They would be placed under hold until Arin arrived.

Before he could express as much, Essiya seemed to steel herself. "I *am* sorry about this."

She struck him, her fist slamming into his jaw with impressive force.

The first blow knocked the wind from him. The second brought with it an unpleasant ringing in his ears. By the fifth, the entire right side of Arin's face had either split or swollen, and he coughed a spatter of bright red onto the ground.

"Sweet Sirauk," she swore. "How are you still conscious?"

"I told…you." Arin was acutely aware that he would soon succumb to the blood loss. "I was built…to survive you."

"Survive a little less effectively, please."

The blows began again.

"Go to sleep, go to sleep, go to sleep," she begged, a tortured mantra for every hit.

Despite the pulsating behind his eyes, the scream of every stitch of skin on his face, Arin lifted his head. As he gazed at her through the one eye that hadn't swollen shut, he planned to say, *You will fatigue before I do, as it appears our training wasn't sufficient to teach you how to knock a chained man unconscious.*

But the taunt curdled on his tongue. The cabinet rocked dangerously behind him as Arin shot forward. The pain, the cheering villagers, the raw skin of his wrists—everything faded into black as Arin's entire being narrowed down to the spot at Essiya's collarbone where her torn tunic had slipped.

"*What is that?*" Arin rasped, harsh with horror.

Essiya followed his gaze and blanched.

A gold vein curled around the ridge of Essiya's collarbone. It hadn't been there when they were grappling outside. It hadn't been there.

"Damn it," Essiya groaned.

This time, her fist slammed Arin's head into a metal bucket sitting at the edge of the shelf.

Agony, and then—

Silence.

CHAPTER THIRTY-FIVE

SYLVIA

I raised a trembling, blood-streaked hand to Arin's nose.
Breathing. Still breathing. The way his head had hit the shelf, I—

I yanked my glove back on. There was no time to drown in guilt or regret. It had to be done. Pushing myself off of Arin's prone form, I ran to the giant hole I'd made in the side of Rory's shop and scanned the scene outside.

The Omalian soldiers who hadn't been killed had immediately surrendered, and I watched the villagers tie their hands behind their backs while the Nizahl soldiers presumably went in search of their Commander. I spotted Namsa and Maia crouched beside Medhat, rubbing his back while Lateef scooped Kenzie's corpse from the ground.

The only person who seemed to notice my absence right away was Efra, who skulked around the Nizahl soldiers like a cat with its tail standing on end. Thank the tombs he refused to use his magic on me—the distress and indecision wafting off of me would have drawn him straight to Rory's shop.

Once Nizahl's dead had been accounted for and the last of the Omalian crown's threat was subdued, they would arrest the Urabi. All but Maia had used magic during the battle, clearly marking themselves as Jasadi. If I knew Mahair, they would not allow the soldiers to arrest the Jasadis who fought at their back. It would be a bloodbath—another set of soldiers, another round of carnage. Except the Jasadis were probably out of magic, and the villagers were weary.

I exhaled slowly, forcing my whirling thoughts to slow.

There was one order that superseded all else; one order every Nizahl soldier was required to obey and put above magic.

The safety of their Heir.

If they saw me leaving with Arin, they would abandon the village immediately. Their one and only priority would be tracking down their Commander. I could take Arin far enough that it would be pointless for the soldiers to try returning to Mahair, since the Jasadis would be long gone by then.

I rotated my palm. The gold vein had gained new friends, thin silver cracks fracturing through my palm and across the space between my fingers. I didn't even want to think what other veins had appeared after I saved Raya.

One last time. I would use my magic one last time, and then not again. Not for any situation, not for anybody.

Dust rose from the floor of the apothecary. My magic pumped, excited to join the fun again, and I caught a glimpse of glowing eyes in a shattered bottle. I looked away instantly, heart pounding, fear so potent on my tongue I feared I might choke on it.

That wasn't my face in the bottle.

Before I could summon the bravery for a second look, my magic barreled over the edge. The dust spun faster, and streaks of color flashed through the whirling clouds. Iridescent veins crawled over my hands. They shaped themselves into the lines of a kitmer's wing—silver on my right, gold on the left.

When the dust settled, two kitmers stood in the center of Rory's shop. Unlike the kitmers from the cliffside, this pair filled up half the apothecary, and they lacked the abnormalities of their older siblings. Shining horns curved several inches above their heads. Clawed feet scraped eagerly against the floor.

Like the others, they had my eyes.

"Hello," I said. "As we will be partners for my latest feat of idiocy, it seems only fitting you should have names."

I pointed to the bigger kitmer, the tiny silver feathers on its chest fanning from its thick neck in a distinct V shape. "Would you be offended if I called you Niseeba?"

It stared at me.

"Great!"

I took an extra minute for the other kitmer. Its wings were the brightest gold I had seen, the long feathers at the ends of its limbs dappled in silver.

"Ingaz," I decided.

Niseeba flapped her wings, sending a shelf of vials shattering on the floor. The quiet from outside unsettled me, and I hurried to lift Arin before someone found the shop, or worse—the Nizahl soldiers turned their attention to the Jasadis in their midst.

Any heightened sense of ego I might have gained at my performance in the battle promptly evaporated when I tried to lift Arin. "Awaleen below," I croaked. My muscles burned as I withdrew and crawled behind his head. I tucked my arms under his shoulders and heaved.

My knee slipped in a viscous ointment, and I slid to the left, crashing into a bench with Arin slumped against me. Frustration shrieked inside me, aching to be given voice.

Something soft brushed my chin. I jerked back, which seemed to upset Niseeba. She growled, then tried again to slide her wing between me and Arin. Dumbstruck, I watched the kitmer as she wiggled the length of her wing under the Nizahl Heir and tilted her shoulders down.

Rovial's tainted tomb, she was lifting Arin's weight so I could roll him onto her back.

Black eyes met mine and narrowed into slits. *Move, you sorry sack of panic*, they seemed to say.

I leapt into motion, heaving Arin with all my strength. Niseeba knelt, the ends of her wing curling in to prevent Arin from slipping. Arin slid between the kitmer's shoulders, his head coming to rest below Niseeba's curling horns.

Shouting broke out in the village. It would be a matter of minutes before they checked Rory's shop. I stripped the blanket from the cushions and wrapped it around Arin and Niseeba, securing him to the kitmer's back. I also checked that every inch of his skin was covered. What a disaster it would be if he accidentally drained Niseeba's magic and plummeted out of the sky.

The Urabi would certainly take my departure as abandonment. Finding one of them to explain my plan would be too risky. I rifled through Rory's drawers and withdrew ink and parchment.

I am seeing our first plan through. Find me where we were meant to go.
—Essiya

Double-checking Arin was secure on Niseeba's back, I climbed on top of Ingaz, who took my weight without trouble. I tightened my legs around the kitmer, fingers digging into the leathery gold feathers at her spine. Dread crystallized in the pit of my stomach, cutting into my insides with each breath. I'd never been airborne before.

Riding a kitmer didn't need to be any more frightening than riding a horse. At least it would be a memorable death, if nothing else.

Ingaz and Niseeba bunched their shoulders, the flap of their wings sending every movable object in the apothecary hurtling into the walls. I spared a thought for the poor souls Rory would recruit to clean up this mess.

"Please let this work," I mumbled, wrapping my hands around Ingaz's horns.

Together, the kitmers rose into the air. I swallowed, pretending the tang on my tongue wasn't vomit-flavored, and tightened my knees.

Ingaz dove through the gap I'd blown through the wall and into the melee. I clutched her feathers and glanced over my shoulder, relaxing when I saw Niseeba and Arin right behind us.

Time for the next part of the performance.

We streaked across the village, flying above blackened patches of dirt and smoking pyres. The ash hit my nose and coated my eyes in a watery haze.

As I had feared, the villagers were crowded around Namsa, Lateef, Maia, Efra, and Medhat, facing off against the Nizahl soldiers. Shouts pelted between the two groups.

Ingaz's wings cast a long shadow over the Jasadis as we sailed toward the Nizahl soldiers. Some of the villagers started screaming; others joined with cheers. I spotted Lateef staring at Niseeba behind me, Arin coiled to her back, and I hoped he had seen us come out of the shop. I hoped Rory was his typical overzealous self and went directly to the apothecary to assess the damage, where he would find the note immediately.

The Nizahl soldiers had seen their unconscious, badly injured Commander on Niseeba's back. I watched horror collectively sweep over them and grinned. "Come and rescue your precious Heir," I bellowed, the invitation rolling over the wreckage with ease. "Before there's nothing left of him to find."

A volley of invectives chased me through the air. I smirked at the soldiers on the ground and tightened my grip on Ingaz. We rushed toward their center, and they scattered in time to avoid Ingaz's claws. Gusts of dirt and ash whipped from Ingaz's beating wings, sending the soldiers flying.

"Pathetic," I seethed. "An embarrassment to your Commander."

I leaned forward, flattening my torso against Ingaz's spine as we shot upward. Niseeba followed close behind. We sailed out of Mahair, the distance between us and the devastated village growing. I checked on Arin again, but he was still secure on Niseeba's back.

Once we cleared the top of Essam, I let myself breathe. The nearest Nizahl holding I knew of was the one Arin had transported me to after the waleema, the same cabin where he'd offered me my freedom to compete as his Champion. If I dropped him off there, it would take the soldiers a day to find him—enough time for me and the Urabi to reach the Omal palace.

Ignoring the cynical part of me that refused to trust such an easy victory, I let the tension leak out of my muscles and relaxed on my kitmer's back.

I had despaired of the vastness of Essam when Hanim made it my prison, but now, the horizon of endless, rolling green filled me with awe. Hirun snaked through the woods, seeming to chase us across the acres. Somewhere north, the river beneath me was pouring through the mountain's mouth, cascading down a cliffside and reuniting with Suhna Sea, where it would start its journey anew. Regenerating again and again, its memories washed away in the tide.

A low growl rumbled in Niseeba's throat. On her back, Arin stirred, groggily twisting against his restraints. I had tied his coat around Niseeba's neck to prevent his face from brushing against her, knotting the sleeves under her chin.

Unfocused blue eyes blinked from Arin's bloodied face. They caught mine and cleared, holding for a long second before moving to the kitmer beneath me. They widened at the sight of the woods passing below us.

"I was hoping you would wake up," I said, raising my voice over the wind. "How many times have you stood over your maps and looked at the world from above, just like this?"

Arin maneuvered an arm out of the restraints and grabbed Niseeba's horn. His jaw worked, the pale column of his throat rippling with—what? Anger, confusion? Awe? Reading Arin was difficult on any given day, and it certainly didn't help that half his face was covered in throbbing bruises.

"Leave your legs in the restraints," I advised. "You're still badly wounded, and you might lose consciousness again."

Working his other arm free, Arin paused to shoot me a glare. I rolled my eyes, remembering the fight he'd put up in these very same woods when I had tried to bandage his wounds from the Ruby Hound.

I wouldn't faint.

"As the mighty immortal man wishes," I muttered.

Before Arin could finish untangling his left leg, his entire body went taut. His gaze flew to the trees, then back to me, and I did not have to try to guess what emotion they contained this time.

Pure, unadulterated alarm.

Ingaz dipped, a terrified shriek tearing out of the kitmer. Her wings bent at the middle, as though trying to lift against thick sand. Niseeba shook her head from side to side, weaving drunkenly through the air.

"What is it?" I shouted, leaning forward as Ingaz careened toward the trees. "What's happening?"

And finally, as the kitmers streaked toward the woods, Arin spoke.

"Hold on!" Steely and aggressive, brooking no argument—the voice of the Nizahl Commander. "The Mirayah is drawing in the kitmers' magic."

The *Mirayah*?!

We plummeted.

CHAPTER THIRTY-SIX

SYLVIA

I coughed myself awake, rolling to my side as water surged out of my throat. Pain pounded between my temples. My entire body vibrated, shaking like a freshly gonged bell.

As soon as I could breathe, I crawled away from the waves lapping at my legs. I raised an arm and squinted into the sun.

Wait. The sun? I'd been flying through the clouds with Arin and the kitmers, markedly missing any trace of the sun. Besides, this was too clear, too blazing, for the season.

"Arin!" I called, staggering out of the water. Why was I at a seashore? The closest shore of Suhna Sea was in Jasad, hundreds of miles away. Questions beat impatient fists against the inside of my skull. "Niseeba, Ingaz!"

I whirled toward the sea, heart pounding as I searched the endless stretch of blue. Waves splashed at my legs, unnaturally warm. His leg was still restrained when we fell. What if he hadn't been able to free himself in time?

"Arin!" I screamed his name, shoving clumps of my drenched hair out of my face. I scrambled for my magic, but it was nowhere to be found. Not absent because it was ignoring me or waiting for the right opportunity, but *gone*. I couldn't feel it at all.

"Your companion left."

I went still. Without turning around, I slipped my fingers into my waistband and withdrew my dagger.

"Now, now. If you kill me, who will help you escape?" asked a singing voice. "Don't you want to know how to leave the Mirayah?"

I twisted around, blade high and knee crooked to pounce.

My teeth came together, hard. The creature had assumed the general shape of a man, but it was the furthest thing from human. Features crafted by an uninspired hand sat above its thick neck—a set of colorless eyes, an upturned nose, a thin mouth. Either laziness or weakness had caused it to forgo the more intricate details—eyebrows, the hollows under the eyes, the ridge between forehead and nose.

What did the details matter when you could shed your skin between one breath and the next?

"Dulhath." I tightened my grip on the dagger. "You're the one that escaped from Galim's Bend."

"Jasadi," the dulhath shot back. "I presume the same Jasadi everyone's been making such a fuss about."

"You said you saw my companion leave. Where?"

The dulhath shrugged, gesturing farther down the shoreline. "He dropped into the water somewhere down there and spent time pacing around, bellowing a name and searching the water. I wasn't sure for what until I saw you roll onto the sand. Essiya, I presume? He seems quite badly hurt, poor thing—I don't see how he makes it back without something else finding him first."

The knot in my chest loosened. Arin was alive. He was alive and strong enough to search for me, which meant he was not too injured to tear apart anything in this tombs-cursed realm that tried to hurt him.

"I don't have my magic here," I warned. "There is nothing for you to eat."

"Ah, but you're wrong, sweet Essiya. The Mirayah does not strip away your magic—it merely renders it…" The dulhath cocked its head back and forth, as if sampling different words. "Ineffective."

The dulhath took a step toward me, lips white and contorted into an eerie grin. "I could indulge myself now and suck the magic out of your marrow. It won't be nearly as tasty or nutritious, but it would slake my hunger. What I am offering you is a fair fight. I will show you out of the Mirayah, and you fight me with that"—he gestured blandly toward my dagger—"instead of your magic."

How stupid did he think I was? Dulhaths were notorious liars, single-minded in their pursuit for their next meal. He would lie with his last breath if it meant he had a chance at my magic.

"As soon as we leave the Mirayah, you'll be able to transform." My waterlogged boots sloshed as I advanced higher up the shore, my dagger aloft. "The last one of you I killed became a giant three-headed spider and tried to impale me on one of its legs."

The dulhath tracked me with his colorless eyes. Poorly masquerading as human or not, dulhaths were an ancient and terrifying predator. They had devoured the magic of Kings, feasted on entire villages and schools. With magic gone from everyone but Jasadis, the dulhaths had lived on the edge of starvation for over a century. They would do anything, say anything, to eat.

"Is that a no?"

"A resounding one."

"Shame," the dulhath sighed. "Imagine how delicious your magic might have tasted outside the Mirayah."

Movement from the corner of my eye drew my attention higher up the beach, where craggy slopes of sand flattened into soil at the edge of the woods. Figures stepped out from between the trees. Five, ten, fifteen men spilled out like flies from rotted fruit. Tattered uniforms clung to their bulky frames. Soldiers' uniforms, Omal's colors... but these weren't the standard Omalian uniform. I should know—I had just seen a horde of men in those uniforms ride into Mahair.

Vacant gazes latched on to me. They lumbered in no great hurry, and why should they? I was trapped between them, the water, and the dulhath.

Trapped without my magic.

As they closed in, I went stone-still at the sight of three circles on the collar of those strange, outdated uniforms.

Two circles at the top, one circle at the bottom, the edges of each overlapping to form a ram's head. In the space where the circles connected were three clear horizontal dots.

These uniforms weren't simply out of fashion. They hadn't been worn in hundreds of years.

"Poor creatures," the dulhath clucked. "They have been in the Mirayah ever since the Siege of Six Dawns. Not a clue who they were or what happened to them."

The Omalian soldiers who'd borne the brunt of Orban's offensive spell... the ones who had turned on their brethren and begun to eat them alive as a result of Orban's forbidden wartime tactic.

Awaleen below, what kind of magic ruled this realm? How ancient were the creatures inhabiting it?

I rapidly weighed my options. Use the dagger to cut down as many of the Omalian soldiers as I could before they swarmed me, or throw the dagger at the dulhath and forfeit the single weapon at my disposal for the slim chance of killing the smarmy little toad.

The knife cut through the air and plunged into the dulhath's shoulder.

I have been many things in this life, but wise wasn't usually one of them.

The dulhath rocked on his heels. A snarl tore across his face, and before I could move, the Omalian soldiers converged upon me.

I thrashed as countless arms pinned me to the ground, clawing and biting at any extremity that came within reach. I tried to gather sand to throw in the dulhath's eyes as he crouched over me, but a soldier jabbed his knee onto my wrist and pressed his forearm to my throat.

The dulhath plucked a strand of hair from my cheek and twisted it around his finger. "Don't worry. You won't feel any pain. By the time it's their turn to eat what's left of you, you will be long dead."

I tried to spit on his sorry attempt at a face, but the soldier's arm was a boulder on my windpipe. The dulhath trailed a curved nail over the inside of my arm and lifted my hand to his face. He ran his nose over my palm, inhaling deeply. "What a true treat you are, Essiya."

His lips curled back, revealing the bladed tip of his black tongue. With a gooey squelch, it split into seven wet slivers, each tip sharper than an arrow and likely capable of winnowing through skin and bone.

Dania's bloody axe, I was going to be eaten. Five years living in Essam and slaying every beast Hanim could conjure only to die in the Mirayah. Jasad would fall because their Malika had gotten herself digested in a place that shouldn't exist.

The tongues sprang toward my arm, and I shut my eyes, bracing for agony.

It never came.

I snapped my eyes open to the dulhath gurgling, clawing at his neck as Arin's blade slid across his throat. With a fist in the dulhath's thin hair, Arin slammed the blade into each of the dulhath's eyes before cutting his tongues at the root, silencing the creature's screams.

Sizzling blood splattered over me and the soldiers. They shot toward Arin as the dulhath's body dropped to the sand, dead at last.

The Nizahl Heir put distance between us, drawing the mutated soldiers away from me. His hair had dried in dark silver waves, falling around the bruises matting the side of his face. Arin picked up the dagger I'd thrown at the dulhath and wiped it clean with the edge of his coat.

Get up and help him, I shouted at my prone limbs. The soldiers streamed toward Arin, leaving me behind like a forgotten pet, but I could not bring myself to do more than sit up in the sand.

I wanted to see him fight. I wanted to see what it looked like when Arin of Nizahl didn't hold back.

At first, I wasn't sure what I was seeing. The soldiers seemed to drop around him untouched, hitting the ground without getting up again. He was barely moving, but they were falling.

Until the next wave of soldiers swarmed him, and I realized they weren't keeling over on their own. Arin struck at a preternatural speed, a blade in each hand, slicing the soldiers at critical points—the pulse at their neck, their throat, the lower right of their belly. One of them threw himself at Arin, knocking him back a step and dislodging one of his daggers. I scrambled to my feet, but Arin had already hurled the soldier like a javelin, knocking him into three other attackers.

My mistake was in thinking an unleashed Arin would fight the way I did. Where I descended into a fog of instinct, reacting as my blade demanded and surrendering to the skill of my body, Arin led with his mind. He was a lightning strike, not a storm. Precise, fatal, and terrifying to behold. His body flowed with a grace and focus I would never master, not in any number of lifetimes.

It was awe-inspiring. Infuriating. Unbelievably attractive.

I wiped some of the sand from my cheek and shook myself. Indecent thoughts about the man currently slaughtering my would-be murderers was a normal reaction to almost being eaten.

No reason to allow Arin to have all the fun. I hurled myself into the fray, leaping onto the back of a soldier rushing Arin and tackling him to the ground.

"Did you enjoy the show?" Arin growled, wrenching a soldier to his knees and snapping his neck. The body listed, spraying sand as it thumped to the ground. In his last seconds, I could have sworn I saw relief in his eyes.

I caught the blade Arin tossed me and grinned. "Immensely."

Between the two of us, we finished off the remaining soldiers in record time. When the last soldier fell, I wiped my forehead with the back of my hand and gazed at the corpses strung along the shore. How many? Fifty? A hundred?

My heart pounded, my breathing erratic from the exertion and the unrelenting heat of the sun. Arin slipped off his coat and threw it over his shoulder. Somehow, his vest had remained unscathed in the melee, the black clasps over his chest buckled tight. Without glancing at me, he strode over the bodies and headed for the woods.

Very mature. I followed him, enjoying the flex of his broad back as he maneuvered around the graveyard he'd created. "Too late to pretend," I called in a singsong. "The dulhath said you went looking for me."

Tension feathered across Arin's shoulders. He was more wound up now than he'd been while facing a small army.

"Where are we going?"

He continued walking at an arrogantly fast clip, and I struggled to wade through the sand after him. Blocking me out was his grand approach, really?

"I don't have my magic here! And I am guessing you found out you aren't able to drain magic, or you wouldn't have needed to kill the dulhath with your knife. We need to work together to get out of the Mirayah, and your theatrics are not helping anyone."

Arin stopped to pick up a rock and wipe it on a dead soldier's sleeve before tucking it into his pocket. Not a glance or syllable in my direction as he strode off once more.

Releasing an embattled sigh, I bent and scooped a handful of wet sand. I patted it into a ball, drew my arm back, and threw.

The ball of sand hit the back of Arin's head and exploded. I had the rare pleasure of watching the Nizahl Heir halt in his tracks as sand dropped in clumps into the collar of his shirt.

"Do you want me to be in your debt? Is that why you keep saving me?" I snapped. "Keep your favors. I can take care of myself."

At last, he turned around. "Debt?" Disbelief sharpened the word to a deadly point.

Fury spilled over him, the sudden rush of it startling me a step back. The white scar on his jaw seemed to glow with his anger. "How do you expect I would collect on this debt?"

Arin advanced, stalking toward me with the single-minded intent of a wolf cornering its kill. "You tie me to a wall and beat me bloody, you abduct me, your kitmers drop me into a cursed realm I have managed to avoid my entire life, and then you allow a dulhath that *you* released to nearly eat you!" By the end of his rant, Arin's voice had risen to a roar. "I *wish* I had a good reason for saving you. I wish it was logical or rational, informed by any semblance of reason. I wish more than anything my first thought when I emerged from the water was not of you, that I hadn't been prepared to tear through every grain of sand and burn every tree in this damned place until I found you."

I stared at him, truly speechless for possibly the first time in my life. Blood rushed to my head, blurring the edges of my vision. Gripped with the same sensation I had felt while watching Arin rip apart the soldier in Mahair who had tried to kill me, two contrary forces struggling to meet in my head.

"I didn't *allow* the dulhath to nearly eat me," I mumbled, dropping my eyes to the sand. "I tried to bite him first."

Catastrophe lay pressed between us. One step forward, and we would dissolve into it.

"You don't have your magic here," Arin repeated, as though my words had only just penetrated.

My throat felt too brittle to contain the forces vaulting for freedom from my chest.

"You sound relieved. Were you afraid you'd lose again?" I said shakily.

Arin stepped into my space, forcing my gaze up. "You torment of my soul," Arin growled. "I am afraid I will win."

Without my magic's pressure against the back of my head, I could hear myself think for the first time in a long time. I could identify the ache spreading through me, burning through the layers of armor I had carefully built around myself from the minute I watched my mother get dragged into Bakir Tower. His honesty undid me; what remained was unbearably fragile. Something raw and ruined that hurt if I tried to pick it up. The last real piece of me, protected for longer than I'd known it still existed to protect.

A thumb grazed my cheek, and my wet eyes flashed open to find Arin mere inches away, his hand curving around my face. With a jolt, I realized he was touching me, bare skin to bare skin.

"Stupid risk to take," I managed. "Even in the Mirayah, my magic could still have killed you."

"Yes." Arin smoothed his thumb over the tear beading in the corner of my eye. "It could have."

Frigid water lapped around my ankles as the tide advanced across the shore. "Do not toy with me. This—this is the last piece of my heart I have left, do you understand? I don't know how to protect it once it is outside my body. If I trust you and then you cast it into the dirt, it will be the death of both of us. What is left of me will kill what is left of you."

"I am becoming oddly partial to your death threats," Arin mused. "I seem to hear in them different words entirely."

"Then you should have your ears checked," I muttered.

"Essiya," Arin sighed. "Look at me."

I sniffed, wiping my nose with my sandy sleeve and swinging my gaze back to him.

Arin undid the top button of his shirt, revealing a triangle of smooth skin. As I watched, Arin wrapped his hand around something beneath his collar. His gaze traveled over my head, as though inspecting a problem manifesting in the horizon. I waited, mystified, until his features settled in weary resolution, and he dropped his hand.

A tiny violet-and-black fig necklace laid against the pale skin below his throat.

The necklace I'd bought off the Omalian merchant during the second trial. The necklace I had gifted Arin the night of the Victor's Ball.

He kept it.

Arin of Nizahl, who did not tolerate a loose stitch or a crooked collar, who inspected every grain of dust that dared settle over him, had been wearing a cheap piece of Omalian jewelry under his punishing layers of clothes. No eloquent words or theories or complex pieces of strategy could explain it.

I never stood a chance.

I grabbed the sides of his ridiculously perfect vest and yanked Arin forward, closing the remaining distance between us. A laugh rumbled through the chest pressed against mine, warming me down to my toes.

I calculated my odds of reaching his mouth, and I was strongly contemplating climbing up his chest like a nisnas when Arin exercised an ounce of mercy and lowered his treacherous, beautiful mouth to whisper, "Tell me what you want, Suraira."

I flushed, my grip on his vest tightening. "I want to pull your arrogant head off your smug should—"

He kissed me.

A hush stole over my mind. The world shrank until only Arin remained. Only Arin and the arm he slipped around my waist, drawing me tight against him. The heat of his mouth, reducing me to ash as rapidly as a feather dropped into a hearth.

I gasped as broad hands gripped the back of my thighs and lifted me. I allowed myself to go pliant, wrapping my legs around his waist. When air became marginally more important than exploring the swell of Arin's bottom lip, I dropped my forehead to his cheek as I caught my breath.

Arin began to walk at a purposeful clip toward the woods. The sun had dropped to the middle of the sky, its piercing glare softening in its descent, burnishing the sky in streaks of blue and pink. White foam crawled higher up the beach as the tide rose, water spilling closer to the woods with each wave. As the tide receded, it devoured. The corpses disappeared into its embrace, sinking beneath the clear blue waves.

"You can't carry me across the sand," I protested. "Put me down before you drop us both."

Arin spared me a scornful glance, and I rolled my eyes. "Have it your way," I grumbled, and set to pressing my lips to the column of his throat.

His grip on my legs tightened, and Arin walked faster.

As soon as we stepped into the woods, darkness enveloped us. The temperature plunged, and I was suddenly glad for Arin's plethora of clothing. The wind carried the acrid scent of recently burnt wood, and a fainter, sweeter smell.

My knees slackened as I slid to the ground. Without exchanging a single word, Arin and I moved in tandem, rotating around each other as we assessed the scene. The ground rumbled beneath us. A shriek pierced the quiet, tearing a gash for the ensuing silence to bleed through.

The beach had vanished. The woods closed around us in every direction, trees stretching as far as I could see.

"This isn't Essam." A statement of the obvious to Arin, but I couldn't let these woods think they had fooled me. Essam Woods had been my home for a quarter of my life; it had sheltered me, hunted me, shaped me. Within it, I had been prey and predator.

In these woods, I was only prey.

"Magic does not govern the Mirayah," Arin murmured. He pressed the hilt of a dagger into the hand hanging at my side, and I closed my fingers around it as Arin and I shifted around each other once more. Every story I had heard about the Mirayah unfolded in the shadows between the trees, every monster and murderer rumored to have fled to the legendary refuge. "The Mirayah governs magic. Don't touch the trees, and do not leave my side."

I supposed I deserved the dig—the last time Arin told me not to touch the trees, I had slapped my hand directly over poisoned sap in Ayume Forest.

"The Mirayah moves from place to place within Essam Woods," Arin continued, his back pressed to mine. "If we can find the edge, we can cross before it moves again."

How were we supposed to find the edge? We had no notion of our location, no landmarks to guide our path.

"I could climb to the top of one of these trees. I might be able to see where the Mirayah ends."

"No."

"Arin—"

"The minute you leave my side, it will whisk you away," Arin snapped. "I can—I can *feel* it. It wants you to itself, and my presence is an obstruction."

I shuddered, wrapping both hands around the dagger. What did the Mirayah want with me?

A guttural growl rolled out from the shadows. I froze as another joined it, then another.

Ten sets of slitted blue eyes appeared in the gloom.

Before I could consider the wisdom of unleashing my scream, Arin grabbed my hand and yanked, dragging me behind him as we ran. "Rochelyas!"

Rochelyas? Kapastra's poisonous pet lizards? I thought Rovial killed them all when he waged war against Omal. Damn it to the tombs, how long had the Mirayah been here, leeching from the magic of the woods?

We sprinted through the trees, weaving between tauntingly low branches and the shifting ground beneath us. Arin's steely grip on my hand dragged me forward each time I faltered.

My chest heaved with the effort of staying upright as we fled through the woods, the injuries I'd ignored in Mahair screaming at my abuse. First a dulhath, then mutated soldiers, then rochelyas? What was next, Ruby Hounds?

I slammed into Arin as he abruptly halted. He caught me with an arm around my middle before I could pitch to the ground, drawing me against him.

"Do you see what I see?" he asked.

We stood at the top of a gently sloping hill overlooking a verdant meadow. I didn't need to glance over my shoulder to know the trees had disappeared. The temperature had shifted again, the light fog rolling over the green plains warm and sticky against my skin. If my hair hadn't already gone through every level of torture known to a scalp, ten minutes in this weather would double it in size. The sun had recently set on this meadow, leaving the sky a morose blue, and night had begun its steady encroachment.

"I know this place," I said suddenly and not entirely of my own volition. Distractedly, I tugged Arin forward, focus narrowing on the single tree in the endless stretch of green around us.

Arin allowed me to lead him across the hill. The grass crunched beneath my feet, entirely too fresh. Even in the best of seasons, none of the kingdoms had so many acres of healthy and undisturbed land. It would have been farmed or built upon.

A small lake appeared on the other side of the hills, stars twinkling over its placid surface. As beautiful as the lake in Ayume, which had thickened around me as I waded into its toxic depths, crushing me slowly.

We would *not* be going for a nighttime swim.

I stopped beside the tree, all thoughts of the Mirayah fading beneath the tide of recognition cresting over the back of my mind. "I have been here before," I gasped. Before Arin could stop me, I sealed my palm to the bark. I knew these striations like I knew the lines on my palm. The spiky layers of the trunk, each thorn of wood curving upward like a corn husk. At the top, red roots sprouted long branches, feathered with thin green around the stem.

"This was a date tree," I said, as I had once crouched in a burning room and said, *The Malik and Malika of Jasad were magic miners*. Absolute. Unequivocal. "It burned."

I glanced at Arin, who was watching me with transparent concern. "We are in Jasad."

Or at least, what would eventually become Jasad.

"We're safe here," I insisted, drawing Arin to the ground beside me. "The Mirayah wouldn't dare."

Arin observed me strangely, as though I had begun to slur my speech or speak in tongues. It was the same look Efra wore when my magic swept through me, scrambling my thoughts beneath its undertow. But my magic wasn't here now. It was just me.

I shivered, wrapping my arms around myself as I leaned against the tree.

Just me.

CHAPTER THIRTY-SEVEN

SYLVIA

The Nizahl Heir was far more industrious than anyone with his looks had a right to be. He set about collecting fallen fronds for kindling, breaking the top layers into pieces to catch the flame. Once the spark had caught, he laid out his coat and gloves beside the fire.

"Are you going to ask me about it?"

Arin paused in the middle of untying the straps of his vest. After a beat, he continued, gaze fixed on the flames.

I wrapped my arms around my knees. The branches shuffled beneath a light breeze, scattering the shadows dancing across Arin's grim face.

"The first one was there when I woke up." I traced the vein on my palm. Without its light golden glow, it resembled a raised scar. "The rest began appearing afterward. Every time I use my magic, I find a new vein."

"Why are you telling me this?"

"The others are hoping this war can be won without my magic, but I am not so optimistic," I said. "I am afraid that I will have to choose—my mind or my people."

Astonishment colored the gaze Arin turned onto me. "You have spent this entire time railing against the notion of magic-madness. You have told me again and again that it was a hoax."

"In Mahair, I saved Raya's life by transferring some of my magic to her. Not through her—*to* her. She woke up with silver-and-gold eyes."

The crackling flames spat sparks into the air between us. In this meadow, on the outskirts of time and reality, the Nizahl Heir went deathly still.

"That isn't possible."

"You said it yourself, Arin." I exhaled, tendrils of mist curling from my lips. "My magic does not behave as it should."

"You cannot *transfer* magic. It has not been done since the Awaleen."

"So I have heard."

"Essiya, magic-madness—" Arin hesitated, a rare enough sight that I raised my brows. "What I said earlier, about the reoccurrence of a case every century. Each one was a Jasadi. It didn't matter which kingdom still had magic or how strong the magic. Every single century, a massacre occurred at the hands of a magic-mad Jasadi, typically a child or adolescent. Magic-madness isn't new; the cases were simply too rare and sporadic for the kingdoms to properly track."

I did not know whether to laugh or cry. It must have taken him ages to filter through the countless texts of scholarly deception to find a trustworthy accounting of magic-madness. He wouldn't be sharing the information with me if he hadn't decided to believe it himself.

"You said it happens once a century. When was the last case?"

The Heir stayed quiet, and it was all I needed to know.

"It's me, isn't it?" I settled on a hoarse laugh, tipping my forehead onto my bent knees. "I am the next magic-mad Jasadi."

"No."

The denial, offered without any room for negotiation, only served to strip more of the protective layers between me and a complete collapse. He must have come to the same conclusion when he saw my vein appear, when he saw the kitmers. He *knew*.

"Magic consumed the others in childhood and adolescence, but what about someone whose magic has been trapped half of her life? She could survive into adulthood before it destroyed her."

I unraveled, the past and future peeling in thick spirals around me. Only the core remained, and in it I saw the truth I'd shoved deep the instant I saw the vein on my palm. The truth I'd kicked into the corner alongside the shards of my memories, the mirrors of my mind waiting to be seen.

"Essiya—"

"If the others are wrong about Queen Hanan..." My voice held steady. "I won't be able to avoid using my magic, and the act will consume me. What will remain is not someone who can be kept alive. It will be someone ruled by power, and anyone in her way will burn. Essiya, Sylvia—they won't exist anymore. Do you understand?"

"Spell it out for me." I stiffened at the coiled wrath in his eyes. "Say it."

"If my magic overtakes my mind, you are the only one who will be able to stop me."

In an instant, Arin's hands were around my wrists, yanking me toward him. I careened forward, joining him on my knees as the fire crackled next to us.

A storm raged over the Nizahl Heir. I'd never seen anything like it before, not on Arin. Nothing had ever truly broken through his ice. Cracked it, perhaps, punched a hollow crater here and there...

Transfixed, I almost missed his lips moving.

"You want me to kill you?" he hissed. "Is that what you ask of me?"

"I don't *wish* to die." In the face of his rage, my own sparked to life, burning my hard-won resignation to ash. I took comfort in its familiar embrace. "If you recall, the only reason Jasadis need my magic is because your father burned our kingdom to the ground, and *you* have dedicated your life to destroying magic."

"I have not declared war," Arin bit out. "I am handling the other kingdoms, preventing the mobilization of any armies, and I—"

When his silence lengthened, I shook my trapped wrists. "What?"

"I have searched for other solutions," Arin said. Slow, almost wary. "Other mechanisms to address the dangers of magic without resorting to war."

My right wrist dropped as Arin reached back, searching in the inner pocket of his drying coat. When he withdrew a shiny, flattened silver slab, I wrenched out of his grip, falling backward in my haste to retreat.

I rolled, grabbing the dagger from where I'd left it by the tree. I scanned for any exit from this meadow, but the sloping hills stretched endlessly around me. We were trapped until the Mirayah decided we weren't.

I had worn those cuffs my entire life. I had seen them every night as I went to bed and every morning as I dressed; scratched at them until my skin broke; traced the runes carved into their surface until I could draw them in my sleep.

"This is your solution?" My lips curled. Anger vibrated through every inch of my body. "Design more cuffs? Suppress the magic of every Jasadi?"

Arin rose without drawing his own dagger. I struggled not to stare at the cuff, nausea roiling in my gut. "Jasadis are already losing their magic. In mere generations, it will be gone, just as the other kingdoms lost theirs. What is the harm in cutting it off now? You would have no need to hide. No need to fear magic mining or losing your mind."

"You said yourself that true magic-madness only occurs once a century." I gestured toward myself with the dagger. "I am the last one! Once I die, it will be over. Jasad's magic will fade within the next century and take magic-madness with it."

Arin threw the cuff to the ground, using both hands to rake

through his hair. "You say you don't wish to die, but you won't accept any solution outside of your death. Do you think surrendering to your magic is bravery? Do you think it will atone for your past?"

I advanced on him, the tip of my dagger pressing into his half-laced vest. Arin did not bother knocking it from my grip, and the insult incinerated the last shreds of my reason. "Instead of worrying about my past, let us discuss Nizahl's. You say that you adhere to the founding laws of your kingdom—when the Awaleen appointed Fareed to oversee magic, was it to prevent magic from existing? Or was it to protect against its abuse?"

I relished Arin's frown for only a second before pressing on. "Your father and the rest of the kingdoms benefited from my grandparents' magic mining. When Rawain decided Jasad's power had grown beyond its parameters, he burned our kingdom to the ground. Is that the decree of Nizahl? When did protecting against the dangers of magic become synonymous with destroying magic itself?"

I hurled the dagger to the ground. It plunged into the grass beside the cuff. "Our magic is part of us. Suppressing it is no better than mining it."

"What would you have me do?" Arin spoke through gritted teeth. "Pretend that Jasad's magic does not have the capability to decimate thousands upon thousands of lives until it has weakened enough to no longer pose a danger? Risk another century of magic mining? Another century of the kingdoms losing resources and land to Jasad because they have no way to fight back?"

"I want you to do what you were appointed to do, Commander. You cannot criticize me for surrendering to my magic when you have surrendered to your fears." Exhaustion crashed through me, a bucket of water dousing my panic at the sight of the cuff. "If you let it, fear will make ruins of the future. You will build the rest of your life on the grave of every good thing you might have had, if only you had let yourself try."

I settled the heel of my boot onto the knife's hilt and pushed it deeper into the dirt. "If the next Malik or Malika abuses their magic, intervene. Honor the principles of Nizahl, of our Awaleen. Use that"—I jabbed a derisive finger at the cuff—"if your theory proves incorrect and another case of magic-madness arises after me. If any rulers who come after me try to mine Jasadi magic, slit their throat or throw them to the Urabi."

"After you." His bitter tone cracked a whip across my skin. "You still expect to die."

"Not if I can help it," I said. "Not if everything goes according to plan." I did not need to mention how little faith I had in this plan.

"And if it doesn't, you want me to kill you. Is that right?"

I drew myself up tall. "It would be your duty. It is your oath to protect against the abuses of magic, and if I go mad—"

"You will not go mad."

"But *if*—"

In a flash, his hand clapped over my mouth. Arin snarled like it was pure willpower preventing him from hurling me into the lake until I stopped speaking. "There is no *if* you survive. There is no future where it is my hand that ends your life." This close, I could make out the austere lines of anguish twining around his rage. "If your magic takes you, I will drag you back. It cannot have you."

I caged my breath. Vaida's voice found me in the meadow, her prophecy a soundless whisper in the dark.

Arin is consumed by what he loves. If asked, he would get on his knees and let it kill him.

A rush of guilt tightened my fingers around Arin's sleeve. My entire life had been measured by the places I fled. I had never settled long enough to wonder about the people I left behind; the lives I destroyed.

I'm so sorry, I wanted to whisper. *I am so sorry I did this to you. I never meant to drag you into my wreckage. I never expected you to stay.*

I gently withdrew Arin's hand from my mouth, my gaze steady. "Then have me yourself."

Whatever concept of time marched outside the Mirayah, it failed to reach us here, in this meadow where Arin traced the lines of my face with his fingertips, traveling over each detail as he might pore over the valleys and canyons of his most precious map.

My mouth went dry as Arin lowered me onto his coat, his body carefully leveraged over mine. He kissed me until I scarcely remembered my name—any of them. His mouth revisited the places his fingers had traveled, pressing against the hollow of my throat, the pulse at my neck, the hasanas under my chin. Heat carved through me like a merciless blade, leaving me shaky with a nameless, devouring need.

I grabbed the edge of my tunic and tried to shove it over my head, but the useless pile of buttons caught on a curl halfway through. Before I could tear it loose, Arin laughed, brushing my hands away to untangle the trapped strand with blood-boiling patience. When my turn came, I sat up and undid each strap of his vest with a restraint my quaking body did not share, working it down his arms and onto my discarded tunic.

I fought through the buttons of Arin's black shirt, my stomach winding itself into tighter and tighter knots. A heavy hand settled on the back of my neck, coaxing my head up.

"Should I put a knife in your hand to calm you down?" he murmured, the amused rumble reverberating in the broad chest beneath my palms.

I scowled. "For someone so fond of insulting my sense of humor, you certainly seem to have developed a terrible one of your own."

A grin broke out on Arin's face, which did very little to soothe my nerves. I braced myself on his thighs, unconsciously flexing my fingers around the same muscles I'd watched kick a soldier halfway across the shore.

He was the single most beautiful thing I had ever laid hands upon, and I was not good at treating the beautiful things in my life gently.

When I finished unbuttoning his shirt, rising to my knees to draw it off the broad cliffs of his shoulders, I had to redirect my gaze from his bare upper half to the fire to give myself a chance to breathe. No wonder this man wore his vests and his coats and his gloves. Without those layers, the world might fall to distraction any time Arin entered the premises.

I shied away from meeting Arin's gaze. He was allowing me a rare opportunity to see his plain thoughts, to peer inside the mind he fought so hard to protect. Baring himself in more ways than one, and I—

I lowered my hands to my lap, unable to do anything other than stare dumbly at the build of a man who had most assuredly never eaten a sesame candy in his entire life. The fig necklace sat beneath the hollow of his throat, framed by collarbones I could crack my skull against.

I beat back the sudden urge to cackle as I dropped my back to the grass, digging my knuckles into my eyes. Arin leaned over me, bracing his arms on either side of my head as his lips ghosted over the furrowed lines at my forehead. His low laugh warmed my skin, and I didn't resist when he tugged my hands away from my face. He'd laughed more in the last day than I had heard him laugh the entire time we'd known each other. "I believe this is the longest you have ever stayed quiet. I find it rather disturbing."

Before I could break my accidental vow of silence with a surly retort, the world spun. Arin flipped our positions, my knees hitting the ground on either side of his hips and straddling his waist. His hands traveled over my legs, curving around the backs of my knees.

I stared down at Arin, and I tried not to feel like a disciple of carnage pinning their sacrifice to the altar.

"You can touch me, Suraira."

I unknotted my fingers from their nervous tangle. *Don't shake*, I warned my hands. *Hold steady.* If Arin thought for half of a second that I was afraid of him, his Awaleen-forsaken vest would be back on before I could blink. He wouldn't believe me if I tried to explain that my fear was for him. For what the sheer depths of my hunger might wreak upon him. If I learned how it felt to touch the untouchable Heir, how could I return to a world where this knowledge would only serve to haunt me?

Perhaps temptation was the Mirayah's great trick. If threats would not compel me to stay, the promise of a lifetime of this very well might.

I gingerly mapped the scars curving along his side from the encounter with the Ruby Hound. Convinced Arin would interfere and get himself killed, I'd used my magic to trap him while I disposed of the Urabi's beast. The injuries from Galim's Bend were hidden beneath his bandages, and I forced away the memory of digging my fingers into his wounds while he bled. His scars were a reminder of a lesson learned; mine were a haunting, a tapestry of failure.

But when he stroked along the damaged skin on my back, I wondered if he read in my scars another story.

Before the nerves could sweep me away again, I slid to straddle Arin's knees and kissed the sharp indent of his hip. He gasped, his stomach flexing beneath my palm. The hands fisted at his sides flew to my shoulders.

I had seen Arin of Nizahl's eyes icy and unyielding, thunderous and terrifying, soft and fond. But never like this—unfocused, hazy, lost in sensation. A man existing in his body instead of only in his mind.

His hand splayed between my shoulder blades, the bite of his fingers a warm and possessive brand, and drew me back up to his mouth.

In the meadow of the ancient realm, I knew my days of running were coming to a close. I could go anywhere I wanted, but my destination would always be him. He had made himself the threshold to a world where it might finally be safe to land. To stay.

Arin turned us over, his body a powerful bow over mine, and I shaped silent promises against his shoulder.

I can't promise to always stay, I said to his skin. *But I can promise to never stop trying to come back.*

A frog watched me from the edge of Hirun.

Awareness speared through the fog of sleep. I sat up immediately, grabbing my tunic from the pile beside me. The meadow had disappeared, taking the lake and lone date tree with it.

Trees surrounded us on every side. A symphony of crickets chirped from rotted logs scattered over the earth, and patches of frost-bitten dirt melted under the weary morning light.

We were back in Essam. The Mirayah had drifted while we slept and left us behind.

Relief melted through me, and I put my head in my hands before I embarrassed myself in front of the frog and started kissing the dead leaves.

Why had the Mirayah let us go? We had fallen asleep between its jaws, and it chilled me to think it could have decided to close its teeth around us as easily as it had decided to spit us back out.

But then, perhaps releasing your prey to the vicious wild was the greater punishment. A lesson to never shake the bars of your cage again.

Beside me, Arin slept soundly. His chest rose and fell with his even breaths, and I spent far too long staring at the smooth curve of the muscles in his arms. I possessed about as much artistic skill as a slab of wood, but I'd never been troubled by the fact until confronted with the tableau of a sleeping, bare-chested Nizahl Heir.

Upon closer examination, I flushed to the very tips of my ears at the crescent nail marks scattered across his neck and shoulders. I had felt every ripple of tension in those arms as he spread himself over me; gripped the back of his neck and lowered his head to mine like a drought-stricken woman reaching for rain. I was afraid to check his stomach for bite marks.

No matter the urge, Arin had indulged me. He had touched me like my pleasure was a sacred decree; unraveled me like he had taken a vow to do nothing else his entire life. I ached with the proof of his singular attention.

I turned my palms toward the sky. The wings webbed on each of my wrists glowed faintly, confirming what I already knew. What I had known as soon as consciousness crept in, carrying with it the too-familiar pressure against the back of my mind.

I had my magic again.

I tried to swallow past the dry lump in my throat. I had known it wouldn't last. How could it? I had a kingdom to save, and he had a war on his horizon. Our paths would cross again, and it was up to Arin which side of the line he would be standing on when that time came.

The frog hopped closer, and my nose wrinkled at the rot and boiled-egg scent of Hirun.

I was going to get up. Just one more minute, and I would cast the same enchantment I had used over Arin in the Meridian Pass. It would protect him from any dangers until he woke. We had landed by raven-marked trees, which meant a Nizahl holding was nearby. Arin would find it, and by the time he reunited with his soldiers, I would be in the Omal palace.

Just one more minute, and I would walk away.

The frog croaked. Before I could toss a rock at the pest, a silver beak speared the earth and swallowed it whole.

I gawked as the kitmer straightened. When another appeared at its side, I beamed in delight. I'd thought the Mirayah destroyed these two after it caught their magic in its net.

Niseeba fluttered her wings, stamping from foot to foot. Beside her, Ingaz rooted through a decaying log in search of crickets.

"I will be just a minute," I reassured them quietly. I prodded around my coat and withdrew a sheaf of papers. Taking a fortifying breath, I folded them into the inner pocket of Arin's coat. The entries had survived my fall into the sea with minimal smudging.

The Urabi would kill me for this. Efra would get to crow from the rooftops about how he *knew it all along.*

Maybe he was right. Maybe the seeds of doubt sown in the Nizahl Heir would never fully flourish. Maybe Supreme Rawain's lies had rooted too deep in Arin's mind for anything else to ever grow.

In the measure of monster or man, what tips the scales?

"Stay out of sight, but make sure he returns to his holding unharmed," I murmured to Niseeba. Between the two of them, the stern kitmer seemed to have taken a liking to Arin. "Keep him safe."

I slid onto Ingaz's back and wrapped my hands around her horns. I took one last look at the fig necklace lying in the hollow of Arin's throat.

The Commander of Nizahl had a choice to make.

CHAPTER THIRTY-EIGHT

MAREK

Hundreds of recruits poured into the compound, a hush of exhaustion silencing any conversation other than which rooms would get first turn at the baths. Buoyant with dreams of collapsing for a long night of uninterrupted sleep, Marek released a groan fit to rattle every window in the Ravening compound when he opened the door to find someone sitting on the edge of his bed, his hand freezing halfway inside Marek's stash of sugar-coated pistachio squares.

Outraged, Marek momentarily forgot he was addressing a guardsman of the Heir. "It took me two weeks to save enough for those! How many did you take?"

Jeru paused, then proceeded to lower the bag to the ground and shift it under Marek's bed. "Not many." A guilty beat. "I'll replace them."

"Right." And afterward Marek would grow wings and fly.

Collapsing onto the rickety chair by the door, Marek kicked his boots out in a sprawl. "Are you not concerned your Commander might notice your repeated visits to the Ravening compound?"

Jeru pushed a couple of rebellious curls from his brow. Troubled grooves had formed in the young guardsman's forehead. "The Heir has too much demand on his time to notice my movements."

Marek snorted, unfastening the clasp of his gunk-stained coat.

"Your liege would notice a mosquito in a storm. Unless he lost his touch?"

Jeru's face hardened. "What did you find at the Shinawy household?"

Dania's dusty bones, what *was* it about that tombs-damned Heir? The guards, Sefa, even Sylvia had fallen victim to his thrall. Marek didn't understand it. When Arin of Nizahl looked at him, Marek's insides tried to evacuate through his shoes.

"Have you found Sefa?" Marek answered Jeru's question with one of his own.

It would be fair of Jeru to ignore Marek, but Jeru was cursed with the tragic trait of being entirely too nice.

"I have reason to believe she's in Lukub."

Marek sat up straight, his coat dropping into a forgotten heap on the ground. Every ounce of exhaustion in his body evaporated. "Where?" If he took a horse tonight, he could be across the eastern border of Lukub in three days' time. The compound was swimming with new recruits; Sulor hadn't noticed Marek arrive while tallying the wagons, so the section leader shouldn't notice him escape. If he did—well, it wouldn't be the first time Marek had evaded Nizahl soldiers.

"Her last known location was the Ivory Palace."

"The—" Marek stopped short. "What? Sefa would never go anywhere near the Ivory Palace. Sultana Vaida is more twisted than the Nizahl Heir. She'd pluck out Sefa's tongue to use as a hairbrush if it suited her."

Marek leaned forward in his chair, clasping his hands between his spread knees. The inside of his mouth tasted vaguely of the bosomat the soldiers had been passing around the back of the carriage. "What reason do you have to believe she is in Lukub?"

Jeru scooted backward on the bed and braced his back against the wall, arms crossed over his chest. His boots dangled over the side in a way Marek would've typically found entertaining. "Does it matter?"

Marek's wash of excitement ebbed, and it salted its retreat with a bone-deep dread.

"That depends. How badly do you want to see what I found at the Shinawy household?"

In another context, Marek might experience a stroke of guilt for putting such strain on the guardsman's face. For Sefa, Marek would put Rovial's tomb itself onto the man.

"There is a...man. Heilan Huz. He has spent the last month yowling about how the Sultana stole his lap girl. The girl he described matches Sefa, down to her mannerisms."

The blood drained out of Marek's face. He stared at Jeru, unable to articulate a response. Afraid, in fact, to open his mouth and vomit directly onto the uniformed guardsman.

"Lap girl?" was the best he managed to produce.

"Keep your head. The man is older than the mountains. High nobles in Lukub like to preen with pretty girls on their arms, particularly during festivals hosted at the Ivory Palace. It seems likely he took Sefa to the Ivory Palace, the Sultana kept her, and Huz is sore that the Sultana stole something he viewed as his."

Sweet Sirauk. Marek didn't know what was worse: the idea of Sefa relying on the generosity of lecherous high nobles to stay alive or the idea of Vaida imprisoning her in the Ivory Palace.

"But she is alive." He could not make it a question. It couldn't *be* a question.

"As far as I know," Jeru said. He studied Marek's rigid posture. "Breathe, Lazur. This is good news."

Swiping the rancid pile of fabric masquerading as his coat, Marek fished around the pockets. He tossed a cuff link at Jeru. "I found this in the Shinawy matriarch's wardrobe, buried behind her massacre of goose-feather gowns. The symbol in the center—is that what you're looking for? Orbanians flew that symbol on their banners during the Siege of Six Dawns, right?"

Pilfering through Mira's belongings after bedding her was not one of Marek's proudest moments, but it also was not among his worst. The cuff link had been the only inconsistent item in Mira's heaving wardrobe. The leather cuff link bore three suns, the spheres overlapping in the shape of a ram's head. Three smaller suns gathered at the nexus where the spheres connected, as though giving the ram three eyes at its forehead.

"Yes." There was a hard look in Jeru's eyes as he traced the symbol. "You should bathe and prepare yourself for travel. Fifteen hundred recruits will be leaving for the southern border of Lukub by dawn." Jeru tucked the cuff link into his pocket, laying an absent hand on his sword. "I should warn you—Sefa may not be in the Ivory Palace. She might have escaped Huz while she was at the palace and fled elsewhere."

"By the mist-damned bridge, I hope she did," Marek said fervently. "She would be safer on the streets than in the Ivory Palace. She knows how to survive as a vagrant, but a royal court? Sultana Vaida's court?"

A shudder slid through him.

"By the mist-damned bridge?" Jeru repeated, a hint of a smile breaking through the somber set of his features. "You sound Nizahlan."

There was a time when hearing that would have sent Marek into a panic. It summoned the whispers of his family, echoing their vile voices in his ear. In Nizahl, he was a failure. The son who fled. Threw the Lazur legacy into the dirt the minute he laid violent hands on the High Counselor, and for what? *A girl who will not marry you, Caleb, who has no father and no name to speak of. Your brothers and sister died so you might be given this chance. So you could saunter to greatness the way you saunter through everything in life, even if this greatness is wasted in hands more familiar with the shape of a woman than the weight of a sword. Is this who Amira, Binyar, and Hani left behind? Is—*

Marek stood abruptly. It had been a long time since he allowed his parents to linger in his thoughts.

A violet raven stared at Marek from Jeru's lapel. The swords clashing beneath it were stitched with a bright silvery thread Marek had never seen anywhere other than on Nizahlan-made clothes.

"I sound Nizahlan because I am Nizahlan," Marek said. "Even if sometimes I wish it were otherwise."

His parents might not be happy to have lost the tally of another hero child to bury, but his siblings—the only family he had cared about—would never have wanted Marek to follow them into the ground.

He was not the Lazur who fled; he was the Lazur who lived.

"I understand," Jeru said, and he sounded like he meant it. "Go ready yourself, Marek. We leave for Lukub at dawn."

Marek had been dropped into this compound with the clothes on his back. He had approximately three belongings, and most of them were edible. "Readying himself" would consist of bathing and trying not to think about what Sefa might have endured at the Ivory Palace.

"What do you need with the cuff link? Livening up His Highness's uniform?" Marek asked. With his imminent—and by the grace of the Awaleen, permanent—departure from the guardsman looming, Marek could afford a little curiosity.

The cuff link crumpled beneath Jeru's tightening fist. "Not exactly."

Several hundred men, half of whom would have stuck a sword through your ear if you tried to remove them from their bed so soon after their return from Galim's Bend, gathered at Fareed Mill to watch a guardsman of the Commander prepare to engage in combat to the death with Sulor, their least favorite section leader.

"Does anyone know what's happening?" Zane muttered, rubbing his giant knuckles into his eyes. At roughly six foot eight, Zane was the largest recruit in the compound, and also the reason Marek had escaped Galim's Bend without becoming a midday treat for a nisnas. Zane had lifted Marek off the ground like he weighed less than a sack of flour and kicked the nisnas clear across the road with his boot. Were Marek a different man, his ego might have suffered a blow, but those different men were probably busy dissolving in nisnas toxins.

It wasn't Marek who answered, but the recruit next to him, a reed-thin noble from Almerour. Marek had only spoken to him a handful of times—Almerour was two towns over from where his parents lived, and though the odds of a boy four years his junior recognizing a Lazur were slim, Marek kept his distance. "His Highness's guardsman issued an arrest for Sulor to be tried for his crime in the high courts of the Citadel. Apparently, our fearless Sulor has been taking bribes from noble families in the eastern quarter to reroute patrols in Nazeef, Tower Row, and Mandara."

Zane and Marek pinned Almerour with matching stares of confusion. "Reroute patrols? Why?"

More importantly, why would a guardsman of the Heir care so much about some side dealings in the noble quarters that he'd lie to his Heir and ask Marek for help?

Almerour seemed only too happy to explain. "The conscription ban. When the Citadel lifted it, noble families started cutting deals with section leaders to hide their eligible children. Pretend Zane is the son of a wealthy eastern quarter merchant. The patrols come knocking on the door to take Zane away, so what does Papa Merchant do? He offers the section leader responsible for recruiting from their quarter a handsome sum to drag a non-eligible child out of the lower villages, call him Zane, and throw him in the compound. Zane's name is recorded as a recruit, while the real Zane gets to stay home and hide under Mama and Papa's pillows until the other Zane finishes his service."

Marek and Zane exchanged a stunned look. Forcing a non-eligible lower villager—someone vulnerable like a child or the sole caretaker of a family or a person struggling with a disqualifying injury—into a military compound under a false name in an effort to line your own pockets?

"That is despicable," Zane growled, Marek's own revulsion echoed in the giant. "How do you know so much about this?"

Almerour shrugged. "Because Sulor offered the deal to my parents, and they turned him down."

Marek winced in begrudging sympathy. If he'd still been in the Lazur house, his parents would've tossed Marek into the wagon themselves.

As the Ravening compound watched, Jeru walked to the center of the field wearing a standard recruit uniform. Marek searched for the guardsman's pin, but he must have removed it when he changed. If Marek had harbored any doubt about whether Jeru intended to fight Sulor, it would've vanished right then. The Heir's guardsmen never removed their pin—even in death, they kept it with them. To take it off indicated a betrayal of their vows. It made them a traitor.

Comprehension slapped Marek across the face.

Aren't you worried about defying your Commander? If you are caught, I imagine he will greet your deception with a nice sturdy noose.

Jeru had been rescued from the lower villages, hadn't he? The story Sylvia told them in the tunnels fogged the back of Marek's mind, and he struggled to call the memory forward. The Nizahl Heir had saved Jeru before an executioner could lop off his head for supposedly stealing a bag of oats. The oats had been stolen by a twelve-year-old boy, but Jeru had taken the blame.

Marek closed his eyes, an exasperated admiration painting the inside of his lids. Jeru had been willing to die to protect a single child in the lower villages. Betraying his Heir—an act Jeru probably viewed as worse than death—for the chance to catch the section leader responsible for accepting bribes from the entire eastern quarter and condemning countless lower villagers?

It was so disgustingly honorable that it made Marek's teeth hurt.

The Almerour boy continued, eager to reclaim Zane's attention. "Before Jeru's men could take Sulor, he started shrieking about invoking his right to Fortune by Four. Can you believe the gumption?"

Zane cocked his head. "Fortune by Four? Never heard of it."

On the field, four swords were driven into the earth like signposts, forming a square border around Jeru and Sulor. Sulor toed off his boots, bouncing on surprisingly lithe feet, and picked up a sword nearly the size of Zane.

Utterly unbothered, Jeru stepped around Sulor's boots and rolled his sleeves to his elbow.

"It's an old rite," Almerour started, and Marek understood why this bookish boy's parents had been so eager to thrust him into a compound, "used to decide conflicts between people from different kingdoms who didn't trust the laws of either kingdom's court to fairly mete out their justice. Goes back to about 400 A.E."

Zane's brows became a hairy ball of bewilderment in the center of his forehead, so the Nizahlan hurried to clarify, "A.E.—after the entombment. Back then, every kingdom still had their magic, so the idea was you could invoke the Awaleen through Fortune by Four and avoid a real trial by fighting your way to freedom. Theoretically, those swords could act as conduits for the Awaleen's magic. An Orbanian could plead for Dania's magic, a Lukubi for Baira's, a Jasadi for Rovial's, an Omalian for Kapastra's, a Nizahlan for any of the four." Almerour pointed at each of the swords gouged into the field. "Not that it ever worked. The Awaleen are asleep in their tombs and we are alone up here, whether some like to accept it or not."

Marek crossed his arms over his chest, watching the guardsman lay a relaxed hand on the hilt of the sword strapped to his waist. Sulor may be a traitor and a coward, but he was a prime fighter. He hadn't been appointed leader of their compound for the sweetness of his temper. Jeru appeared to have the nerves of someone preparing for a leisurely stroll through a meadow. "Why would Jeru accept a trial of Fortune by Four? Nizahl prays to no Awal or Awala."

Almerour shrugged, losing steam now that Zane's attention had returned to the field. "You forget that it was only in the last seventy years or so before the Blood Summit that Nizahl started tightening its grip around the use of magic in any form. The people of Nizahl came from each of the four kingdoms; the streets were filled with the magic of Orbanians, Omalians, Jasadis, Lukubis. We observed these traditions just like everyone else, for a time. Today, the only tradition for the Awaleen that Nizahl participates in is the Alcalah."

With a shout like a wounded boar, Sulor swung his sword at Jeru with a force capable of hacking through ten men. The milling soldiers snapped to attention, and Marek held his breath.

Jeru whirled out of the sword's path. He still hadn't pulled out his own weapon. Was he angling to get his tombs-damned head cut off?

It continued in the same pattern, with Sulor swinging at Jeru and Jeru dancing out of the way. They rotated between the borders set by the four swords, and as they continued, Sulor lagging with the fatigue of wielding the sword's weight, Marek might actually have believed Jeru was being blessed by the Awaleen.

Until Sulor bellowed and changed the direction of his swing, cutting through Jeru's uniform and lancing a bloody stripe over his chest. Jeru collapsed to one knee. Shouts and cheers mixed together from the observers, with some urging Jeru to get up.

Arms pushed Marek back as he jolted a step forward.

Pull out your sword, you arrogant idiot! Marek wanted to shriek.

Sulor raised his arms with a triumphant shout, turning to face the spectators with a victorious sneer that Marek wished to carve off with his thumbnail.

The section leader's knuckles whitened around his sword as he lifted it high. Jeru's head remained bent, and Marek had never been more attuned to the fragility of a human neck.

As Marek braced to see the guardsman's curly head roll across Fareed Mill, his chances of finding Sefa rolling with it, a burst of movement juddered Sulor to a stop.

Jeru had sprung from his crouch and shoved a dagger through Sulor's unprotected throat. The heavy sword dropped to the ground, and Jeru tucked his arms beneath Sulor's as he whispered in the choking section leader's ear.

Jeru dumped an empty-eyed Sulor onto the ground. The section leader's body rolled, lifeless eyes staring across the field. Stunned silence waited beyond the four swords as Jeru retrieved his dagger.

Jeru glanced around. When his gaze landed on Marek, he lifted the dripping dagger to his temple in a salute.

Marek's lone cheer drifted over the stunned crowd. It settled, soft as first snow, and triggered an eruption. The entire compound vibrated, Jeru's name echoing across the fields.

But when Jeru looked down at Sulor's body, there was no victory in his eyes.

Only dread.

CHAPTER THIRTY-NINE

SEFA

It was over.

Sefa leaned over the balcony and watched a rider draw his horse to a stop beside the ruby obelisk.

Even with the crescent moon's lopsided smile tinting the sky, Sefa had a difficult time identifying the rider's features. Though if she had to guess, she would say he was a ridiculously tall man with reddish-brown hair and gray eyes, a peculiar hat balanced above his head.

Someone walked toward the rider, and Sefa didn't need to guess the newcomer's identity. The leisurely gait, the spots of color where flower petals had been woven through her braids. Vaida strolled toward Bausit, the ends of her satin cloak trailing in her wake like a river of blood.

She'd worn one of the gowns Sefa made. It fit her much better than Sefa could have hoped, clinging to the Sultana like a second skin and emphasizing every inch of her towering, imposing frame.

Of course, if the Sultana had chosen any other dress from Sefa's pile, Sefa would already be dead. Vaida would turn the gown inside out and see the words Sefa had painstakingly stitched line by line. Everything Sefa had witnessed, every whisper she had collected, every suspicion—Sefa had recorded it inside the gowns.

Vaida had told her to use her instincts, to be perceptive, and Sefa had listened. She wasn't Marek—she wasn't charming or gorgeous or particularly endearing. But Sefa was steady. Patient. Knitting quietly in the corner of the servants' quarters, Sefa had eventually ceased to garner any notice. A while later, the staff had begun to speak freely, their volley of complaints every night as amusing as it was informative. Sefa had learned when the Sultana met with her counselors; which towns received resources beyond their allotment in exchange for hosting more celebrations honoring the Sultana; which families were under suspicion of Nizahlan espionage; how many gardeners Vaida had tossed into the Traitors' Wells for harming her flowers.

Sefa had learned about the ring.

It wasn't much. Rumors, mostly. Stories stitched together from generation to generation of servants who had served the Sultanas of Lukub. The ring had belonged to Baira, passed down from Sultana to Heir for thousands of years. When Lukub still had magic, the ring could summon Ruby Hounds from anywhere in the land to the Sultana's side. As Lukub's magic weakened, more of the Hounds died off, and the ring became a relic. Ornamental. Powerless, but beautiful.

Sefa thought of Vaida sitting in front of the mirror, cold eyes fixed on her own reflection. The cherries thrown at her portrait. The endless celebrations and cavalier tyranny.

A relic of a ruler.

Bausit knelt before Vaida, and Sefa gazed past them to the expanse of Essam stretching as far as the eye could see. She wished she'd had a chance to climb Baira's Shoulders and see the kingdoms laid out beyond the trees.

She wished she could have seen Marek and Sylvia just one last time.

There was only one reason Bausit would rush to the palace instead of asking Vaida to meet him elsewhere.

Sefa's candle guttered. Wax dribbled over the elaborate lettering carved into the alabaster stone, cooling inside the names of each of the Sultanas who had succeeded Baira.

Sultana Vaida would walk through the mists of Sirauk itself if power waited for her on the other side. She had a ring fused with Baira's magic, an unrelenting desire to start war with Nizahl, and now—the location of a realm full of ancient, untamed magic.

Sefa gathered the gown she had finished this morning, folding it carefully. Across the bottom seam, she traced the final words she had written.

Find Vaida's ring.
Tell Marek and Sylvia I fought.

CHAPTER FORTY

ARIN

Arin was being watched.

He stepped away from the window, letting the curtain fall shut behind him. The prickle of magic at the back of his neck hadn't faded since he woke up twelve hours ago. Woke up *alone*, his hand sliding over the space where a warm body should have been.

"And this is the holding Vaida swallowed under her border?" Arin palpated two fingers against the underside of his jaw, testing for knots. The only benefit of losing four days to the Mirayah was skipping the tedium of healing.

The right side of his face had sunk into a black-and-blue bruise, and his eyes twinged if he blinked too hard, but the damage could have been worse. The most irksome effect was the fuzziness in his head, unraveling the seams of his thoughts before they could piece together.

He wouldn't be surprised if the disorientation had nothing to do with his injuries, and the Mirayah had simply dosed him with magic in an attempt to alter his memories of finding it.

But Arin remembered her. He remembered every detail.

"It is, sire." Jeru paused as Arin stripped off his coat and laid it flat on the table. "Vaida asked to be informed when you woke."

"Did she?" Arin assessed his chest in the mirror. The gashes from

Galim's Bend had already closed. In a week or two, they would be just another scar. The bruises from Mahair, meanwhile, throbbed across his shoulders and chest.

Other marks, much more pleasantly obtained, were scattered across Arin's body. He grazed the bite mark on his stomach, a small smile playing over his lips.

Arin knew his reputation at court and around the kingdoms. They called him withholding. Heartless. Frozen.

Frigid, on their bolder days.

For a time, he had believed them. Aside from Soraya, Arin had spared the lowest level of attention toward pursuing the whims of his body. When Arin decided on a course of action, it was premeditated. Measured and thoroughly considered. Planning was the antidote to passion, and Arin had rationalized himself away from every bed that had tried to invite him in.

Arin leaned forward, bracing his elbows on his knees as he cataloged the marks on his chest.

What they had done in the Mirayah was not premeditated, measured, or thoroughly considered, and it had been the best night of Arin's life.

Vaun materialized beside Arin, his expression a mask of fury as he gestured at Arin's battered face. "I will repay her for each injury she has dealt you twice over, my lord. She will regret ever laying hands on you. You helped keep those ungrateful, insipid villagers alive, and in return she nearly *killed you!*"

Arin flicked a dismissive hand. "Superficial wounds. She was trying to save my life."

Arin's attention caught on Vaun's lapel, where he typically displayed his guardsman pin in flagrant disregard of his own safety. "Did you lose your pin?"

Vaun's hand flew to his lapel. He seemed mystified to find it naked. "I must have dropped it. Apologies, my liege—I will see to getting a new one." Vaun shook his head. "How would tying Your Highness to a wall and brutalizing you save your life?"

Jeru pulled aside one of the excessively long drapes to peer out the window.

Arin withdrew a long-sleeved black shirt and set it aside while he rifled for a new vest. "As long as I was conscious, I was a liability to both of us. The Urabi would try to kill me to prevent me from capturing the Malika, and my soldiers would arrest every Jasadi in the village as soon as the Omalian threat was subdued. But if I am critically injured—"

"Your soldiers have to immediately ensure your safety." Vaun's scowl could carve through steel. "She cheated."

"No." Arin pressed his tongue to his teeth in an effort not to smile. "She played the game."

"They said she flew out of the village on the back of a kitmer." Jeru leaned against the wardrobe. "Riddah and some of the other soldiers reported seeing gold and silver thunderbolts flying from her hands."

The vest Arin had triumphantly located slipped from his fingers. The haze over his thoughts cleared away at last, and Arin went cold.

Every time I use my magic, I find a new vein.

I am afraid that I will have to choose—my mind or my people.

"My lord?" Jeru tentatively picked up the fallen vest. "You have visitors. Layla and Bayoum are eager to confirm your good health, but I can tell them to return at a later time."

Jeru tried to hand Arin the vest, but Arin pushed it away. He drew the shirt over his arms and lagged, staring at the laces waiting to be done.

"I'll require a moment alone." Arin spoke without inflection. "Tell Layla and Bayoum I will be out to see them shortly."

When his guardsmen withdrew, Arin picked up his coat. He couldn't recall if he had returned the pieces of her cuff back into his pocket after showing them to her.

A wrinkle in the inner left pocket disrupted Arin's search. He paused, noticing the slight bump for the first time.

Arin extracted a sheaf of torn pages folded tightly within the heavily lined pocket. The pages were worn in the center from countless folds, their surface faded from the press of too many negligent fingers. The writing wasn't in her hand, so Arin flipped to the last page immediately and skimmed for the signatory.

Binyar Lazur, First General of the Southern Regiment of Nizahl.

Binyar Lazur? Arin's brows drew together. When would Essiya have crossed paths with a deceased Nizahlan general? Arin had met Binyar during his brief stay in the Citadel. A stalwart, matter-of-fact man with stern notions of honor and family legacy. Nothing like his younger brother, whose only commitment in life was to a girl ten times braver than him. Perhaps the younger Lazur brother had given Essiya these pages.

Arin sat on the armchair by the window and began to read.

The fortress fell before the messenger did.

Arin had reread the pages four times, rearranging the pieces of the story over and over again, and failed to find a fit.

Arin brushed his thumb over Binyar's increasingly frantic script. He aligned the pages into a neat stack.

The fortress fell after the Blood Summit. *Because* of the Blood Summit. Nobody fully understood how it had happened, but the most commonly cited theory was the loss of Jasad's entire royal bloodline had weakened the fortress and left it vulnerable to collapse.

Which might have been perfectly plausible if not for Essiya of Jasad. The second Heir of Jasad survived the Blood Summit. Her magic and bloodline had still existed when the fortress fell.

Arin took a measured breath. He needed to look further—to pull new pieces onto his board.

It cost Arin to set aside the death-of-the-royal-bloodline theory. It took a hammer to the ground beneath his feet, and through the cracks, Arin saw flashes of the dangerous sinkhole waiting just beyond the surface.

If it wasn't the death of the royal family that caused the fortress to collapse, then the enchantment must have failed.

The enchantment sustaining the fortress around Jasad was the kingdom's best-guarded secret. The only information he'd been able to find vaguely mentioned the ceremony to refresh the fortress every year. The Qayid or Qayida would recite the enchantment to renew the original magic cast by Qayida Hend thousands of years ago.

Arin traced it back again.

Niphran was Qayida when the fortress fell. She had been Qayida once before, but her parents had stripped her of the honor when they exiled her to Bakir Tower. Niyar and Palia reinstated her sometime around Arin's fourteenth birthday. He remembered the date because his father had accepted an invitation to the festival and left for Jasad the week before. Isra had insisted on staying behind for Arin's birthday, and she had snuck him out of the Citadel to visit the preserved ruins in Ukaz. She'd stuffed his hair under a knit cap and waited patiently whenever Arin's attention snagged on a strange pattern in the carvings or a collection of stones he'd read stories about.

Two years later, she had left for the Blood Summit, and Arin had spent his birthday alone in his chambers, designing the statue that would stand above his mother's tomb in the Citadel's gardens.

Arin's fingers curled. He wanted to rise and cast these pages into the flames. Not every question needed a satisfactory answer. Plenty of people were content with uncertainty; they lived and died without expending themselves to understand anything beyond the corner of the world they occupied.

They would not stand directly over the sinkhole and push *down*.

But Arin could no more halt the turn of his own mind than Essiya could halt the call of her magic.

I bet the Mufsid blamed Hanim for the fortress falling. Richly ironic, if you ask me. Hanim didn't sack Usr Jasad. She might have written the false enchantment, but who read it?

Arin stood, tossing the parchment toward the armchair. The pages fluttered to the ground as he started to pace.

Even if Arin posited that reading the wrong enchantment could destroy a fortress thousands of years old, it didn't explain how Nizahl would have known beforehand. According to Binyar, Nizahl's armies were already marching for Jasad. Thousands of soldiers had been waiting behind the fortress when it fell. How could his father have known the wrong enchantment would be read for the first time in Jasad's history?

Hanim was their leader for a time, you know. Before her exile for conspiring with your father against the Jasad crown.

The cracks above the sinkhole widened. A warning to stop, to step back from the precipice.

But the pieces had begun moving of their own volition, racing into place.

How can you sense magic?

Why would Hanim tell Rawain that she'd given the Mufsids the wrong enchantment? Assuming Rawain and Hanim had conspired together when Rawain was the Nizahl Heir, Rawain had already resoundingly betrayed Hanim by the time he became Supreme. The Qayida may have been monstrous, but she was no fool. She would never risk the fortress unless she stood to gain something immeasurable. Something she had tried to claim through Essiya, the last living Heir.

Jasad's throne.

What had reassured her in the Supreme's word after he had aided her exile and turned his back on her once before?

A piece quaked at the center of the frame. On it, Arin saw Isra's face. He saw the lower village girl plucked from obscurity to marry the Nizahl Commander, the son born too soon after the wedding.

Was your hair black before the curse?

Arin braced himself on the wall as the room spun.

Hanim had to have believed Rawain meant to lay claim to Jasad's throne instead of destroying it. Something had convinced her Rawain would put her on the newly taken throne.

I met your mother at the Blood Summit. Isra knew she was going to die. She walked into that Summit knowing what Rawain planned to do.

To risk the fortress, it would have been more than mere alliance. More than promises. It would have needed to be the same claim she had sought through Essiya.

The strongest claim to a crown was blood. Rawain's son would have become Heir to Jasad and Nizahl.

Rawain's son...and Hanim's.

The sinkhole yawned open, and Arin disappeared.

CHAPTER FORTY-ONE

SYLVIA

Apparently, all it took to infiltrate the Omal palace was a good glamor and a competent understanding of its layout.

Nobody had glanced twice at the servant entering through the kitchen doors at dusk, her head bent low over a pail of chicken feed. She had frizzy brown hair, dull green eyes, and a small mole on her chin.

As soon as I stepped out of view of the guards, I dropped the pail near a couple of children enthusiastically tearing chunks of bread into a long dish. A boy staggered past me with a giant bowl of milk, grains of sugar pebbled around the bowl's rim. He poured it over the bread. Laughing shrieks bounced between the children as hot droplets of milk sprayed their curious little faces.

I swiped an empty tray from the counter and stepped over the puddle. I had loved om Ali when I was younger. I hoped the children remembered to add nuts.

The only soldiers I had seen so far had been strewn around the upper towns. Omal *and* Nizahl soldiers, which had entertained me greatly. Arin wouldn't casually waste Nizahl soldiers on Omal's upper towns. Felix must have irritated him enough for Arin to deliver his bloodless version of a backhand.

A guard glanced at me as I walked into the main lobby, tray balanced on my shoulder. He thrust out a hand when I tried to move around him. "Keep an eye out for the men," he said. "The court drank its weight in ale at dinner. Anything they can drag into their lap, they will."

Typical. I offered a short nod, hoping he wasn't expecting more of a response. Sefa and Marek had once said I spoke without any sort of accent, but how would they know? Apparently, they'd had a Nizahlan inflection the entire time. We had just been three silly chickens clucking in a circle.

The guard stepped aside, and I went on my way. The court was indeed drunk, and the sounds of laughter and raised voices set my teeth on edge. The lower villagers were dying at the hands of the Omal Heir while his court sat here celebrating.

Much as I would have liked to see how many of them I could maim before the guards noticed, time wouldn't allow me my pleasures. Every minute I wasted was another death. Another opportunity for the Urabi to lose hope that I would find them.

The overpowering scent of eucalyptus and cinnamon perfumed the halls. In an ancillary chamber reserved for the young ladies of the court, dreamy swirls had been painted in a pattern reminiscent of leaves dancing in the wind. Pillowy furniture responsible for the murder of at least a thousand ducks per cushion filled the room. Gauzy silk drapes twisted to resemble white and blue clouds swayed from the ceiling.

Markedly absent were any young ladies, who had likely received the same warning I had about the wastrels. Another stroke of fortune.

Every day during our training, Arin would have a guardsman bring a new map to my rooms. My preparation for the Alcalah had included memorizing every hall, hovel, and hole in the palaces we'd be visiting. My success in the trials, he'd said, only mattered if I survived to compete in them.

I counted the blue whorls of paint in the right corner of the room until I reached number seven. Right where the paint curled in, a divot the size of my thumb broke the pattern. At the exact spot Arin's maps had said it would.

I hooked my thumb in the divot and tugged. A click sounded on the other side of the wall. With a groan, the outline of a door appeared against the paint. Wiping the dust from my nose, I shouldered it open.

Ah, lovely—another inhumanely narrow stairway designed by someone with a vendetta against functional spines. I tossed the tray to the ground, the crash muffled by the thick white carpet.

I shut the door behind me, pitching the stairwell into darkness. I climbed, counting each step. One hundred fifty-four was how many it would take to reach Queen Hanan's wing. One hundred fifty-three to find my grandmother.

One hundred fifty-two until I either gained her army or lost mine.

I lost count after eighty. My shoulders stung from scraping against the spiked surface of the stone walls. I tripped on every other step. The pitch black of the stairwell conspired with the limited air to fray the nerves I'd been holding steady since I left the Mirayah. I rationed my breaths, careful not to pull so much that the dust ignited a coughing fit.

My magic hummed, but I didn't dare listen. When the others used their magic, their biggest concern was how long it would take to replenish. How much they could use before they became temporarily defenseless.

I didn't have that issue. I had never scraped the bottom of my well. For all its problems, my magic answered my call, even if not always in the ways I intended.

If I thought about it too long, the irony would plow me over. I had access to a seemingly unlimited amount of magic, but I couldn't use it. Even an act as small as lighting my way through this awful corridor would produce another vein. It would break another mirror in the shadow of my mind, pierce me with the shard of an unexplainable memory.

All magic has rules. Consequences. We just need to figure out what hers are.

I paused, propping my arm against the wall and resting my sweaty forehead in the nook of my elbow. Namsa and the rest of the Aada hadn't abandoned their inquiry into my magic. They were not an easily dissuaded group of people, the Urabi.

They had made a conscious decision to ignore it.

Every time my magic overwhelmed me, Efra felt it. He felt the numbness winding through me like a toxin, even if he didn't know what precipitated it. Even if he couldn't hear the voice behind it.

They knew what it meant for my magic to disconnect me from myself, even temporarily.

This was a race: my mind against my magic. They needed my magic too much to advise me against using it. Still, I knew they didn't want to watch me destroyed—otherwise, they would have suggested raising the fortress during Nuzret Kamel as our first and only option. Instead, we were risking everything to appeal to Queen Hanan.

An effort doomed to fail even before I slipped Binyar Lazur's confession into Arin's coat.

I continued my trek, a light palm on the wall to track the curving stairwell. How ardently would Efra have advocated against me if he knew that I had handed over one of our most critical tools to Arin of Nizahl? Not just Efra—they would all be furious. The Commander of Nizahl, the enemy of magic. A lost cause. A waste of a resource to appeal to someone who viewed magic as the scourge of the earth.

And maybe they were right. I was making my own gamble. Arin's unwavering commitment to logic and truth versus his loathing for magic.

No, I wouldn't call it a gamble. A gamble implied equal odds. It suggested that one outcome was just as likely as the other.

You lied to your father.
This was a theory.

When I finally stumbled out of the stairwell, a fine layer of dirt coated me from neck to knee.

I didn't bother dusting it off. The grime fit perfectly with my new role as bedraggled orphan crawling to her grandmother's knee for a morsel of mercy.

Before I had taken more than a step around the corner, the edge of a frame bumped against my sleeve. I glanced up at the portrait and recoiled.

After several minutes of reeling in my jaw from its drop to the palace kitchen, I took a step closer to the monstrosity.

This portrait hadn't been there the last time I visited. Not only would it have been impossible to miss, but it would have guaranteed Arin's discovery of my true identity.

In the portrait, Queen Hanan and the late King Toran stood side by side, holding hands. Lustrous waves of black hair fell to Queen Hanan's waist, and mirth danced in brown eyes long since gone dull. King Toran, my grandfather, towered over her. I blinked at his fluffy, silver-streaked beard and thick eyebrows, one of which was arched in stern contemplation.

At least I knew where my height came from.

Sitting on the throne, one knee crooked to the side and the other straight forward, was Emre. He had the same wavy black hair as his mother, falling over his forehead and around his ears in a messy thicket. Spectacles perched at the top of his wide nose, and he gripped the arm of the throne as though it might eject him at any moment.

Balanced on one knee, an arm wrapped around her middle, the child version of myself aimed a gummy smile at the artist.

I stepped closer, studying the minute paint strokes as though I could glare them out of existence. They had drawn me at around six or seven, kicking my legs cheerfully on my father's lap. My curls were free and voluminous, tightly coiled as they had only been when I was young.

My father on the throne, his child on his knee. An impossible tableau. A work of fiction. My father had seen me as a newborn and then died in the woods. I hadn't visited Omal a single time until I fled there after killing Hanim—Gedo Niyar and Teta Palia had forbidden me from accompanying them on any diplomatic trips to the kingdom.

Had Queen Hanan commissioned this to fulfill some sick fantasy? To create a universe where she and her husband hadn't happily disinherited me after Emre died?

A sick foreboding twisted through my gut. This portrait would have sent Felix into a rage. It suggested a claim. Legitimacy.

It was an act of defiance against her nephew.

A shadow fell over me. A hard grip caught my shoulder, spinning me around.

"Who—"

My dagger split through the side of his throat, severing everything but his spinal cord. Blood sprayed in a wide arc across the painting.

I stepped over his twitching body and kept moving. Blissfully unaware of my approach, the other two guards played cards in front of the doors to the throne room, a flipped wooden crate serving as their table.

The second guard looked up when blood spattered the cards. His companion gasped, clutching at his slit throat as I loomed behind him.

The cards went flying at my head. The second guard rolled to the ground as my dagger embedded itself in the wall behind him.

It was not a fair fight. The guard slammed his fist into my jaw, tilting forward as he did so. I absorbed the blow and drove my dagger into his heart before he could regain his balance.

Wiping my blade, I took in the bodies scattered on the clean white rugs. Just three guards?

Felix knew we were coming. Had he really been so confident that we wouldn't penetrate the upper towns that he'd left the palace unsecured? Fairel would have been able to dispose of this lot with a single arrow.

I gripped the curved handles of the throne room's doors. My blood beat in my ears.

For the last month, I had imagined the aftermath of this moment. Queen Hanan's rejection, Felix's wrath, the inevitability of raising the fortress and dying in a blaze of magic.

I hadn't given much thought to the possibility of success. The portrait in the hall—it changed the conversation. Maybe Queen Hanan could be persuaded. Maybe Nuzret Kamel and the fortress could be avoided.

My dagger lifting to cut through more guards, I heaved against the doors to the throne room. They groaned, steel hinges fighting ancient wood, and parted.

The groan echoed, ricocheting from the peak of the domed ceiling to the farthest corner of the cavernous throne room.

No guards rushed out to meet me. Aside from the squelch of my boots against the gleaming blue and white tiles, there was no sound at all.

Breathtaking sapphires shimmered in concentric spirals around the glass dome at the peak of the high ceiling.

At the other end of the throne room, a platform rose like an island in the midst of a foaming sea. In the center, the Omal throne.

Were I a more geologically inclined woman, I might wonder what sort of stone the enormous rochelya wrapped around the throne was composed of. The ethereal blue of its scales reminded me of Suhna Sea just before dusk. Its long tail was lashed around the throne's leg, the reptile's head looming above the back of the seat. Empty eyes glowered across the room, and a fearsome jaw unhinged in a silent roar.

Queen Hanan watched me from beneath its shadow.

I sheathed my dagger, taking a tentative step forward. "Your Majesty." I cleared my throat. Should I have called her grandmother or Teta Hanan? I'd spent the later part of my youth in a keep full of village orphans—I had no idea how noble grandchildren addressed their elders in Omal.

I approached slowly, hands raised. There were three exits in the throne room; three places where guards could stream in and completely surround me if she called out.

"I wanted an audience with you, Queen Hanan. When last we met, I was Nizahl's Champion. Today, I come before you as Malika of Jasad, and I—" I swallowed. "I hope to leave as Heir of Omal."

A tiny sound broke the tomblike silence of the room. It sounded like water leaking from a roof.

Plink. Plink. Plink.

Sunlight speared through the dome and scattered against the sapphires, sending arches of brilliant blue light dancing across the walls. They illuminated the blood dripping from the foot of the throne, the sheen of red spreading over the iridescent tiles. I followed the blood to the platform, where a pool had collected around the rochelya's tail.

I climbed the steps to the platform.

She provoked him.

My boots tracked red prints across the river of blood.

Commissioning that portrait had been a message. The first decisive action by a Queen who had moldered for decades.

The first and final.

Queen Hanan stared sightlessly from the throne. She wore a blushing pink gown that stood in sick contrast to her bluish complexion. Knives pinned her hands to the arms of the chair. A deep gash across her throat exposed the sliver of her spine where her neck had been sawed to the bone. The point of a sword breached her forehead. It had been thrust through the back of the throne and into her skull to keep it raised.

Something glinted in the rochelya's open jaw.

Stepping close to the corpse of my grandmother, I lifted the object from between the rochelya's teeth.

A glass crown.

The platform rumbled. Ah—*there* were the guards. An army of them, it sounded like.

I closed Queen Hanan's eyes. With the end of my sleeve, I wiped the blood at the corner of her mouth.

"I haven't held a very favorable opinion of you, Teta," I murmured. The thunder of hundreds of approaching footsteps echoed in the throne room. "I cannot change the past, but I can offer you this: I will choose to believe that you would have said yes."

Three sets of doors burst open. Rows of uniformed Omalian soldiers marched in front of the platform, spears pointed as they filled the room in neat lines. Boots squeaked over the shining marble floor. The chandeliers dangling on long chains from the ceiling swayed. A statue of King Toran in the corner keeled forward, cracking against a pillar.

I turned my back to my grandmother and gazed out at the sea of Omalian uniforms. Too many; far too many. They parted at the center as a lone figure strolled toward the platform. A real crown sat above his feathered black hair. Gleeful hazel eyes shone in his loathsome face, resting over a nose identical to mine.

"Hello, cousin," Felix said.

CHAPTER FORTY-TWO

SYLVIA

I gazed out at the expanse of Omalian uniforms and wondered how many more waited outside the throne room. Felix had to have sent at least four or five thousand to attack the villager armies amassing at the perimeter of the upper town. How many soldiers would be left in reserve? Tens of thousands?

I gestured at Queen Hanan's corpse. "Have you been naughty again, Felix?"

"Me?" The new King of Omal pursed his lips in a mockery of concern. "My dear Essiya, you are the one who executed the Queen of Omal. Your very own grandmother."

When comprehension struck, it brought with it a bolt of begrudging respect. Well, well, well—my cousin had finally cast aside his little boy tantrums and played the game like the rest of us.

The raids in the lower villages had been his opening ceremony. The heralding of his new reign, establishing what fate would come for those who opposed him. Mahair was the last lower village he had targeted. He had wanted to give me enough time to see what would befall the town if I didn't come running to save them.

There weren't many guards protecting the palace because Felix *wanted* me to infiltrate the throne room. I needed to be caught beside the slain body of the Queen so he could claim the throne and my head in one fell swoop.

Even the dullest of minds could be sharpened against a powerful grudge. Felix had never recovered from Arin denying him his right to kill me that day at the waleema. I had stabbed him in the leg, insulted him, foiled his plot with the ghaiba, and then had the audacity to become a threat to his crown. Arin must have told them I was to be taken alive, but who would blame Felix for executing the Jasadi responsible for slaughtering the Queen? His revenge had given him the greater claim to my life.

"You can keep the crown," Felix said magnanimously. "I had it made just for you."

I rotated the false crown between my fingers. "Do you believe in death, Felix?"

The King crossed his arms over his chest. Indulging me in my last moments, it seemed. "Are you certain you wish for your last words to be such stupid ones? You might try begging for your life instead."

"I have never been particularly averse to death," I mused. "I didn't welcome it. I resisted it with all my might. But at the end of the day, it was always a matter of scale. I would rather be a powerless fugitive than dead. I would rather be dead than trapped. I fought so hard against anything that might tie me to this earth—anything that might weigh the scale against death if ever I was trapped again. I cast aside my identity, my magic, my affections. I told myself they were nothing but stones in my pocket.

"I can't fight my way through your soldiers, and I can't die before Nuzret Kamel," I said. "I have to choose living, and the only way I live past today is if I break the scale. If I surrender to my magic and walk into a trap from which there is no escape."

Queen Hanan was dead. Even if I killed Felix right now, if I bypassed her council to reinstate myself to the line of inheritance and claim this kingdom in blood—it would not be enough. My claim would force Omal into war with Nizahl on Jasad's behalf, and with two dead rulers supposedly slain at my hands, the armies would mutiny.

I had known the chances of victory today were slim, but some foolish part of me had held on to hope. *There is a chance*, it would whisper. *Still a chance.*

But a chance was mercy, and mercy was not for those with blood on their hands. For us, there were only choices.

Only the scale.

A true ruler is one who puts their people before themselves. No matter the cost.

I dropped the crown to the ground. The glass crunched beneath my boot. "I make you this promise, Felix of Omal: your name will not be remembered. When your story is told for generations to come, it will be an accessory to my own. Even the hate your people hold for you will dwindle, taking the last seed you've sown into this world with it. When you finally fade, dear cousin, you will taste true death long after you've rotted in your grave."

An enraged flush darkened Felix's neck, and he raised an arm. A row of archers in the back of the room lifted their bows. In the front, hundreds of spears flipped toward the platform. The soldiers in the center withdrew their swords and pointed them at the ground, waiting. He had taken layers of precaution against my magic.

If only it mattered.

How deep can you dig, Essiya?

Bows strained as the archers notched their arrows, and Felix grinned as he stepped behind a throng of his guardsmen.

I couldn't whisper when I called for my magic anymore. What I demanded from it would answer only to my scream.

Mist crept over my skin. When I had summoned my magic before, it was usually a shapeless command. *Protect. Fight. Save.* The means through which it achieved those goals hadn't mattered.

Shouts rang in the throne room as whirls of smoke erupted between the guards. They writhed like fallen storm clouds.

There was nothing shapeless about what I wanted from my magic this time.

Silver wings sliced through the smoke. The shouts matured to howls as hundreds of kitmers materialized between the rows of soldiers. Twice the size of any I had created before, they were near-perfect replicas of Rovial's kitmers. Vicious black eyes blinked beneath curved horns. Feathers sharper than any blade unfurled as the kitmers rose to their full height.

As one, they roared.

Long claws gouged into uniformed chests, eviscerating soldiers where they stood. Anarchy claimed the throne room as attention turned to the kitmers and away from their creator. Arrows flew through the air, bouncing ineffectually against the creatures. One of the arrows went through the eye of the soldier sprinting toward me, and he dropped like a sack at the foot of the platform.

"Make way for the King!" came the order. "Get him out of here!"

"No!" Felix bellowed. "Kill her! Someone kill her!"

Gold and silver veins flowered over my arms, effervescent beneath my skin. He still didn't understand, did he? I was already dead. Sylvia, Essiya, whoever the other faces were—by Nuzret Kamel, they would be gone.

Magic was a greedy conqueror. When it finally laid claim to the rest of my mind, it wouldn't share.

"For Fairel," I murmured. "For everything your people have lost at your hands."

One of the kitmers flew past my shoulder, obeying my silent command. Felix shrieked as the kitmer's claws unfurled. They gouged into my cousin's neck and yanked through muscle and bone. His screams choked off as blood filled his mouth, spraying thick and tacky onto his guards.

"For our grandmother."

When Felix's headless corpse fell to the ground, joining the slew of other carcasses, I felt no joy. I felt nothing much at all.

Blood spattered the serene walls of the throne room. The last of dusk shifting through the glass dome trailed its light over mangled and eviscerated bodies heaped like offerings at the altar of the dead Queen. Between them, moving under the veil of hundreds of beating wings, walked the gold-and-silver-eyed sole survivor.

"Fly to every corner of this land and tell them that the throne of Omal has fallen," I ordered. "Take my voice and tell my people the Malika of Jasad is calling them home."

I shielded my head as the kitmers smashed through the dome, raining glass over the graveyard they left in their wake. A blanket of silver and gold seethed over the darkening sky as the kitmers pooled together above the palace.

I watched through the dome's shattered opening as Jasad's symbol rose above the Omal palace like smoke from a burning pyre.

The kitmers flew apart, shadows streaking into the horizon. Carrying my voice, my message, to every corner of these kingdoms. When Nuzret Kamel came and the fortress rose, every Jasadi needed to be on the other side. War was upon us, and the time to choose had come.

I paused beside Felix's body. His head had flown onto a slop of gore farther away, and I picked it up by its feathered hair. They would want proof, the villagers. They would want a memento to take back to their ravaged homes.

I retrieved his fallen crown, cleaning it off on my pant leg. I set it back on his hair.

"You can keep the crown," I said.

A face reflected out of my cousin's staring eyes, moving when I moved. It belonged to a stranger. A child this time, perhaps eleven or twelve years old.

My heart pounded. A sick rush of fear spread through my chest, spilling into the darkest recesses of my mind. I stared at the face, and I did not scream when I heard the voice.

You see us, my magic whispered. *We know you see us.*

Gritting my teeth, I closed Felix's eyes. If madness was my destination, I would not ease its way.

I walked past the collapsed columns of the throne room. I tore the torch from the wall and touched the flame to the shredded leg of a dead soldier. It licked hungrily over his uniform and leapt to the next body. It would reach Queen Hanan last, but it would reach her eventually. Nobody would be spared.

Nobody except me. Felix hadn't understood—nobody did.

When the dust settled, I would always be the one left standing.

Survival was not the story of my success.

It was my eternal punishment.

CHAPTER FORTY-THREE

SEFA

"Move, you stupid girl!" An elbow caught Sefa in the shoulder, shoving her out of the way.

The kitchen moved at a jarring speed, trays whizzing over heads while the pile of dirty dishes accumulating on the counter grew to staggering heights. Dried stains covered Birta, caking her in the evidence of her long and ardent labor. "There are near a thousand Nizahl soldiers outside our gates for Sedain. Make yourself useful and start carrying out the bowls of bissara while I prepare the goulash."

Sefa obeyed without thought, reaching for the first bowl of green soup she saw.

"That's the molokhia, you imbecile!" Birta howled. "Get out!"

"Sorry!" Sefa swiped the knife lying beside a pile of diced potatoes—the only reason she had stopped by the kitchen in the first place—and left.

Servants scurried along the halls, silver trays stacked with empty plates balanced on their shoulders. Complaints flew between them as frequently as commands.

Sefa glided through the pandemonium without slowing.

"Zahra!" Salwa appeared at her elbow, streaks of dirt on her forehead and her round cheeks. "Aren't you going to come outside? The Nizahl regiment is here. Some of the soldiers are *so* handsome, but they don't speak much. We heard the Commander is here, too—apparently, he's been in Lukub for days!"

Arin of Nizahl was in Lukub? He was *here*?

"Good," Sefa murmured, mostly to herself. "He'll stop her if I fail."

If. Still so foolishly optimistic.

There was not a world where Sefa managed to steal Vaida's ring and escape Lukub unscathed. The best she could hope was to destroy the ring before they caught and killed her.

"I will be out soon, Salwa." Sefa cupped the younger girl's cheek and pressed a quick kiss to her forehead. "Thank you for always being so kind to me."

The young servant blinked, but Sefa was already walking.

The guards stationed on either side of the short hall didn't react when Sefa walked past them. She was the Sultana's personal attendant—who would question her presence in the Sultana's chambers? Who would think to search her for a weapon?

Sefa closed the door behind her and leaned heavily against it. When she could catch her breath again, she settled on Vaida's dressing room chair.

Sefa didn't want to do this.

My palace was built by an Awala who crafted illusions more perfect and persuasive than any reality... If you wish to last in the Ivory Palace, I suggest you fiercely guard that heart of yours. Its softness is an irresistible temptation to those of us with teeth.

Vaida had been taught what it took to last in the Ivory Palace. Maybe there was an age before the Sultana counted herself among those with teeth, when she had just been another girl with a soft heart.

Sefa picked up the chair and moved it behind the door. If she moved fast, she could knock out the Sultana as soon as she walked in. She would remove the ring and run, even if the tombs-damned thing burned through her skin and bones. Vigilance was the key to leaving this chamber alive.

Ignoring the weight of the knife, Sefa waited.

The scent of flowers startled Sefa from her nap.

Inches away, richly lashed dark eyes studied Sefa with languid curiosity. "You shouldn't be here, Zahra," Vaida said. "The other servants haven't sat down in hours. They will think I am giving you preferential treatment again."

Candlelight flickered around the room, shadows dancing cheerily across the walls. Candles Sefa had most assuredly not lit. When did Vaida enter the room?

Sefa had *fallen asleep*. Awaleen below, it was almost a mercy knowing she'd never see Sylvia again. Her friend was the Victor of the Alcalah, a survivor of the Blood Summit, a fugitive Queen. Meanwhile, Sefa had worked herself into such a fit about swinging a chair at Vaida that her body had shut down.

"I—" Sefa hadn't counted on speaking. She didn't have a good explanation for her presence. "Birta wanted me out of the kitchen. I couldn't keep pace with the rest of them."

Vaida's eyes narrowed. "What did she say?"

"Nothing important." Frustrating as Birta's behavior had been throughout Sefa's stay, Sefa was not about to unleash Vaida's ire against the older woman. "She was exhausted, is all."

"Hmm." Vaida wandered toward her bureau and extracted a silk shawl from the top of the drawer. "For a moment, I thought you might be hiding from the Nizahl soldiers."

"The soldiers? No, I only learned today they were here." Distracted, Sefa got up from her chair and edged away from the door. If a scuffle ensued, she didn't want the guards to hear. Given how disastrously this robbery attempt had already progressed, Sefa wasn't going to take any chances.

When Vaida's comment caught up with her, Sefa stopped. "Why would I hide from the Nizahl soldiers? Are they planning something?"

Maybe Sefa wouldn't have to take the ring after all. If the Nizahl Heir had come to quarrel with Vaida about the holding she had swept under Lukub's border, Sefa could find him and warn him about the Mirayah. Arin would listen. He would also have her arrested, but imprisonment would be a blessed fate compared to what Vaida would do if she caught her with the ring.

It glinted against her finger as she approached Sefa, the shawl dangling from her loose grip. Sefa stiffened as Vaida drew the ends of the shawl around Sefa, tucking it around her shoulders. It constrained her arms as Vaida pulled on the ends, tugging Sefa a step forward. "Do you trust me, darling?"

Sefa had to strain to look up at the Sultana. Viscerally aware of the ring's proximity, she struggled not to give away her nerves. Vaida was in a strange mood—a mood Sefa couldn't pin down despite the patterns she had learned to keep watch for.

"The last time I mentioned trust, you said, 'If you're going to say something that silly, save it for a stage.'"

"So I did." Lips painted berry red parted in a smile. "You have an excellent memory. I do, too."

Vaida's grip on the shawl tightened, drawing Sefa another step closer. "I kept waiting for you to betray me. To lie or cheat or even complain about the other servants. But you couldn't make it easy for me, could you?"

Sefa's confusion ripened into pure bewilderment. "Make what easy, Sultana?"

A light perfume overwhelmed Sefa as Vaida yanked the shawl again, bringing Sefa close as she bent to murmur in her ear. "I recognized you from the very first minute you walked into this room, Sefa. Or do you prefer Sayali?"

Sefa's blood ran cold. She tried to recoil, but Vaida had the ends of the shawl in a choke hold, trapping Sefa against her.

"The other rulers wouldn't have known you. Felix and Sorn can barely recognize the shape of the nose at the end of their face. Your glamor at the Victor's Ball was excellent. It hid your true form well." Vaida's breath ghosted over the top of Sefa's hair, and Sefa trembled as the Sultana rested her forehead against hers. "Don't blame yourself. If Arin had thought there was a chance you would cross my path in that glamor, he might have warned you I can see through them as well as he can. I am the descendant of Baira. Did you think there was any illusion powerful enough to fool me?"

Vaida had known. She had known who Sefa was the entire time.

Just as terror threatened to stop her heart, a startling wave of peace crested over Sefa. Why was she surprised? She should have known better than to make herself a pawn on this twisted royal board. Their schemes weren't her, and they never would be.

"You didn't kill me, but you were never planning to let me go," Sefa realized. Vaida had taken her along to the meeting in the alley because she'd known Sefa was never leaving the Ivory Palace alive. Her secret would be safe, and her own vanity would be fed. "You struck a false bargain to keep me around as a contingency in case you didn't find the Mirayah."

Vaida laughed. "I had so hoped you would understand. Ah, the Mirayah. I have been searching for years, Sefa. Expanding my borders into Essam mile by mile, recruiting and executing so many incompetent Jasadi men who made me false promises about finding it. And then Bausit found Kera, and Kera found me the Mirayah. He picked up a trail near Mahair, of all places. He chased the Mirayah to its next location."

Had someone in Mahair gotten swept into the Mirayah?

A slim shoulder rose beneath Vaida's lacy gown. "If Kera had failed, I would have needed a way to prove Nizahl broke the Zinish Accords. The daughter of Nizahl's late High Counselor infiltrating my palace and posing as my attendant? Spying on me on the Commander's orders? It might have been enough."

"Stepdaughter."

"Pardon?"

"I was not his daughter," Sefa said thinly. Vaida gave her a look like Sefa had done a somersault in the middle of a funeral.

"The distinction wouldn't have mattered. Posing under a false identity to enter my service while you had ties to the Supreme? It would have galvanized most of my nobles to whip open those gaudy purses of theirs," Vaida said. "The other kingdoms would have had no choice but to throw their support behind me."

Another question resolved itself in the mist of Sefa's dawning comprehension. The visits to the nobles, the trips around Lukub—Vaida had been parading her around to ensure everyone saw how closely embedded Sefa was to the Sultana. When the time came to scream *spy*, there would be countless noble witnesses.

"Arin of Nizahl is a frustrating man," Vaida said, giving Sefa her back as she strode to the window. "When we were seven, I tore apart his chambers as a jest—flung around his clothes, spilled ink on his maps, set fire to his drawings. Nothing serious. You must understand, he was *impossible* to crack. He wouldn't anger if Sorn insulted him, wouldn't react when Felix followed him around like a stray cat. I wanted to know what it would take to finally crack the ice around that baffling, beautiful boy, but alas. He walked in, took one look at what I had done, and said, 'I have more maps in the antechamber if you run out of things to burn,' before he left. Awaleen below, I wanted to *scream*."

Vaida leaned against the window, observing the frenzy of activity beyond the obelisk. "Then one day, a Jasadi girl destroys a wing of the Citadel. And when I taunt him about her, Arin of Nizahl nearly kills me. He would have done it, too—I saw it in his eyes. He would have dropped my body at his feet and stepped over it without a second thought."

She traced a shape in the thin layer of frost coating the window. The candles cast twisting shapes over her body. "It was euphoria. After all these years, I was proven right. The calm, calculated Commander is just as vicious as I am—just as destructive over what belongs to him."

With all her strength, Sefa lifted the chair and slammed it against the side of Vaida's head.

CHAPTER FORTY-FOUR

SEFA

The Sultana's head hit the window with a sickening crack. She collapsed, the long tail of her gown cushioning her fall.

Thank the Awaleen for Vaida's unbelievable self-absorption.

Sefa dropped to the ground and checked Vaida's pulse. The Sultana groaned, twitching, and Sefa released a breath of relief. She picked up Vaida's hand and with the thickest handkerchief she'd been able to sew, she yanked at the ring.

A blaze of agony scorched Sefa's fingers, just as strong as it had been the first time she tried to pick up this accursed ring. She pulled the second handkerchief from her pocket and stuffed it between her teeth.

The ring wouldn't come off. Sefa's fingers spasmed, and she momentarily paused her efforts to muffle her screams in her elbow as invisible fire chewed through her arm.

All she needed to do was fling the ring out of the window and get out of the palace long enough to bury it in the gardens before Vaida roused and alerted the guards. Even if she just managed to hurl the ring out of the window, it might be enough to delay the Sultana until Arin stopped her or figured out the exact nature of her plans for the Mirayah.

Except the tombs-damned ring *wouldn't come off*.

With every scrap of her attention on the ring, Sefa didn't see the shoe until the heel struck her across the face. An avalanche of lace fell on top of Sefa as Vaida tackled her flat to the ground. Blood trickled from a cut at Vaida's cheekbone and dripped onto Sefa's chin. A ghoulish slash of a smile stretched over Vaida's face.

"Finally," she hissed. "I've been waiting for you to come out and play."

Sefa's gut roiled. She was out of time. If Vaida screamed, the guards would arrest Sefa instantly. With a relic ring in the Mirayah, the possibilities of what she could unleash from the realm's rogue magic were endless. War would tear apart Nizahl and Lukub as it had torn through Jasad, and Vaida wouldn't care a whit about the lives she trampled on her way.

"I'm sorry," she said. Tears burned in her eyes as her hand reached into the folds of her skirt. Into the pocket she had prayed she would not need to open. "I am so sorry."

In a move Sylvia had helped Sefa practice a dozen times in the tunnels, Sefa fastened her hand around Vaida's throat and heaved them to the side.

The Sultana struggled, her nails biting into Sefa's arm and chest, but Sefa was heavier and stronger. She couldn't allow Vaida enough air to scream.

And a small, strategic part of her had never forgotten Vaida's weak grip around her wrist in the wardrobe; the terror in her eyes when she thought she might die.

With her free hand, Sefa pinned Vaida's right wrist under her knee and pulled out the knife.

As soon as Vaida saw it, she thrashed like a landed fish.

"Please don't move," Sefa sobbed. Her vision had gone blurry. "Please."

Sefa prodded the knife against Vaida's fingers to splay them as far apart as they would go and didn't allow herself to hesitate as she brought the knife down with all her might.

The quake of a scream rattled silently beneath Sefa's palm. Vaida's eyes rolled to the back of her head. Finally, *finally*, she lay mercifully still.

Wiping impatiently at the tears streaming down her face, Sefa released Vaida's throat and gingerly picked up her severed ring finger by the nail.

Sefa retched, clutching the leg of a dresser for support. It was all the revulsion she had time for. She stuffed the finger into the pocket concealed within the flaps of her skirt and used the bloodied knife to tear off strips from the bedspread. She had repaired Marek and the girls at the keep enough times to know you never allowed blood to flow freely.

Once she had finished wrapping the wound, she dragged Vaida behind the bed in case the guards glanced over Sefa's shoulder when she exited and caught sight of their prone Sultana.

She checked on the tourniquet to ensure it hadn't loosened. Vaida would be fine. Her wound would heal, and Sefa had managed to avoid slicing into any of her other fingers.

Smoothing her skirts and taking a deep breath, Sefa forced her racing heart to slow. She couldn't act as though anything were wrong.

Leaving empty-handed would look suspicious, so Sefa picked up the washing basket by the door. Balancing it on her hip, Sefa wiped the sweat-slicked curls from her forehead and counted to ten before she reached for the handle.

A chill crept along Sefa's neck. It numbed Sefa's ears as it sank through her clothes and burrowed into her skin.

Before it could reach her spine, Sefa turned around.

Vaida stood on the other side of the bed, milky-white eyes fixed on Sefa.

Not Vaida, something inside her whispered.

A primordial instinct locked every muscle in Sefa's body. Her heart plummeted somewhere near her shoes, but she held still. The reaction of prey in the wild—or a human in the face of something so very clearly inhuman.

"It is all right, little flower." Vaida's lips moved, but it wasn't Vaida's voice. It rolled in deep waves, a storm barreling toward a clear horizon "I am tasked with defending Baira's seal for its rightful inheritors, but she picked you." Vaida waved her bleeding hand toward the door. "Though you had best hurry before she wakes up."

The white orbs shining between Vaida's lashes rolled back, and Vaida collapsed once more.

It took Sefa a precious minute to thaw herself back into motion. When she was sure the creature wasn't rising again, she shoved aside the urge to curl into a little ball and scream for the rest of her life.

If she had had any lingering doubts about the magical potency of this ring, an ancient sentry guarding it on Baira's behalf had effectively obliterated them.

The Lukubi guards didn't budge as Sefa moved between them. Nobody rushed into Vaida's chambers or stuck a dagger into Sefa's side. Each step away from the room eased the weight from her lungs. Nothing mattered beyond putting one foot in front of the other. When the door to the servants' stairwell closed behind Sefa, she tossed the basket and ran.

The servants, still harried from the Nizahlan newcomers, paid Sefa little attention as she sprinted across the kitchen and through the back door.

The vast gardens of the Ivory Palace's northern pavilion teemed with black-and-violet uniforms. The sight temporarily distracted Sefa, and she scanned for any sight of silver hair.

The Commander wasn't here. No matter—Sefa needed to bury this Awaleen-forsaken ring before she tried to find him.

Elbowing through the thick of soldiers, Sefa headed for the ruby obelisk. The guards at the gates had seen her leave with Vaida plenty of times; they wouldn't pay her any mind, especially not with the influx of strangers flooding the Ivory Palace.

"Sefa!"

The world froze.

Sefa knew that voice. Its owner was etched in the tapestry of her soul.

When she whirled around, she had almost convinced herself it was a trick. An illusion by the Ivory Palace to toy with her.

Golden hair ruffled around Marek's petrified face. He was dressed in a Nizahl soldier's uniform. The sight of him summoned the spirits of his brothers so powerfully that Sefa was *sure* it was an illusion and she was back in Nizahl, back at the Lazur house, watching Marek hug his older siblings tightly at the door.

"You found me," she mouthed.

He kept his promise.

Marek's gaze flew past Sefa, and the suddenness with which he sprang into motion bowled over several of his fellow soldiers. "Run!" he bellowed, trying to force through the crowd. "Sefa, run!"

Arms like barrels wound around Sefa. Her feet left the ground as her struggling body was lifted with complete ease.

They swung her around, and Sefa confronted a dozen armed Lukubi guards.

The one in front eyed her dispassionately.

"Take her to the Traitors' Wells," he said. "But first, cut the Sultana's ring out of her skirts."

CHAPTER FORTY-FIVE

MAREK

Several hundred pounds of soldier sat on Marek's back, holding him to the ground while he thrashed.

"Are you trying to get yourself killed?" Zane flipped Marek around, revealing a ring of bewildered Nizahl soldiers hovering over him. The tree trunk of a recruit kept Marek pinned like he was little more than a disagreeable kitten. "Attacking Lukubi guards where everyone can see! The Commander is at his holding a mere mile away—if he hears about this, he'll throw you into a cell!"

"Get off me!" Marek growled. Hadn't they seen the guards picking up Sefa? Cutting at her skirts until a *finger* fell out? Marek had no idea what she had gotten herself involved in, but he knew where they would be taking her. "I need to go to the Traitors' Wells!"

"If you free one of the Sultana's prisoners, you will be executed!" A scrawny recruit crouched beside Marek. The Almerour boy. "The Commander will have no choice but to hand you to the Sultana to punish as she sees fit."

"I don't *care!* I don't care about the Sultana or the Commander or any of these tombs-damned royals! Get off me, Zane, or I swear on Sirauk—"

The giant rolled off of him immediately. Wearing a Nizahlan uniform hadn't culled the superstitious lower villager in Zane.

"Go get help," Zane clipped to Almerour, but Marek was already sprinting in the direction he'd seen the guards carry Sefa.

What had Sefa been thinking, taking the Sultana's ring? As for the severed finger—it couldn't have been Sefa. Not his Sefa, who had followed stray cats into barns to feed them despite being a vagrant herself, who'd thrown up the first time she saw a butcher slit a chicken's neck and drop the thrashing body into a barrel.

None of the Lukubi guards paid Marek much attention as he shoved his way through the gates, but the other Nizahl soldiers cast him various irritated and questioning glances. As guests of Lukub, they were meant to be on their best behavior. Sedain was tomorrow, and despite the closure of Orban's trade routes, thousands upon thousands of visitors from the other kingdoms had arrived to celebrate. The last thing anyone wanted was a fresh Nizahl recruit making a spectacle of himself.

Marek gripped the hilt of the sword buckled at his waist and wished he could discard it. Running with it strapped to his hip would only slow him down, but he might need it against whichever guards were tasked with overseeing the Traitors' Wells.

The din of the festivities faded behind Marek as he jogged away from the glaring eye of the ruby obelisk. He steered himself into Essam to avoid running along the side of the heavily trafficked road.

A little over a mile later, Marek heard it. The special symphony of Vaida's reign.

Wailing from the Traitors' Wells.

Marek veered toward the sound and immediately tripped over a rotted log. The woods blurred as he rolled down a short hill, brambles and spindly roots crunching beneath him.

A pained groan tore out of him when he finally came to a stop. Before Marek could convince himself to rise, a knee pressed to the center of his back.

"Don't move," Jeru murmured. "Wait."

A pair of voices drifted over the hill, accompanied by the unmistakable clomping of hooves. "She didn't tell anyone when she would be back?"

The other rider scoffed. "No, but how long could she be gone? Sedain is tomorrow. She'll return before morning."

"What about the Awaleen-forsaken *horde* of Nizahl soldiers camping on our neck?"

Their grumbling faded between the trees, and the point of pressure on Marek's spine eased. Marek flipped around, angrily swiping at the dirt clotted on the side of his face. At the sight of Jeru's scowl above him, Marek smothered his aggravation before it could shriek out of him.

"How did you find me?" he bit out.

Jeru glowered, rising from his crouch and grabbing Marek's shoulder, hauling him to his feet. "You should be grateful it was me your fellow recruits decided to find instead of someone else. What do you think will happen if you try to pull Sefa out of the Traitors' Wells, Marek? There are Lukubi guards crawling all over these grounds."

Damn Zane and Almerour to the tombs. Marek yanked his elbow out of Jeru's grip and pushed past the guardsman. "I don't care."

"Clearly! About yourself *or* Sefa."

Marek slowed, hesitated. "I can get her out before the guards catch me."

"You can't. Even if you had a rope, you don't have the time. Every guard within half a mile will swarm you as soon as you reach the wells."

Marek spun around. "Then I will kill as many of them as I can! What do you want me to do, Jeru? Leave her to rot down there while we sit around and exchange ideas?"

Jeru pursed his lips and glanced away. "It's complicated. She is half-Nizahlan, but we cannot claim her without also claiming what she's done to the Sultana. The attack would be a breach of the Zinish Accords. The Heir has every reason not to save her."

"Did you think I would go ask the Heir for help?" Marek sneered. He started walking again. "I would have better luck appealing to the well."

"Marek, wait." Jeru's voice changed, became urgent. "Do you hear—"

A point of a sword came to rest at Marek's chest. A row of Nizahl soldiers materialized from the trees, swords aimed at him and Jeru. More soldiers arrived, closing around Marek and Jeru in a large ring. None were from the Ravening compound; these were actual soldiers, not fresh-faced recruits.

"You were right, Vaun."

Marek whirled around.

Standing at the top of the hill, gloved hands tucked behind his back, was Arin of Nizahl.

Light seared Marek's eyes as the sack was torn off his head.

He was on his knees in a cabin, his hands bound tightly in front of him. On his left, Jeru kept his head bent as the sack was ripped off, eyes closed as if he couldn't bear to open them.

At the other end of the cabin, Vaun watched Jeru with such profound malice that Marek impulsively tried to scoot closer to the bound guardsman. The Heir stood by the hearth, a pretty young woman to his right and a scowling man with hair slicked like a banana to his left.

The Commander wasn't looking at any of them. He watched the flames crackle in the hearth with a vacant look in his eyes, a detachment so thorough it chilled Marek more than the frost seeping through the floorboards.

"—collaborating with a wanted fugitive and risking a centuries-old treaty!" The banana-haired man paused for breath while rattling off Jeru's crimes. "Do you comprehend what would have happened if you'd been caught by Lukub's forces? If the Sultana's guards had caught one of the Heir's personal guardsmen trying to rescue Vaida's assailant from the wells?"

The doe-eyed woman crouched next to Jeru, pressing a tentative hand to his shoulder. "Were you threatened, Jeru? Were you forced to assist him under some kind of duress?"

"Enough prevaricating, Layla. What kind of threat could *he*"—the banana man stabbed a thumb in Marek's direction—"have leveraged against the Heir's guardsman? Jeru could have cut him into ribbons at any time."

"I did threaten him." The lie punched out of him, hoarse, his voice roughened from a steady stream of cursing over the last half hour. Marek doubted he'd be leaving this cabin alive, but Jeru might. Jeru would keep Sefa safe—he'd given Marek his word. "He didn't betray his Heir. I forced him to help me. He had no choice."

Jeru's head finally lifted, offering Marek a dumbfounded stare. "He is lying."

"I am *not*." Marek scowled. Even minutes away from bidding goodbye to the union between his head and neck, Jeru wanted to try his hand at honor.

"The traitor visited the Ravening compound a month ago, and he made no report of finding the fugitive masquerading as a Nizahl recruit. During his last visit, he murdered the section leader and, again, made no report of the fugitive," Vaun said.

"Sulor chose a trial of Fortune by Four instead of arrest," Marek protested. "He lost. Under Nizahl's laws, it isn't murder."

"The Heir outlawed the Fortune by Four years ago," Banana Man snapped, seeming revolted at the necessity of addressing Marek. "The guardsman had no right to deprive the courts of finding justice."

Outlawed? No wonder Jeru had looked ill after killing Sulor.

Marek couldn't believe what he was hearing. "They would never have found Sulor guilty! He was taking bribes from royal families, families that pay members of the courts! Rerouting patrols, falsifying records, and conscripting non-eligible children from the lower villages—"

"We are not here to litigate the matter of the section leader's death," Layla said gently. She crossed to Arin, who had yet to blink away from the hearth. "My liege, would you like us to have them both sent back to Nizahl to await trial?"

Marek's heart stopped. If they tossed both of them in a wagon headed for Nizahl, Sefa would die. She would die alone in the dirt, the wails of her fellow prisoners the last sound in her ears. "You can't. No, please, *please*—"

"Untie the boy," the Heir said, the order as disconnected as the rest of him. "Let him try to rescue his friend."

Banana Man's expression cracked with outrage, but he managed to hold his tongue. Vaun looked like he had swallowed a nest of wasps, but he swiped his dagger through Marek's ropes.

Marek rose, rubbing his wrists. "What about Jeru?"

"You should go," Layla said, and her patronizing tone annoyed Marek more than Vaun's glare and Banana Man's catty remarks. "The Heir has granted you your freedom. Don't squander it."

Marek ignored her. "Are you listening to me, you silver-haired bastard? What about Jeru?"

Vaun's fist crashing into Marek's jaw—expected. The furious outbursts from the Heir's advisors and sycophants—also expected.

The sudden burst of laughter from the Heir? Most assuredly not expected.

The cabin went silent. United in their confusion, prisoner and advisor alike watched the Commander bow in laughter as though Marek had tossed out a side-splitting jest instead of an insult.

"Silver-haired bastard," Arin repeated, gloved hands wiping at his eyes. "You Lazurs are cannier than you think."

Today of all days, Marek needed Arin of Nizahl to be Arin of Nizahl, and not this...disengaged impostor. "If Sefa dies, it is on your head," Marek said. "I don't know why she cut off the Sultana's finger, but she would never have stolen that ring if she didn't have a good reason. She is half-Nizahlan—she is owed your protection."

Vague interest flickered over Arin's features. "Ring?"

"The attendant was arrested for assaulting the Sultana and stealing both her finger and the ring," Banana Man said.

The Heir nodded to himself, as though it made perfect sense. Marek wished he could rip into the Heir's skull and wrench out an explanation. What did he see in Sefa's actions that Marek didn't? Marek knew her better than anyone alive.

Before he could speak and earn himself another blow from Vaun, the cabin began to shake.

A mirror tilted forward and smashed into a wooden bench, spraying glass in every direction. The wardrobe rocked, its doors flying open. Layla reached for the Heir's arm while Banana Man shrank behind Vaun.

In the distraction, Marek tried to lift Jeru by the elbow, but the obstinate, tombs-damned man wouldn't get off his knees. "I betrayed an oath, Marek," Jeru snapped in response to Marek's snarled order. "Do you understand that? I know you haven't bothered keeping an oath in your life, but they mean something. To some of us, they are worth dying for."

Stung, Marek stepped away from the guardsman. No matter what he did, Marek would always just be the cowardly Lazur, wouldn't he?

"You broke an oath, and the price is death. My siblings kept their oaths, and their price was death," Marek said quietly. "Judge me for it as you like, Jeru, but I will never apologize for wanting to live. I will never apologize for choosing Sefa. My oaths may look different than yours, but they are no less important."

Jeru dropped his eyes, and Marek let himself believe he saw an apology in them.

The Commander wasn't paying attention to any of them. He shook Layla off without a second glance and strode toward the door.

"Your Highness, it isn't safe!" Vaun pursued Arin, and the rest of them reluctantly followed. Marek spared one last glance toward the bowed guardsman.

Outside the cabin, the wind whipped Marek's hair into his eyes. He raised his arm to shield his face from flying debris. The trees around their cabin swayed, leaning into one another as though clustering for shelter. The ground quaked, pebbles skipping around their feet.

The Commander seemed entirely unconcerned with the prospect of being crushed to death by a falling tree. He had gone eerily still, his gaze tracking the darkness of the woods.

"Sire, what is it?" Vaun demanded.

Layla screamed as the sky broke apart above them. Bayoum hit the ground and covered his head.

Hundreds of kitmers sailed over Essam, the crescent curve of their golden beaks shining brighter than the moon itself. When those beaks parted and Sylvia's voice spilled out, Marek nearly joined Banana Man on the ground.

"People of Jasad, hear me now. I am Malika Essiya, daughter of Niphran. This is a call to the children of Rovial, to those of us from the last kingdom of magic—come home. The enemy cannot defeat us if we stand as one. Together, we are a fortress they cannot break."

Open-mouthed, Marek could only stare in wonder. He was an ant, a forgettable speck in the presence of an all-consuming might.

The call repeated as the kitmers flew past them, and Marek couldn't help glancing at the Nizahl Heir. Surely, even *he* couldn't be cold and removed at such a sight.

The wind had blown the Heir's silver hair out of its tie, leaving it floating around his upturned face. His eyes had gone distant again, but Marek had seen this particular distance before—this was the Heir's mind at work. Spinning webs like a spider crouched in a corner, working in the shadows until its net was ready for its prey.

When the last of the kitmers disappeared, taking Sylvia's voice with them, the Heir looked... exhilarated. The kind of exhilaration Marek experienced when a pretty girl curled a strand of his hair around her finger or he won a risky wager at the tavern. The last time Marek had seen that look, he'd been faking a smile in Omal while Sylvia went on and on about the way Arin sent Vaida to sleep and stole a mold of her ring without alerting the guards.

Marek went dead still.

"You have a mold of the ring Sefa tried to steal!" Marek couldn't believe he had forgotten. "You took it during the second trial!"

He may as well have shouted into his armpit for all the attention Arin paid him. The Heir pivoted in the direction of the Ivory Palace. The top of the ruby obelisk pierced the sky, barely visible beyond the trees. Arin stared at it for a long moment, a spark in his eye that reminded Marek unsettlingly of a flickering match in a pitch-black room.

When Arin turned around, his eyes were clear for the first time since Marek arrived at the cabin. "Vaun, go untie Jeru and tell him to get Sefa out of the wells," Arin ordered. "The boy can go with him. Take as many recruits as you need and restrain the guards who stand in your way. Bayoum, send the signal to the third and fifth quarter regiments to move on the Ivory Palace. Layla, fetch a horse and ride to Orban as fast as you can."

"Sire, what—" Layla moved haltingly, eyes wide. "This would break the Zinish Accords. It would be war!"

"It is already war." Arin strode past them. "Take the Ivory Palace."

CHAPTER FORTY-SIX

ESSIYA

By the time the first khawaga spotted me, it was too late. My flying dagger found its home in the throat of the khawaga who had given the warning shout. The second, his feral dog.

"The dog!" Maia gasped, clutching her dagger with both hands.

"Did you want to try petting it before it ate your face?" Efra snapped.

A flood of khawaga erupted from the Orban castle. Curved swords glinted in the khawaga's eager hands, and bloodshed ripened in the air like a rotted fruit on the vine.

"Step back!" I ordered the Jasadis.

I touched my palms together and slowly spread them apart, a net of gold and silver building between my hands with gossamer threads. My magic pulsed through me, enthusiastic, desperate to obey. I barely had to think about what I wanted before it acted.

"You killed my wife!" he screamed, tears dripping from his mud-streaked chin.

I sighed. "Which one was your wife?"

I didn't need to glance at Efra to see he had gone still. Every time the images returned, Efra sensed it. What did he feel emanating from me? What was his magic reacting to in mine?

Not that it mattered. I had stopped trying to understand the visions.

If this was magic-madness, I would rather not look it in the eye when it came for me.

I pulled my arms back and hurled the giant net. In midair, it splintered into dozens of tiny nets sailing toward the khawaga. Howls hit my ears, the sweet music of bladed nets swaddling the khawaga and their dogs. I kept walking, laughing past each swearing, stuck khawaga. Honey coated my tongue, the sweet aftertaste of my magic making me lightheaded with giddiness. I didn't notice if the others followed.

An enormous bull glowered at me from the doors to the castle.

I smiled, and a line appeared at the bull's nose. With a thunderous crack, the fracture widened, splintering the door. I kicked the hinges and shielded my face as the door collapsed inward, exploding into wood and metal pieces.

"SORN!" I boomed. "Have your manners abandoned you? Come say hello, you drunken weasel! I've come to wake your Champion!"

More khawaga poured from the heart of the castle. I kicked the closest one in the gut and slammed my fist into his throat, disarming him with a savage twist of his wrist.

"Enough! Enough! Lower your swords!" a familiar voice roared. "SORN OF ORBAN GRANTS ENTRY TO MALIKA ESSIYA!"

The last sentence must have contained some magic of its own, because the khawaga immediately went still. I stopped in the middle of a killing strike, tip of the sword poised at the thudding point of the khawaga's neck.

The Orban Heir leaned over the staircase. He met my gaze over the raised blades of his khawaga. A smirk twisted the royal brute's mouth.

"Well, if it isn't the dead coming to beat down my door," Sorn drawled. "Come in, Essiya of Jasad."

Animal heads watched us from the walls. A black stallion, a wolf, a three-headed extinct creature I'd once fought in Essam. Maia shuddered at the ghoulish mounts, clinging to Lateef's arm. Namsa inspected them with a little too much interest.

The servant stopped at a door carved in the image of two rearing bulls. "The Heir will see you inside."

She disappeared, leaving me to turn to the Jasadis with a somewhat sheepish smile.

I hadn't told the Urabi about the voice I'd heard, nor the faces I couldn't stop seeing. When they tracked me down at the edge of the Omal upper towns, I had handed them Felix's head and refused to answer any questions.

They hadn't wanted to come to Orban, but I had insisted we pay Sorn a visit. Orban had blockaded most of the major trade routes after Galim's Bend. What was the point of telling Jasadis to come join me in Jasad if they couldn't even get onto the roads leading to the kingdom? They would have to trek through the paths in Essam riddled with residual magic, leaving them exposed to all sorts of danger.

I slid my hands into the pockets of my cloak. "When we're in front of Sorn, don't contradict me. He might seem like another spoiled, drunkard Heir, but Sorn will gut you like a prize pig at the first sign of weakness."

Gratified by their nervous silence, I pushed into the room.

Or *rooms*, as it turned out.

Sorn's private chambers were an altar to excess. Sconces chiseled from stark white bone held flickering torches, the orange glow lending a dungeon-like atmosphere to the rooms. Soft bear-hide rugs padded our footsteps as we crossed to a luxurious bed fit to sleep sixty.

"Awaleen below," Maia breathed, and I followed her gaze to Sorn's headboard.

Hundreds of bone fragments had been soldered together to form the pale, ghastly headboard looming several feet over Sorn's bed. The bones twisted around one another like gnarled tree roots, rising behind the pillows like a skeletal fog watching over the dead.

"Is your headboard made of skulls?" I clicked my tongue. "You do tend toward the literal."

"Do you like it?" The smile Sorn shot me bordered on feral. "I can get a similar one made for you. You've killed enough of my khawaga to get the base started."

Crude and demented as always. I might have fallen for it if exhaustion hadn't riddled Sorn like mold on wet cheese. His chestnut hair had lost its luster, falling limply over his forehead. Lines fanned out around his mouth and temples, eroded beneath the tide of tension flowing through his face. Though he was still powerfully built, his clothes hung a little looser on his frame. The booming energy, the debauched ennui...gone.

I focused on the source of his trouble—and the reason for our visit.

The still figure beneath the sheets looked even smaller in this room of beastly trophies. I hadn't seen Diya since the third trial. Her hair had grown, the wavy strands tickling the tops of her ears. A waxy tint overlaid her brown skin in a shade Hanim would refer to as death's breath, and I saw the other Jasadis shudder.

My attempt to reach for Diya's shoulder stopped short at Sorn's grip on my wrist and a growled, "What do you think you're doing?"

Breaking his hold took less than a quarter of the effort it had taken to break Arin's. I chose to consider that an accolade for my own skill instead of a reflection on Sorn's mental state. "I came here to help her. Stop getting in your own way."

Sorn's nostrils flared, but he didn't block me from checking Diya's pulse.

Thready and weak. She didn't have much longer.

Any uncertainty about Sorn's feelings for his Champion faded at the sight of Diya's lips. Someone who had slept this long would've had lips more cracked than the Desert Flats. Instead, they looked softer than my own.

"What do you want?" Sorn snapped. My prolonged assessment of his fallen Champion seemed to grate on him.

I sat on the foot of Diya's bed and crossed my legs. "I'm sure you have a guess. Impress me."

Sorn sat back, knees spread in a pointedly masculine sprawl, an arm dangling over the end of his chair. "You want me to open the trade routes so Jasadis can go get killed in Jasad."

Lateef and Namsa shifted. I slid them a quelling glance.

"Is that right?" I cocked my head.

"I saw your kitmers—I heard your call. Thousands of Jasadis would need open roads to travel, no?"

"Open roads." I didn't hesitate. "Protected roads."

"Protected," Sorn repeated. The flames from the torches gave his handsome features a somewhat sinister cast. "You want me to send khawaga to guard the trade routes for your Jasadis?"

"When Jasad rises again—"

"No, no." Sorn lifted a hand. "Save your pretty speeches for more willing ears. I want your plain words or none at all."

I pressed my lips together, briefly impressed. So Sorn *did* have a brain, and it wasn't entirely governed by drink and bloodshed.

"Nizahl will not come after you. Protecting the travelers on your trade routes is Orban's prerogative."

"Tell me more about Orban's imperatives." Sorn stretched each word beyond its limits, heavy with sarcasm.

"Nizahl won't act against you unless you have reason to know those on your trade routes have magic. How would you know? Since the khawaga will be tasked with protecting anyone who travels on the trade routes, Jasadi or Orbanian alike, you won't be in violation of any decrees. The Commander won't violate his own laws."

Sorn laughed. He wiped a hand down his face. By the time it reached his chin, the laugh became a sigh. "I take it you haven't heard the news."

His tone set off a litany of warning bells. "News?"

"Arin broke the Zinish Accords. He and Vaida are at war. Theoretically, of course, since no one knows where Vaida vanished to after her attendant cut off her finger and tried to steal her ring." Sorn shook his head with grudging admiration. "The little rascal made it all the way to the gardens before they caught her."

The resounding silence from the rest of us seemed to delight Sorn. "I see I've upset you."

My eyes narrowed to slits. "Vaida's ring cannot be stolen. It's imbued with Baira's magic—probably as old as relic magic gets. It is impossible to remove from Vaida's presence." I tried very hard not to think of the creature that had overtaken Vaida's body and smiled at me with pure white eyes the night I tried to steal the ring. The gleeful—and perplexing—way it had taunted me.

Nearly there. They tried again and again, but your choices never changed. Who knew this one would meet with success?

"Well, the attendant found a way. She also managed to escape the Traitors' Wells with a Nizahl soldier. Arin and Vaida in the north, you and Felix in the south; my entertainment has been richly provided for. Tell me, do you still have his head?"

"The Nizahl Heir wouldn't break the Zinish Accords unless he had a reason," I insisted. "Where did Vaida go?"

Sorn shrugged. His enthusiasm for throwing startling news at me had waned, and boredom began to creep back into his expression. "How should I know?"

I smoothed the end of Diya's quilt. "Open your trade routes and protect your travelers for the next twelve days. After that, you can sit back and watch the lot of us tear one another apart if you wish." I spread my hands wide. "I know you don't care for pretty speeches,

Sorn. I don't have one to give you. Every step of this will be hideous. It will be brutal, grisly, and bloody."

He arched a brow. "Now you're just trying to get me excited."

"But our magic is not going anywhere," I continued, exhaling my annoyance, "and neither are we. Jasad's time has come. When the bloodshed ends, you can either find yourself with a powerful new ally, or four enemies."

"What happens in twelve days?"

I raise the fortress and die, or I raise the fortress and go mad.

"Nothing you need to concern yourself with."

Sorn scratched his head, curling a short strand absently. "I could change my mind after you revive Diya. You have nothing to ensure I'll stay true to my word."

I shot him a chastising look and tapped Diya's leg under the quilt. "I believe the key to keeping your duplicitous hide in line is lying right here. As easily as we can cure her from this slumber, we can just as easily send her back. Or worse."

I had no idea whether we could send Diya back into her endless slumber. Nor did I particularly *want* to kill the only Champion I'd befriended during the Alcalah. The feasibility of my threat was immaterial. To a man as desperate as Sorn, the threat alone sufficed.

Sorn stared at me a long time. Eventually, he looked over at Diya. I fought back a twinge of reluctant pity for the Heir. Longing and devastation had ravaged him, clear as day in his drawn expression.

Sorn chuckled softly. "Thank the Awaleen you and Arin are on opposite sides of this. The combined force of you could bring the rest of us to ruination."

"Is that a yes?"

"Yes, damn you. Yes. Wake her, and Orban will open the trade routes."

"Just open?"

Sorn's jaw worked. "Open and protect the trade routes."

Finally, a victory. A mostly bloodless win. I struggled not to grin at the Jasadis.

Not a win yet, I reminded myself. First, we had to wake Diya.

"Lateef." I inclined my head toward the sleeping figure in invitation.

Lateef rounded the bed, moving to the side opposite Sorn. He took a deep breath and laid a hand on Diya's forehead. Sorn's shoulders stiffened. It seemed to take considerable effort for him not to smack Lateef away from his Champion.

"His magic is generalized," I explained. "He can use it to heal her."

Moments passed. Lateef's eyes moved rapidly behind his closed lids. Namsa shifted her weight, tension lining her brow.

Not a single twitch from Diya.

With a heavy exhale, Lateef opened his eyes and drew away from Diya. "I checked every organ, every vessel in her body. No ailment prevents her from waking. Physically, she is in perfect condition."

Disappointment, brittle and volatile, tore through Sorn's features. "Thank the tombs you came. I don't know what I would have done without even more useless information!" With a low oath, he shoved his chair back and stood. "Get out, all of you. You failed to uphold your end of the bargain. Leave the premises before I allow my khawaga to finish you off."

I rose, tongue heavy with insults ready for launch. Before I could utter any of them, a quiet voice spoke over us.

"Perhaps I can try."

Maia stepped forward, trembling hands knotted in her tunic. "If it is not a physical malady, the cause of her ailment might be a different kind of blockage."

"Mental, you mean?" asked Namsa.

Maia nodded. "By your leave, Your Highness."

"You want to use your magic to rummage around her *mind*? Absolutely not."

I thought fast. Our opportunity to win Orban was slipping out of reach with each passing second. "It could be the reason, Sorn. The elixir we drank in the third trial was intended to draw us into an illusion. Soraya's poison used magic to redirect the illusion, but since Diya doesn't have magic, she couldn't follow. She might have gotten lost."

Sorn swallowed. "So if she's lost—if she is wandering around her own mind, this girl can pull her out?"

An excellent question, and one I hadn't stopped to consider. The only time I'd known Maia to use her magic was to sever my consciousness before I hurt Efra on the cliffside.

"She is our executioner," Efra said. At Sorn's recoil, he added, "Not that her power is limited to executions, of course."

If Efra opened his mouth one more time, I would pull his lower lip over his head and kick him through the nearest window. Why would he lie? Maia, the Urabi's executioner. Imagine! Baira's blessed bones, it was a wonder Sorn hadn't burst into laughter.

Maia lifted her chin. "My magic allows me to enter a mind and expose its deepest, most closely held fears and secrets. I can alter its reality and convince the mind that it has died. The body usually follows soon after. My magic kills bloodlessly and mercifully. It is truly one of life's foremost marvels, the unknown powers our minds wield over our bodies."

"Marvels," Sorn said, a bit dumbly.

I didn't bother to hide my open shock. She was a lahwa. There hadn't been a lahwa in two hundred years, and nobody had been too sad to see the rare magic die out.

The Urabi and Mufsids must have devoted every resource to chase Maia down when they found out she existed. Not only could a lahwa read thoughts, but if she wished, she could read every thought I had ever had. Twist and reshape them to fit her goals, restructure the inside of my head like a bored parent moving furniture around the house.

I licked suddenly dry lips. I had too many secrets to have a lahwa around. How many other times had she used her magic on me?

"I never use my magic unless I am under strict orders."

I glanced at Maia sharply. Had she read my thoughts or just my face?

The girl's gently resigned sorrow almost did away with my repulsion. Almost. But her type of power had been reviled even before the other kingdoms lost their magic.

"Fine." Sorn sounded like he'd ingested a hive of wasps. "Do it. But if you hurt her—"

"I will do the Champion no harm."

Maia took Lateef's place by the bed. Her uncertainty disappeared, and the delicate finger she placed between Diya's brows remained steady. She was confident with her magic, I realized. Assured.

Maia's gaze tunneled, going distant as gold and silver swirled in her eyes. Sorn blinked at the sight, thrown, and I wondered when he had last seen Jasadi magic on full display.

"She is alone in a cemetery," Maia murmured. "Carving a name into a wooden headstone. L. U. B. N. A."

"Lubna," Sorn said, hoarse. "Her little sister. Awaleen below, you're in her head."

Suddenly, Maia winced. "She is murdering her parents. Quite enthusiastically."

Sorn grinned. "That's my girl."

"She cut them into pieces for selling her sister to the khawaga," I explained to Namsa. The older woman watched Maia with concern.

"She is set to be hanged. A rope is being put around her neck and tightened." The colors in Maia's blank eyes swirled faster. "The Orban Heir is ascending the hangman's platform."

"She slaughtered several of my khawaga before they caught her," Sorn said proudly. "The audience for her execution was substantial, so my father ordered me to see the task done right. But I hadn't expected a woman the size of a thimble to have felled some of my best men. Something about her...the wrath in her eyes...I respected it. I understood it."

"The Orban Heir orders the rope removed. 'There will be no hanging today.' The crowd is in an uproar." Maia tilted her head. "She keeps replaying this moment. The rope loosening. The Heir reaching for her arm. The crowd shouting. Over and over."

Maia jolted. "Sweet Sirauk, she's looking right at me."

"Who are you?"

We all jumped at the growled words. They had come from Diya, though her body remained unmoving and her eyes closed.

"Your Heir sent me to heal you. A poisoned elixir twisted your mind into itself. It appears it forced you to relive your worst moments on repeat."

"These aren't my worst moments." Again, her lips moved while the rest of her remained still.

"I see." Maia's brows furrowed. Reassessing the scene. "Ah." Maia shifted uncomfortably. "She felt an intense animosity for the Heir on the platform. She plotted to kill him as soon as they left."

Sorn continued to grin like a lunatic.

"But he was...charming. Understanding. He sentenced the khawaga who killed her sister to death and pestered his father into changing the law so a guardian responsible for selling off a child would face the Garha."

The Garha? I racked my memory for the term. Sorn spared me the effort. "Butcher shop for those accused of treason. We skin them alive and send the hides back to their families. Then they're dismembered and hung on hooks through the main road. The dogs eat the parts they can reach, and the rest rots in the sun."

Arin's wry voice. *You should see what Orban does to traitors.*

Maia continued, unaware of our conversation. "He makes her feel capable. Strong. She trains with his khawaga and bests them all. He gives her a place in the palace. But his attentions are always friendly. Like a 'proud owner of a prize warhorse,'" Maia recited. "She wonders why his attraction encompasses so many women, but not her."

Sorn flinched as if struck. "What?"

"But she is lowborn, and the hardships of her life have eroded any beauty she may have possessed. She determines her feelings for the Heir are best kept private, where they will not embarrass or burden him."

"That's—why didn't she *say*—" Sorn spluttered.

I sat down and propped my chin on my fist, wildly entertained.

"We're in the third trial," Maia whispered. "They are handing her and Sylvia the elixir."

I blinked at the name. But Maia was reciting Diya's thoughts, and the other Champion knew me as Sylvia.

Maia quieted. "What's going on?" Sorn demanded. "What happened?"

The gold and silver drained from Maia's eyes seconds before they rolled to the back of her head. She collapsed, landing on the rug in a heap. Namsa and Lateef rushed to her.

Sorn swung to me. "Did it work? The incompetence of you lot is galling!"

"The effort of sieving through your Champion's mind will leave her fatigued for *weeks*," Namsa hissed. "Have some gratitude."

"Gratitude? I'll be grateful when one of you bumbling, magic-addled buffoons *wakes my Champion!*"

"Would you all shut up?" Diya snarled. "My head hurts."

The sight of five heads snapping to look at the bed was almost comical. Sorn's anger dissolved. Joy crept over his face like a rising sun. "Diya? Are you—are you yourself?"

She glared. "What kind of idiot question is that? Who else would I be?"

I cackled. "She's fine."

When she glanced in my direction, I casually blew her a kiss. "I figured the reigning Victor of the Alcalah should pay the sick a visit."

"Damned Alcalah. Blast it to the tombs." A scowl stole over her. "I would have won if you hadn't cheated."

"Jealousy can be so ugly."

"Like your face."

I patted her covered foot. "I look forward to when you're in full health and have recovered your wit. It was never much to begin with, but this is just embarrassing."

"My liege," Diya said to Sorn, serious. "Can you pass me that sword?"

But Sorn didn't appear to be listening to either of us. He was simply watching Diya.

Diya sat up, eyeing him. "What did he offer to have you fix me? I imagine it has to do with why you're in a giant, garish, blood-spattered dress."

I plucked at some of the bigger bloodstains. "Orban promised to reopen and protect the trade routes."

"What?" Diya rubbed her forehead. "Orban hasn't closed the trade routes in fifty years. What happened?"

My palm warmed, and a glass of water appeared in my hand. I handed it to Diya. She took in the gold and silver swirling in my eyes and sighed.

"A Jasadi. I should have figured. You were entirely too foolish to have survived until the third trial." She drained the glass. "Good luck with the war. You'll need it."

"Diya." The name fell from Sorn like the plea of a sinner seeking benediction, pained and half-whispered. "Diya, why didn't you tell me how you felt?"

The Orban Champion squinted at Sorn. "Felt about what? My lord, have you taken ill?"

I groaned. Perhaps she and Sorn were well-suited after all.

"Sorn." I waved a hand in front of his face. I never thought I would miss the mountains, but I only had twelve days left to enjoy warm baths and soft beds. I didn't want to waste any more of them. "You won't forget our agreement or bend to pressure from Nizahl."

He turned his chin briefly, meeting my impatient gaze with an irate one of his own. "I already promised. You've gotten what you wanted—now go. The khawaga won't trouble you."

Namsa lifted Maia, carrying her weight without trouble. She frowned at the Orbanian pair, following Efra and Lateef to the door.

Sorn took Diya's hand between both of his. She glanced at me with a bemused shake of her head, and I tossed her a quick smile.

For both their sakes, I hoped Sorn was careful with Diya's heart. If he toyed with it, she'd gut him and any woman within arm's length. Awaleen help the fool who interfered.

With a rueful laugh, I closed the door behind me.

CHAPTER FORTY-SEVEN

ESSIYA

I held tight to Ingaz as we flew over the Meridian Pass. The rust-colored crags rose high in the center of the desert, curving like fangs from the cracked yellow mouth of the Flats. I was tempted to push Ingaz between them and travel over the path we had taken on our way to Orban for the first trial. Was the relic magic that attacked Arin still there? Would I see the Urabi's scattered arrows embedded in the dirt?

Thinking about Arin was a mistake. I closed my eyes against the brutal urge to twist Ingaz to the right, to soar toward Nizahl and crash through Arin's window so I could demand to know exactly what he was thinking violating the Zinish Accords. Arin defied prediction in every way but one: he always operated within the confines of his own rules.

Something disastrous must have happened. I felt it in my bones.

The kingdoms were coming apart at the seams. With the Orbanian protection in place, thousands of Jasadis would be moving into the trade routes toward Jasad. We'd flown over thousands of Nizahl and Lukubi soldiers battling throughout Essam Woods. Omal would be in shambles as the lower village rebellions grew, as it waited for the council to appoint a new ruler in the next twenty days—a formal procedure for which they had no precedent.

I glanced at Efra. The first time we met had been on top of those crags.

Efra lay flat on his stomach, both arms wrapped around his kitmer's neck. He hid it well, but I didn't need his flavor of magic to sense the terror wafting off him. Considering I had ordered my first batch of kitmers to fling him around Suhna Sea, I couldn't begrudge him his distrust.

I guided Ingaz toward Efra and said, "It won't drop you."

Efra forced open an eye to glare at me. "Forgive me if I lack confidence in your promises."

I fell quiet. Why did I try with him? His opinion about me had formed on those crags, and nothing I did would change it.

"Sorry," Efra ground out. "I didn't mean it. You have upheld every promise you've made us, and Lateef is right—I am acting like a petulant child."

I nearly fainted off Ingaz. Was this real, or had the magic-madness finally finished me?

Unleashing his iron grip on the kitmer, Efra slowly sat up on the creature's back and wrapped his hands around its horns. "I hate your family. Your mother, her parents, their parents. You come from a lineage that has slowly unraveled our kingdom, and it is... difficult for me to separate you from that history. I keep thinking, any minute now and her blood will show itself. Any minute now and she'll laugh in our faces and leave us to die, fulfilling her family's legacy at last."

"Do you still believe that?"

He glanced over, conflict clear in his expression. "I don't believe you will leave us."

"But you still believe I might fulfill my family's legacy?"

"Essiya," Efra said, and my grip on Ingaz's horns tightened. Not only had Efra never used my given name before, but I had never heard him adopt such a tentative tone. "We both know I can feel what happens when your magic consumes you. You... you disappear. The only part of you that remains in those moments is your magic, and—it's so angry. It doesn't care about Jasad. It doesn't care about anything but destruction."

I am what remains.

A shiver crawled over me, and I fought to keep my heart from sinking to the bottom of my stomach. Despite the aggravation Efra had caused me, he was the bravest of the Urabi. At least he acknowledged it. At least he said it out loud.

We cleared the Meridian Pass. Namsa and Maia were lagging behind us, but Lateef had shot ahead to dip and weave over the cracked plains of the Desert Flats. The older man delighted in the act of flying on a kitmer's back, and had I been in a more pleasant mood, his childlike giggling would have amused me.

"Do they have a plan for what they'll do if I survive raising the fortress?" I asked quietly.

I did not explain what I meant, and Efra did not ask. We both knew that if I survived Nuzret Kamel, what would be left of me would be far more dangerous than anything that awaited the Jasadis on the other side of the fortress.

They needed to have a plan for how to kill me before I killed them.

He hesitated. "No."

I smiled grimly. "Now who's a liar?"

I pulled on Ingaz's horns, and we dove.

From the sky, the Desert Flats bore a striking similarity to the cracked, stale surface of month-old aish baladi, the thin layer of sand and dust over the plains a near-replica of the flour slapped onto the bread before the baker piled it on top of our wicker trays. We'd been flying over the lifeless expanse for a full day, and I had yet to see any kind of life. What creatures might have once called the Flats home had long desiccated, and even the buzzards had vanished for lack of fresh meat.

Which was why I drew Ingaz to a halt when two tiny shadows moved, interrupting the miles upon miles of nothing we'd put behind us.

"Is everything all right?" Namsa yawned, maneuvering her kitmer into a standstill beside me. Lateef, Maia, and Efra struggled to control their kitmers, looping around us in helpless circles.

I pointed out the shadows. "I think there are people down there."

Namsa followed my finger. "Probably just a couple of rock formations."

"Rock formations wouldn't move." My magic juddered like a wheel caught in mud, fixating on the figures. There was something there.

I swooped lower, searching the ground. No rock formations. The shadows belonged to a man and a woman. Blond and black heads of hair that, even if I couldn't have recognized them separately, were unmistakable when bent together.

I pressed Ingaz's horns down, and we shot toward the ground. I heard Namsa and the others shout behind me, but I didn't slow. It could be a hallucination. Another vision.

The figures swiveled at the sudden whoosh of Ingaz's wings, and the choked noise I released barely registered as human. I cut through the sky like a falling star, heedless of my trajectory.

Ingaz landed hard, and in my stupefaction, I forgot to tighten my hold. I tumbled off her back in an inelegant sprawl, limbs cascading into the hard dirt.

Two faces appeared above me, blotting out the darkening sky.

"Until you landed, that was the most impressive thing I had ever seen," Marek said breathlessly.

"Is it really you?" Sefa's teary brown eyes, warm as a blanket on a winter's day, roamed over me.

The grin spreading over my face couldn't have been stopped by any earthly means. Maybe I *had* fallen asleep on Ingaz's back, and this was just a dream. A wonderful, wonderful dream.

Awaleen below, I hoped I never woke up.

A dry sob heaved through Sefa. "I never thought I would see you again." She moved to cup my face and paused. "Can I touch you?"

It was that question—so benign, so gentle, so *Sefa*—that finally convinced me.

I sat up too fast, tackling her to the ground with the force of my hug. Sefa started weeping immediately, clinging to me as though I might change my mind and throw her off.

A lightly muscled set of arms wrapped around the both of us. Marek laid his cheek on top of my hair. We stayed on the ground, wrapped in a spine-stretching embrace, until someone cleared their throat.

I peered around Marek to see Lateef, Namsa, Maia, and Efra observing us from a safe distance. Efra appeared vaguely constipated, which wouldn't have been worth noting given his general demeanor, except the expression was mirrored on Lateef and Namsa.

I drew away from Marek and Sefa. I took my first proper look at the pair.

"Marek…why are you in a Nizahl soldier's uniform?"

Before he could answer, Sefa pushed her hair behind her shoulder, exposing a row of ruby studs along the shoulders of her clothes.

No, not clothes. *Livery.*

No one knows where Vaida vanished off to after her attendant cut off her finger and tried to steal her ring…She also managed to escape the Traitors' Wells with a Nizahl soldier.

At the look on my face, Sefa winced. "We have much to discuss."

Lateef stepped forward, casting a nervous glance to the darkness spreading over the Desert Flats like spilled ink. "Perhaps those discussions are best conducted at another location."

"We can't take them with us." Efra pinned Marek with a hostile glare and received a wide grin in return. "They aren't Jasadi. One of them is a *Nizahl soldier.*"

"Fake soldier," Marek corrected good-naturedly, not seeming the least bit put off by Efra's attitude.

"They're coming," I said. "Namsa, Maia, do you mind sharing your kitmers? They're a little larger than the others and should support the added weight. It'll take us another few hours to get to the mountain, but we should land by dawn."

Efra tried again. "We can't—"

Five kitmers turned their heads toward Efra, pitch-black eyes fixing on him in the gloom.

"To be clear, Cinnamon," I said affably, "I was not proposing a debate. If you have trouble with the order, feel free to surrender your kitmer and hike your way through the Desert Flats on foot."

Efra's teeth clicked together, his jaw working with poorly concealed fury. He glanced away.

"Friends of the Malika are most welcome," Maia said. She smiled at Marek, who beamed at her with an enthusiasm bordering on deranged.

Once Maia helped Marek onto the back of her kitmer, he released a bitter laugh and said, with no small amount of devastation, "No one is ever going to believe me."

Together, we climbed into the air and flew home.

CHAPTER FORTY-EIGHT

ESSIYA

Sefa and I sat on the floor of the kitchen, watching Marek spin around the dining-turned-dance hall as though he'd known these people his entire life instead of six hours.

I had been braced to return to a mountain brimming with disappointed Jasadis. Not only had I failed to secure the Omalian army, but my decision to divert us to Mahair had cost us Kenzie and Medhat. Medhat may have survived the battle, but he had refused to leave with the Urabi. They'd buried Kenzie in Mahair, and Medhat had chosen to stay and help the village rebuild rather than return to the Gibal without her.

I had expected flails to rain down on me, not kisses. But I barely had a chance to bathe before we were dragged to an evening of celebration and twice as much food as last time.

"Many of them wanted the fortress over the army," Namsa had explained. "Nuzret Kamel is coming, and they can feel change in the air."

I peeled the sliced almond half from my square of basboosa and passed it to Sefa, who licked off the syrup before popping it into her mouth.

"He really told you to go to the Desert Flats?"

"*Through* the Flats," Sefa corrected. We had had this conversation twice already, but she didn't display any of the impatience I would have in her position. "I think he only has a general idea of your location, and he figured you would find us on your way back from the Omal palace if we went through the Flats. Plus, it was the only way to avoid the battles raging across Essam."

Chewing my lip, I scraped the browned top of the basboosa with the side of my fork. I didn't look at Sefa. "How is he?"

The silence that followed was somehow louder than the trills of laughter and tubluh competition on the other side of the room.

"Not well," she said at last. "Don't tell Marek I told you, but he was sure he and Jeru would die in that cabin. The Heir is…different. Something has come undone within him."

Binyar Lazur's confession. Arin knew the truth about the fortress.

I set aside the plate and drew my knees to my chest. The side of me that had scraped her fingers raw trying to loosen a single thread from the perfectly wound Heir rejoiced. The other side, the side who knew how it felt for the pillars supporting your world to suddenly crumble, grieved for Arin.

"Were you aware that he loves you?" Sefa asked, with the airiness of one inquiring after the color of the sky. "Quite irreparably, it seems."

I turned my head, positive I'd misheard. "What?"

She rolled onto her knees to bring down a bowl of kabab halla, accidentally spilling some of the broth onto her skirt. She flipped the chunks of slow-cooked beef to check for fat. "After Jeru and the Nizahl soldiers pulled me out of the Traitors' Wells, Arin rode to us. I don't think the soldiers were expecting him, given the small matter of ongoing insurgency, but he got off his horse and handed me one of his maps. He told us which routes to avoid on our way to the Desert Flats, and then he said, 'If she dies for them, they will die with her,' and strode off."

Satisfied her kabab halla had no white strings, Sefa spooned it over her rice. The Ivory Palace had apparently given her nerves of steel, because my stare boring into the side of her head barely seemed to faze her.

"He means they need me to survive, that's all," I managed.

"You know what he means."

"Arin wouldn't—"

"Kill everyone in the vicinity if you die? Seek revenge on anyone who allowed it to happen? Maybe he wouldn't have before. But I told you—he is coming apart at the seams. When the world stops making sense, you cling to the only thing that does."

"And you think he—you think how he feels about me makes sense?" My laugh was strangled. "Even if we set aside our titles and our histories, it wouldn't make it any more sensible. Someone as precise and calculating as Arin—who despises a loose thread on his vest and loses sleep if he has an inefficient day—would despair of me by week's end. I can't count the number of times I've walked out of my room in stained clothes or brought someone to tears because I was in a bad mood and they were in my way. I thrive in chaos; Arin suffocates in it." She had offered me the proof herself. In what world would Arin of Nizahl choose revenge over reason? My death would hurt him—I was not delusional enough to think it wouldn't. But Arin would have to be utterly unmoored from himself to sink into the kind of rage you needed to sustain revenge.

"Not if you help him breathe," Sefa said. "Not if you are his air in the chaos."

Awaleen below, I had forgotten how hard Sefa's particular insight could land. I exhaled roughly, dropping my forehead to my knees to block out the revelry taking place on the other side of the kitchen counter.

"How do you do it, Sefa?" I muffled my question against my knees. "You have endured an absolutely harrowing two months. If Marek hadn't found you in time, you might have died in the Traitors' Wells. How do you stay so calm through it all?"

Across the room, Marek shouted our names pleadingly. Sweat glistened on his forehead, and his hair had been mussed into a feathery gold nest on top of his head. Our contented isolation baffled him to no end.

Sefa wrinkled her nose at Marek. "Do you remember what Raya would say when I would moan and groan about whether my dresses would sell at market?"

"'Save some stupid for tomorrow,'" Sefa and I said in unison. We exchanged a grin.

"Today, everyone I love is together and alive. Tomorrow, that might not be the case. I understand how easy it is to dwell in the aftermath of all your worst fears. To spend every day bracing for tomorrow's pain. But, Essiya, you can't survive in the future. You don't exist there yet," Sefa said. "How do I stay calm? Simple. I recognize that I am afraid because I still have something to lose, and if I'm afraid, then it hasn't been lost yet. It means I have a chance to change the outcome." Sefa's hand settled over mine and, when I did not pull away, tightened. She held up our joined hands. "Did Sylvia ever think she'd be sitting here, letting me hold her hand without recoiling?"

I huffed, avoiding her knowing look. "I am not convinced I'll keep letting you do it now."

"Thank you for making the present worth fearing the future."

Her sincerity would kill me before the night's end. "Keep your thanks to yourself."

Sefa's laugh faded into quiet sobriety. She covered my hand with her other one. "Do not let the future reach you here. Do not let it torture you before its time."

We watched children laugh as they gave chase through the throng of dancers; drummers' fingertips, orange with garlic and oil, leave greasy impressions on the surface of their tubluh; Lateef pick up Namsa by her elbows and spin her around the dance floor as her short legs aimed for his knees; Efra eye Marek like all the ills of the world had been birthed alongside him.

And for a wonderful evening, the future failed to reach us.

CHAPTER FORTY-NINE

ARIN

The ice clinked around Arin's empty glass as he watched the door.

It had been approximately two hours and seventeen minutes since he'd returned from Lukub. Twenty of those minutes had been spent sitting inside the empty carriage and staring at the Citadel. The tower that had been home to generations of Nizahl's most powerful, to those bestowed with the sacred duty to protect the kingdoms from the horrors of misused magic. Supremes and their Commanders, fathers and sons, lineage upon lineage dating back to Fareed himself.

All a lie. An elaborate degradation of every value, every commandment, every principle Arin had been taught to uphold.

In the darkness of his chambers, Arin filled his glass and waited. Not much longer, now.

The knock came as the last drop of talwith slid down Arin's throat.

"Enter," he said.

Outside the window, the clouds shifted. Moonlight spilled into the room, its bluish hue illuminating the haggard guardsmen shuffling into Arin's chambers.

"Sweet Sirauk," Jeru whispered, taking in the wreckage of Arin's room with wide eyes. The top of Arin's bed had been shredded to slivers. Long scorch marks had eaten away at the carpet. The cabinet had been upended, ancient weapons and glass scattered on the windowsill and ground.

If Arin hadn't opted to open the talwith, he might have started testing his weapons on the furniture in the ancillary rooms.

Vaun had gone stock-still, having noticed the object sitting center on Arin's map table. The blood drained out of his face.

Jeru followed the trail of destruction to the map table and promptly blanched.

"Is that…" Jeru choked off, his fist flying to the hollow under his throat. He might as well vomit all over the carpet—it wasn't as though Arin cared anymore.

Wes's head stared at them from the center of the map table. Clouded gray eyes gazed into the distance, fixed on a point none of them could follow.

"I found him there," Arin said. He crossed his legs, balancing the empty glass on top of his knee. "A message from my father, I imagine."

"Why—why would the Supreme kill Wes?" Jeru had turned a fascinating shade of yellow.

A silly question, but Arin indulged it nonetheless.

"I asked Wes to follow my father." Arin rolled the glass between his palms. "How familiar are you with magic mining, Jeru?"

"Not very, my lord." The guardsman was visibly struggling to speak, his attention split between Arin and the disembodied head of his colleague.

Jeru was a good man. A decent man Arin should have left alone, far from the reaches of the Citadel. From the reaches of Arin.

"Most texts will tell you that magic mining is a profane practice and the reason the Blood Summit was called. What they won't tell you is how magic mining dates back hundreds of years. They'll neglect to mention that the rulers—all of them—had been mining their people's magic for their own use long before their favorite resource began to decline, and then they decided to trade it. An entrepreneurial sort, our ancestors."

Arin's eyes had gone dry and stiff, but he couldn't close them. Each time he blinked, and the world went blessedly black, Arin would forget what awaited him on the other side. And each time he opened his eyes and remembered, it became more and more difficult to convince himself to do it again.

Only three more tasks left. Three more tasks, and he could stay in the dark as long as he wanted.

"Eventually, the other kingdoms lost their magic, and Jasad became the sole miner left. Perfect leverage for the throne to act with impunity—who would stop them? Who would get up from that bargaining table when they had become reliant on mined magic to sustain them through hard winters and endless rebellions?" Arin's lips twisted into a rueful smile. "But Jasad's magic weakened with every generation, and it was simply a matter of time until Jasad stopped coming to the negotiation table and started hoarding. They had turned their thoughts to their own border. What would happen to the fortress when magic eventually left Jasad? The fortress was the only obstacle between them and the kingdoms they had spent their entire reign toying with."

Arin flicked the bottle to the ground and stood, ambling around the map table to stand with his back against the window. A thick, opaque slime had soaked into the maps beneath Wes's head. The names of Nizahl's provinces had bled into one another to form a meaningless streak of ink.

"You'll have to forgive some speculation on my part," Arin said, resting his forearms on the raised edge of the table. "The details… blur. My father is an industrious man, as we all know, and he saw an opportunity in the Qayida of Jasad. A woman named Hanim Werda, renowned for her brutality in battle and her disdain for the

Jasad crown. Hanim was also the leader of the Mufsids. Yes, those same rebels my father had executed before I could get anything useful out of them. As the story goes, she and my father conspired for years to overthrow the Malik and Malika, but Hanim was caught and exiled."

Jeru approached the map table, gazing at Wes's head like it might animate if only Jeru hoped hard enough. Vaun hadn't moved an inch since he first entered.

Walking through the ruination of his entire existence was strangely relaxing to Arin. He wasn't wandering in the mist anymore, each new unexplainable piece of information striking like a fist in the dark. The sun had finally risen, burning the skies clear, and Arin could see again. He could see everything.

"After they killed Niphran, the Mufsids sacked Usr Jasad and tried to reinforce the enchantment on the fortress. I suppose they were nervous someone might take issue with them raiding Jasad and killing the Heir. In any case, the enchantment had the opposite effect. The fortress collapsed. On the other side, waiting to charge, were our armies. Two days before the Blood Summit. Two weeks before the rest of the kingdoms sent their armies marching into Jasad alongside ours."

"How?" Jeru croaked. "How did the Supreme know?"

Arin snapped his fingers, startling the guardsmen. "Excellent question, Jeru! How did my father know? He was away at the Blood Summit, ever so tragically fighting for his life as the Malik and Malika slaughtered hundreds of royals.

"Traitors are a fascinating sort," Arin continued. He settled his gaze upon his unmoving guardsman. "Hanim betrayed her own kingdom out of a misguided belief that my father, the same man who allowed her exile and abandoned her to Essam, would put her on the Jasad throne. After all, she had given him a half-Jasadi Heir who could lay claim to both the Nizahl and Jasad crown—there was no need for war, was there? No need to decide magic was the core of all evil while you collected it for yourself in the shadows."

Distracted, Arin grazed his thumb over the curling corner of the map. It wouldn't straighten, so Arin tore it off. Goodbye, Dar al Mansi!

"Half-Jasadi..." Vaun spoke for the first time, and Arin remembered he was there. "Sire, you cannot mean to say...But you don't have magic."

"No, I don't," Arin mused. "I can drain it. I can sense it. But I have none of it myself. Odd, isn't it? A musrira's curse fails and, instead of killing me, conveniently allows the Nizahl Commander to detect and extract the very same thing he was trained to destroy. Where had my magic gone? How had it been taken? I tormented myself with the questions until I realized I was asking the wrong ones."

Mining magic, draining it. Same thief in a different hat. What matters is not what is taken, but where it goes.

"As I said, my father is an ambitious man. Like the Malik and Malika, he too foresaw the end of magic coming. The destruction of a resource all the kingdoms had long relied on. Mining magic was a short-term solution. The procedure is catastrophically fatal, and you can only extract someone's magic once. But what if you had a tool capable of draining magic slowly, siphoning it across a person's entire lifetime? A spigot you could shove into a river and—"

Arin stripped off his gloves. The lanternlight flicked warm colors over the pale canvas of his skin. "Drain with a single touch."

"Sire, it isn't possible," Vaun said, dismissing Jeru's attempt to nudge him away from the map table. "Your father would never expose his Heir to the horrors of magic-madness."

Arin settled his gaze on Vaun. "You know so much about what my father would and wouldn't do, Vaun. It is thanks to you that the last piece of this puzzle presented itself to me."

Reaching into the pocket of his vest, Arin locked his shoulders beneath the crushing weight of every misstep that had led him here. If he had dismissed Vaun from the Citadel after the Alcalah. If he hadn't told Wes to pursue his father.

If he had looked up from his carefully charted maps long enough to see that the world on paper was nothing like the world around him.

"You have been a guardsman for so long, you have forgotten how to be a soldier. You forgot a rule we teach the recruits in their first week." The same rule Arin had revealed to Sylvia as they stood in a cabin with a dead Nizahl soldier between them. For her, it had been a handful of black curls in the soldier's pocket. Wes had been much more helpful.

Arin extended his palm. Sitting in its center, a raven's head had been embossed onto a pin with the letter *V*. Jeru had an identical pin tucked under the lapel of his uniform with the first letter of his name.

"When defeat becomes a possibility, what are our soldiers trained to do?"

It was Jeru who answered, grief slowly mottling into rage. "Collect evidence of their killer."

"I found this under Wes's tongue." Arin flipped the pin between two fingers. "It was a wasted effort, Vaun. He had already sent the letter. All you did was cost me the only loyal guardsman I had left."

Vaun raised his chin, meeting Arin's gaze without flinching. "I will not apologize for protecting you and this kingdom as I always have. As I always will. The Supreme gave me an order, and I obeyed."

Protecting him. It would be laughable if it weren't close to the truth. The two of them had grown up alongside each other. Vaun had been Arin's shadow since they were children, a steady and reliable presence in a court of shifting faces. It struck Arin, in these last moments of Vaun's life, that he barely remembered whether Vaun had had a family before coming to the Citadel. Vaun's existence had always been an appendage to Arin's.

"You filthy traitor!" Jeru spat. "You killed the Heir's guardsman! Your—he was your superior!"

An infected appendage put the entire body at risk. Arin should have recognized those first signs of rot back in the tunnels. He should have been strong enough to pick up the knife and sever it at the root.

"As you know, there is no formal court procedure for royal guardsmen. You are mine to punish as I see fit, up to and including forfeit of your life." Arin gently laid the pin by Wes's head. "Pick up your sword, Vaun."

The guardsman straightened his shoulders, tucking his hands behind his back. "I will not fight you, my liege."

"Sire, I am happy to stand in your stead." Fury vibrated from Jeru's every pore. He was wild with anger and devastation, which meant it would take Vaun little effort to catch him in a mistake and cut him down. Skill was only half the component of success. The other was focus, and Jeru currently had none.

Arin came around the table and brushed Jeru to the side. "Your sword, Vaun. I will not repeat myself a third time."

Vaun didn't move, and Jeru swore. "Fight him, you coward," Jeru hissed. "Or do you only hurt those who cannot see you coming?"

Steel whispered against leather as Arin's sword slid free of its sheath.

It took one lie for you to lose faith in me. Tell me, Your Highness: How many will it take until you lose faith in your father?

She had asked the wrong question.

Vaun swallowed. "Sire—"

Arin's sword split through Vaun's chest before it could expand with more air to waste on the next word. The next lie. The sword went through Vaun's back and into the cabinet behind him. Arin pushed the hilt through the resistance of bone and oak. When the hilt scraped the front of Vaun's uniform, Arin didn't immediately release it. Vaun slumped over the sword in his chest, pinned to the side of the wardrobe like a bird caught by a powerful arrow. Tears welled in Vaun's eyes as he raised his head.

She should have asked him how many lies it would take for Arin to lose faith in himself.

For twenty years, Vaun had stood by Arin's side. Up until the end, he had thought he was serving on behalf of Nizahl. On behalf of his rulers. The crown had consumed Vaun, so Arin paid him the mercy of holding his eyes as the last of Vaun's life drained out of them.

Arin released the sword and gave the dead guardsman his back.

"Tell my father to meet me in his study," Arin told Jeru.

Two tasks left.

CHAPTER FIFTY

ARIN

There was a spot of blood on Arin's sleeve when Rawain found him in the study.

That bothered him. Everything else was in place. Everything else had been precisely arranged.

Everything except the spot.

"Arin!" Rawain crossed toward him in five rapid steps. His father's grip on his shoulders startled Arin, so much so that he forgot to resist when Rawain yanked him into his arms. The Supreme squeezed Arin tight, the hand holding the scepter digging into Arin's back. "Thank the Awaleen. You cannot imagine how worried I have been. When did you return from Lukub?"

Stiff in the Supreme's embrace, Arin bit back a bitter laugh. Rawain knew something was amiss, so he chose the angle of concerned, loving parent. The approach had successfully disarmed Arin too many times before.

How long had Arin's father been learning how to fight him?

A not-insignificant part of Arin wanted to relax into his father's hold. That same instinct had Arin's arm lifting and stopping just short of hugging his father back.

The future split into two clean paths before him.

In one of them, he allows his arm to settle around Rawain and accepts his father's embrace. He remembers the many moments of his life where an accomplishment wasn't real unless Rawain declared it so. How he pushed himself day and night to be a son worthy of being Commander to Rawain's Supreme.

On this path, Arin realigns his world to match his father's version of it. He never has to confront what he's done, because he no longer entertains a world where it matters.

On the other path, Arin drops his arm, and there is only darkness.

He could only see as far as the first step before it plunged into millions of possibilities. It terrified Arin to his core, the depth of the unknown waiting behind that first step.

But on this path waits a girl, and maybe a man who deserves her.

I've told you before, my liege—life is not an equation you can calculate over and over again. Every choice won't be perfect, but you still have to make it.

Arin pulled away from his father and plunged himself into the dark.

"What happened?" Rawain demanded. "When we received word that Nizahl had taken the Ivory Palace, I was sure Vaida had done you some terrible harm. I feared the worst, Arin."

Arin inclined his head with polite interest. In his pocket, he rolled the edge of the portrait under his thumb. "The worst?"

Rawain frowned, studying Arin closely. "You look unwell. Have you been to the healers? Why did it take you so long to come back from Lukub?"

"I had business to attend to," Arin said, and flattened the portrait against the table.

Rawain looked at the portrait for a long moment. "Should I know who this is?"

The woman in the portrait had high cheekbones, cut in the same slant as Arin's. Midnight dark hair spilled past her shoulders. She was unsmiling in the portrait, as though the very act of sitting still invited her to violence. Her eyes...they were a different shade of blue, but they were unmistakably Arin's.

"I should think you would recognize my mother," Arin said.

It had been an inordinately challenging portrait to track down. Understandably so—why would any library or archive keep the portrait of a disgraced and exiled Qayida of the Scorched Lands? Fortunately, Vaida's mother had hated Rawain, and in her never-ending quest to spite Nizahl, she kept a portrait of the woman he'd been caught conspiring with as a reminder of his dishonor.

The Supreme sighed, the sound laced with disappointment. "I see your ill-fated intervention in Mahair gave the Jasadis enough time to sink their claws into you. I would think of anyone, you would be best equipped not to fall prey to their lies. Were you not immune to their magic, I might worry they had extended their influence over you."

Arin couldn't help a small smile. Such an elegant threat. Anything Arin claimed to the council, to the rest of Nizahl, could be instantly cast into doubt at the suggestion of magical manipulation. After all, to the world, the Nizahl Heir's resistance to magic remained rooted in rumors and wishful thinking.

"If you would humor me," Arin said, "I am still settling the last pieces."

His father adopted a patiently amused mien, as though Arin was a small child trotting out his schoolwork. "What is it, son?"

Arin perched on the desk, bracing his hands on either side of him. "I understand most of it, you see. The young, ambitious Heir hoping to herald his reign with the destruction of the long-loathed fortress of Jasad and the supposed extermination of magic. Not immediately, of course—something Hanim Werda didn't understand when she offered to help you. She had no idea how patient you are; how willingly you will wait for the seeds you plant to bloom. Eighteen years, in this case—from the time you met Hanim until the moment you orchestrated the Blood Summit."

At the last part, Rawain's expression finally wavered. "Arin, you cannot possibly think I had anything to do with Isra—"

"Stay with me, my liege," Arin said pleasantly.

"What I struggled to understand was how. You couldn't have used mined magic to cause the carnage at the Blood Summit—you were all there to beg for more magic from Palia and Niyar, and even if you had some saved, it wouldn't have been nearly enough to inflict devastation on such a scale. Besides, you would never have eliminated Palia and Niyar if you still needed them. But you didn't need them anymore, did you? You had created your own source of magic."

Rawain arched a thick brow. "Please, don't stop. It has been too long since I heard proper fiction. What was my new source of magic?"

The same question Arin had nearly broken his mind trying to answer. How could Arin, born half-Jasadi, not possess a trace of magic?

The answer hadn't been in Lukub this time, but in the Citadel's own library. Arin had walked past the answer thousands of times, openly admired its statue carved over the council room.

"Me." Arin tilted his head, matching his father's patronizing patience with a smile. "You did to me what the Awaleen did to Fareed. You used every drop of mined magic Nizahl had traded over the years to make me your conduit. I imagine Hanim helped—turning an infant into a conduit is a procedure that requires incredibly delicate magic, after all. At least, if you don't want to kill the child right away."

If Arin had known what he was looking for sooner, it would have been painfully obvious. The only recorded conduit in history was Fareed—he'd had his magic stripped out of him by the Awaleen and anchored to his two favorite swords, which had later become part of Nizahl's symbol. Ironically, it was impossible to *be* a conduit without being born with magic yourself. Your body never stopped seeking what was taken from it; it drained every magic it touched in hopes of filling the gaping void left behind.

And for every conduit, there was an anchor. The place where Arin's magic had been tied, where the magic he drained flowed.

"Which brings me to my first question. Did you intend to get her with child, or was it an accident?"

Arin posed the question with only slight interest, as though it hadn't haunted him every night since he discovered the truth. Many sleepless hours later, and Arin still didn't know which was worse: that his father had planned to sire a half-Jasadi child with the intention of subjecting them to a near-fatal procedure to strip their magic and turn them into a conduit, or the alternative—Rawain had seen Arin, held him, and decided he would rather watch him die than raise this half-Jasadi son.

Rawain's mask of confusion and concern disintegrated. A bone-chilling blankness replaced them, and Arin knew his time was running out.

The discovery had proceeded much like the unveiling of an exquisite painting. Attention not only for the whole of what it was, but for the individual brushstrokes bringing each detail to life. Details like Nizahl's prisons, always bursting with Jasadis awaiting their trials. Prisons Arin routinely visited to drain the magic from the detained. Arin had thought his father merciful for prolonging the fate of the sentenced Jasadis. For allowing them to live on for years after capture.

Have you considered, in that infinite mind of yours, that the truly brilliant people are the ones who understand the realities we build were already built for us?

"I tried so hard with you, Arin." Rawain shifted his weight onto his scepter, leaning heavily against it. "Even when you questioned, when you pushed back, I reminded myself you were a child. You were learning. When you became Commander and undid half of my policies, I told myself it was a sign of great leadership. You had a strategy, and as long as I held on to the assurance that we shared a vision for our world, it did not matter to me how you sought to achieve it. At every step, I trusted you. And at every step, you doubted me."

The Supreme swung, so quickly Arin only saw the blur of the scepter before it collided with the side of his head. The force knocked Arin off the desk. He caught himself on the wall, teeth coming together in time to prevent a hiss from slipping out.

"I raised you better than this."

The sparks hadn't faded from Arin's vision when the next blow came to the back of his head, taking him to his knees.

"You make a mockery of the gift I went to the ends of the earth to give you. The magic you drain from these oh-so-poor Jasadis, do you think I hoard it for my own pleasure? Do you think I *wish* to possess it?" The end of the scepter pressed into Arin's neck, keeping him down. "Unlike the Jasadis you draw it from, the magic I wield doesn't run in my veins. It holds no chance of corrupting me, and I can prevent others from using it for evil. I can use it to make Nizahl strong—to make this *family* strong. If it weren't for me, you would have died at sixteen, slaughtered at the hands of that Jasadi murderer you allowed into your bedroom."

Rawain's speech, delivered with ire and put-upon frustration, barely penetrated the buzzing in Arin's ears. Blood matted the side of his head. Pain pounded between his temples, but at least he didn't feel any fractures.

With an edge of a humor he thought Essiya might appreciate, Arin noted that at this point, he probably had more bumps and craters on his skull than the roads of Mahair.

Arin's jaw popped when he opened his mouth to speak, mellifluous and calm. "Slaughtering nearly everyone at the Blood Summit with magic I stole for you, blaming Niyar and Palia, and then using the bloodshed as an impetus to rally the other kingdoms into destroying Jasad? My lord, forgive my skepticism, but what corruption might magic offer to a soul that has never known anything else?"

The weight of the scepter vanished from the back of Arin's neck. He raised his head. Rawain had the scepter raised high as he stared at Arin with a coldness Arin could never, if he lived a thousand years, manage to replicate.

"I always feared you would become like your true mother," Rawain said. "I stayed vigilant for what you might have inherited from Hanim. In my worst nightmares, I never thought you would take after Isra. As weak and—"

"Weak is not a mother who throws herself between a boy with none of her blood and the wrath of the man who made him." Arin wiped the blood dripping onto his lashes. "Weak is a ruler who holds a match to the world and then blames it for burning."

The scepter swung. With the height of the swing and the speed, the blow would surely knock Arin unconscious.

So this time, Arin caught it.

Rawain inhaled sharply, trying and failing to yank the scepter from his grasp as Arin stood.

"I could have stopped you at any time. I could have stopped you a decade ago," Arin said. It was hollow. Exhausted. "I should have known you would never stop yourself."

Footsteps rang out before Rawain could answer. A shadow in uniform emerged from the corridor, stepping into the small study.

"Arrest the Heir," Rawain commanded. "Magic has taken him."

"Is it ready?" Arin asked Jeru.

Jeru nodded.

"Hold him."

As soon as they grabbed Rawain, he began to struggle. A gag went between Rawain's teeth, and Jeru wrapped his arms around Rawain from behind, pinning his father's elbows to his sides.

"My guardsman," Arin said. "The one you kindly deposited on my map table. He sent me a message before you ordered Vaun to execute him."

Arin pulled out a scrap of parchment no larger than his palm and lifted it for Rawain to see.

No mines. The scepter.

"He found you out, didn't he?" Arin murmured. "He saw you use magic from the scepter."

The hateful beady eyes of the raven glared at Arin. For two decades, the scepter had symbolized Rawain's power, but it had always been Arin's magic behind it. Arin's magic anchoring everything he drained into his father's scepter. Arin's magic facilitating every horror they were oathbound to prevent.

Rawain's grip on the scepter refused to budge, no matter how hard Arin pulled or how tightly Jeru held.

"Wait." Arin gestured at Rawain's robe. "Lift his sleeve."

Looking faintly ill, Jeru drew back Rawain's billowing sleeve.

At the sight of a thick metal cuff around Rawain's wrist, welding him to the scepter, Arin laughed. "Clever."

"There is no clasp or latch of any kind," Jeru said, distressed. "It cannot be removed."

"Of course it can," Arin said. "Take out your sword."

The scepter went taut as Rawain began struggling in earnest. Jeru strained to hold on to the Supreme.

Arin dragged the scepter forward, drawing his father's hand flat to the desk. The cuff around his wrist scraped the wood.

The moment Rawain registered Arin's intent, it happened.

A spark lit in the glass orb behind the raven. The ember swirled faster, growing into streaks of gold and silver. Rings of light spun around the head of the scepter, the brightness forcing Jeru to look away.

Arin was transfixed. There it was—the truth. The root of every darkness that had scourged the kingdoms over the last twenty-three years.

Arin's magic.

Arin laid his hand atop Jeru's flagging grip on his father's arm, pinning it down. As the scepter's magic expanded to a searing peak, Arin swung.

Blood landed on Jeru in thick splatters, spraying across the desk. His father screamed behind the gag. A touch dramatically, in Arin's opinion. It was a conservative cut; he'd only taken Rawain's hand.

Arin steadied his shaking fingers over the scepter. It was his father who had lost a hand, yet Arin's heart reacted as though he had given up something, too.

The Supreme staggered back, grasping the desk for balance. He'd lost all color, and his wild eyes weren't on his missing limb, but on the scepter. He tore the gag from his mouth. "It can't be reversed," Rawain spat. "You will never regain your magic."

Arin lifted the scepter, the Supreme's hand still clenched within the cuff. "Regain?" How painfully predictable for his father to assume Arin wanted the scepter to bolster his own power. "I have no use for this magic, my liege. But I know someone who might."

A fist pounded against the desk as soon as Arin turned around.

"Do you think your precious Jasad Heir is any different from those who came before her?" Rawain snarled. "Do you honestly believe she won't resume magic mining *as soon* as she reestablishes her kingdom? And what will happen to us if she does, Arin? She won't trade with us, and without my scepter, without the magic you draw, we will have nothing!"

Arin thought of the girl he'd met crouched over a dead Jasadi's body, mumbling death rites with a vexed expression. The girl who'd exposed her magic to him by throwing a dagger at Felix's thigh after he hurt the little orphan girl. The magic she'd spilled every time Sefa or the boy were in danger. The same girl and the same magic that had stopped the Ruby Hound before it could shred Arin apart.

"She is nothing like them." Arin glanced at the blood coating his gloves. He couldn't tell if it belonged to Vaun or to his father. "Nothing like us."

"You would choose her over your own kingdom? Over your own family?" Rawain sounded stunned.

Jeru opened the door, and Arin spared his father one last look before he walked through it. Blood slicked the surface of the desk, dripping onto the carpet. Rawain had wrapped the end of his robe around his bleeding limb, but his eyes were glassy, his skin the color of wax.

"Yes," Arin said. "I choose her."

One last task.

The oars slipped into the water. Night had deepened, and the moon hid its face behind the trees. Essam Woods bordered the river, trailing branches skimming the surface of Hirun as the trees shivered with the rising wind. Hirun wound through the woods like a dark ribbon, its current gently rocking their boat.

They had been rowing for close to three hours before Jeru finally spoke.

"What happens now, my lord?"

Arin set his knees apart as he leaned forward, the ends of the oars tucked under his arms. The long bundle between his and Jeru's feet seemed more ominous than the shadows flitting between the trees.

"I am not your lord anymore," Arin said. "I will be stripped of my titles under guilt of treason. My armies will become my father's."

Jeru paled. The boat slowed as the guardsman's grip on the oars went slack. "But—but your father will send your armies to Jasad. It will be a slaughter."

"No," Arin said. "He needs magic to sustain his own hold on power, and the Jasadis have the last of it. But even if he wants to, his attentions will be soon diverted toward the attack from Lukub. It will buy us time."

"Attack from Lukub?" Jeru looked bewildered and embarrassed, as though Arin had caught him in the middle of failing a test he should have studied for.

"The Mirayah never stays in the same place for very long. Every report of it our soldiers have brought back indicates it rotates between five places in Essam. Depending on the latest location, it would take Vaida twelve to twenty days to reach it. She has been gone for seven."

Jeru's eyes were the size of saucers. "I thought the rumors about the Mirayah were just superstition. How long have you known it was real?"

"Long enough," Arin said tersely. "Vaida would never have surrendered the Ivory Palace unless she knew it was temporary. Unless she had a greater plan in motion."

Between the war with Lukub, the rebellions raging across Omal, and Orban's khawaga protecting Jasadis on the trade routes, his father's armies would have no choice but to separate. Even if he did send regiments south, he would not be able to spare enough to battle the volume of Jasadis Essiya's kitmers had likely galvanized toward their kingdom.

Arin picked up the oars and pushed, the soreness in his arms barely registering. He was dimly aware he hadn't eaten or slept in days.

Numb wasn't the right word for it. Arin just felt...distant. As though most of him had stepped into another room, and the sounds coming from behind the door were too muffled to make out.

"Your Highness—" Jeru murmured.

"I am not your Heir." Arin turned the oar. His last task would only take three days, if the winds favored. Three days until he reached the mountains. Three days until he reached her.

"I am nothing."

CHAPTER FIFTY-ONE

ESSIYA

Dreams passed over me in gentle waves.

I stand on Sirauk, my old cloak billowing around me.

"You came back," the mist says.

I swing my legs over the side of the bridge, observing the great nothing below. Deep in the darkness, they watch me. Waiting.

"I shouldn't have."

I pluck a red burss from the ground and stroke my thumb over its curling tail. It will be nice to have company again.

Niphran pats my curls with a contented sigh. I sit in her lap, playing with the dolls Dawoud had attempted to confiscate.

"How was your day, ya umri?"

"Soraya wouldn't take me into town. I tried to sneak into her carriage, but she caught me," I whine. I twist the doll's twine hair into a series of miniature braids. "She always catches me."

"You should listen to Soraya."

I pause, digging my nails into the doll's tummy.

This wasn't right. It hadn't happened like this.

I turn my head to stare up at Niphran. "Soraya came after the poison made you mad. You should be in Bakir Tower."

Niphran smiles, but it isn't Niphran anymore. Her skin churns, eyes liquefying into ruby pools; she whispers, "It's time to come home, darling."

Two shadows rise behind her, their arms outstretched.

I scream.

Water splashed over the side of the bucket as Efra forced my head deeper into the water.

I clutched the edges of the bucket and strained against his hold until my vision dimmed. When he released me, I flopped back onto the carpet, sputtering. Water poured out of my nose and mouth, and I hacked with a force that might've broken a rib.

When my demise no longer seemed as imminent, I sat up, wiping my face with the dry parts of my sleeves. Efra crossed his arms over his chest.

"Thank you," I muttered.

"Don't thank me," Efra said. "Holding your head underwater three times a day? The privilege itself is a gift."

"Then you're welcome, and get out." The water was still sloshing inside the bucket. I'd need to refill it again.

It was late, and I did not want to risk anyone seeing Efra leave my chambers at this hour. Bad enough I had had to kick Marek and Sefa into their own room, but how could I explain Efra's comings and goings? I couldn't offer an excuse without explaining that the symptoms of my magic-madness had begun to arise with alarming regularity, and only Efra could sense it in time to burst into my room and dunk my head beneath the water.

"Is it just the visions?" Efra asked, crouching in front of me. There was genuine, if reluctant, interest pooled in his green eyes. "Does it interfere in any other way?"

"I told you about the veins already." The vulture had caught me at a low point, shaken from another unexplainable vision. Besides, the only reason to hide the veins was to hide the encroaching madness, and Efra was all too aware of that already.

Efra just waited, watching me drip water onto the carpet and attempt not to shiver. He was remarkably bold for someone in the proximity of a woman with seemingly bottomless magic and a tenuous grasp on her mind.

"There are impulses," I said flatly. What did it matter? Maybe once I was dead, they could use my symptoms as a guide to managing this condition if Arin was wrong and it occurred again. "They don't feel like mine."

"Whose do they feel like?"

"Your mother's," I snapped. "How should I know?"

To my surprise, Efra remained somber, lips pressed tightly together.

"If your madness consumes you before Nuzret Kamel, we are lost."

"It won't." I hoped. "I can last for ten more days."

"We won't be strong enough to kill you if you succumb," he reminded me, as if I needed reminding. As if half the visions weren't devoted to the myriad of ways my hands had maimed and murdered in realities I shouldn't exist in.

"Get out, Efra," I said tiredly. "Or I might not wait until I'm magic-mad to kill you."

Still looking thoughtful, Efra left. I squeezed the tunic around the ends of my hair and used the last of my energy to crawl back into bed.

I had been expecting the world to end. Preparing for it, in fact.

I just hadn't expected it to end the very next morning.

Maia burst into the Aada room where I had absconded after breakfast, her ponytail askew and cheeks flushed.

"Mawlati," Maia choked out. "There is, uh… Nawar rode ahead to let us know—that is, we need to prepare for an arrival. Two arrivals, in fact."

Lateef and I glanced at each other, equally mystified. "Arrivals." I straightened, dropping the missive I had been reading onto the maps laid open across the table. A nebulous dread formed a knot at the base of my spine.

"What arrivals, Maia?" Lateef demanded.

Eyes brimming with guilt and uncertainty found mine, and I went stiff.

No. It wasn't possible. I had told them hundreds of times they were never to bring him into the mountains. Maia and Lateef startled as the table's ledge cracked beneath my hands. My veins were rigid inside my skin, glowing with my fury.

I might kill them. I might truly kill them.

"He's here?" I forced out, my throat raw from the effort of swallowing down the shriek I wanted to unleash. "They brought him here."

"Nawar only told us he'd been captured at the mountain's edge with one of his guardsmen. I don't know any more," Maia said, and she sounded genuinely sorry for it. "I came to tell you right away."

I was too furious to be grateful. Maia moved out of my way as I stormed out of the room, and I raced through the corridors.

He was here. He was here, he was here, *he was here.*

My blue abaya fluttered behind me, falling open around my black pants. A bottleneck of bodies choked off the entrance to the enclave, shoulders bumping against one another as people craned for a glimpse of the door.

Unbelievable. Disobeying my most important order wasn't enough; they needed to be here for the evidence.

"All of you—out!" I roared. Heads spun, finding me at the rear of the crowd. My fists shook at my sides, nails biting into my palms to restrain my magic. "Go to your rooms and close the doors. Nobody leaves until I have given my permission."

For a long minute, nothing happened. I wasn't backed by Lateef or ringed by Namsa and Maia. This time, it was my word—my authority—on its own.

You could force them to listen. The whisper curled like steam from a kettle around my anger, cooling it into sharp crystals and shredding me from the inside. *We could make them regret the day they made a mockery of you.*

Nausea swelled through me as my magic showed me precisely what could be done to the Urabi gathered in the enclave. How I could bring the roof crashing down above them with a single flick of my hand. How I could press my palms to the wall and encircle them in flames, watching as they screamed and rammed into one another like ants in a hole.

I pressed my back to the wall. The cool stone seeped into my overheated skin, and with great effort, I shoved the images to the back of my head.

"By your leave, Mawlati," the head Visionist said, offering me a short bow. She moved past me, the rest of her cohort slinking close behind.

One by one, the corridor emptied, until only Maia, Sefa, Marek, and Lateef remained.

Two large hands captured my shoulders. Marek held me at arm's length, expression unreadable. "This is your dominion, Malika Essiya. Whatever you wish to happen will happen."

"I—" I was going to be sick. I didn't know what to do. Why, *why* had Arin come here?

The door rattled, silencing us. The knock came: three hard raps, followed by two quick ones.

"Essiya?" Maia prompted. "Do you want to get it?"

I couldn't move. My heart accelerated to a feverish pace, battering itself against my ribs.

When my petrified stillness continued, Lateef wrenched the door open, shielding his face as a vicious cold front swept in.

Namsa came in first, rubbing her hands together. The wind had slapped a red flush on her cheeks, and I wished I could slap another one. I would, if I could just regain control over my limbs.

Guilt-ridden eyes immediately slid to me, and Namsa spoke fast. "Mawlati, I understand you wanted to keep the Commander away from the Gibal. We intended to honor your wishes, but…he had compelling evidence for why we should bring him to you alive. He wasn't followed. We checked. We left Asim and George in Essam to ensure nobody tries to track him to us."

She flinched at my bitter laugh. "Yes, because the Nizahl Heir, a man who knows every tree, squirrel, and puddle in Essam, suddenly wandered right in front of our perimeter without any reinforcements. What evidence could be compelling enough for you to bring him here against my orders?" I pried my teeth apart with difficulty. "You call him the Silver Serpent, for Sirauk's sake. How frequently does a serpent sidle right into a hunter's net?"

Namsa's mouth opened and closed. My neck prickled. The air in the room shifted, and I sensed him before I heard him. The world narrowed down to the tall shadow shifting into the enclave.

"I don't believe serpents are much for sidling," a smooth, achingly familiar voice said from behind Namsa. "We much prefer to slither."

CHAPTER FIFTY-TWO

ESSIYA

Rain darkened his hair. Water dripped onto the broad line of his shoulders, soaking into his cloak. A black blindfold covered Arin's eyes, another testament to how little his captors knew him. Arin's mouth was the real danger. He could persuade a balding bird to give up its last feather, and they had left him without a gag.

His scar looked harsher, cutting his throat and jaw and disappearing into the faint bruises coloring the side of his face. The bruises I had given him in Rory's shop.

Arin wove his fingers together, entirely unbothered by the ropes encircling his wrists. The corridor, so spacious mere seconds ago, barely seemed able to contain him.

The mighty Nizahl Heir, caught at last.

Efra stamped the rain from his boots behind Arin, squeezing around Lateef to peer at me warily. "How angry is she?" he asked out of the corner of his mouth.

Namsa shook her head. Another blindfolded figure appeared behind Arin. I had seen such a robust mop of curls on one man, and one man only.

"Jeru!" Sefa exclaimed. She rushed toward the guardsman only for Efra to thrust an arm out.

"He is a prisoner of the Malika." Efra shot Jeru a distasteful glance. "Keep your distance."

I heard Marek call my name, but I didn't turn. I couldn't focus on anything other than Arin, who stood still as the mountain itself. Arin, who couldn't walk into a room without visualizing every potential method of assassination, had been left blindfolded and bound in a corridor with Jasadis. I expected to see tension. The furrow of his brow as he listened to the voices and counted how many people were in the room. The careful scuff of his boot on the ground, testing for soil or cement.

He did none of it. Arin simply stood there, and it was one of the eeriest things I had ever seen.

"Enough arguing," Lateef demanded, and my gaze clicked over to him when he moved behind Arin. "We need to contain the newcomers and convene an Aada about what to do with them. Have they been searched?"

Namsa shook her head. "We didn't have time."

Lateef moved toward Jeru. "I'll take him."

Before Efra could so much as breathe in Arin's direction, I stepped forward, cutting him off. "I will search the Commander."

"Your magic—"

I gestured at my gloves and abaya, then at Arin's layered uniform. "I won't come into contact with his bare skin." I had asked the seamstress to create a pocket in every piece of my clothing specifically designed to fold a pair of gloves.

I thought I heard Efra mutter, "Let's keep it that way," before he stepped aside.

The world muted as I stepped closer to Arin. "Raise your arms to the side," I murmured.

What had he been thinking? What could possibly have compelled him to come to the mountains in search of me now? For months, he'd known I was here. He could have easily tracked me down in Jasad, his armies in tow. It was reckless. Foolish. All the things Arin was not.

Arin raised his arms.

I tried to touch him brusquely, efficiently. Efra would be scanning my emotions with a fine-tooth comb, searching for any evidence of my feelings for the Heir. The Aada would accuse me of partiality. They would decide what to do with Arin without my input if they thought I had been compromised.

My hands moved to his shoulders. I ran them along his chest, over the strong planes of his stomach, circling to the small of his back. It brought us nearly chest-to-chest, close enough for his soft exhale to stir the hair at my ear.

Without forcing me to utter it aloud, Arin pushed his feet apart. Heat crept along my neck, and I didn't linger as I swept over his thighs and calves.

I straightened and stepped away, staring at the floor. "No weapons."

Lateef nodded, releasing Jeru.

"What was the compelling evidence the Heir brought with him, Namsa?" I crossed my arms over my chest, jerking my chin toward the weaponless Commander. "Or was that another excuse?"

"It wasn't, Mawlati! He brought—"

Efra cut her off. "We can discuss what he brought with the Aada. Rest assured, Namsa is telling the truth."

Rovial's tainted tomb, how I wanted to strangle Efra. I settled for an acerbic laugh. "I should rest assured, should I? The Commander and his guardsman arriving without a single weapon between them. Almost as though they wanted to ensure they'd be taken alive into the mountain."

Namsa ran a tired hand through her hair. "The decision to take the men was a joint one."

"Then you're all fools."

I tapped Arin's shoulder in warning twice before I put my hands on his blindfold.

Efra grabbed my wrist and wrenched me away. "What do you think you're doing?"

I didn't get a chance to respond. At the sound of my pained hiss, Arin—who had remained perfectly still and serene until then—moved. Before I could pull my wrist out of Efra's grip, Arin kicked out the back of Efra's knee and slammed his bound hands into the side of the other man's head.

It took seconds. Efra crumpled to the ground, and I darted in front of Arin, throwing my arms in front of him as Lateef and Namsa pushed toward the Heir.

"He can see!" Efra shouted, clutching his knee.

"He can't, I am sure of it," Namsa protested, worrying her lip. "I wrapped the blindfold in three rounds."

Still groaning, Efra rolled onto his side.

I wanted to weep with frustration. This was precisely why I hadn't wanted them to bring Arin here. They had all ignored me, convinced by Efra that my emotions had clouded my judgment, but my *emotions* had wanted the contrary of what I recommended. I knew what the man behind me was capable of. "He is the Commander of the most powerful kingdom in the land. Do you think cutting off one of his senses will deprive him of the others? His hearing is better than all of ours combined. He heard Efra move, noted the position, estimated where to kick based on Efra's height. It's why I wanted to take his blindfold off. It serves no use. The minute you led him into this mountain, you compromised it forever."

"Then it is a relief indeed we do not intend to release him from this mountain alive," Efra spat, rolling to his feet. He strode toward Arin, and I spun toward him. My magic flooded me faster than it had since the battle in Mahair. My skin stretched beneath my rigid veins, and the bottom of my stomach disappeared.

Behind me, Arin finally tensed.

"Are you going to attack a man while he cannot fight back?" I growled. Ridiculous, given Arin had flattened Efra not one minute ago, but the *principle*—

"Move aside, Suraira."

The soft command brushed the top of my hair. I tilted my head back to look at Arin. "You aren't the one who gives orders here, Commander," I whispered back.

Jeru stepped forward. "I thought the Urabi had rules about how they treated their hostages," he said, reasonable in the face of the circulating tension.

"We do." Eyeing Efra warily, I lowered my arms. "Namsa and I will take them to the cells."

"Let us go gather the Aada," Lateef said, taking Efra's elbow in his firm grip. The older man shepherded a scowling Efra into the corridor.

As soon as Efra and Lateef vanished, a weight shifted off me. "I'm taking his blindfold off," I told Namsa. "Do the same for Jeru, please."

Namsa, wisely withholding her comments, stood on her tiptoes to reach for Jeru's head.

Thumbs gentle on Arin's cheekbones, I eased the tight blindfold off inch by inch. It slipped right over his hair, dropping to the ground behind him.

Silver lashes lifted. Pale blue eyes ringed in shadow met mine.

"Hello again," I said.

His gaze roved over me, assessing, then drifted idly over the top of my head.

My brows drew together. Something was wrong. Terribly, terribly wrong. When he didn't frown at the blindfold heaped on the ground or the giant tear in his coat, my concern tripled.

What happened after the Mirayah?

Namsa cleared her throat. "Essiya, we should go. The Aada will be waiting."

Right. I had a measly trickle of time left before I needed to explain to the Aada why abducting Arin of Nizahl days before we headed to Jasad for Nuzret Kamel might be highlighted in history as the peak of human stupidity. Though if I did, they would argue for executing Arin on the spot.

I didn't hold on to Arin like Namsa did to Jeru as we walked. He wouldn't try to escape. We had already given him what he wanted.

But I was beginning to think what he wanted might not be exactly what I thought.

Darkness enveloped us at the head of the stairs. Dust motes tickled my nose, and I paused with a hand to the wall to sneeze. I shook my head, cursing the general sediment of mountains, and rubbed at my watering eyes.

Naturally, I did so while descending the next step, and my heel skidded straight off the edge of the stair.

I collided into a solid wall of muscle, saved from tilting right off the edge of the banister-less stairs. The scent of ink and rain flooded my nose. I tipped my head back—to thank him, or maybe to gauge his thoughts about the inefficiency of mountain architecture.

But as soon as he had steadied me, Arin stepped back, putting distance between us. Again, he stared clear over my head.

The spark of concern became a flame. I glanced at Jeru, hoping for an answer, but the guardsman kept his head down.

We continued to the cells without further incident. We placed Jeru in a normal cell, and Namsa insisted on putting Arin in the cell at the far right. "The bars are warded. It is our most secure cell."

"Take Jeru's restraints off. I will deliver the Heir to his cell."

Namsa glanced at Jeru uncertainly. I sighed. "Jeru, will you attack Namsa if she releases you?"

He blinked. "No."

"There we are. Namsa, you have magic, and he's beaten and exhausted. If he manages to best you, then you deserve to lose."

With a chuckle, Namsa waved me off and withdrew a knife for Jeru's ropes.

Arin and I rounded the corner. No sooner had we disappeared from Namsa's view than I spun around and grabbed his coat, hauling him into the wall. He didn't resist, bone-chillingly pliant against me.

"What are you doing here?" I hissed. "I have to walk into a room and spend a good portion of my day convincing them not to kill you. Do you know how long it will take to persuade a mountain full of Jasadis that their worst enemy should be spared?"

Arin shrugged. I thought his shoulder was falling off for a second, so off guard did the lazy motion catch me. "Then spare yourself the trouble and let them do as they please."

I scoured his face, utterly baffled. What was he doing? I thought I understood the rules of our game, but this—I didn't see the purpose, the objective.

My tone shifted to take on a plaintive note. "Arin, what's wrong?"

It was the wrong question. Breathtaking grief fractured in the eyes he rapidly shut. He twisted out of my grip like a tiger shaking off a fly. "Just take me to the cell. Please."

I stared at him, hurt swelling in my chest. Namsa appeared in the next instant, preventing me from coming up with more sensible questions than *what happened to you, who did it, and where can I find them?*

"The cell is just up there," she said, once again exercising wisdom by ignoring the obvious tension. "Shall we?"

Arin followed her without so much as a glance my way. As I scowled at his wide back, my attention snagged on the ground. A folded rectangle lay where I had slammed Arin into the wall. It must have slipped from his coat.

Awaleen below, I had done a detestable job searching him.

I picked it up, unrolling it carefully as I caught up with Namsa and Arin. As soon as he stepped between the three walls, alternating silver and gold bars slammed down, the wards radiating heat.

"Excellent." Namsa wiped her hands on her hips. "We should hurry."

I didn't hear her. I wouldn't have heard if she had yanked me down and shrieked it directly into my ear. Noise filled my head, a loud buzzing growing louder and louder the longer I stared at the portrait.

"Namsa," I said, surprisingly even toned. "I have stretched your goodwill thin. Know that I appreciate your patience. I will put one last demand upon it and ask you to wait for me at the top of the stairs. I'll just be a minute."

"Please make haste," Namsa sighed. "A minute, Essiya."

She glanced at the portrait in my hands disinterestedly and departed.

The eyes were just as I remembered them. A chilling blue, the color of frost creeping over rushing water. Her black hair was long and silky in this photo, wavy instead of frayed and short. She looked regal. Queenly. The woman she might have become if I hadn't ruined her.

I crumpled the portrait, fighting the urge to tear it into pieces. A sum of paint strokes and dabbled water. All it took to bring a nightmare to life.

I took a deep breath, trying to still my trembling hands. Perhaps he had a rational explanation. What was I thinking? Of course he did. They were his specialty.

"Why do you have a painting of Hanim in your coat?"

CHAPTER FIFTY-THREE

ARIN

It had all been going according to plan until he saw her.

Fear had been plain in her features as she pushed the blindfold from his head. He could count on one hand the number of times he had seen Suraira afraid, and the dismay of causing it had been the first thing to pierce him since he'd fallen into the void twelve days ago.

He shouldn't have brought the portrait. He should have burned it or tossed it into Hirun on his way here. If he had, it would never have had a chance to put that stricken look on her face. Before he could ward it off, the memory forced its way through Arin's defenses. Essiya on her knees, wrists tied on the other side of the tree as Hanim raised a whip to her bare back.

Hanim, Arin's mother. Hanim, Essiya's tormentor.

Sinking to the ground, Arin leaned his head back against the wall. "The letters you left with me were useful. Perhaps more useful than you expected."

"You mean Binyar Lazur's confession?" Essiya stepped toward the bars, wrapping her hand around a silver one. "What does that have to do with the portrait of Hanim?"

"You once asked me if my hair was black when I was child."

Essiya rubbed the heel of her hand into her eye. "Yes, you said it was black until the musrira cursed you."

"No, not because of the musrira." The cold seeped into him from the floor. He barely felt it. As long as he didn't look at her, he didn't feel much at all. "Because I wouldn't have survived if he waited until I was four."

She stayed silent, clearly waiting for him to elaborate. When he did not, she released an aggravated sigh. "Arin, I am occasionally fond of your winding way of speaking, but today is not one of those days."

He flinched at the sound of his name. It was a terrible power she held—the power to make Arin real. Yank him from his head and anchor him into being, skin and bones and the horrors in between.

He could see her shaping his name once more. It couldn't be allowed to fall from her lips.

"I don't look much like her now, but I took after my mother until I was two years old. My real mother." Arin's gaze flicked down to the crumpled portrait.

She did not react—not at first. The Jasad Malika squinted at Arin as though waiting for something. When it never came, Essiya stumbled away from the bars. Watching the truth detonate through her, shattering pieces of her along the way, threatened the void once more.

He was in no condition to speak to her. Anything he said would only bring her pain.

"Hanim couldn't have been your mother. She was a Jasadi. Rawain wouldn't have…he hated…" Dust flooded the air as she sank to her knees, her legs folding beneath her. The pieces he'd put together were slotting into place for her, too.

She shook her head, speaking in a daze. "In the third trial, Soraya showed me a vision of the fall of the fortress. Soraya asked one of the Mufsids why Hanim would ever think Rawain would allow her to take Jasad's throne. Why she would risk bringing down the fortress for Nizahl's armies."

She pressed her hands to her stomach, tears gathering in her eyes. "It was you. Her son. She believed Rawain would give her Jasad's throne because they shared an Heir. She gave Soraya the wrong enchantment on purpose."

Essiya raised her head to stare at Arin, and he forced himself not to look away. She was owed more than the void. She could have whatever she wanted of Arin while he still had it to give, and he would not deny her.

"Hanim's son." She made a sound between a gasp and a giggle. "No wonder she hated me so much. Rawain took *you*, and she was stuck with me. She was watching you rise to command scores of men by sixteen, and I was an Heir with no throne, no magic, and a broken mind. I could never have pleased her, because she was measuring me against you. Rawain took her son. He had her future, and she only had her monster."

She brushed her hair behind her ear. Thin gold and silver veins snaked up the side of her neck, disappearing into her tunic.

"I'm going to die raising the fortress Hanim brought down. I killed her, and she'll kill me. She wanted our line off the throne, and the line burns with me."

Arin's gaze jerked from the veins on her neck. "Raising the fortress?"

"Mawlati!" The call echoed from the other side of the cells.

"Don't worry." Essiya climbed to her feet, the bottom half of her abaya covered in a layer of beige dust. "It is a good plan. You will like the symmetry of it. I'll die, but so will my magic."

She laughed again, her fingers braced on the wall as she wandered toward the other woman's voice.

I am afraid that I will have to choose—my mind or my people.

Arin stared after her, unmoving. Unmoored.

And when seven sneering men sauntered into his cell some time later, Arin did not put up a fight.

CHAPTER FIFTY-FOUR

ESSIYA

The sight of Rawain's scepter tossed on a cushion in the middle of the floor, Rawain's severed hand still attached, had done wonders to improve my mood.

I huffed, darkly amused. Well, at least I understood how Arin had managed to persuade them to bring him into the mountain. Stealing the Supreme's scepter was a convincing argument on its own, but paired with his hand still in its cuff?

"He lies about having Jasadi blood. We would have known. Someone would have seen him perform magic as a child," Efra argued. They'd been going in circles for hours. I'd told them what Arin said about Hanim and watched the implosion from afar.

"When would we have seen him use magic, Efra? The Malika said it was stripped from him at two years old." Maia had firmly situated herself on Arin's side.

Namsa gnawed on her lip. "What about his sensitivity to magic? It isn't natural, and we know it could not have been a musrira."

"Curses were more of a Lukubi specialty," Lateef agreed. "Sustaining them is arduous work, and it requires the caster to expend magic throughout the lifetime of the curse. A failed curse would have killed the musrira *and* her victim."

They went round and round. I should have been part of the conversation, analyzing theories alongside them. I shouldn't have been sitting in the corner like a child, clutching my stomach as I sank through the sands of a different crisis.

Hanim's son. Her *son*.

I tried to see the resemblances, and to my distress, they came readily. The silky fall of her hair, the sharp cut of his jaw. His tendency to fixate. Her strategic mind.

I thought of the dreams I'd had after Soraya stabbed me in the Ivory Palace. Isra blocking Rawain's path in the nursery, where a black-haired baby slept in his bassinet.

He won't survive it. Please, Rawain, you have to wait.

What do you care what happens to my son?

He is mine just as he is yours.

I kneaded my knuckles into my chin, willing myself not to emit the sounds brewing inside me. Hysteria would help nobody.

I killed Arin's mother.

Lateef cleared his throat. "Mawlati, do you remember when you asked me the difference between draining magic and transferring it?"

Focus. I had to focus. Arin's life hinged on my success in this room. If I disintegrated, my authority went with me.

I forced myself to think through the fog. "You said the only person capable of sensing and draining magic was Fareed. You said the Awaleen gave him that ability to protect the kingdoms against abuses of magic."

"Exactly!" Lateef said, and I couldn't help a small smile at the pleased note in his voice. "I regret my phrasing—it was not entirely accurate. You see, the Awaleen didn't *give* Fareed an ability so much as they took one away. They stripped out his magic and anchored it to his weapons, so that any magic he drained would flow into the two swords we know to be Nizahl's symbol. In short, they turned Fareed into a conduit."

I stared at Lateef. "Are you trying to say Rawain stripped out Arin's magic and used it as a funnel to pull magic into some sword?"

"Not a sword."

Everyone's heads swiveled to the scepter.

"How?" Namsa rasped. "Only the Awaleen can create a conduit without killing the intended target."

Arin's aggravated admission to Wes the day I had manifested in Essam. He had to have been talking about the magic mines.

I cannot figure out where they are. I have spent days scouring my maps, but I would have felt them. I should have felt them.

"If Rawain bartered for mined magic from Jasad, and if Nizahl had stored enough of it from their centuries of the trade…" I looked at Lateef. "Could it have been enough power to create a conduit without killing him?"

Lateef blanched. "I… it is possible. Only if the subject was very young."

I wouldn't have survived if he waited until I was four.

Arin was a conduit. Which meant he had not only brought us his father's scepter—he had brought us the source of his magic.

"The Silver Serpent's lineage is of no consequence," Efra interrupted. "We have four days until we leave for Jasad. His presence ensures our route will be compromised, since every Nizahl soldier under the sun will be out searching for him. Not only is he too dangerous for his fate to be left to chance, but he cut off the Supreme's hand and stole the scepter. He will be branded as a traitor to his crown. They'll want to execute him."

I inhaled sharply. Execute him? Surely, Arin would be able to make Nizahl's council understand why he had acted against the Supreme. What Rawain had done violated every tenet of Nizahl's laws.

I took a deep breath. Here was where the test came. Where I discovered whether the last two months had earned me any goodwill among my people, or if I would always be the Heir who failed them.

"I think the Nizahl Heir will help us."

Several heads swung in my direction, not all of them friendly.

"For the last ten years, Arin of Nizahl has been our enemy," I said. "Since the moment he took his title at sixteen years old, he has fought against magic. With every fiber of his being, he believed magic led to destruction and death. *Magic-madness*, they told us. Magic came at the price of sanity. We were destined to repeat the carnage Rovial inflicted on the earth. Our Awal's curse was our curse." I raised a hand to ward off the protest I could already see forming on Efra's face. "I do not say this to defend the Nizahl Heir. What he has done, he will carry for the rest of his life. We have lived in terror of his power, of his mind. But here, we have the opportunity to utilize those same terrors against our enemies. The Commander brought us the Supreme's scepter. His own father's hand. Efra just said it himself—if he is caught by Nizahl, he will be found guilty of treason and executed. He had nothing to gain and everything to lose by coming here, and yet he came. What if he has come to reclaim his magic? To join us? Nobody knows the geography of these kingdoms better than him. The points of weakness in the trade routes we've been arguing about for days? He could probably find them in his sleep."

I believed what I was saying, but even as I spoke, a part of me held itself stiff in doubt. By the time Arin made one move, it meant he had already mapped twelve moves ahead. What was his plan for coming here?

"And if we decide he is too great of a threat to be kept alive?" Efra leaned back in his seat, arms crossed. "Would you abide by our decision to execute him?"

You err by giving them a decision to begin with, my magic whispered. *This is your kingdom. Your throne.*

It showed me a vision of Efra flying back into the wall. His bones breaking in the collision, the unnatural way his arms and legs would fold beneath him as he fell.

Efra pressed two fingers to his temple, derision fading into unease. He'd felt it—the voice's presence. If only he could hear what it said, what it wanted. He might think twice before suggesting the execution of Arin of Nizahl.

"Of course," I said.

If they killed him, I would bury this mountain in the sea.

"What if he tricks you?" Maia asked, peering up at me with earnest brown eyes. "What if this is all part of a larger ploy?"

This time, I answered honestly. "Then I will kill him myself."

When the meeting finally ended, I didn't head toward the dining hall with the rest of them.

Much as I wanted to change out of these clothes, I couldn't risk stopping by my room. Marek and Sefa had undoubtably taken vigil there, waiting to pounce on me with questions I had just spent the last four hours answering.

In the empty hall, I stripped off my gloves and wiped my palms on my thighs before sliding them back on. How did Arin tolerate wearing gloves every minute of the day?

I nodded at Shawky, the guard they'd assigned to the cells.

"Mawlati?" Shawky shuffled awkwardly, not moving from the front of the door. "Aren't you headed to supper?"

I raised a brow. Shawky hadn't spoken to me once since my arrival. A close friend of Efra, I'd gathered.

"Not yet. I'm checking on the prisoners."

Shawky stayed in place, scratching his collar with studied nonchalance. "Perhaps it would be best to eat first."

I narrowed my eyes. "Step aside."

The guard took too long to move, so I shoved him aside and forced my way into the dimly lit stairwell, descending two steps at a time. No amount of blinking dispelled the blanket of darkness over the hall, and I kicked myself for forgetting to snag a lantern. With an impatient flip of my wrist, a flame appeared in my palm.

My chest twinged; Medhat had shown me how to do it.

I reached Jeru's cell first. The guardsman had his head in his hands, shoulders drawn. I dropped the flame into one of the torches lining the grim corridor, but he didn't react at the burst of new light.

"Jeru. Are you hurt?" Soft, so as not to startle him.

He raised his head. Tears had carved clean tracks across his dust-covered cheeks. "They didn't come into my cell. I think they wanted me to listen."

I lurched back. They?

I bolted down the rest of the empty cells and turned right. At the end of the corridor, I heard, "Someone check for a pulse."

I couldn't remember the last time I had run so fast. Maybe the night I killed the Nizahl soldier, when I had run back to Mahair and brought Sefa and Marek to help me bury the body. Possibly not even then.

I skidded to a stop in front of Arin's cell. Seven men crowded the tiny space, looming over the still figure on the ground. Blood spattered their shoes, their clothes. None of it theirs—not a single man had a scratch on him.

On the ground, Arin lay unmoving.

Red clouded my vision. Between one blink and the next, every vein in my body lit into an inferno. But the men only saw the magic swirling in my eyes before they found themselves hurled back into the wall, their bodies pinned by an invisible force against the gray stone.

I dropped to my knees beside him. My hands hovered uselessly, trying to assess the damage. They'd broken his right arm. Certainly cracked his ribs, if his rattling breath was any indication. His face— his beautiful, barely healed face—had been battered into a mess.

I gently peeled a lock of hair from a gash on his forehead. Arin could have disassembled every man in this cell blindfolded with a hand tied behind his back. I'd watched him cut down a swarm of magic-rotted Omalian soldiers like he was brushing his hair.

"He didn't fight back," I whispered. It echoed in my head, bouncing across the edges of my shock until it became a roar. My magic clawed for release, and I did not resist it. The rush of power quieted the grief howling in my chest.

He didn't fight back.

I stood slowly, palms open at my sides. The pinned men squirmed against the wall. Helpless. Pathetic. "You attacked a hostage in his cell. Seven against one. When you saw he wasn't fighting back, you thought what? You'd have a nice story about cornering the Nizahl Heir to carry back to your wives? I recognize how difficult it must be for you to excite your women in bed, but this story doesn't end well for you. In fact, this story ends you."

I placed two fingers on the throat of the first man. His eyes bugged, limbs jerking unnaturally. "Hmm." I tilted my head, the glow from my eyes casting light over his paling features. "How long does it take a tongue to melt? Let us find out together."

The red-haired man's screams filled the cell until they petered into a guttural groan. His head lolled forward as he fainted, blood pouring from between his parted lips.

The next man started screaming before I even touched him. My brows rose. "Now, now. No need for theatrics." I tapped his nose. His skin began to undulate, his flesh stretching into grotesque bubbles under his skin.

The bubbles popped, and ants poured from the seeping wounds into the man's eyes, nose, and ears. He choked on them as he tried to scream. "How many ants does it take to chew from skin to bone? So many questions we're answering today."

I had just shifted in front of the third when a strong arm wound around my stomach. Arin had drawn himself up from the ground, his chest heavy against my back. He yanked me away from the man. "Stop it." Haggard, barely audible.

"But we are having such fun," I insisted. "Right, gentlemen?"

The second man screamed again, and the ants seized the opportunity to flood his mouth a second time. Tsk. What did I tell him about theatrics?

"Suraira. Enough."

Arin staggered, the arm around my stomach tightening for a different reason. I caught his waist, immediately forgetting anything other than the injured Heir in my arms. "Arin?"

I held him tight to keep his head from skimming the wall as we collapsed to the ground. The arm around me never went slack, keeping me firmly pressed to his side. We landed in a heap.

"You didn't fight back," I said, and it came out small and childlike. "Why?"

"Their magic was drained...as soon as their skin came into contact...with mine." He swallowed, his throat working to gather his words. "Their magic went to the scepter.

"Let them..." He stopped to breathe, the same horrible rattling sound accompanying the action. "Go."

I seethed. They did not deserve to leave this cell whole and intact. "They drained their magic when they hit you—fine. What does it matter?" I recoiled as a sudden thought occurred to me. "Please don't say you allowed them to attack you out of a sense of *fairness*. Arin, they would have been at a disadvantage with or without their tombs-damned magic!"

Arin raised his brows silently, not ceding any ground. "Let them go."

We glared at each other. Finally, I swung my head toward the pinned men, my glare hot upon them. "Remember this. This is the mercy of the man you brutalized. It is because of him your lives will not end in this cell."

I waved, releasing them from their holds. They sprinted out, shoving one another in their hurry. One of them stopped to haul the unconscious first man over his shoulder.

"At least the one with the ants lost a decent layer of skin," I said sullenly.

Arin coughed, but he might've been trying to laugh. "How much tongue does the first one have left?"

I sniffed. "Just the root, I hope."

Agonizing minutes passed while Arin caught his next breath. "You can't harm a Jasadi on my behalf. They will lose faith..." Another long moment. It hurt to watch him try to draw air. "In your impartiality. In your leadership."

He'd prevented me from filleting the men who did this for *my* protection?

That did it. Tears I hadn't noticed building spilled onto my cheeks. I covered my face, embarrassed to be the one crying when Arin had about half an inch of unbruised skin left.

"You should not spend your tears on me."

"They are yours anyway, you idiot," I sobbed. Months of fear and loneliness poured out of me, ruptured by the sight of Arin lying still in pools of his own blood. "Why did you come here? I was ready to die. I was ready to be honorable and brave and self-sacrificing for the first time in my miserable life. I had made my peace. I would restore Jasad, burst into flames, and enter history as a savior instead of a coward. Simple."

"You are not going to die."

"Of course I am! I was always going to die—my time has been borrowed ever since the Blood Summit. I've been trying to be brave about it. To be like *you*. But then you come here, and you make me want to be selfish. You make me want to be a coward." I wiped my nose on my sleeve. "You make me think I have a choice."

"Look at me, Suraira."

I raised my puffy eyes. His gaze seared through me, focused and intent. Finally *Arin*, and not whatever listless creature Efra had brought in.

"I could spend the rest of my existence apologizing to you, but I will never be sorry that you survive. Not for a single…second."

As soon as he finished his last labored sentence, his eyes rolled to the back of his head. I caught him as he slumped to the side. With as minimal disruption to his wounds as possible, I pulled him against me. His blood had soaked through my tunic and coated my arms. The puddles of it on the cell floor hadn't dried.

"What does it take to make the Nizahl Heir finally faint?" I traced the bridge of his nose, following it to a silver brow. "Just losing four times the blood of an average man."

I inhaled as far as his weight against my chest would allow, then screamed for Namsa.

I crossed my legs on the bed, watching his chest rise and fall. The healer's magic had passed right through him, so we'd had to include nonmagical remedies. The sight of Arin with his arm strapped to his chest, black-and-blue bruising covering him from temple to chin, a plethora of bandages over his body—it tore at me. I wanted to rewind time and finish what I started with his assailants.

Assailants who were, in a delightful little twist of irony, now in the cells themselves. Efra had begrudgingly agreed to place them down there in punishment. I personally thought it was a generous deal. They stayed in the cells until we left for Jasad, and I would refrain from skinning them with a potato knife.

I also won Jeru in the bargain. The Nizahl guardsman had been relocated to a room next to Marek and Sefa's. Easier on the sentries, I'd argued.

My hands twisted restlessly in my lap. The bandages the healer had placed on him were suffused with enough magic to heal an army. The hope being that in his current condition, he would drain it slowly enough that the magic would have a chance to heal him before it disappeared.

I wouldn't do either of us any good by sitting and fretting. I padded across the room, slipping a billowy black abaya over my shoulders. I shut the door behind me and patted Niseeba's head. They had found her screeching outside the mountain, hopping around the door Arin had entered through, and she hadn't settled until I brought her to him.

"Keep him safe for me," I murmured.

The guard at Jeru's door stepped aside as soon as he saw me, which was an excellent reminder that I needed to find Shawky and have him thrown into the cells with his worthless friends.

I cracked the door open, relieved to find Jeru wide awake. He was sitting in bed, his back braced against the wall with one leg straight and the other drawn to his chest. His dinner tray remained untouched by the door, and I picked it up as I entered.

The rest of the room came into view, and I heaved a giant sigh as I spotted Marek and Sefa watching me sheepishly.

"You two aren't supposed to leave your room! How did you get past the guard?"

Sefa pointed at Marek immediately. "He told them you sent us to keep an eye on Jeru."

Ignoring the betrayed frown Marek shot Sefa, I approached a silent Jeru.

"Existential agony is much more effective on a full stomach," I advised, sliding the tray next to him. I perched on the edge of the bed. "Besides, you have about twenty seconds before Marek tries to steal it."

"Make it ten," Marek said.

Jeru didn't say a word. Goodness, I had had about my limit of morose, moody men.

"He had to listen to the men beating Arin to a pulp," I told Sefa and Marek. "They've been punished, but apparently Jeru isn't quite finished punishing himself."

Jeru exhaled, the end of it curling into a defeated laugh. It raised the hair on the back of my neck. "He didn't fight back."

My brows furrowed. "I know."

"You don't know. You don't know anything." Jeru tugged on the ends of his curls, which had already been pestered into a tangled frizz. "He came here planning not to fight back. He came here *ready* not to fight back."

I stared at Jeru, something dangerous shivering in the back of my head. He couldn't mean what I thought he meant.

"He came here to restore his magic," I said, and even as I said it, I heard how foolish it sounded.

Arin didn't just distrust magic—he despised it. He had led a life premised around magic creating unspeakable horrors wherever it went.

I wanted to cover my ears as Jeru opened his mouth. I wanted to knock his teeth down his throat. I wanted to do anything but sit still, frozen, racked with horror.

"The Heir came here to die."

CHAPTER FIFTY-FIVE

ARIN

He opened his eyes to darkness.

Had it not been for the pain radiating through his body, he might have mistaken the serenity for death.

Arin flexed his fingers, testing the extent of the damage. He vaguely recalled a healer attempting to fix him by steeping bandages in her magic instead of pouring it straight through him. It had worked to some extent—his broken arm was fixed, sore but not agonizing. He drew in air, and his ribs barely complained. The healer must have used every drop of magic at her disposal.

What a *waste*.

The bulk of the healer's magic had gone straight to Rawain's scepter.

A light snore came from Arin's right. He wasn't alone in the bed.

Her hair coiled in a bun above her head, hands tucked under her cheek, Essiya slept facing Arin. Her oversize sleeping gown was rucked around her knees, revealing gauzy white pants. She had gone to sleep with gloves on and a scarf tied around her neck, neither of which Arin imagined were comfortable.

Her furious tears were the last sight he recalled. She hadn't understood why he did not fight back. Why, when Arin could have disassembled each of those men and stacked their limbs in a corner like firewood.

He had considered it. When the blows kept coming, when the taunts began to cut their way through the void, Arin had wanted to react. But their one advantage was stolen, their magic gone as soon as they touched Arin's skin, and Arin was the Commander. It was not fair. It was not *just*. His magic had tipped the scales.

Essiya stirred, her lashes fluttering with restless movement. Part of him wanted to strangle the fools who had allowed her to be alone in a room with him. Even if she believed he wouldn't hurt her, the rest of them had no reason to share the sentiment. Leaving her here, unguarded... how carelessly they treated the woman poised to risk everything for them.

How carelessly she treated *herself*, sleeping next to him. Utterly, ridiculously confident in her safety.

No number of nightmares would ever terrify Arin as much as the sight of her standing in the middle of the cell, drenched in gold and silver light from hundreds of veins crisscrossing her body, glowing eyes mottled with fury. Essiya had killed before. More than once. But she had never done so with absolute disregard for the weight of the action. If he hadn't interceded, she may very well have commanded the third man to eat his friend and watched in elation while it happened.

If my magic overtakes my mind, you are the only one who will be able to stop me.

In slow and steady slices, Essiya's magic was consuming her humanity.

Arin watched her sleep for a long time. He counted the black eyelashes resting above her cheeks. Drew a map between the hasanas dotting her throat and chin. In the tunnels, he had memorized her as one might the mechanics of a particularly dangerous weapon: understanding it solely in the event it was ever turned against you. He hadn't lingered on the pulse feathering in her throat. The slight unevenness of her brows where they arched at the ends. The way six strands of her hair hung a little shorter than the rest.

At that moment, without matches and without moving, Arin set fire to every map he had ever created. He watched the world he'd built—the world he'd believed—burn to ashes, and a new one rise to take its place. One that began with a girl sleeping at his side and ended with her alive. It was the only world he cared to participate in. The only world he would die to secure.

Arin slid his legs over the side of the bed. The carpet brushed his feet, startling him.

As odd as it sounded to admit even in the privacy of his own head, he had forgotten what sensation felt like. The warmth of the bed, the prickliness of the carpet. The sore twinge in the muscles of his stomach. Since the cabin in Lukub, everything had been muted. He had moved through the hours only under absolute necessity, and had it not been for that necessity, Arin was not certain he would still be here.

Arin allowed himself a moment to appreciate the irony. He had come to the mountains to give the Jasadis the scepter and to do the same thing Essiya aimed to accomplish by raising the fortress: use his death to undo some of the damage he'd done while he lived. Killing him would absolve her in her people's eyes. It would bolster Jasadis across the kingdoms. Their lost Malika, slaying the enemy of magic. Dealing Nizahl a debilitating blow. Death would find him anyway, in a poisoned chalice or a prison cell, and Arin wanted his to count for more.

So it was, in Arin's opinion, cruel of his mind to decide it could feel carpets again.

The bed shifted. Essiya wriggled into the spot where he'd lain, relaxing into the leftover warmth.

Arin stretched out on the carpet, staring at the shifting shadows on the ceiling.

This war would not end with her life. It would not cost her sanity.

A weight lifted from his chest as Arin began to plan. If his death would not save her, then what he had left of his life would. She would not raise the fortress. Rawain would not ruin Nizahl in his supposed war against magic, even knowing that if Essiya did raise the fortress, Nizahl didn't have a hope of overcoming it. Rawain would gladly leave the Jasadis trapped within their kingdom while Nizahl lost more and more of its children to the maw of Rawain's wars.

Eventually, Arin lapsed into a restless sleep. At some point, he roused to find Essiya curled beside him on the carpet, her head pillowed on his sleeve. Fast asleep again.

She'd followed him to the ground. Arin regarded the ceiling, caught between exasperation and amusement. He challenged anyone to find a more stubborn woman walking the earth. He could rap his knuckles against that hard head of hers and pull away with five broken fingers.

He closed his eyes again, the knife wedging deeper while Arin bled and bled, and never had a man found such peace in the shadow of his death.

The next time Arin woke, he was suffocating.

Shoving himself upright with one arm, Arin assessed his surroundings while he fought to pull air into his body. A lantern burned in the corner of the room. In its dim light, Arin saw Essiya bowed over a bucket, the irksome Urabi man pressing her head beneath the water.

A man who screamed like a newborn when Arin rolled to his feet and drove a dagger into his shoulder.

Arin shoved the man out of the way and crouched beside Essiya, drawing her out of the water. Her eyes were half-lidded, crescent moons of silver and gold flicking wildly beneath them. The veins on her neck had expanded to the bolt of her jaw, curling behind her ear and disappearing into her dripping hair. He lifted her sleeve, only barely remembering to keep his bare hands from skimming her skin.

Veins. They throbbed over her entire arm in a brilliant lattice.

"You need to put her back in the water," the fool boy behind him growled. "She needs to wake. Her magic controls her when she dreams."

She was drowning in her magic. So much of it that Arin—across the room and in his sleep—had suffocated under its tide.

"Take the knife out of your shoulder and prepare to use it. If I linger for longer than a second or if my eyes turn black, slit my throat."

"Slit your—"

"You are not strong enough to stop me if her magic overwhelms me," Arin snarled with the last of his air. Only she would be strong enough to stop him, and she might not have the chance.

It was a bittersweet decadence, this choice. In the end, Arin picked her cheek.

His bare thumb skated over the ridge of her cheekbone, and fire engulfed him.

CHAPTER FIFTY-SIX

ESSIYA

I opened my eyes to Efra aiming a knife at Arin, who violently shook as he coughed blood onto the carpet.

Scrambling toward Arin, I barely registered the wet slap of my hair or the water soaked into the collar of my tunic. "What happened?" I demanded. I wrapped my arms around Arin's middle as his back bent over a new round of coughing. Less blood this time, at least.

"He...touched you." Efra seemed too bewildered to remember his hostility. "Not even a touch—he barely grazed your cheek with his thumb. I felt your magic recede, and then he just—" Efra gestured. "He told me to slit his throat if his eyes turned black or he lingered for longer than a second, but he threw himself off of you before I could."

Aghast, I pressed my forehead to the center of Arin's shuddering back.

"He also stabbed me, if you consider that of note," Efra grumbled. "You might have warned him about my visits."

I laughed against a wing of Arin's shoulder. How had he managed to hide a knife through multiple searches?

I could only imagine what Arin had thought, waking to find Efra pushing my head into a bucket of water. I shut my eyes in mortification. "When would I have had the chance?" I groaned.

"Whatever magic he pulled from you seems to have accelerated the healer's magic," Efra said. "His bruises are gone."

It was true. He wasn't struggling when he coughed, which meant his ribs had also healed.

"His body probably stopped draining the magic infused in the bandages because it was busy trying not to drown under the magic he drained from me. How could you let him gamble with his own life like that?"

Efra regarded me as though I had begun to bleat like a goat. "What do I care what the Silver Serpent does with his life?" And then, with no small amount of displeasure, he added, "His strategy worked. It staved off your magic long enough for you to regain control."

"It doesn't matter. There are other ways to push my magic back. This will not be one of them. Not ever again." There wasn't a point discussing this with Efra, of all people. "Go see to your shoulder, Efra."

At the door, I stopped him with a reminder. "I am relying on your discretion. Be advised I will not take it kindly if my faith is misplaced."

He rolled his eyes. "They have been expecting you to stab me since you arrived. Nobody will ask questions."

The door closed behind him. The coughing had slowed, but Arin's body was ice cold against mine. What would have happened if he hadn't been wearing the healer's bandages? If there hadn't been magic in place to heal him? Would it have only taken that single touch for my magic to kill him?

Eventually, his body relaxed against mine. I leaned back, arranging his head into my lap. I rolled my sleeve, holding my arm under his nose until a warm puff of air brushed over my skin.

He had saved me—again. I had almost killed him—again.

The Heir came here to die.

We had nine days until Nuzret Kamel. Nine days for me to undo twenty-six years of Supreme Rawain's poison and prove to Arin that having magic was not the end of his world. All he had ever experienced of it was pain and anguish.

I had nine days to show him it could be so much more.

"To reiterate: You want me to jump?" Arin glanced from the waves crashing against the cliff to me, arching a silver brow.

"Not jump. Slide." I gestured impatiently. "Just hold on."

I rubbed my temples, feeling like a premiere fool. I had been trying to summon the Sareekh for the last fifteen minutes. So much for *you may call upon me at any hour of need*. Even the fish were lying these days.

Arin didn't know why I had brought him up here, only that I wanted him to see the rest of the mountain. We hadn't discussed last night.

"If you're trying to figure out how to push me over the side, I don't think anyone would stop you," Arin said.

A joke. He is joking. Don't react. Do not—

"Including you?" I demanded.

The second brow jumped to join the first, high on his forehead.

I dragged a hand down my face, turning away. I couldn't stop thinking about what Jeru had implied—the risk Arin had taken by touching me.

Arin caught my arm, spinning me back around. He stared in steadily rising disbelief, holding fast when I tried to wriggle away. "Essiya, I am not going to throw myself off this cliff."

"No, you would have me do it for you." I wrenched free. "Is it so horrible, being Jasadi? You would rather *die* than have magic?"

Arin's eyes widened. His lips parted, but before he could speak, the ground rumbled beneath us. Salt water misted the air, massive waves slapping against the side of the mountain.

"Took it long enough," I groused. The sea rippled as water sluiced off the rising island, the Sareekh's scales shimmering bloodred under the shafts of sun.

You summoned. Loudly.

I pointed at the Nizahl Heir and thought, *I want to show him magic can be beautiful. He knows little of what it can do besides kill and cause chaos. Help me.*

I am not your personal amusement.

Please? I channeled it as pathetically as I could. *I did not call upon you frivolously. He matters to me.*

A long, sullen vibration. I glanced back at Arin. The Nizahl Heir had slid onto his haunches, watching the Sareekh with open-mouthed awe. "This is Sareekh il Ma'a," he said. Wonder colored his voice. "I read about it when I was a child. The stories...did not do it justice." He glanced up at me, and I would have dealt with the Sareekh's attitude a million times over if it meant seeing more of the pure astonishment in his eyes. "Did you summon it?"

I rocked on my feet, strangely shy all of a sudden. "It likes me. I am theoretically allowed to call upon it when I am in need, but we're having a debate about the circumstances of such need."

Oh, fine.

Two spindles shot through the air. The cages closed around my and Arin's middles like bony corsets, hoisting us into the air.

A credit to Arin's ironclad control—he didn't shout. He didn't wrestle. The Sareekh reeled us over the side of the cliff, and Arin's single admission of stress was in gritting his teeth.

My hair whipped in the wind, and I kicked my legs with child-like glee. The Sareekh's parted spinal column revealed the bundles of spiky bones, curled into buds beneath a gelatinous layer. They sealed as it drew Arin and I down, leaving only the two extended sets of bone cages.

"Don't be frightened!" I shouted over the whistling wind.

Arin's glare intensified under my maniacal grin. His hair blew around him like a wrathful cloud, and it only entertained me further.

The Sareekh sank beneath the waves. The first glimmer of unease cracked through Arin as we raced toward the churning waters. I should have warned him what I intended to do. Surprises were not the way to endear magic to Arin.

I heaved myself to the right and grabbed his hand, resenting the gloves more than ever. I wanted to feel his skin. Trace the light veins on his hand with a soothing thumb. He weaved his fingers through mine and held on tight.

Brace yourselves.

We crashed into the water. Our hands flew apart as we submerged, sinking at dizzying speed. The shock of cold faded faster than the disorientation, and I struggled to adjust to the darkness.

Your magic. The purpose of this lovely excursion, no?

Right. The veins lit one by one as magic flooded my body. I opened my mouth. Gold and silver bubbles floated from my lips. The first of them found Arin and quadrupled in size, merging to form a translucent barrier around him. The rest did the same to me. Our chests lifted with air at the same time, and I laughed, the sound swallowed by the still water around us.

But Arin didn't look excited. The opposite, in fact.

On reflex, I glanced down at myself. Silver and gold veins blazed over my body, wrapping around every inch of exposed skin. I had grown so accustomed to the sight, it barely registered how much they had spread.

He just needed to see. If he understood what magic could do, the wonder it might create, he wouldn't be so unsettled by the veins. He wouldn't have the words *magic-madness* swimming in loops around his mind.

He just needed to see.

I wrapped my arms around myself. I shaped the silent intent, viscerally aware of Arin's attention. My magic heated, hungry for more. Always hungry.

I threw my arms wide. Light poured over us, searing as an implosion of the sun. The rays pierced across the water, lighting distances and depths I couldn't begin to comprehend. They rotated around us, illuminating, exposing the life waiting mere inches away. Schools of fish swam beneath our legs, their scales casting glittering shadows as they passed. A silver creature with a fin on its back chased the smaller fish, its tail cutting naturally through the water.

I did not point out the monsters hovering behind Arin.

They were the same ones that appeared my first time underwater, crowded curiously behind the Sareekh's head.

They will not come closer.

They are already too close.

As a single force, the creatures wriggled back, putting space between them and Arin.

They obey me, and I obey you. They will not harm what is yours.

Bewilderment cut through my relief. I hadn't dwelled on it too much the first time, but now, the Sareekh's proclamation puzzled me. It sounded so certain, so assured.

But why? Why would a creature like you obey me?

It is what I was created to do.

You were not created to obey some random Heir to a throne that doesn't exist anymore.

The Sareekh hummed, but did not reply.

I moved closer to Arin, careful not to reach him too quickly. I didn't want to consider how it would feel if he recoiled from my magic.

"Look behind you," I murmured.

A muscle jumped in Arin's jaw. "A most comforting sentence," he muttered. Holding tight to the Sareekh's ribs around him, he turned.

"Do you know their names? I imagine they dislike me referring to them as 'the monsters.'"

Arin seemed completely unfazed by the primordial creatures floating in front us. "Your point has been made, Essiya."

"I didn't have a point. I had a question." I nodded toward the spherical pink creature near the front, its glossy flesh puckered with bright blue pods. "Is this an Arnabeet?"

The Sareekh rumbled another laugh in my head.

Arin shot me a thoroughly unamused look. "It is called a Khawfa."

"Khawfa?" I widened my eyes, the very manifestation of innocence. "Is it new?"

The fact that Arin knew exactly what I was doing didn't stop him from falling victim to the urge to correct me. "Of course not. Its existence can be traced to 350 A.E., when a group of Lukubi sailors dragged one to shore. The Khawfa exuded a gas that killed everyone in the vicinity. It turned the sand pink as it died."

He shook his head, curiosity flaring brightly before caution snuffed it. "I never thought I might see one in the flesh."

"Magic," I said lightly. I pointed to the next fish. "What about the shiny black one, with the rotating fins?"

So it went: Arin relenting to the pressure of his curiosity, relaxing to the magic wrapped around him, while my nails bit into my skin to combat a different pressure in my veins, beating harder and harder.

Marek chattered away, the only voice in the resoundingly silent mess hall.

It had seemed like a good idea, bringing Arin, Jeru, Sefa, and Marek along for supper. I wanted the others to get accustomed to the Nizahlans' presence, and it would be best to do so before we began the journey to Jasad. Arin had already received one shock to his system today—what was one more?

But the *stares*. There would be less attention on our table if I had stripped naked and tried to juggle bananas with my nose.

Marek's most reliable offensive strategy was turning into a golden-haired beam of charm, and he'd chosen to target Lateef first. The elderly man was clearly taken aback by the waves of unrelenting conversation unleashed upon him, but they'd eventually settled on a spirited debate over the best methods for shearing sheep.

In the center, Arin sat rigid and straight-backed between Maia and Namsa. The women had taken three bites the entire meal. Maia's husband sat on her other side, darting glances at Arin over his wife's head.

I didn't blame him. I doubted they'd been spared the one pervasive thought rotating in everyone's heads, exchanged in hushed glances.

The Silver Serpent had found his way into the nest.

"Namsa, have we received any word from Yara about the trade routes?"

Namsa startled at her name, dropping her spoon with a clatter. A pea flew from her plate and landed on Arin's vest.

"Oh, bloody Sirauk, I'm so—I can wipe—" Namsa waved her hands helplessly around the pea, clearly too panicked to remember anything other than not to touch the Nizahl Heir.

Arin picked it up between two fingers and deposited it on the table. "It is quite all right." The measured cadence of his voice, the most I'd heard of it in hours, immediately soothed my nerves.

It seemed to have the opposite effect on Namsa. She gave him a pained smile before hurriedly returning to me.

"About the routes," Namsa said delicately. Lateef set down his fork and pinched his beard.

I lowered my spoon, momentarily wishing I had my own beard to pinch. Maybe I could find a couple of long chin hairs. "What?" If Sorn had reneged on his promise, I would hollow the bastard's head and pin it on his wall of trophies. We were relying on those roads. Thousands of Jasadis had already begun their journeys.

"The rebellions in the Omalian lower villages and deaths of Queen Hanan and Felix appear to have inspired similar unrest in Orban," she said. "Sorn hasn't stripped all the protections from the trade routes, but King Murib has forced him to divert a significant number of khawaga toward combating the unrest."

I put my face in my hands. "Is Murib going to fight the rebels?"

"It appears he is hoping to negotiate," Namsa said. "I would guess he wants to avoid meeting the fate of the Omalian crown."

"I can divert my kitmers toward the trade routes," I said. "They won't do much against armies, but they might be enough to supplement what we're missing from Orban."

"If Nizahl moves toward the trade routes..." Maia glanced at an impassive Arin. "Should we start sending out our parties? The mountain is still full, and if we move at once, our presence will be much more conspicuous on the roads."

"Nizahl has their hands full with Lukub," I muttered. "Nobody knows where Vaida is, but I expect Rawain is turning every stone trying to find her."

"I fear Lukub may not be enough of a deterrent. The Supreme knows the Jasadis are moving. He'll send forces south to guard the border," Lateef said.

"No," Arin said.

I lifted my head. With two fingers, Arin pushed aside his plate as though it were a guest that had overstayed its welcome. He folded his hands in the empty space.

"Rawain will not risk his hold on the Citadel by scattering his armies." Firm and absolute, Arin's tone left no room for argument. "Not without the scepter."

"Do you think he's been using the scepter to bolster his armies?"

"I know we have never lost a battle during his reign. I know Essam has never proved inhospitable to us, even during the bitterest of winters. We have fed, clothed, and sheltered our soldiers without raising the levies on our nobles." Arin's expression was inscrutable. "I know I survived an injury at sixteen which should have proved fatal."

"There could be other explanations," I said.

"There could be."

The thought of Rawain draining Jasadi magic to bolster his own armies—an army that existed to protect against people exactly like Rawain—was too nauseating to contemplate.

"Why do you think he will be reluctant to lessen the protections around the Citadel without the scepter?" Lateef asked when my silence lengthened.

"My father believes in a certain balance of life when it comes to leaders and their subjects," Arin said. "He will devote a significant number of his remaining forces to protecting the Citadel. If he sends forces south, they will most likely be composed of new recruits."

"Recruits?" Marek's outburst nearly startled Sefa into dropping her soup. She righted her bowl at the last minute. "Most of those recruits have never even been in a fight!"

"I am well aware," Arin said, clipped. "The goal is distraction. The sheer volume of them will slow you down until he gains enough of an advantage over Lukub to send his real army toward Jasad."

"Distraction." Marek's derision was palpable. "Disposable, you mean."

"As I said." Frost crystallized around Arin's features. "He believes in a certain balance."

Apparently, Marek's time hiding in a Nizahl compound had given him a tender outlook on the plight of the poor Nizahl recruits. I had too many Jasadis to keep alive to care about the unfortunate backgrounds of the men Rawain would be sending to battle. It did not matter if the hand holding the sword wanted it there or not—it would kill me just the same.

Sefa set down her spoon with a loud clatter, finally looking up from the depths of her soup. "What Vaida has planned will not run its course in eight days. She spent years searching for the Mirayah. Whatever relic magic Baira left her, it will either obliterate us all instantly or far outlast this particular war."

I met Marek's gaze in a moment of shared bewilderment. Sefa wouldn't speak much of her time at the Ivory Palace. I hadn't known how to broach the topic beyond surface-level questions. What I did know for certain was Sefa would never have inflicted an act of violence against anyone—even the Sultana—unless she had had no other choice. Unless she had known without a doubt that leaving the ring with Vaida would invite deadly consequences.

"There is no war. Not yet," Lateef said. "Only the Commander can declare war."

The bolt of Arin's jaw tightened. "Not necessarily. There are... exigent circumstances to my authority."

He may as well have knocked me clear across the hall. Hanim's ghost rose more viciously than it had in months, and suddenly I was in Essam, gutting the fish for our dinner while Hanim flicked over my notes.

"*The Rule of Rulers*," she mused. "I suppose you could have chosen a worse title."

I bit back my smile. "Thank you."

"What did you learn?"

I finished cleaning Hanim's fish and skewered it over the fire while I considered my practiced response. "The Rule of Rulers is that for every supposed absolute, there is an exception. I found twenty-nine instances of the phrase 'imminent risk' and seventy-six of 'exigent circumstances' in the laws of all five kingdoms."

"Tell me about each of them," Hanim said, taking the skewer I offered her. She peeled the flaking skin from her fish. "Then you can eat."

"The Nitraus Vote," I gasped. "You committed treason when you took the scepter. The council will hold a Nitraus Vote to instigate war without your authorization."

The grim set of Arin's features lifted briefly, replaced by a spark of appreciation. He was always disproportionately impressed by knowledge of obscure information. "Yes. In all likelihood, they have already held it."

"Nitraus Vote?" Lateef repeated, frowning. "I'm not familiar."

I explained quickly, struggling to prevent my disquiet from veering into panic. Thousands of Jasadis were headed toward our kingdom on *my* command. I had promised them a fortress, protection. If Nizahl had mobilized for war, Orban might renege on its promise to protect the trade routes.

If we reached Sirauk Bridge only to find armies waiting for us, Jasad would drown in more of our blood.

I blew out a breath. Across the table, weariness and trepidation marked every face, shoulders stooped like birds tucking their wings against the storm.

Arin met my troubled gaze with his own. The first sign of a battle lost was the *belief* it was lost.

I clapped my hands together, once again startling Sefa into sloshing her soup.

"Who wants to fight the Nizahl Heir?"

Arin set his feet, waiting.

Even after clearing the tables, the dining hall hadn't accommodated the influx of people rushing to take turns fighting the Nizahl Heir, so we had moved to the cliffside. My first set of kitmers circled overhead, chasing the sunlight as it receded over the sparkling surface of Suhna Sea. Everyone sat cross-legged in the valley between our mountain and the neighboring one, the frozen lake where the Visionists had conjured the attack at Galim's Bend not far behind us.

Maia's husband took the sword Lateef handed him and swallowed. He glanced at Arin's discarded sword and then at Maia, who was rocking on her heels with dizzying velocity.

Maia's husband set his sword on the ground. "Commander or not, I will not use a weapon against an unarmed man."

Arin had yet to use the sword I'd handed him. He'd set it behind him and had not reached for it in the last seven challenges. With his coat off and his sleeves rolled to his elbows, there was no difference between him and a man enjoying a moonlit stroll.

"I admire your honor." The suggestion of a smile touched Arin's lips. "Perhaps the memory of it will keep your wife warm after you're dead."

Arin struck as jarringly fast as he had with the others. Maia's husband barely had a chance to react before Arin swept his legs out from under him. Instead of rolling away from Arin's boots, the husband rolled in, hurtling his weight against Arin's legs. The crowd stirred, curious to see if the Nizahl Heir might finally lose his balance. So far, no one had been able to knock him down. Maia's husband was a man of impressive height and build—if anyone could tangle Arin, it would be him.

So they thought. I leaned against Sefa's shoulder, scooping a spoonful of sugared pomegranate seeds out of her bowl. On her other side, Marek and Jeru were observing the proceedings with matching looks of consternation.

"How many more is he going to fight?" Sefa sighed. Maia's husband had gotten back on his feet. We watched him swing at Arin's head and miss.

"As many as are stupid enough to challenge him."

Without a vest, only the thin barrier of Arin's shirt obstructed my view of his chest as it flexed. I drank in his twisting torso, the strip of his back where Maia's husband had grabbed at Arin's collar and rucked up his shirt. Rovial's tainted tomb, Arin without his layers was obscene.

"Please get that look off of your face," Sefa said, the strained request startling me from my reverie. "I feel an urgent need to throw you into the lake."

"The lake is frozen."

"And yet I doubt it'll be cold enough." Sefa shuddered. "I thought Marek had exposed me to the full range of human depravity, but Awaleen below, Essiya…unless you want everyone to know you'd like to eat the Heir alive, take a firmer hand with your lust."

I flashed her a crude smirk. "I'll tell you who I'd like to take a firmer hand with my lust."

I erupted into peals of laughter as Sefa started shoving me toward the lake.

Maia's husband hit the ground a third time, and he raised his hands in defeat. "I surrender. I need my spine in working order to survive the journey to Jasad."

Arin extended a hand toward Maia's husband. I stiffened, jerking away from Sefa. I couldn't remember Arin extending a hand to anyone other than me. The Urabi were already paranoid about his abilities, about coming too close to him. If Maia's husband rebuffed the gesture, all the goodwill Arin had spent the last hour fighting for would be destroyed.

He had taken a calculated risk, and it proved worthwhile when Maia's husband clasped Arin's glove.

I exhaled, belatedly noticing I had crushed the pomegranate seeds in my fist. Ugh. I reached around Jeru to wipe the sticky red mess on the back of Marek's shirt.

"You're nervous," Sefa murmured, soft brown eyes roving over my features as though my emotions had been written in a special ink only she could read. "You want them to trust him. Do you think he can't take care of himself?"

"It isn't about capability." We watched Lateef walk in front of Arin, hand him a glass of water, and promptly put as much distance between himself and the Heir as possible. A fighter, Lateef was not. "Arin is not willing to defend himself. If they try to kill him, he'll—" My throat closed, the memory of finding him in a pool of his own blood on the cell floor still fresh. "He will let them."

"He certainly does not seem to be letting them now."

She was right. When Arin entered the mountains, the emptiness had leeched the life from every glance, every word. Arin's entire identity had been cast to the flames; the order of his world obliterated into formless chaos. I knew better than to think my display with the Sareekh had convinced the Commander of Nizahl of the wonders of magic, but it was clear a shift had taken place.

"He is hiding something." I studied him and did not flinch when he glanced over his shoulder, meeting my gaze with a piercing one of his own. "He has a plan."

"Doesn't he always?"

When Arin had dropped seventeen Jasadis to the ground, I stepped forward.

Amusement warmed the eyes fastened to my face. "Do you never tire of trying to spill my blood, Suraira?"

I quirked a brow. "Everyone needs a hobby."

Picking up the sword, I raked a quick glance over the crowd. They had risen to their feet, conversations faltering into a thick silence across the cliffside.

"I hope you fare better than you did in Mahair," I said.

"Play without cheating and I might." Arin finally picked up the sword he'd left to collect dust, and I grinned.

"I won't need my magic to put you on your back."

Catching Sefa's knowing stare over Arin's shoulder, I flushed a shade similar to the pomegranate on the back of Marek's shirt. Arin could have easily replied that *he* hadn't needed magic to put me on my back, but then again, he probably knew how to take a firmer hand with his lust.

Arin twirled his sword once and beckoned me. Ah. He wanted to give them a show.

I pretended to crouch to tie my boot and scooped a pile of dirt and rocks. Springing to my feet, I flung it at him and took the opening of his momentary distraction to ram into him at a dead run.

However, I had done this twice previously, and Arin was prepared. The bastard managed to twist us around at the last second. In a flash, our positions were reversed, my back against his chest, the sword pressing into the skin beneath my chin.

The scent of rain and ink tickled my nose, achingly Arin, before his breath brushed against the side of my head. "Is this all you have to offer me?" Tight against him, I could count every beat of his heart, pounding inside his chest.

I kissed the edge of the sword, feather-light, as gold and silver gleamed in my eyes. The second most dangerous thing I had ever kissed. The first tightened his hold behind me.

The ground beneath Arin quaked.

The Commander pitched forward, momentarily unsteady as the cliffside shook. I slipped under the sword and grabbed Arin's collar, yanking him to me.

"Cheating again," Arin murmured, but there was laughter in his voice. I was using my magic, and for the first time, it did not draw a veil of dread over him.

We fought for years. Centuries. Reality passed around us, but it could not penetrate through us. In a space separate from time, our swords clashed with the music of a ballad. Our bodies moved around each other like stars voyaging across the night, permanently aligned. Not a single drop of blood was shed, because the truth was the mightiest force between us: the next time we aimed to hurt the other, it would be real. It would be his sword at my neck if magic-madness swept me where no one could reach; it would be my dagger in his heart if he betrayed me.

Arin maneuvered me against the side of the mountain, his sword inches away from the soft side of my belly. He braced his elbow by my head, the curve of his arm hiding my face from the other Jasadis. "You are out of training," he said. "Use your magic."

I tried to catch my breath, determined to spew a variety of outraged denials. I may not have been able to train in the mountains, but I hadn't needed to. I was a better fighter than everyone here, and according to the Alcalah, better than the best of the other kingdoms.

My chest deflated. Out of training, I might still be better than everyone, but I wasn't better than him.

He didn't want me to lose in front of the Urabi, but they would know if he threw the fight. Both scenarios reflected poorly on their Malika.

"This does not count as cheating," I warned. I flicked my gold-and-silver gaze to his, elated when Arin didn't flinch. If anything, he drew closer, as if caught in the tide of the colors swirling in my eyes.

Too caught to notice the weight of my fist—tripled under my magic—slamming into the side of his head.

Arin shook his hair out, arching a taunting brow as he flipped his sword. I hid my grin, vigilant of the attention on us. I still had a limited range of what I could do with my magic; I lacked the intuitive connection most Jasadis developed in their adolescence. I hadn't learned any tricks in classes or studied magical strategies with my tutors. Hanim's focus had been entirely devoted to releasing my magic, not teaching me how to use it once freed.

Still, I learned quickly, and my time in the Gibal had not been without its lessons.

I pressed the tip of my index finger to a crack in the ground. Fire burst like a gushing river and raced toward Arin's boots. The Jasadis cheered as Arin twisted out of the fire's path. It leapt, hopping in the fractures of the dried ground, molten veins winding tighter around him.

A screech sent the Jasadis to the ground as Niseeba swooped low, the flap of her wings extinguishing half of the flames. Her shadow crossed Arin like a protective caress, and I scowled at the kitmer as she rejoined her younger siblings in the sky. Perhaps favoring Arin was her revenge for being named *disaster*.

With magic at the helm, the fight raced toward its inevitable finish. I could have snapped Arin's bones like a stick of bosomat. I could have melted his tongue into a thick syrup down his throat.

For the first time, I understood how he could look at magic and see more than another tool. What sword could have stopped me? What mortal weapon might have slowed me down?

I pressed the tip of my sword to his throat.

"Don't move."

The fire snaked in fluid lines around us. Even with his chin tilted back and a knife digging into the delicate skin of his throat, Arin's composure never faltered.

Cold blue eyes met mine in a challenge. This was the Arin I met in Essam, the Arin who hunted me in Mahair. The famed Commander of Nizahl, trapped against my blade.

"On your knees."

Not a single person dared breathe.

"Get on your knees, Commander," I repeated harshly.

For an awful second, I thought he wouldn't move. I thought he would knock the sword out of my hand and cut me down in front of the watching Jasadis, done with the facade. This would be where he drew the line: the last frontier he would not surrender. Efra was right, and Arin had been toying with me all along. The Silver Serpent had infused his venom into me, and I was nothing more than another in a long line to fall prey to—

In a sinuous motion, Arin knelt.

Shock reverberated from our audience, so strong it threatened to shake the very mountain itself. I didn't dare move beyond keeping the sword aimed. The beginnings of a tremor worked through my arm.

All of Nizahl's power knelt before me. All of Rawain's strength and might. The strongest Commander in centuries, gazing up at me with utter tranquility.

"Arin of Nizahl. For ten years, you have been the enemy of magic. You have hunted us. Harmed us. Done your best to break us. In the service of the Supreme, you have perpetuated the lie he fabricated ten years ago to justify our annihilation. Magic-madness, they said. A disease. An inevitability. A death sentence."

The air changed, threaded with a dangerous pulse. If I wasn't careful, righteous anger would fall way to vengeance.

What secret irony it was that Arin had been right. Partially right, as I had been partially wrong. Magic-madness *did* exist, and he was looking at it. He had seen my veins, suffocated beneath my magic, but nobody knew about my magic's voice. About the hallucinations, the shifting figures.

The figures who now stood in a ring around me and Arin, holding vigil to the truth. Dozens of them, some faces I'd seen before and others I hadn't, invisible to every eye but mine.

"The innocent blood on your hands does not care for what cause you shed it, Commander. For what you have done, death would be a just consequence."

I didn't dare look at Jeru.

"But you carry the magic of Jasad in your veins. You are of us, and we are of you. Today, we show you mercy. We offer you a choice."

Arin's words from the cabin, offered so long ago, came to life between us.

I offer you a new life.

"Swear yourself to the throne of Jasad. Swear your loyalty to magic and to those born with it. Swear yourself to us, and you can live."

Please want to live, I didn't add. *Please want to stay.*

"No."

My lungs collapsed.

Murmurs broke out immediately, followed by the shuffle of dirt as everyone shoved in for a closer look.

"Thrones fall. Magic fades." Arin's level voice cut through the din. "I will swear my loyalty, but not to Jasad's throne, nor to its magic." A black gloved hand pressed against the tip of the sword, lowering it to aim at his heart.

"I swear my loyalty to Jasad's Malika."

I couldn't breathe.

"Everything I have is hers to command. What she wills, I will create. What she hates, I will destroy. I am the weapon of the Malika, and it is her alone I pledge myself to."

Speechless, I stared at Arin.

I'd had a plan—a good plan, damn him. I didn't know what to do with this. What game was he playing, suggesting something so ludicrous? I'd offered him a pledge everyone would consider reasonable, but who would believe Arin of Nizahl had vowed himself to the Malika of Jasad?

Unless it wasn't a game.

I stepped back. Arin simply watched me. Sword pointed at his heart, on his knees, and terrifyingly sincere.

What was he thinking? Arin of Nizahl, subject to *my* will? My whims? It was stupidly dangerous. He knew about the veins. He knew what would happen if I survived raising the fortress.

"Do you accept?" Arin asked.

"I—I—"

The figures shifted around us, their silhouettes blending into a shroud of darkness whirling around me and Arin, separating us from the Jasadis. They wanted this. They wanted to claim the Heir as they had claimed Raya.

I lowered the sword and exhaled.

"I accept."

CHAPTER FIFTY-SEVEN

ESSIYA

The following three days were the best I had spent in the Gibal. Sefa fussed over me in ways I would never allow from anyone else. How much I ate, what I wore, how long I had slept. The attention from Namsa or Maia would have fallen falsely, even if its roots were true. My purpose to the Urabi was first and foremost a weapon. You might clean your blade and sheathe it lovingly for years, but once it cracked, you would be a fool to do anything other than melt it down and forge a new one.

Sefa asked because she'd been burdened with the unfortunate defect of caring about me. Cracks and all.

In the evenings, Marek and Sefa joined me on the cliffside while the Urabi prepared for our departure from the Gibal. I enjoyed watching my kitmers circle the sun as it set over Suhna Sea, their silver wings dappling the horizon with the fiery colors of Jasad. Marek regaled us with tales of his time in Nizahl's Ravening compound. Zane, the kind giant who rescued Marek from a nisnas, possessed a love of beans that had resulted in gratuitous amounts of flatulence; he also prevented Marek from throwing himself on the Lukubi guards who arrested Sefa. Almerour, whose real name he had forgotten, wouldn't know how to aim a spear if you brought the target to the end of his nose, but he could apparently talk about the history of the kingdoms until everyone in the bunks fell asleep.

Sefa spoke about Lukub only once. Quiet and subdued, she told us about saving the Sultana, about realizing her options were to either die looking for us or to finish what she and I had started during the Alcalah. When she spoke of Vaida, her tone tightened with discomfort, as though she knew what Marek and I were thinking. As though we might hold her in judgment for showing kindness to a woman who manipulated her; think less of her for enjoying an adventure with someone who threatened to cut out her tongue and had her thrown in the Traitors' Wells.

When it was my turn to close the gaps of my time since the Victor's Ball, the seams of my story were loose and uneven. I couldn't tell them about standing in the waterfall while hallucinations danced around me. Nor about Raya's glowing eyes, swirling with Jasadi magic. Killing Felix and signing my death sentence in the same motion. The constant cacophony of my magic, an ever-growing pressure within my veins.

Neither I nor Arin had forgotten what awaited me when I left these mountains.

Since the moment he had declared himself to my service, Arin had been a force of unrelenting, unstoppable action. Every Jasadi with unusual magic had been accounted for, and Arin had divided the Urabi into groups. Half of them pursued tasks aimed at preventing the war, and the other half prepared to win it. The only task he had assigned both sides was the scepter.

"He thinks using it to raise the fortress will keep me from using my magic," I explained to Sefa and Marek.

"Do you disagree?" Marek watched me closely.

"I have less faith in Rawain's sense of moderation. I suspect he used the magic in his possession frequently and generously, and there will not be much waiting for us inside his ugly scepter."

Every order Arin issued, he did so under my name. He taught the Urabi how to swing a sword or dispatch an armed opponent. He advised what kinds of food would survive a long campaign toward Jasad and what would perish. No details evaded his inspection, and no question chafed him into irritation. We were more organized, more purposeful, than we had been since my first day at the Gibal, and he attributed it all to me.

An outright lie, of course. Leadership exhausted me. I was a performer on a stage, and I had memorized my steps, but I took no joy in the motions. The rhythm of it did not flow naturally through me. And more and more frequently, I simply wanted to sit down and catch my breath. Wipe the sweat from my brow and rub my aching feet.

What drained me, revitalized him.

On my worse days, I wondered whether Arin was right, and I had resigned myself to death to hide the fact that I was still Sylvia. I was still the girl who wanted to run, who would watch this mountain burn and turn her back on the flames. Death meant I would atone for my past, but it also meant I could never fail in the future. I would not need to sit on a throne I hated or break beneath a crown I could not carry. This escape—this one permanent escape—was the only place I could run where failure would not trail behind me like a chain around my ankle.

There were moments when I thought Arin knew. When he entered our chambers after I had just settled into sleep, the brush of leather as he moved my hair from my cheek. He would sit at my side, motionless for the first time since his burst of activity in the morning, and I wondered if even in the dark he could see right through me.

Do you think surrendering to your magic is bravery? Do you think it will atone for your past?

But he never mentioned atonement again, and I avoided discussing anything that might summon that hollow emptiness back to his eyes. It had vanished after his first night in the Gibal, but I doubted it had disappeared entirely.

Arin's mind was a maze with no beginning or end. The scepter, the preparations—they were merely passages toward his ultimate plan. The scepter would not be enough to raise the fortress. The Urabi would never be trained to the same level as an army of Nizahl soldiers, not even new recruits. He had a destination at the end of this maze, and for whatever reason, he didn't want me to know where it led.

But he kept my secret, so I kept his.

Arin paced around the table, his brow furrowed nearly to his nose. He shuffled four documents to the right. A pause. Two documents returned to the left.

"Is he going to talk anytime soon?" Namsa mumbled, draining the last of her yansoon. "I would ideally like to sleep before sunrise."

"No one is holding you here," I said, not unkindly. "There's more than enough of us already." Lateef had taken a seat after twenty minutes of uncertain hovering near the maps, and now he joined the rest of us, nibbling at his atayef and watching the Nizahl Heir circle the table.

Legs outstretched beside mine on the ground, Maia offered me a handful of sunflower seeds. I shook my head, and she hesitated before extending her arm past me, holding out the seeds to Marek.

Marek beamed. "Oh, you beautiful, wondrous thing," he said, scooping half the seeds from Maia's palm. His fingers lingered on hers a beat too long, casually scanning the woman on the other side of the seeds. "Thank you."

"I can go fetch more, if you'd like," Maia said, blissfully unaware she had fallen straight into Marek's crosshairs.

"These are perfect, Maia. Just...perfect." The last part emerged so lascivious and heated, it was a surprise the seeds didn't roast right then. It also sailed past Maia, who flashed him a smile and turned back around.

I sighed. Marek's inability to accept kindness without trying to offer his body in return needed to be part of a longer conversation—ideally one he had with Sefa and not me. Pointing out Maia's current marital status wouldn't help. Marek had invited many a wedded woman into his bed, regardless of how many times their husbands tried to murder him.

I placed my chin on Marek's shoulder as though I were about to kiss him on the cheek. "She's a lahwa. The Urabi's executioner."

Marek blinked, turning slightly to meet my gaze. His attention dropped to my mouth. "Hmm?"

Awaleen below. He was hopeless.

A mean-spirited idea came to me. One I would have normally cast aside as pure pettiness, if I hadn't already had my fill of stubborn Nizahlan men to last a lifetime.

I brought my mouth closer to Marek and whispered, "A lahwa kills bloodlessly. Elegantly. All she has to do is reach into your mind and draw out your greatest nightmare. Submerse you in your terror until it stops your heart and ends your life."

I doubted he heard a word. The intrigue had fled from Marek's features, replaced with a cross between unease and confusion. He regarded my lips like they were coated in poison.

My attempt to move closer met with resistance. Marek planted his hand over my face and pushed my head back. "Not funny."

I swatted his sweaty hand away, wrinkling my nose. "Avoid gambling on a prize you don't want to win."

Rolling his eyes, he cracked a seed between his front teeth. "Too much has passed between us. Too many occasions where I watched you sniff the end of your braid and pick dirt out of your nails with a knife. My nightmares echo the sound of you clearing the phlegm from your throat in the morning."

My jaw dropped. How dare—oh, he was a dead man. We would see whose morning sounds were more disgusting when I shaved off all his nice, shiny hair and stuffed it down *his* throat.

"Besides," Marek said wryly, inclining his head toward the table,

"I might take my chances with average husbands, but even I am not fool enough to bed the Commander's... whatever you are."

I followed Marek's amused gaze to the table, where Arin had stopped scrutinizing the maps to stare at us. At my sheepish grin, he shook his head and returned to his task.

"See?" Marek said, altogether too pleased with himself.

"I see nothing. Eat your sunflower seeds."

"He still calls me 'the boy,'" Marek griped.

"It's affectionate."

"It's patronizing. Might I remind you, he and I are only three years apart."

"Wrong. You are an infant," Jeru snapped. "Pay attention."

We startled. I'd forgotten Jeru was on Marek's other side. The guardsman hadn't uttered a word all day.

At the table, Arin stopped pacing. He braced his palms wide across the table and bowed over the maps. Marek and I exchanged meaningful glances, and I pushed to my feet.

Standing at Arin's shoulder while he loomed over a table covered in maps stirred a bittersweet nostalgia. The first time we'd been in this position, it had been over a map with the words *Scorched Lands* over Jasad's former territory. It had never crossed my mind that months later, Arin of Nizahl would be bent over another map—only this time, on behalf of the rebels he had spent years chasing.

"Hello," I said, standing entirely too close.

He tilted his chin and studied me for a fraction of a second, as though waiting for bad news. When I continued to just smile like a drunken fool, his face softened. "Hello."

"What do you think of our maps?"

He gestured at the spots he'd marked. "Not nearly sufficient for what we are attempting. I could draw better maps from scratch."

We. I beamed. Not even Marek's giant eye roll could ruin the effect that one word had on me.

Arin raised a palm before Lateef could speak, anticipating the elder's indignance. "I do not mean it as a slight. In fact, you should consider it a compliment. I had maps much more sophisticated than these, and yet I continuously failed to capture you."

"Hmm." Appeased, Lateef reclined in his chair once more, legs crossed and a bowl of yellow tirmis in his lap. He squeezed a slice of lemon over the beans. "I'll consider it as such, then."

Arin had crossed out three of the major routes we had originally planned to take to Jasad. "Without Orban's protection, these roads will be compromised at every major juncture."

"What about Tareek il Hadi?" I tapped the sliver of road at the hills of the Blood Summit, its path cutting across Orban, the south of Lukub, and winding through Essam to Jasad. "My grandparents took this when we rode for the Summit."

"Your grandparents also took a retinue of trained Jasadi soldiers. Tareek il Hadi hasn't been safe for anyone since 1500 A.E. It is saturated in old magic."

"Then it is only fresh magic you prefer to siphon?" Efra asked, leaning against the other wall.

Gold and silver flicked into my eyes.

Under the table, Arin stamped on my foot. Hard.

I yanked my incensed glare away from Efra. Arin pointedly lowered his gaze to the veins glowing over my skin, pulsing in tune to my heart.

Arin's ability to see the veins could not be more inconvenient. The one person capable of speaking reason to my rage, even when I did not want to be reasoned with.

"As I was saying," Arin continued, as though he hadn't just saved Efra from an evening coughing up his fingernails, "Tareek il Hadi is not ideal, but it may be the only choice. None of the kingdoms can spare the resources to send more than a handful of soldiers to patrol it."

"Thank you for the insight, Your Highness." With a stern glance at Efra, Lateef dropped another translucent tirmis peel onto the pile by his foot. "We can reconvene tomorrow and finalize a course of action. It has been a long day, and any further work we put forth tonight will not be our best."

As soon as the dismissal left Lateef's mouth, everyone stampeded for the doors. Marek grabbed Jeru's arm and dragged him from the room, muttering some joke about Heirs being left to their affairs.

Lateef stood slowly, working a piece of tirmis between his teeth. The bean shot out and hit Namsa square in the forehead. "Off you go," he told her, passing over the bowl.

She wiped her forehead with a scowl. "You could have used your words."

"I did," he said. "The second time, I use my tirmis."

She stomped out, leaving me, Lateef, and Arin by the table.

Lateef's air of geniality vanished as soon as Namsa did. "Essiya, are you *trying* to discredit yourself?"

I balked. "What?"

Lateef rubbed his forehead. "I forget you are a mere twenty and one. And you"—he waved at Arin—"twenty and six. The fate of our future rests on the shoulders of children." Lateef sighed. "Broken and brave children."

Arin and I slid each other glances, mutually baffled.

"You must exercise greater care when you interact with each other," Lateef said. "Do not make it impossible to ignore what is already glaringly obvious."

I crossed my arms. "I do not interact with the Heir any differently than the others do. If you mean they will think I am too friendly, that I should be calling him Silver Serpent or sauntering around like Efra—"

"Friendly? Awaleen below, I would give my left leg for friendly. I would even accept affectionate. Essiya, it is impossible to watch you two and not recognize how deeply in love you are."

CHAPTER FIFTY-EIGHT

ESSIYA

Oh no.

Heat flushed through my body, reducing my caustic remark to a crisp. I became viscerally aware of Arin's proximity.

Lateef's gaze bounced between us. He heaved another sigh. "Children."

Neither of us spoke as the door swung shut behind the elder Jasadi. I tried to negotiate with my jaw. If it moved and produced speech—any speech—I would give it anything it wanted. I would stop clenching my teeth before bed. I would stop sucking the marrow out of beef bones. I would use my miswak before and after every meal.

"On the cliff, you asked if I would rather die than have magic. If existing as a Jasadi was too abhorrent for me to bear."

Arin stared straight ahead, the lines of his body coiled tight with a pressure that must have bordered on painful.

"What was too abhorrent to bear was the hypocrisy," Arin said, eerily flat. "The lies." His laugh chilled me. "How often I cast you as a liar, when I was nothing more than the custom sword my father forged through magic to fight against the method of its own creation."

I forced myself to slow down and choose my words with care. "Do you recall what I told you in the tunnels? The night Vaun dragged me into your chambers and you asked me how I could read Nizahl's old language?"

"Vividly." Arin cast a wry look my way. "I spent a significant amount of time after the Victor's Ball reviewing the many missed opportunities to uncover your identity."

I rolled my eyes. "Then you remember what I said. What I still believe. We build our reality on the foundation our world sets for us. You are not to blame for being planted in poisonous soil, Arin. Our choices come when we realize what we have grown into; when we look at the world around us and recognize our role in it. Only then, when you decide whether you will grow roots or tear yourself free, can you be truly held to account."

Arin pushed his fingers through his hair, features as impenetrable as stone. "Quite a forgiving perspective. Do you think the Jasadis I drained, imprisoned, and executed would agree?"

"Your death is not a penance. It does not balance the scales," I said.

"If I told you the same, would you listen?"

Thrown, I took a second to recenter myself. "That is different."

"You haven't forgiven yourself, either."

"For what? Turning my back on Jasad?"

"No." He glanced over, and I found myself held at the knifepoint of his gaze. "For surviving."

The air left my chest. Arin's unvarnished honesty was always an arrow to the throat. A clean and quick kill, leaving no shadows to hide behind.

I released a tremulous laugh. "What a pair we are. The magic-mad Malika and the magic-stripped Heir."

"You are not mad."

Yet. It lingered between us, another arrow neither of us was ready to aim.

"Even if I survive, what then? What do you think will happen after the fortress is raised? The Awaleen-damned fortress. The others are so preoccupied with restoring it, I doubt they've given much consideration to what happens after. How will we rebuild Jasad without help from the other kingdoms? How will we trade if our fortress keeps out merchants? There are Jasadis like Adel, who have lived in other kingdoms their entire lives. Started families in Omal or Lukub or Orban or Nizahl. Jasadis whose great-great-grandparents left the kingdom centuries before the Jasad War, who have almost no magic and even less interest in returning to a scorched land they weren't born to. Will they be forced to continue living in hiding, fearful of losing their lives over any innocent act of magic?"

I shook my head. "We need you. *I* need you. Just this morning, Namsa asked me about the number of wells around Usr Jasad and if we would need to dig more."

"Twenty-seven, and yes."

I groaned, covering my face. "If you have made it your new life's mission to outdo me at every turn, consider it satisfied."

Arin's lips twisted. "You give me too much credit."

"I give you exactly what you deserve," I pointed out. "If you'd like me to list your flaws, I am happy to oblige. We can start off with your sense of fashion. Do you own coats without ravens? You could choose to have a new coat specially tailored for you every day for the rest of your life, and it would hardly scrape the surface of your ridiculous wealth. Does every single one *need* ravens?"

Arin leaned in, bracing himself on the table and pinning me between the borders of his arms. "I didn't realize you paid such attention to my wardrobe."

Arin's gaze traveled over me with aching slowness, trailing heat everywhere it landed. "What else is on your list?"

I swallowed. I had not seen him look like this since the Mirayah.

"Your hair. If I went to sleep with my hair down, I would wake up with half of it stuck together and spend the next bath negotiating each curl apart. You go to sleep with your hair down, and it takes you one lazy swipe of your fingers to tame it again."

"I see." My mouth went dry as he twisted one of my curls around his finger, winding it into a spiral. "I can shave my head, if you would like."

"No!"

Arin's quiet laugh brushed the side of my neck, raising goose bumps on my skin. I gasped as he gripped my hips and lifted me onto the edge of the table, positioning himself between my knees.

"Is this part of the game?" I asked shakily. "If it is, it is thoroughly unfair. I am at a disadvantage of experience."

Arin arched a brow. "Did your previous experience leave something to be desired?"

I shoved his shoulder, cheeks flaming. "You know what I mean. I don't want…" I'd rather strangle myself with a serrated chain than reveal the extent of this gnawing insecurity. "I do not want to disappoint you."

I may as well have slapped him across the face. Arin withdrew, silver lashes ringing thunderous blue eyes. "I beg your pardon?"

Coherency evaded me, slipping like water between my sifting fingers. "I just mean, I know you have had others. I—I enjoyed myself, uh, greatly, but for you it might not have been as—what I mean to say is—"

The ripple in Arin's mouth sealed mine shut. Mirth had lit through him like stars in a dusky sky. I hid my face in his shoulder, groaning softly.

A heavy hand came to rest on my neck. His thumb slipped into the collar of my tunic, soothing a circle against the hilt of my spine. "Any advantage of experience I might have evaporates the minute you touch me, Suraira." His voice was firm. "Since it seems I have been less than clear: the advantage is yours. You unravel me utterly."

Molten fire flooded me, more than if he had uttered barroom filth. I could have handled that better. A thousand tiny tremors worked through me. "How cruel of you to say such things to a dead woman."

His grip on my neck tightened painfully for a fraction of a second, then relaxed. "If you live—if we both do—what life do you see for yourself?"

"I haven't envisioned anything," I said. Strange, how ardently I had once fought to ensure I could exist for another day, another week, another year. I had rarely looked to the future, because I didn't need to. The details might change, but I wouldn't. I would be there.

Now, the future burst with colors and potential, but none of the possibilities included me.

"Lazy," he chided.

I blinked, struggling to focus on something other than the trail of his fingers along my hips. "I do not see the point of giving myself over to fanciful musings of a future I won't experience."

Again, Arin reacted with unsettling calm. "Indulge me, then." His eyes went hazy as I carded my gloved fingers through his hair, succumbing to the impulse I'd been pushing off for days.

Arin slid an arm under my legs and another behind my back. He carried me to the sleeping pallets on the other end of the room, left over from an overnight meeting the Aada held a few weeks ago.

He settled me onto a pallet and dragged a quilt over us, covering my shoulders. "There are other ways to keep me warm," I pointed out.

In a second, I was soundly enfolded against him, tucked away from the world and all its horrors. I pressed my cheek to his vest. I was convinced he had brokered a deal with the seamstresses to produce an endless supply of vests for him in the mountain.

"Answer my question."

I sighed. Once Arin caught on a question, he would not budge until he'd untangled a satisfactory answer.

Knowing he wouldn't drop the matter, I seriously considered it. What would my life look like if I survived raising the fortress?

"Once Jasad is safe, and my best utility is not in front of an army or beneath a crown, I think I would want to travel," I said, surprising myself. "I thought about it often as a child. Exploring. I would beg Dawoud and Soraya to take me to their wilayahs. Usr Jasad felt enormous to many who passed through its doors, but it always felt so limited to me. I climbed the trees in the gardens every day, looking down at the world and wishing I could be part of it." I chuckled. "I practically screamed myself hoarse until Gedo Niyar and Teta Palia agreed to take me to the Summit with them. I think they only said yes because they worried I might use their absence to spend more time with my mother."

I cleared my throat, turning my cheek into his arm.

"And if you were in Nizahl, I would come visit. You could show me your favorite places, and I would pretend to understand why they are an architectural marvel." I shut my eyes tight.

His breath stirred the top of my head. He sounded worn. "Suraira, I cannot fathom how to make you believe me. Anywhere you are is my favorite place."

I winced, rolling away from him. I tried for a lighter note. "In that case, I hope you are fond of graves."

"It is no bravery to pretend life is cheap to you," Arin said. "It is no bravery to push out all the things that make it worthwhile."

It had been ages since I remembered that my death was not a tragic inevitability, but a choice I was making. A necessary choice, but a choice nonetheless. Of course, Arin would be upset.

The choices I made always left him alone.

After a strained minute, he said, "Go on. Tell me of the rest of your life."

Lying on my back, I subjected the ceiling to intense and unwarranted scrutiny. "Eventually, when the world was safe again, I would want to settle. Probably in Jasad, but...there is a blue cottage in Mahair, not far from the keep. It has a garden and space for Marek and Sefa. I would replant my fig tree, and Marek would probably keep it alive for me, because plants seem to like him better. I would open an apothecary, or maybe a keep like Raya's. I'd teach young girls the best way to gut a man and how to braid your hair without looking in a mirror. Fairel has yet to master the latter."

My restraint reached its limit, and I burrowed into Arin's shoulder once more, eyes drifting shut. Sleep had been crawling over me, and its weight swiftly became too strong to resist—though I tried. What could it offer me when my waking hours had already woven me the sweetest of dreams?

"In the evening, I would come home to you."

When sleep finally stole me away, it whispered its apology.

CHAPTER FIFTY-NINE

ARIN

He tucked the note into her clenched fist and drew the blanket over her shoulders before he stood.

And continued to stand, fixed in place.

Arin had always considered it a requirement of any leader to delineate their areas of strength and weakness. What could be more imperative than understanding where you might be tested and fail?

But as Arin watched Essiya wriggle into the empty pallet where he'd lain, her chin jutting out from under the covers as she burrowed deep, Arin did not know whether the ache coring him from the inside was strength or weakness. It destabilized him. Unraveled him with every minute spent in her presence.

But it also gave him the strength to turn around and walk away.

Carving her out, pretending that leaving her side did not shatter pieces of him as he walked, was not a viable option. If she weakened him, so be it. Arin would be twice as strong.

The guard at Jeru's door jerked awake at the sight of Arin heading toward him. He glanced behind Arin, searching for an escort, and leapt to his feet at the sight of the empty hall.

"You can't be here," the man said, panicked. Silver and gold swirled in his eyes, but Arin struck faster, locking an arm around his neck.

The first guard slumped just as the second guard rounded the corner carrying a clay ula and a plate of ruz ma'amar. Both fell at her feet at the sight of Arin carefully laying the guard on the ground.

A smart one; she did not attempt to fight Arin directly. Someone needed to sound the alarm, and she swung around, chest expanding with the beginnings of a scream.

It would have worked were Arin not already in motion. One of the guards' chairs sailed across the short hall and slammed into her back.

A minute later, Arin dragged her unconscious form next to the other guard's.

At least they had not wasted their magic on a useless attempt to hold him off.

Jeru glanced up at the sound of the creaking door, wide awake. At the sight of his Commander, Jeru nodded to himself. "I thought so."

Without prompting, the guardsman followed Arin out of the room, stepping over the slumbering bodies at his threshold.

They had made their way around the corner when Marek stumbled out of his room, hair mussed in every direction and sleep hanging over him. He was holding an empty ula. When he spotted Arin and the unconscious guards, the sleep vanished. Comprehension dawned onto the farmhand.

"You cold-blooded traitor," he breathed. "You're abandoning her. She gave you every secret they have, and you're leaving."

"Marek, it is not what you think." Jeru grabbed the boy's arm. Marek tore free, and Arin had the foresight to grab the front of Marek's shirt before he could sprint down the hall and finish what the second guard had started. Arin shoved him through the door he'd emerged from, stepping into the dark room with Jeru close behind.

"The Commander isn't betraying the Malika," Jeru said, glancing toward Sefa's still outline on the bed. "He is trying to help her. If he returns to Nizahl, he can recall the soldiers from Jasad. Remove the blockades from the trade routes the Jasadis need to reach their kingdom. He can prevent his father from sending recruits to die. Marek, if Arin returns, Jasad will have Nizahl at its side."

Reluctantly, Marek's attention slid to Jeru. "What about the Supreme?"

Arin abruptly released the boy and wiped his gloves on his pants. "My father is my responsibility. As is Vaida."

The lump beneath the covers sat up, and Sefa regarded the three men in her bedroom coolly.

"Are you going to kill her?"

A thin shaft of light from the hall cut across Sefa's silhouette. Despite the boredom in her tone, a warring mixture of regret and consternation simmered beneath the surface of Sefa's sleep-lined features.

Arin briefly wondered which of her ever-shifting collection of faces Vaida had shown Sefa. After Sefa cut off her finger, the Vaida Arin knew would have had each of the girl's limbs tied to a different tree while a pack of starved mutts ripped her apart. Leaving her in the Traitors' Wells mere miles from Arin's holding? If he didn't know any better, Arin might have thought Vaida *wanted* the seamstress saved.

Arin answered Essiya's friend with the honesty she deserved. "I hope not."

"Good," Sefa murmured. She melted back into her covers, pausing halfway to peer at Arin. "I never thanked you for the High Counselor."

"Then be relieved that I have no interest in your thanks."

A private smile played on Sefa's lips. "You and her really are perfect for each other."

The strange half-Lukubi, half-Nizahlan girl disappeared beneath the covers, leaving Arin staring after her.

"All right," Marek interjected, smoothing the wrinkles Arin had left in his collar. "Say I believe you about the Supreme. How exactly do you plan to overcome a charge of treason?"

Jeru dug his elbow into Marek, but Arin scarcely noticed.

"Murder is only treason if left unfinished," Arin said. He tucked his hands into his pockets and turned to the door. "When I am done, they will call it succession."

CHAPTER SIXTY

ESSIYA

The hours ticked past me as I sat in the center of the Aada. Different people took turns shouting, but they had given up directing their ire toward me. No amount of vitriol had coaxed a response. Throwing rocks at a wall loses its appeal quickly, so they had turned on one another.

In theory, I was listening to them. In theory, I looked blank and taciturn.

In reality, I strained to contain my magic as it howled inside me, slamming against my shoddily erected barriers. What no one in the Aada could see were the veins pulsing in bright silver and gold, an inferno of color burning out of me.

When I woke this morning and read the note in my hand, the veins had completed their conquest of my throat and crawled to my jaw. They throbbed over my body, straining to reach the rest of my face.

If I relaxed even an inch, my magic would slam through my control and slaughter everyone in the vicinity. It would swallow me in the blaze, leaving a creature from the nightmares of the Awaleen crawling out of the ash. A creature with no interest in fortresses or creation; a creature with the singular purpose of destruction.

The torn top half of the note fluttered at the center of the table, where it had passed between dozens of hands.

Take Sareekh il Ma'a to Jasad.

The second half of the note, tucked inside my tunic, had not been shared with the masses.

I will find you again, Suraira.

I stood abruptly, startling the quarreling groups into silence. Unclenching my teeth took longer than I anticipated, the muscles in my jaw resistant to the sudden movement. "We begin our leave for Jasad tomorrow. I will ask the Sareekh how many of us it can carry at a time and how long it anticipates the journey around Nizahl to take. We can send a small search party to ensure our landing location is free of soldiers."

A wave of protest followed, but I cut it off with a raised hand. "I have listened to your arguments, and none of them include an option that allows us to safely reach Jasad in time for Nuzret Kamel. The Jasadis in other kingdoms have no choice but to risk the trade roads in order to reach our kingdom; we have the benefit of travel by sea. Ignoring it without good reason is a recipe for death.

"I understand your doubt in my decision-making. I understand why you might hesitate to accept the suggestion of our sworn enemy. But in four days, Nuzret Kamel will lift the mist from Sirauk Bridge. Records show it lasts a mere hour or two. We cannot allow spite to govern us. We cannot miss our window of opportunity to raise the fortress."

"Why would we listen to him after he betrayed you?" Efra shot to his feet. "He came into this mountain, learned all of our plans, played the part of reformed villain—and then escaped!"

Just as the disgruntled rumbling threatened to devolve into another hour of shouting, a quavering voice spoke up for the first time.

"He left behind the scepter," Maia said. Doe-like brown eyes that were more suited to a poet than a lahwa flicked to the corner of the room, where Supreme Rawain's scepter still rested. "If he had really betrayed us, wouldn't he have taken it?"

"He must not have had time," Efra snapped.

"If any of you come up with a better idea for reaching Jasad, you can find me at the cliffside." I left the room swiftly, closing the door behind me. As soon as I turned the corner, I broke into a run.

"Do you think the rest of us do not wrestle with the darkness our power brings?" she cries out. *"Do you think we don't understand?"*

I laugh. "What darkness do you wrestle?"

A third figure grips the teary-eyed woman's arm, holding her back. "We are too late. Resign yourself to apathy, and atrocity will surely follow. You cannot wring sympathy out of stone."

"You wound me," I drawl. "Allow me to return the favor."

Our magic ruptures.

Eight colors stripe the sky, mingling with the dusk.

When I blinked back to my body, I was outside, teetering on the edge of the cliff.

You remember.

I took a shaky step back from the edge and shook my head. None of it was real. It couldn't be.

I see.

I took a deep breath, focusing on the unbroken horizon of blue stretching far beyond the Sareekh. The sun shone through the hazy clouds, diamonds sparkling over the waves lapping around the Sareekh. A beautiful panorama by any standards. How unfortunate the only person present for it could not be warmed by beauty.

"There are eight hundred of us in this mountain. How many trips would it take you to transport us to Jasad, and how long would it take?"

It will take twenty trips to transport eight hundred. Two revolutions of the sun to finish.

I ran through the calculations. Twenty trips, eight hundred people, two days. Each trip would take a few hours. A speck compared to our other options.

"The first set leaves tonight."

I will be here.

"Thank you," I said. "For everything."

I found Maia and Namsa and asked them to assemble as many of the Jasadis to the cliffside as they could. "I would like them to see one last thing before we go."

Twenty minutes later, I once again stood at the edge, half the Jasadis in the mountain milling before me. Maia and Namsa stood on either side of me, a silent support.

I faced the crowd. Power threaded through my voice, amplifying it across the mountainside. "When many of us think of war, we imagine the battlefield. Swords singing through the air, horses galloping over burning terrain. War is known only for its physical violence." I gazed out across the sea of Jasadis, anchoring myself in their attention. "But there is a consequence of war worse than any sword. More violent than any bloodshed."

I spread my fingers and dragged them across each of my eyes. Gold and silver threads followed my fingers, connected to the pulsing points at my temples. I twisted my hands, wrapping the threads around my wrists like gossamer bracelets.

"The first fatal consequence of war is our voice."

The magic encircled my arms, looping around my neck and torso in steadily winding ropes.

"I spent my life frightened by the sound of my own name. I folded the parts of me the world did not want into as small a piece as I could manage, and I hoped time would take it away. Magic is not all we are, but it is all they were willing to see. Their fear tore us apart, and our fear destroyed what remained."

The threads wove through my hair, rippling along my curls. The sky darkened as my kitmers circled overhead, their cries echoing between the silent mountains.

"Today, we turn their fear against them. We reclaim what was taken, and we do it loudly. We will not shrink. We will not hide. Hear me well, and hear me true: this will not be another Jasad War."

My boots left the ground. The threads spun faster, twirling around me by the thousands. The light brightened, searing hotter than the sun. My magic howled, its joy pulsing in each thread around me. I was the heart of magic. The axis of power.

"This is our siege."

I spread my arms wide. The threads expanded behind me, spinning together a golden shadow with me as the spindle.

I laughed, golden tears dripping from the corners of my eyes, as agony cleaved through my body. Enormous silver wings burst from the shadow. The cliffside shook as the Jasadis screamed.

Gleaming horns punctured the air as the kitmer raised its head, black eyes moving with mine. Torso, legs, spine—the threads tightened around the kitmer until it tore away in a mighty flap of its wings. The kitmer shrieked, the sound thundering across the horizon, and I knew they would hear it for miles.

The scream of a scorched land rising from the ashes.

My smaller kitmers rose to join it, a flurry of silver and gold wings blotting out the sun. I shielded my face as the wind scattered around them.

Efra stepped toward the cliffside, mesmerized. The kitmer I'd conjured at the Victor's Ball, returned at last.

I inclined my head, and it wheeled over the surface of the sea, its wings spreading as it flew toward Essam. It would sear the sky gold and silver over the trade routes—protect them, remind the Jasadis enduring the journeys to our kingdom of what waited for them on the other side.

Home.

Pandemonium shook the mountain. Jubilation spread like wildfire. Groups of children escaped their parents to chase the cliffside, seeking another glance of the kitmer.

My fault, waiting so long to prove the potency of my magic to them. They should know who led them. They should know what kind of magic supported them.

"Essiya, are you all right?" Namsa crouched next to me, worry emanating from her.

"Certainly." I lifted my head. Glowing and dry eyes met Namsa's stunned ones.

"And you should refer to me as Malika."

CHAPTER SIXTY-ONE

ARIN

They arrested him and Jeru ten miles from the Citadel.

Arin's cooperation as they tied him and Jeru to the back of the wagon only furthered the soldiers' unease, and by the time they arrived on the Citadel's grounds, the soldiers had been engaged in three hours of furtive whispers.

From them, Arin learned his father had not disappointed Arin's predictions. Experienced soldiers had been sent to secure the territory between Nizahl and Lukub as well as hold the Ivory Palace. Layers upon layers of protection stood between the Citadel and Lukub, whereas every recruit in every compound had been pulled out of training and ordered to march south.

Toward Jasad.

Jeru had looked faintly ill at the news, but Arin was unmoved. Two days had passed since he escaped the Gibal, and Arin had no illusions of the kind of chaos he had left behind him. The Jasadis would not have wanted to heed the advice he had written to Essiya. They would have fought her on it.

She probably wanted him dead more than everyone in that mountain. She would be incandescent with fury, or worse—she would cut off her pain with the sharp end of her magic.

In either case, she would have taken Arin's advice. It was good advice, and Sylvia of Mahair had never turned her back on a tool that might keep her alive, no matter whose hand offered it. The recruits would need to march to the lowest of the southern wilayahs for the war.

All Arin needed to do was reach Janub Aya before his soldiers.

The first gate parted for their wagon. Rows of recruits watched Arin and Jeru pass with varying degrees of shock. The news of Arin's arrival would reach the Citadel long before he did, and sure enough, Bayoum was waiting on the Citadel's grounds when the wagon stopped.

The soldiers helped Arin and Jeru out of the cart. Bayoum's face soured at their overly solicitous behavior.

"You came back," Bayoum sneered. "Why? Do you think you have a chance at a trial after you brutalized the Supreme? Plead your case in our courts? The fate of traitors lies in the hands of the betrayed."

"Hand," Arin said.

"What?"

"He only has one hand. I took the other."

Bayoum turned the color of a beet. He spun to the soldiers. "Take the traitor to the Capsule and throw his guardsman in one of the cells beneath the tower. If the traitor escapes—if you allow him to talk his way out of his restraints—I will execute you and everyone you have ever met."

Jeru glanced at Arin as he was led away and nodded, a resolute set to his hard features.

In that moment, Arin forgave him every lie, every duplicity. Of course, Jeru had tried to save Marek. Of course, Jeru had used Marek to bring a corrupt compound leader abusing his power in the lower villages to justice. Unlike Vaun, who had followed Arin's orders to the very last syllable, Jeru obeyed the principles of the Commander Arin aimed to be. And when Arin deviated, Jeru stayed the line. He held firm.

Even if it meant following Arin to his death.

Low clouds veiled the top of the Citadel's tower. The wings of the Citadel curved around the tower in steel crescents, the glass halls connecting them to the tower frosted from the cold. Black stones gleamed around windows washed gold with candlelight.

Arin knew the Citadel was not particularly warm. Visitors from other kingdoms, even other parts of Nizahl, often joked the Citadel had been built to inspire foreboding in all who gazed upon it.

But then, Arin was not particularly warm, either. The Citadel had always been a part of Arin—the steel in his spine, the stone around his heart. The axis around which his world spun.

As Arin had taken the shape of the Citadel, so too was it time for the Citadel to mirror its master.

Stone for stone. Steel for steel.

Ruin for ruin.

The soldiers handed him off to two of his father's guardsmen, who were markedly less shaken about transporting Arin like a common prisoner. They were also familiar with the Capsule, having escorted Arin to and from his punishments as a child.

"Rauf. Zach." Arin inclined his head. "This must feel all too familiar for you."

Rauf cleared his throat, opening his mouth only to cut himself off at Zach's sharp look. Rauf had always had a slightly softer touch than the rest of his father's guardsmen, and age seemed to have exacerbated the problem.

After climbing for five floors, they stopped halfway up the next set of steps. Zach swung his elbow at the uneven blocks of gray stone. Instead of cracking his bones, the block beneath his elbow exploded in plumes of dirt. Zach pushed his arm through the empty space and reached down.

The stones shifted, heaving inward to reveal a dark passageway clouded with dust. The passage was too narrow for more than one person to walk at a time, so Rauf stepped in front of Arin while Zach trailed behind.

The passage ended in a pocket of darkness carved into the wall. It ended in the Capsule, in nothingness—a black hole where neither light nor shadow could reach.

Arin's teeth ground together. He had underestimated how strongly his body might react to the Capsule, regardless of the years.

Without prompting, Arin stepped over the foot-high threshold and into the hole. The guards watched him for a minute, perhaps waiting for the facade of cooperation to snap.

Arin settled at the back of the hole and stretched his legs in front of him, crossing them at the ankle.

Eventually, their footsteps faded, leaving Arin to contend with his old nemesis.

The void.

The Capsule only existed thanks to the forces of paranoia that had governed Supreme Ghashli, Nizahl's ruler five generations after Fareed. Supreme Ghashli had been convinced his enemies were in the walls coming to kill him. He hired dozens of Laeyim from Omal to build passageways throughout the Citadel in an effort to find the voices. Laeyim were excellent builders, but their magic came with an unfortunate side effect: the passageways were hidden from everyone, including Supreme Ghashli. Not only was he convinced there were enemies waiting for him behind the walls, but now he had granted them passageways that led directly into various wings of the Citadel.

Supreme Ghashli disappeared shortly after the Laeyim finished construction. It took them years to find his body. One of the passageways to the Capsule had mysteriously opened for the Supreme, and it seemed he had never found his way out again. They discovered his corpse in the exact spot where Arin was sitting, a grotesque smile fixed on what flesh remained on his skeleton.

Arin leaned his head back, the wisp of white air leaving his lips the only evidence of life in the nothingness. The only difference between Arin and the lingering ghosts of his childhood, all of whom had died a strange sort of death in this hole.

Arin breathed. He waited.

He closed his eyes and thought of a shy smile curving against his shoulder. He filled his ears with the sound of her laugh, the way it burst uncontrolled from her chest and smothered itself behind her palm.

In the evening, I would come home to you.

Arin sat among his ghosts and dreamed of his future.

CHAPTER SIXTY-TWO

ESSIYA

Someone peeled open my eyelid.

"Her magic hasn't lapsed once. It's been churning since she sent off the kitmers," Namsa murmured.

"Do we know—could it be—" Quiet and uncertain. Maia.

"What do you think?" Efra snapped. "We have to manage the symptoms before it takes her completely. Help me drag her to the lake. The bucket won't be enough to revive her this time, and we need to go. The Sareekh will be back for us by tonight."

I laughed without opening my eyes. Metal clanged as feet shuffled back, a litany of gasps ringing in the room.

"The four came first and slipped through mists of story," I hummed in the voice that wasn't mine. "Children of silver, beware, beware! Those legends of lies and glory."

I slipped away.

CHAPTER SIXTY-THREE

ARIN

Arin wasn't sure how much time had passed before a thud on the other side of the passageway roused him from his light slumber. It couldn't have been more than a day.

Light scorched the inside of Arin's eyes, and he raised his hand against the torch moving toward him from the other end of the hall. When it stopped in front of the Capsule, illuminating the person on the other end, Arin found himself momentarily stunned.

"Layla?"

Tears had dried in streaks down Layla's round cheeks. The gold bracelets around her wrists shivered beneath the unsteady hand holding the torch aloft.

Blood coated the front of her gown.

"They're coming. I told them they were coming, and they didn't believe me," she gasped, and Arin moved fast to catch the torch before she could drop it on herself. "I was out by one of our holdings, and I saw—"

"What is it?" Arin caught her elbow, drawing her upright. "What's coming?"

"The Ruby Hounds." A wet sob. "She brought them back. The Sultana—she left the Mirayah with hundreds of Hounds at her back. The Ivory Palace has been retaken, and she marches toward Nizahl as we speak. I watched her slaughter an entire regiment.

The Hounds just—they just shredded through the soldiers, and I couldn't help any of them, I couldn't—"

Behind his alarm, a reckless burst of wonder spilled through Arin. She had really done it.

"A Ruby Hound." Dancing shadows moved across the walls as he stood, twisting with the path of his torch. Layla dropped to a seat at the high edge of the Capsule, gripping the stone. "Good."

"Good?" Layla gaped at him. "Their coats are made of pure gemstone! Our swords cannot harm them. Nothing can!"

When Arin didn't react with the appropriate fright, Layla reared back. She regarded Arin with dawning horror. "Did you know what the Sultana would do?" she demanded. "Did you know she would bring an army of Ruby Hounds down upon us?"

"I knew it would be an army."

She will never win a war with Nizahl. Not if she spends three lifetimes preparing.

"I did not know an army of what."

Something has convinced her she can.

"So you have a plan?" Layla reached out, catching his sleeve. Arin dropped his gaze to the point of unwelcome contact. "I knew you would."

As he watched Layla lean toward him, the familiar clash of fear and fascination playing out over her expression, Arin's long-brewing frustration finally edged out his manners.

He pulled his sleeve away. "What would you have done if I had ever returned your interest?"

Layla blinked. "My liege—"

"Layla. At this very moment, I am not your liege. Consider this a narrow window to speak to me freely." Arin studied the blood-splattered diplomat. In many ways, Layla would have been his ideal match. She enjoyed unraveling the twisting politics of court and handling frail-tempered nobles. Kind and even-handed, she would have softened Arin's image to his people and helped rule with a firm hand.

She would also have led a life of singular misery with a husband whose nearness she yearned for and feared in unequal measure.

Layla was an essential component of his plan, which made the timing for Arin's patience to finally hit its limit less than ideal. "You collect these bracelets from your suitors and speak of how you long for the perfect match. I have listened to you say time and time again how your only wishes are a peaceful love with a good man." Arin crouched, the bottom of his coat settling into a black pool around his boots. "My love would never have been peaceful for you. How could it be, when you find peace in nothing else about me?"

When Layla flinched, clearly poised to protest, Arin tried another tack. "Why did you come to free me?"

There was no hesitation this time. "You are the Commander. Nizahl is under attack, and we need you."

Arin smiled.

"That wasn't the right answer, was it?" she whispered. "I should have chosen differently."

"It was the perfect answer." He was her Commander. Her Heir. "It is only that I love a woman whose choices are not so perfect." Who found her peace in Arin even when Arin found nothing peaceful in himself.

Arin straightened from his crouch, drawing himself to his full height.

Enough of that. The Capsule had already had its chance to cannibalize its favorite morsels of Arin, and he would offer it no fresh bites.

"Is the council convened?" Arin asked.

"Y-yes. In the war wing."

They'd need to hurry. In the best of scenarios, the council's courage would last until the first gate was breached.

"Have the soldiers release my guardsman from beneath the

Citadel," Arin said. "Meet me in the war wing when you are finished. Jeru will not join you—he has his own orders."

Without waiting to see if Layla would follow, Arin crossed the passageway. Even if the defenses Arin had set in place worked, Ruby Hounds had once been able to travel at three times the speed of a horse. Vaida would be at the gates of the Citadel by nightfall, if not sooner.

Ruby Hounds. Arin stepped into the stairwell, grudging humor tightening the corners of his mouth. Like a true prodigy of these blood-soaked courts, Vaida had known she needed a way to win a war against Nizahl without the other kingdoms' support.

When Vaida came, Arin would be prepared.

He was a prodigy of these courts, too.

CHAPTER SIXTY-FOUR

ARIN

The doors to the council room flew open beneath Arin's hands. As expected, the council was already on their feet, their shouts clearly heard from down the hall. A moment later, and Arin might have caught them in the midst of making their escape. The Citadel was the target of Vaida's attack, and it had been too long since any of these soft-boiled nobles had fought a battle they were not assured they could win. Years since they reckoned with the true meaning of their mortality.

Heads swiveled to Arin, and he was amused to find that only Bayoum seemed furious to see him freed from the Capsule. Relief rippled over the others.

Rawain watched him from the head of the table, entirely unsurprised at his son's appearance. The glow of health his father had carried throughout his fifty-some years had waned into a sickly gray. Even his shoulders seemed to have shrunk, smaller than usual beneath the heavy fabric of his robes. The place on the table where his scepter would typically lean was noticeably empty.

"Arrest him!" Bayoum roared. "Who allowed this traitor free?"

"He is your Heir!" Sama snarled. "The Commander of this kingdom."

"Titles do not outlast treason!"

Arin ignored them. His father watched Arin, and Arin returned the attention in kind.

Had he played out this coup in his head already? In another world, Arin might have spent time explaining to the council what Rawain had done—the Blood Summit, the mined magic, the truth of Arin's heritage. Arin would have wanted the straightforward approach, guided by facts and reason.

However, in that scenario, the council would need incontrovertible proof, and Arin did not have it. Meanwhile, the proof of Arin's treason was covered by the sleeve of his father's robe. Readily available and undeniable. A decision would be made, and it would not be in Arin's favor.

Perhaps Rawain would be proud. Arin's new strategy had been taken directly from his father.

"It will not be long before Vaida arrives at the gates of the Citadel with the Ruby Hounds," Arin said. The din of argument died. Bayoum still glared, but he had clearly been outmatched. "Ruby Hounds cannot be cut down by modern swords. No armor will shield against them. They follow the Sultana and the Sultana alone."

Arin crossed to the windows and flipped the lock pinning the two sides together. The window opened outward, delivering a refreshing breeze entirely at odds with the gravity of what lay behind the dark outline of Essam Woods.

"The tower's alarm has not sounded," Sama said, wiping her forehead on the inside of her wrist. "If Nizahl were in true danger, wouldn't it have warned us?"

"Vaida hasn't crossed through Nizahl's borders yet." Arin traced the wall, following her path through the map inside his mind's eye. "She will have gone north first to retake the Ivory Palace and expel our soldiers. I imagine my father sent thousands of soldiers to barricade the Citadel for fifty miles out, at the very least. She will use the bulk of her army to tear through those soldiers, and the rest she will send around the mountains." Arin's finger moved over the wall. "Where they will enter Nizahl through the lower villages."

"Awaleen save us." Gersiny sat heavily upon his chair, his cane crooked beneath his white-knuckled grip. "It will be a massacre."

"Yes." Arin inclined his head. "But it needn't be."

Gersiny raised his head, hope spilling over his greenish complexion. "Do you have a plan, Your Highness?"

Gersiny's deference snapped the last of Bayoum's pathetic restraint. "Have we forgotten the traitor disappeared with the Supreme's scepter? That he is suspected of collaborating with the Jasadi rebels?" The counselor slapped his hand onto the table. "Who knows what magic his Jasadi whore placed—"

Bayoum's scream shattered the night's serenity. The other counselors shielded themselves from the splatter of blood as Arin's dagger drove into the hand Bayoum set on the table. It wedged deep through wood and bone, the hilt resting an inch beneath the counselor's middle knuckle.

Arin allowed himself to take some pleasure in the spectacle of Bayoum pinned, baying like a stuck boar. The counselor writhed in Arin's hold as he grabbed Bayoum by the collar and pulled out the dagger. Arin hauled him across the table, knocking over inkwells and empty chalices.

When Arin hoisted Bayoum's head through the window, the counselor began to plead. Incoherent babbling, a stream of pitiful appeals. Arin didn't hear a word of it. His head pounded, the edges of the void he'd managed to subdue in the Gibal straining against its restraints. The darkness tore open at the back of Arin's mind, and from its depth, reckless rage burst free.

Arin lowered his mouth to the counselor's ear. "Tell High Counselor Rodan I said hello."

Nobody intervened. Nobody stepped toward Bayoum's defense.

The counselor's shrill scream bounced between each wing of the Citadel as Arin heaved him through the window. When he landed, a small, still speck on the lawn of the Citadel, Arin and the raven mounted above the tower looked down upon the late counselor, both pairs of eyes cold and unmoved.

"As I was saying." Arin turned back to the remaining counselors, withdrawing a handkerchief to clean the blood from his dagger. "The bloodshed is not inevitable. I can prevent it."

Layla's arrival did not distract the council, though her bloodstained gown won itself a smattering of raised brows. She responded to Arin's questioning glance with a nod.

"How?" Sama demanded. "What means do you have to fight hundreds of Ruby Hounds?"

Faheem waved Sama aside. The High Counselor came around the table, ignoring the streaks of blood Bayoum's hand had left across the surface. "What do you require, my lord? We can reinstate your inheritance. You can be Nizahl's Heir again."

"I have no interest in being the Heir," Arin said. "My price for your lives is Nizahl's crown."

The council stopped short. Even his father, who had been watching the proceedings with an inscrutable expression, snapped to attention.

"You wish to be Supreme?" Faheem asked, as though he might have misheard. "Your Highness, it isn't—your father—"

"My father is the traitor," Arin said. "As Bayoum so succinctly put it, titles do not outlast treason."

"We can supersede the laws of inheritance in a state of emergency. The Nitraus Vote isn't just for the removal of a sitting Commander—it also permits the advancement of their title. He needs three votes," Layla said. A calculating gleam sparked in the emissary's eyes, and Arin remembered why they had gotten along so well in their youth. Layla loved devouring every morsel of knowledge about the kingdoms' political framework, no matter how abstract or ancient. "For the Nitraus Vote to advance a title, he would need the High Counselor's vote and two others."

When Rawain stood, the counselors jumped. His father's presence, always so preeminent, had shrunk considerably. "He is bluffing," Rawain said calmly. "Everyone in this room knows how Arin favors those lower villages. He forbids their conscription, empties our treasuries for their little nimwa system, appoints their vagrants to his personal guard. Do you truly believe he will allow them to die if the power to stop it is in his grasp?"

Arin leaned back against the windowsill, wrapping his hands around the squared ends. "Do you remember what you told me after Galim's Bend?" The words had been emblazoned into his core. "You said I have the most aggravating habit of measuring the worth of my life as equal to those around me."

Movement across the horizon caught Arin's eye. The tops of the trees rustled, rows upon rows bending beneath an invisible pressure. The movement rippled toward the gates with the unstoppable force of a wave barreling toward shore.

"Consider the habit broken," Arin said.

Metal screamed as the wave reached the first gate. Arin did not flinch at the siren's sudden wail. The piercing cry razed across Nizahl as the first gate to the Citadel fell.

Dress strategy in the right clothes, and it transformed into prophecy. As Arin had promised, Vaida had arrived at the gates. What, then, of the lower villages? The noble towns lying just behind, where their families lived?

Faheem knelt at Arin's feet. "I am High Counselor Faheem Giran of Nizahl. My vote lies with the Commander, Supreme Arin of Nizahl."

The blood drained out of Rawain's face. He looked at Arin as though he had never seen him before.

"He is lying!" Rawain shouted. "He will not sacrifice the lower villages!"

The next to kneel was Layla. "I am Layla Ayud, diplomat of Nizahl, and my vote lies with the Commander, Supreme Arin of Nizahl."

Gersiny, the oldest counselor in the room, shrank beneath the wail of the siren. Sama chewed her lip, and Arin knew she wanted an answer to her question. She wanted a *how*, and the presence of Vaida's Hounds at their threshold did not alter her skepticism.

"I have grandchildren in the lower villages," Gersiny finally gasped. Frail hands cupped his cane as he implored Rawain. "They are all I have."

Rawain clasped the old man's arm. "He won't allow harm to come to them. I swear to you on my crown, Arin is *lying*."

But Gersiny was shaking his head. "The Nizahl Heir has never lied to us before." Faheem helped the counselor free himself from Rawain and take a knee before Arin. "I am—" He swallowed. "I am Gersiny Biyad, once High Counselor to Supreme Munqual, present advisor to Supreme Rawain, and my vote lies with the Commander, Supreme Arin of Nizahl."

Screams floated through the window as the second gate shrieked beneath the horde of Ruby Hounds.

"Thank you," Arin said. He settled his gaze on his father. "I accept."

The rest happened with satisfying speed. The guards were called in, and Arin allowed the counselors to take refuge in the Citadel's basement. Rauf and Zach were to watch over them, but should his father's guardsmen attempt to leave the basement, they were to be killed.

When only his father remained, Arin stopped the last guard with a wave. "Wait by the door. When I leave, take him to the Capsule."

The guard bowed as he retreated, closing the door behind him.

His father's gaze remained steady as Arin approached. "How strange is love," Rawain mused. "You betray me, you manipulate my council into stealing my throne, and yet my anger is rivaled by my pride. Within a year, you accomplished what your mother and I failed to do in our entire lifetimes. The Nizahl crown and the Jasad Malika—yours. Both thrones under your name."

At Arin's silence, Rawain laughed. "Surprised? Please, Arin. I made the mistake of betting on Hanim, and her love was useless to me. But Essiya of Jasad? Her love is worth a kingdom. When she is your wife, Jasad will be yours."

"I will never sit on the Jasad throne," Arin said. "The Jasad crown will belong to my wife, and my wife alone."

Wisps of smoke curled into the room. Vaida had arrived at the third gate.

Rawain tipped his head, a laconic smile twisting the corners of his mouth. "I see the specter of my wrathful son behind the mask of the merciful new Supreme. Which is true, I wonder?"

"Which is true, indeed," Arin said. He raised a hand to the side of Rawain's face. A scratch sliced along Rawain's cheek, and Arin pressed the edge of his thumb against it. Not enough to draw blood, but enough to show he could. "I imagine you will have much to think about in the Capsule, but allow me to give you one more."

Leaning in, Arin whispered, "You were right. During the Alcalah, I took a mold of Vaida's ring. As soon as the Jasad Heir destroyed the Victor's Ball, I had every blacksmith in Nizahl engrave the sigil into our swords, our shields, our arrows. I barricaded the path around the mountains to our lower villages with the same sigil—a sigil I believe can kill the Ruby Hounds. In the event I was mistaken, I diverted two thousand soldiers to begin evacuations of the lower villages before I left Nizahl. The Ruby Hounds will not penetrate our kingdom past the Citadel."

A breathless laugh caught on the edges of Rawain's teeth. His eyes shone, and until the day Arin died, he would never know whether it was with hate or pride.

When Arin left, the guard swiftly entering behind him to whisk Rawain to the Capsule, he spared a glance toward Fareed's statue above the war room. The first Supreme; the first conduit.

Beneath the archway of Nizahl's founder, Arin made one last promise.

"I will do better than him."

CHAPTER SIXTY-FIVE

ESSIYA

The Sareekh loosened its hold around my middle, and my feet touched Jasad for the first time in eleven years.

Some of the Jasadis were crying. Others had dropped to the ground to vomit—a mixture of traveling with the Sareekh and relief, I guessed. The sea chopped against the shores of Janub Aya as the Sareekh's red scales curled inward. Waves flared over one another in their rush to shore, crashing against my ankles.

"Thank you," I murmured. The debt I owed the Sareekh wasn't one I could ever repay.

When you remember what you lost, come back for me. The vibrations of the Sareekh's voice were wistful. **The sea is emptier than it used to be.**

The churning water closed over the Sareekh. With one last ripple, the surface once again lay smooth.

The steep climb up the sandy hills sloping from Suhna Sea to Janub Aya had tested the mettle of the arriving Urabi. Hundreds of footprints lined the hills on every side. Heaving a sigh, I traipsed to the top of the hill, ignoring the breeze and its sand-swept kisses.

Wiping the grains from the corner of my eyes, I trailed my watering gaze over the ruins of Jasad's southernmost wilayah.

Unlike the upper wilayahs, where the wealthy had bought acres of land to build multistoried family estates, the homes in Janub Aya weren't much different than Mahair's. Many of them looked to have fallen into shambles long before the war. Squat buildings with swathes of gray cement streaked across their mudbrick sides, attempts at paint long worn away. The dirt roads had caved toward the center from the number of horses that must have thundered along these paths, forming shallow gulleys. A clothesline fluttered from a half-destroyed balcony, as though waving hello.

I spotted Maia peering into a woven basket, the handle roped to the third-story balcony of another abandoned building. I had seen those baskets in Mahair, too—the patrons on my route would let down the basket with money inside and pull it up with whatever they had ordered from Rory.

It was bizarre, seeing how this corner of Jasad matched the village I had called home for years. I had never been south of Har Adiween. Janub Aya and its tiny population might as well have been the other side of the world.

A horse clomped from around the remains of what might have been a butcher's shop, led by a smiling Namsa. I dusted the front of my tunic to avoid her searching gaze. After summoning the final kitmer, my magic had overwhelmed me. I did not remember anything between raising the kitmer and gasping as I burst through the surface of the lake.

Namsa jerked her chin at the clouds draped low over the wilayah, a fine white mist trailing beneath them. "In case you're wondering, no. The clouds never go away. Between the sea and Sirauk Bridge, we were lucky to get twenty days of sun a year down here," Namsa said. She patted the neck of a white-and-brown mare. "Amu Dawoud would always joke that growing up in Janub Aya meant I'd never wrinkle. The moisture keeps you young."

I threw my leg over the mare and hauled myself up, tightening my knees against its quivering torso. Thinking of Dawoud here hurt in an unfamiliar way, raking at a wound I'd forgotten to properly cauterize.

"He is buried at the top of the hill in Silsilit Abeer," I said without looking at Namsa. "You can visit him."

Namsa's head whipped toward me. Disbelief spilled over her features, pooling into a pained whisper. "Amu Dawoud died in Omal. Silsilit Abeer is in Alb Safi."

He will be buried in a spot where the grass still grows.

"The hill is the highest spot where the grass in Jasad still grows."

I spurred my horse forward, leaving Namsa to scramble onto her own mount. I wouldn't allow her or Dawoud or anything else to carve away at the calm I had finally achieved.

In two days' time, Nuzret Kamel would clear the mist from Sirauk and I would raise the fortress. For once, I didn't need to worry about the consequences—I wouldn't be around to bear them.

Cornered by Sirauk and the sea, Janub Aya's only points of entry were from Eyn el Haswa to its right or Ahr il Uboor to the north. The tiny wilayah had been the last to fall in the war solely due to the sheer inconvenience of accessing it.

"The scorch marks have strange patterns," Namsa murmured.

I glanced up, scanning the dilapidated buildings looming above us. Scorch marks devoured the frame of every door, licking to the outer walls in black stripes. For most, the roofs had collapsed in, but the structural integrity of the rest of the house remained intact.

"The glass. It exploded outward." I nodded to the warped hinges of a window, shards of glass buried in the dirt beneath it. "The residents set the fires from inside."

It took nerve to leave your life blazing behind you and ride into the unknown. Despite their less-than-flattering reputation in the northern wilayahs, Janub Aya had had the bravery to do what no other wilayah would once they realized defeat was imminent. They burned their crops, destroyed their homes, and dammed their waters as their final message to the other kingdoms.

They had left in a blaze, and they would return in one.

By mutual agreement, those of us from the Gibal had decided to sleep on the ground. Someone suggested seeking shelter inside one of the empty barns and received grumbles in response.

"It doesn't feel right to disturb anything," Mona, a girl with permanently sad eyes and hair the brown of granulated honey, murmured. "Not yet. Not until we've won."

Shining mist washed over the valley, spools of white curling over the dry plains. The hairs on the back of my neck stood on end, and I didn't have to glance around to know the rest felt it, too.

Magic.

Like dew glistening on a blade of grass at dawn, the magic-charged mist settled over the slumbering Jasadis.

"If the mist is so strong from miles away, imagine how it must feel on the bridge," Mona reflected, curling into herself around the fire. "I always thought the stories about people who tried to make the crossing were exaggerated. Who would be so stupid?" Her eyes slid shut. She inhaled deeply. "I should've held my tongue."

I offered to keep watch.

"You need your rest," Namsa protested.

"I slept plenty before we left the Gibal," I lied. "Let's not waste more energy debating it."

Namsa didn't need to know I hadn't slept in days. It would worry her, and her worry annoyed me.

Besides, I wasn't alone.

The mist isn't safe, my magic whispered. *It hides other dangers.*

I smiled, leaning back against the prickly bark of a decaying tree.

I counted each sleeping Jasadi, my vision perfectly clear despite the dark.

The most dangerous thing hiding in these mists was me.

I pressed my palm to my stomach, forcing down my churning unease.

At the bottom of the hill, Jasadis stretched as far as the eye could see. They wrapped around the edge of Sirauk Bridge, swarming the border to Ahr il Uboor and disappearing around the valleys leading to Eyn el Haswa. Thousands upon thousands of Jasadis crowded into a wilayah capable of hosting a third of their number.

"Awaleen below," Namsa marveled. "It worked. Your kitmers led them home."

"Some of them." I assessed the crowd. They had arranged makeshift huts from shaved tree bark and boulders. Hundreds of little fires danced across the horizon. The smell of cooking meat sweetened the lingering whiffs of rotted wood. "I imagine there are still plenty fighting their way through the trade routes or coming down from the north of Jasad."

Agitation burned the film of confidence around my heart, and I swallowed a surge of bile. If I failed, this was it. The last of Jasad, destroyed. Our people annihilated, our legacy ended.

And if I succeeded, the fortress would protect them from the outside, but there would be nothing to protect them from the magic-mad Malika on the inside.

Death lingered over the merriment like the hum of a coming storm, raising the hairs on the back of my neck.

"Essiya!" Lateef rounded on a group of children Fairel's age and grabbed the nearest one by the scruff, pulling him toward us. "Take the horses to feed," Lateef ordered.

The boy pouted and snatched the reins from me and Namsa.

Lateef clicked his tongue, a sharp sound inside his teeth. "Children these days. No discipline. Go on, you two, go get yourselves a meal and an empty spot to sleep."

The others rushed forward without a second's hesitation. Huh. I should be hungry, too, shouldn't I?

When was the last time I ate?

Lateef shuffled in my direction, flicking a glance around us before murmuring, "I left the scepter with your friends. I suggest you keep hold of it."

I looked at him askance. "Any particular reason?" None of the Urabi had succeeded in eking out any of the magic within the scepter. It was useless, and I did not want it in my sights.

He scowled. "Does nobody listen to the word of their elder anymore? Rovial's tainted tomb! Just go."

I huffed. Lateef and Rory would have been the best of friends.

Dried husks of empty date palms crunched beneath my boots, and I rapidly drew my hood when a woman glanced in my direction. Nobody would recognize me by my face alone, but the magic that had not stopped swirling in my eyes since I raised the last kitmer would surely give my identity away.

I shifted into the head of my kitmers as I walked, seeing through their eyes. A handy trick the Visionists had taught me. I had been tracking the kitmers' progress since I left the mountain. A dozen of my littlest ones dipped over a colorful town with tiled roads and lamps swaying from red rope fiber.

Lukub. Ha! The Lukubi nobles were screaming louder than the prisoners in the Traitors' Wells.

Still in the kitmer's head, I jerked my chin to the left. As pleasant as I found the prospect of infuriating Vaida, the odds of finding hidden Jasadis in the noble quarters of Lukub were slim. Most of those families had been entrenched in their wealth and prestige for centuries, making it nearly impossible for anyone other than old-blood Lukubis to exist among them.

Through the eyes of another kitmer, I saw countless bodies crushed throughout Essam. Nizahlan uniforms, Lukubi uniforms. The khawaga waited in the trees, leaping onto any convoy that stopped a wagon in the trade routes regardless of the color of their uniforms.

Sorn had kept his promise.

I maneuvered into the head of a kitmer in Orban. It swooped, its left wing catching on a string of lanterns. The lower villages were left in pitch black as the kitmer flew into the starless sky, a rope of sputtering lanterns trailing behind it, the flames winking out one by one.

In the head of a kitmer flying above the Ivory Palace, I nearly shocked my poor creature out the sky at the sight of Ruby Hounds prowling beneath the obelisk at Vaida's front gates. Nizahl soldiers raised their swords into the air, but I couldn't imagine how any simple steel might pierce the hard shell of those beasts. More of them were moving across the woods, weaving a red trail across Essam's constellation of shadows.

Well, at least we knew what Vaida had done in the Mirayah.

A hand at my elbow snapped me back into my own head, and I jerked away from Efra. He raised his hands apologetically. "I called your name several times."

Which name?

"What do you want?"

"You shouldn't waste your energy where it is not absolutely needed," he said. "If your magic takes over you again, we have no way to bring you back this time."

My stony silence seemed to perturb him. He cleared his throat. "Are the kitmers coming?"

"They will be here by midday."

He hesitated. "And the large one?"

I narrowed my eyes. Efra's obsession with the large kitmer verged on disturbing. "Tomorrow."

"Good, good." He raked a hand through the brown waves of his hair, which had grown out considerably since I first met him. "There is one more thing."

If he asked me about another kitmer, I would instruct them to eat him.

"The Nizahl Heir was right."

I hadn't looked in the mirror since I raised the last kitmer, but I had witnessed the colors in my eyes unnerve more than their fair share of people. Efra joined their ranks when he stepped away from the full force of my gaze.

"There are roughly two thousand Nizahl soldiers descending from the north. The largest regiment was last spotted in Alb Safi, but our rider said there was evidence of another regiment coming through Essam Woods."

My teeth ground together, my veins giving a single, dangerous pulse. It would take a dedicated Nizahl soldier perhaps seventeen hours to get from Nizahl's southern border to Jasad's. A regiment of two thousand would need considerably longer, which meant they must have started moving at the same time the Nizahl Heir arrived at the Gibal. As he had predicted, Rawain must have emptied out the compounds, filling Jasad with the youngest, greenest recruits he could spare.

"Don't tell Marek," I said. If he was forced to face former colleagues on the wrong side of the battle, he might waste time appealing to me on their behalf.

Anyone entering Jasad with a sword raised against us would die on that sword.

"Keep the others away from me. I'll track the soldiers so we can make our preparations." I would find a quiet spot between the buildings to disappear. "And, Efra—if you touch me again, you had better mean to kill me."

CHAPTER SIXTY-SIX

ESSIYA

Dawn striped the sky pink and orange on the last day before Nuzret Kamel.

The sun crawled over the ruins of Janub Aya, fighting the mist for every inch. Pale flecks of light shimmered over the sleeping Jasadis. Some stirred, pulling the weapons they'd slept beside closer. A few roused just enough to sense the bitter cold, their violent shivering as effective an alarm as a kick to the head.

My attention stayed fixed on the outline of Sirauk Bridge. A nameless dread had throttled me throughout the night, and it wasn't until I filled my chest with freezing air did I realize I couldn't remember the last time I breathed.

Something terrible was waiting for me on that bridge. Something worse than death. Worse than madness.

Run, my magic whispered, over and over and over again. *Leave while they sleep and get away before the mist falls.*

I crouched over the basin and splashed cold water on my face. The time for running was over. The kitmers I had sent to spy on the Nizahl recruits were in Ahr il Uboor, which meant it was a matter of hours before the army arrived in Janub Aya.

The water in the basin settled. The reflection of a blue-eyed adolescent girl gazed back at me, her lip curling with contempt.

The hallucinations had been steady and frequent. I could scarcely turn my head without spotting one lurking in the periphery, watching me. They were in every reflection, in every shadow.

My time was running out.

Sefa yawned as she stretched awake. A stripe of sunlight cut a diagonal across her face, melting her bleary brown eyes into a warm honey. She drew herself up into a seated position, sliding Marek's lolling head to her lap without waking him.

"Did you sleep at all?" Sefa asked. I dipped my fingers into the basin, dissolving the sneering girl.

"Since I was keeping guard, I certainly hope not."

"When was the last time you slept?"

I didn't flinch. "The night before."

She nodded, glancing away. Her jaw tightened, as if her teeth had come down on something bitter and hard. "Hmm. You know, you and Marek keep saying you don't understand how I survived in the Ivory Palace. A place built on duplicity and twisted truths, smoke and mirrors. The answer is very simple: I decided that even if I had to lie to the entire world, I would not lie to myself. If the only place I could be true was in my heart, then I would guard that truth fiercely."

I sighed. I had forgotten how exhausting Sefa's unique intuition could be. Didn't she need breakfast before she launched into a lecture? A sip of water?

"Are you implying I am lying to myself?"

Sefa studied me for a long, disconcerting moment. I tied my hair into a knot at the back of my head and swept the stray strands behind my ears. My attention returned to Sirauk.

"I don't know," Sefa said, and the raw note in her voice caught me. "Since you raised the kitmer, there are moments where I cannot tell who I am speaking to. Whether you are Sylvia or Essiya or someone else entirely."

Thrown, it took me too long to compose myself.

"You have more aliases than I do, Sayali."

"That is not what I mean and you know it. My identity—my soul—does not shift from name to name."

Magic singed my palms. "Maybe it should. What is so special about your soul that it must always remain perfectly pristine? Souls are made to be marked. To fracture and break. We spend lifetimes repairing them, and by the time you go to your grave, your soul should look nothing like what you started with."

"I agree." The mournful words doused the lit end of my anger. "But the essence of who you are does not change. The essence of who you are is what determines whether you keep repairing your soul or simply leave it in pieces each time it breaks."

"Ugh," Marek grumbled, turning his face into Sefa's thigh. "Can we philosophize about our souls after breakfast?"

The leaf next to Marek shifted. Tiny pebbles danced on the dirt. I flattened my hand on the ground, absorbing the minute trembling.

Something was coming.

"Up! Up!" Efra broke through the trees, the other sentries on his heels. His wild cries lashed the Jasadis into full alert. We were on our feet in seconds. Efra's shout echoed through the deathly silent camp. "Nizahl soldiers from the woods—several hundred at least—"

Pandemonium.

We had prepared for the possibility of some of them coming from Essam, but Namsa and the others were still pale with terror as they ran between groups, handing out weapons and snapping off instructions. I watched her shove an axe into the limp grip of the wide-eyed boy who had mouthed off to Lateef last night.

Gazing at the legions of terrified Jasadis, it occurred to me I might very well raise the fortress over a sea of the dead. The border of magic would become nothing more than a shiny headstone to commemorate the corpses stacked behind it.

"You should leave while there is still time," I told Marek and Sefa distractedly. My veins tightened painfully as I rerouted a kitmer from Orban. We would need every last one of them to hold off the Nizahl soldiers, new recruits or not. "Find somewhere safe to hide."

"Why would we hide?" Sefa crept closer to me, as though the mere suggestion repelled her.

"This is not your fight."

"Your fight is our fight," Sefa said. "We will not leave you."

"You may have noticed we love you," Marek added, accepting the bow and arrow hastily thrust in his direction. "Despite your most valiant efforts."

There it was again. The same nameless, debilitating force I had succumbed to in the Victor's Ball. Rising, roaring, gathering force. The sheer magnitude of it stole my breath.

No one is meant to be alone for so long.

Dawoud was buried in Silsilit Abeer, but he may as well have been whispering in my ear.

"I—I—"

Sefa squeezed my shoulder, silencing my stammer. "It's okay. Go—they need you."

I took her and Marek's hands. "Don't make me mourn you," I said, punctuating it with a hard glare. "If the soldiers overtake us, surrender. Run into the woods. Do anything but die."

Marek pressed a kiss to my knuckles. "You first."

I stood alone at the front of the crowd, facing Hirun. Behind me, hundreds of small kitmers darkened the sky.

Fog shrouded the river, coasting over the water in timid plumes. This close to Sirauk, the current churned and wept onto the shores.

Reality had split neatly in two. On one side, I flew with my last kitmer, the trees of Essam spread beneath us, the bony branches of its trees locked together, as though Essam couldn't help but shield its ugly innards. The river wound between the trees like a flicking tongue.

On the other side, I watched the bridge while I waited for the soldiers to dock their boats. For annihilation or salvation or a savage marriage of the two.

A presence at my elbow ticked into the second reality. Maia rolled on her heels, restless. "Take a knife, at least. This one is so small."

She offered me a dagger with a blade roughly the length of my wrist. The silver and gold roiling in my eyes glittered off the blade's edge.

"I won't need it."

"Nevertheless." Maia nudged it toward me, a silent plea.

I took the knife and tucked it into my boot. "Go back to the tree line. Your magic is useless against so many soldiers. Climb to a high vantage point and do what you can to warn the others."

Maia's mouth puckered around a protest, but she left without freeing it.

A low, long whistle pierced the quiet.

The soldiers had landed.

My instructions to the Jasadis had been clear, but I couldn't resist raising my hand as a reminder. Their obedience was vital. They needed to trust me, however sour it might taste, or suffer the consequences.

In one reality, the boats knifed through the fog, sharp-nosed and austere as they butted into the shore. Soldiers in black and violet splashed into Hirun as they climbed onto the western perimeter of Janub Aya. Arrows stretched in taut string. Swords hissed free of their sheaths.

In the other, my largest kitmer folded its wings and dove.

The initial wave of soldiers multiplied, wet boots leaving mud tracks in the dirt as hundreds marched forward.

More than anything—their boats or their uniforms or their useless weapons—those mud tracks scraped at an infected wound inside me. We stood in the mouth of Janub Aya's destruction, and ten years later, they came to track mud in a wilayah they weren't fit to lick the dust off of?

I started to walk.

The soldiers at the front exchanged unsettled glances. Whatever they had expected, it hadn't been this. A lone woman walking over a rocky plain, an armed audience unmoving in the background. A flurry of kitmers circling patiently in the sky.

What their pathetic mortal eyes couldn't see were the veins rich in color on my face. Pulsing, twisting beneath the hollows of my eyes, tangling at my temples.

By the time they realized they were looking in the wrong direction, it was too late.

A great shadow blotted the clouds. An ear-splitting shriek pierced across the wilayah. Trees bent and snapped beneath the gales forming beneath my last kitmer's beating wings.

I broke into a run, a giddy laugh whipped from my lips as the wind raced and the air thinned behind the kitmer. It flew above me, keeping pace as I ran faster than I ever had. Faster than the night I killed the Nizahl soldier. Faster than when Arin chased me to the edge of the river. Faster, even, than I had in the Alcalah's first trial, with a pack of rabid dogs and the Lukub Champion at my heels.

They tried to turn back, to escape, but their own numbers worked against them. Pathetic little ants, bumping and jostling one another, swords greasy in their grips. Seventy or so men in the rear were clever enough to turn around and dive into the river.

My two realities blended into one. I crossed my arms over my chest, and the kitmer flattened its wings. I slid to my knees in a long skid, and the kitmer dove ahead, its torso nearly skimming the top of my head.

The kitmer unfolded its wings, and I threw my arms wide as it collided with the front of the Nizahl incursion.

Jasad's symbol roared one last time.

Together, we burst into flames.

The lucky soldiers were thrown in the blast—hurled into trees and Hirun, but spared the fate of those directly beneath the kitmer. Then again, the ones directly under the kitmer had the benefit of dying quickly, spared the scent of their flesh burning as they desperately crawled toward the river. Bloodcurdling howls joined the stampede of flaming bodies careening toward Hirun.

When the last of the kitmer's magic burned off, the flames dancing over my body died with it. The earth quaked under me as the Jasadis surged toward the remaining soldiers.

Someone dropped to the ground beside me, grabbing my face with frantic hands. "Oh, thank the Awaleen!" Sefa choked out.

"I told you she was all right," Marek said from somewhere behind me, suspiciously hoarse. He cleared his throat. "Killing the moon is easier than killing Essiya of Jasad."

Sefa shook me. "You neglected to mention that when the kitmer burned, you would burn with it!"

I looked at her unblinkingly. "Of course. It is of my magic, and my magic is of me."

A volley of screams came from the north. The regiment of soldiers traveling through Ahr il Uboor had arrived.

I pried Sefa's hands off and stood. "Both of you get back. Now."

Magic sang in the air as the Jasadis threw everything they had against the soldiers. Hayagan whipped their magic toward the horses, sending riders flying off their backs. The Sahirs handed out weapons as fast as they could fashion them. Four had already collapsed and been dragged back to safety. Those with generalized magic were more subtle. Their movements were just a little faster. Their artless swings, a dash more graceful.

I spun toward the next wave of soldiers from the north, and my magic laughed as I did.

The cloud of kitmers above me flattened their wings as they barreled toward the swarm of black-and-violet uniforms, the tips of their wings catching on fire. My fingers burned as their feathers became ash, the flames traveling over me and my creatures in tandem.

Being *Essiya* did not make me hard to kill.

Being *of Jasad* did.

CHAPTER SIXTY-SEVEN

ARIN

The third gate of Nizahl fell, and through it, history spilled onto the Citadel's grounds.

The Ruby Hounds were nothing like what Arin had imagined—nothing like the sorry impression the Urabi had conjured in the woods. Rising on legs high as his shoulders, they loomed taller than the gates they had crushed beneath their powerful paws. Jagged coats of raw ruby glinted under the waning moonlight.

The soldiers around Arin held firm, but terror saturated the air. No amount of training prepared you for witnessing a horde of legendary beasts barreling toward you.

What training did was keep their swords aloft and unwavering. It meant when Arin raised a hand, he did not have to glance behind him to know the seventy-three men leaning out of every window and roof of the Citadel had angled their bows in preparation.

Dirt kicked into the air as the Hounds pounded across the lawn. A Hound twice as large as the others cleared the fallen gate in a single leap, and Arin finally saw her.

Sultana Vaida leaned forward on the back of her Hound. A silk ivory dress flowed around her lithe figure, slitted on either side of her legs. A large white flower was woven through the thick braid draped over her shoulder.

That was where the similarities to the Vaida Arin knew ended.

The skin of her shoulders had been replaced by glittering ruby shards, winding down her arms like scales. They jutted over her shoulders and along her collarbone. Bloodred eyes scoured the Citadel's field, searching.

When Vaida saw him, Arin dropped his hand.

Arrows whistled across the courtyard. A normal arrow would have snapped on impact, and it was clear Vaida expected as much.

So when they sank into Vaida's beasts, cleaving through their coats, Arin had the satisfaction of watching her cringe as the Ruby Hounds reared back with an earth-shaking roar.

Another fleet of arrows flew.

Do you think they will be necessary? Vaun's voice lingered in Arin's head for the first time since he had executed the guardsman. He had been the only witness to Arin's preparations for this battle, and Arin supposed he should be glad the guardsman had kept at least one secret from Rawain. One last echo of loyalty, ringing longer than Vaun's life.

In minutes, the Hounds would be upon them. Arin extracted the wooden splint from his pocket and raised it to one of the torches flaming cheerfully against the Citadel's walls. Soldiers parted around him as he walked forward.

Vaida saw what Arin meant to do seconds before he did it. She shouted, but Arin had already lowered the burning splint to a line of thin white dust nearly invisible between the tall blades of grass.

The flame caught and erupted, racing over the lines Jeru had meticulously drawn. Together, the lines connected to form the sigil of Vaida's ring.

The fire surrounded the Ruby Hounds, melting through their rubies like butter placed upon a hot pan. Baira's relic magic turned against the source of its own power.

Arin heard the first dying scream of a Ruby Hound.

The barricade of fire flashed red as Ruby Hounds leapt through the flames. The minute the paws of the first Hound landed on the other side of the white lines, hundreds of black-and-violet uniforms swarmed toward the flames. Ruby and steel met, the sound shrieking to the top of the watchful eaves of the Citadel.

A sword smoothly cut through the flank of a Ruby Hound, and though the Hound ripped the soldier's throat open with a swipe of its paw, the damage was done. The next soldier slashed her sword across the staggering Hound's chest, and it dropped to its side.

Despite utilizing every blacksmith in the kingdom, Arin had only been able to secure six hundred and seven swords with Baira's sigil carved into them. The arrowheads had been faster to make, and they flew through the carnage as Arin walked, finding a home in the sides of the half-melted beasts bursting through the flames.

Vaida appeared through the carnage, the ash of her white flower dusting her braid. Black scorch marks had devoured the bottom of her ivory gown.

Never in any lifetime would Arin purport to understand the Awaleen, but watching Vaida barrel over burning bodies astride a snarling Ruby Hound, Arin had the sense that in a long line of powerful Sultanas, Vaida would have been Baira's favorite.

The Sultana drew to a stop in front of Arin, her Hound's nostrils flaring inches from Arin's sword. She descended from its back, approaching Arin with her hands spread. Rubies studded her knuckles.

"Darling." The musical cadence of Vaida's voice had roughed, as though her throat had shed layers since the last time they met. "What a pleasure to see you."

"I wish I could say the same." The Mirayah might have used the relic magic from Baira's ring to produce the Ruby Hounds, but it had exacted its own price from Vaida.

The Sultana approached, and Arin stayed still as she brought her fingers close to his mouth. One of them was not of flesh—a sliver of ruby had pierced through the socket where Vaida's severed finger had grown.

"What have you done to yourself, Vaida?" Revulsion and dismay joined forces to boil over the peaks of Arin's control.

"The Mirayah would only extract Baira's magic from the ring if I gave up what I held most dear," Vaida said offhandedly. "I fed it my beauty. Oh, don't look so aghast, Arin. I knew the price when I entered."

In a strange turn, she appeared thoughtful. Wistful, even. "The Mirayah could have glutted itself on your beauty. Your frightful, frustrating beauty. If I had been planted among flowers instead of thorns, I might never have known to guard myself against dark and hungry things—not if they had a face like yours. I might have let you consume me whole."

Another arrow whistled close to Vaida, missing her head by inches. She stepped toward Arin, equal parts ploy and playfulness. An arrow could not find her without finding Arin, too.

Arin gazed into her red-streaked eyes. "Am I a dark and hungry thing?"

"The darkest." Vaida leaned in, arching her toes to whisper in his ear. "The hungriest."

Screams rang out as the Ruby Hounds converged on the first of the recruit compounds housed within the Citadel's acres. Arin did not turn.

"I didn't think you would be here with the hive of Jasadis marching toward their kingdom. I spotted a couple of her kitmers on the trade routes—marvelous, isn't it? So many of our kingdoms' storied creatures returning again." Vaida patted Arin's vest, observing Arin with an emotion she almost passed off as worry. "You know she will kill you if you don't kill her first."

Arin's voice remained cool. "Worried she would come for you next?"

Vaida trilled a laugh. "My dear, I am positively terrified of that girl. The most volatile power is the kind that doesn't recognize itself, and Essiya of Jasad could crouch over her own corpse without knowing its face. Without realizing she is her own killer."

A chill went through Arin's spine.

Around them, Vaida's Hounds were slowly overrunning Arin's soldiers. For every dead Hound there were a dozen felled Nizahl soldiers.

"You can still end this, Vaida."

The rubies glittering in place of the Sultana's eyes were as haughty as her real ones. "End it? My dear, I am only just beginning."

Before Arin could react, Vaida stepped back through the flames and disappeared.

For the thousandth time, Arin reminded himself what waited on the other side of this battle.

By now, Jeru would have gathered Ehal and his own horse. They would be fed and rested, prepared to ride straight for Sirauk Bridge as soon as the Citadel was secure. Nuzret Kamel was tomorrow, and Arin would need to ride through the night for any hope of reaching her in time.

Essiya wouldn't need the fortress if she had Nizahl, and Arin *was* Nizahl. Commander and Supreme; sword and crown.

I am the weapon of the Malika, and it is her alone I pledge myself to.

Arin pushed his sword through the maw of a Ruby Hound, using both hands to twist through its skull. Around him, Lukubi soldiers wove between the Ruby Hounds to clash against the Nizahl soldiers, their atrocious battle skills bolstered by the beasts at their sides.

If their ranks flagged, if the flames died down, if the Hounds managed to tear through their formation and flood into the towns beyond the Citadel, if he didn't reach Essiya before the mist fell... the possibilities balanced like a scythe on the back of his neck.

By the time he found Vaida again, blood had molded his sleeves to his arms, and his vest lay in tatters.

Vaida stood on the perimeter of the dying flames, her gaze fixed on the Citadel.

As Arin peeled off his right glove, dropping it to the grass, he wished he had had a chance to understand. Why dedicate her life to violating the accords drafted by her ancestors to prevent this very carnage? What was it about the Citadel—about Nizahl—that Vaida had so desired?

Foolish questions, his father would say. The answer was one and the same.

Power.

What Vaida specialized in was an art even Rawain could never master. Comfort wrapped in barbed wire. Luxury and decadence dressing a hollow kingdom, consigning its people to a poverty of any genuine pursuit, any true passion. Gutted by generations of rulers who cared more about presentation than purpose, who suffocated scholarship, led by the whim of the day.

Arin couldn't deny how masterfully Vaida had turned Lukub into the perfect illusion. No rebellions, no dissent—just quiet disappearances and a Champion striking a bargain for his sister's life; spies and empty libraries and skinned faces pinned to the inside of the Ivory Palace.

With Nizahl's armies, there would be nothing she couldn't conquer. She wouldn't need to limit her expansions to Essam Woods. She would never be forced to rely on a treatise like the Zinish Accords for support again.

Vaida lowered her gaze when Arin dropped the second glove, still walking toward her at a measured pace. She laughed. "I think this is the first time I have seen you bare those hands of yours since we were children. Shall I commemorate the occasion by testing how quickly those fingers will snap between my Hound's teeth?"

"I do not want to do this." Arin stopped before reaching her. "Baira cursed the Sultanas when she left behind that ring. The Awaleen were capricious and cruel—their gifts have always come with consequences."

Ruby thorns pushed out from Vaida's eyebrows, thin and sharp like the obelisk at the front of the Ivory Palace. Red lips stretched into a smile. "No gift comes freely, Arin. Besides, now we can both be cursed. Silver hair for you, ruby eyes for me. It's exactly what we dreamed about as children, remember?"

Arin did remember. He remembered being ten years old and hiding from Sorn in the servants' stairwell. He couldn't tolerate listening to the Orban Heir babble about hunting for one more minute, and Arin had yet to master the art of politely freezing out a conversation. Vaida had tracked him down and spent the next two hours making shadow creatures with her fingers to entertain him, regaling Arin with made-up stories of their adventures. In exchange, he'd taken her for a walk around the Citadel's gardens and carried the basket while she filled it with her favorite flowers.

He remembered letting her rub a tincture of pomegranate and beetroot into his hair at the brilliant age of eleven because she had cried that he had the hair of an old man and she didn't want to be stuck with Sorn when Arin died.

He remembered Vaida finding him the hour before his mother's funeral and forcing him to misbutton his coat.

"You look too prim, darling. The vultures need a spectacle," she'd whispered. "They want to feed. Give them something obvious to peck at, and they won't dig much deeper."

A year later, he had ordered thousands of her favorite blossoms sent to the Ivory Palace after her own mother's funeral.

Vaida was his first friend, and his very favorite foe.

"Here's what will happen when I touch you, Vaida." Arin stepped toward her, folding his hands behind his back. The handle of the dagger tucked into his waistband bumped into his wrist.

"Every ounce of the decayed relic magic Baira infected you with will drain from you and into my father's scepter. The Hounds will wither and disappear. I will take you into a dungeon beneath the Citadel to await a tribunal for violating the Zinish Accords. You have no friends among the kingdoms. King Murib and the Omal intermediary council will find you guilty. They will sentence you to death, and I will bury you in the gardens of the Ivory Palace. The head of your council or your designated inheritor will be seated on your throne, breaking the chain of Baira's descendants."

Another step. Vaida watched him, her hulking Ruby Hound snarling behind her shoulder. A scream rent the air, abruptly silenced with a crunch.

Vaida's lips pursed in delicate amusement. "All from a single touch? My, my."

"The alternative is this: you allow me to drain the curse and I allow you to go home," Arin continued as though she hadn't spoken. "You will sit on the tribunal sentencing my father. You can be his judge and his executioner through the formal procedures."

"I want your father's throne *and* his head, Arin." Vaida beamed. "I will have a tapestry of his robes commissioned to hang over Lukub's gates."

"I can give you his head and his robes."

It earned Arin a pause and a bewildered blink. Vaida knew Arin would not lie to her—not even in a moment like this.

"I want Nizahl."

Arin's gaze moved over the torches mounted across the stone walls around the Citadel. The mist circling over the kingdom had dissipated, and the moon hung low over the massacre raging within the Citadel's borders.

"I cannot give you Nizahl."

"Make it one of your choices." She crossed the final steps toward Arin, her Hound's nostrils flaring. It bared its teeth as Vaida played with Arin's collar. "The other two don't suit."

For all the devastation she had wrought, Vaida was not a fighter. She never learned that it wasn't the weapon she should fear, but the opponent wielding it. That battles were not won by the number of Ruby Hounds or shiny spears, but by the fate of a single mistake.

When Arin had the swords and arrows forged, he had also requested the sigil be engraved into a single dagger. A dagger he would only be able to use if he stood close enough to the Sultana to share breath.

When it slid into her chest, it seemed to take Vaida an eternity to understand what had happened.

"This wasn't one of your options," she said in a small voice. "You tricked me."

A flurry of arrows cleaved into the Hound rearing over Arin. Arin ducked out the path of its flailing paw. The ground shook as it slammed into the ground beside them. Vaida's eyes moved from the dagger to Arin. Swaying, she grabbed Arin's arm as he released the hilt.

"If you die, the Hounds die with you." He caught her as she slumped into him, lowering her gently to the ground. "It was not an option I wanted to exercise."

Vaida coughed. "Sneaky."

Blood lined the seam of her lips. Arin didn't resist when she tugged him close. "Would you really have given me Rawain's head?"

Arin carefully pulled a blade of grass from Vaida's hair. "Yes."

Vaida withdrew the dagger from her chest. Blood flowered beneath the silk over her heart. "Do you think I will meet Baira when I die?"

Arin knelt beside her.

"Lie to me, Arin," she whispered. "Just this one time. I want to imagine it."

So while the Hounds from the Ivory Palace to the Citadel began to die, Arin wove Vaida a story of a reunion with her Awala, as vivid and distracting as the stories she would create for him in their secret stairwell. As the Nizahl soldiers surged forward against the Hounds and the flagging Lukubi forces, Arin listened to Vaida's breathing turn shallow.

"I'm scared," Vaida whimpered. Crimson tears poured over the ruby studs embedded in her temples. "Arin, I'm scared."

The ache in Arin's chest spread through the rest of him. He laid down beside Vaida, his shoulder pressed to hers. "The night before your twenty-fourth birthday, you came to the Citadel and asked me a question."

"I did?" Soft and lethargic.

"You asked me what I would do if I hadn't been born Arin of Nizahl. Who I would want to be."

"I must have been drunk."

"I told you I couldn't imagine a reality where I am not who I am."

She tipped her head to the left, half-lidded gaze unfocused as it settled on him. "A vexing answer, as usual."

Arin chuckled. "Yes, and I have since reconsidered. Do you remember what you said?"

Her eyes slipped shut. "Mm."

"You said, 'I would have been a flower.'"

Vaida's lips twitched. Arin thought she might have been trying to smile. "Definitely drunk," she whispered.

"You can still have a life. A good life," Arin said. "Take my hand before the rest of the magic dies. If there is enough left, drawing it out might heal some of the damage."

It seemed to take unspeakable effort for Vaida to open her eyes again. Faintly, so faint Arin could barely catch it, she said, "But your options."

Arin had watched so much end in the last month of his life. So much destruction. What compelled Arin to say what he did next was as much mercy as it was spite. Spite for the forces responsible for leading them to this battlefield, for the control they had tried to wrest away from Arin.

"There is a fourth option, Vaida. A future you choose. A future where no one will ever know if you died on this field or if you were pulled back to the Mirayah, because your body will disappear with the Hounds. A future you get to build in a realm as intelligent as you are, where your power is limited only by what you can imagine."

A roar of victory swept over the field as the Citadel's siren finally fell quiet. The Hounds had fallen. A breeze blew Arin's hair from its tie. The kitmer who had carried him out of Mahair and watched over him in the Gibal circled overhead. Niseeba landed on the ledge of a balcony and waited.

Maybe Arin wouldn't need Ehal to reach Jasad in time.

The Sultana's last breaths misted in the air between them.

"Always with your pretty words," Vaida sighed, slim shoulders melting into the grass. Blood drenched the front of her dress. "Okay, Arin. Take...my hand."

It might be too late. It was probably too late.

Arin closed his hand around Vaida's anyway.

CHAPTER SIXTY-EIGHT

ESSIYA

Bodies littered Janub Aya, and smoke choked the air. I picked my way around the charred corpses of the Nizahl soldiers. The imprint of my kitmer was burned into the ground around them. The surviving forces had retreated to the border of Ahr il Uboor once the sun set, and I had sent three kitmers to stand sentry over their camp. If they moved, I would know. More likely than not, they were waiting until morning to resume the siege.

The morning, when the mist over Sirauk would fall for Nuzret Kamel's anniversary.

I scanned the dead for familiar faces. I had already checked in on Sefa and Marek. Marek was shaken; apparently, one of the regiments Rawain had sent to their doom was the Ravening compound, where Marek had been hiding. He had yet to encounter anyone he recognized, but I had spotted Sefa with her arms around his rigid frame, stroking his hair.

I froze at the sight of Maia's husband, head twisted at an unnatural angle on the ground.

"She doesn't know yet," Lateef murmured, appearing beside me. His eyes were red-rimmed, and patches of blood had soaked through his clothes. "She's still looking for him."

I gazed at Maia's husband. He had died here, and with him

he would take half of Maia's heart. He would take her bouncing feet, her ever-present smile. The dead rarely left this world empty-handed.

"Have him carried to the river with the others. She can perform his death rites. Do not let her wander through the night, calling his name."

I returned to Sefa and Marek. Sefa was huddled against the side of an overturned wagon, hiding behind the giant wheel while Marek paced in front of her.

"Well?" Marek asked as soon as I approached. "How many?"

"I don't know," I said. "They will count the dead after Nuzret Kamel. There is more dying to do tomorrow."

Sefa drew her face from the inside of her arm. Her lower lip trembled.

"Is this your magic speaking, or you?"

I grazed the rough surface of the wagon's wheel and stayed silent. It was a good question, and I did not have a good answer. My magic's voice had stitched itself across my thoughts with the finest needle, its presence twined through the very fabric of my mind. I couldn't see the seams anymore.

"You don't have to raise the fortress tomorrow," Marek said. I twisted away from his reaching arms, ignoring his pleading face. "Arin is coming back. If you have Nizahl, the other kingdoms will stand down. You will not need the fortress."

I stiffened. Since when did Marek call him *Arin*?

"You are a fool if you believe he is coming back," I said. "Just as I was a fool to think he would stay."

"He only left to prevent this from escalating into war, he told us—"

"Where is the scepter?" I interrupted.

"Sylvia..." Tears spilled onto Marek's cheeks. "Please. We need you."

Efra's quiet warning mingled with Marek's plaintive whisper, shuddering down my spine. Instead of sinking through me, it encountered the solid barrier of my magic. The margins where I began and my magic ended had narrowed, making it so I could only catch glimpses of the emotions I was meant to feel.

We both know I can feel what happens when your magic consumes you. You... you disappear.

Once again, I realized I could not remember the last time I had breathed.

"I—" Moving through my magic was impossible. We were intertwined across every fiber, every stitch of my being.

Marek pulled my rigid frame into his arms, holding me tight. "I lost my family on the battlefield. Everyone I ever loved died to protect someone else's throne. You and Sefa are all I have."

My arms hung loose at my sides. I tried to bring them around Marek, but they wouldn't obey.

"I might not die."

Sefa spoke up, using the wagon to pull herself to her feet. "You will die in every way that counts."

Ugh, I couldn't think about this. I had tired of convincing everyone that I had no particular appetite for death—that I had, in fact, dedicated a great deal of effort toward avoiding the fate of my family. "I have no choice! If we miss Nuzret Kamel, the mist will not fall for another ten years. I cannot rely on the slim possibility of the Nizahl Heir wresting away his father's throne."

I left my other reason unspoken.

My magic would not give me another ten years. One way or another, it would overpower me. At least when I raised the fortress, the madness would have been worth it.

Marek allowed me to disentangle from him, his lips pressed together. "Promise us that if the Nizahl Heir arrives tomorrow, you will not raise the fortress."

For once, my magic and I were in agreement. Neither of us wanted to think about the Nizahl Heir. He had brought my heart to carnage, and there was little left capable of holding faith a second time.

"I promise," I said. "Get some rest."

The sun rose over Sirauk Bridge on the last day of my life, bringing the cries of the resumed battle with it. I watched with dry eyes as the Nizahl recruits streamed into Janub Aya, colliding into the wave of Jasadis whose magic had not been drained by yesterday's fight. The others took positions in the back, prepared to cut down anyone who made it through the first frontier.

"Go toward the sea," I ordered Marek and Sefa, refusing to waver at their stricken expressions. "You will see them coming if they try to cross the sand hills. Hide until the fortress is up."

"Essiya—"

I strode away, heading toward the spot they had buried the scepter. I couldn't handle another plea. My magic already wanted me to leave the bridge and run—to vanish before the mist fell. If they convinced the rest of me, I might very well abandon the Jasadis here to die. Abandon the thousands still on the trade routes.

I dug out the scepter. The raven's wings curled high around the orb, somehow even more vicious without Rawain's hand around it.

The mist clung to the bridge stubbornly, refusing to lapse, and I grappled with the sudden thought that perhaps it never would. The records on Nuzret Kamel were inconsistent and fragmented. What if it was nothing more than a tale stirred in the bored minds of villagers in Janub Aya, a story told to entertain one generation after another reared alongside the mist?

I traced the raven's frozen wings. This was a piece of Arin. A piece Rawain had stolen, corrupted possibly beyond repair.

Damn it. Damn him.

I checked that none of the fighting had penetrated the first wave of Jasadis before I closed my eyes. I had made a promise to Marek and Sefa, after all.

The kitmers I had sent to spy on the Nizahl soldiers sailed over Jasad. There were a dozen routes he could have taken to get to Janub Aya from the Citadel, but I didn't have the time to check each of them. The kitmer traveled over the wreckage of Usr Jasad, past the grim profile of Bakir Tower. A silver-haired rider was nowhere to be seen.

A familiar scream snapped me out of the kitmer's head.

A slew of soldiers barreled over the sandy slopes leading from Suhna Sea, penning in the Jasadis from behind. Magic tinged the air as the Jasadis poured every last ounce to hold the new onslaught back.

But none of that registered, not at first.

The scream that had drawn me from the kitmer was Sefa's.

One of the recruits had spotted Sefa behind the wagon, her sword held in her grip like a dead fish, and thrown his spear.

If I hadn't been on the other side of the clearing, maybe I could have sprinted to her in time. If I had seen it a fraction of a second sooner, I might have been able to stop it. I could have frozen the spear as I had once frozen a dagger aimed at Sefa; I could have diverted its path or even slowed it.

But I did not see it a fraction of a second sooner. I saw it as Marek slammed into Sefa, throwing her out of the spear's path. I saw it as the point of the spear cleaved into Marek's chest, the force hurling him to the ground.

I froze. The scrawny soldier who had thrown the spear also froze. He blinked rapidly, his face transforming into a mask of horror. "Marek?" He blanched and whirled around. "Zane! I need help!" The soldier took off toward the others.

As though it mattered.

As though it wasn't too late.

Because I was a coward, I wanted Sefa to stay on the ground a little longer. I wanted her to spend more time dusting the pebbles embedded in her cheeks and fighting her dizziness. I wanted her to enjoy her last minute of peace. I wanted so much more for her than what was coming. I ran toward them, but I knew. I already knew.

Sefa pushed to her elbows, rolling onto her knees with a pained whimper.

When she screamed, I clapped my hand over my mouth. It was the kind of scream scraped from the very bottom of a soul, impossible to hear without experiencing a visceral urge to turn away. It turned your skin cold and clammy, forced your heart into your throat and your stomach to your feet. It was the kind of scream that time would never scrub from my memory.

Marek's spine contracted weakly, spasming with the muscles in his torso. Blood drenched his entire front, darkest around the place beneath his ribs where the spear protruded.

"Oh no. Oh no, no, no, *no no no*—" Sefa's cries grew incoherent as she crawled to Marek. "No, Marek, please. Please!"

I could almost hear Marek's heart slow. I felt the effort it took for him to twist his lips into a smile for Sefa. I thought he might have been trying for a joke, perhaps a glib remark about Sefa's peripheral vision or how blood actually improved this shirt.

Whatever he might have said, it would have been for Sefa. It had always been for Sefa.

But Marek choked, blood pouring from either side of his mouth. Sefa tried to turn him onto his side without jostling the spear, her slim wrists struggling with Marek's weight, though she'd be more likely to let them break than give up.

When she rolled Marek onto his back again, the once-bright green eyes we had watched dance with humor, eyes that had stolen hearts and frequently broken them, eyes that would scour any room until they found Sefa, were fixed and staring. Dull in a way Marek could never be.

He was gone in less than a minute. My magic could fight back death, but it could not give chase once death had claimed its prize.

I stopped in front of the pair, scepter clenched in my bloodless fist. The last Lazur—gone. The man who never wanted to be a soldier, whose life had twined with Sefa's and never let go—dead on a battlefield like the rest of his siblings.

The sounds leaving Sefa chilled me to my core. The raw agony of a heart breaking, never to be the same again. An entire life turning to ash in your hands.

A chill swept over my skin. I turned from the sight of Sefa bowed over Marek's body.

The mist had fallen.

I didn't look back at Sefa or Marek's body. I didn't look at the Jasadis flagging beneath the surge of soldiers closing in on all sides.

I walked toward the bridge, my magic thrashing in resistance inside me, and I began to recite.

I recited the enchantment again, and I did not notice the blood dripping from my nose.

I recited the enchantment a third time, and the pain bursting between my temples was a mere flicker in an inferno.

I recited the enchantment a fourth time, and my veins burst. Gold and silver spilled inside my skin, spreading like a bleeding palm plunged into a river.

Screams erupted behind me as the ground quaked. A stream of gold rippled across an invisible line in the earth and burst upward.

The fortress rose to my waist. I imagined it stretching from here to Usr Jasad, brilliant and solid and beautiful. The sixth time I recited, I smiled widely, undeterred by the metallic tang of blood in my mouth. More and more figures stepped toward the border and recited with me. The figures from my hallucinations joined hands and stepped toward the fortress.

My magic imploded through every corner of my being. It spiraled in my lungs, settled in my belly. Wrapped its fingers around my heart. It reminded me of losing my cuffs, except my magic's first freedom had felt far more overwhelming.

The second liberation settled me. Light crawled over the broken shards I'd swept into the back of my mind, and like a beleaguered mother confronting her child's laziness, began to piece them back together.

It knew exactly how they fit, where they should go. Shard by shard, my magic built me back. For each piece I reclaimed, a figure stepped into the fortress. I watched them dissolve into bolts of silver and streak across the surface of the fortress, glittering trails chasing them through the resin.

When I recited the enchantment a seventh time, the black-haired man from the waterfall was the only one left at my side. He stepped into the fortress and began to break away in fragments of blazing gold, racing across the fortress like shattered stars.

And I remembered.

"Stay with us," Dania said. Tears glistened in her eyes. "Just until you find your place here."

We shook our head, cupping our sister's face. "How will I ever find my place if I stay in your kingdom? I will sink into the comfort I find among you all, and I will never create my own corner in this world."

A slim arm wove through ours. Attached to it was a face more lovely than the stars we'd abandoned in the heavens, as dark and luminous as the night we'd shaped for them to shine within.

"Let me come with you. We do not even know for certain what awaits you in the east. What magics roam free on that side of Hirun."

We kissed Baira's forehead. "What could it do to me? Any magic that roams is a magic of ours, even twisted or decayed or forgotten. It will love me as dearly as you do."

"So stubborn," Kapastra sighed. A baby rochelya curled around her shoulders, nestling its flat head against her collarbone. She petted its scaled ear absently. "You know our kingdoms are yours, too. What is of us is of you, Rovial. Our magic is one."

We smiled.

"I know."

We stood in Hirun, trailing the tips of our fingers over the rushing current, and listened to the world's heartbeat.

"Why 'Jasad'?" Dania asked. She stood on top of the hill, hands on her hips. Surveying our newly claimed corner of the world with the efficiency and tactical analysis she never quite managed to suppress. There was not yet much to see. The meadow stretched around us in endless green hills, not a sign of life to be seen. "A bit ambiguous, is it not? Morbid, even."

We plucked a cracked date from a bed of burs. Ants spilled out from the tender inside of the fruit, fleeing over our fingers and along our wrist.

We pressed the ruined date into the soil beneath the tree and whispered a promise to it.

"Ambiguity is not morbid. Ambiguity is a question, and our existence is the answer," we said. "Yes, *Jasad* means body. Yes, it also means corpse. What this kingdom becomes—whether it breathes or suffocates, lives or dies—is a question only it can answer."

Dania rolled her eyes. "Not sufficiently dramatic enough for you to say you like the way the word sounds?"

We caressed the fresh dirt over the buried date and laughed. "I also like the way it sounds."

Breathe, little date. Breathe, and I will build a world for you.

Thunder growled over the horizon. Blue light forked through the sky, striking the earth like the flick of a serpent's tongue.

We closed our eyes and smelled burning. Hundreds of miles away, a hut had caught fire. The entire village was in flames.

We tried again to command the rain to fall, and again we crashed into a barrier. Kapastra had locked the sky after her villages had flooded thanks to Dania's attempt to lift the drought from her own kingdom. A drought we had punished her with only after her callous mistake killed hundreds of our children in the south.

Their screams rang in our ears as if we stood in the center of the burning village. We sank to our knees, covering our face with our hands and rocking. Helpless to do more than feel the panic of mothers reaching into their children's beds splintering our chest, howling alongside the farmers fighting to herd their sheep away from the blazing fence. Their farm, their pride and joy, their life's work. The roof caved, and their hearts caved with it. Donkeys and mules choked the only safe passage out of the village, and a child fell beneath the rampaging hooves. Each bone she broke fractured in our own body.

We sobbed until hands found our shoulders, shaking us.

"Rovial, what is it? What's wrong?"

What was wrong?

What was *wrong*?

We placed the thinnest wall between ourself and the collapsing village. A wall just thin enough for us to find the strength to shove off Kapastra's hands and glare through bleary eyes.

"Get out of my kingdom," we snarled.

A date fell on our shoulder.

With a hand against the trunk, we tipped the tree over and set the exposed roots on fire.

"I heard you made a man," we said, leaning against Baira's door. She jumped, and in the distance, half of a mountain splintered and slid into the open sea.

The surprise in her eyes cooled to stiff disdain. "I am not in the habit of making men these days."

"True. Breaking them is more your style."

"What are you doing in Lukub? I told you. I am on Dania's side in this war of yours."

"Lukub. Lukub, Lukub." We toyed with a carved stone chip, smirking at the inscription. Another discarded lover fancying themselves a poet. Pathetic and lost, like everything Baira touched. "Tell me, did Dania give you an earful about what you decided to name your kingdom, or was that judgment reserved for me alone?"

We stepped forward, tossing aside the chip. It landed on a pile of leathery skin Baira's weavers must have forgotten to collect. By tomorrow, the carefully flayed flesh would be sewn into the tapestry at the front of the Ivory Palace. A parting gift for the families of traitors; were they so inclined, they could visit the tapestry and identify which patch of skin belonged to their loved one.

A howl turned Baira's head. A second and third joined it. The mournful howls became a symphony, twisting through her kingdom.

Baira shoved the drapes apart, throwing open the door to her balcony. "What did you do to my Hounds?" she gasped, frantically scanning the moon-drenched expanse of Essam Woods. "I can feel—what did you *do*?"

We followed her to the balcony and stepped onto the ledge. "Worry less about the Hounds and more about your subjects in their proximity. Flesh tears much easier than ruby."

Baira's nails bit into her scalp as she shook her head back and forth.

"Why? Why?"

"Our magic is one, remember?" The kitmer sailed toward us, sparks of our kingdom's colors trailing behind it. The smile faded from our face. "When you stripped the magic out of that man, I felt it. I felt you corrupt the very nature of what we are. Whatever you have created, it is a threat to the essence of our world, and it must be fixed. That man—what is he? Lukubi, Omalian? I would like to do him the honor of burying him in his home."

Ruby and ivory bloomed vicious petals in Baira's eyes. "Then you will not have to travel far," Baira spat. "The man you call a corruption was a Jasadi before we took his magic. Before we made him a *King*. Fareed will be the first to rule a kingdom that isn't loyal to our blood, isn't beholden to our magic. He will fight against you."

We leaned close to our sister's face, wiping the opaque red tears dripping down her cheeks. "My beautiful Baira," we whispered. "Make a King? You could barely make a shiny dog."

We stepped off the ledge, landing on the soft neck of our kitmer. Wind rushed through our hair as it climbed higher, taking us home.

Behind us, Baira's scream joined her Hounds'.

We stepped onto the bridge and crossed our arms. Dania had insisted on this meeting spot, claiming it served as neutral territory between our kingdom and Kapastra's.

She had some manner of mischief planned. She wouldn't be Dania if she didn't. But what?

We screamed as our siblings tore us apart. Baira broke our bones, wrenching us into pieces on the bridge, and Dania plunged her arm into our chest. Kapastra's hands clutched our skull, holding us prisoner to the endless agony.

"Hurry!" Baira shrieked.

Dania's fingers grazed our magic at its very core. Her hand closed around it, and her screams of agony joined ours.

"Don't do this!" we pleaded. "Sisters, please!"

"You will find us again," Kapastra whispered, blue-and-white eyes gazing down at us with the implacable wrath of the heavens. "At least, what remains of you will."

They tore our magic from our destroyed body and cast it down into the river flowing beneath the bridge. We collided with the surface of the water, and the sky fractured into gold-and-silver fire as the rest of our limbs were reduced to ash.

We flowed into Hirun and searched for home.

We are a young girl who loves to cup bees from her growing hive. By the time she is twelve, our power has grown too much, and she burns her hives with the same torch she laid upon her sleeping parents' hut.

She is executed, and we return to the river once more.

Once every hundred years, when the river slows, we are reborn. Sometimes we stay for twelve years, like the first girl, and sometimes we stay for twenty, like the young man who slaughtered his village with the monsters he created.

The story always ends the same. The wrong choices. The scourge of our magic on their mind.

We consume them, and we return to the river once more.

We are a green-eyed girl in a modest town, the pride of our family's life.

We—

For the second time, reality disappeared.

CHAPTER SIXTY-NINE

ARIN

Arin cradled her face as magic scoured through him, screaming as it tore out of Essiya.

His was an incomplete agony; a partial evisceration. Because on the other side of it was the gold and silver draining out of Essiya's eyes, replaced by precious dark brown. On the other side was a beautifully human terror coloring them as she realized what he had done.

"Have you returned?" The echo of a conversation tucked away in a tunnel, hidden beneath the earth. A single bolt of time. An eternity.

Chin trembling, she said, "I never left."

"Yes, you did."

And he would never allow it to happen again.

Arin kissed her.

CHAPTER SEVENTY

ESSIYA

I knew better. I knew better, but I didn't care.

My hands knotted in his vest, drawing him tight against my body. Arin kissed me with scorching ferocity, like a man brought back from the brink. His hand gripped my hip with bruising force, the other sliding over the braid lying against the back of my neck.

The first time Arin kissed me, I had lost myself. I had wanted nothing more than to abandon my mind, to cast aside my worries and fears and find peace against him.

The last time he kissed me, I found myself.

I became aware of the sounds around me. The dampness seeping into my shoes. The ache in my lower back. I breathed in the smell of the river lingering on him, nearly overpowering the scent of ink and rain he could never quite shake. I felt… I *felt*. The sand in my tired eyes; the pitch in my ears; the anger of watching the Nizahl soldiers march onto Janub Aya; the guilt of killing them so viciously; the anguish of fearing that Arin had only pretended to believe me and all along he had planned to pick up his father's mantle; the terror of watching the mist fall.

The scream of grief bottled inside me, because Marek was dead. Marek was dead.

As my magic drained, something inside me gasped back to life. Resurfacing from its slow and steady suffocation, howling back to power. Every heart beating inside Jasad echoed behind my own. The land murmured, weary and low, then seemed to realize I was listening. I was finally listening, so it started shouting.

Arin drew back, leaving his forehead pressed against mine.

"I thought I would be too late." He gripped my shoulders, my arms, my waist. Reassuring himself.

As soon as he finished, he collapsed.

I moved instantly, catching his head seconds before it could bash against a cropping of rocks. His skin had taken on a blue tint I'd never seen on anything living. I dragged him away from the rocks, terror turning my grip rough. "Arin? Arin?"

I glanced around for help, but the battle still raged around us. The Jasadis had been beaten back almost all the way to the tree line, and I forced myself not to look at the bodies strewn over the dirt. Some of the Nizahl soldiers were glancing around in confusion, and I followed their gazes to Jeru, who was chasing the soldiers on horseback and waving a Nizahl flag, bellowing for their attention. Niseeba screeched above us, looping around the scorch marks of her dead siblings.

I raised a shaking wrist to Arin's nose and waited. When a puff of warm air ghosted over my skin, the relief was too much. It was all too much. Each death pierced me through, an embroidery of agony with me as its needle. Each scream rang double in my head. The clouds complained about the sand in the air, the trees sobbed for water, and the earth I'd scorched with the kitmers—it *shrieked*, over and over, blade of grass by blade of grass.

My magic had eroded me nearly to the core. I felt it in every bone, every breath. I could no sooner disentangle myself from it than I could rearrange my organs. Carved into my skull were the memories of a thousand lifetimes. People I had been, places I had seen, lives I had ended. My magic roiled with it, a furious storm slamming into the thin barrier I had erected between us.

I did not have magic-madness. I *was* magic-madness. Every single person since Rovial had had my magic. Rovial's magic.

I sobbed, shaking Arin's shoulder. "Wake up. Wake up so you can laugh with me."

The Nizahl Heir stirred, and the relief nearly killed me. Air rushed out of my desiccating lungs, and I looked for the other wayward piece of my heart. I couldn't risk leaving him to find Sefa, but I didn't need to. I could move to Sefa as I had once moved to Arin, leaving my physical body behind. It was as simple as closing my eyes and opening them next to her.

A shadow stretched over the kneeling girl, a pair of boots stopping by Marek's body. She stared at the shadow through a glassy, unseeing gaze. Rocking back and forth, her bloodied hand pressed to Marek's wound and another curved around his pale cheek.

Tears shimmered in Jeru's eyes as he knelt beside Sefa. "Sefa, I am so sorry. I am so sorry, but we have to go."

Sefa kept rocking.

Jeru reached for her, and Sefa recoiled violently. "No! I won't leave him. Don't you understand, I've never left him? I've never left him!"

The ache in Jeru's face surprised me. His voice was ragged. "You never left. I know you never left, and so does he. But Marek isn't here anymore, Sefa."

Sefa fought Jeru with an exceptional ferocity when he picked her up, but he was a soldier and she was a grief-shattered girl. "Put me back!" she screamed, writhing like a snake caught in a trap. "I won't leave him!"

"You will not die beside him!" Jeru roared, and Sefa finally went still. The guardsman didn't stop walking, didn't look at Sefa. I walked beside them, quiet as the wind and as insubstantial. Jeru headed toward Arin. My body remained bowed over the Heir's, and I quickened my step, eager to rejoin it. "Do you understand what he went through to find you again? What he endured to keep you safe?

He needs you to bury him. He needs you alive to remember him, to honor him."

"You don't understand," she whispered. Jeru tensed, and we both glanced at her tear-stricken face. "What life is left? I can't mourn him longer than I loved him. I am not strong enough for this."

"Nobody is," Jeru said. "You do it anyway."

As soon as Jeru dropped to the ground beside Arin, setting Sefa down, I slid back into my body.

My sudden motion startled Jeru in the middle of checking Arin's breathing. He was slightly less blue, but my stomach still twisted with unease at his pallor. I brushed his hair with the back of my hand.

"He's alive. Keep him that way," I commanded.

I turned to Sefa and took her face in my hands. She barely reacted, still and unresponsive once again.

"He died," she said, and I was not sure who she was speaking to. "He wasn't supposed to die before me. He wasn't supposed to die because of me."

I doubted she would hear me now, but I hoped the words would linger somewhere in her subconscious. Somewhere she could retrieve them when the time came.

"I love you, Sefa." I wanted to cry, but I didn't quite remember how. "I love you, Sayali. I love you, whoever you will be next. You don't deserve this, but you will survive it."

I grabbed the scepter and rose to my feet. Battles still raged around us, but it had begun to slow. More and more Nizahl soldiers were joining the group of confused, uncertain soldiers dropping their weapons to their sides. Most of the Jasadis had drained through their magic stores, turning the fighting mundane.

It was nearly over.

The fortress lingered at half the height of its predecessor, but it was still too high to climb. Too high for him to scale.

The mist around Sirauk hadn't returned, but I could feel the chill of it grazing the back of my neck.

Not long now.

"When he comes after me, stop him," I told Jeru.

"What do you—"

The mist crawled, and I disappeared.

When I materialized on the bridge, I was dressed in a long abaya striped with silver and gold, fastened at my middle with a pin in the shape of a kitmer.

I supposed my magic understood we'd need to be well-dressed for this particular reunion.

Ugh, still with the *my magic*. As though it was a stray cat I'd found and reluctantly taken in, something separate and discordant from myself.

My magic was me. The hallucinations, the visions—all me. Each life we'd lived, stacked in thin layers on top of this last one.

Time's brutality had spared Sirauk Bridge, leaving it as endless and ethereal as the day I had died on it. Rot had not dared approach the perpetually damp wooden planks beneath my feet, nor had rain weathered the thick ropes on either side. Beneath it lay darkness and the quiet hum of Hirun River.

I placed my hand on the fortress. It vibrated, jubilant at my touch.

Inside me, dread turned leaden.

I remembered my magic's previous lives as one might remember a childhood story. The details had blurred, but the endings were always the same. The madness that caused Dania, Baira, and Kapastra to kill Rovial and cast themselves into an eternal slumber would catch up to my mortal mind and consume it. Thousands had died at the hands of my magic-madness, entire populations wiped clean. Even now, the barrier between me and complete surrender shivered beneath my magic's onslaught, fine cracks forming on its surface.

I pressed my fingers to my lips, holding back a wholly inappropriate laugh. I hadn't wanted the responsibility of being the Jasad Heir, and all along, I had had the magic of the Jasad *Awal*? If I hadn't grown up with the cuffs suppressing my magic, I might very well have gone mad before I reached adolescence, like most of the others. They hadn't had the chance to remember who they were before the magic ripped through their minds. They hadn't had a beautiful conduit siphoning away the worst of its effects.

What had the creature protecting Vaida's ring said that night in the Omal palace? *Nearly there. They tried again and again, but your choices never changed. Who knew this one would meet with success?*

She may as well have spelled ROVIAL in large letters on my forehead.

A drop of blood hit my chin. I wiped my nose with a scowl. My magic had been restrained for fourteen years. Surely, another couple of minutes did not merit such a tantrum.

Once the barrier in my mind cracked, I would go mad. The damage I would unleash would be rivaled only by Rovial's, and this time, Arin's abilities would not be enough to pull me back from the brink.

Without that knowledge, I would have walked straight through the fortress to Sefa and Arin. I would have let myself dream of keeping this life, of seeing it through to the end. Arin had come for me, which meant Nizahl would stand beside Jasad. None of the kingdoms could harm us with Nizahl at our side.

I could walk through this fortress and find Arin. We could have a life together. A future.

He and Sefa wouldn't be alone.

In the measure of monster or man, what tips the scales?

Lives unfinished flitted through my mind's eye, playing before me like the last vision of the dying.

Rovial, the mad Awal. Essiya, the cruel Heir.

And Sylvia. My first and favorite lie.

The tide of my magic broke through a portion of the barrier, and I forced myself to swim. To keep my head above water and remember it all. Fairel's laugh. The smell of Rory's favorite mint tea brewing on a foggy morning. Sefa's dazed giggles when she'd been working on a project for five hours straight without blinking. Marek's endless chatter whenever I grew moody and sullen, too stubborn to leave me alone and too restless to stay quiet.

And the memories that hurt. The memories my magic had kicked to the corner and lit ablaze.

We—I—had loved my siblings once. I had loved them before I knew what the word meant or how fatal its corruption could be. I had loved Dania's inability to go anywhere without her axe dangling from her hand or her waist. Kapastra's obsession with shining each individual scale on the newborn rochelyas and giving them names more fitting for an inappropriate suitor, like Amar Arba'tashar and Helywa.

And Baira...nobody could tell a story like Baira. Everyone in this age remembered her for her beauty and her skills of deception, but the Lukub Awala had so much more to offer. She could turn a walk from one tree to the next into the grandest of adventures, whisk you into action with nothing more than the turn of a phrase.

And I...

I am what remains.

I opened my eyes, and the fortress had risen to its full height.

Standing on the other side of it, barely holding himself upright, was Arin.

CHAPTER SEVENTY-ONE

ARIN

Magic never stayed still.

It was a detail Arin had taken for granted. Magic always swirled or churned when a Jasadi used it; it never lingered too long.

The rings of gold and silver in Essiya's eyes had settled into irises. The colors shaded the dark of her eyes in still pools of silver and gold, and Arin had never been more scared in his life.

She glanced past him disapprovingly. "You knocked out Jeru in the middle of a battle?"

Arin slammed his fist against the fortress. It refused to give, as solid as steel despite its fluid appearance. "Enough. You did it—you raised the fortress. The fighting has ended, and it will never renew. I am Supreme, and there will be no war. You are *done*. Get off the bridge before the mist returns."

As soon as the mist rose, Sirauk would devour her. And Arin would be stuck on the opposite side of this damned wall, pounding his knuckles bloody.

Her chin jutted out, her features taking on a stubborn set. "Why should I take orders from someone who nearly killed himself kissing me? You can barely stand, Arin."

"I do not need to stand, Essiya," Arin snarled. "Do you want me on my knees again? Do you want me to beg?"

Essiya set down the scepter, and Arin startled. He hadn't even noticed it when he kissed her. She wrapped her fingers around the orb, hiding the raven's beady gaze.

"Essiya," she repeated with a wan smile. "The almost-Heir. The sort-of Malika. I suppose their annoying little test wouldn't have been complete without the temptation of total power."

Arin took out his dagger and started hacking at the fortress.

"The stories are wrong, you know. Mostly wrong. They trapped me on the bridge—that much is true. But I didn't 'scream so loud that the skies crashed down,'" she scoffed. "Kapastra did. They also didn't draw runes on my forehead. What a silly notion. What effect would runes have had against my magic? Also—and this is by far the most aggravating—I was *not* the 'kind and compassionate' Awal. Perhaps I was compared to those three, but I was also impatient and short-tempered, and I once tried to stab my sister for stealing all the mangoes out of my trees as a jest."

It took a beat for Arin to hear her.

She tapped her nails against the glass of the scepter. "The most consistent part of the story is the ending. I am dragged over the side of the bridge, trapped in eternal entombment. Satisfying, isn't it? I understand why nobody examined the ending too closely. After all, the alternative was unthinkable. The alternative meant the mad Awal might have walked away. Rovial, roaming the kingdoms, alive and well while the only people capable of fending against him slept beneath Sirauk. An unbearable conclusion."

"What. Are. You. Saying." Arin could scarcely force out the words.

"They didn't drag me down." She sighed. "We fought, and they killed me the only way they could."

Arin took a step back. He couldn't begin to process the concept—the very idea—

No. No, her magic had muddled her, and she would be fine as soon as she distanced herself from that infernal bridge.

"Halfway killed me, really. They tore out my magic and cast it down into Hirun. Then they ripped Rovial apart. The truth is not so pretty as the story, I'm afraid." She shrugged. "You were right about the rate of magic-madness. Once every hundred years, with widespread devastation. Rovial's magic reincarnated every century, and every century it would meet the same fate." She tapped her temple. "I feel every single life layered over mine, though they don't feel as though they belong to me. Neither does Rovial's. But the magic... the magic has always been ours."

The world tilted onto its ear, burst into flames, and suffocated Arin in the smoke.

"If you don't want to be trapped, why are you still on the bridge? The mist will take you." Arin was barely audible to his own ears, but of course, she heard it.

"You cannot begin to imagine how much I want to stand on the other side of this fortress with you," she said. Her resignation, the stark defeat, clawed back Arin's panic with a vengeance. "But there is a reason Rovial's magic has killed its host every time. That kind of power has no place in this world anymore. What kingdom could thrive beneath a leader who could never die? A leader who could decimate them with a spare thought?"

Her breath hitched, and Arin saw a spark of terror behind the facade of calm. "I can barely hear myself think behind this magic. If I walked across this fortress, it would only be a matter of time until it extinguished what was left of my humanity. My control."

She took a step back. "I will not let it win again. I will not let it trap me in my own mind."

A wisp of white curled around her ankle. Arin hammered at the fortress with a force his body shouldn't have been able to produce.

She was going to do it. Join the Awaleen in their entombment and lock her magic away beneath Sirauk.

"Let me go, Arin. I can't cross the fortress, do you understand?

If I choose to stay, it will not mean the death of a few hundred or thousand. It will spell the end of our entire world. Nobody but the Awaleen could stop Rovial's magic, and they are in the middle of enjoying their eternal slumber. This is the precise power you have fought your entire life to prevent. The exact madness you feared."

"I can find another way," Arin said, and it was the truth. "Give me time. We can mitigate your magic, seal it off. I have the cuff—"

"No! Cutting myself off from my magic was never the answer. Sefa and Marek were the answer. Dawoud, Raya, Fairel, Rory."

Softly, "You."

It was the last straw. Arin dropped his fists to the fortress, his fingers spreading against it. "If you will not stay, then take me with you." The mist wound faster and higher around her legs, threading between the rickety boards of the bridge. "Do not dare tell me I owe a duty to these kingdoms. I swore myself to *you*. My father will receive his justice. Every leader who helped facilitate the Jasad War is already dead or out of power. Someone else can handle what comes next."

"Yes, and if there is any benefit to finding out I am in possession of eternally fatal magic, it is that the person handling what comes next will not be me."

She took another step back. The mist had risen to her waist. "And why would I drag you to your death when a new life is beginning for you?"

The hand on his father's scepter contracted, crushing the orb. Glass rained into the mist and bounced off her skin harmlessly. She snapped off the raven and let the scepter drop to the ground.

For some reason, the sight of her hand without a single nick from the glass ruined the remaining ounce of disbelief Arin had clung to.

Rovial. She had *Rovial's* magic.

She balanced the raven on the flat of her palm. "I think this belongs to you."

Essiya blew gently on the raven, and Arin jerked back as the wretched pile of feathers suddenly moved.

It fluttered its wings and hopped off Essiya's palm, flying toward him. Instead of smashing against the fortress, the raven sailed straight through.

The raven slammed against—and into—Arin's chest.

The Nizahl Supreme fell to his knees, and he burned.

CHAPTER SEVENTY-TWO

ESSIYA

My time was nearly at an end. The mist had risen to my chest, and I did not want to risk Arin recovering in time to negotiate with me again. If anyone could persuade me to gamble on a matter of life or widespread extinction, it would be him. The mist had hidden him from my sight, and I accepted the harsh mercy for what it was.

I trailed my fingers along the fortress, the beat of my heart frantic against my tightening chest.

I had imagined different scenarios for the aftermath of raising the fortress. Option one: burn to death. Not ideal, but at least it would have been fast and final. Option two: go mad. Again, not ideal, but I had assumed the combined force of the Urabi would be enough to execute me before I caused any real damage.

Eternal entrapment had not been one of my scenarios. If it had been, I might have escaped in the waterfall that first week in the Gibal.

What I could not bear was the thought of leaving Jasad trapped behind me. Barricaded behind this fortress as they had been for hundreds of years, their magic dwindling on the other side, cut off from the kingdoms during the most widespread political upheaval the land had seen in centuries.

I thought about Raya opening gold-and-silver eyes, my magic coursing through a woman with purely Omalian roots.

A crack thundered across the surface of the fortress.

So much magic had been poured into this fortress. Magic that would do nothing for the people on the other side but isolate them for however much longer Jasadi magic lasted.

You can spend your entire existence frozen in one spot, squinting into the future, or you can decide to move. Pick a path and never look back.

Cracks raced over the resin surface of the Jasad fortress. The splinters grew, a low rumble sending tremors through the land.

I slammed my fist into the fortress, and it imploded.

Streaks of silver and gold rained over the crowd. Specks of it twirled in the air like bright dust, twinkling cheerily. Streaks of color raced across the sky as the magic inside the fortress crashed onto the people inside Janub Aya, subsuming them. Some of them dropped to the ground beneath the onslaught, while others started heaving. The Jasadis recovered fastest, their stores of magic revived in double, its colors shining brightest in their eyes.

Jasad's future would not be spent in hiding. It would not languish, isolated and afraid, suffocating as its magic drained away.

Without the fortress, nothing but mist stood between me and Arin.

He was bowed forward, bracing his knuckles against the ground. The raven had torn open Arin's vest and shirt, and I saw its dark imprint settling over the Commander's heart. A raven etching against his skin to match the ones on his coat.

Jeru appeared behind Arin, bending to his new Supreme. Silver and gold flickered in the guardsman's eyes. I checked behind him for Sefa and spotted Maia and Namsa, petting Sefa's hand and nudging a water pouch against her unmoving lips. My magic had crashed into her and settled like a tepid pool, forgotten beneath the storm of her grief.

The Jasadis and Nizahlans had begun to collect their dead. I saw Lateef arguing with a soldier next to Marek's body and had to turn away.

A noise of guttural agony tore out of Arin. Jeru stumbled back as gold and silver rushed through Arin's veins.

The Supreme began to change.

His skin, always sickly pale and nearly translucent, took on a healthier glow. The cuts and scrapes on his body disappeared—including the scar on his jaw from Soraya's murder attempt.

Arin threw his head back, vines of magic winding up his throat. Arin's hair—the beautiful silver hair floating around his face like his personal storm cloud, the hair that declared him anywhere he went, the hair I had twisted in my fingers in abandon—began to darken. Hair dark as the blackest night replaced the silver storm cloud, framing his lovely face.

Hanim's hair. Odd to think that if it hadn't been for Rawain draining Arin's magic, Arin might have grown up the spitting image of his mother.

Still gorgeous. Still Arin. We were both a new and old version of ourselves, now.

"Rovial's tainted tomb," Jeru whispered, awed.

I snickered.

The mist swirled around my chest. I called Jeru's name, and when he met my gaze, a new panic seemed to spark in him. I shook my head and pointed to Arin. I hoped my message was clear. I hoped he understood.

When he comes after me, stop him.

I drank in the sight of Arin one last time.

I chose you, I thought. *Even if it might not seem like it now.*

I retreated into the mist. Gripping the rope for balance, I found the spot where the Awalas had torn out Rovial's magic lifetimes ago. A part of it had died here, furious and betrayed and ravenous for revenge.

I allowed myself to listen to Jasad as I never would again. I listened to Jeru shouting for help as Arin shoved the guardsman out of his way and stormed toward the bridge. The soldiers' pounding footsteps, tackling their Supreme to the ground in a number even Arin could not overcome. The slow and sluggish rhythm of Sefa's heart, still beating despite its wounds. Efra, of all people, joining Lateef to shove the Nizahl soldier away from Marek's body and snap, "He is one of us. He died on Jasad's side. He is ours."

Warmth spread through me. I gripped the rope, leaning over the edge. They would survive this. They would be all right.

I closed my eyes and tipped over the side of the bridge.

CHAPTER SEVENTY-THREE

ESSIYA

"Is this normal? Did we sleep this long the first time?"

"Stop slapping her, Dania. She'll wake up and set us on fire."

"Again," a familiar voice groused.

I grabbed the hand resting on my arm. My eyes flashed open. They shrieked, skittering away from me like roaches under a freshly lit lamp.

I sat up, massaging my scalp and squinting. When I had my vision after Soraya stabbed me, I'd stood amid four thrones cast in darkness and suspended over a gushing river. I had expected to land somewhere grim and dark, suited toward an eternal mind brimming with regret.

Instead, I was in Essam. Lush trees around us, their branches heavy with leaves unmarked by disease or pestilence. The rotten egg smell of Hirun had disappeared, replaced by a faint lilac fragrance. The slivers of sky I could make out above the trees were clear blue.

A frog leapt onto my knee, and I needed no further evidence.

This Essam was not my Essam. A frog would never approach me in the real Essam. They had learned better.

Dania, Baira, and Kapastra stood a distance from me, watching with expressions ranging from mild distrust to naked hope. My magic's memories and my own bled together, my awe and confusion, its rage and regret, churning in the sea of history between us.

I leaned against the tree and petted the frog's head, crossing my ankles together. "So, what do we do for fun down here?"

Surprisingly, it was Kapastra who took the first step. She slid to the ground next to me. "This, mostly. We roam and we remember. Between the three of us, we have amassed quite a storage of memories to relive."

I glanced around Essam and laughed. Of course—this was my memory. My sisters had been long entombed by the time the woods looked like this. "I see."

"Sometimes, we can hear what happens in our kingdoms," Baira offered, coming to join Kapastra on the ground. It was startling to see Baira again and realize how closely she resembled Vaida.

It was strange. Half of me had started shrieking as soon as I opened my eyes to the Awalas of our kingdoms, overwhelmed at encountering the most powerful figures to ever exist in my time or any.

The other half saw three agitating siblings.

"Why did you come here, Rovial?" Dania remained rooted to the spot. "Why now?"

"It seemed like a good time." I rubbed the heel of my hand against my heart. "Rovial is gone. I have his memories, but they are piled against thousands of others. They belong to my magic, but Essiya belongs to me."

"You are your magic."

"Would you calm down, Dania?" Kapastra snapped. "She just had seven thousand years' worth of memories shoved into her head."

Good to know several millennia's worth of sleep had not done much to improve everyone's temper.

Dania rolled her eyes. "Fine."

"Don't listen to Dania," Baira said in her lilting, breathy voice. "She felt incredibly guilty for killing you. We all did. We kept hoping your memories would catch up to your magic someday."

"Hoping and fearing," Kapastra corrected. "But you seem less intent on murder and destruction, which is a relief."

Dania scuffed her foot on the dirt. Perhaps it was not too terrible of a blend, my magic's memories and my own. Through the former, I saw a petulant little sister too prideful to admit her guilt. Through the latter, I saw one of the young wards in the keep, standing outside my door to confess their theft of my sesame seed candies.

"I have too many grudges in this life to keep track of the ones from previous lives," I said. "Besides, I vaguely remember planning to kill you at the time."

Dania settled on the grass with a sigh. "Fair enough."

The tension broken, the Awalas regaled me with stories of their lives in eternal slumber and peppered me with questions about their kingdoms. They already knew about the faded magic, but the political turmoil of the last century or so had gone largely unnoticed.

They were, in a word, displeased.

"You could have done a *little* more killing while you were up there," Kapastra complained. "Nobody would have mourned a tin-brained buffoon like Felix."

"I killed him eventually," I reassured her.

Even as I spoke about my life, I could feel it receding, drawing away like a tide recalled to sea.

It would have scared me more had I not just recovered an ocean's worth of lost memories. The tide would always return.

I told them about the Alcalah and Dawoud. About Arin and the kitmer. Speaking of him was like chewing glass, and I quickly skipped to waking up in the mountains.

"Fareed was handsome," Kapastra said at one point. "If his descendant looks anything like him, I wouldn't mind my magic sending him into minor catatonia for a kiss."

Baira threw a handful of torn grass into Kapastra's face. "Stop. It is obvious thinking of her lost lover hurts her."

Dania and I wrinkled our noses in unison. *Lover,* she mouthed, and I shoved her shoulder, the two of us exchanging a grin.

"I suppose there's no way we can ever go back?" I asked mildly. "Dania, the last time I saw you, you were talking to Kapastra about a prophecy."

My sisters glanced at one another. A delicate wariness descended over them.

"We came down here to protect our kingdoms from the dangers of what unchecked power could create." Dania's speech was too measured to be anything other than rehearsed, and I wondered how frequently they had recited it to one another. "While we ruled, we plunged our kingdoms into war after war. We cannot die, nor can we be killed. The people in our care mattered less and less, because eventually they would die. Their lifetime of misery was a blink of an eye for us. At the time, entombing ourselves seemed to be the only solution."

My chest constricted. "But not now?"

"Our kingdoms don't have magic anymore," Baira said softly. "They are barren in the one resource we carry in excess."

"The only way we can rejoin their world is if our magic is equal to theirs and not greater," Kapastra said.

The frog on my knee leapt off with an offended huff as I curled my legs into my chest. "What do you mean?"

"We would drain our magic—"

"Absolutely not." I barely recognized the chilling rage in my voice. "You will not separate me from my magic again. It's *mine*."

Baira raised placating hands. "We aren't taking away your magic. We would just... give it a boundary. Right now, our magic knows no limits. It is a fountain with no basin."

"A well without a bottom," I mused.

Kapastra jumped in. "But Dania thinks we can pump magic back into our kingdoms. Drain the excess out of ourselves and funnel it back into our people."

"You mean transferring our magic?" The fortress. Raya.

"Exactly."

"Overspending magic is what devoured my humanity the first time," I pointed out.

"We do not intend to spend it. Consider it…repurposing. It won't regenerate. In either case, if it proves a flawed strategy, it isn't as though we are in a position to harm anyone."

"How long would it take?" I asked. "I want—I don't want to emerge when everyone I love is dead."

Too many already are, I almost added.

At the hurt look on Baira's face, I quickly amended, "Everyone mortal, I mean."

"I cannot offer you a definitive date," Dania said. "But we have no other demands on our time here. We can easily devote the whole of our days toward accomplishing this."

"It is only a theory," Kapastra said.

"Excellent," I said. "I love a good theory."

I burst into tears.

My sisters immediately crowded around me. Dania wrapped her arms around my shoulders, leaning her head against mine. Baira pulled my palm to her cheek and drew soothing circles on the back of my hand. Kapastra, who hated touch as much as I once had, patted my knee and attempted to distract me by asking questions in various dead languages.

I wasn't alone. I might not be where I wanted to be, but I was not alone.

"Tell us about everyone you love," Dania murmured, drawing a curl away from the warpath of my tears. "Tell us about the lives of Sylvia and Essiya."

"We have plenty of time," Baira added.

I laughed, wiping my eyes with the heels of my hands.

"You can show us, too, if you'd like," Kapastra said. My most somber sister gestured at the scene around us. "We can help you remember this time."

And they did.

LUKUB
ONE MONTH AFTER THE ENTOMBMENT

Sefa sat before a council of strangers in a shoddily sewn dress, and she read the scroll set in front of her a fourth time.

"This isn't right," Sefa said, also for the fourth time. "Can this even be done?"

The sour-faced man by the name of Biyad, who had summoned Sefa to the Ivory Palace with a vague and threatening letter, gestured at the three men beside him. "She had it written, witnessed, and signed two weeks before Sedain. There is no law in Lukub preventing the crown from being passed to someone outside the line of inheritance, and the line died with Sultana Vaida. She chose you for Lukub's throne, and it is our duty to uphold her wishes."

"We don't know if she is dead," Sefa said. "Her body was never recovered."

Biyad sighed. "We did not summon you until we had exhausted every effort to find the Sultana."

Sefa traced the dainty signature at the bottom of the scroll. Sefa was not fit to rule a room, let alone a kingdom. What had Vaida been thinking?

Sefa could scarcely convince herself to put food in her mouth. Dark circles cratered the bottom of her sunken eyes, and she had lost any sense of time. She rarely left the bed Lateef had offered her in Jasad, and making the trek to Lukub had only worsened her sleeping issues.

Her body might be sitting here, but the most important parts of Sefa had buried themselves beside Marek. His chest lay still, so she stopped breathing. He decayed, and so did she.

If any meaningful part of Sefa had tried to survive, the reminder of Essiya's fate slaughtered it. Sefa had drawn a shroud over her remaining scraps, laid down, and stayed still for a very, very long time. It wasn't until Jeru poured water over her head that Sefa had spluttered back to life.

"I made him a promise that no harm would come to you," he'd said, tossing the empty bucket onto her bed. "I intend to keep my word."

As Sefa shrank before the Lukub council, the cavern of the unknown future cracking open in her chest and threatening to swallow her whole yet again, a hand settled over her shoulder.

Jeru scanned the scroll. "Give her a chance to think."

"Lukub is in turmoil," Biyad said. "Our Sultana is gone, the palace is in disrepair, and the rise of the Jasad crown is cause for grave concern."

An arrow of anger pierced through the shroud of numbness around Sefa. "Lateef—Malik Lateef," Sefa corrected, "has done nothing to earn your grave concern. Jasad has done nobody harm."

"Their magic—"

"Does nobody harm," Sefa hissed. "I have it, too. So does Jeru. So do hundreds of Nizahl soldiers. Do we all intend you harm?"

Tears suddenly choked her. How dare they? After everything.

Sefa had asked Lateef what his magic felt like, and he described a gentle rhythm, pulsing in tune to his own heart. Easy to ignore, but easy to find if you went searching. The bits of magic Sefa had absorbed from the fortress felt like a finger she had suddenly grown out of her elbow, and she had not quite figured out what to do with it.

Meanwhile, Jeru used the magic he gained on the battlefield of Nuzret Kamel regularly and enthusiastically. Just this morning, he had drained his stores trying to turn his horse's coat the same color green as the trees. "For camouflage," he had insisted.

Sefa stared at the scroll, the neat handwriting so at odds with the woman who had penned it.

My palace was built by an Awala who crafted illusions more perfect and persuasive than any reality.

I think knowing what is real is beyond the reach of mortals and Awaleen alike.

The age of illusions was over. Lukub would not spend the rest of its existence staring into a mirror, struggling to understand what was real. No Ruby Hounds and hollow power, no spies and wells.

It would not hide itself behind shrouds.

"I accept."

Biyad blinked. Jeru's hand flexed in surprise, but he gave no reaction otherwise.

Sefa raised dry eyes toward Lukub's council. "I accept the crown of Lukub."

One week later, on an unremarkable summer day, Sefa became the Sultana of Lukub.

Thousands attended her coronation, eager to witness the marvel of a fugitive and former vagrant ascending to one of the highest seats in the land.

The new Queen of Omal came. An upbeat woman with an impressively square jaw and hands familiar with hard labor had been selected by the lower villages to sit on Queen Hanan's empty throne. The Omal council, outnumbered and outmatched, had approved the appointment. She shook Sefa's hand enthusiastically, chattering about her first childhood visit to Lukub until a servant carrying a tray of talwith tempted her away.

Sorn and his new wife came. Though Sefa had passingly encountered the Orbanian Champion at some point before the third trial, she barely recognized the new Diya of Orban.

It was rumored Sorn would soon ascend to his father's throne. His marriage to Diya, a lower villager, had won him temporary amnesty from the rebellions across Orban. His new ordinances aimed at curbing the unchecked power of the khawaga and resuming trade with Jasad had quelled the remainder of the unrest. Of all the kingdoms, Orban experienced the least bloody transition of power.

Diya stopped by Sefa's dais, studying the ruby spires of her crown. "Is it heavy? It looks heavy."

Sefa startled, touching the rays absently. "No, not really."

"Hmm," Diya said. Light brown eyes studied Sefa with disconcerting attentiveness. "I liked her. Sylvia." She adjusted the axe hanging from her belt. "Orban will not turn its back on Jasad."

The future Queen of Orban left before Sefa could scrape together a response, the warrior's firm stride carrying her out of sight.

Malik Lateef could not attend, but he sent Sefa his congratulations and a reminder that Usr Jasad was always open to her.

Supreme Arin of Nizahl did not show.

OMAL

TWO YEARS AFTER THE ENTOMBMENT

Fairel trailed her fingers over the languid surface of Hirun River. School started tomorrow, and she most decidedly did not want to go. Why did she need to learn about yet another battle between the kingdoms? What did it matter if she knew how to calculate sums off the top of her head? Fairel would much rather help Rory around the shop and spend her breaks shooting arrows from the highest spots she could climb.

A splash caught Fairel's sleeve as a frog leapt out of Hirun, its little legs blurring in its panic. Another joined it, then four more.

Fairel sat up, the basket of ingredients beside her forgotten. What on earth?

The surface of Hirun bubbled, and Fairel shrieked as hundreds of frogs shot out of the river. Before she could scramble away, streaks of pale blue surged over the water's surface.

Fairel snatched her hand from the river, but it was too late. The blue coated her hand, sinking into her skin.

Hirun churned again, and Fairel grabbed her cane, raising it toward the river. Why had she left her bow and arrow at the keep?

Raya was always chastising her about carrying them around. She was going to feel *so* guilty when a swarm of crazed frogs murdered Fairel because she wasn't allowed to bring her bow and arrows.

What emerged from the river was not a frog.

Four stout legs hefted a reptilian creature out of the water. Its blue-and-white scaled body stretched as long as the trees behind Fairel, glittered as brightly as diamonds cast across the sunlit surface of the river.

Petrified, Fairel clutched her cane and watched the beast slither out of the river. She had seen renditions of this creature twined around Kapastra's shoulders on every mural in Mahair. She had studied the fatal effects of its venom in class—the same class she was now certainly going to miss, because she would have the excuse of being dead.

The rochelya aimed a slitted glare at Fairel. Her blue hand turned crushing around her cane.

A strange feeling passed through Fairel. It was almost like falling asleep. Black dots swam in Fairel's vision as the glow around Fairel's hand traveled up her arm and disappeared under her sleeve.

In the river's reflection, Fairel's eyes swirled blue and white.

She gasped as her cane twisted in her grip. In its place, a bow materialized, shinier and bigger than the one she left in the keep. Two arrows lay across her lap, waiting to be notched.

Magic? Had she just—yes. But how?

She lifted the bow to her shoulder, fingers tight around an unloosed arrow. Fairel tracked the rochelya as it meandered up the banks of Hirun, following the terrified frogs into Essam.

When she was sure it was gone, she lowered her arm and stared at the river in disbelief.

"Nobody is going to believe me."

JASAD

SIX YEARS AFTER THE ENTOMBMENT

"Are you sure about this?" Sefa murmured.

Lateef was glad the Sultana had been able to travel for the festivities. He had missed the sad little seamstress.

The grief permanently clinging to the Sultana had shifted since the last time she visited. The density of it had eased, allowing sparks of humor and interest to occasionally surface from the drowning darkness. He imagined in time, he might even be able to look at her without seeing it etched in her eyes.

"I am," Lateef answered. Attending the Summit in Orban had not been without its challenges, given the circumstances of the last Summit. If the Supreme and Sultana had not been in attendance, Lateef would not have made the journey. "Magic has returned across the kingdoms. We have traded peacefully for years, and the other rulers have opened their borders to us. Signing the new accords simply memorialized the terms of peace."

"Have you seen him since the Summit?"

Lateef did not need to ask who she meant. "No."

Children ran up the translucent steps of Usr Jasad, climbing for a better view of Qayida Namsa as she soared over Usr Jasad on the back of her kitmer. A halawany pushed his cart of sweets through the crowd, passing out sesame seed candies and chunks of halawa.

"Have *you* seen him since the Summit?" Lateef couldn't help asking.

"Yes, about two months ago. I visited the Citadel for his birthday." Sefa pushed a strand of hair behind her ear. "I didn't want him to spend it alone."

"He seemed well at the Summit."

Her gaze tunneled, going somewhere Lateef could not follow. "He does what he needs to do, and nothing more," Sefa said quietly. "It is like watching the sun take its rotation across the sky. He is sure and steady, but nothing…touches him. Nothing moves him. If it weren't for Ehal and Niseeba, I think he could go years without interacting with another living creature."

Niseeba. Lateef snorted, amused each time he heard the kitmer's name. The Jasad Malika may have been an odd woman, but nobody could accuse her of a bad sense of humor.

"He is an excellent Supreme," Lateef said solicitously.

His own relationship with the Nizahl Supreme had been a fraught one. The young man was brilliant, as clever and determined as the stories had suggested, but Lateef had been present when Essiya vanished into the mist. He had seen Arin after he recouped the magic his father had stolen from him. Lateef had witnessed dozens of soldiers throw themselves on top of their ruler to prevent him from running onto the bridge. Most importantly, Lateef had never forgotten seeing the Supreme fight his way out and tear through every soldier who stood between him and the bridge. If Sefa herself had not stepped into his path, Arin of Nizahl would surely have vanished into Sirauk's mist six years ago.

She had never told Lateef what she said to Arin that day in Janub Aya, and Lateef had never asked.

Efra elbowed his way through the crowd, Maia hoisted on his shoulders. She cheered Namsa's name as a fleet of kitmers joined the Qayida, their wings beating in perfect synchrony.

"He will recover," Lateef said. "It will not always be like this."

Sefa's quiet laugh broke Lateef's heart. "Do you promise?"

Lateef wrapped his arm around her shoulders. "I promise."

The Sultana leaned her head against him. "Will you come to the Citadel with me for his next birthday?"

"I will," Lateef said. He paused. "What kind of gift does one purchase for Arin of Nizahl?"

The kitmers sailed parallel to the steps of Usr Jasad, the cheers of a thousand spectators chasing them through the air. The first of Essiya's festivals, and the first time Sefa's smile did not carry the ghost of grief behind it.

EPILOGUE

ARIN

TEN YEARS LATER

Arin had never given much thought to what he might face if love ever found him.

It was a word he vaguely understood, upon which people seemed to place great importance, and the combination had been a recurring point of frustration in his otherwise organized understanding of human nature.

He knew the general shapes of it—the back of his mother's hand on his brow when he fell ill; rainy childhood days spent in his father's chambers, working on his maps while Rawain read, their breathing the only sound for hours; Isra's worry and Rawain's pride when Arin excelled above his peers. He had thought if love found him, it would be more of the same. Just another bruise—something fleeting, painful if pressed, easy to hide.

Nobody warned him.

Why hadn't they told him that love was not a soft and gentle wind, but a storm determined to rip you apart and build its home in the wreckage? That it brought with it uninvited guests, new fears and worries and paranoias beyond the reach of any reason.

How in those early days, before he knew what was happening,

he would lose his breath at the thought of a future without her. A future where the guests would be gone, but so would his new home. The home she had carved inside him, where the air smelled like her hair and the bells sounded like her laugh. A place where he could rest until he was old and weary, where he could only sleep with his hand settled over her heart, because even so many years later, that steady pulse was the only pillar Arin would ever lean on.

Death, he learned, did not change anything. It didn't destroy their home; it simply barred Arin from entering. It meant years waiting on the steps. Days where Arin's wrath would flare out of his control, and he would ride into Essam until he became safe for others to be around again. Nights where, if he managed to go to sleep, he would just as often wake up gasping.

Maybe nobody warned him because they hoped they would never have to. Maybe they knew Arin's love, like everything else about him, was made to frighten. Maybe they understood that if it found him and he lost it, what would be left of Arin would not be worth salvaging.

You don't warn an injured horse before you swing the axe. Maybe that was why nobody warned Arin what he might face if love ever found him.

As usual, Ehal came to a stop a few paces away from the front of Sirauk Bridge. Wheeling above them, Niseeba crowed in victory. Arin usually took his excursions to Sirauk by flight, and he suspected the kitmer was jealous he had chosen Ehal for this journey.

Arin slid from his mount, patting the horse's neck. "Ignore her. You took me much farther than any other horse would."

Arin didn't mind the added travel time of coming on horseback. It gave him the opportunity to stop by the market in Har Adiween and buy out the stock from the vendor selling sesame seed candies.

She liked to joke that Arin's one visit to Sirauk every year kept her in business.

She'd been surprised to see him this time. Understandable, since he had already made his trip to Sirauk four months ago, on Sylvia's birthday. Essiya's birthday had passed more recently, and he'd spent it with Sefa.

Arin's gratitude at having the bridge to himself came striped in resentment. As soon as magic had begun to trickle back into the kingdoms, they had forgotten about the anniversary of a day they claimed changed history. They turned the page on Nuzret Kamel and never looked back.

Arin laughed softly. Perhaps he was simply jealous. Time had continued to turn after Nuzret Kamel, and everyone turned with it.

Everyone except Arin.

The life Arin led had not been touched by anything as merciful as time. As Supreme, he had propelled his kingdom toward a future their founder would be proud of—a future better than the one his father had intended. As Commander, he had helped navigate the nebulous future after Nuzret Kamel, forging bonds with Jasad and the newly appointed rulers in Lukub, Omal, and Orban. He had done his best to keep his promise to Fareed.

But in every other sense, Arin had not taken a single step beyond this spot in ten years.

The mist swirled against his boots. Ten years ago, the fortress had stood where Arin was. Where it had fallen, the grass grew in brilliant blades of gold and silver.

No one had ever emerged from the mist.

It had been repeated to him more times than Arin cared to count. As though he were some delusional child or pining fool. As though he didn't *understand*.

He understood perfectly. Nobody ever emerged from the mist. Sirauk Bridge did not entertain survivors. This was reality.

Arin had deliberately decided it would not be his.

He didn't know if the mist would fall today. Malik Lateef had barred any travel toward Sirauk for the entire week, concerned people would forget that the mist might only fall for a total of two minutes during Nuzret Kamel, leaving them stuck on the bridge if they flocked onto it in great numbers.

To Arin, he had written a short note: *We also remember her today. Be careful.*

Arin pulled his necklace from under his vest and wrapped his fingers around the worn beads of the fig. It never left his neck, dangling inches above the black raven etched over his heart.

Sefa had wanted to come with him today. Arin rarely refused the Sultana of Lukub anything, but under no circumstances would he bring her to the site of Marek's death. Ten years, and his ghost still haunted the Sultana. Arin would not deliver her to her grief.

He also did not want to bring along someone who believed Essiya dead. No matter what she claimed, Arin knew she only wanted to come because she was worried. She worried every time he visited.

"She is not coming back, Arin. Nobody who enters the mist returns," Sefa had shouted once. "Every year, you wait. And every year, you come back from the bridge as broken as you were that first day."

Arin had not spoken to her for eight months afterward.

Arin's kingdom thrived. His people were fed, sheltered, and safe. The kingdoms had not seen a significant conflict since the previous Nuzret Kamel, and Arin had spent years working with rulers he barely tolerated to ensure a smooth transition for the widespread return of magic, both within the kingdoms and between them. He had done everything that needed to be done, dedicated the whole of his time and attention to their people's shared success, and Sefa could not grant him one day a year?

A splatter of mud on the side of the basket caught his eye, and

Arin swept it clean with the handkerchief in his pocket. Arin never used his own magic. He frequently found himself wishing Essiya had just taken the scepter with her. She had given Arin back a piece of himself that could not fit into any corner Arin cast it into.

Tightening his grip on the basket, Arin stepped onto Sirauk Bridge. The mist billowed around him, pale breath winding beneath his coat and through the black strands of his hair.

He was not as woefully tragic as Sefa and Jeru believed. He knew the Awaleen had been entombed for thousands of years. He knew it was almost impossible they would rise again, let alone within his lifetime.

But it should have been almost impossible for magic to return to the kingdoms.

It should have been almost impossible for the Nizahl Heir to find the Jasad Heir hiding in a tiny village in Omal.

It should have been almost impossible for him to fall in love with a woman who maddened him at every turn.

It had taken Arin too long to recognize that the best parts of his life existed in the *almost*. They existed here—beyond the reach of certainty, on the outskirts of doubt, swaying over the cliff of catastrophe.

His coat hung so heavy with frost, Arin did not notice when some of the warmth returned to his stiff limbs. He did not register the rays of sunlight piercing the thinning mist, golden pools gathering over the damp boards of the bridge. The boards he could see again for the first time in ten years, connecting Sirauk Bridge to the dense thicket of trees on the other side of the swaying planks.

Arin watched the mist dissipate, and he feared Sefa might have been right. His heart had begun to thump erratically, beating stronger than it had in a decade.

Ten years he had spent navigating the nexus of duty and despair, learning to balance himself on its fractures. Ten years in constant motion, never allowing anything as dangerous as hope to rise between the cracks long enough to change the path forward into a cliff.

In the center of the bridge, the mist melted around four figures.

One of them took an unsteady step toward him, curls catching on the rising wind. A slow grin spread over her face. Dark eyes fastened on to him as the sun cleared the last of the mist from Sirauk Bridge.

And Arin finally allowed himself to fall.

"Welcome home, Suraira."

ACKNOWLEDGMENTS

There are so many people to thank for pushing this book—and me—across the finish line.

Thank you to my rock star agent, Jennifer Azantian, who champions my work (and listens to my increasingly rambling voice notes) every step of the way. To Alex Weiss and the entire ALA team, who never stop making moves and bringing the coolest news to my inbox.

To my wonderful editor, Alyea Canada—I can't begin to thank you enough for the patience, enthusiasm, and keen insight you've offered me and *The Jasad Crown*. Working with you has been a joy.

A huge thank-you to the Orbit team for their passion and hard work! Angela Man, Rachel Goldstein, Kelley Frodel, Alexia Mazis, Natassja Haught, and so many more talented individuals helped bring this book to life. Thanks to the immensely talented Lisa Marie Pompilio and Mike Heath, who created the most gorgeous covers for the Scorched Throne series. To the fantastic Jenni Hill and the rest of the Orbit UK team—I am endlessly grateful to have your support and enthusiasm.

To Nivia Evans, I am forever thankful to you for seeing the heart of *The Jasad Heir* and launching this journey with me.

They say it takes a village, but this book? It took an entire galaxy, and I've been so blessed to have a constellation of amazing people in my life. Jess Parra (Javert, Lestat, and Claudia stickers and twenty-minute voice notes are a necessary part of my day); Hannah V. Sawyerr, who always asks "Okay, but what if?" whenever I try to rationalize away my dreams; Ream Shukairy and Maeeda Khan, you guys make navigating this industry so much more fun (retreat when?); Abby H., who's been rescuing me from rabbit holes since we were eighteen.

To my family, to my family, to my family. My mom, who spent days in 2023 packing preorder incentive envelopes while I took the bar exam. My dad, who'll troubleshoot plot ideas with me when I can't sleep. To Hend (insisted on more Arin/Sylvia in *The Jasad Crown*), Yusuf (will roast fiction as a whole and then proceed to set up my monitors and build my bookshelves), and Hanan (I miss looming over your shoulder while you read)—I am lucky to have you guys as my ~~minions~~ siblings.

To every reader, bookseller, and librarian who picked up *The Jasad Heir* and connected with these characters, who shouted about the book and stuck around to see the journey through—so many of my dreams have come true at your hands. There aren't enough pages to describe what it meant to me to see all the love you've shown for *The Jasad Heir*: the memes, messages, goose-related content, recommendation videos, mood boards, character art. Sorry for making your favorite characters suffer.

الحمد والشكر لله

extras

meet the author

SARA HASHEM is an American Egyptian writer from Southern California, where she spent many sunny days holed up indoors with a book. Sara's love for fantasy and magical realms emerged during the two years her family lived in Egypt. When she isn't busy naming stray cats in her neighborhood after her favorite authors, Sara can be found buried under coffee-ringed notebooks.

Find out more about Sara Hashem and other Orbit authors by registering for the free monthly newsletter at orbitbooks.net.

if you enjoyed
THE JASAD CROWN
look out for
THE FOXGLOVE KING
The Nightshade Crown: Book One
by
Hannah Whitten

In this gilded, gothic, and darkly romantic new epic fantasy series from New York Times *bestselling author Hannah Whitten, a young woman's secret power to raise the dead plunges her into the dangerous world of the Sainted King's royal court.*

Lore has been living by her wits since she was a child, running poisons for the cartel that took her in, avoiding the attention of the law, and keeping her affinity for death magic a secret. Because Mortem is a rare and illicit commodity, and using it could mean death.

When a job goes wrong, Lore suddenly finds herself thrust into a lavish court where no one can be believed and even fewer can be trusted. There, Lore must navigate an intricate web of politics, religion, and

extras

forbidden romance to solve a mystery more dangerous and twisted than she can even imagine.

CHAPTER ONE

No one is more patient than the dead.

—Auverrani proverb

Every month, Michal claimed he'd struck a deal with the landlord, and every month, Nicolas sent one of his sons to collect anyway. The sons must've drawn straws—this month's unfortunate was Pierre, the youngest and spottiest of the bunch, and he trudged up the street of Dellaire's Harbor District with the air of one approaching a guillotine.

Lore could work with that.

A dressing gown that had seen better days dripped off one shoulder as Lore leaned against the doorframe and watched him approach. Pierre's eyes kept drifting to where the fabric gaped, and she kept having to bite the inside of her cheek so she didn't laugh. Apparently, a crosshatch of silvery scars from back-alley knife fights didn't deter the man when presented with bare skin.

She had other, more interesting scars. But she kept her palm closed tight.

A cool breeze blew off the ocean, and Lore suppressed a shiver. Pierre didn't seem to spare any thought for why she'd exited the house barely dressed when mornings near the harbor always carried a chill, even in summer. An easy mark in more ways than one.

"Pierre!" Lore shot him a dazzling grin, the same one that made Michal's eyes simultaneously go heated and then narrow before he asked what she wanted. Another twist against the doorframe, another seemingly casual pose, another bite of wind that made a curse bubble behind her teeth. "It's the end of the month already?"

Michal should be dealing with this. It was his damn row house. But the drop he'd made for Gilbert last night had been all the way in the Northwest Ward, so Lore let him sleep.

Besides, waking up early had given her time to go through Michal's pockets for the drop coordinates. She'd taken them to the tavern on the corner and left them with Frederick the bartender, who'd been on Val's payroll for as long as Lore could remember. Val would be sending someone to pick them up before the sun fully rose, and someone else to grab Gilbert's poison drop before his client could.

Lore was good at her job.

Right now, her job was making sure the man she'd been living with for a year so she could spy on his boss didn't get evicted.

"I—um—yes, yes it is." Pierre managed to fix his eyes to her own, through obviously conscious effort. "My father... um, he said this time he means it, and..."

Lore let her expression fall by careful degrees, first into confusion, then shock, then sorrow. "Oh," she murmured, wrapping her arms around herself and turning her face away to show a length of pale white neck. "This month, of all months."

She didn't elaborate. She didn't need to. If there was anything Lore had learned in twenty-three years alive, ten spent on the streets of Dellaire, it was that men generally preferred you to be a set piece in the story they made up, rather than an active player.

From the corner of her eye, she saw Pierre's pale brows draw together, a deepening blush lighting the skin beneath his freckles. They were all moon-pale, Nicolas's boys. It made their blushes look like something viral.

His gaze went past her to the depths of the dilapidated row house beyond. Sunrise shadows hid everything but the dust motes twisting in light shards. Not that there was much to see back there, anyway. Michal was still asleep upstairs, and his sister, Elle, was sprawled on the couch, a wine bottle in her hand and a slightly musical snore on her lips. It looked like any other row house on this street, coming apart at the seams and full of people who skirted just under the law to get by.

Or very far under it, as the case may be.

"Is there an illness?" Pierre kept his voice hushed, low. His face tried for sympathetic, but it looked more like he'd put bad milk in his coffee. "A child, maybe? I know Michal rents this house, not you. Is it his?"

Lore's brows shot up. In all the stories she'd let men spin about her, *that* was a first—Pierre must have sex on the brain if he jumped straight to pregnancy. But beggars couldn't be choosers. She gently laid a hand on her abdomen and let that be answer enough. It wasn't technically a lie if she let him draw his own conclusions.

She was past caring about lying, anyway. Lore was damned whether or not she kept her spiritual record spotless. Might as well lean into it.

"Oh, you poor girl." Pierre was probably younger than she was, and here he went clucking like a mother hen. Lore managed to keep her eyes from rolling, but only just. "And with a poison runner? You know he won't be able to take care of you."

Lore bit the inside of her cheek again, hard.

Her apparent distress made Pierre bold. "You could come with me," he said. "My father could help you find work, I'm sure." He raised his hand, settled it on her bare shoulder.

And every nerve in Lore's body seized.

It was abrupt and unexpected enough for her to shudder, to shake off his hand in a motion that didn't fit her soft, vulnerable narrative. She'd grown used to feeling this reaction to dead things—stone, metal, cloth. Corpses, when she couldn't avoid them. It was natural to sense Mortem in something dead, no matter how unpleasant, and at this point she could hide her reaction, keep it contained. She'd had enough practice.

But she shouldn't feel Mortem in a *living* man, not one who wasn't at death's door. Her shock was quick and sharp, and chased with something else—the scent of foxglove. So strong, he must've been dosed mere minutes before arriving.

And he wanted to disparage poison runners. Hypocrite.

extras

Her fingers closed around his wrist, twisted, forced him to his knees. It happened quick, quick enough for him to slip on a stray pebble and send one leg out at an awkward angle, for a strangled "*Shit!*" to echo through the morning streets of Dellaire's Harbor District.

Lore crouched so they were level. Now that she knew what to look for, it was obvious in his eyes, bloodshot and glassy; in the heartbeat thumping slow and irregular beneath her palm. He'd gone to one of the cheap deathdealers, one who didn't know how to properly dose their patrons. The veins at the corners of Pierre's eyes were barely touched with gray, so he hadn't been given enough poison for any kind of life extension, and certainly not enough to possibly grasp the power waiting at death's threshold.

He probably wasn't after those things, anyway. Most people his age just wanted the high.

The dark threads of Mortem under Pierre's skin twisted against Lore's grip, stirred to waking by the poison in his system. Mortem was dormant in everyone—the essence of death, the power born of entropy, just waiting to flood your body on the day it failed—but the only way to use it, to bend it to your will, was to nearly die.

If you weren't after the power or the euphoric feeling poison could give you, then you were after the extra years. Properly dosed, poison could balance your body on the cusp of life and death, and that momentary concession to Mortem could, paradoxically, extend your life. Not that the life you got in exchange was one of great quality—half-stone, your veins clotted with rock, making your blood rub through them like a cobblestone skinning a knee.

Whatever Pierre had been after when he visited a deathdealer this morning, he hadn't paid enough to get it. If he'd gotten a true poison high, he'd be slumped in an alley somewhere, not asking her for rent. Rent that was higher than she remembered it being, now that she thought of it.

"Here's what's going to happen," Lore murmured. "You are going to tell Nicolas that we've paid up for the next six months, or I am going to tell him you've been spending his coin on deathdealers."

Fuck Michal's ineffectual bargains with the landlord. She'd just make one of her own.

Pierre's eyes widened, his lids poison-heavy. "How—"

"You stink of foxglove and your eyes look more like windows." Not exactly true, since she hadn't noticed until she'd sensed the Mortem, but by the time he could examine himself, the effect would've worn off anyway. "Anyone can take one look at you and know, Pierre, even though your deathdealer barely gave you enough to make you tingle. I'd be surprised if you got five extra minutes tacked on for *that*, so I hope the high was worth it."

The boy gaped, the open mouth under his window-glass eyes making his face look fishlike. He'd undoubtedly paid a handsome sum for the pinch of foxglove he'd taken. If she wasn't so good at spying for Val, Lore might've become a deathdealer herself. They made a whole lot of money for doing a whole lot of jack shit.

Pierre's unfortunate blush spread down his neck. "I can't— He'll ask where the money is—"

"I'm confident an industrious young man like yourself can come up with it somewhere." A flick of her fingers, and Lore let him go.

Pierre stumbled up on shaky legs and straightened his mussed shirt. The gray veins at the corners of his eyes were already fading back to blue-green. "I'll try," he said, voice just as tremulous as the rest of him. "I can't promise he'll believe me."

Lore gave him a winning smile. Standing, she yanked up the shoulder of her dressing gown. "He better."

Pierre didn't run down the street, but he walked very fast.

As the sun rose higher, the Harbor District slowly woke up— bundles of cloth stirred in dark corners, drunks coaxed awake by light and sea breeze. In the row house across the street, Lore heard the telltale sighs of Madam Brochfort's girls starting their daily squabbles over who got the washtub first, and any minute now at least two straggling patrons would be politely but firmly escorted outside.

"Pierre?" she called when he was halfway down the street. He turned, lips pressed together, clearly considering what other things she might blackmail him with.

extras

"A word of advice." She turned toward Michal's row house in a flutter of faded dressing gown. "The real deathdealers have morgues in the back. Death's scales are easy to tip."

❦

Elle was awake, but only just. She squinted from beneath a pile of gold curls through the light-laden dust, paint still smeared across her lips. "Whassat?"

"As if you don't know." Lore shook out the hand that had touched Pierre's shoulder, trying to banish pins and needles. It'd grown easier for her to sense Mortem recently, and she wasn't fond of the development. She gave her hand one more firm shake before heading into the kitchen. "End of the month, Elle-Flower."

There was barely enough coffee in the chipped ceramic pot for one cup. Lore poured all of it into the stained cloth she used as a strainer and balled it in her fingers as she put the kettle over the fire. If there was only one cup of coffee in this house, she'd be the one drinking it.

"Don't call me that." Elle groaned as she shifted to sit up. She'd fallen asleep in her dancer's tights, and a long run traced up each calf. It'd piss her off once she noticed, but the patrons of the Foghorn and Fiddle down the street wouldn't care. One squinting look into the wine bottle to make sure it was empty and Elle shoved off the couch to stand. "Michal isn't awake, we don't have to pretend we like each other."

Lore snorted. In the year she'd been living with Michal, it'd become very obvious that she'd never get along with his sister. It didn't bother Lore. Her relationship with Michal was built on a lie, a sand foundation with no hope of holding, so why try to make friends? As soon as Val gave the word, she'd be gone.

Elle pushed past her into the kitchen, the spiderweb cracks on the windows refracting veined light on the tattered edges of her tulle skirt. She peered into the pot. "No coffee?"

Lore tightened her hand around the cloth knotted in her fist. "Afraid not."

"Bleeding *God*." Elle flopped onto one of the chairs by the pockmarked kitchen table. For a dancer, she was surprisingly ungraceful when sober. "I'll take tea, then."

"*Surely* you don't expect me to get it for you."

A grumble and a roll of bright-blue eyes as Elle slinked her way toward the cupboard. While her back was turned, Lore tucked the straining cloth into the lip of her mug and poured hot water over it, hoping Elle was too residually drunk to recognize the scent.

Still grumbling, Elle scooped tea that was little more than dust into another mug. "Well?" She took the kettle from Lore without looking at her and apparently without smelling her coffee. "How'd it go? Is Michal finally going to have to spend money on something other than alcohol and betting at the boxing ring?"

"Not on rent, at least." Lore kept her back turned as she tugged the straining cloth and the tiny knot of coffee grounds from her cup and stuffed it in her pocket. "We're paid up for six months."

"Is that why you look so disheveled?" Elle's mouth pulled into a self-satisfied moue. "He could get it cheaper across the street."

"The dishevelment is the fault of your brother, actually." Lore turned and leaned against the counter. "And barbs about Madam's girls don't suit you, Elle-Flower. It's work like any other. To think otherwise just proves you dull."

Another eye roll. Elle made a face when she sipped her weak tea, and sharp satisfaction hitched Lore's smile higher. She took a long, luxurious swallow of coffee and drifted toward the stairs. There'd been a message waiting for her at the tavern—Val needed her help with a drop today. It was risky business, having her work while she was deep undercover with another operation, but hands were low. People kept getting hired out from under them on the docks.

And Lore had skills that no one else did.

She'd have to come up with an excuse for why she'd be gone all day, but if she woke Michal up with some kissing, he wouldn't question her further. She found herself smiling at the idea. She liked kissing Michal. That was dangerous.

The smile dropped.

extras

The stairs of the row house were rickety, like pretty much everything else in the structure, and the fourth one squeaked something awful. Lore winced when her heel ground into it, sloshing coffee over the side of her mug and burning her fingers.

Michal was sitting up when Lore pushed aside the ratty curtain closing off their room, sheets tangled around his waist and dripping off the mattress to pool on the floor. It was unclear whether it was the squeaking stair or her loud curse when she burned herself that had woken him.

He pushed his dark hair out of his eyes, squinted. "Coffee?"

"Last cup, but I'll share if you come get it."

"That's generous, since I assume you need it." He grumbled as he levered himself up from the floor-bound mattress, holding the sheet around his naked hips. "You had another nightmare last night. Thrashed around like the Night Witch herself was after you."

Her cheeks colored, but Lore just shrugged. The nightmares were a recent development, and random. She could never remember much about them, only vague impressions that didn't quite match with the terrified feeling they left behind. Blue, open sky, a churning sea. Some dark shape twisting through the air, like smoke but thicker.

Lore held out the coffee. "Sorry if I kept you awake."

"At least you didn't scream this time." Michal took a long drink from her proffered mug, though his face twisted up when he swallowed. "No milk?"

"Elle used the last of it." Lore shrugged and took the cup back, draining the rest.

Michal ran a hand through his hair to tame it into submission while he bent to pull clothes from the piles on the floor. The sheet fell, and Lore allowed herself a moment to ogle.

"I have another drop today," he said as he got dressed. "So I'll probably be gone until the evening."

That made her life much easier. Lore propped her hips on the windowsill and watched him dress, hoping her relief didn't show on her face. "Gilbert is working you hard."

"Demand has gone up, and the team is dwindling. People keep getting hired on the docks to move cargo, getting paid more than Gilbert can afford to match." Michal gave the room a narrow-eyed survey before spotting his boot beneath a pile of sheets in the corner. "The Presque Mort and the bloodcoats have all been busy getting ready for the Sun Prince's Consecration tomorrow, and everyone is taking advantage of them having their proverbial backs turned."

It seemed like Gilbert was doing far more business during the security lull than was wise, but that wasn't Lore's problem. That's what she told herself, at least, when worry for Michal squeezed a fist around her insides. "Must be some deeply holy Consecration they're planning, if the Presque Mort are invited. They aren't known for being the best party guests."

Michal huffed a laugh as he pulled his boots on. "Especially not if your party includes poison." He rolled his neck, working out stiffness from their rock-hard mattress, and stood.

"Be careful tonight," Lore said, then immediately clenched her teeth. She hadn't meant to say it. She hadn't meant to *mean* it.

A lazy smile lifted his mouth. Michal sauntered over, cupped her face in his hands. "Are you *worried* about me, Lore?"

She scowled but didn't shake him off. "Don't get used to it."

A laugh rumbled through his chest, pressed against her own, and then his lips were on hers. Lore sighed and kissed him back, her hands wrapping around his shoulders, tugging him close.

It'd be over soon, so she might as well enjoy it while it lasted.

Despite Michal's warmth, Lore still felt like shivering. She could feel Mortem everywhere—the cloth of Michal's shirt, the stones in the street outside, the chipped ceramic of the mug on the windowsill. Even as her awareness of it grew, a steady climb over the last few months, she was usually able to ignore it, but Pierre's unexpected foxglove had thrown her off balance. Mortem wasn't as thick here on the outskirts of Dellaire as it was closer to the Citadel—closer to the Buried Goddess's body far beneath it, leaking the magic of death—but it was still enough to make her skin crawl.

extras

The Harbor District, on the southern edge of Dellaire, was as far as Mortem would let her go. She could try to hop a ship, try to trek out on the winding roads that led into the rest of Auverraine, but it'd be pointless. The threads of Mortem would just wind her back, woven into her very marrow. She was tied into this damn city as surely as death was tied into life, as surely as the crescent moon burned into the bottom curve of her palm.

Michal's mouth found her throat, and she arched into him, closing her eyes tight. Her fingers clawed into his hair, and his arm cinched around her waist like he might lift her up, carry her to their mattress on the floor, make her forget that this was something finite.

The fact that she *wanted* to forget was enough to make her push him away, masking it as playful. "You don't want to be late."

He lingered at her lips a moment before stepping back. "I'll see you tonight, then."

She just smiled, though the stretch of her lips felt unnatural.

Michal left, that same step squeaking on his way down, the windows rattling when he closed the door. Lore heard Elle heave a sigh, as if her brother's job were a personal affront, the thin walls making it sound like she was right next to Lore instead of all the way on the first floor.

Lore stood there a moment, the light of the slow-rising sun gleaming on her hair, the worn silk of her gown. Then she dressed in a flowing shirt and tight breeches, made her own way down the stairs. She had a meeting with Val to attend.

Elle was curled up on the couch again, a ragged paperback novel in one hand and another mug of tepid tea in the other. She eyed Lore the way you might look at something unpleasant you'd tracked in from the street. "And where are you going?"

"Oh, you didn't hear? I received an invitation to the Sun Prince's Consecration. I wasn't going to go, but rumor has it there might be an orgy afterward, and I can't very well turn that down."

Elle rolled her eyes so hard Lore was surprised she didn't strain a muscle. "There is something deeply *off* about you."

extras

"You have no idea." Lore opened the door. "Bye, Elle-Flower."

"Rot in your own hell, Lore-dear."

Lore twiddled her fingers in an exaggerated wave as the door closed. Part of her would miss Elle when the spying gig was up, when Val had a different running outfit she wanted watched instead of Gilbert's.

But not as much as she'd miss Michal.

She couldn't miss either of them for long. People came and went; her only constants were her mothers—Val and Mari—and the streets of Dellaire she could never leave.

That, and the memories of a childhood she was always, always trying to forget.

With one last glance at the row house, Lore started down the street.

Follow us:

f/orbitbooksUS

𝕏/orbitbooks

▶/orbitbooks

Join our mailing list to receive alerts on our latest releases and deals.

orbitbooks.net

Enter our monthly giveaway for the chance to win some epic prizes.

orbitloot.com